Avenging Storm

Maurice Mayben

"Warning – you will NOT be able to put this book down!
Fast paced, lots of twists, and a great ending – I loved it!"
— Diann Tonnesen

Robert D. Reed Publishers　　　•　　　Bandon, OR

Robert D. Reed Publishers
P.O. Box 1992
Bandon, OR 97411
Phone: 541-347-9882; Fax: -9883
E-mail: 4bobreed@msn.com
Website: www.rdrpublishers.com

Cover art by Keanan Morgan
Author photo and cover design by Cleone Reed
Interior design by Corryn Hurst

ISBN: 978-1-934759-26-4

Library of Congress Control Number: 2008943539

Manufactured, Typeset, and Printed in the United States of America

To Donna,

Dedication

I dedicate this book to my brother Thomas, suffering the ravages of bone cancer. Be with God, my brother. You are always on my mind. My prayers are for you.

And to the memory of my father Al, who passed on many years ago from throat cancer. Be with God.

Acknowledgements

I thank the following wonderful people who helped make this novel possible:

First, thanks to my wife Marcia, whose valuable encouragement, unwavering support and perseverance made the concept for this story possible.

Next, I wish to thank my editor, Mr. Jared Rosburg of Tucson, Arizona, for his professional work and unabashed critique of my writing and helping to develop the story.

I also thank my mother, Dolores, my departed father Al, my brothers and my extended family. Blessings upon you all. You mean the world to me.

I also wish to thank Steve and Duretta Lorang, Diann and Glen Tonnessen, and Ricki and Jeff Rosenthal for their encouragement and critique.

Special thanks to my Kung Fu San Soo master, Sifu Patrick Daniel Cleary, the inspiration for Derek Storm.

Thank you from the bottom of my heart and may God always bless you and yours. I love you one and all.

Thanks & God bless.

Maurice

Maurice Mayhew

15 Oct 2009

CHAPTER I

THE MERCHANTS

Persian Coast, December, A.D. 1294: Niccolo didn't like the view through the looking glass. A dark spot that had appeared on the southeastern horizon the previous dusk had grown in size. Just after their fleet weighed anchors at daybreak, it loomed larger on a constant bearing from them. And now it was more than one spot, it was three. The spots grew larger, their silhouettes gained definition. As Niccilo had suspected, they were ships. He had no further doubt.

"As I feared, brother, they close distance and show no sign of veering off. Pirates. Have a look." Niccilo passed the looking glass as his brother Maffeo swung around the sail rigging to grab it.

Placing the glass to his eye, Maffeo gazed in the direction of the oncoming threat. He could distinguish three vessels under sail approximately five to six miles away, making good headway, judging by the spray of sea foam from their bows. He could also distinguish several cannon on each vessel and decks crowded with figures preparing for brigandage. The ships bore no banners.

"It seems the Almighty presents us with another challenge," agreed Maffeo. "I see cannon and many crewmen busy about their decks. They most definitely aren't merchant vessels, brother."

Their sea voyage from China had begun nearly two years prior, their fleet of fourteen merchant vessels stocked to their brims with stores, provisions, and valuable cargo intended for the markets of Venice. They had left port in China with their accumulation of wealth from decades of enterprise and a Mongol princess, Kokachin, seventeen years old, and her entourage of dozens, destined to be married to Persian prince Arghun. The brothers had brought Christian scholars and oil from the Holy Sepulcher in Rome two decades ago, to honor the Khan's request from their first visit, so he had magnanimously provided this fleet of ships, crews and warriors who accompanied them. They carried passengers as well as warriors for protection.

The brothers were very proud of the wealth they had amassed and the cargo they were bringing back to Venice and Pope Gregory X, and they were honored that the Khan had appointed them as the Imperial Masters and his personal representatives.

Their cargo consisted of a thousand pounds of several dozens of exotic spices, eleven tons of beautiful porcelain dishes and cooking vessels, several hundred bolts of brightly colored and patterned silk, nine hundred weight of gold, several tons of asbestos cloth and raw asbestos, six tons of raw bronze, thirteen hundred weight of silver, beautiful red rubies and green emeralds, and seven dozen glimmering, polished pieces of the finest jade, many carved or inscribed with the work of China's finest artisans, among them the famed Lao Tse Te. The brothers hoped to dazzle the Pope and their fellow Venetians with the splendor of their bounty.

Their route from China had taken them southward around Indochina, then westward past Siam, Burma, India and now the southwest coast of Persia. The fleet rarely got out of sight of land during the day and they sought safe harbor, or at least calm anchorage, every evening before dusk. They did no sea navigation during hours of darkness. There were too many unknowns on the open oceans.

Their voyage had been plagued with mishaps nearly from the outset. More than one hundred crewmen and passengers had perished or deserted. Storms had battered their ships and crews, delayed them five months in Sumatra, rough seas had cost them a fourth of their precious cargo and disease had taken a heavy toll among the crew, and consequently, morale amongst the crew had suffered, leading to more than two dozen desertions. Their fleet of fifteen merchant ships had been reduced to eleven. One had foundered at sea during a storm, another had struck a reef in the low light of dusk. One vessel had to be abandoned in Siam due to mast damage; inhospitable natives had prevented the crew from getting ashore for lumber to replace it. Fortunately, they had managed to transfer the cargo to other vessels. Another ship had burned to the waterline during a mysterious fire, the ship's first officer suspected of inciting a mutiny, but he and half the crew were never seen again. The captain and warriors of that vessel put down the insurrection, but had to be taken aboard a neighboring ship, theirs having been lost to the depths along with its precious cargo. Now they would have to face the onslaught of pirates, for they were far beyond the range of their worldly benefactor's protection.

Their heavily laden vessels had deep draughts, sitting low in the water, making them slow and cumbersome to maneuver. Each vessel was one hundred sixty feet in length, nearly thirty feet at the beam with masts sixty feet high. Each carried a basic civilian crew of thirteen, a few fare-paying passengers, and a contingent of eight to ten Chinese or Mongol warriors with personal armament. The merchant ships bore no cannon but officers and ships captains carried single-shot matchlock pistols. Bearing only light weapons, the warriors would be no match for the cannon-armed marauders gaining from astern. It was clear that the small fleet would not reach its intended destination.

"We must turn the fleet northeast and find safe moorage along the coast, or those damnable devils will be upon us within a few hours," declared Niccilo.

"Agreed."

"We should consider lightening the load. Perhaps we can reach a port before they overtake us. What say you, brother?"

Maffeo considered and nodded concurrence, regretful about losing more of their cargo. But he quickly grasped the reality of their situation. They stood to lose it all, perhaps their lives as well.

Niccilo and Maffeo discussed which cargo to jettison first. They agreed on the bronze and silver and then, if necessary, the porcelain. Should more weight need to be shed, then the spices and possibly the valuable asbestos would follow. They elected to keep the gold, silk, jewels and carved jade.

"Good. We are in agreement. I'll inform the Captain to have the crew begin. If you would be so kind, brother, tell Commander Sun to signal the other vessels."

Maffeo dashed across the deck, grabbed their interpreter, Su, then both made straight for the Fleet Commander. After listening for a full minute, Commander Sun Dek Li nodded to Maffeo and immediately issued orders to signalers and crew of his command vessel, *Sea Crane*. Shouted orders erupted along the length of the ship as officers and crewmen leaped into action. Signalers waved colored banners as trumpets blared a cacophony of commands to the nearest vessels.

The signals were rapidly relayed down the lines to the trailing ships, the furthest of which was two miles astern. It took ten minutes to get acknowledgement from the fleet and get them turned to the northeast toward the closest land.

The decks became chaotic. Crates and trunks were heaved overboard. Boxes of spices were tossed, piles of asbestos cloth followed. Stacks of poorly packed porcelain dishes crashed and tumbled across the decks before they could be heaved overboard. Bolts of beautiful silk cloth unraveled over the decks and gunwales as they streamed into the ocean. Heavy bars of silver and bronze splashed into the waters to become glistening curiosities for the fish. Several frightened passengers tripped on rigging and went over with the cargo; they were left behind, noticed in the frenzy, but not saved.

Observing the pandemonium, Maffeo yelled to his interpreter to save the jewels, jade and gold. Su relayed the command to the Fleet Commander, who received it and puzzled over the priorities. Just the same, he commanded the crew to comply. The signalers again waved multicolored banners and blew their horns in a coded pattern, relayed down the line and acknowledged back to *Sea Crane*.

∞

Two hours of strenuous labor had sapped the energy of the weary crews. Lightening the loads was having an immediate effect. The fleet's speed had increased by several knots and the marauders closed the distance at a much slower rate. But they were still closing and might intercept one or two of the trailing junks before they could reach landfall. At least the leading element of the merchant fleet stood an excellent chance of making port before being intercepted. The coastline grew steadily closer on the horizon but at an agonizingly slow pace.

With mariners glass in hand, Niccilo sought out Fleet Commander Sun. After again assessing the closure rate, he tapped the Commander on the shoulder and pointed toward them as he handed over the glass. Commander Sun peered through the optic for two minutes. Commander Sun nodded in affirmation, mostly to himself, mumbled something not understood by Niccilo and stuffed the glass into his belt. He faced Niccilo, bowed slightly and walked past him toward the bow.

Commander Sun shouted more commands. The intensity of the cargo dumping slowed and several of the crew and warriors turned their attention to other tasks. The fleet signalmen again transmitted orders with their horns and banners. Crewmen adjusted sail riggings while the warriors prepared for inevitable battle. Pistols were charged with powder and shot, archer quivers donned and crossbows made ready. Broadswords, hook-swords and lances were honed and readied. Leather and iron body armor was donned. Fire urns were stoked until they glowed amber.

Noting the sudden change of status, Maffeo approached his brother, "What do you suppose the Commander has in mind?"

"I'm not certain. He observed the pirates through the glass then began issuing orders. I hope he has ..."

A loud explosion sounded in the distance, rolling like thunder across the sea and cut off Niccilo in mid-sentence. Then another boom. Two splashes emerged abeam one of the trailing merchants, *Sea Spray.*

The signal trumpets sounded again and the three leading fleet vessels veered toward the command ship. The command vessel slowed slightly as the crew reefed sails to half-mast. The trailing vessels spread out, attempting to make a line-abreast formation.

More cannon shots from a pirate ship followed, exploding harmlessly into the sea aft and starboard of *Sea Spray.* Su and Fleet Commander Sun approached the merchant brothers.

"Masters, the Commander has a plan." Su turned to face the Commander and listen. The Commander spoke forcefully and rapidly, but briefly, then paused for Su to interpret.

"The Commander says he is transferring all warriors of the four lead ships to *Sea Heaven.*" Su paused for the Commander to speak again.

"Commander Sun will take those warriors onto *Sea Heaven* and engage the marauders. The Commander requests the Masters to remain aboard *Sea Crane* and guide the fleet to safe harbor while he provides such protection as is possible." Su paused again for the Commander to speak.

Su's face saddened as he turned back to the brothers. "The Commander will leave your crew aboard and take only his warriors. He says he will take *Sea Heaven* and the remainder of the fleet to delay the pirates while the Masters and their nephew seek safety ashore. He says it has been an honor to serve you, Masters, and may the name of the mighty Khan be revered."

The finality of the statement set in. They all stood silent for the moment, only the sounds of wind and breaking waves were heard. The brothers silently glanced at each other.

Maffeo broke the silence. "Please tell the mighty Commander that his name will be held in high esteem, recorded so in our logs and may

Almighty God protect him and his warriors."

Su translated for the Commander, who obviously was honored and bowed deeply toward the brothers. Immediately upon rising, the Commander strode rapidly for the port side, shouting orders to his warriors.

More cannon shots roared from the pirate ships, this time one finding a target. The main mast on *Sea Spray* shattered near its mid-point and came down, fouling the sails and making a tangled mess of the rigging. Splinters from the shattered mast pierced crewmen and passengers alike. One crewman was harpooned through the head and died instantly. Two others were gored in their backs and went down screaming. Other crew and passengers absorbed numerous smaller splinters. The upper deck of *Sea Spray* quickly became a bloody mess as crewmen and passengers scurried about to assist the wounded. The eight warriors aboard benefited by the protection provided by their thick leather and metal armor and began firing their crossbows and pistols at the rapidly closing pirate ships. *Sea Spray* quickly lost speed and two of the pirate ships converged on her. All three marauders focused their cannon fire on the upper deck and masts of the stricken *Sea Spray*. They avoided firing shots near her waterline. They didn't want the vessel to sink before they could pillage her cargo.

Meanwhile, two of the lead merchant junks, *Sea Legend* and *Sea Crane,* had pulled abeam opposite sides of *Sea Heaven*. The Fleet Commander barked orders for his warriors to secure the three ships together as they sailed at full speed a mere ten feet apart. As a legendary leader, Commander Sun was the first to slip over the side and cross a connecting line to *Sea Heaven*. He wrapped his powerful legs around the thick hemp line, rapidly advancing hand-over-hand as the ships tossed in the choppy waves. Following their commander's example, warriors from both outboard ships quickly crossed the lines to *Sea Heaven*. In an amazing display of agility and determination, every warrior crossed without mishap, in spite of being heavily laden with armor, weapons and being tossed around on the heaving lines.

After assessing the status of *Sea Heaven*, Commander Sun ordered all its remaining cargo jettisoned, all passengers transferred to the other ships and all warriors to make ready for combat. The passengers aboard *Sea Heaven* attempted to cross to the other ships as the warriors had done. Two frail men were lost into the ocean between ships, but with the vessels under full sail in the choppy sea, their only hope of survival was rescue by the trailing merchants while on the move. The Fleet Commander could not afford to slow the fleet because it was his duty to see the Masters and the princess safely to their destination. This he had sworn to the Khan in person. As the last passenger on each line was pulled aboard, that line was cast off.

With all passengers away and all lines cast off *Sea Heaven*, the Commander observed *Sea Spray,* straddled between two marauder vessels. The warriors aboard *Sea Spray* were fighting valiantly, cutting swathes through the pirates as they swarmed aboard the junk from both sides. The crewmen were also fighting for their lives, having varied measures of success against the hoard of vile encroachers. Some crewmen fought well, either from previous training or just abject terror. Others succumbed to the pirate onslaught without inflicting any damage. Even the passengers fought with any weapon they could find.

Observing the desperate struggle and carnage aboard *Sea Spray* from his perch on *Sea Heaven,* Commander Sun could stand for no more delay. No true warrior runs from battle while his brothers stand and fight. In the mind of a warrior, it is better to die with honor than exist in disgrace.

The fourth of the leading merchant junks, *Sea Willow,* tried to close with *Sea Heaven* to transfer its warriors, but Sun amended his previous order and waived them off. He knew *Sea Willow* had Master Niccolo's son and the princess aboard and he was not about to have her slow down to transfer warriors. The Masters would require protection once reaching landfall and the small contingent of eight warriors aboard the *Sea Willow* were under the command of Sun's most competent junior officer, Chin Moon Kick. *Sea Willow* veered away and ran line abreast, full sail, with *Sea Crane* and *Sea Legend*.

Sun shouted more commands. Colored banners waved and the horns blared again.

The three lead junks raced for the coast as *Sea Heaven* came hard-about to port and tacked into the wind. The six trailing line-abreast junks split into two groups and reversed course in opposite turns, back toward the besieged *Sea Spray*.

"*Enough of this running,*" Sun thought. It was time to be offensive.

∞

The third marauder ship, not fast enough to beat the other pirate ships to *Sea Spray,* continued at full sail and changed course to intercept the next closest merchant, *Sea Wind*. Its cannon fired as the target was broadside in a starboard turn. The shot found its target, not on the top deck, but on the hull close to the waterline. The shot pierced the hull, shattered planking and a crossbeam, slammed into the cargo of gold ingots below deck and ricocheted out the same side of the hull, further forward below the waterline. The stricken junk took on water rapidly and quickly listed to starboard, going down by the bow. Knowing he couldn't save the ship with its heavy cargo and catastrophic hull damage, *Sea Wind*'s captain gave the order to abandon ship. The passengers and crew began going over the sides, but the ship's eight warriors looked at each other with that aura of contempt for the enemy that only warriors understood. They simultaneously drew arrows from their quivers, loaded their crossbows and loosed them at the pursuing marauders.

The marauder leader was irate with the cannoneer for his poor aim, causing them to lose valuable plunder. The grungy, bearded foul-mouth strode up to the head gunner and, while screaming gross vulgarities at him, thrust his dagger into the bungler's throat. The man's blood splattered back onto his face, but he didn't react. He didn't even a blink. His bloodlust heightened but not satisfied, he screamed orders to kill any survivors. As his archers prepared their bows, eight arrows from the sinking junk split the air and found vulnerable targets on the marauder ship, one of them being the right temple of the merciless pirate leader. Another being an archer pierced through the throat and another pirate skewered through the groin. Then eight more arrows from *Sea Wind* quickly struck more pirates; chests, arms, legs and backs received the pointed messages from the Chinese warriors.

However, the pirates were undeterred by the meager resistance. They raised their bows to return fire but were overwhelmed by an unexpected fusillade of arrows… from *behind.* Twenty arrows showered their deck from the direction opposite the sinking junk. Many arrows found flesh to penetrate and the deck became slippery with the life-blood of the pirates, oozing into its crevasses and creases. Screams of agony pierced the air as those pirates yet uninjured turned to face the unexpected attack. Another merchant junk, *Sea Heaven,* was approaching rapidly from behind, with another wall of Chinese arrows leading it. Another dozen arrows found flesh and organs to skewer amongst the sea-going vermin: more screams, more geysers of blood, more death. The pirates were cut down by the dozen by the reinforced contingent of warriors aboard *Sea Heaven.*

The third wave of *Sea Heaven's* arrows came, but not gently like before. This time they came with fire... and gunpowder. The flaming arrows struck the pirate vessel on its deck, mast and sails. Upon striking any hard target, the gunpowder wrappings burst open and the flames ignited the powder into explosive fireballs. Sails, rigging, clothes and human flesh were torched and the stench of charred hemp rope, smoldering wood and cooking human flesh quickly filled the air. Another wave of flaming arrows from *Sea Heaven* soon had the pirate vessel burning everywhere above the waterline. Many of the pirates abandoned ship without order, showing the lack of discipline typical of their ilk. Others tried to fight the fires, but to no success, as each consecutive wave of flaming arrows from the *Sea Heaven* rained down more carnage like fiery meteors from the heavens. The pirate ship and its lawless contingent were destined to burn to the waterline and sink.

∞

Aboard *Sea Heaven,* Fleet Commander Sun had ordered his crew to tack upwind until they were behind the pirate ship pursuing *Sea Wind*. He had ordered his warriors to prepare flash arrows with deadly, explosive gunpowder charges. The men worked at a brisk pace, knowing their comrades were depending upon their talents. It was a matter of honor to them. They had wrapped the small charges of gunpowder tightly inside rolls of parchment, tamped them and twisted the ends closed. Each compact charge was then tied tightly to the shaft of an arrow, just aft of the point.

It wasn't long before the marauding ship closed and fired upon the next junk. Sun had seen *Sea Wind* take a cannonball through the hull near the waterline and was alarmed at how quickly she was going down and urged his warriors to quickly prepare the flash arrows.

Sea Heaven had finally come upwind of the attacking marauder and Sun ordered hard port and full sail to close on the pirate vessel. The warriors had completed only a few of the flash arrows, so Sun had half of his archers make ready on the starboard bow with their crossbows, and two spare crewmen help make additional flash arrows. His warriors gave the untrained lads a crash course, and they rose eagerly to the challenge.

Sun observed the crew of *Sea Wind* abandoning their sinking ship and wondered how *Sea Spray* was faring. He glanced south and saw *Sea Spray* being looted by the other two pirate crews. *Sea Spray's* complement was nowhere to be seen. Sun knew there was nothing he could do for them. But right now, he could save the crew of *Sea Wind*.

One of Sun's warriors approached and reported they had forty flash arrows ready and the crewmen were making more.

"Excellent," declared Sun, "all archers to starboard. We'll fire two volleys of standard arrows and thirty flash arrows. Burn those bastards."

Sun was pleased the pirates had their attention diverted away from his ship. It allowed *Sea Heaven* to close unobserved from behind, within crossbow range. Sun grinned with pride as he saw his eight *Sea Wind* warriors loose two volleys of arrows at the pirates and exact their lethal price. He turned to his archers, gauged the moment, then commanded the archers to loose. The first wave of projectiles inflicted its toll on the backs, legs and necks of the unsuspecting pirates. The second barrage proved more effective. Pirates fell on the deck, over the gunwales, screamed in agony and bled to death. Two successive waves of flash arrows torched the pirate vessel and its crew. Sun took delight in seeing the murderous scum suffer.

It also relieved the pressure on the survivors, who clung precariously to drifting debris, thrashing to keep above the choppy waves. The warriors had expended their arrows, stripped their heavy armor and abandoned ship. To their credit, each retained his broadsword.

Sun ordered *Sea Heaven* alongside the floating debris from *Sea Wind*, furl sail and pick up survivors. He had spotted shark fins breaking the surface even before the battle started, so he was anxious to get the survivors out before the sharks sensed blood.

Pirates from the burned ship also waved for rescue as *Sea Heaven* sailed past. But Sun would have none of it. He ordered his warriors to leave them until all of the *Sea Wind* survivors were rescued. If the sharks got to them first, then it was karma, the way it was meant to be. He walked to the bow to appraise the approach to his survivors. As he peered over the port bow, a knife thrust from below the gunwale and slashed his left cheek to the bone and punctured his eye.

Two pirates had grabbed one of the mooring lines and climbed up the hull to get out of the shark-patrolled waters. The Fleet Commander's face, suddenly appearing over the gunwale, had surprised them and one reacted instinctively.

Sun fell backward onto the deck in agony, blinded in his left eye. Blood streamed from the gash as his warriors ran to his aid.

They found the two intruders hanging on the bow line, cowering like puppies caught peeing in the palace. Officer Wang, second in command, took charge and ordered them hauled aboard. He decided they would fertilize the sea floor as shark feces after his warriors beat them senseless.

One of Sun's personal staff anxiously pushed his way through the others, urging them to make way so he could attend to Commander Sun. Warriors stepped aside, knowing the Commander's best chance of recovery rested with their most skilled healer, Chang Li Suk. Upon reaching his wounded Commander, Chang gripped both sides of the Commander's head and assessed his condition.

"Commander, be still. I am here," Chang spoke calmly to the Commander, who tossed and rolled from the physical torment. "You will be well. This wound will heal."

Chang un-slung a large leather pouch from his shoulder and searched through the contents. He pressed wadded cloths over Sun's wound and instructed a crewman to hold them firmly. He prepared a mixture of herbs and oil, soaked a small piece of bread in it and forced it into the Commander's mouth.

"Commander, chew and swallow the bread."

Sun complied, mumbling about its awful taste. Chang wrapped his hand with an asbestos cloth and grabbed an iron stoker from a fire urn.

"You, and you," he said, pointing at two crewmen, "hold the Commander steady. I must seal his wound." Chang knelt, placed his mouth next to Sun's ear and whispered, "Please forgive me, Commander. I must seal your wound by fire. The men are watching."

Sun reached up with his left arm and firmly gripped Chang's shoulder, giving it a squeeze of acknowledgement. He firmly ordered, "Save the survivors. Don't waste time staring at me. Get to it."

His crisp order had the desired effect. The mesmerized crewmen snapped out of their haze and set out to obey. Survivors of *Sea Wind* were brought aboard as seven warriors pounded mercilessly upon the two captured pirates.

Chang nodded to the crewmen to firmly hold the Commander, then he pressed the hot stoker into the Commander's wounded eye and slowly drew it across the slashed cheek. Pain gripped the Commander like a vice, but his yell sounded not of pain, but of rage. The pungent smell of his own charred flesh and the sound of sizzling blood, coupled with the intense pain, relieved the Commander of his perceived obligation to be strong and he slipped into blissful unconsciousness.

The civilian captain of *Sea Heaven* approached officer Wang and informed him that all *Sea Wind* survivors were aboard, but one was lost to sharks. Wang nodded and saw several men congratulating a surviving warrior, his tunic dripping seawater, who had fought off a shark with his broadsword, thus saving himself and two other crewmen. The wounded shark became the meal of choice for the others while the survivors swam for their lives.

"Thank you, Captain," acknowledged Wang. "Signal the other ships to prepare flash arrows and surround the other pirate vessels. Do not allow them to escape. Then make sail to join them. The Commander's plan is to burn them like rats and we will carry out his orders."

"Immediately, sir." The Captain walked off and shouted orders. The banners waved and horns blared. Crewmen scurried about the decks and raised the sails. *Sea Heaven* caught the wind and began to make way.

Wang walked to the bow, where the group was tending their unconscious commander. He overheard Chang giving instructions to the crewmen to take the Commander below, cover him with blankets and tend to the anticipated fever. The crewmen carefully lifted the Commander and shuffled toward the stern.

"How is the Commander?" inquired Wang.

"Sir, I believe he'll be unconscious for several hours. The wound seemed to seal properly and the bleeding has been stopped. But I wager he'll be meaner than the red dragon when he wakes."

Wang chuckled. He knew the temperament of his commander. "I will not take that wager, Chang. Now, let's rescue *Sea Spray.*"

∾

The combat aboard *Sea Spray* hadn't lasted long. The eight warriors, thirteen crew and nine terrified passengers were overwhelmed by the sheer number of invaders. The warriors had launched all ten-dozen of their arrows and fired their pistols, but the pirates rapidly closed on them. Dozens of grappling lines from two marauder vessels were tossed over both gunwales of *Sea Spray.* Crew, passengers and warriors alike cut through many of those lines but there were just too many. Pirates from both attacking vessels pulled their ships closer to *Sea Spray* until the beams of all three were pounding against one another on the waves, with *Sea Spray* trapped in the middle. Scores of marauders opened fire with pistols and loosed arrows at the merchant defenders, while dozens more boarded with weapons of every description.

The eight mighty Mongol warriors of *Sea Spray* had been a sight to behold. Their intensive combat training was evident in the way they had hacked, sliced, and thrust their way through the throng of pirates. The warriors had charged in four paired teams, echelon formation with one warrior slightly behind and offset of his partner. The lead warrior charged into the throng, slashing the weapon-bearing arm of an attacker, and then moved on to the next one. The supporting warrior provided the death strike to the disabled victim, a thrust through the abdomen or a deep diagonal slash across the neck. If the lead warrior engaged an adversary for more than a few seconds, the support warrior intervened with the killing blow and advanced to the lead position. This method allowed the teams to alternate quickly, gaining initiative and sustaining offensive momentum vital to mortal combat. In this manner, the enemy's momentum could be diminished, perhaps even defeated.

But not this day. The invader numbers had been too great and the eight warriors had slowly succumbed, pierced by arrows, lances or pistol shot. In the aftermath, the pirates noticed that these eight warriors had killed seventy adversaries. These warriors had been very effective, very dangerous men.

The pirates ransacked *Sea Spray*, pillaging all manner of manufactured good, object of value and item of interest. The few cargo crates that remained were broken open, gold bars and jewels pocketed while the wine and liquors were consumed with hearty gusto. The pirates were disappointed there were no wenches for their taking and consoled themselves with the rich bounty.

The dead bodies of the *Sea Spray* contingent were searched for valuables, stripped of their colorful silk tunics, then heaved overboard for the sharks. The unusual Mongol weapons proved to be so effective that interest over them inspired short, bloody fights. Arguments also broke out over division of the gold, jewels, jade carvings and anything else of mutual desire. The brutal, bloody chaos on the decks of both the pirate vessels and the captured junk was a sight no respectable warrior would tolerate. These vulgar pirates were not respectable men. They were not honorable men. In the vengeful eyes of the silently approaching Chinese and Mongol warrior brethren, they weren't even men.

∞

The six remaining merchant ships tacked upwind and silently eased their way toward the chaotic gaggle, *Sea Heaven* trailing but gaining rapidly. The other five junks each had eight warriors aboard. *Sea Heaven*'s contingent was twenty-eight warriors. Sixty-eight combat ready warriors plus the element of surprise should be enough to vanquish the unsuspecting pirates. So believed officer Wang.

He had observed the bodies of his brother warriors heaved overboard from *Sea Spray* and the disgusting frenzy of the sharks as they devoured them. His blood boiled at this disgrace to their honor and he silently vowed upon their spirits that they would soon be avenged. He instructed his signalmen to use only banners for commands, no horns. Wang wanted to bring the small fleet within crossbow range, undetected, before the pirates could bring their cannon to bear.

His assessment of the liquid battlefield gave him reason to grin. The three ships were still lashed together, drifting on the current and the wind, their sides clashing against one another while cresting the short, choppy waves. The wind had caught the beam of one vessel and swung all three tethered ships broadside to the stalking Chinese junks. The pirates were focused on the captured *Sea Spray*.

He turned to the signal crew. "Signal *Sea Mist*. Have Captain Wu lead *Sea Jade* and *Sea Fish* around the stern of the group. They will open fire on our signal."

The signal officer nodded and flashed the banners at Captain Wu's ships. He received immediate acknowledgement and reported so to Wang.

"Now," Wang continued, "signal *Sea Search* and *Sea Crab* to join us. We will sail straight at that nearest pirate ship and on our signal, turn port all at once and loose the flash arrows from our starboard sides." The signaler relayed the orders to the other ships and reported acknowledgement.

"All warriors to starboard. Make ready the flash arrows," Wang commanded. The men hustled to their posts, eager to rain fiery destruction on the defilers of their brethren. The fire urns were stoked until their coals glowed hot amber and the odor of burning coal and raw gunpowder wafted over the deck. As if by the Almighty Khan's hand, the sea swells lightened and made for steady aim.

Captain Wu's ships made excellent progress and slipped astern the drifting gaggle. The high stern of *Sea Spray* blocked the view of the pirates on her lower foredeck. The marauders were so intent upon fighting amongst themselves, they made no notice of the stealthy approach of their soon-to-be flaming demise.

Wang headed his three ships directly at the three-ship gaggle. He glanced down at his archers and recognized Chan, the most experienced.

Chan glanced at Wang, then back at the target, estimated the range and timing, then glanced back at Wang and nodded.

"Signal our ships to come hard to port and loose the arrows," commanded Wang. "Captain, bring us hard to port." All men steadied themselves as the sails were furled and the ship heaved hard to the left while rolling into a starboard list.

All three of Wang's ships turned in unison, bringing their starboard sides parallel to the target. At the appropriate moment, Wang drew his broadsword and commanded the archers to ready their bows. The flash arrows were set into the crossbows and set aflame. All archers braced their stances and took aim.

"LOOSE!" Shouted Wang, as he sliced the air with his broadsword. "Signal Captain Wu to loose his arrows."

The flaming arrows arched smoke trails across the blue sky, streaking toward their targets with their explosive messages of flaming death. Even before they had struck, the next wave of the barrage was readied for delivery.

Several of the arrows fell short, splashing harmlessly into the ocean, but the majority found solid or flesh targets. The hull, rigging, and sails of the nearest marauder ship were quickly set ablaze and dozens of the sea scum went down, dead or horribly disabled. One flash arrow struck into the neck of a pirate and exploded, decapitating him and wounding several others as his body fell to the deck, spewing a crazy arc of blood. Another arrow found a leg to blow off, another a back, another a shoulder, and so it went. Bodies, alive and dead, were aflame on blazing decks. By the sixth wave of flash arrows, every pirate on the vessel was dead or wishing for its merciful release. The whole vessel quickly became an inferno.

Satisfied, Wang needed to see how matters fared on the far side of the gaggle. He instructed the captain to bring his vessel around the bows of the drifting ships and signal *Sea Search* and *Sea Crab* to follow.

As *Sea Heaven* cleared the bow of *Sea Spray*, Wang could see the battle still continued on the other marauder vessel. Those marauders still on the *Sea Spray* were hacking at the grappling lines holding the ships together. The ships on both sides were aflame and they were desperately attempting to cut loose from them.

Wang astutely assessed the situation. He ordered his warriors to concentrate their fire on the bow of the second marauder ship to keep the pirates from manning their cannon. Without cannon they were no match for his warriors and archers. With one pirate ship already sunk, another completely aflame and uninhabitable, the third partly aflame and denied the use of its cannon, he felt confident of victory.

An explosion erupted on the portside marauder vessel, hurling flaming debris into the water and onto *Sea Spray*. Wang rightly surmised the vessel's gunpowder had torched. He considered the pirates still aboard *Sea Spray*. They had successfully cut away from the burning hulk of the portside marauder ship and were attempting to accomplish the same on the starboard one. The two dozen pirates still aboard Sea Spray had no cannon, no longbows, only swords and light weapons. They had no masts to raise sails and maneuver. He decided to enjoy the luxury of dealing with them later and returned his attention to the remaining marauder.

Wang ordered the crossbow fire of all six merchants concentrated on the remaining pirate vessel. In short order, it too was a blazing pyre. Vermin, both rodent and human, deserted the ship, taking their chances in the shark buffet. Wang and his warriors took glee at seeing them hurl their burning bodies into the cool ocean, only to become shark protein, screaming in anguish as the frenzied marine eating-machines chewed off huge chunks.

The three ships now drifted separately. There was only minor fire aboard *Sea Spray* and the pirates were tending to those. Wang elected to let them extinguish those fires before securing the ship. He ordered all ships to kill any pirates that attempted rescue from the waters and all acknowledged.

The screams of the dying were slowly coming to an end and cheers of victory resounded amongst the fleet. Both pirate hulks had burned to their waterlines and were allowed to drift off and submerge into the briny underworld. The six merchant junks surrounded *Sea Spray* to prevent her drifting away. Lookouts were posted on all ships to monitor the pirates and given specific orders to immediately and ruthlessly kill any who attempted escape or surrender.

∞

After two hours, the remnants of pirate scum on the *Sea Spray* realized they had no hope of escape. Furious but unintelligible arguments could be heard across the water as several wanna-be leaders and their factions vied for control and engaged in fighting that proved mortal for some. Several white flags appeared from the besieged pirates, only to have arrows shot through them by Wang's warriors. Surrender was an option not made available to the scum who had defiled their warrior brothers. Five pirates raised swords and shouted defiant words at the surrounding warriors. They were immediately dispatched with arrows through their chests, heads and groins. Observing this, others jumped ship and attempted to swim for the merchant vessels. They too succumbed to an onslaught of arrows from the vengeful brotherhood of warriors. The last two pirates, seeing the ruthlessness of the Mongol warriors, reached a mutual homicide pact and simultaneously thrust their swords into each other's gullet. Their deaths were quick, but not painless. Their cries of dying agony echoed over the water.

Wang ordered the Captain to bring *Sea Heaven* alongside *Sea Spray* and directed his warriors to prepare to board her. It was time to survey the damage.

∞

The coast was desolate but still a beautiful sight to the brothers. *Sea Crane, Sea Willow,* and *Sea Legend* had reached the coast together. Maffeo had sighted a likely anchorage slightly to the north and the ships tacked toward it. Niccilo observed several smoke columns rising above the horizon astern and feared they had lost the remainder of their fleet. They were too distant from the battle and too weary from their torturous journey to think differently. They had no way of knowing the heroics of the Mongol and Chinese warriors had saved most of their vessels and cargo. Not until that evening would the merchant brothers discover the results.

The suspected anchorage was more than it first appeared. It proved to be an outlet to the ocean and, following it upstream, they discovered a port. Strangely dressed natives appeared along the riverbanks and stared at the unusual vessels as they pressed upriver. Both brothers had the feeling they had been here before.

∞

Commander Sun awoke to a horrible headache and incredible pain on the left side of his face. He was feverish and carefully being tended to by a crewman with moist cloths, providing a modicum of relief. He brushed aside the crewman's hand, slowly struggled to his feet and headed for the daylight of the cabin door, which he could only make out through the blurred vision of his right eye. He came to the sudden realization that he would never have the use of his left eye again. He exited to the deck and called for Wang, who came running.

"Commander Sun, I am thankful you have recovered. Congratulations on your victory. Your plan defeated the pirates. What are your orders, Commander?"

Sun contemplated what he had just heard. He recognized a crock of manure when he smelled it.

"Wang, my plan could not have succeeded without superior leadership and tactical cunning. And since I was unconscious during the battle, just who supplied the leadership and cunning?" The rhetorical question, delivered with a knowing wink and a wan smile, was not meant to put Wang on the spot, but to give him praise in front of the men. The troops understood their Commander's intent and began to cheer the junior officer, whose decisive actions had brought victory from almost certain defeat. Wang blushed and bowed repeatedly to the Commander and the troops. The applause was allowed to flourish for several minutes. Then Sun placed his arm over Wang's shoulder and whispered into his ear. Wang nodded understanding. The Commander turned away and walked to the beam to view *Sea Spray.*

Wang issued orders to several warriors to search *Sea Spray*. The warriors bowed and slipped over the gunwales onto *Sea Spray* and spread out toward the cabins at the rear and the cargo hold amidships. They searched with torches and lamps for twenty minutes and returned with several small crates and trunks. Wang nodded grimly at the paltry remnants recovered from the looted ship and had his troops return aboard *Sea Heaven* with it. Once back, Wang ordered the troops to set *Sea Spray* adrift.

There were only two hours of daylight left, it had been an extremely long, bloody day, and landfall by dark was improbable if they tried to take *Sea Spray* under tow. She was now a burned, worthless hulk. It was best to set her adrift and reach landfall before dark with the remainder of the fleet than risk being caught on the open sea. Perhaps they might even catch up with the Masters.

The fleet unfurled sails and made way for land. Off to the northwest drifted *Sea Spray,* void of crew, void of stores and void of cargo; she was void of all but the small wooden chest in a hidden compartment beneath her deceased Captain's bunk.

CHAPTER II

DESERT STORM

February 24, 1991, Southern Iraq: A cold, strong wind blew across the desert, gusts driving gritty sand into flapping jackets and maps. The squad leaders of 2nd Platoon, Bravo Company gathered on the lee side of a Bradley infantry vehicle. The temperature was low forties but wind chill made it freezing. The wind ripped into their flesh like the talons of a bird of prey. That's why they referred to it as the "hawk." Some of the troops used their gloved hands to shield their eyes from the glare of the setting sun, others blew warm breath onto their bare hands. The smoky sky from flaming Kuwaiti oil fields was made even more ominous-looking by the dark orange of the waning sun.

U.S. Army Staff Sergeant Derek Storm listened intently as his platoon leader, Lieutenant Sikes, briefed the upcoming movement into the Iraqi interior. "Our platoon will move northward shortly after sunset, to the Euphrates River. We'll parallel the river northwest until we reach phase line Celia, here, forty clicks northwest. Once there, we'll establish defilade positions and prepare to defend against counter-attack. 2nd Armored is our armor support and Delta Troop Cav will provide helicopter gunship support."

Lt. Sikes paused, bit into his grease pencil, turned a page of his notepad, then continued. "The first day of the ground war has gone well. We've taken substantial ground and are pressing the attack north. The Iraqis are in full retreat and their command and control structure has been obliterated. However, Division Intel reports there are still organized Iraqi armor units to the north, cut off from their supply lines. We need to get to phase line Celia by 0200 and prep for counterattack. If there is one, we'll deal with it and get some rest. Any questions?"

The Lieutenant glanced around at his Sergeants. There were no questions, which struck Storm as odd. Usually, one of them had a question or quip.

"Okay. We move out as soon as refueling and re-arming are complete. It's going to be dark within an hour, so let's hit it." The Sergeants exchanged salutes with their Lieutenant, secured their gear and returned to their squads.

Storm approached his Bradley as the squad finished refueling. "The ammo reloads done?" he inquired of his right hand man, Specialist Eric Martin.

Martin turned, grinned, and in his typically short manner, replied, "Yep. All done, Sarge." He tossed two freshly loaded M-16 magazines to Storm. "The twenty-five mike-mike is chock full. So's the 7.62 and we got one more TOW missile," referring to the twenty-five millimeter anti-aircraft, anti-armor gun on the Bradley's turret with 7.62 millimeter coaxially-mounted machinegun and the tube launcher for the anti-tank missile. The system was very effective. All three weapons were operated with the same sighting system and could be used for firing upon aircraft, troops, bunkers, vehicles and even tanks. The tracked vehicle itself was lightly armored and carried a nine-man infantry squad, including their personal weapons and equipment. It had top hatches for the driver, the track commander, the gunner, and a rear cargo hatch. The rear side of the vehicle could be lowered and used as a ramp for rapid entry or deployment.

"We got grenades, 40 millimeter rounds for the 203's and some 9 millimeter, too. The water cans are full and we picked up another case of rations," added Martin.

"What's the status of the vehicle?"

"Good to go."

"Hoo-ah. We'll be moving out as soon as all the tracks are refueled. Get the lads gathered around for brief-up." Martin nodded and hustled around the vehicle to muster the squad.

Martin admired and respected his squad leader. The twenty-three year old Storm had joined the Army five years previous and had risen steadily through the ranks. He was a natural soldier. He loved the physical conditioning, the hard regimen of infantry training, the exhilaration of tactical exercises and now, leading a squad of eight other men whose lives depended upon him. He had qualified as "Expert" marksman with every weapon the Army had ever put in his hands. He excelled in hand-to-hand combat due to his martial arts training since early childhood, under the expert tutelage of his father and later, Master Chin. There wasn't a soldier in the battalion willing to take him on after the legend of Hargerstein's Bar had made the rounds.

Martin recalled one night a year ago, while out with some buddies, including Storm, intoxicated soldiers from another unit made disparaging remarks about their manhood. Shoves and verbal threats set the stage, but the confrontation was ended within seconds. Storm had single-handedly launched into the loudmouths with the fury of a category five hurricane, his fists, elbows, knees and feet targeted groins, temples, throats and kidneys. His buddies just gaped in awe. All six of the drunkards were on the deck, unconscious, or balled up clutching their guts and groaning. By the end of the following day, word had gotten around the Battalion that Storm was not a man to screw with. He had managed to talk his way out of trouble with his Commanding Officer as his buddies confirmed it had been a matter of self-defense.

At five feet ten, Storm was not impressively tall. Nor was he impressively handsome. But he was good-looking in a rugged, manly way that women found intriguing. His 180 pounds were solid muscle, his middle slightly thickened from years of hard training and his leisure pastime of amber brew. His forearms, upper arms and legs were extremely strong from years of Kung Fu training, thanks to the hard discipline instilled by Master Chin. He moved with the agility of a large cat in the hunt and his reflexes were equally sharp. He sported light reddish brown hair, blue-green eyes and a face that betrayed his predominantly Irish ancestry. The redness in his hair and his intermittently intolerant disposition had earned him the nicknames of "Derek the Red" and "Red Storm." Although his average looks didn't cause women to swoon, his ruggedness and erect, confident stature and sense of humor appealed to women and he rarely suffered for lack of female companionship. He prided himself on being a competent lover, not just in the manner which most men imagine, but that women had told him so.

Storm pulled his map from his pocket, laid it on the sand beside the track and the squad clustered around him, some with enthusiasm, some with apprehension. Combat drew various reactions from men. A few were looking forward to kicking some Iraqi ass; others became withdrawn and uncertain. Storm believed he had a good squad. They would do their jobs. They had all fired weapons at the enemy that first day and had been fired upon. They had the confidence to fight and win.

"Make sure everyone has a full canteen and basic load of ammo. As soon as we mount, run a clean patch down your rifle bore and check all your equipment. I don't want any screw-ups. I want this squad ready to fight. Oh, good news. The First Sergeant says there'll be hot chow tomorrow morning." Light-hearted cheers issued from the troops. Their last hot meal had been three days previous. They had been eating cold rations, called MREs (meals, ready-to-eat) since their departure from base camp in the Saudi desert.

"We're moving out at dusk, up to the Euphrates River, then northwest to phase line Celia, here." He indicated that point on his map. "We should reach the objective by 0200, then prep for counter-attack. Hopefully, hot chow in the morning. Right now, Jefferson and Renaud, break out the night vision devices. Ruck up." The men broke and mounted the track, grousing and bantering.

Storm made a head count as they mounted, then raised the ramp and sidled forward to the commander's hatch. Martin was in front of him heading for the gunner's turret. The diesel and oil fumes, plus the aroma of nine men without showers for three days, assaulted his nostrils and he blew his nose as soon as his head cleared the hatch. He observed Martin check the 25mm cannon and made a routine inspection of his personal gear. Satisfied, he ducked inside to check on the squad's progress. All were ready, so Renaud passed him the Night Vision Scope to mount on the 25mm. Storm passed the scope topside to Martin, who mounted the scope, checked the batteries and the alignment, then racked a high-explosive (HE) round into the chamber. HE rounds were effective against bunkers and vehicles but were of questionable value against tanks. Storm wished his squad had been issued the depleted uranium anti-tank rounds. They were extremely effective against heavy armor and could chew a tank into a blazing steel wool pad in a heartbeat. Unfortunately, those rounds were terribly expensive and there weren't enough to go around. What they did have was the Tubular-launched, Optically-guided, Wire-controlled (TOW) anti-tank missiles, formidable tank busters. The missiles were set into twin tubes mounted on the top of the vehicle, with four spares carried below in the hold.

Storm heard the Lieutenant's vehicle start, so he donned his helmet and checked the cord. There was no chatter on the platoon FM frequency. Over the vehicle intercom, he ordered the driver to start their track. The huge diesel engine sparked to life within seconds, spewing a small rooster tail of exhaust into the fading twilight. The rumble of the other platoon vehicles added to the cacophony. *"Not long now,"* Storm thought.

He gave one last glance into the crew compartment, noticing several of the men breaking open their MRE's while others tried unsuccessfully to find a comfortable position to catch a few winks.

Storm kept a watchful eye on the Lieutenant's vehicle, waiting for the hand signal to move out. The radios would not be used until dark or they made contact with the enemy. Until then, all routine commands were visual signals.

The signal came. Storm commanded the driver to move out and his Bradley, call sign Sword two-one, moved into the lead as the other Bradley's maneuvered into echelon formation. The noise from the diesels increased sharply as they powered across the desert dunes and around gullies. The air filled with oily exhaust fumes, further reducing visibility. Not having had a chance to chuck down an MRE, Storm peeled open a snack bar, one of several he usually kept in his pockets. He munched as he scouted the terrain ahead, issuing instructions to the driver as the need arose.

Just as the sun settled below the western horizon, Storm noticed two flights of USAF A-10 Thunderbolts, green camouflaged, twin engine, twin boom-tailed tank busters. They were headed southbound and Storm assumed they were returning to base after a daylight mission of pummeling Iraqi tanks with their Maverick missiles and depleted uranium 30mm rounds. It wouldn't be long before the Air Cavalry showed up to provide nighttime air support with their Hellfire-laden Apaches. The night vision equipped gun-ships with their Hellfire antitank missiles and mini-guns provided an awesome airborne firestorm the likes of which Storm was glad not to be on the receiving end. The burned out hulks of Iraqi tanks and personnel carriers, strewn across the terrain and surrounded by dead Iraqi soldiers they had passed earlier in the day, stood as grave testament to the lethal firepower of the A-10s and Apaches. He felt relieved knowing the A10s had obliterated the Iraqi army in front of them.

The wind velocity dropped off shortly after dark but the air quickly became colder. The blowing sand diminished and a one-quarter moon provided nearly one mile of visibility to the unaided eye. Every ten minutes or so, Storm switched on his night vision scope and scanned the forward horizon for any indications of enemy activity. He hunched up his shoulders and bundled his wool scarf tighter around his neck. Fortunately, the vehicle's heater kept his lower half warm.

Storm noticed bloated corpses of camels and their nomadic jockeys as they drove past. All men; no women or kids. The thought of civilian noncombatants being chopped to pieces gave him pause. He had no qualms about squeezing a trigger on enemy soldiers but the sight of dead civilians bothered him. At least he could sleep at night knowing he wasn't responsible for their deaths. He gave thanks to God.

After three hours of progressing northward, his platoon reached the Euphrates River. Moonlight shimmered off the waters and several cormorants took flight. Fish rippled the river surface and then quickly vanished.

Lt. Sikes's voice broke the squelch on the platoon FM net for the first time that evening, "Sword element, this is Sword two-six. Security out and element leaders rally on me. No acknowledgement."

Storm quietly told the driver to leave the engine running, removed his com helmet and ducked into the squad bay. "Okay, wake up. Security out, no lights. I'm going to the Lieutenant's track. Martin, you're in charge. Use night vision."

Martin nodded affirmation, then posted the sentries. Storm jumped down the rear ramp, M16 in hand and hustled back to the Lieutenant's track. Its rear ramp opened. Other squad leaders approached and quickly shuffled up the ramp as Sikes's men deployed for security. The squad leaders clustered around Sikes as he focused his red-filtered flashlight on his map.

"GPS shows us here, at this bend in the Euphrates. We're twenty-two minutes ahead of schedule. Good job. We're gonna turn northwest, about three-two-five degrees magnetic, and advance to phase line Celia. The scout element has encountered a minefield ahead and Division engineers are being moved forward to clear several lanes through. We'll be here for about an hour or until the lanes are clear. Shut down the tracks, save fuel. Rotate security shifts. I want at least four men outside at each track using night vision. How's our status?" He glanced up at the Sergeants. Each reported his squad's status of fuel, ammo and equipment. There didn't seem to be any major problems. Batteries were needed for some night vision devices. They quickly squared that away and headed back to their vehicles.

Storm trotted to his track and waved the mount up signal to his troopers. The men rose from the cold sand, relayed the signal and hustled toward the warmth of the track.

Again, Storm took a headcount, mounted the track from the side and told Pvt. Vrisigian to raise the ramp. Storm scurried across the top of the vehicle and dropped into the commander's hatch.

"Tommy, move us into hull defilade behind that sand dune to our left," Storm yelled to the driver, "then shut down the engine and get some sleep. That's an order." The driver, Tom Harley, was a good trooper and had been pushing himself harder than the other squad members, almost as hard as Storm. Storm knew Tommy was groggy. He turned to the rest of the squad as the vehicle lurched left and then forward, coming to rest at the position Storm had indicated. "Okay, four men for outside security, two on each front side of the vehicle. One-hour shifts, use NVGs and the SAW. Martin, you're in charge. Did you get a nap?"

"Yeah, I managed an hour or so."

"Good, I'm gonna check my eyelids for holes. Wake me up in an hour or if Sikes tells us to move out." Storm was grateful for the break. He hadn't had more than four hours sleep per night for the past seventy-two hours and it was beginning to catch up to him. This lull provided a rare opportunity to snatch a combat nap.

The four men selected for the first guard shift grumbled as they bundled up against the cold. They gathered their weapons and equipment and exited through the rear hatch. Martin secured it behind them, checked his Indiglo watch, then assumed his post at the turret. Storm removed his Kevlar helmet, unclasped his flak vest and sprawled out on a side bench. He pulled his scarf over his head and closed his eyes. Others did the same. A couple of the men lit cigarettes. It was quiet, relative peace. Storm drifted off to sleep.

∞

"Sarge, wake up." Martin's voice came into audible focus as Storm was shaken to awareness. He removed the scarf from his head and rose to gather his senses. His nap was almost into REM stage, but not quite.

"How long was I asleep?"

"Almost two hours, Sarge. You were out so deep I didn't want to wake you. Sikes's runner just told me the platoon's movin' out in ten minutes."

Storm wrapped the scarf around his neck, rubbed his eyes and yawned. He sat up and stretched as much as space would allow.

"I've recalled the guards," Martin informed him. "The runner said the engineers have cleared two lanes for the Battalion to get through. Our platoon will be the second unit down the east lane, marked in green. Third platoon is in the lead."

"Okay. Get everyone mounted and get a headcount, weapons ready." Storm crouched and moved forward to the driver. He shook Tommy several times. "Time to roll, lad. Get ready to crank her up." Storm moved back to the commander's turret, checked his weapons and donned his com helmet. He mentally prepared himself and stood up through the hatch. The cold wind was still there with an unmistakable bite. *"Yup, that's why it's called the hawk."* He got a thumb-up from Martin as he emerged through the gunner's turret and switched on his intercom.

"Tommy, we ready?"

"Any time, boss."

Storm heard Sikes's track start and ordered Tommy to crank her up. The noisy diesel turned over and spewed exhaust fumes. The other platoon tracks were up and running, ready to roll.

Sikes's voice came over the radio, "Sword element, move out."

"Okay, Tommy. Back her away from the dune and turn right. Once you clear the corner, bear left until I give you a visual bearing." The track lurched rearward a few feet and then pivoted right around the end of the sand dune. Storm studied the luminous glow of his compass, checked the GPS and gave the driver a visual reference to drive toward. Again, with his track in the lead, the other platoon tracks maneuvered into an inverted V formation. Storm turned on the night vision scope and scanned forward. Third platoon was on the move already.

Eight minutes later, Storm saw the third platoon collapse into single column, half a mile ahead. He could make out the ghostly green day-glow chemical light sticks of the combat engineers marking the entrance to the lanes through the minefield. He radioed this information to Sikes and heard the Lieutenant command the platoon to collapse to column formation. Storm instructed Tommy to maneuver two hundred meters astern the last Bradley of the third platoon.

A glow flashed over the northern horizon. The rumble of explosions could be heard from the distance. Storm counted the seconds between the flashes and the rumbles and estimated they were three miles away. Two Apache helicopters were back-lighted by the flashes, circling and launching missiles at ground targets.

"Tommy, button up," Storm yelled. Tommy lowered his seat, his helmet vanished below the deck and he slammed closed the hatch. This gave Martin, the gunner, full traverse of the weapons turret without impediment from the driver's hatch. The driver navigated the vehicle through periscopes arranged around the forward edge of the hatch.

Storm's vehicle entered the minefield lane two hundred meters behind the last vehicle of the third platoon. Renaud tugged on Storm's trouser leg from below, inquiring about the explosions. Storm yelled back that he could see Apaches engaging ground targets a couple miles ahead. The men nervously thumbed the safeties on their weapons and rechecked their equipment. They were all awake and wide-eyed.

The marked lane appeared to end three hundred meters ahead. Storm was anxious to get through the lane so they could maneuver. They didn't dare stray outside the lane for fear of hitting an antitank mine, which would kill the lightly armored Bradley and probably everyone in it. The Bradley was designed to transport Infantry troops and protect them from small arms fire. It could not withstand a direct hit from a tank cannon, missile or antitank mine.

Their Bradley passed the final lane marker and Storm had the driver swing right toward the riverbank and slow down so the rest of his platoon could catch up and resume tactical formation. Three of the platoon vehicles had cleared the lane when a flash one thousand meters ahead caught his attention. A green-tracer tank round arced across the horizon, slammed into a vehicle of the third platoon and obliterated it in a massive, brilliant fireball. Storm felt the concussion. His ears and sinuses were blocked by the sudden change in air pressure. Fragments of smoldering debris rained down. Then another shot, then another. Within seconds, six more enemy cannon rounds arced toward targets, their green tracers defining their paths. Two vehicles of the third platoon were ablaze just two hundred meters away and Storm saw one American soldier running around, his uniform on fire. As he dropped, another American soldier appeared out of the smoking chaos and smothered the flames with a field jacket and sand. Machinegun and cannon fire ripped the air, streaming trails of phosphorous light. A third platoon TOW missile shot from a launcher tube, the motor ignited brightly and it zoomed toward an Iraqi target. The remaining vehicles of the third platoon maneuvered, seeking any available terrain depression for cover. The TOW missile impacted on an Iraqi T-72 tank and blew the turret off the hull. Storm felt the concussion from that explosion, too. The blaze illuminated several other enemy vehicles. An Iraqi T-72 blasted another round toward the third platoon, but it missed, impacting harmlessly into the desert hundreds of yards beyond.

Air Cavalry Apaches swept in from the north, darting like wasps seeking revenge and launched their Helllfires at the Iraqi tanks. Even without NVGs the enemy vehicles were identifiable. Their tracers were green while the US forces used red. The T-72 that had fired the last round exploded from a Hellfire missile impact, setting off secondary explosions of fuel and ammo. The first of the American Abrams tanks cleared the minefield and began lighting up the Iraqis with its laser range finder and huge cannon. It fired two rounds and destroyed two tanks with single-shot kills in less than ten seconds. Machinegun tracers arced through the night as infantrymen and tankers from both armies slugged it out. Two more Hellfire missiles and another TOW added their shrieking messages of destruction. Three more Iraqi tank crews died instantaneous explosive deaths. The air began to reek of cordite, burning fuel and torched flesh as numerous explosions blasted the desert air with flash and concussion.

Storm peered through his scope, seeking a target to engage with his 25-millimeter cannon. He saw an Iraqi T-72 slewing its turret toward them. He immediately realized that the enemy tank had the drop on them and there was no way to get his weapons turret around to engage it before it could take a shot.

"Tommy, hard right, hard right! Hammer down! Max speed!"

The Bradley pivoted right and lurched forward, throwing the squad around in the hatches and aft compartment. Excited yells issued from within.

"Make for that dune to your left, Tommy. Get behind it. Fast!" Storm raised up on his toes, bracing his arms on the turret, to peek above the sand dune, but before he could visually acquire the T-72 an explosion tore through the left bottom of the vehicle. A brilliant flash illuminated the interior of the track as intensely hot flames shot up through the floor. The left track separated from the vehicle and the concussion threw Storm from the turret as the vehicle raised up several feet on its right track, then slammed back down. Flames erupted from the open turret and commander's hatch as well as the engine grill cover.

Storm was ejected heels over head. Slow motion from temporal distortion took hold and it seemed to take forever until he struck the ground. Sounds lost volume, time seemed to slow down, tunnel vision encroached. He impacted the ground like a sack of wet cement. He felt a horrible crunch and lancing pain from his left arm and shoulder. The earth around him rumbled and he struggled to suck air into his lungs. As he regained his senses, he realized his legs were on fire. The sharp pain in his left arm wouldn't let him beat out the flames. Racked with intense pain, he acted on instinct. He tunneled his legs into the sand and used his right hand to scoop sand onto his burning legs. He managed to extinguish the flames in seconds but it seemed like an hour. He saw and felt other explosions around him as the firefight continued. His blazing vehicle continued toward the riverbank, its momentum taking it over the edge, out of sight. He tried to raise himself but a racking pain in his back sucked the wind out of him and brought him back to the ground.

Realizing he could be run over by one of his own vehicles, Storm rolled onto his stomach, carefully avoiding the torso twisting agony he had previously experienced and crawled toward the riverbank. He had to find cover. Every muscle in his body seemed to rebel, his head pounded and his heart felt as if it would burst. He struggled to force saliva down his parched windpipe but he got a mouth full of sand instead. He used his right arm and scorched legs to crawl toward the river, every movement accentuating the pain in his shoulder, arm and legs. The thick smell of cordite and scorched flesh, the pain, all combined. Nauseated, he vomited into the sand. He wiped his mouth on his sleeve and heaved again.

Storm struggled to maintain consciousness as he crawled the remaining forty meters to the embankment. Thrust after painful thrust, he determined to make it, to seek cover and live.

Reaching the embankment, he peered over the edge and saw his track burning in the gulley below. He eased himself over the edge, attempting to slide feet first down the slope. It was steeper than he thought and he encountered a hard object about halfway down. He tripped and tumbled to the bottom. The pain of his injuries spiked as he rolled and tumbled, striking other hard objects near the bottom. He knew he had suffered a concussion and was losing control: intense pain, dizziness, tunnel vision, sounds fading…

∞

Storm was vaguely aware of being alive. He blinked his eyes slowly, fighting for focus. His vision was blurred and his head throbbed. He could feel pain in his shoulder, arm and back. His legs felt alternately cold, then hot. Slowly, he focused and discovered he was face down in sand staring at wooden planks. He sensed it must be morning, judging by the angle of the shadows. He tried to move his left arm to see his watch but the pain proved to be too much. He used his right hand to remove the watch, noted it was 0837 hours, and stuffed the watch into his right trouser pocket. He carefully assessed his injuries and determined he had a back injury that caused intense shooting pain if he twisted his upper torso. Keeping his spine as straight as possible and avoiding rotation seemed to be bearable. His shoulder hurt like hell, as did the fracture of his left forearm. He knew he had burns on his legs, probably first degree, but some blisters on his left leg were probable second-degree burns.

He didn't have any treatment for the burns other than water but there was something he could do about his arm. He looked around for things to use as a splint and sling. He decided his scarf would serve as a sling and he could strip pieces of cloth for ties, but he needed something about a foot long, stiff and thin to use as a splint.

Storm assessed his surroundings. He was lying in a huge trench, 100 yards wide and several hundred yards long and almost thirty feet deep. It was not the riverbank or a wash, as he believed last night. He peered both ways along the gulley. The more he studied it, with its overlapping half-spherical sides and bottom, the more he came to deduce that he was not in a gulley or wash, but in a chain of connected bomb craters. He guessed it was the work of the USAF B-52s carpet-bombing before the ground war started. Only a huge bomber could deliver a single-pass footprint such as this. The dimensions of the trench amazed him. "Poor bastards," he mumbled, referring to the pulverized Iraqis who had been on the receiving end.

Storm examined the wood planks behind him. They were old, partly exposed, imbedded in the sand. With his good hand, he felt one. It was rotted, yet oddly strong. He used his bayonet to pry at the plank but couldn't break off a piece the size needed for his splint. It kept splintering into unusable slivers. Frustrated, Storm dug around and was rewarded for his effort. He uncovered another wooden object and began digging around it. It appeared to be a small wooden chest with metal corners, clasp and hinges. This wood was old also, but the size of each slat was about right for his intended purpose. He smashed at the edges of the chest with the pommel of his bayonet and they gave way. He pried loose three of the slats and thanked God.

After cutting a few strips of cloth from the legs of his burned trousers, Storm placed the thin, narrow planks around his broken arm. Using his good hand and his teeth, he tied four strips around his arm and the planks, two above the break and two below, firm but not enough to cut off blood circulation to his left hand. He eased his arm up into the sling. He took several deep breaths to alleviate pain and rested.

Sunlight pierced the inside of the small chest and reflected off of something shiny and green. Using his bayonet, he enlarged the hole in the chest and saw several pieces of shiny green stone and a thin metal tablet. Storm reached into the chest and removed three objects. One was a tarnished thin metal tablet inscribed with oriental characters, about twelve inches in length, three inches wide and half an inch thick. Another article was an intricately carved green stone displaying a three dimensional oriental building and similar characters. The third piece was a carved green disc-shaped stone approximately four inches diameter with oriental characters inscribed on both sides. Storm brushed the sand from the articles and studied them, thought they might have value and stuffed them into his jacket pocket. He suspected the green stones might be jade and the characters must be Chinese because for many years he had trained in Kung Fu San Soo, a Chinese martial art from southern China. He recognized a few of the characters but not enough to glean any sense of their meaning. If nothing else, they'd make neat souvenirs of his adventure. Yet, a nagging thought rattled around in his pain-afflicted brain. *"Oriental characters buried in a box in the Iraqi desert? What the hell is that about?"*

"Later. First things first," he said aloud without realizing it.

His burned out track was further out into the middle of the bomb trench, laying on its right side. Storm eased himself up and cautiously walked to it. The fire had thoroughly burned out the interior. Storm peered inside and wished he hadn't. Every member of his squad was dead, burned crisp. The heat from the explosion had cooked off the ammo and fuel, making the interior an inescapable inferno. Storm walked around the other side of the track and saw the impact point of the explosion. He deduced that it wasn't a tank round that had hit them, but an antitank mine. The left track was missing and there was a jagged four-inch hole in the hull just inboard of the front left road wheel, breeching the hull bottom. The explosion had pierced the hull just behind Tommy, the driver, thrown Storm out the top hatch and killed the others. Fire and secondary explosions had done the rest.

Storm was saddened at the loss of his men, all of them good men, most of whom were good friends. Particularly Tommy and Martin. He would grieve for them at an appropriate time, but now he had to concentrate on survival and rescue. He was obviously not fit to walk out of Iraq on his own. He had to be at least sixty miles from the line of departure, where the Division support elements were. There was no way to know where his platoon or battalion HQ might be. With the squad radios torched, he had no way to contact them.

He assessed his available assets. The only usable item from the vehicle was one of the water cans. He un-strapped the can and placed it on the ground, being careful not to twist his spine. Not one of the M-16 rifles was usable; the stocks were melted, their actions fused. Likewise for the machineguns. All the MREs were burned up. He had his compass, binoculars, a few snack bars, five gallons of fresh water, a singed map, a lighter, some matches, survival mirror, and two-quart canteen. His 9 millimeter Berretta, three 14 round magazines and his deadly Kung Fu-trained hands comprised his entire arsenal; it was nowhere near enough to defend himself if he were spotted by an Iraqi patrol. He decided to maintain low profile and sharp lookout during daylight.

He looked for a spot to hide and noticed that the array of planks had a definite shape. It wasn't just a hodge-podge pile of planks; it had form. The bomb blasts had apparently blown enough of the sand from around the wood that Storm could make out the rough outline of an old ship.

"Geez. It looks like those boats in Hong Kong harbor in the Kung Fu movies," he mumbled. "How the hell did a Hong Kong boat get buried in the Iraqi desert?" And what were the chances of bombs uncovering it without destroying it? The proverbial hand of God? He shook his head in disbelief.   "Yeah, right. A Chinese ship in the Iraqi desert. I can see it now, trying to explain it to my friends, 'No shit. I found a Chinese ship in Iraq. Yeah, sure. Say Sarge, aren't you due for a drug test?'"

Storm decided he could use planks for a rescue signal. Splinters could be used as tinder to start fires for signals and warmth. At night he would dig a small cavern into the sand, next to the boat wreck, shielded from the outside to hide the glow.

Storm set about surviving. He downed all of his remaining snack bars and drank his fill of water from his canteen. He spent his first hour slowly dragging loosened planks into the middle of the trench and placing them in the shape of a large H, signaling that a survivor needed help. The dark rotted wood, laid out end-to-end until thirty feet in length, contrasted nicely with the sand and should be easy to spot from low flying aircraft. He spent a few more minutes erecting a small pile of splintered wood near the H and prepared tinder to set it ablaze on short notice.

Then he referred to his charred map and attempted to fix his position, not an easy thing to do without GPS in a desert with few landmarks. One sand dune looks like the next and they all move with the winds over time. He determined he would have to climb out of the trench to get a better view of his surroundings. He filled his canteen from the five-gallon can. It was very difficult balancing the heavy can with his good arm while holding the flimsy canteen between his knees. Half of the water made it into the canteen, the other half spilled over his legs and into the sand. The water felt good on his burned legs but he made a mental note to fashion a funnel for next time. He couldn't afford to waste that precious fluid, not knowing how long he might be stranded.

He chambered a round into his Berretta, then struggled to the far side of the trench, lugging the water can to the base of the shallowest incline. Leaving the can, he carefully climbed up the slope on the eastern side of the trench. It took four long minutes to negotiate the grade.

Storm eased to the ground as he approached the crest, careful not to present a silhouette. Cautiously, he peeked over the edge and surveyed the terrain. He could see the Euphrates River a hundred and fifty meters to his northeast. He knew he was south of phase line Celia and north of last night's rally point. He used his compass to get reverse azimuths from several points along the river and mentally triangulated his position on his map, but made no marks on it; less to explain during interrogation should he be captured. Through his binoculars he scanned the horizon and sky. There were no signs of human life anywhere, friend or foe. Just burned out vehicles, some still ablaze. Only high altitude wispy contrails and the dissipated roar of jet engines high overhead broke the whisper of the winter wind. Several cormorants flocked at the edge of the river. At least the sun was warm, he thought, and then wondered what cormorant tasted like. *'Probably like chicken. Everything else did.'* Maybe he'd find out in the near future.

Storm decided to stay near the top of the trench during daylight hours, in the hope he could signal friendly forces and maintain surveillance for enemy soldiers. At night, he would descend back into the trench to shelter from the cold and build a small fire that would be unobserved from above the rim of the trench. Storm kept an eye out for possible rescue opportunities and unexpected threats as he buried himself partly in the sand for camouflage. He readied his signal mirror.

As the day wore on, his mind drifted back to better times: Kung Fu training with his father and Master Chin, old girlfriends, high school, basic training, church and other matters. Those memories seemed preferable to his present predicament. The pain from his burns was occasionally eclipsed by the twinge in his back or the agony from his broken forearm. What if he was presumed dead and they left Iraq without him? After all, the firefight had been at night and to his knowledge, no one had seen him ejected from the vehicle. He was probably considered KIA, along with the others of his squad.

The day passed without any hint of rescue. At nightfall Storm decided to return down the incline, retrieve the water can and seek shelter amongst the rubble of the ancient vessel. He spent an agonizing hour covering his footprints in the sand, digging out a small shelter at the shipwreck and piling the sand around himself, leaving several ventilation holes. He used splintered planks to build a small fire. It cut the evening chill and made the night bearable. He remembered the jade objects and pulled them out to examine them in the flickering firelight. They were quite beautiful, definitely oriental. *"How had they come to be in Iraq? Buried in a box in a Chinese ship in the damned desert?"*

Storm drifted off to sleep, not deep, but the combat sleep of soldiers, waking at every odd noise or smell. The night progressed slowly as Storm conserved his energy and attempted to ignore his pain.

The high-pitched whine of a low flying aircraft woke Storm. His watch indicated 0652. He shoveled aside the sand and crawled out. He attempted to signal the aircraft, thinking it was piloted, but the white, unmanned Predator drone headed northwest and turned into a speck on the horizon, never altering course.

Storm collected his water can, took his fill and secured the lid tightly. He eased his way to the far incline and climbed to the crest again, covering himself in sand. His eyes were never at rest, constantly scanning the terrain and the sky for movement. The hours wore on as they had the previous day, interrupted by only one moment of excitement. Storm had dozed off shortly after noon and was awakened by something crawling across his arm. The Sergeant opened his eyes and found himself staring at a large black scorpion, its tail curled ominously. He managed to shake the thing off before it could strike and brushed it away with his binoculars. He watched the ugly creature scurry off.

A glint of light over the southern horizon caught Storm's attention. He focused his binoculars and searched. Forms began to take shape. One object became two, then became four. They were flying a course that would bring them close to his position and they were down on the deck, maybe a hundred feet above ground. The spots turned into A-10s as they rapidly closed on him. Storm readied his survival mirror, noted the angle of the sun, aligned the shiny surface toward the aircraft and began flashing and praying.

∞

USAF Captain Mike Starr piloted his A-10 aircraft, call sign Crush four-one, as he led his four-ship northwest, bound for their assigned patrol sector. They were out to smash Iraqi armor further north and provide air support for the advancing Infantry. En route, they were paralleling the Euphrates and searching the river and highway for targets of opportunity.

"Crush four-four has a signal mirror, left nine o'clock, four miles." The UHF radio call came from his number four wingman. Mike clicked his microphone switch twice to acknowledge and looked left. Sure enough, someone on the ground was signaling. No telling whom it could be, but it appeared to be signal flashes from a survival mirror. He glanced down at his navigation chart, estimated the position and noted the bearing and distance from the reference point they called "bulls-eye."

He switched to the UHF emergency channel and transmitted, "Signaler at Bulls-eye, three-three-zero for sixty-five miles, this is Crush four-one on Guard. Come up voice." Mike signaled his wingmen and began a hard tactical turn around the ground signal and his wingmen adjusted their positions to maintain a tactical spread formation. Mike hoped the signaler would come up on the UHF radio emergency channel and identify himself. After several transmissions and no response, Mike told his number three wingman to switch to rescue frequency and see if there were any aircraft down. The wingman acknowledged as the flight climbed to a higher tactical orbit over the site. A minute later the wingman reported back that there were no known Coalition aircraft down but there had been ground action near that location two nights previous.

Mike had to make a decision. The signaler was persistent, constantly flashing at them, the radar warning receiver didn't show any missile threats and no enemy troops could be seen in the area. Either this was a friendly who wanted to be spotted or an ambush to lure the A-10s into range of anti-aircraft guns. Mike decided to take a chance.

"Crush four-one is going down for a closer look. Three, you have the lead. Hold high and fast. If I draw fire, roll in hot and smoke 'em."

"Crush four-three has the lead. Ninety-left, now. Combat spread." The number three wingman took lead of the flight and adjusted the formation. Mike increased speed as he nosed over the Warthog, so nicknamed by Air Force pilots, owing to its ugly profile, and headed for the deck. He kept his speed fast as he flew past the signaler at low altitude. He could see a man waving boldly. He appeared to be an American soldier, alone and not far from several burned out armored vehicles. A large H was on the ground not far from his position. There wasn't any ground fire coming up at him, the situation was stable.

"This is Crush four-one. I have one friendly on the deck. No sign of enemy or hostile fire. I'm going in low and slow for a better look. Keep high cover."

"Crush four-three, roger."

Mike extended his flight path out and slowed his airspeed, then turned back to fly over the signaler. He was definitely an American soldier. As he passed directly over the soldier, he pulled up and executed an aileron roll to let the signaler know rescue was on the way.

"This is Crush four-one. I'm gonna be off freq to notify Search and Rescue."

"Crush four-three, roger."

Starr switched to rescue frequency as he climbed to rejoin his wingmen.

"Smack niner-six. Smack niner-six. This is Crush four-one on frequency Amber."

The response from the orbiting Command and Control C-130 came immediately. "Crush four-one, this is Smack niner-six. Authenticate Lima-Tango."

Starr checked his code page for the proper response. He keyed his radio, "This is Crush four-one. I authenticate Quebec. Over."

"This is Smack niner-six. Authentication Quebec confirmed. Go ahead Crush four-one."

"This is Crush four-one. One friendly in need of pickup at Bulls-eye three-two-niner slash sixty-three. I say again, one friendly for pickup, Bulls-eye, three-two-niner slash sixty-three. How copy? Over."

"This is Smack niner-six. We copy. Bulls-eye. 3-2-9 slash 63. We have Smack zero-six available for immediate. E-T-A four-zero minutes. Do you have voice contact with survivor?"

"This is Crush four-one. That's a negative but he definitely looks like one of ours and is using standard visual signals. No sign of hostiles. LZ looks safe."

Starr rejoined his flight, changed frequency to the AWACS mission controller and reported the situation. He was instructed to provide cover for the soldier and the rescue chopper. Starr acknowledged, resumed lead of the flight and they orbited in tactical formation overhead. Now their job was guardian angel.

∞

Storm thought the A-10s hadn't seen him and were flying away. But they turned in a sharp box-like pattern around his position; their flight paths crossed so closely, Storm thought he was going to see a mid-air collision. A minute later, one of them descended and came screaming across the desert about thirty feet off the deck and four hundred miles an hour. Storm waved at the attack aircraft as it passed yards away.

Storm watched as the jet turned back around and came right back over him at slower speed. Just as it passed over, the pilot pulled up and did a slow roll. Storm felt relief. He had been found. Search and Rescue would come to get him. He watched the jet climb back up to altitude and orbit, apparently to mark his position or provide cover for the rescue chopper. He wasn't sure which and he didn't care. The good guys were now his personal protectors. Storm dropped to his knees, clasped his hands as best he could, and gave thanks to God for deliverance. He made his way down the incline to light the signal fire. Rising smoke would provide a discernable vertical signal above the rim of the trench to the inbound, low-level rescue chopper. He flashed his mirror at the A-10s occasionally to make sure they didn't lose interest. Then he sat down slowly, nursed his wounds, hoping the Rescue showed up soon... with hot chow.

∞

The rhythmic whop-whop-whop of a large helicopter echoed through the trench and Storm absentmindedly twisted, being rewarded with a breath-sucking protest from his back. The rotor thumps grew louder from the direction of the battle two nights ago. Storm carefully raised to his feet and plunged his morphine injector into his hip; he had reserved it until he was certain of rescue, not wanting to be groggy should enemy soldiers come upon him. With the A-10s overhead and the rescue chopper closing, he felt elated. A whirlwind of rotor wash advanced over the trench embankment, blasting sand downward and outward for thirty yards below the huge Air Force helicopter. Storm could see two pilots through the windscreens and a man hanging out the side door. Until now, he had not liked helicopters. To him they were overly complicated contraptions; thousands of fast-moving parts in close formation and easy to shoot down. But this one had an aura of precious life. It was the best damned flying machine he'd ever seen.

The chopper set down in the trench about fifty yards from Storm and the engine retarded to idle speed, letting the sand settle enough to allow Storm to walk toward it. Two helmeted men jumped out of the side door and jogged toward Storm, each aiming an M-16 rifle. Storm waved wearily at them. One of the men signaled Storm to sit on the ground. He did so, gingerly.

They identified themselves as Air Force Search and Rescue. Storm noticed the multitude of subdued blue Air Force enlisted stripes on their sleeves. One had five stripes, the other had six. These were senior Air Force Sergeants. The higher-ranking Sergeant spoke first, his southern drawl obvious.

"Looks like y'all had quite a ruckus out here. There's two burned up Bradley's and seven smoking T-72s and a dozen flamed BMPs topside. You boys kicked ass."

Storm, giddy from the morphine, drawled back, "Well, I'd 'a cleaned up the place if I'd known you were comin'."

The rugged Rescue Sergeants chuckled and assessed Storm's injuries. Storm told them where it hurt and they went to work. Their discussion of his injuries and treatment went mostly in one of Storm's ears and out the other. This was the least amount of pain he'd felt in thirty-six hours. They treated his burns and decided to leave the field splint in place on his arm.

"Y'all did a mighty fine job with that splint, Staff Sergeant," complimented the senior.

"Shucks. 'T weren't nothin'."

One of them placed a brace around his neck while the other returned to the chopper. He was back a minute later with a backboard. They placed the board on the ground and told Storm to roll over onto it. Eagerly, but gingerly, Storm complied. The Sergeants strapped him to the board, then lifted him and shuffled to the chopper. As they neared the rotor wash, Storm closed his eyes to keep the swirling sand out. They slid the board into the chopper and secured it to the floor with tie-downs. Next came an IV drip. Before long, Storm slipped into blackness.

∞

Overhead, Mike Starr saw the Rescue chopper lift off, turn southward in a hover, then climb for altitude. He was curious.

"How's our boy doing, Smack?"

The chopper responded with Storm's status and known injuries.

"Where you taking him?"

"Papa Sierra," meaning Prince Sultan Air Base.

"Is he enlisted or officer?"

"This is Smack zero-six. PJs tell me he's E-6, Army."

"Thanks much. Take care of our boy. I'll find you at the O-Club tonight and buy you guys a few."

"Sounds like a deal. Smack zero-six, out."

Mike made a mental note to track down the Rescue guys back at base and keep his promise. He also wanted to know who the survivor was, but business first. His flight still had ninety minutes of station time remaining and there were still Iraqi assets to be hammered. He banked his Warthog northward while monitoring his wingmen and transmitted, "Crush flight, go to frequency Gold."

∾

Four days later, with the war over, Storm lay in bed at an Army field hospital. When he had first regained consciousness three days ago, he was in the Air Force hospital at the Air Base, naked under the sheets in a comfortable bed, a cast around his left arm and upper torso. It was a superior facility compared to the Army Field Hospital. He had been in an air-conditioned room in an air-conditioned building in a real hospital bed with clean sheets. There was even a radio in the room airing the Armed Forces Network. The Air Force doctors and staff had been great. They had treated his burns, set his broken bone and cast his arm, relocated his shoulder and had run X-rays of his back. The doctor informed him of his condition. The shoulder had been reset and should heal just fine, same for his arm. His burns were mostly first degree and would take several weeks to heal, but the second-degree burns on his left leg would give him pain for some time and take longer. The X-rays showed damage to his lower spine. An MRI would be required to more clearly define the extent of the injury, but that would have to be done in Germany. Back surgery would probably be necessary. He was looking at six to eight months of convalescence and rehab.

The day after that, Storm was transferred to the Army field hospital, a bare bones tent operation out in the sand. No more air-conditioned rooms for this lowly grunt soldier. There was heating and air-conditioning of sorts, but in a tent in the blowing sands it wasn't very effective. But all things considered, he was thankful for the attention to his wounds. He saw one soldier several bunks down who was missing a leg and thanked God he was whole.

The second day after he arrived at the Army tent hospital, he discovered he'd lost track of his personal items, uniform and equipment. Initially he felt anger, then worry, finally depression. The Army staffers were too busy tending wounded Iraqi soldiers captured during the coalition offensive to take time to track down his personal belongings. Then to make matters even more depressing, a Major from Battalion S-2 Intelligence section showed up with his lap dog Lieutenant and debriefed him. The debrief was anything but brief. It took hours, repeatedly going over what he knew, which was almost nothing. By the time it was over, Storm felt like a load of laundry after spin cycle.

Storm had lots of time to reflect. The loss of his friends hit him hard by the third day. He felt guilty about being the only survivor of the squad. His men were dead. He wasn't. It was his fault. He was responsible for them. There must have been something he could have done differently. Why his men? And why had God spared him? The same questions rebounded in his mind through that day and evening. The doubts slowly ebbed. Realization that he couldn't have changed events became a sobering reality.

"Sergeant Storm, you have a visitor."

Storm looked toward the beckoning voice at the doorway and saw a man's silhouette walking toward his bunk. Out of the glare emerged an Air Force pilot, a Captain, walking erectly and confidently, carrying a small duffel bag.

"Are you Staff Sergeant Derek Storm?" asked the Captain with an unmistakable Bostonian accent.

"Yes, sir. Sorry I can't get up."

"That's okay. Relax. I'm just here for a friendly visit." The Captain extended his right hand to Storm and introduced himself. "I'm Captain Mike Starr. I was leading a four-ship of A-10s a few days ago near the Euphrates River and we spotted a mirror flash from the ground from a lone soldier. Was that you, by chance?"

Storm gripped the offered hand and returned the firm, manly handshake.

"I think so. How…what…how did you track me down?"

"It was pretty easy. The Rescue team told me the survivor was an Army Staff Sergeant and they were taking him to the hospital at Prince

Sultan. I ran into the chopper pilots at the Officers Club and they gave me your name. When I checked with the hospital, they had no problem tracking you down and told me you were transferred here. Simple."

Storm was surprised that an Air Force officer would go out of his way to track down an average infantry grunt. He was flabbergasted.

"Sir, that was you who spotted me?"

"Actually, it was one of my wingmen."

"Then you guys orbited over me the whole time. I'm so grateful…" Storm choked a little. "I…I don't have the words to thank you enough. I was worried about being left behind in Iraq while the whole Army went back to the States."

The Captain grinned and patted Storm on his good shoulder. "No chance of that. Once we spot a survivor, we make every effort to recover him. I'm not going to leave a man behind unless I know in my heart I've done everything within my power to recover him. I couldn't look at myself in the mirror otherwise."

Storm lowered his eyes and nodded agreement. "Thank you, sir."

"You're welcome, Sergeant. Besides, if I was shot down and you found me, you'd rescue me, wouldn't you?"

"Absolutely, sir. But thanks again, just the same."

"How are your injuries?"

Storm related his condition and likely prospects of surgery and therapy. The conversation shifted to more mundane matters: families, hobbies, etc. Storm related the incident of the cute nurse back at the Air Force hospital, who had her tush groped by a horny wise-ass Infantry Sergeant and how the wise-ass ended up with sore testicles. Starr grimaced in sympathetic pain as they laughed.

After the laughter subsided, Starr hefted the small duffel bag onto the bunk.

"I almost forgot. They gave me your gear. It looks like it might be the clothes and equipment you had on when they admitted you at the Air Force hospital."

Storm was elated. He struggled with the duffel's clasp with his good hand. Starr lent a hand. Storm rummaged through the contents while thanking the Captain. "I was worried that I'd lost this stuff. I want to show you something… if I can find them." Storm shifted the contents around while Starr held open the duffel. Storm found one of the articles. He pulled out the largest of the three artifacts, the carved jade palace.

"Look at this, sir."

The Captain gazed at the magnificent jade sculpture. "That's beautiful. Where'd you get it?"

Storm related how he had discovered the pieces. He rummaged around in the duffel, found the others and showed them to Starr. Storm noticed the Captain was fond of the large jade sculpture and made a decision.

"Captain. I'd like you to have that sculpture. It's the least I could do."

Starr was dumbstruck. Now it was his turn to be speechless, which wasn't often. "That's very kind of you, Sarge, but it's not necessary."

"I insist, sir."

"I didn't come here for a reward. Besides…"

"It's for saving my life, it's…"

"..it might be really valuable.."

"…not a reward, sir. It's a symbol of my gratitude and I would be deeply offended if you refused my gift." Storm managed to get the last word. The Captain realized this was an honorable and generous young man. To refuse his gift could insult his honor. He curled the ends of his mouth up into a tight grin and looked away from Storm, considering his response.

"Sergeant Storm, you're quite a piece of work."

"Hoo-ah."

"Hoo-ah back at ya." Starr decided to accept the Sergeant's gracious offer, with conditions. "Storm… Derek, I accept your generous gift on the condition we keep in touch after all this. Agreed?"

Storm offered his hand and they shook, knowing they would be in touch in the future. For another two hours they exchanged stories and personal information. Starr had plans to take an airline job on the east coast after his combat tour.

Storm planned to remain in the Army and apply for Special Forces. He had no way of knowing that the future held other prospects for him, daring and dangerous prospects.

CHAPTER III

THE DOCTORS

Portland, Oregon, February 2002

MEDICAL MONTHLY: The Official Publication of the National Organization of Medical Professionals

DDCG: Key to the Cure? Recent developments from the research laboratory of the Flynn Medical Group, Portland, Oregon have raised the hopes of thousands in the search for the cure for cancer. Extensive enzyme research by Dr. Peter Flynn, Ph.D., a biochemical engineer and his brother Dr. Daniel Flynn, oncologist, partners of the Flynn Medical Group, have discovered an approach to boosting the metabolic rate of specific enzymes that may be used to literally "eat" cancerous cells within the human body, then be expelled through the normal metabolic and excretory processes.

"This is an exciting discovery and I believe we are on the verge of a breakthrough in cancer research," stated Dr. Peter Flynn. "Our new compound, DDCG, used in conjunction with certain enzymes, has shown dramatic results. I look forward to the day we can cure cancer without the debilitating side effects of radiation and chemotherapy."

The Doctors have been engaged in cancer research in their private facility for five years, taking avenues previously not researched. For further information on DDCG and the Flynn research, log onto our website at www…"

It was a typically busy day at the medical offices of the Flynn Medical Group and a typical Portland day in February: forty-two degrees, overcast, cold rain and dreary. Dreary, but busy. The medical needs of the city didn't slow down for a rain shower. Far into the afternoon, patients poured into the office with the cadence of a fine Swiss watch.

The Flynn Medical Group had been in operation for three decades, expanding as successive generations of Flynn family doctors filled in the practice begun by the grandfather, Dr. Fergus Flynn. It now occupied its own city block near University Hospital, its four-story building jutting prominently above its manicured grounds.

The medical group performed most of their own laboratory work and pharmacology, which helped fund their cancer research laboratory. The first floor hosted their in-house pharmacy as well as various storerooms. The second and third floors housed the heart of the operation. Here, eight doctors and their staff handled the hundred plus patients they saw every working day. The fourth floor housed a medical lab, which handled their X-Ray, blood and urine analysis work, and their Cancer Research Laboratory. All totaled, the group employed forty-eight medical professionals including doctors, nurses, physician assistants, lab techs, pharmacists, office workers and receptionists.

Dr. Peter Flynn glanced up from his work in the Cancer Research Lab and gazed outside. The early dusk was beginning to spread over Portland, indicating it was near time to close shop.

Pete was one year younger than his brother, Dr. Daniel Flynn, the oncologist whose office was on the third floor. The brothers had been in medical school at the same time decades ago when their father was starting the practice. After completing their internships, both melded into the practice. Now their kids were aboard.

Pete was not a medical doctor. He had earned his Ph.D. in biochemical engineering from Notre Dame and for thirty-years had been engaged in research into the human gnome, DNA analysis, and now, cancer research. He was fifty-five years old and still had all of his own hair, even though the grayness lightened his wavy brown locks. He carried his five foot ten inch height on a one hundred sixty pound frame, kept in shape by frequent jogging and racquetball; that and spending most of his working days on his feet.

He launched himself into cancer research in 1997 after losing his wife, Katherine, to ovarian cancer. He knew he couldn't bring her back but he believed he could find a cure for the malady that had ravaged her beauty and her life. Tens of thousands of people died each year from this malady. A cure had to be found and Pete was determined to do it.

The research lab on the fourth floor was a large open space, secured by an electronic cipher lock on its only door, and equipped with hundreds of thousands of dollars worth of research equipment, pharmaceuticals, specimens, test animals, supplies and one large steel, fireproof firearm vault internally bolted to both the floor and the wall. Pete and Dan had spent weeks evaluating various vaults and decided that this particular gun safe was best suited to their needs. It was large, climate-controlled, rugged, fireproof and immovable.

Pete concentrated on the readout of his most recent enzyme analysis. The latest results were promising. The enzyme consumption rates were greatly increased by using a chemical compound he had developed. He was attempting to get the enzymes to literally "eat" cancerous tumor cells at such a fast rate the cancer would be consumed before it could infiltrate healthy tissue. His special compound, doxodigallocatechin gallate, or DDCG, was mixed in solution with a proteolytic enzyme called matrix metalloproteinase, which was known to break down cancer cells, but not fast enough to keep them from invading healthy tissues around the tumor, in effect helping the tumor to grow. The enzymes alone didn't eat the cancer cells fast enough. But with a significant metabolic boost, the enzymes could theoretically devour the cancerous cells, then be de-boosted and evacuated through the body's normal cleansing process. But there were still side effects to be tested before he could expand upon his recently published findings in Medical Monthly, the most widely read medical periodical on the continent.

Alvin Hayes, Pete's forty year old, rotund lab assistant, looked past Pete's shoulder at the analysis. Al, a biochemist in his own right, though not a Ph.D., had been working with Pete for three years, using this job as a resume builder. Al had aspirations of his own, namely, snagging a research job at a major biochemical company. He enjoyed his work with Pete, liked the affable man, but the pay and benefits at the big labs were far superior and he would take any reasonable job offer.

"How's it look, Doc?"

"Well, there appears to be another marginal increase in the rate, but I'm not sure it'll be enough."

"So what's your next step?"

Pete sighed and contemplated before answering. "We'll probably have to play with the concentration ratios; see if we can find a mix that yields an optimum rate. But this is the best results we've had."

Al grinned and nodded.

"Tell you what, Al. Let's get squared away and call it an early day. I could sure use one, that is, if you're up to it."

"Okay, you got it, Doc. You don't have to ask me twice."

Al and Pete went through their twenty-minute routine of securing the lab for the evening. Al rounded up the used beakers and placed them in the sterilizer, stowed the lab animals in their cages and straightened up the lab. Pete shut down the electronic equipment and stored the most expensive pieces in the vault along with the test data and computer CDs. Only the most sensitive research data went into the vault. Only Pete and Dan knew the combination. Routine files were stashed in the metal file cabinet or left on file in password-protected computers.

Al bid good night and headed for home, passing Dan just outside the door. Dan managed to catch the door before it latched and stepped into the lab. Pete greeted him with a soft smile.

"Hi, Dan. How'd rounds go today?"

"Sad day. Mrs. Hopkins's lymphoma has taken a turn for the worse and Mr. Morrison finally succumbed. May he rest in peace."

Pete sympathized with Dan. It wasn't easy watching patients die slow, painful deaths. Lord knew how difficult it had been for Pete to watch his beloved, beautiful Katherine waste away.

"Dan, even as good a doctor as you are, you know you can't save them all. Some things are just out of our hands."

Dan nodded solemn acceptance. "I know that, but it still gets to me sometimes. It's not possible to turn it off every time."

"Well, at least there's good news on the research side." Pete   told Dan of his latest successful test of DDCG with enzymes. The discussion sparked Dan's interest and took his mind away from the morbid suffering of his patients.

Dan was five feet eleven, with graying, wavy brown hair and light brown eyes. He too carried his one hundred seventy pounds on an athletic frame, often squaring off with his brother on the racquetball court. He also managed an occasional round of golf, preferring to walk. Dan had a pleasant face that conveyed his gentle nature and caring attitude. One look at the two and one could easily see they were brothers.

Pete summarized, "After all the unsuccessful trials at inhibiting heterocyclic amines and the endothelial growth factors, I was beginning to think there was no end to the dark tunnel. But if I can get this boosted enzyme theory to work *and* find a substance that can inhibit ornithine decarboxylase, we'll have something to develop."

Dan nodded and gently slapped his brother's back in congratulations. They walked out together, stopping on the third floor at Dan's office, making arrangements for their next racquetball challenge. Pete left for the evening while Dan tended to his patients. The office bustled for another hour, then staffers filtered out as their shifts ended. Dan was the last to leave the building, as usual. He checked the doors were locked, dimmed the lights and exited by the rear door after arming the security system. He extended his umbrella and made his way to his car. He climbed into his vehicle and drove for home. He pulled into the rush hour traffic, not noticing two stocky men in dark gray suits who emerged from a faded blue Toyota just around the corner and confidently walked to the rear door of his building.

Boston, Massachusetts: The National Organization of Medical Professionals, NOMP, made its headquarters in Boston. The forty-year-old organization was a professional association of medical workers that established standards for medical personnel, reviewed medical procedures and exercised considerable lobbying power across the nation, but especially in D.C. Its membership consisted of most medical professions: physicians, nurses, therapists, radiologists, and lab technicians. The hundreds of thousands of members contributed funds monthly, many directly through payroll deductions, providing the organization with millions of dollars for their operations and lobbying efforts.

The thirty-six members of the Board of Directors sat around a huge polished mahogany conference table in the dark stained, oak paneled boardroom. The medical professions were represented on the board in proportion to the membership, but the chairmanship, vice-chairmanship and all national committee chairmanships were reserved for MDs. The other professions could hold the national offices of treasurer, secretary or director of the national districts or serve as vice-chairman of the national committees. All of the MDs on the current board had been previous hospital administrators but none had seen the inside of an examination or operating room in more than a decade. They were now paper-shufflers, more involved with lobbying than actual medicine.

NOMP was most noted for its massive successful lobbying campaign during the nineties to defeat proposed national health care legislation that threatened medical workers with being charged with crimes for providing private medical services to patients. They astutely saw the threat to their livelihoods and the care of their patients and countered the threat with every resource at their command. The radical, proposed government takeover of the health care industry, which comprised one-seventh of the national economy, was soundly thrashed before it could even make it out of committee.

The current Chairman of the Board, Dr. Leon Sampson, was a likable man in his late sixties who had not seen a patient in twenty years but did genuinely care for the health needs of the public. He was very skilled at administration and organization, chaired an orderly meeting and gave each board member an equal opportunity to present his or her thoughts.

The current matter before them had been placed on the agenda by board member Melanie Taylor, one of two board members representing the therapist members. There was in progress orderly, but heated, discussion over the admission of other health care fields into NOMP. Melanie was concluding her presentation and preparing for the avalanche of protests and questions that were sure to follow.

"In conclusion, based upon the data, I suggest NOMP open our membership to health care workers of alternative treatments to cancer." Melanie paused briefly at the conclusion of her presentation and addressed the chairman.

"I'm prepared to entertain questions and comments, Dr. Sampson."

Sampson thanked her and opened the floor to questions. The first to signal was Dr. Ardmore Rushton, a cynical, six-foot tall, swarthy-looking MD in his mid-forties, who was the political nemesis of the non-MD professions; he was arrogant and egotistical. He was also the Executive Director of Operations, calling the daily shots on the national operations and lobbying efforts. He was recognized.

"Thank you, Mr. Chairman and thank you for that splendid presentation, Ms. Taylor. I'd like to point out that we have considered this matter before and it been resoundingly defeated several times and, in my opinion, it would be an ineffective use of this board's time to delve into redundant discussion on this matter. I move we table this until we have empirical data that conclusively shows these alternative treatments are effective. Otherwise, we'd just be admitting quacks and charlatans, diminishing our image and prestige."

Sampson considered the comments. "I'm aware the board has

previously rejected similar proposals, Dr. Rushton. However, some of the new evidence, particularly that from Dr. Flynn in Portland, seems to have marginal credence. I think we should take a few minutes to evaluate the data and its implications. I don't consider his research to be quackery. It may actually hold some promise. Do you have questions, Dr. Rushton?"

"Yes, Mr. Chairman." Rushton turned to Melanie, "Just how do these alternative treatment methods advance the mission of NOMP?"

Melanie referred to her notes, "Dr. Rushton, and fellow board members, recent test data from Portland, Norway, Mexico and Germany suggest certain alternative cancer treatments have equivalent or better success rates as compared to radiation and chemotherapy, without the side affects of either. That being the case, shouldn't we consider giving status to the service providers of these methods, granting membership into NOMP, thereby expanding our organization?" Melanie played her deep pocket card, knowing that the board members would seriously weigh the effect on the bottom line, even though she personally wanted to see certain alternative medicine treatments recognized. She was the genuine article, a true health care professional who considered it her life's career to provide the most effective treatment available to sick people, even if those methods didn't fit the mainstream.

Another board member, Roberta Salerna, a representative of the Physicians Assistants, posed a question. " Melanie, exactly which alternative *disciplines* are you considering with this proposal?" Her sarcasm was blatant.

"For one, the providers of diet and nutrition treatment, such as in Mexico. Two, those that provide preventive measures with immune system co-factors. Also, the electrolytic immersion therapy for toxin removal seems effective and they may be considered as well."

Several members took the floor in turn, commenting on the quackery of alternative methods, treating patients with leeches and voodoo. A few though, weighed in on the affirmative side. Drs. Rushton, Raas, and Nurse Miller pushed for an immediate vote by the board.

With discussion concluded, Dr. Sampson asked the board for a motion. Rushton immediately made a motion for a vote. It was quickly seconded. The chairman called for a show of hands in favor, then against. The ayes won.

"On the matter of recognizing providers of alternative health services for admission to NOMP, all in favor raise your hands."

Thirteen members voted yes. The board secretary noted the count as Dr. Sampson continued, "All opposed?" Twenty members raised their hands. Two abstained.

"The motion to recognize and admit has failed, twenty to thirteen with two abstentions. Motion is denied. Alternative medicine methods and the providers of those services will not be recognized as medically qualified providers of health care and will be denied admission to NOMP. This matter is closed. That being the final item on the agenda, I'll entertain a motion to adjourn."

"I move we adjourn," piped up Miller.

"I second," added Salerna.

"All in favor say aye."

"Aye," responded the overwhelming majority.

"Meeting adjourned."

The board members gathered their documents and brief cases and streamed out of the room. Melanie and others made plans for dinner while Rushton, Raas and Miller retreated to Rushton's office.

After closing and locking the door, Rushton instructed his secretary to hold all calls. He turned to Raas, who was mixing drinks at the elaborate mirrored wet bar. He swirled the drinks and passed them to Rushton and Miller, then took his own and sipped the scotch as he sat on the couch. Miller was already seated and Rushton sank into his high-backed, leather swivel chair and leaned back arrogantly, placing his feet on the desktop.

Raas broke the silence. "That Taylor is a pain in the ass. What are we going to do about it?"

Miller added, "She refuses to see the economic impact. Thousands of radiologists and chemotherapists will be out of work. Where would that leave the NOMP? In the toilet. I've tried to convince her, but she's just too goody-goody to be swayed."

Rushton was pensive, staring at his office wall. Finally, he chipped in. "I'm not really concerned about the alternative methods as much as I am about the enzyme protocol being developed in Portland by, what's his name…Flynn?"

"Yeah," answered Raas.

"If this ParaZyme 2000 has anything to it, the radiologists and chemotherapists will be out of work anyway. Oncology will take a different course and thousands of medical workers could have their life-styles drastically changed, of course, seriously impacting our status here."

Raas interjected, "And that fool Sampson keeps giving credence to Taylor and her cohorts. Each time he does, they gain votes. First they had five, last time nine, today thirteen with two abstentions. They're gaining ground. If we don't take measures soon, they could control the board after the national elections next week."

"Don't fret," assured Rushton. "I have a plan. Right after the national elections, we'll unseat Sampson from the chairmanship and replace him with someone more to our liking."

"Like, maybe, you?" quipped Miller.

"The thought had crossed my mind," replied Rushton, with an egotistical sneer. "I have a plan and once we have control of the board, we'll have more discretion with the funds."

"Right now, what are we going to do about this enzyme protocol?" inquired Miller.

"We need to suppress it, at least until we figure out how to get a piece of the action. For the time being, just think of it as a work in progress. I've got some people on it." Rushton kicked his feet from the desk and swiveled to gaze out the window, anticipating a call from Portland.

Portland, Oregon: Pete reached to the night stand and pressed off the alarm on his clock radio. He didn't have to look at the digits; it was 5:31 a.m., the same time he awoke every morning, even weekends. Pete lived in a modest apartment, keeping the bare essentials of furniture and furnishings. A college sophomore would have felt right at home. After Katherine had passed away, he sold their house, not being able to sleep in it without her.

He went through his morning ritual and ventured out to the porch to fetch his the newspaper. He padded into the kitchen for a couple cups of green tea as he read the paper.

Finished with the paper, he jogged on his treadmill for thirty minutes, then cooled off and prepared his usual breakfast of yogurt, granola and toast. Then he hit the shower.

An hour later, Pete parked his three-year-old Bonneville in his reserved spot, locked his car with the electronic fob and walked to the rear door. Being the first to arrive, as usual, he disarmed the security system and took the elevator to the fourth floor. He turned on the hall lights and headed for the research lab. He rounded the corner and was shocked, the lab door was wide open, the cipher lock was disassembled and hanging from the wall by its wires. He cautiously approached the doorway, wary.

He didn't see or sense any one else, so he assessed the damage. The equipment had been smashed; glass covered the floor, along with files from the rifled cabinet. One of the computer stacks was missing. The monitors and keyboards were smashed and there were pry marks on the gun safe, although it hadn't been breached. The lab animals were dead. The refrigerator was wide open and all samples were missing. Reference catalogs were scattered across the room, the bookshelf upended and a table overturned.

Pete returned to the hallway and checked the medical lab. Nothing seemed out of place or missing. He thought it best not to touch anything, so he used his cell phone to call the police. After a brief discussion with a dispatcher, Pete canvassed the remaining floors, alert for intruders. Finding every other office intact, he returned to the rear entrance to await the police.

A patrol car with a single officer arrived, lights flashing, seven minutes later. The tall, immaculately uniformed officer questioned Pete about the scene, asking pertinent questions and making suggestions. Then the officer called for the detective squad to investigate. After that, he secured the entrances with yellow tape.

Employees started to arrive, curious about what had happened. Pete told the story numerous times while holding the employees outside the building in the parking lot. He had several of them go around to the front and advise the first arriving patients that they would have to reschedule their appointments after the police completed their work.

Dan arrived, puzzled by the congregation. Pete related his findings as he approached.

"How bad was the damage?" inquired Dan.

"Most of it can be replaced. Fortunately, they couldn't get into the vault. But it's still a hell of a loss. It'll take at least thirty grand to replace the stuff. I hope the insurance covers some of it."

Finally, an unmarked detective car arrived with two plain-clothes officers. They spoke briefly with the patrol officer, then approached Pete and Dan.

"Dr. Flynn?"

"Yes," answered both brothers in unison as they extended their hands. The detectives appeared confused.

"We're both doctors. I'm Pete Flynn. I discovered the break-in. This is my brother, Dr. Daniel Flynn." The four men shook hands and got down to business. The detectives asked them if they had any idea of who might have motive to do the break-in, if they had any enemies or had any threatening or suspicious phone calls recently. The doctors could think of no specific candidates.

"What puzzles me," stated the older detective, "is why would someone break into a building with an advanced, monitored security system, trash the lab, but leave all of the drugs in the pharmacy and treatment rooms, then rearm the system when they left? It's obviously not the work of druggies. It took technical know-how to override the security. Druggies don't have that kind of finesse."

"Considerate research burglars?" Dan posited.

"What kind of research are you working on, Doctor?" asked the second detective.

"We've been researching a cure for cancer called ParaZyme 2000," answered Pete. "It's still in the research stage, far from production, and it was only made public last month."

The detectives glanced at each other then back at the brothers.

"That could explain the timing of the break-in. Was your name specifically mentioned in the press release?"

Pete nodded. "As well as our location."

"Doctor, is it possible a competitor or pharmaceutical company wants to steal your research?"

Pete thought about it. "I suppose so, but if that's the case, there are thousands of suspects. I don't see how you could possibly run down every one. Nor could I expect you to."

The detectives agreed then excused themselves to go investigate the alarm system and the lab.

The brothers discussed their options.

"Pete, if the detective is right, the lab isn't safe here. They could come back at night when you're alone and hurt you. I don't want that on my mind, or my conscience."

"Yeah. You're right. It could place the employees in jeopardy, too."

"They could just keep destroying the lab time and again until we lose our insurance or go broke. It would have the same effect."

Pete grimaced. He knew Dan was right. "I'm the single guy, no house, the kids are grown, and besides, I'm the one doing the research. I think the best option is for me to move the lab to a secret location. Only you and I will know."

"Moving the lab is a good idea. But to keep it secret, don't even tell me where it is. I suggest you select a good location, keep in touch by encrypted e-mail and we'll get funding to you through a blind trust with a Post Office Box. Pay everything through the trust; don't open any personal accounts in your name or social security number. And get rid of your cell phone. Use only e-mail or pay phones. Remember that."

Pete nodded.

The detectives emerged through the rear door and approached the doctors.

"We'll have our forensics people go through the place, but given the precision and discipline required for this job, I doubt they'll find anything substantial as evidence. Do either of you have firearms available for any future occurrences? Concealed Carry Permits?"

The doctors both carried firearms in their vehicles and had others at home but neither would admit it to a cop. They just returned blank stares.

The detective sensed their reluctance to answer. "Well, if you don't have some type of defense, you might want to consider getting some," relayed the senior detective, with a wink. "Our job is to apprehend criminals. We don't provide security services. That's the responsibility of the citizen."

The doctors nodded, understanding exactly what the detective had just said.

"How long do you think your forensics team will need to be inside?" asked Dan.

"I'm guessing it'll take them most of the morning."

Dan was concerned about his scheduled patients. "Detective, the damage seems concentrated on the fourth floor. If I have one assistant go inside to gather up the appointment schedules from the second and third floors, without touching anything else, would that create a problem? We need to notify our patients to reschedule."

The lead detective thought about it and relented. "Okay, Dr. Flynn. Choose two assistants, one for each floor. Detective Cranston and I will accompany them to get your schedules."

"Great. Thank you." Dan turned to his brother. "Pete, may I have your cell?"

"Sure." Pete handed his cell phone to Dan.

Dan hustled off with his and Pete's cell phones in hand. He recruited two staff assistants to go inside with the detectives, gather the appointment schedules, and then contact the patients. The staffers gladly walked off with the detectives.

Dan addressed the loitering employees. "Gang, it looks like we're out of business for the morning, so come back at one this afternoon. Hopefully, the police will be done by then." Noticing the questioning looks, he assured, "And yes, we'll pay you for showing up this morning. See you all at one."

The employees scattered for their vehicles.

Dan had another thought. He walked back to Pete, "Did you check my office, too?"

"Yeah, but I couldn't determine if anything had been disturbed. You might want to have a look yourself."

Dan walked rapidly to the rear entrance, ducked under the police tape and went inside to the elevator. It was already on its way down to the lobby. The door opened and his efficient, pretty staff assistant, Julie, stepped out with Detective Cranston.

"I have the appointments right here, Dr. Flynn."

Dan noticed the young, handsome detective assessing his pretty staff assistant, not ogling, but admiring.

"Good. Would you reschedule them for us, please? Thanks, Julie."

Dan addressed the detective, distracting him from a short daydream as he admired the retreating Julie. She had that effect on men. "Detective, perhaps I should take a quick look into my office on the third floor to see if anything's missing."

" Uh…okay, Doctor. I'll go with you." Dan saw the young man blush slightly. He appeared to be embarrassed. Dan smiled.

The men stepped aboard the elevator and rode to the third floor, then made for Dan's office. The door was unlocked but Dan thought nothing of it, since Pete had mentioned he'd opened it. Dan eased the door open as Detective Cranston peeked past him into the room. The detective politely but firmly pushed Dan aside.

"If I may, Doc. Let me go first, just to be on the safe side."

Dan immediately saw the wisdom and stepped aside as the detective, hand on his holstered revolver, entered the office, looking and listening for any possible threat. The office was not large or ornate and there were few places a perpetrator could hide. The detective stepped across the office to a large wardrobe cabinet, extracted a handkerchief from his pocket and grabbed the handle. He jerked the door open, finding the space behind unoccupied. Then he glanced under the desk. Satisfied, he waved Dan inside.

Dan headed straight for his desk. The detective extended the handkerchief to him. Dan took the cloth without speaking, understanding that the detective wanted him to use it on anything he touched. Dan checked his desk thoroughly, finding nothing amiss. He did the same for his file cabinet and the wardrobe.

"I don't see anything missing or out of place."

Cranston nodded. "In that case, Doc, let's leave and wait for forensics."

They returned to the elevator. Dan was satisfied nothing was missing from his office. He would have been less satisfied if he'd known about the undetected items that had been added to his office; the electronic bugs in his phone and desk lamp. And the one in the research lab.

∞

The spartan storefront office was just that. In a small strip mall in a run-down part of the city, this bare-bones operation sufficed as the Operations Center for some shady characters. The outside was bland, with a trash-strewn parking lot that begged for resurfacing. Windows were cracked and taped, others boarded over. Spider webs cluttered the eaves. There were no advertising signs or logos in the windows and the blinds were drawn closed.

The interior? Little better. It had minimal furniture: a desk, two old chairs, a filing cabinet and a credenza with a copier/fax machine on it. There was a hard wire telephone on the desk, a lamp, a CLOSED sign on the door and not much more. The trash basket was filled with fast food wrappers. The office also had a small unisex bathroom, seldom cleaned, and a storage room. The rent had been paid in cash six months in advance and the utilities listed to a corporation that no one had ever heard of.

Drew Kress, a six foot two, two hundred thirty pound hulk of a man with a scarred left cheek, ran his hand through his thinning brown hair as he waited for the telephone to be answered. After fifteen seconds, he was rewarded by a familiar voice on the other end.

"Yeah, it's me," he said. "The research project was conducted last night. We got some data you might be interested in, but I don't think it's the really juicy stuff you wanted. But I'm no doctor. You'll have to look at this stuff to see if it is." Kress paused for a response.

"Yeah, I think there's more, but we couldn't get it without a cutting torch. Who knew the bastard had a fireproof gun vault?" Kress recoiled from the loud insults being launched at him through the phone line. He wasn't accustomed to that kind of reaction and he didn't like it one bit.

"Be reasonable, Doc. What normal doctor keeps a freakin' gun vault in his office? Do you? We'll go back in a few days after the heat cools down and burn our way in with a cutting torch." He paused for another stream of insults.

"Look. I'll fax this stuff to you. Who knows, maybe the stuff you want is here. If not, we'll go back." Another pause.

"Yeah, the surveillance equipment is in place and we're already wired in. If they mention anything pertinent about the project, we'll keep you posted." Another pause, he silently mimicked the jerk on the other end of the line, his "employer." "Yeah, we took care of the equipment. It'll take them some time to get it all back together." More insults and a warning from the jerk.

"Okay, yeah, yeah…I need to hang up so I can fax you this stuff, or you gonna spend all day talkin' my goddammned ear off?"

Kress hung up.

"What an asshole!"

He stood up and stepped to a closed door behind the desk. He swung the door open. Another large man, dressed in a rumpled off-the-rack suit, sat at a table, wearing headphones and monitoring a tape machine.

"How the bugs workin', Charlie?"

Charlie flashed a thumb up.

∞

FOUR DAYS LATER: It was cold as Dan and Pete stepped outside the twenty-four hour coffee shop into the early morning darkness, each holding a cup of steaming brew.

The plan to move the lab was underway. During the weekend, Pete had removed the most important equipment and data disks from the lab and transferred them to a safe storage. He had everything he needed to move on. He'd given thirty days notice to his landlord and cancelled his utilities, packed his personal belongings, retrieved all of the data and equipment and loaded his Bonneville to the brim. For security, he stayed at Dan's home in a secure, gated community. He had withdrawn six thousand dollars cash from his accounts, electing to use that so his credit cards couldn't be traced. He canned his old cell phone and started a new service under the name of the blind trust that Dan's attorney had set up. His car packed and fueled, Pete was ready to hit the road. He decided to head south for a warmer climate but hadn't told Dan exactly where, as Dan wished. The two-thirty a.m. chill caused them both to shiver slightly as they sipped the hot coffees.

"Well, Dan. I guess it's time to hit the road. I'll be in touch by e-mail."

"I'm sorry that Al's not going with you."

"It's for the best. He wants to move on to a corporate job. Besides, it'll be easier to keep the lab a secret if I'm the only one who knows where it is."

"Right." Dan looked down at his feet, saddened that he might not see Pete for some time. "You be careful. Who knows how rough these bastards could get?"

"I will. I plan to drive around the city, switch back a few times, make a few circles, go in and out a few parking garages, you know, just in case of a tail. Only when I'm sure will I hit the freeway. And I'll only use the cell phone for dire emergencies."

The brothers shook hands and embraced.

Pete climbed into the Bonneville as Dan watched gloomily. A minute later, Pete's Bonneville was on the road to ... wherever.

∞

"Dammit!"

Kress was fit to be hogtied. He and Charlie were standing in the dark, dressed like cat burglars, inside the fourth floor lab of the Flynn Medical Group. Or what used to be the lab.

The lab door was wide open as they wheeled the cutting torch bottles into the room, eager to cut into the gun vault and collect the other half of their pay. But their flashlights revealed a wide open vault door; it was empty.

Boston, Massachusetts: "The national election results are in. Four of the current board members will be replaced next week," stated Rushton, "and three of them were sympathetic to Melanie Taylor. We have a good chance to unseat Sampson at the next board meeting."

"When's that?" inquired Miller.

Raas interjected, "Next week."

The group smiled at the prospect of having majority control of NOMP. They could shape it to their wishes and appropriate funds for whatever operations or lobbying they deemed fit. The membership would pay the assessments almost without question. They toasted, gloated and chuckled.

"What's the status on the ParaZyme 2000?" asked Raas.

Rushton snorted his disgust. "The fools botched it. They didn't get it and I've just learned that the lab is no longer there."

"What? They shut down?"

"No. I think they moved it. But we don't know where."

The conspirators glanced at each other, struggling for an answer of what to do next.

Miller was the first to offer an opinion. "I think we need to get more serious about this. We need some professionals."

Raas added, "I agree. I think we need to go hard press. These petty thugs can't get the job done."

Rushton nodded and contemplated.

"Hard press. Yes, I agree. We'll have to find some real mercenaries, special ops or former CIA types. There's too much at risk. I'll get working on it. Who do we know that has that kind of information? Who do we have in our pocket in congress right now?"

Las Vegas, Nevada: The left punch came at Storm's face quickly, followed by an immediate right elbow toward his left temple. But the sixth degree black belt quickly stepped to the right, outside of the punch, blocked it with an up-windmill, cross-stepped behind his opponent, punched his right fist into the man's left kidney, hooked his right arm under the opponent's right arm from behind, then quickly pivoted counter-clockwise as he threw the adversary onto the flat of his back at Storm's feet. Storm grasped the extended right arm, manipulated the wrist, twisting outward and pressing down until the opponent tapped the mat to signify submission. Storm's workout partner and right hand man, Mark Long, lie at his feet rubbing and flexing his abused wrist. Such was the open workout style of Kung Fu San Soo, an ancient martial art, having its origins in the rugged highlands of southern China.

San Soo is a vicious form of self-defense, savage in intensity and practical in the real world. In fact, in San Soo philosophy there were no rules, no prohibited maneuvers or manipulations, no fancy, flowery names for movements or imitations of animals. Just savage, brutal counter-violence without remorse. The simple techniques worked best. They were easy to remember, easy to practice, savage and lethally effective. Considerable effort had gone into the development of the art over thousands of years in China before it had been brought to the States.

Long twisted his legs in a break dance motion as he swiveled his hips, then arched his back as he pushed with his shoulders and sprang upright onto his feet, then launched another attack on his Sifu, his teacher. The hopping front kick nearly caught Storm's head, but a quick duck, followed by a downward left punch into Mark's cup-protected groin stopped the assault and Storm's reverse spin kick swept out the only leg Mark could land on. He slammed flat onto his back again, legs apart and both arms smacking the mat to help absorb the impact. Sifu Storm slid between Mark's sprawled legs like a hockey skater, pressed his knees outward on the inside of Mark's knees, exposing the groin and stomach to further punishment. At the submission, Storm allowed Long to recover and rise to his feet.

Storm glanced at the wall clock and noticed it was time to close shop for the day.

"Good workout, Mark. Thanks for stretching me a bit today."

"My pleasure, Sifu." The young man rubbed his stomach and shrugged his shoulders to stretch his abused back muscles. Mark Long was a young firebrand who practiced San Soo with a vigor and discipline that Storm appreciated. That's why Storm had promoted him quickly over the last four years. He was currently Storm's highest-ranking student, his newest black belt, his right hand man and his assistant instructor.

"See you tomorrow morning for the eight o'clock class?"

"Wouldn't miss it, Sifu."

The two men regularly sparred for twenty minutes during the late afternoon after the day's classes were completed. Storm was relieved he didn't have an evening class scheduled tonight. He was looking forward to having the night off, especially since his girlfriend recently bailed out on him; the lack of commitment issue. *What is it with women? They date you for two months then expect an engagement ring and a house. What ever happened to dating just for the sake of dating?* He was a little bummed out over the whole thing, but, hey, there were other fish in the sea, especially the huge sea of beautiful women in Las Vegas.

The years since being medically discharged from the Army proved to be both struggle and blessing for Storm. The back surgery in Germany proved successful, but not one hundred percent. He still encountered a painful twinge from his lower back on occasion, so he'd been medically discharged with a twenty percent disability in 1993. Fortunately, his left arm and shoulder healed without any complications and the burns on his legs healed with minimal scarring. But his Army career was over, crushing his chances to get into Special Forces.

He immersed himself into Kung Fu again, having cherished the times he'd had with his first teacher, his father, now deceased from cancer, as was his mom. Storm had found a San Soo Master in a small town in the high desert of southern California and studied under him for four years, then another Master in San Bernardino trained him an additional three years, promoting him to his current level of sixth degree. Only two more levels to go and he would be a Master in his own right.

Storm had operated several Kung Fu studios during those years, eventually establishing his current one in Las Vegas. This studio had been in operation for five years. In the interim, Storm had trained and promoted several other students to the rank of Black Belt. The first had died in a car accident several years ago. The second, now a world traveler on a huge motor yacht, had moved on just several months ago, and Storm missed his loyal companionship. Now, his newest Black Belt, Mark Long, was an asset to his studio and could be trusted to competently instruct the classes in the event Storm couldn't show.

Mark gathered his gear and stuffed it into his gym duffel, saluted his Sifu, then strolled out the door. Storm retreated to his office in the rear of the studio. It was time to get out the monthly billing.

Just as Storm got the computer program going, he heard the front door squeal of metal scraping metal. He looked up from the computer on his cluttered desk to see a familiar face smiling brightly at him.

"Uncle Pete!"

"Hello, Derek. How have you been?"

Storm rushed across the thick studio mat and grabbed his uncle's extended hand for a firm handshake and a hug. "Boy it's good to see you, Pete. It's been too many years."

"I guess it has. Katherine's funeral, if I recall. How've you been doing, Derek? You look fit." Pete's departed wife, Katherine, had been Storm's aunt, his mother's sister.

"Just great. Yeah. Running my own studio full time. Even managing to make a living at it. What brings you to Las Vegas? Vacation?"

"I wish. Actually, I'm on an adventure of sorts. I was in the area and thought I'd stop by to visit, maybe buy you dinner if you're free tonight."

"It just so happens I am free tonight and dinner sounds good. You don't have to buy, though."

"No, I insist, Derek. I want to discuss some things with you regarding my research, but we'll get to that over dinner."

"Okay. Sure. Let me close up shop and we'll get moving." Storm walked back toward his office with his uncle along side. "This is the first time you've seen my studio, isn't it?"

"Yes. Most impressive." Pete gazed at the array of Chinese weaponry hanging on the walls and neatly stacked in the corner stands. "Are you proficient in all these weapons?"

"Almost all of them. I'm still working at mastering the three-section-staff." Storm removed a curious looking device from the wall. It consisted of three two-foot long sections of bamboo joined at the ends by sturdy swivel chains. "This gizmo is the dickens to master. It takes quite a few raps on the skull and shins to learn to use it properly. But it's coming along. Stand back about ten feet and I'll show you."

Pete complied and watched in admiration as Storm began swinging, rotating, and manipulating the sections with adept skill. He blended kicks with the staff striking and blocking motions, the individual sections contorted wildly into a frenzied dance of malevolent aggression.

"Wow!   I don't think I'd want to be on the business end of that."

Storm chuckled. "That's why my Army buddies called me Derek the Red."

"Yeah. I can see why."

Storm replaced the staff and pointed at his office. "Let me shut down the computer and lock up."   He stepped toward his office and asked, "Where are you staying while you're in town?"

"Oh, I haven't decided yet. I'm sure there's a hotel room somewhere in Vegas that can put me up for the night."

"Nonsense, Pete. If you don't already have arrangements, stay at my place. I've got a spare room and it's clean and comfortable."

"Are you sure I wouldn't be imposing? I don't want to inconvenience you. And I didn't come here for a free night's stay. I really need to talk with you about some business and family matters."

"Look, Uncle Pete. How often do I get to see you? I'd be honored to have my uncle, Dr. Peter Flynn, as my guest. Please say yes."

The doctor blushed slightly, honored by his nephew.

"Okay. Done. But I spring for dinner, okay?"

"Okay. Dinner and home it is. But I need to go home for a shower first. We don't have one here."

"How far is your place?"

"Just fourteen minutes south of here, up the hill. I've got a nice two-bedroom apartment in a gated community. You can follow me in your car. The code to get into the gate is two-one-seven and I'm in apartment two-one-seven. Easy, huh?"

Pete nodded as Storm shut down the computer. The billing could wait until tomorrow. They headed for their vehicles and Storm locked the studio door behind them.

∞

The waiter nodded as he jotted down the order. "Your salads will be out shortly."

As the waiter hustled off, Storm's curiosity kicked in.

"So, Pete. What's up with the business and family?"

Pete's smile faded as he sighed. "Derek, I've been researching a cure for cancer since Katherine passed away." Storm nodded as he listened intently. Both of his parents had died of cancer and he took immediate interest.

Pete took a sip of wine, set down his glass and folded his hands on the table. "We've made some significant breakthroughs by combining certain anti-cancer drugs with certain enzymes that can eat cancer cells. The research was going pretty well until last week."

"What happened last week?"

"Our lab was broken into: equipment destroyed, samples stolen. It was a mess. Fortunately, no one was hurt and the thieves didn't get hold of the most important equipment or the research data. I had those stored in a vault. Dan and I thought it best to move the lab to a secret location so I can continue the research. I left Portland the night before last. Since I was passing through Vegas, I thought about you and decided to see if I could enlist your help."

Storm nodded solemnly. "Absolutely, Pete. How can I help?"

"Nothing specific right now. But a time may come when I'll need a bodyguard or a ... *special* courier. I can't think of any one more qualified or loyal than you. Would you be willing to do it?"

Storm took note of his uncle's emphasis and understood the potentially hazardous implications. "To help my uncle in the quest for a cure? Anything. You just name it. That crap killed my mom and dad. If there's a cure, I want to help."

"Thanks, Derek. You don't know what a relief that is."

"Any idea who broke into your lab?"

"No. The police suspect it may have been a competing researcher or a pharmaceutical company, but I'm not so sure, now that I've had hours on the road to think about it."

"What makes you say that?"

"First, every researcher I know is a genuine scientist, interested in discovering the cure. Sure, they'd like the credit for the discovery, but not a one I can think of would even consider doing anything to inhibit the discovery. As for the pharmaceutical companies, they stand to lose huge profits if the discovery should be suppressed. They would want to buy the rights to produce it and make a fortune. No, this is the work of some sick, perverted people bent on preventing the cure from being discovered or mass produced."

Storm became pensive. Pete sipped his wine again.

The waiter came to the table with their salads, placed them and retreated. Both diners remained silent until the waiter was beyond earshot, sipping their wine and glancing around the restaurant.

Storm broke the silence. "You have any possible suspects in mind?"

"I have only a hunch, but I don't want to say anything without proof."

The men picked at their salads and sipped their wine for a few minutes. This time Pete spoke first. "I'll be moving on tomorrow morning, Derek. I'll be searching for a secure location for the lab. I'll be pretty much incommunicado except for encrypted e-mail, so I'll need your e-mail address to keep in touch. I'll forward the encryption program to you once Dan's set up."

Storm gave his uncle the address and told him to be sure to stay in touch.

"One more question, Pete. What makes you think you'll need a bodyguard? Have you received any threats?"

"No, not yet. But if my suspicions are correct, the people behind this may not be satisfied with simply wrecking my lab."

Boston, Massachusetts: The shrill female voice on the phone told Rushton his request for information was not welcomed.

"You want my help now? Why should I help you after the mess you people made of our national health care proposal? You made us look like fools."

Rushton was prepared for the challenge. He grinned smugly as he removed his glasses and responded. "Dear Ms. Congresswoman, congressperson, whichever you prefer. Your group's proposal would have ruined the entire health care industry in this country. Besides, it's ancient history. We're talking about the present, which means you should check with your political action committee to see who the recent contributors are and the level of their generosity."

There was a pregnant pause on the line.

"So, Doctor, you're saying we're in your organization's good graces again?" inquired Congresswoman Iris Stakemore, fifth term representative from a district near San Francisco. Iris had been instrumental in the congressional legislation eight years previous that had failed overwhelmingly, due to NOMP. She took the failure hard and was reluctant to be of service. However, money was money, and she needed lots of it for her political activities. So, maybe she could overlook their past differences and lend a hand ... if they paid for it ... handsomely.

CHAPTER IV

THE CRUISERS

Cabo San Lucas, Baja, Mexico, February 2002: The white ball rolled uphill along the lush green surface, slowed, curved right and gently plopped into the hole without touching the sides. It was a perfect thirty-foot putt.

Lucien "Luke" Hale gaped in awe as it dropped and bounced around the hole. He shook his head and grinned at his wife, the beautiful Heather McAulay Hale, ladies golf champion.

Luke Hale was a pit bull of a character, a distant descendant of Nathan Hale, the American patriot spy hanged by the British during the American Revolutionary War. He was also, regretfully, a distant relative of Samuel Hale, the Tory cousin who exposed Nathan to the Brits. Physically, Luke appeared average at five foot eight on a one hundred seventy pound, muscular frame. He had graying brown hair, balding at the crown, so he kept it short and wore brimmed hats to avoid looking like a circus clown.

Luke had served in the Army, assigned to an Armored Cavalry Squadron, eventually becoming the Troop's Operations NCO and distinguished gunner on the M-551 Sheridan Assault Vehicle, a lightly armored reconnaissance vehicle that resembled a small tank. Luke then served as a weapons and demolitions expert in Special Forces while he finished his college education. He graduated with honors in 1978 with a business degree in Finance, but the only jobs open back then for fresh college graduates were for the average twenty-one year old whose biggest responsibility yet in life was to organize a fraternity beer bust. Luke had already had more responsibility in the Army than most of these college kids would ever see in their lifetimes. Luke sought a real challenge to feed his need for the adrenaline rush of parachuting, playing with explosives or mountain climbing.

He checked into the military flight programs. The Navy and Air Force both sent him for testing. One week later, Luke received a phone call from the Air Force recruiter and learned he had scored the highest of all the applicants and the commander, a Major and a pilot himself, wanted him in that afternoon for an interview. Luke readily agreed and at the end of the interview, the Major told Luke that he was getting the first pilot training slot available.

The Navy called the very next day and offered Luke a pilot training slot at Pensacola. Luke politely informed them he had already accepted the Air Force's offer. Thirteen months later, Luke graduated pilot training at the top of his class and was assigned to fly F-4 Phantoms. He spent the next seven years in the USAF Tactical Air Command having a supersonic ball. His final two years were spent as an F-4 instructor pilot.

Luke loved the high-speed, low altitude, gut-twisting G-forces, as well as the camaraderie, and he logged a thousand hours in the Phantom by the time he departed the Air Force to search for an airline position. In 1986, he took a job with a major airline. For fifteen years he traveled North America, becoming a Captain in 1998, the same year he earned his black belt in San Soo.

In the aftermath of the 9-11 atrocity, Luke and Heather assessed their finances and agreed he should take an early retirement, sell all of their properties, buy a huge yacht and cruise the world.

Heather was full-blooded Scot. She was fair-skinned, five feet five inches on a one hundred twelve pound athletically sculpted frame of beautiful proportions. Her blazing auburn ponytail and infectious laugh were recognizable for hundreds of yards and her effervescent personality assured her of many friends. Luke often referred to her as a social butterfly, flitting about from one social flower to another.

Luke and Heather were married eight months after they met. Each had children of their own from previous marriages, four in all, grown and independent. They were also blessed with three beautiful granddaughters, who they visited frequently.

Heather had an uncanny ability to make money with real estate. During their ten years of marriage, she had increased their assets tenfold through rental properties and re-sales. Combined with Luke's stock investments and commodity futures trading, plus his retirement from the airline, they had amassed a nest egg of millions. So, in October of 2001, they sold their properties and went in search of a huge motor yacht.

In December, they found their floating retirement home docked in Newport, California. It was a magnificent steel-hulled vessel with a triple-decked fiberglass superstructure, one hundred thirty feet long and thirty feet across its beam. A near-bankrupt dot-com company in southern California had put it up for sale. The Hales jumped at the opportunity to buy it for half of its value.

The beautiful eight-year-old vessel gathered double-takes from every boating enthusiast who gazed upon her. She was streamlined, elegant, and powerful where it counted. She featured eight lush staterooms, six crew berths, two salons, a gourmet galley, wet bars, formal dining salon , large spa, barbeque and a helipad on the aft top deck. There was also a small gymnasium and a machine shop, as well as state-of-the-art communications and navigation gear.

The Hales took possession of the vessel the day before Christmas, the ultimate Christmas gift. They re-named her *Serene Vixen* and retained the services of the original crew: six deck hands, the mechanic, the chef and the Captain. Two of the deck hands were married to each other and shared one of the staterooms. The Captain, being due the respect a Captain should have, also occupied a private stateroom.

Luke bought a two-seat helicopter, took a few lessons and flew it to the ship.

Two days after Christmas, they headed south to Cabo San Lucas for the winter. They had the Captain moor the ship two miles off shore in the Gulf of California, shielded from the Pacific Ocean. Magnificent cruise ships anchored nearby.

Several times each week, the Hales flew ashore to play golf. Most of the country clubs welcomed them and allowed Luke to land near their parking lots. Attendants would always rush out with a golf cart since Luke tipped generously.

Their golf round was over. Heather had beaten him again, by eight strokes. Usually it was ten.

"Even par. Looks like you owe me another fantasy," she said smugly.

Luke shook his head and chuckled. "You're gonna have to teach me how to do that."

"What, give me a fantasy?"

"No. Putting, you sexy Scottish wench."

They giggled and embraced, sharing a delicate, affectionate kiss. Luke replaced the pin, gathered their clubs and they walked hand in hand to the cart. They had a solid relationship that most other couples envied.

As they drove past the clubhouse, Luke slowed the cart and signaled one of the attendants to hop on the back. Once he was aboard, Luke drove to their helicopter. The young Mexican attendant cleaned their clubs, stowed them, gratefully acknowledged Luke's tip, then drove the cart back to the clubhouse. Luke prepared the chopper for the flight back to the *Vixen* as Heather buckled in.

Luke started the engine, scanned three hundred sixty degrees for obstacles, then lifted the vibrating copter to a hover, rotated into the wind and climbed to five hundred feet. He made a lazy left turn and set course directly for the *Vixen*, seven miles across the water.

Via intercom, he said, "I believe it's time for lunch and some afternoon delight."

Heather grinned coyly and winked as she placed her hand on his thigh. Luke could feel the heat.

Boston, Massachusetts: Rushton waited anxiously at a table in the coffee house. He was early for his clandestine appointment with a man whose moniker and phone number had been provided by Congresswoman Stakemore's haughty personal assistant.

It was blustery cold and the sky overcast, depressing. He sipped his mocha latte and watched the door, expecting his appointment to arrive at any moment. He checked his watch every two minutes. The noontime lunch crowd was on the streets, bustling to and fro, all bracing their collars against the cold wind. All except for two burly men in beige overcoats at opposite street corners. They were casually looking at magazines, but otherwise scanning the surroundings. Rushton wondered if either of them might be his appointment.

Rushton glanced at his Rolex for the sixth time, now nine minutes past the scheduled appointment. "*Doctors aren't supposed to be kept waiting like this.*" Patients didn't like waiting either, but they accepted it. Doctors, however, should never, ever, be kept waiting. He returned his attention to his latte, deciding to allow until quarter past the hour for contact. The minutes dragged by and his anxiety increased as his unilateral deadline neared. The crowd outside thinned, but the two men in trench coats were still on the corners.

At the deadline, Rushton headed for the door, not noticing the tall brown-haired man in a business suit that approached behind him. As Rushton stepped outside, a firm, low-toned voice behind him said "Please step into the van, Dr. Rushton." A gray van without panel windows pulled up to the curb directly in front of him, the side door slid open and a firm hand on his back pushed him toward it. Rushton tensed as he noticed the two trench coats approaching rapidly.

The voice behind said, "Relax, Doc. I'm your rendezvous. Just step into the van and tell me what's on your mind."

Rushton almost pissed his pants; he didn't have the nerve for cloak and dagger drama. He reluctantly approached the van, cautiously looked inside and was roughly pushed in from behind. The two trench coats piled in followed by a third man, presumably the voice, who slid the door closed and locked it. The van pulled out into traffic.

Rushton silently assessed his predicament. He was in a strange vehicle without rear windows, with three strange, large men, four counting the driver, and he had no contact with any one at his office. If he tried to use his cell phone, they could easily use him to fill a hole in the Charles River. He forced himself to remain calm.

The two trench coats each grabbed an arm and frisked him, even in places a doctor might be embarrassed. They weren't gentle about it, either.

"What's this about? Who are you?"

"Relax, Doc. We're just taking a few precautions. It's necessary in this line of work. If you're clean, we'll introduce ourselves and discuss business." The stern expression on the hard lined face informed Rushton that these men were very serious about their business and he would do best not to do anything that might give them reason to fill that hole in the Charles River.

The man with the deep voice was well over six feet tall, perhaps six feet six, with wide shoulders and arms thicker than Rushton's thighs. *"This guy could be a lineman for the New England Patriots."* The man had dark, piercing eyes and his weathered skin told him that he was no desk jockey. Nor were the others.

"He's clean," stated one of the trench coats as he handed Rushton's wallet to the ringleader.

"Dr. Rushton, you may call me Colonel Bravo. Your voice mail message mentioned certain references from congress and that you had a need for some … technical appropriations work. We had you investigated to make sure you aren't some federal plant or an undercover crusading reporter looking for a network headline. From what we can tell, you appear to be genuine." Bravo studied Rushton's driver's license intently, then offered the wallet back to him as he flipped it closed.

"So you're the mysterious Colonel Bravo. How.." Rushton gulped, "..how can I be sure you aren't some federal plant or crusading reporter. Can I see your ID?"

The men chuckled at the absurd request.

"Doctor, in our line of work, real names and ID's are a handicap. You will only know me as Bravo. You will not enjoy the privilege of knowing the names of any of my people. I will be your only contact and you mine. No one else is to attempt contact with me or even know that we exist. It's necessary for security and it's the only way we do business. If you don't accept that, then we have no business to discuss." The unspoken threat, "or else," was tacitly understood.

Rushton considered the conditions. These professionals played their cards close to the vest and that's the way he surmised it had to be. If he didn't accept their conditions, he'd have to find others, and the odds were high that the next group would require the same conditions. He couldn't afford to lose the time in the search for the Flynn lab, nor did he relish the thought of repeatedly exposing himself to more cloak and dagger treatment. The next group he tried might be harsher than these guys, or worse, incompetent. He reasoned that these men had to be the professionals he'd contacted. Stakemore, he rationalized, wouldn't set him up for fear of losing her juicy contributions.

Rushton decided to take the chance. "All right, Mr. Bravo. I guess I can see the need for security. Shall we discuss your compensation package?"

Bravo grinned for the first time. "Not yet, Doctor. First, tell me what you want. Then I can assess the equipment and manpower needs, risks, transportation, et cetera. Then we can discuss our … compensation package." He didn't mention the thirty percent markup for Stakemore's kickback. She referred to it as a campaign contribution, but it was a kickback, plain and simple.

"Do you mind if I check you for wires?" asked Rushton.

The trench coats looked at Bravo and laughed. The big man opened his jacket, revealing an ugly black, huge-caliber pistol holstered on his hip. One of the trench coats produced a switchblade so rapidly it was at Rushton's throat before the click subsided. Rushton pissed his pants.

"It seems you don't understand the program, Doc. You aren't in control. I am. We conduct business my way, or no way. Is that clear?"

The blade pressed harder against his throat.

"Y...yes. Yes. I understand. Please. Remove the knife. I get the picture." That hole in the Charles River was getting closer.

The big honcho nodded and the switchblade was withdrawn. Rushton could feel a trickle of blood on his neck. He gulped and nodded compliantly.

"Relax, Doc. You're fine. Just remember, you called me. I'm the one who needs to be suspicious. Why the hell would I be wired? Huh? Think about it."

It took Rushton a moment to collect himself. His crotch was soaked with urine and his right foot was immersed in the puddle in his shoe.

"You're not really cut out for this kind of work, are you, Doc?" teased the mysterious honcho, as he peered down at the doctor's wet pants. "So, if you want something done, lay it out for me. It'll get done and you can go home and change your underwear."

Rushton regained his composure. "Okay, Colonel. Here's what I need."

Mojave Desert, California: The real estate agent drove along a meandering road northeast of a little resort community named Silver Lakes in Helendale, halfway between Victorville and Barstow, just off the old Route 66. It was an odd place for a resort community, in the middle of the desert, but there it was: two large man-made lakes surrounded by a mix of a semi-custom homes, condominiums, twenty-seven hole private golf course, tennis courts, community center, lodge, shopping center, and post office; it was an oasis sixteen miles from the nearest civilization.

"Well, Doctor," explained the agent to Pete, "the property is now owned by a rancher named Charlie McKeon. His father bought it from the U.S. government just after World War II and the section that's for sale sits on the southeast corner. All the land you see to your left is owned by Charlie. Quite a spread, eh?"

Pete glanced at the expanse of desert. "That's quite a bit of property," agreed Pete.

"Now keep in mind, Doc, this section we're going to has been abandoned for decades. The Army used it for something or other during the war, built an underground bunker there, then abandoned it and sold the property. Old man McKeon sealed off the bunker to keep kids and drifters out. It hadn't been opened for decades until Charlie decided to sell it. He opened it up for me to have a look-see when he put it on the market. The bunker's pretty large inside and there wasn't any trash. It seems to be in pretty good shape. You have plans for it?"

Pete gave the agent the story he had concocted. "Our trust has some assets of unusually large dimensions and we need a secure place out of the public eye while they're being developed. It might fit our needs." Pete was intentionally vague about the assets. The less anyone knew of a the lab, the better.

Pete had already purchased a three-bedroom condo, using the name and funds of the blind trust Dan had set up. His name would not appear anywhere on the deed or closing documents since Dan's attorney had handled the transactions by wire transfers and faxes.

The agent maneuvered onto a dirt path leading uphill to a chain-link fenced area. Pete could barely distinguish the entrance to the bunker. The agent stopped just short of the fence and popped the trunk lid from the inside. The agent continued his sales pitch as he retrieved two flashlights from the trunk. Pete allowed him to blather, avoiding answering questions.

The agent unlocked the gate chain and swung the gates inward enough to step inside. They made their way up the slope and over a slight rise to the bunker doors.

The steel doors were huge, large enough to drive a Mack truck through. The agent unlocked the chain on the doors and asked Pete to help him open the left door. It took the efforts of both to move the heavy, rusted door. It screeched as it protested the upset to its massive inertia. The men struggled to fully open it and repeated their effort on the right door; it too protested. The entrance was huge. An eighteen-wheeler could be driven inside. They flicked on their flashlights and scanned the tunnel. It was empty and dirty, but cavernous.

The agent kept talking and Pete kept ignoring. He was focused on his needs for the lab. Two cars could easily park inside the entrance. As they walked down the ramp, Pete noticed a loading dock with stairs. He followed his light and the agent followed him. Spider webs cluttered the corners and black widows scurried from the spill of the lights. A faint odor of skunk was discernable. Pete made a mental note to have the whole bunker sprayed by an exterminator. Black widows, brown recluses and skunks had to go. A squeaking mouse scampered past his feet, crawled into a space that seemed far too small for its body and disappeared; mousetraps too, noted Pete.

They climbed the steps onto the dock and opened another rusty door, revealing a long corridor and several more mice. Scanning with their lights and brushing away webs, they walked slowly down the corridor. Several chambers were off the sides. Pete envisioned one chamber as the room for the lab animals. Another would serve nicely as a storage room, another the lab itself, and the fourth as a safe room. Pete envisioned an environment where he and an assistant could sustain themselves for a week if they were under siege. That would mean fresh water, electricity, ventilation, heat, communications, sewage, lavatory, supplies, fire suppression and firearms.

Pete assessed the property and calculated the work that would need to be done to get it functioning. He figured he could have it in shape in four or five weeks.

But he would need help, the kind of help who could keep a secret.

Cabo San Lucas, Mexico: The white launch eased alongside the anchored *Vixen* as Paul Thomas, one of the deck hands, skillfully coasted it toward the boarding ladder. His wife, Caroline, also a deck hand, tossed the forward line from the launch up to Luke Hale, their boss. Luke snatched the line from mid-air, pulled it taut and secured it to a bollard. He stepped toward the rear to catch the aft line from Paul.

"Did you get it?"

"Sure did, Jefe," answered Paul, using his Mexican term for boss, as he pointed to a cardboard box on the aft seat. "They were most accommodating." Paul tossed the rear line up to Luke and retrieved the box as Luke secured the aft line. Luke assisted Caroline over the gunwale then received the heavy package as Paul boosted it from below.

"This thing weighs about sixty pounds, boss. Careful with it."

The men gently maneuvered the container into the cockpit as Paul climbed aboard.

"Mind if I ask what's in it, Luke?" asked Caroline.

"Not at all, dear. It's a multi-phased, synchronized array, encrypted GPS data-link system for the helicopter." It was obvious by her expression she had no idea what the gizmo was. Luke and Paul snickered like a couple of high-school kids, knowing she had little understanding of electronic gadgetry. She was a marine biologist by training and understood fish and crustaceans, not gizmos. But she was cute, intelligent and energetic, part of what made her and Paul a joy to have as crewmembers.

Paul was a Navy-trained marine engineer and had a good understanding of "technical stuff," as Caroline referred to such. The young couple were in their mid-twenties, had lots of vitality and were part of the original crew. They were happy to be retained since the Hales planned to cruise the world. The year prior to that, they didn't get much travel because their foundering company couldn't afford to take the vessel out on excursions and they were worried about losing their jobs, which weren't high-paying anyway. They wanted the benefits of the job, not the money. To them, as with most of the young crew, the benefits of travel aboard a luxury yacht far outweighed the landlubber lifestyle.

The only crewmember who earned a respectable salary was the Captain, Walt "Salty" Skibba, who preferred to be called "Skipper." Salty was in his early sixties, six feet tall and medium build. He kept his hair cropped short and was almost never seen without a hat. He had a neatly trimmed salt and pepper beard and a commanding presence that demanded instant respect, and deservedly so. Salty had served as a career Navy officer aboard numerous ships and had spent most of his adult life at sea. He had retired from the Navy at the rank of Captain after twenty-nine years of service and numerous campaigns such as Panama, Viet Nam and the Persian Gulf. He had lost count of how many times he'd been around the world. Salty had hired on as the Captain of the *Vixen* shortly after she took to sea and he seemed to know every weld and bolt in her. Twice divorced, he sometimes ribbed himself about not learning the lesson the first time. He spent his spare time reading technical manuals, playing golf and enjoying the company of various females ashore. Luke imagined he could be quite the rascal when it came to the ladies, as worldly a man as there ever was. Luke admired Skibba's macho and swagger, his supreme confidence and his skill as a Captain. The *Vixen* was in the best hands possible.

Caroline recovered from the boss's techno-speak and not to be mistaken for a dumb blond, said to her husband, "Would you translate that into English or should we talk marine biology?"

Luke and Paul snickered as Paul explained it was a Global Positioning System, a GPS, that operated from satellites and used electronic signals to guide Luke's helicopter to the ship in bad weather. Caroline nodded, but she wasn't fooling the two wise guys.

"Thank you, lover. I'll go see if there's some lunch for us while you two… get technical." She glided away in a haughty, sexy shuffle, her nose in the air, reciting from memory the characteristics of some rare tropical fish as the two men chuckled at her expense.

"You're beautiful when you're angry," Paul shouted after her. Caroline flipped her wrist into the air without looking back. "God, I love that woman."

"Ah, to be young and in love." Luke stuck his little finger into his mouth, then placed the wet tip into Paul's ear, giving him a wet Willy. Paul recoiled from the prank and laughed. "Let's unpack it here, Romeo. It'll be easier to get it topside."

The men opened the package as Salty Skibba approached. The Skipper chomped on his ubiquitous Cuban cigar, puffed a few times then asked in his gruff, raspy voice, "What in Neptune's blazes is that contraption?" He stuffed the huge cigar back between his lips and puffed a dense cloud of aromatic smoke.

"Howdy, Skipper. It's a multi-phase, synchronized array, encrypted GPS data link system. The synchronized array provides relative bearing and range displays of the chopper and the *Vixen*, with displays on both, and the encryption is similar to IFF Mode 4 interrogation so we can electronically tell good guys from bad guys, even if I'm out of radio range. It bounces the data off the UNIVOR NAVSATs. This system should keep me from getting lost, especially in limited visibility."

The skipper nodded approval. "Whatever it takes for the ship's Master to make it home. I won't ask what it cost but I would like to know what's in store for us, sir."

Luke sensed the Skipper's concern. "No drama, Skipper. It's just to keep me from getting lost if I get caught in foul weather." Luke, also an aficionado of fine cigars, distracted the Skipper. "You got another Cuban on you, Captain?"

The Skipper, noting his boss's use of his formal title, knew he shouldn't ask any further questions and produced a Cuban Excalibur for Luke, knowing the boss would bring back a whole box for him the next time he went ashore. "Here you go, boss. Enjoy," he said with a tight grin on his lips.

"Thanks, Skipper. Help yourself to my humidor." Luke bit the cap off, spit it overboard, then rolled the tip in his mouth. Skibba produced his butane blowtorch.

"Aye-aye. Thanks, boss." However, the Skipper had no intention of invading Luke's tobacco stash, even with permission. He ran the ship's operations but he knew his place and Luke was the boss. Skibba respected his authority.

The two aficionados puffed heartily on their Cuban delights, billowing a huge, dense cloud that drifted right at Paul, the non-smoker. Paul huffed and waved the cloud away. "How can you guys stand that stuff?"

The Skipper chuckled. "Sonny, some things in life just beg for indulgence. The sea is one, amorous ladies is the second and this, young man, is another, followed, of course, by an excellent single malt scotch."

"Or a vintage port wine," added Luke, as he puffed heartily. "The Skipper's right about the sea and the ladies, too."

Paul just shook his head and grinned, put in his place.

"How will you get this gadget installed, boss? I don't believe Dave has the training to handle this kind of job." The Skipper was referring to the ship's mechanic, Dave Welch, the second highest paid member of the crew, handling all of the mechanical and power plant repairs on the vessel.

"Well, my son Pierce has vacation this week, so I'm flying him down from Los Angeles to do the installations. He should be at Del Cabo airport in an hour. After we get this stuff topside, I'm heading for the airport. He's been to trade school for these kinds of applications; autos mostly, but he does marine work too. He thinks he'll have it done in two days and then he can enjoy the rest of his vacation with us. It's a win-win."

With all of the components unwrapped, the three men pre-positioned them for Pierce's arrival.

On his way to the chopper, Luke detoured through the main salon. As he entered, he observed a shapely, female derriere pointed in his direction as its owner bent over a storage locker under one of the cushioned seats. Luke switched into stealth mode and silently stepped toward the exposed target, gave the left buttock a soft pinch and a firm pat.

"Where's that no account husband of yours?" he softly whispered.

The woman raised slightly without glancing at her assailant and whispered back, "I don't know, so you better make your move before he finds out about us."

Luke wrapped his arms around her as she turned into his embrace. Their lips melded into a passionate kiss as they caressed.

Luke gazed into Heather's green eyes, lovingly stroked her cheek and planted a soft kiss on her forehead. She hugged him tightly and buried her head in his shoulder as he stroked her hair.

"I'm off to the airport to get Pierce. We'll see you in a few hours. Love you, babe."

"And I love you. Fly carefully."

Caroline Thomas entered the salon and cleared her throat. "You two need to get a room."

The Hales chuckled and turned toward her.

"Is this the pot calling the kettle black?" teased Heather.

Caroline blushed. She had the mobile satellite phone in her hand, extending it to Luke. "You have a call from a Derek Storm. The Skipper asked me to track you down."

"Thanks, Caroline." Luke accepted the device and held it to his ear.

"Derek, many moons pass, no see."

Luke paused. He smiled and laughed at some clever quip. "I miss you too buddy. How's the Kung Fu studio doing?"

The next pause was longer and Luke listened intently.

"Well, Derek, this is quite a coincidence. Pierce will be here in two hours. I was just about to leave to get him at the airport. We can call you back."

Luke signaled Heather for paper and pen. Caroline cut her off and gathered them for Luke.

"Yeah, okay, Derek. Give me your new e-mail address and we'll contact you as soon as we get back to the ship."

Luke scribbled then tossed the pen down, stuffing the paper into his breast pocket. He looked puzzled as he listened to more.

"Encryption program? Why do we need to download that? What are you into, pal?"

Luke looked concerned as the voice on the other end continued. The women looked at one another inquisitively and Heather simply shrugged her shoulders.

"Okay, Derek. Whatever you say. We'll contact you via e-mail. You be careful and check six, hoo-ah?"

Luke nodded then shut down the satellite connection. He handed it to Caroline. "Would you return this to the wheelhouse, Caroline, and ask the Skipper to have the chopper made ready?"

"Yes, sir. And if I may, is there anything I can do to help… I mean with regard to the call? You seem concerned about something."

"No, but thank you just the same, dear."

Caroline nodded and headed for the bridge.

Heather waited until she was out of earshot. "What's going on?"

"He wants to speak with Pierce about some secretive installation work and needed his phone number. He didn't want to say what the job was over the phone and insisted we contact him only by encrypted e-mail." Luke crossed his arms and rubbed his chin. "And he said to keep it on a need-to-know basis. There's something serious in the works, if I know Derek… and I do know Derek."

Las Vegas, Nevada: Storm replaced the phone. It did him good to hear his friend's voice, even if it was slightly distorted. He reminisced about the six years that Luke had trained with him. Luke had come to Storm as a martial novice at the age of forty-three and trained until reaching the rank of Second Degree Black Belt. The two men, though half a generation apart in age, developed a strong bond. They had a lot in common with their Army service, attitudes, humor and tastes in literature, movies and the like. As much as Storm was a teacher to Luke, Luke was a mentor to Storm about life in general. Luke had helped Storm through a rough period in his life, while other alleged friends turned a deaf ear.

They weren't rowdy drinkers but they did enjoy good banter at the bar. The only time Luke had ever seen Storm in a fight was at one such bar trip. A patron took one of Storm's jesting comments the wrong way and confronted him. Storm apologized and offered to buy the big guy a beer, but the man misinterpreted his gesture as a sign of weakness and pressed the issue. Storm tried to avoid a fight but the guy just kept pressing, finally taking a huge cowboy style windup in preparation to throw a punch. The huge, telegraphed motion was so slow, Luke thought he would have to refer to a calendar to see it delivered. Storm hesitated until the final instant before the punch landed, then in a flash, he sidestepped the punch, kneed the guy in the groin, then pivoted as he hammered down on the back of his neck with his fist. The guy dropped to the floor like a sack of lead, unconscious. Luke cleared Derek's back to make sure that none of the guy's playmates jumped him from behind. Fortunately, the rowdy didn't have any friends. One patron and the bartender even applauded Storm for decking the guy. Luke squared up their tab as Derek apologized for the mess, then they went on their way, leaving the unconscious rowdy on the floor.

Luke and Derek also enjoyed target shooting. Both of them were expert marksmen. Luke was the better shot with a rifle, having been an A Team sharpshooter in Special Forces, but Storm was the better marksman with a pistol and often practiced engaging targets at ranges considered to be beyond effective pistol range. It was not uncommon for him to score a headshot at sixty yards. Likewise, Luke had been known to score headshots at six hundred yards on a calm day with his scoped Bushmaster rifle.

Their intensive training and frequent saloon excursions bonded them into a strong friendship and each trusted the other with his life. Both had expressed to the other that if they were ever engaged in the most dire firefight of their lives, they wanted the other to be in the foxhole with him, covering his back.

It was a sad day for Storm when Luke informed him that he and Heather were moving away and searching for a yacht. They enjoyed another two months of companionship before the Hales embarked on their cruise. They kept in touch by phone every three or four weeks, but it wasn't the same as having Luke in the studio while they punched, kicked, leveraged and threw each other around on the mats, telling jokes, laughing at their mistakes and generally having a great time. Derek missed him.

Cabo San Lucas, Mexico: The helicopter touched down gently. A crewman scampered under the rotor blades and chained it to the pad as Luke shut down the engine. Luke emerged with his youngest son, Pierce, twenty-one years old, five feet eleven, short blond hair and hazel eyes. Luke introduced the crewman, Ed Kovack, to Pierce. They shook hands.

"Have a nice flight, boss?"

"Yes we did, Ed. Thanks." Luke threw his arm around the taller Pierce as Ed unlatched the cargo bin door. Pierce reached in for his luggage and Ed offered to help.

"Let me show you where your stateroom is, Pierce, then I'll give you a tour of the ship."

"Is that it, Dad?" Pierce pointed at several electronic components at the side of the helipad.

"Yeah, those are the components for the chopper. The rest are up on the bridge."

Pierce dropped his suitcase. "I'm curious to see what these things look like."

Ed hefted the bag and asked, "Which stateroom, boss?"

"Oh, uh… number eight. Thanks, Ed." Ed shuffled off with the luggage. Pierce examined the components.

"All four of these go in the chopper?"

"That's the plan."

Pierce glanced at the chopper and assessed the amount of space he had to work with. "I don't know if it will all fit, Dad. I'll have to get a better look inside."

"You can do that later. Mom's anxious to see you. Come on."

"When's dinner?"

"I see your priorities haven't changed."

Father and son headed for the main salon with their arms on each other's shoulders, ribbing each other and cracking jokes. They found Heather mixing Pina Coladas at the bar.

"Look who's here," announced Luke.

Heather looked up from the noisy blender and rushed around the counter.

"Come in. Sit down and relax, Pierce. I'm mixing Pina Coladas. Want one? Are you hungry?" Ever the mom, Heather was. "How are you doing? Work going okay? How's your girlfriend? Did you have a nice flight?" The pleasant interrogation went on until Heather was satisfied Pierce was doing okay.

Eventually, Pierce was able to express his desire for a sandwich and they headed for the galley, a tour of the ship and an introduction to the crew.

"We're having a welcome aboard party for you tonight," announced Heather.

"Really? Thanks, Mom." Pierce gave her another hug and a peck on the cheek.

Luke chimed in, "Half of the crew is ashore right now, so you'll meet them at the party tonight. You'll like them, they're all good people."

Pierce was flattered.

"Dad, you said Derek wanted to talk to me about some work?"

"Right, geez, I almost forgot." Luke fished through his pocket. "Let's go to the office." They headed for the stateroom one deck below that Luke had converted into an office. Luke turned on the computer while Pierce munched on his sandwich. Soon, Luke was into the e-mail program, searching for a message from Derek. He found it. It had an attachment; it was a 128-bit encryption program. Luke clicked the download button. It took four minutes to process. Luke opened the next message from Derek.

The screen turned into a crazy jumble for several seconds as the contraption munched on the decryption. A message popped onto the screen in an unusual format, but it was easier to read than regular e-mail.

It stated:

"Luke,

My uncle's cancer research lab was ransacked several weeks ago. He has moved it to a secret location. He needs special installations done but they, and the location of the lab, have to be kept a secret.

Need Pierce to do this. He'll be well paid.

Have Pierce get in touch with me as soon as possible.

Hope all is well on your cruise.

Your loyal friend,

Derek"

Pierce read the message over his Dad's shoulder. Luke made room for him at the computer.

Pierce put down his drink and sat at the computer. He composed a return message and sent it. Within minutes, another message from Derek appeared. It gave information on the general location of the lab, his uncle's e-mail address and a pleading to have the work done as soon as possible. Pierce replied to that message, also, agreeing to contact his uncle. Then he sent a message to the uncle, introducing himself.

"It looks like somebody wants to make trouble for Derek's uncle. Let's hope he can keep it secret," stated Pierce.

Luke nodded, suspecting this wouldn't be the end of it.

Portland, Oregon: The jetliner cleared the runway and taxied in the darkness. A light rain shower spilled on the field. Six large brawny men sporting crew cuts, dressed in gray suits, peered out the first-class portholes. Lights of various colors reflected off the wet ramp surfaces. None of the men was impressed by the weather.

As soon as the seat belt sign was turned off, all six retrieved their beige trench coats and bags. They waited patiently for the cabin door to be opened, they said not a word. Their stoic expressions told everyone they were not open to chitchat, so the flight attendants left them to themselves.

It had been a long day for the men. They headed for the baggage claim as a group, then two of them split off for the car rental counter.

The other four rounded up their luggage.

Two gray Buicks pulled curbside and the trunks popped open. The men loaded their luggage and equipment and two men climbed into each vehicle.

Closing the passenger door of the lead vehicle, Bravo commanded, "Safe house. Go."

Cabo San Lucas, Mexico: Pierce read the return e-mail from Derek's Uncle Pete.

"It looks like my vacation's gonna be cut short."

"Why?"

"Derek's uncle has a high-priority installation he needs done and he's offering me top dollar. I can't afford to turn it down. I told him I could start by the end of the week. I'll have your installation done by Tuesday. Don't worry."

Luke nodded as Pierce shut down the computer. "I'll reschedule your flight for Wednesday morning. Are you sure you can finish by then?"

"Oh, yeah. No problem."

"Well, I'll fly you and your girlfriend down here again when you get some spare time. It's the least I can do for you."

"Thanks, Dad. Let's get started on it. It'll be good to see Derek, again. He'll be there to help his uncle."

The break-in at Portland and all the secrecy about the new lab concerned Luke. He wondered if his son might be placed in danger. Time would tell.

"Tell him to get his butt down here for some vacation when you see him. He's been taking Kung Fu too seriously. He could use a week or two aboard the *Vixen*. Anyway, by the time you come again, there'll be some special modifications to her."

"Like what?"

"You'll just have to wait and see."

CHAPTER V

HARD PRESS

Portland, Oregon, March 2002: Drew Kress grew more frightened by the second. A tall ugly black guy had walked into the office through the back door a minute earlier as if he owned the place. When Charlie confronted him, the big guy kicked him in the nuts and shoved him into a chair, never taking his eyes off Kress. When Kress reached for the pistol in his desk, the thug pulled out a portable artillery piece and aimed it directly at Kress's nose with single-handed steadiness. The bore looked to be about a thousand millimeters wide from Kress's perspective. Kress's heart nearly jumped out through his throat. He abandoned any thought of taking the guy down. Charlie was almost unconscious.

"You Kress?"

"Wh… who wants to know?" Kress felt obligated to play tough guy.

That irritated the big man. "I said, are you Kress?" The black man smoothly cocked the hammer on his hand cannon, his aim never straying. Kress could see the cylinder rotate a huge hollow point round in line with the barrel.

"Yeah, I'm Kress. Wha… uh, what's on your mind?"

The black man nodded, de-cocked the hammer smoothly as he kept aim at Kress, and walked around the desk, reached inside the open drawer and extracted Kress's puny .32. He looked at it and scoffed.

"Couldn't afford a man's gun? This pea-shooter's for pussies." He stuffed the little pistol into his coat pocket, searched the other desk drawer and frisked Kress.

Kress didn't respond and Charlie just moaned.

"Your former employer sends his regards and I'm to inform you that your services are no longer required."

"Nobody told me."

"I just did, pinhead. You got a problem with that?"

Kress didn't respond and Charlie moaned.

"Your employment is terminated. The boss says your contract is paid in full."

"No. No. No it's not. That son of a bitch still owes me…" The re-cocking of the hand cannon and the feel of its cold unforgiving steel suddenly stuffed under his nose cut him off. It was time to reconsider. "Okay, okay man. I get the idea. We're off the job. I guess you're takin' over?"

"That's none of your concern, butt wipe." The black man's saliva splattered onto his face but Kress didn't dare move to wipe it off. The big guy's temperament might have a hair trigger. So might his cannon.

"Right. Yeah, none of my business. What the hell was I thinkin'?"

"You're to turn over all the tapes to me. If you're good, I might pay you a little something for them. If not, I'll just take them, capice?" The ugly man tilted his head slightly to emphasize his point.

Kress didn't respond and Charlie moaned.

Kress followed the thug with his eyes as he circled in back of him, then emerged on the opposite side. The big guy kicked the door to the monitoring room. It smashed into the wall with a loud thud. The tape machines were right there. There was no use lying about them or the taps.

"Okay, mister. I get your meaning. You can have the tapes and the machines."

"I don't want this Jurassic junk, just the tapes, butt wipe." Kress was treated to another saliva bath.

Kress nodded. He watched helplessly as the big man, his cannon still focused on him, extracted the tapes and dropped them into his pocket. He flopped an envelope onto the desk and walked toward the rear door as Charlie rose from the chair. The thug kneed him in the nuts again and pushed him back into the chair.

He turned back to Kress and used the revolver like a pointing finger. "You just had your going out of business sale. You're shut down. You got that?"

Kress nodded and Charlie moaned.

The big guy disappeared through the rear door, closing it softly behind him.

Kress, sweat and saliva dripping from his forehead, felt compelled to get to the toilet.

Boston: Eleven board members convened in Rushton's office. It was crowded but Rushton didn't anticipate the meeting would last long. All of the members present were incumbents and Rushton had a handle on their loyalties.

"Ladies and gentlemen, thank you for coming and thank you for tolerating the crowded conditions. This meeting shouldn't take long and we'll have you on your way as soon as business is concluded. Dr. Raas?"

Raas took the floor. "Our next board meeting will determine the chairmanships of the national board and committees. For the past six years, the current chairs have held the power of NOMP in their hands. We've had some good times, but we've also suffered setbacks and there are a good many of us that believe it's time for a change of leadership. That's why, at the next board meeting, I'm nominating Dr. Rushton for the position of Chairman. We're counting on your support. Is there anyone willing to second Dr. Rushton when the vote comes?" Several hands rose.

"Thank you," said Rushton. "At the meeting, I will nominate Dr. Raas as Vice-Chairman. Is anyone willing to second? Several more hands were raised. Both Rushton and Raas thanked them.

Rushton continued, "We need nineteen votes to win and we have twelve confirmed with five probable and one possible. That's not good enough. If you all would be good enough to lobby the undecided board members, especially the newly elected ones, we'll have an excellent chance to win and get this organization back to a pro-active posture. I can assure you that your efforts will be rewarded with the most prestigious committee positions. I thank you all in advance. Any comments or questions?" All members shook their heads, more interested in getting out of the crowded office than engaging in political maneuvering.

"In that case, I thank you all again for coming and appreciate your support." At that, the members filed out.

Melanie Taylor exited the elevator and noticed the procession leaving Rushton's office. She had a hunch Rushton and his cronies were up to something underhanded. She spotted one particular nurse leaving the office and determined to approach her later to elicit information.

Miller and Raas remained behind. As usual, Raas mixed the cocktails and passed them around. Raas and Miller sipped their drinks and sat down as Rushton checked the hall for eavesdroppers, closed the door and locked it. He returned to his chair and elevated his feet on his desk.

Miller broke the ice. "The finance committee will have its quarterly report to the board in three weeks. I hope you win this election for Chairman, otherwise we'll have a hard time explaining that $250,000 contribution to Congress-critter What's-Her-Name."

"That's nothing," replied Rushton. "We can always create a viable scenario for political schmoozing. I just hope they don't find out about the $200,000 we had to spend for the... professional services. That's when the shit will really hit the fan."

"Two hundred thousand?" Miller was incredulous. "I thought it was only one hundred."

Exasperated, Rushton responded, "The one hundred thou' was the down. The other half is due upon completion, assuming there are no further complications. That's our agreement with the professionals, professionals we all agreed to hire."

"Are they on the job yet?" inquired Raas.

Nodding, Rushton answered, "I spoke with the man last night. They're already in Portland and have terminated the services of the amateurs. Unfortunately, all of Kress's tapes proved worthless. There wasn't a single mention of the new lab location on any of them. Peter Flynn hasn't been seen in over a month. We don't even know if he's still in Oregon. I instructed the new people to take more aggressive measures."

"What kind of measures?" inquired Miller.

"I didn't specify and I really don't care. This ParaZyme 2000 protocol has to be brought under our control or we could all lose our jobs. The very existence of this organization is threatened. But if we can get a piece of the action before it hit's the FDA, we can retire as very rich people."

The grinning greed mongers raised their glasses and drank.

Portland: Kress was pissed, really pissed. *"All that effort wasted, and for what? So that son of a bitch could screw me? Yeah, well nobody treats Drew Kress like that. Nobody. That bastard just screwed the wrong guy."*

Without a pistol jammed in his face, his ego demanded a response.

Kress was glad he had the foresight to make duplicate tapes. The big black thug had overlooked the copies in the filing cabinet. The doctor would have to pay dearly for them if he wanted them. Otherwise, they just might be delivered to the FBI.

Kress had Charlie head for home while he closed shop. For what he had in mind, he'd have to disappear for a long time. He decided to pawn all the office equipment and cancel the rent on the office and take the cash. Then he could disappear for a long time. Revenge would be so sweet. He wondered what Fiji was like. Smiling, he thought it would be just fine.

Helendale, California: Pete decided his Pontiac wasn't adequate for his needs and was a liability, a trail right to him. He had Derek drive the vehicle to Las Vegas and donate it to charity, then purchase a used Chevy S10 pickup, paying cash and registering it to Corridor Holdings at a private mail box in Henderson, Nevada. Derek had delivered the truck to Pete the next day.

The bunker was coming along nicely. Several weeks of clean-up and installations had transformed it into a workable, secure laboratory. Derek had helped. It had taken three days just to get the rooms clean enough to begin installations. Pete had Derek's friend, Pierce Hale, install an elaborate security system. There were numerous closed-circuit cameras viewing the fences and gates, two for the entrance tunnel and dock, one for the hallway and one in each room. They could all be monitored from the safe room. Motion sensor spotlights covered every square yard out past the fence line and light beam sensors connected to two separate alarms criss-crossed the entrance tunnel, dock and corridor. Pete also concealed a handgun in each of the rooms plus a 12-gauge shotgun in the safe room.

It had been quite a challenge selecting a crew of deliverymen who would be discreet about the location of the lab. Pete decided to hire a crew of Mexicans, none of whom spoke a word of English. He suspected all of them of being in the country illegally, and escorted them to the stores where he purchased his furniture and equipment. Then he had them deliver the cargo to the bunker, unload and paid them cash.

Finding the skilled craftsmen he needed was a different matter. He needed an electrician, plumber and a carpenter, but didn't want to reveal the lab to that many people. He got lucky by finding a local handyman with all the experience necessary. Some of the work might not satisfy the county building inspectors, but as long as the electricity didn't short out or the plumbing leak, Pete was satisfied. The county inspectors weren't going to set foot in here, anyway. The man installed a back-up generator, a septic tank, sinks and drains, a huge water heater and a potable water tank. Pete paid him under the table, in cash, and provided him with a generous two hundred dollar tip to deny any knowledge of the bunker if asked. And if asked and he said, "No," there would be an additional generous gratuity.

With Derek's help, Pete put special emphasis on equipping and provisioning the safe room. It already had a thick steel framed door set into reinforced concrete walls. He had Pierce install an electronic cipher lock and all of the equipment necessary for monitoring the security systems. The handyman installed two large sliding steel deadbolts that could only be operated from the inside. It would take a bazooka to penetrate the safe room.

Pete locked all the doors and climbed into his S-10. He backed out of the main tunnel and hit the remote to close the huge steel doors. The massive doors eased their way as the new electric hydraulic pumps pressurized them closed. Once he cleared the gates, he hit another button on the remote and they glided along their new tracks and electrically locked together. A press of another button activated the security system.

He took a circuitous route home, eager to begin his work again. *"Tomorrow we'll be one day closer to the discovery."*

Portland: Dan Flynn felt exhausted as he crossed the University Hospital parking lot to his car. It had been one of those days. The office had been incredibly busy during the morning and an emergency had occupied his time during the afternoon, making him two hours late for his scheduled rounds at the hospital. Now it was six-thirty already and he hadn't even had lunch. His stomach protested his neglect as the sky opened up and released its over-laden moisture. Dan quickly extended his umbrella as he ran to his car.

He started the vehicle, turned on the wipers and navigated through the lot for the exit.

"Call home," he announced to his voice activated car phone. The audio suddenly switched from soft music to harsh dial tone and ringing noises. Dan entered the freeway and headed eastward, moving with the tail end of rush hour traffic. Four rings later, his wife answered.

"Hello?"

"Hi, Kate. It's me. Don't pay the ransom. I just escaped."

"I was wondering if I'd ever hear from you again."

"Oh, yeah. You couldn't chase me away with a stick. Look, I just got done at the hospital and I haven't had a bite since breakfast. Could you whip up something for me? I'll be there in half an hour."

"You sound tired, dear. Would you rather I meet you half way for dinner out?"

Dan thought about it, "I was hoping for some of your leftover lasagna. Is there any left?"

"I believe there is. I guess that means no dinner out?"

"If it's okay with you. How about I take you out for steaks or seafood tomorrow night and we'll go dancing after?"

"Hmmm. Well… since you put it that way, how can I refuse?"

"You're the best, Kate. Thanks. I promise to take you out tomorrow. I'll see you in thirty minutes. Love you."

"Love you, too. Bye."

The dial tone sounded as Dan commanded the phone to hang up, then the audio automatically resumed the soft music from the CD player.

The drive home took him along the highway for twenty minutes then southward on a winding road leading up the hill to a remote, prestigious gated community in the woods, Hampton Manor. It was the same route he took every night. Driving in the dark, Dan had to slow down considerably on the rain slicked, tree-lined road so he could negotiate several sharp switchback curves. There were occasionally small boulders in the road, having fallen from the steep cliff sides. Just another reason to take the curves judiciously.

As Dan rounded the final switchback, his headlights illuminated a white Jeep Cherokee that had apparently taken the curve too fast. Its front wheel was hanging over the roadside gulley. He didn't recognize the vehicle but he did notice a man lying on the side of the road, not moving.

Dan immediately pulled to the side of the road, parked and turned on his emergency flashers. He used his cell phone to call home and alert his wife of the accident, informing her that he was only a mile down the road and requesting her to call an ambulance. Leaving the engine running, he popped the trunk lid from the inside, deployed his umbrella and grabbed his medical kit from the trunk. The man made no sound or movement as the doctor approached.

"I'm a doctor. I'm going to help you," he announced, just in case he was conscious. He didn't want to alarm the victim. Dan knelt beside him, placed a finger to his neck and found a healthy pulse. He bent over to get his ear next to the man's mouth to check his breathing but never got that far. The last thing he remembered were quick, soft footsteps behind him. He felt a jolt on his neck and everything went black.

∽

It was damned cold out here and the wind-driven rain wasn't helping. They had been through this many times during their military and mercenary careers and had learned to ignore it; it was just one of the conditions of the job. At least they had anticipated the weather and had dressed appropriately. The trees provided some limited shelter.

Yankee, Rebel and Trigger, three of Bravo's henchmen, had arrived at the site three hours previous and had scouted the area, selecting the final switchback curve as the optimum place for the abduction. The target vehicle would be traveling slowly, they had a good view of the switchbacks leading into the last curve, there were trees and brush for concealment, and the vehicles had enough room to maneuver for quick extraction.

Another of their crew, Slash, was tailing the doctor from an inconspicuous distance in one of the crew's Buicks and kept the hillside team informed of the doctor's progress by cell phone. They had portable radios for back up. As a last resort, Yankee took the Jeep part way down the road to a turnout so he could overlook the canyon and warn the others of the doctor's approach.

The doctor's maroon Cadillac proved easy for Slash to tail. He reported that the target had exited the freeway. Yankee drove the Jeep back to the ambush site, eased the front wheel over the edge of the gully, then got out and laid at the edge of the road, enduring the cold rain and wind. Rebel and Trigger hid in the tree line.

The Cadillac slowly traversed the switchbacks, its headlights sweeping the trees and cliff faces that lined the road. The noise of its powerful engine and the splash of water from its tires grew louder as it rounded the last curve. As expected, the Caddy came to a halt right behind the Jeep, its trunk popped open and the target climbed out.

Rebel and Trigger held their positions as the target walked toward Yankee, his back toward them. With the forest soaked by days of rain, the few leaves and twigs in their path were not a worry. They were so wet and the wind so noisy, their footsteps would be masked. It was perfect infantry weather. Just the same, the mercenaries employed their best stealth approach to the target, too professional not to do so, as they readied their stun guns. They were on top of the target in seconds and Rebel put the stun gun to the doctor's neck before he could turn around. The target went down unconscious.

"Okay, Yankee. He's down, you can get up," advised Trigger. The soaked mercenary rolled over and clasped an extended hand that assisted him to his feet.

"Okay. Let's get a move on before anyone spots us," commanded Yankee, Bravo's right hand man. Yankee and Trigger hefted the doctor and placed him in the back of the Jeep and covered him with a tarpaulin. They piled duffels and sporting gear on top. Yankee climbed into the back seat to monitor the doctor as Rebel took the driver's seat. Trigger tossed the medical bag into the Caddy's trunk and slammed the lid down, then took the driver's seat in the Caddy.

The noise of another vehicle alerted them as it rounded the curve, its headlights off. It was Slash. Rebel gave him a thumb up signal, then engaged the four-wheel drive on the Jeep and backed it out of the gully. The three vehicles reversed course and headed down the hill with their prize.

∞

The doorbell surprised Kate. She was expecting Dan at any moment and he never used the front door. He always parked his Caddy in the garage and came into the house through the kitchen. And he never rang the doorbell.

Kate was even more surprised when she opened the door. There was a security guard, two police officers and a paramedic.

The security officer spoke first, "Sorry to bother you Mrs. Flynn, but the police insisted on speaking with you."

"No bother, officer. What is it you wish to speak about?"

The police officer with a stripe on his sleeve addressed her. "Mrs. Flynn, 9-1-1 received a call from you half an hour ago claiming there was an accident at the curves on Hillside Drive and requesting an ambulance. We just came from there and there's no vehicle or anyone there. Have you heard from your husband? Did he drive the victim to the hospital?"

Kate was stunned. Dan certainly would have called if he was delayed or caught up in an emergency. It wasn't like him to not keep her informed. She began to fear for him, recalling the break-in at the office last month. Her lips quivered. Her hands began to shake. Her eyes began to tear, smudging her perfect make-up. "What do you mean no one's there? Dan called from there on his cell phone. He said he was at the top curve and there was a white Jeep stuck in the gully and a man lying in the road and to call 9-1-1 for an ambulance. What do you mean he's not there?"

The officers braced her arms and ushered her into the house and set her on a chair. "Mrs. Flynn… Mrs. Flynn, here. Sit down. Try to be calm and talk to us. What is your husband's cell phone number? We'll give him a call."

Kate composed herself enough to provide them with both his cellular and car phone numbers. The officers called both numbers, receiving no answer, just his voice-mail. They asked the model of vehicle he drove, its color and registration number. She was distraught, unable to hold back the tears.

The officers realized Kate's distress and didn't press her. They summoned the paramedic inside to attend to her while they radioed headquarters for information on the doctor's vehicle. The security officer informed them he had that information on file at the office. He knew Dr. Flynn drove a new maroon Cadillac and he could look up the registration in just a few minutes. The police thanked him as they headed for the security office.

After obtaining the registration, the police returned to the site of the reported accident. Something wasn't right. Doctors just don't make prank calls to 9-1-1 or leave the scene without notifying someone. There had to be some kind of evidence back there.

Minutes later, using the cruiser's spotlight, the officers spotted a tire track going off the road just uphill of the top curve. They pulled to the side and stepped into the rain, splitting the darkness with their powerful flashlights. They searched for other evidence. There were no signs of a struggle, no blood, no disturbed foliage, only the wheel mark and a smeared tire print. But a doctor was missing, perhaps another man, a white Jeep, and a maroon Caddy. That's all. It was time to call the detectives.

∾

The left side of his neck felt as if he had a severe burn and he had one hell of a headache. Dan was groggy and couldn't focus. It was dark and he felt as if he was suffocating. He could hear noises: ringing bells, large motors, trucks, and sea gulls. He deduced he was close to the riverfront.

There was a musty odor. A cloth sack was over his head. Hell's bells, no wonder he couldn't see and the air stank. He sensed a presence nearby and listened intently, trying to determine where and what it might be. He let his head sag slowly back to its formerly unconscious position. Fear gripped him and he had to force himself to keep from shivering. His throat felt parched, his nose began to run and thirst and hunger added to his discomfort. His wrists and ankles were secured, by tape he guessed, and he was taped to a chair of some sort. He was cold and perspiring at the same time and realized he was in shock. He had no idea how long he had been unconscious or what time it was.

The shuffle of a shoe on a cement floor came from behind. A creaking noise, probably from a chair, came from the same direction. Footsteps approached and halted right behind him. A firm finger poked him in the neck, right on the burn. Dan recoiled from the pain, wishing he hadn't. Now he or they knew he was awake. He swallowed hard, afraid. His mind toyed with his emotions. Fear was the most potent. What did they want? What would they do to get it? His mind created horrible scenarios.

"Welcome back to the world of the living, Dr. Flynn." The voice seemed cold and detached. The sack was yanked off and bright incandescent light blinded him. A hand grasped his hair and jerked his head back. A cloth was rammed into his mouth and forced into his throat far enough to stifle his yell. Dan gagged. The hand pulled the cloth out of his throat just far enough to let him breathe through his nose, but he couldn't yell. He choked repeatedly as the sack was yanked down over his head and it seemed like an eternity before he could adjust his breathing to compensate for his half-blocked windpipe.

The footsteps walked away, a door opened, then closed. Then silence. Dan concentrated on his breathing and struggled at his bindings, but no luck. He attempted to stand but couldn't.

The door opened again and several sets of footsteps entered. The door closed as one set of steps approached. Dan's head hung at an odd angle, the better for him to breathe.

"Dr. Flynn, we are in need of some information. If you cooperate, we'll see that you're returned home safe and sound. If you don't, well… things could get ugly. Nod your head if you understand." The deep, menacing voice came from high above him. When Dan didn't respond within a suitable time, he was punished by a firm backhand on his head and a kick in the shin. He moaned and struggled to scream, but the gag choked him.

"Dr. Flynn, if you don't cooperate, I'll have to get rough. Is that what you want?" Dan didn't respond and was pummeled again.

"Doctor, don't you get it? You're not leaving here until we find out where you moved the lab. Where's your brother? You are going to cooperate, aren't you?" Dan tried to tell them he didn't know, but the gag prevented his response. He shook his head to signify such but they mistook it for resistance and began hitting him again. Dan screamed but the cry never got past his throat. He felt blood flooding from his nose, making his breathing more labored. His left ear felt like it had blood escaping and he knew he had several cracked ribs. He knew the human body wasn't built for this kind of torture. His self-preservation instinct took over, pain and fear being the victors. He nodded his head up and down, accentuating the motions, hoping the tormentors would recognize he was acquiescing.

"Good," remarked the deep voice. The sack was pulled from his head; the blinding light assaulted his vision, making him close his eyes as his head was forcefully yanked back like before, the gag was removed. Dan coughed. He felt nauseated and tried to force saliva down his parched throat but there wasn't any.

"Water," he begged softly.

"No water, food or sleep until we get the information we need, Doctor." The same deep, stern voice did all of the talking. "Now, where is the lab?"

Dan attempted to gulp saliva again with the same negative result. Sensing he was about to be beaten again, he answered, "I don't know. That's the truth."

That answer didn't satisfy the men and they beat Dan again for several agonizing, painful minutes. A wave of nausea came. A small amount of vomit splashed on him and the bare concrete floor, the acidic bile made him feel worse. He heaved repeatedly as the men sidestepped the spew.

"Why are you doing this?" Dan whispered. "I told you, I don't know where my brother moved his lab. That's the truth, damn you."

The deep voice commanded, "Cut his shirt off. Let him shiver. It'll keep him conscious." Dan heard the click of a switchblade and rough hands grabbed his shirt, viciously pulling it. The blade shredded both his dress shirt and tee shirt. They were yanked from his torso and left dangling from his taped wrists. The cold air penetrated him. It eased his nausea but it would soon induce hypothermia. Cold water was splashed on his back from behind, immediately inducing shock and uncontrollable shivering. Dan's vision adjusted and he tried to glimpse at his assailants. They were wearing black ski masks and only their eyes were visible. They were Caucasian was all he could tell, big, muscular Caucasians.

"Doctor, you can give us the information or you can suffer. You're in control, don't you see. Give us the location of the lab and we'll take you home. It's that easy."

Dan shivered. His senses betrayed his mind as he fought for control. "Please," he begged, " I don't know where the lab is and I don't know where my brother is. That's the way he wanted it. That's the absolute truth. I can't tell you because I don't know. I don't know! Damn it, I don't know!" He sobbed. "I don't know!"

There was silence for a moment. The beating started again. Fists smashed into his body. Dan finally, thankfully blacked out.

Bravo grabbed Dan's hair and yanked his head upright, exposing the bruised, bloody mess. The doctor was unconscious.

"This guy can't handle our interrogation protocol," huffed Bravo. "Cover him up so we don't lose him to hypothermia. When he comes to, give him some water. I'm not through with him."

Slash nodded as Bravo headed out the door. He went to a small office in a corner of the rented warehouse where another of his crew, Sparks, a geeky computer/electronics wizard, had set up their operations center. Sparks was on the computer, grimacing and shaking his head.

"What's up, Sparks?"

Sparks looked at Bravo, his expression turned from frustration to fear. "Uh,… well Colonel, I've scanned the credit card purchases for Daniel Flynn and Peter Flynn… and, uh…"

"What are you telling me, Sparks?"

Being new to Bravo's crew, Sparks found it difficult to make eye contact with him. Bravo's commanding presence intimidated him, a lot. He glanced at the floor, "Well, sir… I haven't been able to find any unusual credit card purchases for either of them or his wife. Just local routine stuff: restaurants, golf shop, department stores. There's nothing unusual."

"Shit! This is going to take longer than I thought. I'll have to call in a marker. I hate calling in chips for penny-ante shit like this."

Sparks was relieved. Bravo wasn't taking his anger out on him. He returned his attention to the computer to look busy. He made entries on his keyboard and avoided looking at Bravo.

"Sparks, give me the bat phone." That was Bravo's term for his special encrypted cell phone for communication with his shadow community contacts. Sparks passed the phone and resumed his work. The Colonel pressed several buttons and placed it to his ear. In a few seconds, he began a discussion with a party unknown and Sparks pretended not to hear a word.

"This is Titan, key two-four-seven-four-two, I need to speak with Bole Weevil, priority Sierra." Bravo used a low-level priority to avoid arousing suspicion from the screener. Another minute passed before he spoke again.

"This is Titan. I have a request, standard priority." Bravo listened, then resumed, "I need a search for an individual, his purchases, vehicle registrations, current location, credit cards, the usual. I also need a phone tap. I'll have my COM specialist give you the particulars. Ready?" Sparks looked up from the computer at the mention of his tasking and Bravo handed him the phone. "Give him all the data you've got."

Sparks nodded as he jammed the phone between his ear and shoulder. He read data into the phone as Bravo headed back to the interrogation room.

Slash had the unconscious doctor covered with blankets.

"Get the sodium pentothal," commanded Bravo. Slash retrieved a small leather carryall and prepared a hypodermic needle and laid it on the table.

"We'll soon know if he's telling the truth."

"What if he is?" asked Slash, so nick-named for his extraordinary skills with bladed weapons.

"We'll drive off that bridge if we come to it."

The doctor began to stir, his headed bobbed slightly. Bravo nodded. Slash swabbed Dan's arm with alcohol, then inserted the syringe and injected the serum.

Dan was in pain and his left eye was swollen shut. He was unable to resist and he realized he had soiled in his trousers. That realization was so denigrating, he screamed inside . He felt a pinch in his right arm and the internal rush of fluid from a hypodermic syringe. "*Probably not morphine.*" His grogginess increased. He felt light-headed, approaching euphoria, and his will to resist had deserted him. He would tell them whatever they wanted to know.

The deep voice of his antagonist returned to torment him. "Doctor Flynn, we have injected you with a truth serum. Very soon you will tell us the answers to all our questions. No more evasion. Now, I want you to lie to me about your name. Is your name Dr. Daniel Flynn?"

"Yes," answered Dan softly, his head rolled slowly from side to side. Bravo glanced briefly at Slash, who nodded. Apparently the serum had taken effect.

"Are you an oncologist?"

"Yes."

"Is your wife's name Kate?"

"Yes."

"Where do you live?"

"Hampton Manor."

"Is your brother Dr. Peter Flynn."

"Yes."

"Is he a biochemical engineer?"

"Yes."

"Is he the same Dr. Peter Flynn who formulated DDCG for the ParaZyme 2000 protocol?"

"Yes."

"Did your brother shut down his lab?"

"Yes."

"Did he stop his research into DDCG?"

"Yes."

"Does he intend to start his research again?"

"Yes."

"Where?"

"I don't know."

"Is he still in Portland?"

"No."

"Where is your brother now?"

"I don't know."

"How do you know he's not in Portland?"

"I helped him pack his car."

"What kind of car does your brother drive?"

"Pontiac Bonneville."

"What color is it?"

"Bronze."

"What year is his car?"

"Uh… not sure. 1999 or 2000."

That information didn't matter. Sparks had already hacked into the Oregon DMV records. Bravo was being certain of the serum's effect.

"When he left Portland, which way did he go?"

"I don't know."

"Then how do you know he left Portland?"

"We agreed it was best to move the lab out of Portland."

"Where did you agree to move the lab?"

"We didn't."

"Do you know what state the lab is in?"

"No. Only Pete knows."

"How does he contact you?"

"E-mail."

"Where do you get your e-mail from your brother?"

"At home."

"What's your e-mail address?"

Dan gave his e-mail address as Slash wrote it on a pad. Bravo read it back to Dan and had him confirm it. Then Bravo demanded to know Pete's e-mail address. Dan complied and Slash wrote that down too. Bravo was disappointed to see it was an address that could be used to send and receive e-mail from almost any online computer in the world. It would be difficult to track down.

"Does your brother contact anyone else?"

"Yes."

"Who is that?"

"My attorney."

"What is your attorney's name?"

"Harold Morrison." Slash wrote that down.

"Is his office in Portland?"

"Yes."

When questioned, Dan gave them Morrison's office address and e-mail address, which Slash obligingly noted.

"Does your brother stay in contact with anyone else?"

"I don't know."

"Where is your brother now?"

"I don't know."

"Does your attorney know where your brother is?"

"Uh... I don't... no."

Confused by the answer, Bravo attempted to clarify, "You don't know or the attorney doesn't know?"

Now Dan was confused. "I... I don't know." Bravo interpreted that to mean that the doctor didn't know if the attorney knew and made a mental note to find out.

"Is your brother still in Oregon?"

"I don't know."

"Is anyone helping your brother with his research?"

"Yes."

"Who?"

"I don't know."

"Is it a male or female?"

"I don't know."

"How do you know he has help?"

"He said he found a research assistant."

"Where does your brother have his bank accounts?"

"He doesn't have any."

"He must have funding. How does he get money?"

"Through a blind trust."

"Where is this trust?"

"Portland."

"What's the name of the trust?"

"Corridor Holdings."

"Who are the trustees?"

"I am."

"Any others?"

"Yes."

"What are their names?"

"Harold Morrison."

"Any others?"

"No."

That confirmed it. Bravo's team would definitely have to visit the attorney's office. This job just became a lot more expensive for a certain doctor in Boston, in more ways than one.

Boston: The Board meeting had been a success in Rushton's eyes. The voting went in his favor. All of the important national positions were now in his hands. He could now focus on the Flynns and their DDCG threat.

But not everything was going well. He just had an e-mail from Bravo, a snag would cost $500,000; another $150,000 now, the remainder upon completion. And they still had no idea where the lab was. Bravo was convinced that the target had no knowledge of the lab's location and had an alternative plan to find it, but it would involve some extreme measures; the kind that could get people the electric chair. Even though he balked, Rushton made it clear that success was paramount and he wouldn't tolerate failure.

That wasn't the worst of it. Kress was attempting to blackmail him for $2,000,000, or he threatened to turn over duplicate tapes of the illegal taps to the FBI.

During his years on the Board and the national committees, Rushton had used his influence on medical and pharmaceutical issues. Of course, the persuasion included bribes and a modest fee for his services. Over time, his fees amounted to more than eight million dollars, tucked away in an offshore bank.

The problem now was Kress. Rushton could pay off the vulture, but he had a hunch that wouldn't be the end of it. Nor could he ever be assured that other duplicate tapes existed. He couldn't go to the FBI without incriminating himself. There was only one solution, a Colonel Bravo solution.

Helendale, California: The young lab assistant was superb.

Pete had interviewed six candidates for the position, meeting all of them miles away from his condo and the lab. He wanted someone willing to work and interested in biochemical cancer research, preferably with experience, but mostly someone who wouldn't mind working in the remote desert. He also wanted an assistant that was free of family entanglements: single, no kids, no relatives nearby. He found a jewel.

She was definitely easy to look at. It was nearly impossible not to look at her. Her beautiful Asian-American face, long dark hair, high cheekbones, brown eyes and smooth skin formed a vision worthy of immortalization by a Renaissance master.

She was quite intelligent, too. She was a Medical Doctor and wanted to be away from men, having recently severed a long relationship in Los Angeles. The man she parted with continued to harass her with calls, letters, and e-mails for months after the breakup, even duplicating keys to her apartment and car. She informed the police that she was being stalked but they couldn't do anything except insist he relinquish all keys to her property. That he did, but it didn't stop the harassment. She decided to get out of Los Angeles and hide. That's how she came to be in the high desert in search of a job.

She was Dr. Lisa Chen, born in San Francisco twenty-nine years ago to a second-generation Chinese-American businessman and his lovely American wife, a former Miss Nevada. She had graduated from medical school at UCLA and completed her residency in South Central. Having had enough of gunshot and stab wounds, she decided to focus on the research and treatment of cancer. When she saw Pete's add in the newspaper, she sent a reply. Pete called her, surprised that an M.D. would be willing to work as a research assistant to a biochemical engineer. He was impressed and decided to meet her in person.

This was Lisa's second day at work and they were getting into the specifics of the research.

"So tell me again what this DDCG is."

Pete exaggerated his inhale, like a pitcher taking his windup. "It's doxodigallocatechin gallate, a special compound I formulated. We're going to experiment with mix ratios of matrix metalloproteinase, inject it into cancerous tumors and monitor the heterocyclic amines and VEGF, the Vascular Endothelial Growth Factor. We want to determine the optimum mix ratio to minimize the amines and VGEF. I had some success with this and published in the North American Medical Monthly."

"I think I read something about that," stated Lisa. "Yes, I recall. You're using metabolically boosted enzymes to eat the cancerous cells before they break down and infiltrate healthy tissue. But how do you stop the enzymes from eating into healthy tissue?"

"Excellent question, Doctor. That's our research. We need to identify a compound that can subdue the enzymes and give the body's excretory system time to evacuate them safely."

"That's a lot to pull together, Doctor. I'm looking forward to the challenge and I can see I'm going to have to study up on doxodi…"

Pete grinned and pronounced it again. "Doxodigallocatechin gallate."

"Doxodigallocatechin gallate. Got it."

"Well, what do you say, Doctor? Shall we make medical history?"

"Absolutely, Doctor. Lead the way."

Portland: The detective vehicle pulled into the elegant circular drive of Dan Flynn's residence. Dr. Patricia Flynn, one of Dan's daughters, observed the plainclothes officers emerge and approach.

"The detectives are here, Mom."

Patricia opened the door before they rang the bell. She waved them in as they produced their badges and IDs. Patricia showed them to the living room. Kate and her other daughter, Dr. Karen Flynn, rose to greet them and offered them a seat.

The older detective began his report. "Mrs. Flynn, I'm Detective Krenna and this is Detective Lewis. We want to apprise you of our preliminary investigation and ask you a few questions. Do you feel up to it?"

Kate nodded.

"We've searched the road all the way down to the highway. We found a tire mark near the location you mentioned, but there is no trace of your husband or his vehicle. We've got the whole police department on the lookout for them. Our forensics people made a cast of the tire mark and we'll try to get a match. If it's Jeep tire, that'll give us more to work with. We're also looking for the white Jeep. We found several sets of footprints on the opposite side of the road at the edge of the woods, but the rain washed away the identifying features. We can't even guess at the type of shoes or their sizes, but it does indicate there were some people in the woods. As I said, we've got the entire force on the lookout."

The women sobbed and held each other. He continued somberly, "Mrs. Flynn, I'm sorry for what I'm about to ask, but I have to ask it for the record."

The women looked agonized as they waited in suspense.

"Mrs. Flynn, were there any marital difficulties between you and Dr. Flynn?"

The women looked appropriately shocked. The daughters were insulted and Mrs. Flynn broke into tears, then slowly composed herself.

"Detective, my husband and I have a wonderful relationship. We love each other dearly and there have been no episodes of infidelity on either part in the thirty years of our marriage; no money difficulties, no family disputes. No Detective, I'm certain he has *not* abandoned his family."

The detectives nodded.

"Thank you, Mrs. Flynn. That eliminates that possibility, so let's consider kidnapping. Have you been contacted by anyone demanding ransom?"

Kate sobbed and wiped her eyes. "No. What does that mean?"

"Nothing at this point, Ma'am. Usually, it takes a while to hear from kidnappers and there are a couple of considerations here. One is, you might be contacted with ransom demands. Second, the FBI gains jurisdiction within forty-eight hours, if it is kidnapping."

Patricia couldn't help wondering about another motive. "What if it's not a kidnapping for ransom?"

The detectives glanced at each other then back to the women.

"Dr. Flynn, we have no reason to believe that any harm has come to your father. Are you aware of any incident or anyone who might want to do him harm?"

The women looked at each other. Kate answered. "My husband's office was burglarized last month. The research lab was torn apart, Pete said it was a mess."

"Who's Pete?" inquired the junior man.

"I'm sorry. Dr. Peter Flynn, my husband's brother. He's the researcher and in charge of the lab."

"What kind of research was he doing?"

"He's researching a cure for cancer," intervened Karen.

"Was this burglary investigated by our department?"

"I suppose so. The office is across the street from the University Medical Center. Is that your jurisdiction?"

"Yes, Ma'am. It is. We'll check with burglary section to see if there's a link." The women nodded and thanked them.

"One last thing, Mrs. Flynn. We'd like your permission to tap your phones in the event the kidnappers make contact. Would that be agreeable to you?"

"Certainly. When? How many people will be in the house?"

"We'll arrange for it as soon as we return to our car and there won't be anyone in your house. The phone company can tap in and we can monitor the line without invading your home. Once the need for it has passed, it'll be disconnected. So we have your permission?"

"Yes. Of course."

"Thank you, Mrs. Flynn. We've bothered you enough for one day, so we'll be on our way." They rose and shook hands with Kate. "No need to get up, Ma'am. We'll find our way out."

"Thank you, Detectives. Please find my husband."

"We'll do our best, Ma'am. Good night."

The detectives made their way out. As they left the house the junior detective asked, "What if it's not kidnap for ransom?"

The senior man glanced down, shaking his head. "I'm afraid to think about it."

∞

Bravo read the e-mail as he hunched over Sparks's shoulder. Their employer wanted additional services from them. Bravo shook his head, amazed at the implications. He stood upright and rubbed his chin. The request presented a distraction from their assignment but it was necessary for security. Kress could blow the whole operation and implicate Rushton, cutting off their revenue. On the plus side, it was another profit opportunity for his crew, but it would require help from certain government sources and that meant serious bucks.

"Okay, Sparks. Send this. 'Assignment accepted. Contact our connection and request cooperation of Treasury Department. From you, we need $300,000 cash in used, unmarked one hundred dollar bills. From Treasury, we need $1.9 Million in marked bills. Need info to contact pigeon. Have all delivered by express courier. Operation will proceed upon receipt'."

Sparks typed, clicked the mouse a few times and reported, "Done, Colonel."

"Excellent. Now have Rebel rig a remote and a bomb that will fit inside a packet of money, large enough to kill the man holding it."

Sparks grinned.

Bravo chuckled as Sparks headed out. Bravo stuck his head out the door and whistled at Trigger. Trigger tossed his cigarette away and approached.

"What's up, Colonel?"

"Trigger, I need you to handle a bag drop, extortion money for that weasel Kress. You've seen him face to face. There'll be a bomb in the bag. You'll drop it off, then remote detonate it once he takes it. Can you handle that?"

Trigger smirked, "Piece o' cake, Colonel."

"Good. There'll be a little something extra in your paycheck. Find Yankee and tell him I want to see him."

Trigger snapped a sloppy salute and walked off, passing Rebel and Sparks coming the other way.

"What did you have in mind for blast radius, Colonel?" inquired Rebel, their demolitions specialist.

"Five meters should do it. Remote-detonated and small enough to hide inside a stack of bills. It'll have other stacks of money around it. Is that doable?"

Rebel huffed. "I thought you had a challenge for me. Sure, it's doable. When do you need it, Colonel?"

"Tomorrow night"

"Can do easy. I'm on it, Colonel." Bravo nodded as Rebel trotted off.

"Sparks. I've got a job for you and Yankee tonight."

Washington, D.C. "That's a tall request, Doctor," said Stakemore, exaggerating the difficulty factor. In fact, when Congress members made requests, feds jumped. "That will take substantial effort and time."

Rushton understood she was fishing for another contribution, because people who expend substantial time and effort need to be compensated substantially.

"Well, Congresswoman, as the new Chairman of NOMP, you are assured we will fully support your efforts for re-election in the manner appropriate."

Stakemore answered, "I'm looking forward to your support, Doctor. You may count on our assistance. I'll turn you over to my staff assistant to arrange the particulars. Thank you for contacting my office. Now, here's Gail, my assistant."

Portland: The warm sunlight through the windshield felt good to the chilled detectives as they made their way toward a downtown multi-level parking garage. Their unmarked car led a four-vehicle convoy in search of Dr. Dan Flynn's maroon Cadillac.

Krenna learned that most new Cadillacs were equipped with an onboard device that could be activated from Cadillac central operations and its location pinpointed through satellite tracking. Krenna had called Mrs. Flynn to obtain her permission for the police to contact the Cadillac center and activate the device. The operations center had located Dr. Flynn's vehicle in a four-story parking structure near the financial district. Krenna notified the forensics lab and they joined the detectives and two police cruisers to find it.

The four vehicles pulled into the parking structure and stopped bumper to bumper at the attendant's booth as Krenna flashed his credentials and explained what they sought. Without question, the attendant raised the barricade. As each vehicle reached its assigned level, they reported to Krenna they were ready.

"All units stand by, we'll be ready in one minute. As soon as they reached the top level, Krenna nodded to Lewis, who had his cell phone against his ear.

"Okay, operations, this is Portland Police, activate the vehicle's alarm."

Both detectives rolled down their windows. A moment later, they heard a car alarm, but it wasn't on their level.

The radio crackled, "Unit forty-three, I've got it. Second level."

Krenna grabbed the radio mike, "Roger, all units converge, second level." He replaced the mike to its holder and spun the wheel as Lewis informed the operations center to cut off the alarm and unlock the vehicle's doors. By the time they reached the spot, two uniformed officers were taping off the area. The two forensics specialists were already unloading their equipment.

"Christ, Kren, that car looks like it just came off the showroom floor," observed Lewis.

Krenna nodded, disappointed. "Yeah. How much you want to bet it was put through the car wash just before it got dumped here?"

The detectives climbed out and stepped over the yellow tape to search for evidence. Lewis pulled his pen from his shirt pocket as Krenna put latex gloves on and opened the doors. Lewis pushed the trunk release button with his pen, the lid popped open and they scanned the cavernous compartment. The trunk had been recently vacuumed. Krenna lifted the cover to the spare tire compartment and found nothing unusual, not even a scrap of paper or a twig.

The detectives checked the pockets on the seatbacks and doors, then the glove compartment. Empty. The whole interior had been vacuumed and wreaked of rubbing alcohol.

"Smells like a hospital, Kren. They must have rubbed down the whole interior with alcohol to destroy DNA evidence. And look, the driver's floor mat is missing. All the others are here."

Krenna frowned. "They probably trashed it."

He summoned the uniformed officers. "I need you to search all the trash containers on this level and the one below. We're looking for a tan floor mat. If you find it, don't touch it. Just notify the forensics guys, okay?"

"Yes, sir," both answered and moved off.

"Can we start now, Sergeant Krenna?" asked one of the forensics specialists.

"Yeah. All yours. Lew, let's check the trash containers on the upper levels. We need that floor mat."

∞

"You losing your touch, man?" teased Sparks as Yankee fiddled with the office building alarm system. "Usually you've got these things disarmed in thirty seconds."

"Can it, jerk-off." The alarm system arming light suddenly extinguished and the door latch released. Yankee smirked as he flipped the door open and it caught Sparks on the knee.

Sparks rubbed his knee as Yankee checked his watch.

"Thirty-seven seconds, Sparks. Let's see you beat that."

"Mea culpa, my friend."

The mercenaries slipped inside and closed the door behind them. They slipped around a hallway corner, staring down a dark corridor. They donned night vision goggles and crept down the hall in search of the office of Harold I. Morrison, Attorney at Law. Sparks spotted it first and pointed. As they reached the door, Yankee burst out laughing.

"What's the deal, man?"

"This guy doesn't have any security on his door. Just that silly handle lock. Not even a dead bolt. What a dork." Yankee pulled out his lock pick and had it open in ten seconds. He pushed the door in, stepping aside, bowing and ushering his partner in as if Sparks was royalty.

The office was a simple one-room operation with minimal furniture. Sparks went immediately to the desktop computer and powered it up. Yankee went to the file cabinet and laughed again. He stuffed his lock picks away.

"He doesn't even have a locking file cabinet. What a bozo." Yankee opened the top drawer, stowed his night vision goggles, switched on his red-filtered flashlight and searched the files. He wasn't having any luck; neither was Sparks.

The computer was password protected. Sparks couldn't even access the desktop.

"Dammit. Everything's password protected. Help me find the password. He's probably got it written down here somewhere." They shuffled through drawers and papers. Sparks found a paper with names and data on it and tried those; access denied. He tried phone number combinations; access denied. He tried several combinations of birth dates; access denied. Fifteen minutes of experimenting failed to achieve any results.

"Yankee, this isn't going anywhere. We'll take the stack with us."

"You losing your touch, man?"

"Touché. But be advised, this guy's password is twelve digits, alphas *and* numerics."

"Get what you need, then help me finish searching the files. There's got to be something we can use."

∞

Kress slouched into a chair in a coffee shop that provided Internet access for its customers. He had spent the night scouting his entry and escape routes. He planned how he would conduct the money drop and make his getaway.

He hooked his laptop into a wall jack and powered on. The usual Monday morning gentry began to fill the place.

The computer alerted him he had e-mail. He found an e-mail from Rushton. He was accepting Kress's terms and he would be contacted by e-mail to arrange delivery. Sure enough, the very next message, from an address Kress didn't recognize, stated that a courier was ready to execute the delivery and suggested a time and place.

"Yeah, right. Like I'm a cabbage head, letting them dictate the conditions." He composed a curt reply and sent it into etherspace. His message made it clear that he was going to set the time and place for the exchange and they should monitor their e-mail at 0200 hours tonight. Kress planned to reveal the details at the last minute, preventing the couriers from conducting any reconnaissance beforehand. If the couriers didn't show or attempted to apprehend him, he'd have the tapes and a sworn affidavit sent to the FBI.

Several minutes later, a reply came. The courier had acquiesced, not that he had any choice.

∞

Sparks was anxious to get re-acquainted with his sleeping bag as he tapped out the Colonel's acknowledgement to Kress. He had been up all night attempting to hack into the attorney's computer. He had managed to hack the password, only to discover that most of the files were encrypted and the decryption program was password protected too. He worked on that for an hour, when the computer alerted him to Kress's incoming e-mail.

Bravo was disappointed but not surprised that Kress had rejected his suggestion and instructed Sparks to acknowledge.

Bravo was on the phone with Bole Weevil, his covert source inside a federal alphabet agency. Which agency was anyone's guess.

"Yeah, got it. Titan out." The Colonel slapped the device closed and hooked it onto his belt.

"Good news, Colonel?"

"Nope. There isn't a trace of Peter Flynn. Not even in the Financial Crimes Network. The good doctor has made a deep hole and covered it well. We'll have to go through with the extortion drop. If that doesn't work, we'll go to scenario Echo."

Sparks didn't like the sound of that. He was working on scenario Charlie, hacking into the attorney's computer. Scenario Delta was the drop. If neither of those worked, scenario Echo required arrangements for a funeral.

Bravo left the office and checked Rebel's progress with the demolition charge. The explosives technician had completed the diabolical device, using the remote controller from a small toy racecar.

"Where we at, Rebel?"

Rebel answered without looking up. "Just getting ready to test it, Colonel." He inserted batteries into the remote as Bravo and Trigger watched. "Okay, everybody clear. Fire in the hole." He uncovered the guard and pressed the button. Across the warehouse, a loud crack sounded as a bright flash and a tiny smoke cloud emerged from under an inverted pail. The punctured pail ricocheted off the ceiling and slammed around the warehouse as echoes reverberated off the bare walls. To anyone outside it was no louder than an empty pallet dropped from several feet above the floor, not unusual around the busy docks.

"I used a blasting cap and a pinch of Semtex. I know the charge will go if the detonator and cap work, which," Rebel grinned, "they do." Rebel removed the batteries and placed them on the bench. "The main charge is ready, Colonel. Trigger hollowed out a stack of money; the Semtex is glued inside. The receiver antenna is a thin wire wrapped around the bundle. Tonight, all I have to do is rig the blasting cap, load the batteries and this little lady will be ready to please. You just give me the word and I'll make her dance."

"Your mama," interjected Trigger. "If I'm the one carryin' a live bomb, you can bet your ass I'm the one holding the detonator."

Rebel and Bravo looked at each other.

Bravo stated, "I believe our friend has a point."

Rebel looked at Trigger in mock disbelief, "And after all we've been through. I'm crushed."

Bravo slapped Rebel on the back. "Good work. Have it ready to go by midnight."

∞

Kress walked inconspicuously along the sidewalk, carrying a large canvass duffel. He meandered toward the drop site. Even though it was 1230 in the morning, he didn't appear suspicious because he wore his old security guard uniform. Anyone observing him would think he belonged there.

He was en route to a building he had worked at previously as a security guard. He was very familiar with the floor plan, the security systems, the closed circuit monitors, the security office and the janitorial schedules.

The day prior, Kress had visited the security office on the pretense of seeing his old pal Bucky. Kress entered the security office with a dozen doughnuts, just to pass old times and shoot the breeze. After some time, Bucky headed for the restroom, leaving his trusted friend Drew in the security office. It had taken Kress all of four seconds to find the security code for the alarm system. Kress hung around for half an hour more, then bid farewell, promising to visit again soon.

The twelve-story building was monitored from the premises during business hours. After hours, it was guarded only by the alarm, connected to a remote monitoring service. The service would only be alerted if the alarm was tripped, so all Kress had to do was disarm the system, unlock the door with the master key he copied before quitting the job, and reset the alarm once inside.

The janitors rarely ever worked past eleven p.m., so Kress was confidant the building would be vacant. It was. Only the hallway lights were on. All of the office lights were extinguished.

Kress ambled to the rear door, keeping his face hidden from the exterior camera and entered the disarm code, quickly unlocked the door, entered with his duffel, closed and locked the door and re-armed the alarm. He rounded the nearest hallway corner, out of sight from the street and the nearest closed circuit camera, then opened his duffel. He pulled out an oversized jumpsuit and slipped it over his guard uniform, tossed his hat into the duffel and donned a black ski mask. He donned rubber gloves for his hands and plastic booties for his shoes.

Kress hefted the duffel and went to the security office on the bottom floor, gaining entry with his master key. He disconnected a security monitor and placed it with his duffel, then connected a signal generator to an unused closed circuit. He gathered the monitor and his duffel and trotted to the elevator lobby. He summoned all three lifts. The doors of the farthest elevator opened first, so he entered and hit the emergency stop button and retrieved the duffel and monitor.

He summoned the remaining elevators and as each opened, he sent them to the top floor and quickly stepped back out. He returned to the farthest lift, released the emergency stop and rode to the sixth floor. Kress pressed the emergency stop and jammed two large screwdrivers into the doors.

He ran to suite 604, entered with the master key, grabbed a chair from the office and carried it to the end of the hallway, placing it under the exposed closed circuit camera. He trotted to the opposite end of the hall, retrieved the monitor and a signal tester from the duffel and brought them back. He placed the monitor on the chair, stepped up, reached for the camera and disconnected its cable. He attached the signal tester to the cable and confirmed it was receiving the signal from the generator in the security office. All good. He disconnected the tester, pulled the excess cable from the wall and connected it to the monitor. He pulled the chair as far down the hall as the cable would allow, positioning the monitor so he could watch it from the elevator.

Satisfied, he grabbed his duffel and went back to suite 604. He placed the duffel at the window, swapped the signal tester for his laptop and searched the room for the phone jack. He disconnected the office phone, connected his computer and powered up. While it was going through startup, Kress removed a cordless drill from the duffel and drilled a half-inch hole into the wooden window frame, then tossed the drill into the duffel. He took a steel lag bolt eye hook from his coverall pocket and twisted it into the hole, using a large screwdriver as a lever for the last few twists.

Into the duffel went the screwdriver and out came one hundred feet of quarter inch steel cable attached to a collapsible grappling hook. Kress twisted the hook prongs and secured them, ran the loose end of the cable through the eyebolt and knotted it. He cautiously lifted the window blinds as he checked the dark alley below. Certain it was clear, he opened the window, wrapped an old sweater around the hook, then heaved it across the alley to the rooftop of the adjacent three-story building. The muffled hook made a slight noise as it skidded along the flat, tarred roof and collided with a vent hood. Kress ducked back inside and observed for any reaction.

He saw his computer was ready. He tapped a few commands and pulled up his e-mail program. He composed several short test e-mails to himself and sent them into etherspace.

He checked the alley and rooftop again. There wasn't a soul around. He reeled in the excess cable and dragged the hook toward the edge of the roof. As planned, the prongs caught on the brick parapet capping the roof perimeter. Kress grabbed a ratchet device from his duffel and rigged it around the cable, pulling the excess cable through the eyehook and back through the ratchet. He tightened the cable, then clamped the lever to crush the two strands of cable together. He ratcheted the cable tight, then attached thick twine to the end of the locking lever. He tossed the spool of twine across the alley, clear of the cable.

Next, he mounted a dual-wheel pulley to the top of the cable and attached a heavy-duty strap with a snap-link to the bottom. He strapped a nylon harness around his hips and attached another snap link to the front. He clipped the two snap links together and kicked his feet out to test the cable with his full weight. It held.

Kress regained his feet and disconnected the snap links, then secured the pulley. He returned to the elevator with an empty gym bag and two walkie-talkies, pulled the screwdrivers from the doors and went to the top floor. On the twelfth floor, he jammed the doors open, then forced open the doors to the other two lifts, hit their stop buttons, then un-jammed the third one and rode it down to the lobby.

Once there, he tested the radios and placed one and the empty canvass bag next to a trash can between the elevators. He went to the security office, disconnected the signal generator and connected a spare cable between the wall outlet and the VIDEO OUT port of a security monitor. He switched on the closed circuit video and checked the monitor. The recording system was off. All good. He stuffed the signal generator into his leg pocket, then selected the video monitor to view the camera overlooking the elevator lobby. The signal should now be relayed to the monitor he had installed on the sixth floor.

Kress went to the alarm control at the rear door, disarmed it and unlocked the door. He returned to the elevator and rode back to the sixth floor, forced open one outer door of the middle elevator and jammed it open. The vacant shaft was now exposed. He sent the functional elevator back down to the first floor and checked his watch. He was ready with twenty minutes to spare.

Kress returned to suite 604 and stowed all of his gear into the duffel, then composed an e-mail to the courier. He sent the e-mail and awaited acknowledgement as he gathered the extortion tapes for the exchange.

The e-mail acknowledgement came back in a few minutes. Kress disconnected his laptop and stowed it in the duffel. He headed for the elevator with the tapes.

Now all he had to do was wait.

CHAPTER VI

TRAIL OF TEARS

Portland: Bravo's crew was on the road by the time Kress's e-mail arrived. They cruised the city, Rebel and Trigger in one vehicle, Yankee and Slash in the other. Bravo and Sparks remained at the safe house.

Kress was clever. He had waited until the last minute to reveal the location for the exchange. The e-mail gave the location and his conditions. They had thirty minutes to show with the money. If they tried to screw him, the incriminating tapes would be sent to the FBI.

Sparks notified the crew by cell phone. Each unit acknowledged. They were minutes from the site.

The vehicles converged and slowed to assess the area. It was a moonless night and the sky was clear. The building occupied an entire city block with dark alleys on each side. They drove around back into a parking lot and checked for threats.

Yankee radioed, "We'll cover the front and the west alley. Unit two, drop Trigger and cover the rear and east alley." He turned to Slash, "I'll drop you here. Watch the parking lot. I'll watch the west alley."

Slash nodded. He snugged his collar and stepped into the darkness. Yankee drove to the corner and parked in a shadow. He shut down and lowered his window.

Rebel dropped Trigger at the rear door and parked in a dark corner of the lot. He turned off the engine, climbed out, chambered a round into his .45 and holstered the piece. He bundled himself inside his fatigue jacket and reported ready.

Yankee checked his watch. They were on schedule.

"Okay, let's do it."

Trigger acknowledged, "I'm goin' in." He opened his bomber jacket for access to his Beretta, grabbed the moneybag and opened the door. He peeked inside and entered. He cautiously stepped into the main lobby, peeking around each corner. There was no one in sight, no unusual sounds or odors. He hugged the wall to minimize his exposure.

"SQIIXXZZK."

The sudden noise startled him. It came from a radio.

"Pick up the radio, pea brain."

∞

Kress saw two Buicks enter the parking lot. He saw four men, one of them the black thug that had invaded his office and kicked Charlie in the nuts. One Buick drove out of sight. The other parked in a shadow after dropping off the black guy.

The black guy, carrying a gym bag, appeared on the security monitor. Kress snickered. *"Let's play ball."* He pressed the transmit switch on his radio and scraped a screwdriver across the mike, knowing it would cause a high-pitched squeal on the radio in the lobby. Kress saw the guy jump. *"Good, he's nervous."*

"Pick up the radio, pea brain," Kress radioed.

The henchman looked around.

"Down here, on the floor at the elevators."

The mercenary crossed the lobby and picked up the radio.

"Okay, ass wipe," came the reply, "let's party."

"Open your jacket." The man opened his jacket, but not enough to satisfy Kress.

"Take it off. Now!" He removed his jacket and dropped it, releasing the gym bag only to switch hands. That was a good sign. It meant there was something valuable in the bag. Kress noticed the guy was packing serious firepower.

"Open the elevator and throw your gun inside."

Trigger reluctantly drew his pistol and pressed the elevator button with the end of the suppressor. The doors opened and he tossed it inside.

"Now lift your pant legs." A smaller pistol was strapped inside his left ankle.

"Toss that in, too. Now!"

The guy hesitated.

"Do you want those tapes to go to the FBI?"

The thug reached down for his backup piece. He tossed it into the elevator.

"Any other weapons?"

"No."

"There better not be. Show the money." Kress observed the thug open the gym bag and hold it up.

"Take it to the camera and show me." The guy complied. It looked like real money on the monitor.

"Good. Now take out the money and put it into the canvass bag on the floor near the elevator. No tricks."

The black man returned to the elevator and transferred the money. When finished, he radioed, "All set. Now what?"

"Toss the money into the elevator and press every button to send it to the top floor. You stay in the lobby. If it skips any floors or you try to come up, you know what happens."

The thug nodded and disappeared into the lift, emerging seconds later without the bag. The doors closed. Kress monitored the thug as the elevator ascended.

"Where are the tapes?"

"They'll be sent down as soon as I get the money."

∞

Trigger spoke into the collar mike for his team radio.

"The bastard disarmed me and the money's on the elevator. It's heading for the top, stopping at every floor. I can't tell which floor he's on and he's got me on video. If I leave the lobby or he finds the device, the op is blown." Trigger subtly pushed the down buttons for the other elevators but they didn't move.

"He's got the other elevators locked on the top floor."

Yankee needed more information. "Can we reach the stairway without being seen?"

"Yeah. Come in the rear door, take the first left and the stairwell is across the hall."

Yankee made a quick decision. "Slash, go in the back door. Did you copy Trigger?"

Slash was already at a full run as he pulled his pistol. "Roger, I'm on the move. Trigger, tell me when the elevator stops at each floor."

"Roger. It's on the fourth floor now. It takes about fifteen seconds per floor."

Slash rounded the corner like a base runner rounding third to win the World Series. He barely managed to break his momentum without overshooting the door. He eased inside, trotted around the corner and up the stairs.

"I'm in the stairwell." He bounded the stairs two at a time.

"It just stopped on the fifth floor."

Slash passed the third floor. His radio reception was fading and he was getting tired.

"Sixth floor," reported Trigger, but Slash, climbing one step at a time now, was panting too heavily to hear the fuzzy transmission.

∞

The doors opened. Kress saw the pistols on the floor as he grabbed the moneybag. He used his metal detector to scan the bag. There was a strong signal. There shouldn't be one at all.

Kress cautiously opened the bag and scanned each packet of bills. The elevator doors closed and it headed up. He got a strong signal from one packet and sifted through it, finding the bomb. He tossed it down the open middle elevator shaft and heard it hit bottom. He scanned the remaining packets. They were good. He stuffed the detector into the bag, grabbed the wedged screwdrivers from the middle elevator doors and tossed them in too. The middle doors closed, sealing off the shaft. He decided to keep the tapes and tossed them into the moneybag. He zipped the bag and ran for suite 604. He thought he heard footsteps in the stairwell.

∞

In the lobby, Trigger heard something thud inside the middle elevator shaft as the ascending one reached the seventh floor.

"It's on seven, Slash. Do you copy?"

Exhausted, Slash passed the sixth floor and thought he heard a transmission. He stopped on a landing to catch his breath and requested Trigger to "Say again."

"The elevator is on seven."

"Roger... almost there."

Yankee heard Trigger transmit, but not Slash. Trigger relayed for him.

Trigger put his jacket on and fingered the detonation transmitter.

∞

In suite 604, Kress shouldered the moneybag and hooked the duffel to his waist. He unlatched the pulley and snapped the links together, gave one test bounce on the cable then lifted his legs clear of the window. The pulley slung him outside and across the alley. He accelerated toward the adjacent building. The pulley made noise. Kress bent his knees, anticipating impact against the brick parapet. He hit harder than expected and it knocked the wind out of him. In seconds, he recovered and got one leg over the parapet and hauled himself over the top. He unhooked the duffel and opened it. He ran to the spool of twine and gave it a tug. The lever released, the ratchet and cable arced across the alley and smacked into the wall. Kress hauled up the cable and ratchet, feeding it into the duffel. Two gunshots cracked. Kress felt the shockwave of a bullet pass his head. Another ricocheted off the parapet. Then there was an explosion inside the office building.

Slash caught up with the elevator on the eighth floor, but there was no one there. In the hallway, he could hear the team radio better.

In the back lot, Rebel heard a clacking noise coming from the alley; he approached with caution. The alley was too dark; he donned night vision goggles. Several rats and a stalking cat were all he could see. He heard something metal hit a wall. He saw something being hoisted on a cable. Rebel looked up and saw a man pulling up the cable. He looked at the target building and saw the open window on the sixth floor.

"This is Rebel. I've got action on the rooftop across the west alley."

Slash caught up with the elevator. "The money is gone!"

Yankee heard that loud and clear. "Rebel, shoot! Trigger, blow the wad! Slash, hustle back down! I'm bringing the wheels to the west alley."

Rebel drew and fired two rounds at the silhouette, both missed. The head disappeared over the rooftop before he could get off a third. He heard an explosion. But it wasn't where he expected. It was inside the target building. *"What the hell?"*

Trigger had pushed the detonate button and was rewarded with a blast of shrapnel through the middle elevator doors. He took hits in the legs, chest, arm and neck as the concussion threw him against the opposite wall. He was bleeding in six places; they burned and he struggled to breathe. A ragged two-foot diameter hole was in the elevator door and the odor of exploded Semtex permeated the lobby. A fire alarm was going full blare and several automatic sprinklers spewed water over the lobby.

Slash rode the elevator down to the lobby and was soaked as soon as the doors opened.

"Trigger is down! Rebel, meet me at the rear door with the car!"

Rebel acknowledged and dashed for the car. He jumped in, cranked it and drove to the rear door. A moment later, Slash exited with Trigger slung over his shoulder. Slash opened the back door, dropped Trigger inside, then jumped into the front seat.

"How's Trigger?"

"He'll live. But we better find those tapes or the Colonel will have our balls for breakfast."

The Buicks careened around corners as sirens grew closer.

∞

Kress crossed the roof to another building and crossed that roof, too. He ran over the top of an elevated walkway to a third rooftop, crossed it, then went down a fire escape ladder into a dark alley and to a parking garage where his old Toyota was parked.

Sirens and air horns pierced the night. Kress unlocked the trunk and tossed in the bundles, removed his waist harness, ski mask, jumpsuit and tossed them in, too. He grabbed his guard cap, closed the trunk and unlocked the driver door. He tossed his cap onto the passenger seat and started the car. He drove slowly out of the garage, careful not to arouse suspicion. He headed north on the Interstate. Olympia, Washington would be the first stop. Vancouver, British Columbia would be a good point of departure for Fiji.

∞

The detective squad room was unusually bright for 7:33 a.m. The aroma of freshly brewed coffee filled the air as several detectives and their Captain gathered at the coffee bar. Jocular jousts bantered back and forth amongst them.

"Kren, are you interested in a white Jeep Cherokee?" asked the Captain.

"What?"

"The white Cherokee you A-P-Bed the other day. They found one last night in the alley behind the Eager Beaver."

"The strip joint?"

"Yeah. It's in the impound lot. Forensics will be going over it this morning."

"There won't be any evidence, I bet."

"Why not?"

"A hunch."

"Where are we on the Flynn case?"

Krenna sighed. "It looks like a kidnapping, but not for ransom. The doctor's Caddy was so clean the forensics guys found squat. I'll bet the Jeep turns up the same. There haven't been any ransom demands. The phone taps have been useless and there's been no sign or contact from Dr. Flynn. There were no marital or money problems, but there was an incident last month that could be the motive."

"The burglary?"

"Yeah. Cranston investigated. He told me the Flynns moved the lab to a secret location to protect some cancer cure they've discovered. They think there's someone trying to find the lab and that's why Dr. Flynn is missing."

The Captain nodded. "We've only got another twelve hours before the FBI gets jurisdiction. If we hand it over, give them everything you've got. I don't want any heat from the D-As office or the press. Clear?"

"I hear you, Cap. I don't have crap to work with, anyway. Maybe the FBI can find something." Krenna detested handing work over to the feds. Sometimes they were exceptionally good. Other times, toilet paper provided a better wipe.

The Captain turned to Detective Gosselman. "Goss, I want you and Bostick to investigate an explosion at the Hennessey Building."

Cabo San Lucas, Mexico: Salty eyeballed the approaching skiff as it headed directly for the *Vixen*. He could see three figures in the shoddy vessel, but he didn't recognize them from a distance. He raised the binoculars. He saw two strange men in plain clothes, standing, a third seated. It was Paul Thomas. And he was handcuffed.

The skipper went to the weapons locker and pulled out a Colt .45 handgun, Luke's favorite, and a 12-gauge shotgun. He racked a round into the chamber of the .45, engaged the safety and stuffed it into his belt, hefted the shotgun and grabbed a portable radio.

"What's up, Skipper?" asked Terry Pell, the *Vixen's* helmsman.

"Trouble. Prepare to get under way and monitor channel six. I'm going to find Luke." The Skipper trotted to the helipad. Luke was there, fiddling with some electronic component in the chopper. He had seen the skiff also.

"Boss." The skipper handed Luke the .45. "I don't know who those guys are, but they've got Paul in handcuffs. Can't be good news, so I brought your peacemaker. It's cocked and locked, safety's on."

Luke took the weapon, checked the safety and tucked it into the belt behind his back.

"Thanks, Skipper. What do you make of it?"

"Don't know. They're not wearing uniforms, but Paul's in cuffs and he doesn't look happy."

"Okay, I'll go down and find out what's up. You cover me from the deck above. Keep the shotgun hidden unless I have to pull out the persuader. We'll play it from there."

"Okay, sounds good. I've got the bridge on radio and Terry can have us ready to move out in few minutes. Paul was the only crewman ashore. Everyone else is accounted for."

"Thanks. I don't know what I'd do without you."

"All in a day's work, boss."

The small boat slowed and pulled alongside the *Vixen* at the aft cockpit as Luke descended from the helipad.

"Ahoy, Mr. Hale," yelled the driver.

"*Ahoy? Who the hell says 'ahoy' in the twenty-first century?*" "Yeah. Back at ya."

The other man tossed a line up to Luke. He snatched it and secured it.

"What's this about? Why is my crewman in handcuffs?"

"We'll explain that when we come aboard."

"Well, I've got news for you. You're not coming aboard until I know who you are and why you have my crewman in cuffs."

The men looked at each other, one short and fat, the other of medium height and build. The fat man seemed to be their spokesman.

"Sir, we're DEA and we apprehended your man trying to make a drug deal."

"That's bullshit, Luke," yelled Paul. "I was just lying on the beach when these two goons tried to sell me some cocaine. I told them to buzz off and they jumped me and ..."

"Shut up," yelled the tall guy. "You're under arrest."

"Show me your ID," insisted Luke. There was something not kosher about these two scruffy-looking yokels. The fact they didn't want Paul to talk made the hair on Luke's neck bristle. The fat man flashed his credentials and started to replace them in his back pocket.

"Nice try, gordo. Show me your ID. Now!" The edge in Luke's voice could have cut steel.

"Look, Hale. We're the DEA..."

"That's *Mister* Hale to you. And I don't give a shit who you say you are. Until I see your ID, you're nothing but a smelly scumbag trying to board my ship without permission. Toss your ID's up here."

The men looked at the deck above, where the Skipper was, removed their credentials and tossed them to Luke. Luke noticed Salty peering over the rail, his shotgun hidden. Luke examined the IDs and memorized the names and badge numbers. Neither fed appeared to have shaved in three days and their clothes looked like they had just climbed out of a hamper.

"Mr. Hale, like I said, we arrested your man for trying to buy drugs, but we're willing to overlook his offense if you'll cooperate with us."

"*Aha, now the hook.*" "What do you mean by 'cooperate'?"

"Well, sir. We're working on a major sting to nail a South American drug lord. We'd like to use your yacht to setup a sting. If you let us use the boat, we'll overlook junior's little indiscretion and we won't turn him over to the Mexicans. It'll be our secret. What do you say?"

The fat man's smirk rubbed Luke the wrong way. There were several things that Lucien Hale had no tolerance for. Corrupt cops were at the top of the list, especially federal rogue cops.

"Paul, what really happened?"

"Mr. Hale, he's under arrest…" the fat man started to say, but got cut off.

"Don't interrupt me again, fat ass." The chill in Luke's voice could have extinguished a blowtorch. He had no fear of the federal cops. Not only that, he detested them. He suspected they entrapped Paul so they could look good to the desk monkeys in Washington.

"We just want your cooperation, Mr. Hale. We're federal officers…"

"…which means you work for me." Luke hissed and tossed their credentials back. "Bring Paul aboard and we'll talk."

The agents pocketed their credentials and gathered Paul. They pushed him over the transom into the cockpit.

"Take the cuffs off," demanded Luke.

"No way. He's under arrest." The arrogant fat man smiled smugly as they climbed aboard.

Luke was not about to be bettered by a couple of bottom-of-the-barrel federal vermin. "Since we're in Mexico, what authority do have to arrest anyone? As far as I can tell, you've abducted an American citizen in a foreign country where you have no jurisdiction."

"You're not cooperating, Mr. Hale."

"It's my right and duty to resist federal officers who've abused their authority."

"Mr. Hale, if you don't cooperate, we'll turn junior over to the Federalis and tell them we suspect you're trafficking in cocaine. Your ship could be confiscated. Know what I mean?"

Hale got the meaning.

"Well, Mr. Hale?"

"I'm thinking." Luke couldn't believe Paul would go looking for a cocaine deal any more than Heather could. It was preposterous.

"Mr. Hale, you've got ten seconds to decide or we're takin' junior for a ride."

Luke held up his open right hand and lowered his gaze as he shook his head, "Okay, you got me." His left hand flashed from behind and leveled the .45 at the fat man's nose. The unmistakable sound of a 12-gauge shotgun pump caught their attention. Salty had the drop on the tall agent. Luke stared at the fat man.

The feds stammered as they reached for their pieces, but they reconsidered and froze.

"I've made my decision. No, you can't use my ship and no, you're not taking Paul in on trumped up charges. Put your arms up."

The feds slowly raised their arms, alternately watching the .45 and the shotgun. Luke casually pulled a long Cuban cigar from his pocket, bit the cap off and spit it into the porker's face as he pressed the barrel of his persuader under the man's jaw. Without looking away, Luke calmly struck the flint of his lighter and slowly, luxuriously, lit the aromatic tobacco rod and blew the smoke into the jerk's face, eliciting a cough.

After several hearty puffs Luke said, "You've been answered. Where's the key to the cuffs?"

The fat man was defiant. "Mr. Hale, you're assaulting federal officers and that carries severe criminal…"

Luke jammed the Colt harder into his jaw. Through clenched teeth, he whispered, "I don't think you grasp the severity of the situation, Mr. Fed. You have a Colt .45 Auto with a hair trigger aimed at your brain, just three pounds of squeeze from blowing your head off. Now where's the key? I won't ask again."

The fat man relented. "Mario has it."

Crewmembers gathered to observe the commotion. They were all surprised to see their boss jamming a gun into a man's neck and being extremely mean doing it. This was a side of Luke they hadn't seen before.

"Well, Mario. Are you going to give me the key or do I blow your partner's brains overboard. Of course, if I do him you know what'll happen to you. I'll find the key anyway."

The junior fed looked at his partner. The fat man nodded.

"It's in my right pocket."

"Paul, get the key."

Paul fished through his pocket.

"Got it."

"Free yourself and throw the cuffs overboard."

Paul gladly complied.

"Okay, Paul, go tell the Skipper to make way. It's time to leave."

Paul hustled up the ladder. The Skipper had already heard the order and radioed the bridge.

Luke continued the pressure. "Now gentlemen, left hands only, throw your pieces overboard." The agents slowly complied.

"Now throw your back-up pieces over." The fat man reached slowly behind his back as Luke grabbed him by the shirt collar. The fed removed a small caliber revolver and tossed it. The tall guy reached to his ankle for a .32 automatic and chucked it.

Luke yelled to Salty, "Cover me, Skipper." The old salt chomped his cigar and nodded. Luke frisked the fat man, finding a switchblade and a straight razor. He found the same arsenal on the younger agent. Their weapons and IDs went for a swim.

"You're gonna regret this, Hale," threatened the fat guy.

"Maybe so. But I'm doing the American public a favor ridding them of agents that give our government a bad reputation. Do you guys feel like a swim? Form is optional. And you can look forward to an Internal Affairs investigation. I hope you have a gentle proctologist."

The men glanced at the shore. "The beach is two miles away," complained Mario.

"Yeah, but at least you have to swim through the sharks."

"Hale, if you think you can ever get us in front of an Internal Affairs board, you're high on drugs. We'll bring so much heat down on you, this ship will melt."

"Shut up, Carlo," hissed Mario.

Luke reasoned he had no choice. He shot the fat man's hip.

The round fractured his pelvis, blood and bone chips exploded from his buttock as it knocked him down. Porky howled and everyone, except

Salty, gaped in awe as Luke put his next round into the thigh of the other agent. They writhed in agony.

The ship's anchor chain rattled as it reeled aboard. The yacht's engines sparked to life.

"Where to, boss?" yelled Skibba.

"Southwest. The Pacific beckons."

"Aye, aye." The Skipper radioed the helm. The engines revved and the massive yacht eased forward.

Luke tossed towels to the scoundrels. "Here. Plug your holes with these and behave yourselves, or I'll be back to give you a real spanking."

The crewmen were astounded. But not Heather. She'd been married to him for eleven years and knew he had this dark, malevolent spirit whenever his liberty or loved ones were threatened. She also knew he would die to protect her and the crew.

Dave Welch, the mechanic, came bounding down the ladder. "Boss, what about their skiff?"

"Cut it loose."

The *Vixen* headed southwest for open waters. It was imperative they clear Mexican territory.

"Luke, what about the launch? It's still at the marina."

"Damn. I forgot about that. C'mon, Paul. We'll take the chopper. I'll drop you at the marina and you'll have to intercept the *Vixen* while she's under way. I'll cover you from the chopper."

Dave loosed the line and the shabby skiff fell astern. Salty descended the ladder and gave Dave the shotgun.

"Keep those two covered, I'm going topside with the boss." The Skipper chased after Luke and Paul.

"Hey, boss. Where we going?"

"Heather has always wanted to visit Fiji."

"Fiji it is. What about the bloody guys?"

"Keep them under guard. If they make any trouble, shoot them. I'll clean the mess when I get back."

Boston: Rushton's cell phone rang.

"Doctor Rushton."

"This is Bravo. The exchange didn't happen. The merchandise never showed up and the perp got away."

"Dammit! I thought you guys were professionals. What the hell am I supposed to do now?"

"This guy is smart. It'll take time to find him. I suggest you call in some markers and squelch this until we corner him."

There was a long silence.

Bravo continued. "On the primary matter, the location of the objective is still unknown. Our source proved worthless and his attorney is out of the country."

"Shit! Bravo, you get that damned data. Do whatever it takes. Am I clear?"

"Crystal."

"Get me that data, fast. I'll pull some strings."

Portland: Bravo snapped shut his phone. He was pissed. They had lost the money, the contract got away, they didn't get the tapes, Trigger was injured, Dan Flynn had no idea where the lab was and Sparks hadn't cracked the encryption yet.

They were running out of options. The only ways to find the lab were to crack the encryption or implement scenario Echo.

"Slash, tend to Trigger. Have him ready to travel in three hours, conscious or not."

Slash nodded and moved out.

"Rebel, Sparks, pack up the equipment and sanitize this place. We're moving out."

Bravo drew his Beretta and attached a suppressor. "Yankee, get a large sheet of plastic and a roll of duct tape."

"How large, Colonel?"

"Large enough to wrap a body."

Olympia, Washington: The sunrise beckoned. It was time to get coffee and inventory his loot. Kress pulled over and parked.

He locked the car and stretched as he headed to the coffee shop. After draining his bladder and fetching a cup of brew, Kress headed back to his car and opened the trunk. He noticed most of the bills were marked with dye. They were worthless. Only one hundred grand was usable. *"Son of a bitch."*

Kress separated the currency and closed the bag. It was time to send an express package to the FBI.

Cabo San Lucas, Mexico: The helicopter vibration made it difficult for Paul to focus the binoculars. Luke flew at thirty feet above sea level.

They were a mile from the marina.

Luke, Salty and Paul had worked out a plan.

Paul finally had some success with the focus and scanned the marina.

"Boss, there's a man searching the launch. There's another guy on the dock right beside the boat."

"Are they wearing uniforms?"

"No. I can't tell who they are."

"Well neither can I. They must be thieves or vandals, right?" Luke gave a smirk that affirmed he was scheming something outrageous. Paul set down the binoculars and readied the 12-gauge.

Luke outlined his plan. Paul acknowledged. They were three hundred yards from the dock and closing at ninety knots. The rotor noise alerted the suspicious men and they looked directly at the chopper.

Luke pitched the nose down, bringing the swirling rotor blades dangerously low to the dock as he maneuvered directly over the launch and at the man on the dock. The man on the dock realized he was about to become the main ingredient of a flying blender. He jumped from the dock, his arms and legs flailing comically.

"Oh, poor form. The Russian judge will penalize that," Luke joked as he swung the chopper around to rotate Paul's door toward the launch. The intruder was crouched low inside the launch, his arms covering his head as the rotor downwash showered debris on him.

Paul leveled the shotgun at him. Luke eased the chopper down on the dock as the man rose. Paul fired a warning shot over the guy's head and quickly racked another shell into the chamber. The man raised his hands and yelled something. Paul stepped out and advanced, using a sure-footed shuffle, his shotgun never wavering from his target.

Paul yelled at the man and Luke saw the guy jump overboard. Paul hustled to the launch and freed the lines, throwing them aboard haphazardly. He jumped in, fished the key from his pocket and started the engine.

The engine cranked and Paul fire-walled the throttle, nearly hitting the intruder in the water. A huge wake diffused from the stern, overpowering the floating perpetrator and causing other vessels to bang into the dock.

Luke lifted off. Plexiglas shards sprayed into his face as a spider-webbed bullet hole appeared in the windscreen. Luke flinched, the chopper twisted in mid-air. Luke regained control and flew over the water. He felt three more impacts along the helicopter's frame. He quickly checked his flight controls and engine instruments as he skimmed the water, changing heading and altitude every four seconds to present a difficult target. The bullet impacts ceased before he got a hundred yards from the dock.

"*Must have been pistol fire.*" If it had been a rifle, the shots would still be coming.

Luke slowed the chopper and rotated to face the dock. There were two men on the dock holding pistols. The guys in the water were climbing out. The dry men helped the wet ones onto the dock and all four ran to a boat. Within seconds, they were underway, making hot pursuit of Paul.

Luke tuned the radio to channel six. "Scooter, this is Eyeball."

"This is Scooter," came Paul's reply.

"Scooter, you've got four armed bandits in a high-speed craft on your six o'clock, one mile, hot pursuit. Whip those gerbils."

"Scooter, roger." Paul jammed the throttle full forward. The launch surged forward, bouncing hard on the choppy breakers at the mouth of the gulf. Paul hung on for dear life as the boat pounded the crests at thirty-six knots, the spray soaking him and the interior.

Luke climbed to five hundred feet at maximum power. He could see the launch two miles ahead and the *Vixen* eight miles beyond that. They were both making good speed for international waters. Luke scanned the area for other pursuit vessels. There were none.

Luke transmitted to the *Vixen*, "Sanctuary, this is Eyeball."

"This is Sanctuary. Go ahead."

"This is Eyeball. How far are you from the line?"

There was a brief pause. Luke knew the Skipper was calculating the exact distance to international waters.

"Eyeball, this is Sanctuary. We're exactly four point four nautical miles from the line, ETA eight minutes, forty-eight seconds."

"Roger. Break, Scooter, this is Eyeball, how many knots are you turning?"

"About thirty-five knots."

Luke did some quick mental calculations.

"Scooter, this is Eyeball. Keep turning at full revolutions. The bandits are keeping pace. Sanctuary will cross the line two and a half minutes before you. You'll have to make it all the way past the line. Acknowledge."

"Roger that, Eyeball. Scooter is balls to the wall making for the line."

"Sanctuary, this is Eyeball, over."

"Go ahead, Eyeball."

"Make full speed for the line and don't slow down until you cross it. About a mile past, turn her broadside and slow for Scooter to catch up. Keep the intruder package out of sight and silent. Prepare a reception committee. Acknowledge."

"Aye-aye. Sanctuary out."

Luke raced the chopper parallel to the speeding launch. Every mile, Luke circled the chopper to check on the pursuers. Paul had widened the gap. The pursuers were persistent, though.

The Skipper reported the *Vixen* had crossed the line. Luke saw the ship turn to port and slow, perpendicular to Paul's course. Luke saw Paul head straight for the stern. Luke circled the chopper again. The pursuers were still coming.

"This is Eyeball. Bandits are still in pursuit. Sanctuary, I'm going to trail Scooter. Let me know as soon as I cross the line."

"Roger that." The Skipper referred to the new GPS display. "Less than one minute to the line, Eyeball."

"Copy that. Call me at the exact line."

Seconds later, "Eyeball, this is Sanctuary. You just crossed the line."

Luke slowed and circled. All of the cruisers were in international waters.

The pursuit boat sped past the helicopter. Two of the pursuers fired wild pistol shots at Luke as they passed below. None hit, but it pissed off the already pissed off millionaire aviator.

"This is Eyeball. The bandits are hostile. They just shot at me. Prepare the reception committee."

"Sanctuary copies. We're ready. You just get back in one piece. Tomorrow's payday and everyone's broke."

Luke chuckled. "Thank you for the touching sentiment. I'm inbound, ETA two minutes. Have my tool ready at the pad."

"Way ahead of you, boss. It's awaiting your tender caress."

Luke flew past the pursuit boat and headed for the helipad. Paul came abeam the *Vixen* and secured the launch. Luke landed and cut the engine. As he emerged, he noticed oily smoke coming from a bullet hole in the engine cowling. Now he was really pissed.

Skibba was at the pad holding an FN/FAL rifle with a twenty round magazine and Luke's favorite, a Bushmaster 17S scoped rifle with a thirty round magazine.

"Good to see you, boss. The bogeys are a mile out and closing fast.

They've hailed us on the radio but we haven't responded."

"Good! I'm gonna deal with these bastards right now."

Luke walked to the port side and watched the rapidly approaching boat with a cold, harsh glare.

"Boss," interjected Skibba, "the launch is secure and Paul's aboard. He's anxious to shoot someone."

"Can't say I blame him, Skipper."

"Not in the least. I'd be pretty riled up too."

Luke thumbed off the safety and cocked the bolt. He opened the scope covers and swiveled his cap around. He was ready for some serious rock and roll.

The pursuers slowed and approached, waving credentials and yelling.

Luke raised his rifle.

"We're DEA. Who are you?"

"I'm the Master of this vessel. We're in international waters and DEA has no authority here. Why were you shooting at me?"

"You have a suspect aboard. His name is Paul Thomas. Turn him over and we'll leave."

"I told you, we're in international waters. No one on this vessel has committed any crime, so beat it."

"Where are the two DEA agents that came to your boat this morning?"

"How should I know? I'm not a babysitter. Did you check the whorehouses in town? They're probably eating the mints out of the urinals, or maybe they're studying for a piss test." Luke couldn't hide his disdain for the corrupt bastards. Heather and Caroline had them under guard. Luke was sure the women had threatened to shoot their balls off if any harm came to their husbands.

"You're harboring a suspect, and…"

"Enough of this bullshit," yelled Luke. "Shove off right now." He took careful aim. The DEA men looked at each other in disbelief, perhaps considering whether or not to call his bluff.

"Wrong response," Luke mumbled.

Crack! Crack! Crack! Crack! Crack! Crack! Six sharp blasts spewed from Luke's Bushmaster as supersonic steel-tipped projectiles zipped between their legs and pierced the fiberglass hull. Arcs of seawater streamed into the vessel as the agents raised their pistols. The racket of seven more rifle bolts slammed into chamber caused them to look around. The agents saw they were heavily outgunned. Eight high-powered rifles trained on them from widely separated parts of the ship.

They were sitting ducks. They lowered their pistols and glanced at the growing puddle of water in their boat.

"I should drill you bastards right now for shooting up my helicopter. But I'm going to be magnanimous for the next ten seconds. If you stay here, your boat will sink and you'll have a long swim. If you try to board my vessel, you'll be shot. Decide quickly. Every minute you wait is an hour swim through the sharks."

The agents looked at their leader.

Crack!

Luke put another round through the hull. It had the desired effect. Their leader holstered his pistol and ordered the driver to head for shore. He told the others to start bailing. The boat's motor roared as the driver gunned the throttle.

Luke secured his rifle and cleared the chamber. He pulled a cigar from his pocket, chewed off the cap and ever so slowly puffed it to life as the Skipper held up his torch. The Skipper lit his cigar right after Luke. The crusty veterans savored the aromatic pikes as they watched the slowly sinking boat speed away.

Luke puffed a huge cloud of smoke and flashed an impish grin. "What's for lunch?"

Portland: A reflection at the river's edge, eighty feet below, caught the attention of Gary Porter atop his dock crane. It looked like a huge roll of plastic, but that didn't seem possible; such a roll wouldn't float. Porter called the crew on the pier and asked them to see what it was.

The foreman radioed back, it was something wrapped in plastic and duct tape. Porter saw the men pull it to the pier with gaffs. It was too heavy to lift. One man descended a ladder. Another moment passed before there was news. It was a dead body.

∞

A patrolman arrived ten minutes after the discovery. The foreman had already roped off the area. The police officer gathered the workers and took their statements.

Minutes later, detectives arrived. They questioned the longshoremen and examined the body. A pungent odor assaulted them as they peeled open the plastic cocoon. The body appeared well preserved, having been in cold water. It hadn't been dead long.

The corpse was bare above the waist and there were bruises on the torso and face. There was a burn mark on the left side of the neck. The detectives found a money clip and a wallet.

"The motive wasn't robbery. There's six hundred dollars here, three platinum credit cards and an ATM card. The names on the cards say Flynn Medical Group and Daniel Flynn, MD. The driver's license says Daniel Flynn. I think we've just found the missing doctor. Get a diver into the river to search for evidence."

The senior detective noticed the fingers on both hands were bruised around the knuckles and appeared broken.

"The poor guy was tortured. His fingers are broken, he's got burn marks, bruises, abrasions, maybe even a few busted ribs. His face is barely recognizable."

The detective turned over the body and noticed a hole in the back of the head. "And they shot him in the back of the head. Looks like a single shot, maybe nine millimeter."

"Why do you think they wrapped him in plastic?" asked the junior detective.

"They wanted it to float, so it would be found."

The coroner's wagon arrived. An unmarked detective vehicle came screeching around a corner with its beacon flashing. It skidded to a halt ten feet from the crime scene. Krenna and Lewis emerged. A rehash of the statements and findings transpired. Krenna took charge.

The coroner's staff carefully placed Dan's corpse into a body bag and tagged it. They placed it into the rear of the coroner van.

"When will the autopsy be done?" Krenna inquired of the coroner's assistant.

"The physical pathology will be done by tomorrow. The lab work might take another day. As for the ballistics, who knows?"

"Okay, Bobby. Ask Doc Phillips to get the autopsy report to me as soon as possible." Krenna turned to Lewis. "Now for the heart-breaking part, notifying the widow."

Pacific Ocean: *Serene Vixen* cruised southwest over the calm waters, headed for Fiji with the autopilot engaged. Luke was at the helm by himself for the first time. The crew enjoyed a feast in the dining salon. Luke had spent many hours learning to pilot the elegant yacht under the superb tutelage of Salty Skibba. The solitude gave him opportunity to reflect.

Immediately after the confrontation with the DEA, Luke had relieved

Heather and Caroline and told them to go get lunch. Once they were gone, Luke locked the stateroom door.

The prisoners were barely conscious, having lost a lot of blood. They were pale and frightened. It was something Luke had seen before, during a classified Special Forces mission in South America. The men struggled briefly at their duct tape bonds, to no success.

"The Master of a vessel at sea has nearly unlimited authority to deal with crime and punishment aboard his vessel. I hereby convene this Master's Mast, a hearing to determine your guilt or innocence of the following charges: charge one, conspiracy against citizens rights; charge two, deprivation of rights under color of law; charge three, felonious false arrest; charge four, attempted extortion; charge five, attempted piracy. How do you plead? If you plead guilty, nod your heads; not guilty, shake your heads."

Both shook their heads.

"Okay, gentlemen. I'll accept your head shakes as pleading not guilty, so let's examine the evidence. One, you two arrested my crewman and accused him of buying drugs. But you showed no proof. Also, Paul consented to allow me to search him and his stateroom and there was not even a hint of illicit narcotics. However, I did find this packet of white powder in your pocket, fatso. I don't know what this stuff is, but it was in your possession, not Paul's. Two, you both premeditated, therefore conspired to deprive Mr. Thomas of his God given rights to life, liberty and due process of law, and three; you did so under the color of law, abusing your status as DEA officers. Four, you attempted to extort the use of my property by offering to overlook Paul's alleged wrongdoing. Five, you attempted to pirate my vessel by threatening my crew's lives and liberty with lies to the Mexican authorities."

The miscreants tried to yell and struggled, but their screams were muffled.

Luke displayed several documents. "I have obtained Mr. Thomas's sworn declaration that you attempted to entrap him in a crime for which he had no knowledge or involvement. You arrested him and discussed in his presence, your plans to commandeer the *Serene Vixen* to conduct illegal activity. I heard you utter those very intentions right after you came aboard. With my sworn declaration and Mr. Thomas's sworn declaration, as well as the sworn declaration of Captain Skibba, who also overheard and witnessed your threats, I have no choice but to find you both guilty on all five charges. In the old seafaring days, the guilty were often keelhauled. They dragged the convicted man under the barnacled hull of the ship; their skin would be ripped to shreds and they'd bleed to death, if the sharks didn't get them. But I'm not that cruel. I hereby sentence you both to death. May God have mercy on your souls. This Mast proceeding is now closed."

The convicts thrashed about, but only Divine intervention could have saved them. Luke hammered both on the backs of their necks with his closed fist. After confirming they were unconscious, he grabbed each man's head, then rapidly and without remorse, twisted it violently. Each neck snapped like a dry twig, a more merciful death than most methods.

Luke confirmed they were dead. He left the bodies in the stateroom, locked the door and hung the DO NOT DISTURB sign. He would dispose of them later.

The Skipper entered the bridge and assessed the ship's status as he handed Luke a Mai Tai.

Luke snapped back to the present. "Thanks, Skipper. How was lunch?"

"Terrific, boss. Your lady sure knows gourmet cooking. You should get some while it's hot. I'll take over."

Luke glanced down as he reflected on the morning's events. "Skipper. Thanks for backing me up this morning."

The fatherly Skibba emerged. "Let me tell you something, Luke." It was the first time the Skipper had ever addressed him by his Christian name. "I'm sixty years old and I've been around the world nine times and in some rough scrapes. I've known a lot of good men, and I know a good man when I see how he reacts under pressure. You're a good man."

They smiled as the Skipper patted Luke on the back.

"Thanks, Skipper. That means a lot to me."

"Go get some chow. I've got the con."

Luke headed for the dining salon.

The cacophony was deafening and the aroma of Heather's rosemary chicken filled the air. Luke sipped his Mai Tai as he sat down and Heather prepared a plate for him. It looked and smelled wonderful.

"There's ice cream for desert, sweetheart," Heather mentioned, as she placed the plate in front of him and pecked him on the cheek. Luke smiled and silently gave thanks for having such a wonderful wife. He would go to the ends of the earth for her.

"Should I prepare some food for the gentlemen below?" she whispered.

Luke shook his head and smiled. "They don't have much of an appetite."

Boston: Raas and Miller entered Rushton's office and locked the door. Rushton instructed his secretary to hold all calls. This time, Miller mixed the drinks.

"How are the new committee assignments coming?" asked Raas.

"I've given those more thought," answered Rushton. "Melanie Taylor took Sheila Peterson to lunch yesterday and asked about our political contributions. I don't want her getting into the PAC or the special operations files. I want her isolated from the operations department and the lobbying committee."

"She'll get suspicious," challenged Miller.

Raas provided the answer. "I'll transfer her to the finance committee. We can pass it off as a promotion. Once she's out of operations, we'll change the security lockouts."

"But the finance committee?" Miller questioned testily. "She'll be as big a threat there as in the operations department."

Raas had the answer. "We can transfer the PAC functions from the finance committee to the special operations division. Of course, we'll transfer the key people in the PAC section as well. Then we'll tell do-gooder Melanie that we need her to straighten out the mess in the finance committee. Hopefully, she'll think she's been promoted."

"Very clever, Raas."

"Thank you, Claudia." He hoisted his scotch and grinned.

"Shit!" Rushton was glaring at his computer screen.

"What's up?" inquired Miller.

Rushton glanced up. "Kress sent the tapes to the FBI. We have to squelch this before it lands us in prison."

"When did he send them?" asked Raas.

"Today, according to this e-mail. He's demanding more money since he discovered the cash was marked. Any ideas?"

Raas gulped his Scotch and slammed the glass onto the coffee table. "How the hell are we supposed to deal with this?"

"Easy," soothed Miller. She grinned coyly as she sipped her martini and plucked out the olive. She teasingly sucked it from the plastic stick. She knew something the others didn't.

CHAPTER VII

INTROS AND FAREWELLS

L as Vegas: The phone range. "Storm's Self-Defense Studio, this is Derek."

"Derek, it's Pete."

"Hi, Pete. Your new lab working out okay?"

"Uh, yes, but that's not why I'm calling." Storm could hear distress in his voice.

"What's going on?"

"Have you heard about Dan?"

"No. What's the matter? Was he in an accident or something?"

There was a pause, and sobbing. "Derek… Dan has been murdered."

"What? Did you say murdered?"

"Yes. He disappeared a few days ago. Some dockworkers found his body in the Columbia River yesterday. The police said he was murdered."

Storm was in shock. His Uncle Dan was one of the kindest individuals on earth. His life had been devoted to caring for the sick. He had funded critical research. Now he was gone. His friendly face would never grace another family reunion.

"My Lord. That's awful. Is anyone with Aunt Kate?"

"Her brother is there. Your cousins are a mess, too, but they have Kate's side of the family nearby to help."

"Pete, I'm going to Portland to help out. Are you going?"

"I want to, Derek," answered Pete through his sobs, "but I'm afraid to go."

Storm was puzzled. It wasn't like Pete to bypass the family at such a grievous time. Something was drastically wrong.

"Pete, what's going on? Tell me so I can help."

Pete struggled to regain his composure. "Derek... I think Dan was murdered... because he couldn't reveal the... location of the lab." Storm felt the pain.

"Pete, there must be some way I can help."

"Keep a check on your e-mail. Kate's family will notify us of the funeral arrangements. I think the funeral is the day after tomorrow."

Storm checked his calendar. "Pete, I'm going. I'll fly up tomorrow afternoon. Come with me."

There was a pause. "Derek, I think Dan was killed because there are some evil people trying to locate the lab. If I go to the funeral, they could do the same to me."

"Who murdered him, Pete?"

"I have my suspicions, but I don't have proof. I think it's the same people behind the lab break-in."

"Do you have a firearm?"

"Uh... yeah. I've got a revolver."

"Good. Get some training and practice. If this is as serious as you think, you might need it."

"Okay, I'll do that."

"I'll express your condolences to the family."

"That would be kind of you. Thanks. You're a good nephew."

"It would be my honor." There was another long pause. Storm could hear someone in the background. Storm couldn't make out the discussion and wondered to whom Pete was speaking. The voice sounded sympathetic.

Finally, a strange voice came on, a melodious female voice with a slight Asian accent.

"Hello, Mr. Storm, this is Lisa Chen. I'm Pete's new assistant and I've convinced him to send me in his place. I think it's important so I can relate the condolences of the other family members when I get back."

"Well, it's nice to speak with you Miss Chen. I have another question for Pete. Is he still there?"

The lady seemed nonplussed. "Well, yes, he is. Just a second."

"You have another question, Derek?"

"Yeah. Who is this Lisa Chen? Your research assistant?"

"Right. I hired her a couple of weeks ago. She's a sweet lady but I'm reluctant to send her. She could be in danger."

An idea came to mind.

"Pete, why doesn't she come to Vegas and fly to Portland with me. I'll be her bodyguard. What do you think?"

Pete spoke with Lisa and repeated Storm's proposition. They discussed the matter and Pete informed Storm that Lisa agreed. It would be Storm's responsibility to see her safely back to the lab. Since no one outside the family could connect Lisa to him and Storm escorted her, she would be safe.

"Okay, Pete. Agreed. I'll escort the lady to Portland. Give her directions to my studio."

"Right. And Derek, have a look at Kate's security. I'm worried about her."

"Roger that." Storm couldn't resist asking, "Pete, what does she, you know, Lisa… what does she look like?"

Pete hesitated. "Well, you can't miss her. She's four foot nine, two hundred pounds, nappy hair. And she has a dynamite personality."

"Terrific," replied Storm facetiously, "I'm looking forward to meeting her. Send me an e-mail with the flight information and when to expect her."

"Okay. I'll be in touch."

"Goodbye, Pete." Storm hung up and stared out his office window. He felt grief and anger. He didn't have answers to the questions that gnawed at his spirit, but he'd get them. And once he found out who murdered Dan, he or they were dead. They just didn't know it.

Portland: Krenna stared at the closed file on his desktop. The label read FLYNN, DANIEL, MD, Autopsy Report of the County Coroner. He opened it.

He skimmed over the technical jargon and concentrated on the pertinent matters: cause of death was a single nine-millimeter bullet wound through the back of the head, striking the top vertebrae and fragmenting into the medulla oblongata causing instant death, along with seven broken ribs from at least two assailants having different size fists, the smaller fisted assailant predominantly left handed, no jewelry imprints, four broken fingers on the right hand, two broken digits on the left, numerous bruises on the upper torso and face, burn mark on the left side of his neck, probably from a stun gun, numerous burn marks on both arms and abdomen, probably from a soldering iron.

"Good God!"

Lewis came up behind and peered over his shoulder.

"What's the matter, Kren?"

Krenna shook his head. "I just got the autopsy report on Doctor Flynn." He gave it to Lewis.

Lewis read through it, his jaw dropped open.

"There were traces of sodium pentothal in his blood. It must have been an interrogation. But why kill him? If he gave in, they could have let him go. Ditto if he didn't know what they were searching for. Why kill him? What's the motive? And why dispose of the body in such a way as to be quickly found? It doesn't make sense. We're missing something."

"Did he have gambling debts?"

Krenna shook his head. "I don't think so. I ran the doctor's arrest record. He doesn't have one, not even a parking ticket. His credit is spotless."

Lewis shook his head and sat at his desk, facing his partner. Krenna's phone rang.

"Detective Krenna." He listened while nodding occasionally. Lewis swigged his cola as he waited. Krenna bid farewell and replaced the phone. He looked disappointed.

"What's up?"

"That was forensics. The tape and plastic didn't have any prints. The bullet was a frangible round. It was a nine-millimeter but it split into eight pieces and none of them is big enough to get a rifling pattern. Nothing for DNA evidence either. The divers didn't find anything. The tire print matches the standard equipment on damn near every Jeep Cherokee in the country. The lone footprint is a size eleven combat boot, a very common size and obtainable at any Army surplus store. The only deduction forensics could put together was that the wearer was about two hundred twenty pounds, probably six foot to six foot two." Krenna sighed, exasperated. "We need a miracle."

Las Vegas: Lisa Chen turned into the strip mall lot, located Storm's studio and parked her SUV.

She took several minutes to brush her hair, touch-up her make-up and spray perfume. Satisfied, she emerged and smoothed her dress, ensuring the slit hit her thigh at just the right height; not too high as to appear slutty and definitely not low; it was just the right amount of too short.

Lisa turned it on. She swayed toward the studio, determined to melt any male in the place with her classy sensuality. *"Two hundred pounds. In your dreams, Pete."* Lisa paused at the door, noticed the CLOSED sign, took a deep breath, rose erect and pushed the door open. It made a loud squeal, nearly breaking her focus.

It smelled like a sweaty men's gymnasium. It was dark inside, too. She removed her sunglasses. There was only one man in the studio, in the dark, wearing a traditional Chinese outfit. The jacket was black, trimmed with a white collar and cuffs and white rope ties down the front. The pants were also black. A black sash was tied around his waist, draping down his left side. His long hair was tied in a ponytail.

He was wearing a blindfold and wielding a Chinese broadsword with red and gold streamers attached to the hilt. He slowly carved, sliced and thrust the sword at imaginary targets as he gracefully cross-stepped, shuffled, back-stepped, hopped, twirled, kicked and crouched. His form and grace were beautiful. She was in awe.

"We're closed for lunch. I'll be with you in a moment," came the confident voice of Derek Storm. Lisa recognized it from the phone.

"Please continue. It's magnificent. I'll wait," she replied in the sweetest tones she could summon. Storm froze in mid-step, the sword over his head. He abandoned his practice and lowered the weapon.

"I haven't heard a voice that beautiful since yesterday. Would that be Lisa Chen?" *"Okay, Derek. Be a gentleman."*

Lisa walked toward the muscular, barrel-chested man.

Storm slowly eased the blindfold from his eyes and noticed the aroma of her perfume.

"Your perfume is delightful. May I ask what it is?"

"It's called Mistress. Do you like it?" That melodious voice and Asian accent intrigued him.

He slid the blindfold higher and smiled. As the blindfold rose, Storm noticed very sexy high-heeled shoes attached to some exquisitely shaped feminine legs. The blindfold rose higher, revealing a stunning red slit dress clinging to perfectly shaped hips, a narrow waist and an athletically toned, flat stomach.

The next increment revealed porcelain smooth skin on arms framing her bosom. Storm couldn't stand it any more and removed the blinder completely. The creature standing before him was the most beautiful woman he'd ever seen in his life. She had long, straight jet black silky hair cascading down her front left side to her waist. Her face was gorgeous, with high cheekbones, dark absorbing eyes, perfectly trimmed eyebrows, luscious lips generously adorned with red lipstick and a strong, but feminine jaw line.

Lisa took in Storm's expression. She coyly tossed her hair over her left shoulder to drape it across her breast as she pretended to admire the weaponry adorning the studio walls.

As she glanced away, Storm drank in her stunning profile, showcased by the sunlight through the windows. Lisa knew his eyes were probing her and she loved it. She knew he was expecting someone from a comedy show and instead meets a genuine China doll. *"Maybe Pete knew what he was doing after all?"* She turned away as she strolled along the wall, giving him an opportunity to appraise her from behind.

He did, too. The lyre-shaped curve of her hips where they invitingly melded into her shapely buttocks was accentuated by her sexy stroll and her clingy dress. Storm had seen all he needed to see to convince himself that this woman was, bar none, the most beautiful woman he had *ever* seen. If her personality was nice, the trip to Portland would be bearable. He wished they could have met under better circumstances.

"You know, these weapons all originated in the country of my ancestors," she stated.

"So you're Chinese?"

"Half. My mother is American. She's a former Miss Nevada."

"Well, that would explain her gorgeous attributes." He approached Lisa. She faced him as he extended his hand.

"I'm Derek Storm, Pete's nephew. My mom and he were siblings, as was Dan."

Lisa offered her hand to the handsome goateed Irishman. "I'm Lisa Chen. It's nice to meet you. I'm sorry about your uncle."

Storm took Lisa's hand and placed a tender kiss on the back of it. "It's my pleasure, Miss Chen. Or should I call you Doctor?"

"Call me Lisa."

Storm glanced at the wall clock. "What time is our flight?"

"Four-thirty. Do we have enough time?"

"Sure. But I need go to my apartment for a shower and grab my luggage."

"Shall I follow you?"

"That's good. I hope you don't mind waiting while I take a shower.

There aren't any facilities here and I guarantee that I normally smell a lot better than this."

Portland: "How you doin', Trigger?" inquired Bravo.

"Better, but I still can't stand." Trigger had bandages on his left side from his head to his ankle. The two largest were on his leg.

Slash entered, chewing on a sandwich and offered a second sandwich to Trigger. "Here you go, amigo, roast beast and cheese."

Trigger sat up, grabbed the sandwich and bit off a quarter of it, as if he hadn't eaten in a week. Slash pulled a cola can from his pocket and gave it to him. Trigger popped the lid and guzzled half of it, followed by a long belch.

Slash remarked, "He's back."

Bravo grinned. "How long before he's on his feet?"

"Couple of days, at least. Then he might be able to get around with a cane. I had to cut pretty deep. But he's a strong bastard. Could be sooner."

"Are you insulting my mother again, cracker?" Trigger wasn't pissed. It was just banter.

"That depends, boy. Do you know who your father is?"

"Get well, Trigger. I'm gonna need you," encouraged Bravo over his shoulder as he exited the room. The garage door opened. Sparks and Yankee entered.

"Did you finish the recon?"

"Done, Colonel." responded Sparks.

"Good. Let's have a look."

The mercenaries gathered around a large table as Yankee spread out a huge hand drawn diagram; it depicted the cemetery where Dan Flynn would be buried.

"Rebel's not back yet?" asked Yankee. Bravo had sent Rebel to recon the church where the memorial services would be held. Bravo didn't expect him back for another hour.

"Not yet. Show me what you've got."

Yankee laid out the sketch and several dozen snapshots of the cemetery. "Sparks also took some video."

The mercenaries studied the exhibits as Yankee talked. He pointed to each feature of the sketch and the corresponding Polaroids as he went. "This is north. Here's the plot location, oriented east/west. It looks like the head of the coffin will be east. The mourners awning is here, so the best angle for video would be from here, at the edge of this tree line."

Bravo pointed at an alternate spot. "Why not here? It's closer."

"There's a small ridge line right here." Yankee traced a line on the sketch. "It's just high enough to obstruct the view. The other location is better."

"Okay. Go ahead."

"These are the exits, the roads and the parking areas. There are lots of trees and shrubs close to the site but Sparks still thinks we'll need zoom lenses."

"Are our lenses adequate, Sparks?"

"Yes, sir."

"Okay. Where do we park the van?"

Sparks pointed at a parking area. "Here, Colonel. One man here with the sound equipment. The video cam here, camouflaged. I'll rig a remote and run it from the van while the other guys get photos and audio.

"Will we have data link from the van?"

"Good to go."

"Good. What's the weather forecast?"

Slash tossed the morning paper onto the table. "Weatherman's calling for overcast, light rain, forty-five degrees, light winds."

"Okay. As soon as Rebel gets back, we'll plan. Let's hope Peter Flynn shows up."

Las Vegas: The drive to Storm's apartment was easy. Lisa parked her SUV in a covered stall. Storm escorted her to his second floor apartment and offered her a cola while he took a shower.

Lisa sipped as she perused Storm's lodging. It was typically male décor. Oriental weaponry hung from the walls and numerous inexpensive pieces of oriental art complimented them. Lisa was impressed by how clean and orderly it was.

"I didn't know a single man's apartment could be so clean. My compliments to your housekeeper."

Storm stuck his head out the bedroom door. "Thanks. I'm the housekeeper."

"That's hard to believe. My brothers were slobs. You sure there's no girlfriend who comes in and cleans up?"

"Sorry, Miss Busybody, but I don't have a girlfriend. Just because I'm single doesn't mean I have to live like a pig."

Lisa smiled. He didn't have a current love interest. Storm crossed the hall, a towel around his waist. It was Lisa's turn for an appraisal.

She peeked around the corner and assessed his physique. She noticed burn scars on his left side, but everything else was quite appealing. He had broad shoulders and muscular arms and legs, well-developed pectorals and a strong jaw line. The darned towel was hiding his buns. *"What a shame."*

Storm closed the bathroom door and climbed into the shower. Lisa inspected the weapons and artwork in the living room. He had all manner of swords, knives, axes, lances, chains and sticks. She wondered if he knew how to use them.

A metal tablet on the mantle caught her attention. It had Chinese characters inscribed into its hard, shiny surface. Lisa held it. It had inscriptions on both sides. Her Chinese was rusty.

There were numerous characters she didn't recognize but she tried to interpret them in context. Her interest piqued. Her mouth hung open. This couldn't be. Where did this come from?

She heard the shower stop. She approached the bathroom door, tablet in hand. "Derek?"

"Just a second. I'm drying off."

She resisted the urge to open the door. "Derek, the metal tablet on your mantle; where did you get it?"

"Oh, that? It's a little souvenir from Iraq."

"Iraq?"

"Yup. I found it when I was in Desert Storm. Why?"

"Well, it has an interesting medical inscription on it. Did you know that?"

Lisa could hear Storm moving about inside. "I meant to have it translated but I never got around to it. Can you read it?"

"Some of it. You don't know what it says?"

"No. Tell me."

"It seems to be a medical record, a journal of a village healer from somewhere in China."

Storm opened the door and stood face to face with Lisa, a damp towel around his waist. He appealed to her from this angle, too.

"A medical journal, huh?" He shook his head as he gently touched her shoulder and stepped past her. A shiver excited her.

"I was hoping it was a Chuan Fa technique from some ancient Kung Fu master. So what does it say?"

"I don't recognize all of the characters. But basically, it says, 'I, Chang', …something or other, 'healer of', …I don't know the next characters, 'inscribe this report of the internal growth disease peculiar to our city to any who are of concern. May these tablets last the ages and benefit our descendants with good health and long life'."

"Tablets? Plural? Go on."

"'For many…' don't know, 'and generations, the people of..' don't know, 'have suffered an illness inside their bodies. Strange growths, begin small and grow, attack internal..', I think it means parts or organs.' The growths enlarge and stop blood, air and energy to the lungs or cause sufferer to breathe heavy and have heart surrender. Growths transfer from one,' I think it's part or organ, 'during time passes and cause suffering in next... part or organ'."

Storm nodded thoughtfully. "Lisa, I'm going to close the door so I can get dressed. I'm not being rude, just modest. Keep reading. Please."

"Oh. Of course."

Storm closed his door as she continued.

"'One generation seen, most those working or living near city…', I think this next character means 'asbestos', but I'm not certain." She paused briefly as she read the next few characters. "Okay, that makes sense. 'near the city asbestos market suffered. Those people living far from the market did not acquire the internal growth disease. Many of people working at the market and lived far from the market acquired the growth disease but their families did not. No other area of city affected. This would show some element in the making of…' I think it's 'asbestos… may be cause of disease. Maybe this element is carried on the air or maybe the food. Some healers believe growths may be caused by spirits of the ancients, but not Chang' whoever he is."

Lisa could hear Storm shuffling about inside the bedroom. "Are you getting this?"

"Yes. Keep going. It's interesting."

"'My observing as city healer of three hundred thirteen'…don't know…'of the moon as I inscribe tablets, I have revealed a treatment to prevent and part of time make smaller these internal growths. Some people disappear the growth complete and never acquire back. This treatment serves the people and healers well and is plentiful in city. Steady consume each day…'" Lisa stopped abruptly.

The bedroom door opened and Storm emerged with a suitcase and hanging bag. "Steady consume each day what? What's he talking about?"

Lisa stammered. "I… that's the end of this tablet, but I think he's referring to asbestos cancer, Mesothelioma. If I'm correct, this healer,

Chang, has discovered a possible cure for Mesothelioma. Do you realize how important this tablet is? It says there's a cure and it's plentiful, at least it is… or was, in China."

"But what's the treatment? Did it say?"

"No. It must be on the next tablet. Do you know where it is?"

Storm walked to the living room, set down his luggage and sat on the couch. He gestured at Lisa to have a seat as he related the story of how he found the small wooden chest containing the tablet.

"…and I found two jade sculptures with it. There was a carved jade sculpture. The other jade piece was this." Storm held up a four-inch diameter, round jade piece suspended on a leather thong around his neck.

"Can I see that?" Storm removed the necklace and handed it to her. She studied the medallion and seemed disappointed.

"What does it say?"

"Well, this side says, 'By the strength of the eternal Heaven, holy be the Khan's name. Let him that pays him not reverence be killed'." She turned the medallion over. "This side says 'something Khan'."

Storm stared at her.

"Were there any other tablets, Derek?"

"I don't know. I was wounded, in a lot of pain. I didn't spend a lot of time searching. I had other priorities."

"Have you ever had these authenticated?"

"I never got around to it. I had no idea they were important."

"Tell you what. Let me call my brother Lawrence. He's an art historian and assistant curator at an Oriental art museum. Maybe he can verify their authenticity."

"Okay. Go for it."

Lisa fished her cell phone from her purse and dialed. Storm went to the kitchen and returned with two bottles of light beer.

"Then you agree, Pete. It could be Mesothelioma?" She nodded and handed her phone to Storm.

As Storm took the phone, she uncrossed her legs and poured some beer. She leaned back and crossed her legs in the other direction. The gesture wasn't lost on Storm.

"This is Derek." It was Pete and after a brief discussion Storm agreed to have the artifacts authenticated immediately after his return from Portland. Storm cut the connection and returned the phone to Lisa, who was delicately sipping her beer and leaving sexy red lipstick marks on the glass.

"Well. That settles it. With two professional opinions, I need to have these things authenticated. Did you say your brother could do that?"

"If he can't do it himself, he'll know who can. I'll call him right now."

"I suggest we head for the airport and you can call him on the way."

∽

Lisa contacted her brother and described the artifacts to him. He seemed interested but insisted on examining them first hand. She informed Lawrence that Storm would visit him in San Francisco. She introduced Storm to Lawrence over the phone. After Storm finished with Lawrence, he returned Lisa's phone. He guessed that Lawrence was gay but didn't say anything.

The flight from Las Vegas to Portland had been quite interesting. Once they had boarded the airplane, they learned a little about each other. Storm learned that she was thirty years old. Her grandfather had escaped China with the family in 1947, during the communist revolt. Her grandparents and uncles learned English and became American citizens. They lived in the San Francisco area. Lisa's father was born in the U.S. and was CEO of his own international air freight company. Her mother was a former Miss Nevada and later a Las Vegas show promoter when she met her father. Lisa had two brothers and two sisters and she was the middle child. Lisa had never been married and studied medicine at UCLA. She interned at a cancer ward, which was hard on her emotions, especially seeing children die. After her internship, she went into cancer research. She had had several serious relationships but had not yet found Mr. Right. Her most recent beau turned out to be a controlling, possessive jerk who had stalked her. It drove her from Los Angeles. That's when she hired on with Pete. Her favorite color was red and she loved flowers and taking long, hot bubble baths.

Storm revealed his history, too. He had trained in Kung Fu since he was six years old. His father, a former Army Ranger with two tours in Viet Nam, was his first teacher. By the time he took the art seriously, he was in his late teens and his teachers considered him to be quite talented. He was now a sixth degree black belt with a goal to be Master in two years. Both of Storm's parents had perished from cancer, two years apart. He had one brother, whom he hadn't heard from in six years, and one sister with whom he had a good relationship. Storm told Lisa he was thirty-three and had been married once, but it didn't work out. He related the story of having been a soldier in Desert Storm and how his vehicle struck a land mine, killing his crew and wounding him, his discovery of the buried ship and the Chinese artifacts and his rescue, his back operation, rehabilitation and medical discharge. He had been teaching Kung Fu since then, making a decent living and having fun. His favorite color was green and he had an interest in history.

After arriving in Portland, Storm called his Aunt Kate to offer his condolences and arrange a time to visit her. He hadn't specified the reason. He wanted to comply with Pete's request to check on her security. Lisa checked out their rental car while Storm was on the phone with Kate and by the time he was finished, so was she and they went to their hotel. Their check-in was painless and each had a separate room on different floors. They agreed to meet at the hotel restaurant at eight p.m. for dinner.

Storm arrived at the restaurant ten minutes early and tipped the hostess to get a table in a quiet, cozy corner near the fireplace. The hostess accommodated and gave him a coy smile. Storm let her know he was expecting a lady with long black hair, then positioned his chair to observe the entrance. A cocktail waitress appeared and he ordered an Irish coffee.

There was something about Lisa that captivated him. It went beyond her beauty and her intelligence. Her personality was magnificent. She was caring, thoughtful and independent.

She appeared at the restaurant entrance. He didn't think it was possible but she looked even more stunning than the first time he had seen her. She wore a long, tight, green and white silk dress that hugged her curves and draped to the tops of her slender ankles. A long slit in the left side of the dress ran from the hem to her mid-thigh, emphasizing her pretty legs atop their high heels. The dress had a high, closed collar that resembled a choker. A beautiful mink jacket covered her shoulders. Her hair was woven into a braided bun, exposing the creamy smoothness of her neck. Her makeup made her complexion glimmer and her long dark eyelashes called attention to her absorbing brown eyes.

Storm saw the hostess point in his direction and he rose to greet Lisa. After escorting her to the table, the hostess departed and Storm took a few seconds to appreciate the vision.

"I must be dreaming."

Lisa smiled. "You're a charmer, Mr. Storm."

"You look lovely. I had no idea any woman could be so beautiful."

Lisa blushed and glanced away, unable to look Storm in the eyes.

She was accustomed to being complimented but she found Storm's admiration nearly overwhelming.

"May I take your wrap?"

"Yes, thank you, Derek." He liked hearing his name coming from her lips. He eased the mink from her shoulders, revealing the dress's long, elegant sleeves. The back of the dress, well, there wasn't a back. The dress disappeared just below the collar and didn't reappear until her waist. Her shoulders and back were exposed. They were delicate and smooth without a single blemish. "*Absolute perfection.*"

He draped the mink over the back of her chair and pulled it slightly away from the table. Lisa gracefully slid onto the seat as Derek adjusted it for her. He sat across the table and stared into her eyes. She blushed again. "Are you going to stare at me all night?"

"I could die a happy man right now if you're the last thing I see."

She appraised Storm's attire. He was wearing a camel hair sport jacket with a green dress shirt opened at the collar and charcoal gray slacks with black leather shoes and belt. His reddish brown hair was pulled back into a ponytail and his goatee was meticulously trimmed, framing that crooked smile.

"I just don't know what to say, Derek, except maybe that there's more to me than meets the eye. You look very handsome." She gazed right back into his eyes, now sure of herself.

"Shall we order some wine or do prefer a cocktail?"

"Wine sounds lovely, thank you. Cabernet?"

"Cabernet it is." Storm raised his hand to attract the waitress's attention. The attractive young waitress immediately noticed.

"Yes, sir. What can I get you?"

"The lady would like a glass of cabernet sauvignon, please, and we're ready for the menus."

"Very good. May I tell you about our special this evening?"

"Yes, please," interjected Lisa.

The waitress faced Lisa and made hand gestures for emphasis. "The special this evening is Spinach Ziti Alfredo. It's a blend of fresh, chopped spinach with a touch of diced tomato in a low-fat cream sauce served over a bed of al dente Ziti pasta. It's the chef's specialty."

"Oh, that sounds delicious. I'll have that," said Lisa.

"Make that two."

"Very good. A glass of cabernet and two Ziti specials. Would you like a drink, sir?"

"Please bring us a bottle of your best cabernet." The waitress nodded with a smile and walked off.

Storm turned back to Lisa. "Lisa, do you really think there's something to those Chinese tablets? How do they tie in with your research?"

"Pete has made a significant finding with his doxodigallcatechin gallate enhancement for enzyme rate regulation."

Storm gave Lisa a blank stare. His knowledge of biology and chemistry went no further than high school level. His strongest subject had been world history. "In English, for the benefit of the bio-chemically challenged."

Lisa snickered. "Okay. I forgot." She took a few seconds to compose a layman's edition. "Pete has invented a compound called DDCG. His approach involves enzymes."

"Enzymes. Right. Isn't that what they use to clean up oil spills?"

"That's right. Enzymes dissolve things. They help digest our food, they dissolve grease and oil, and they're even used in household cleaners."

"I'm with you."

"Well, Pete thinks we can get enzymes to dissolve the cancer tumors without the side effects of radiation and chemotherapy; they make the patients very sick. Sometimes they cause more damage than the cancer, well, until the final stages. The problem is the enzymes don't consume the cancer fast enough to prevent its spread. You see, when the cells break down into sub-cellular particles, they can still invade healthy tissue before they're fully consumed. The second problem is getting the enzymes to stop before they eat into healthy tissue. If we can solve those two problems, we have a good chance at curing cancer."

"So how does DDCG function in all this?"

"The DDCG regulates the rate of enzyme consumption. At low ratios the DDCG speeds up the process, but not enough. At higher ratios it decreases the rate to nearly zero, barely measurable. But it also destroys surrounding health tissue. Now we need to find an inhibiting agent or ratio, then we can stop the enzymes at will. But we're still searching for the key."

"I see. That tablet made reference to a potential treatment. If we discover that treatment, you're saying it can be used as the inhibiting agent?"

"Exactly! It's exciting. Mysterious, too, don't you think?"

"Mysterious?"

"Just think. The cure may have been discovered seven centuries ago, but was lost. Along comes the dashing Derek Storm and discovers the tablets, only he doesn't know their significance. But there's at least one tablet missing, begging to be found."

"Yeah, in a country that's about to be blasted to kingdom come in another war."

"Don't you see, Derek? We may have to go find those other tablets. Exciting, isn't it?"

Storm's face had a faraway expression. He was somewhere else. The memories of the pain, hunger and isolation returned. He felt the sorrow of losing his squad, the vision of their charred bodies haunted him.

"Derek. Did I say something that upset you?"

Storm snapped back. He smiled. "Sorry. I was somewhere else."

"Iraq?"

"Yes. It's not a pleasant memory."

"I'm sorry."

The waitress returned with their wine and poured it. They tasted it and thanked the young lady. Storm waited until she departed before speaking.

"You have nothing to be sorry for, Lisa. It's just a memory." He sipped his wine "So, you think I'm handsome and dashing?"

∞

The weather was exactly as forecast and provided excellent cover for Bravo's team. Their hooded raincoats protected them and concealed their radios and earpieces.

The team had arrived at the cemetery two hours early. They immediately set up their equipment and located their assigned stations. Slash and Rebel were equipped with digital cameras with zoom lenses. Yankee had a handheld acoustical dish with headphones. He was stationed inside the tree line seven yards from the video camera. The video cam was operated from the van by a wireless remote.

Sparks had everyone's equipment set up and tested in short order. There were only a couple of minor snags but the team was ready with an hour to spare. The mercenaries retreated to the warmth of their vehicles to await the motorcade. The team radio was silent except for the occasional radio check.

Rebel noticed the motorcade and elbowed Slash. Slash nodded and keyed his radio, "Curtain call."

"Roger. Posts. Acknowledge when ready."

The men exited their vehicles and flipped on their hoods. They leisurely walked to their stations as if visiting the grave of a loved one. Each man acknowledged when in position.

The motorcade turned up the narrow road toward the burial site. A man in a black overcoat emerged from the lead vehicle and began directing vehicles. The vehicles scattered and Rebel saw the police car leave.

"PLAYERS have departed."

"Roger."

Rebel and Slash took photos of the mourners and their vehicles. Sparks activated the video cam and focused on the group as they walked toward the awning. The mourners were covered with hats, hoods and umbrellas, making it difficult to get clear facial images. Yankee activated the acoustical dish and randomly sampled conversations.

It was obvious who the grieving widow and daughters were. They were dressed in black and led by their forearms by close male members of the family. The widow wore a black veil. Eighty people gathered under the awning.

Sparks scanned individual faces as he studied the monitor and manipulated the controller. Bravo watched intently over his shoulder. Sparks paused a long time on one male who resembled the image of Pete Flynn in the photograph taped above the monitor.

"What do you think, Colonel?"

Bravo studied the image. A woman to the subject's left whispered to him.

"Close. Maybe he's had a nose job." Bravo keyed the radio, "Yankee, second row back, fifth seat from the left, the man in the dark gray overcoat with the gray scarf and black hat. Focus the dish on him."

"Aye-aye."

Sparks reached to another control panel and turned a dial. Garbled acoustics filled the van as Yankee aimed the dish. Within seconds, Yankee had the dish positioned on the subject and the whisperings of the gossipy woman came through without distortion. The woman referred to the subject as Tom several times.

"That's not him," stated Bravo. "His nose is different and the woman keeps calling him Tom. Just the same, designate him Alpha and assign Slash to tail him."

Sparks nodded and informed Slash. Sparks scanned more faces. The rain came down harder. It made scanning difficult and muddled the acoustical feed. Sparks had to spend more time zooming and focusing to get the sharpest image. Bravo seemed impatient but understood the difficulties.

"This is Rebel. I've got a candidate."

"Go ahead."

"Standing behind the last row, third from the right. Man in beige trench coat holding a brown umbrella."

Sparks slewed the camera and adjusted. A face came into focus. The man did bear a strong resemblance to Peter Flynn.

"Can you zoom in tighter, Sparks?"

"I'll try, Colonel." Sparks adjusted the zoom and focused.

"That's the best image I can get in this rain, Colonel."

"Okay. That may be good enough." The Colonel gave Sparks a congratulatory pat on the shoulder as he leaned closer to the monitor. The hair color was wrong and he couldn't see the man's jaw line.

"This is Slash. I think that guy standing in the back is one of the mortuary staff. He was driving one of the funeral vehicles."

"Are you sure?"

"About ninety percent, boss."

Well, that leave's ten percent doubt, reasoned Bravo. "Okay, Sparks. Designate him as subject Tango." He keyed the mike, "Rebel, your candidate is designated Tango and he's your assignment."

"Rebel copies."

The rain diminished. Scanning became easier. Sparks had scanned two-dozen faces when Bravo gripped his shoulder.

"Freeze there, Sparks. No, back one. Yeah, that one." Sparks slewed the camera back to the left and fine-tuned.

"Colonel, I don't mean to question your judgment, but I don't see the resemblance."

Bravo stared intently. The monitor displayed a rugged looking man sporting a neatly trimmed goatee and a reddish brown ponytail, blue eyes and a square jaw. The subject didn't look the least like Peter Flynn, but the Colonel had an intense interest in him.

Bravo leaned closer and nodded. He snatched the bat phone and hit speed dial. "Yeah, it's me. I need a bio workup on one Derek Storm for the past ten years; marriages, kids, work history, pets, bowel movements, the works. Storm: S-T-O-R-M, first name Derek: D-E-R-E-K. 24th Infantry Division, Persian Gulf War. Soon as possible. Right." Bravo slapped the device shut and clipped it to his belt.

"Who is he, Colonel?"

"Someone I recognize from the Gulf War. He's ten years older but I'm pretty sure that's him."

"Is he trouble?"

"Can't say. What's he doing here? Sparks, you got that family tree?" As part of their research, Sparks dug up the Flynn family tree to see if Peter Flynn had any brothers or sisters that could be providing him with safe haven. His only brother had been capped by Bravo himself and his only sister had died of cancer.

Sparks shuffled through a folder. He found the document and handed it to Bravo. "Amazing what one can find on the Internet, huh? Better espionage through technology."

Bravo snatched the paper. "Put a lid on it. Scan the people next to him."

Sparks returned to his work as Bravo scanned the sheet. A name jumped off the page. Storm's mother was Pete and Dan Flynn's sister. He was their nephew!

Sparks had the video cam focused on the little old lady to Storm's left. She was a short, gray-haired woman in her seventies. Tears streamed down her wrinkled cheeks. An arm of the elderly man to her left was draped over her shoulders and patting her.

"Okay, nothing there. Move to his other side."

Sparks slewed the video to the right, centering a slightly blurred image on the monitor. He adjusted the focus, bringing into view a face so lovely he stared at it with his mouth agape. The image showed a beautiful woman, mid to late twenties, Asian descent, long black hair, smooth complexion and flawless makeup, not that she needed the stuff. She was naturally gorgeous. She was wearing a black dress with a mink jacket and a small black hat.

"Who's that?" asked Bravo.

"Wife or girlfriend, maybe?"

"They don't seem lovey-dovey." Bravo keyed his radio, "Yankee, new target. Fourth row back, third and fourth seats from the left. The man with the goatee and ponytail and the Oriental bimbo next to him."

"Got 'em."

Sparks adjusted the speaker again as Yankee aimed the dish at Storm and Lisa. Nothing was coming through except background noises. They weren't speaking. They seemed attentive to the burial service.

Bravo's bat phone rang and startled Sparks. Bravo answered and listened. He stared at the monitor. Bravo finally said, "No, I don't need his social security number. Good work, Clete. Your check is in the mail." Bravo snapped the phone closed and replaced it.

"So who is that guy, Colonel?"

"That is former Staff Sergeant Derek Storm. He was in the 24th Infantry during the Gulf War. We've met in person, so he'd probably recognize me. He was a top-notch squad leader and the toughest son of a bitch in the battalion. Nobody dared mess with him after he creamed six soldiers by himself. I was battalion S-1 when that happened and his Company Commander nearly issued him an Article 15. He taught martial arts in his spare time. He was awarded the Army Commendation Medal, the Good Conduct Medal, Purple Heart, the Soldiers Medal and the Combat Infantry Badge. He was rated Expert with rifle, pistol, grenade, machinegun and anti-tank weapon. He was a damned rugged soldier until he was medically discharged for a back injury. There's a gap in his history after he was discharged, but recently he's been running his own Kung Fu business in Las Vegas. He was married once but divorced. No kids that we know of. He's not currently married according to the VA disability files, so this broad must be a girlfriend, although she looks to be way above his pay grade." Bravo studied Lisa's face. "That is one classy piece. Have they said anything?"

"Not a whisper."

"If you were Pete Flynn and you wanted to hide, and let's say you had this Army combat veteran Kung Fu expert of a nephew, your siblings were dead, who would you chose to be a confidant?"

Sparks looked up and grinned. Bravo's concept had just been validated. "Designate Storm and the toots as Foxtrot."

Bravo keyed the radio, "Yankee and Rebel, new assignment."

"Yankee, go ahead, chief."

"Rebel's ready."

"I want you both on the couple in the fourth row back, third and fourth seats from the left; the man with the goatee and the China doll next to him. We know the man's identity. Find out the babe's name, their lodging and their itinerary. They are designated Foxtrot. Copy?"

"Yankee copies."

"Rebel, roger that."

"Do not approach or engage this guy. He's more dangerous than he looks. Keep the survey loose but don't lose them."

Both acknowledged.

"That gives us three candidates. But I'll bet my pension that Storm knows where Peter Flynn is."

∞

The ceremony concluded with prayer. Storm and Lisa queued in line to offer their condolences to his aunt and cousins. The mourners filed past Storm's aunt, offering their condolences and help. It tore at Storm's heart. When it came to his turn, he hugged his cousins and kissed their foreheads.

"This is Lisa Chen," he said softly. "She's Pete's research partner."

Lisa extended her hand. "Hello. Pete wanted me to express his condolences and let you know he's okay."

The sisters thanked Lisa and hugged her. Tears welled in Lisa's eyes, too.

Storm hugged Kate and kissed her cheek. Her skin felt cold and clammy. She was shaking and sobbing, tears poured from her blue eyes, now reddened. Her hands trembled as she raised her kerchief under her veil.

"I'll see you at four o'clock, Aunt Kate. Get some rest, okay?"

Kate nodded meekly. As Storm was about to introduce Lisa, Kate turned pale and swooned. Storm caught her, other mourners gasped. Storm lifted her and carried her toward the parking lot.

"Is there a doctor here?" he yelled over his shoulder. Several men ran ahead of him to clear a path and start the car. One of the staff opened the rear door and helped him place Kate on the rear seat.

"Let me to her, Derek." It was Lisa. Doctor Lisa! He forgot she was an M.D. He felt like an ass.

Lisa checked Kate's vital signs. "Lay her down so the blood can flow to her head." Derek eased her down.

Lisa assessed Kate. "She'll be okay. There's nothing physically wrong. It's all emotional. It's best if she's taken directly home and put to bed."

"I'll take her home," said one of the men.

Derek looked at Lisa, who was observing Kate. Her eyes teared. "Thank you, Lisa."

She looked up with sad eyes, smiled and placed a soft hand on his cheek. "I'm a doctor, you adorable fool. And don't you forget it."

∞

"Did you hear that?" asked Yankee.

Bravo answered as Sparks said, "Bingo."

"Roger that. Confirm it was Foxtrot female who said it?"

"Affirmative. They mentioned her name, too."

"It's on tape. Don't use their names any more. Yankee, you and Rebel get on the Foxtrots, now. Slash, skip Alpha. Back up Yankee. All survey on the Foxtrots."

Bravo was disappointed, but not surprised, that Pete Flynn didn't show. But they had the next best thing, his research partner.

∾

Storm and Lisa drove back to their hotel, unaware of two gray Buicks in their wake. They parked below ground.

They decided to meet in the lobby for lunch. After that, Storm would drive to Kate's house and scope out her security.

∾

The mercenaries easily tailed the blue Ford. It led them to the Hollister Plaza Hotel and pulled into the underground parking. Yankee got to the elevator and monitored its progress. It stopped at the lobby level before moving up. Then it made five stops on its way to the top floor. There was no way to tell which floor their room was on.

"Shit."

"Shit what, Yank?" Slash came trotting up.

"I couldn't tell what their floor is." Yankee pulled his cell phone from his pocket and checked for signal. There wasn't any.

"Shit."

"Shit what, Yank?" Rebel came running up.

"What are you two, stereo?"

Rebel and Slash looked at each other and Rebel shrugged his shoulders, not getting it. Slash laughed.

"No signal down here. Anyone remember their names?"

They shook their heads.

"We need to call the van." Slash pressed the elevator button and they checked their cell phones while they waited. None of them had a signal.

The elevator doors opened. The mercenaries stepped aside to allow people to exit, hustled inside and rode to the lobby. As soon as the doors opened at the lobby, the cell signals came in strong. Yankee speed dialed Bravo as they strolled to the bar. The place was empty except for the bartender.

"This is Yankee. Foxtrots are at the Hollister Plaza but we don't know what room and I can't recall the name." Yankee listened as they bellied up to the bar. Slash ordered three beers.

"Sparks has to replay the audio to get the chick's name. The guy's name is Derek Storm." Yankee listened again and nodded. "Got it. Thanks, Colonel. We'll keep you posted." He snapped the phone closed and shoved it into his pocket.

"The chick's name is Lisa Chen. She's a doctor."

The beers arrived and Slash tossed a twenty on the bar. They hoisted their mugs.

"No better way to spend an eleven a.m., quaffing a brew," elaborated Yankee. They swigged their beers in unison. "Any ideas on how to find out what room they're in?"

An idea struck Slash. He leaned over and whispered. Yankee grinned, sauntered to the house phone and dialed the front desk. "Yeah, hi. This is room service. We got an order here for Lisa Chen but the printer screwed up and we can't read the room number. Can you give me her room number so I can get this to her while it's still hot? Yeah, Chen. Two rooms? Well, I'll be. Give me both numbers. Thanks. She isn't checking out today, is she? Tomorrow? Okay, thanks Brenda. You're a sweetheart. Bye."

Yankee grinned as he sauntered back to the bar.

"You got their room number," deduced Slash.

"Room numbers, with an S, plural. They're in separate rooms, 614 and 712."

Yankee pulled his cell phone again. He speed dialed Bravo and waited.

"This is Yankee. They're in separate rooms. I don't think they're a gossip item. Both are under the chick's name and they checkout tomorrow at noon. What do you want us to do, Colonel?"

Yankee listened. "Yes, sir. We'll keep you posted." Yankee closed the cell phone and dropped it into his pocket. He leaned closer.

"The Colonel wants their itinerary, even if we have to break into their rooms. He said to avoid contact with Storm and don't spook them. Don't leave any traces in their rooms." Yankee took another swig.

"All right, Yank. You're the sneaky entry expert. How do we get in?"

Yankee swigged the remainder of his beer and signaled the bartender for another round. "Do we have a suitcase in the car?"

∞

Lisa arrived first, dressed casually. She wore black slacks, low heels and a tight, lavender turtleneck sweater that emphasized her figure. She wore a pink jacket, lavender wool cap and matching scarf. Even her lipstick was lavender. She looked like a fashion model.

She scanned the newspapers as she waited for Storm. She noticed the admiring stares of men as they passed. She had grown accustomed to it during her teens.

A tap on her shoulder caught her attention. Storm had silently walked up behind her. She greeted him with a pleasant smile and appraised his attire. He wore a blue dress shirt that enhanced his eyes, black slacks and the camel hair sport jacket.

"You look nice," she said.

"So do you. Do you have a preference for lunch?"

"You choose."

"Okay. I'm in the mood for some exquisite Chinese." His crooked grin amused her and she giggled, not sure if he meant Chinese food or if he was making a clever double-entendre.

"Chinese sounds good. Maybe the concierge can recommend a good restaurant. Or did you have something else in mind?"

Storm didn't realize his statement could be taken two ways. "Did I say something wrong? I hate it when I do that."

"You missed your own joke?"

Storm looked puzzled.

"'Have some exquisite Chinese for lunch?' Were you referring to food... or me?" Lisa toyed with him and smiled coyly.

Storm's puzzled expression disappeared, replaced by a blush. "I was referring to food but believe me, I find you supremely attractive."

She smiled with affection. "That was the perfect answer. Chinese sounds wonderful." She folded her arm under his and they approached the concierge.

After getting directions, they walked arm in arm and headed for the restaurant, two blocks distant.

They reached the Chinese-Thai restaurant within minutes and were seated immediately. The décor was dark and typically oriental. The lighting was dim and the table placements cozy.

Storm seated Lisa and sat next to her. He didn't want to be across the table. It seemed too far away. Lisa took note.

The waitress provided menus and asked for their drink orders. They reached a consensus on sweet and sour pork.

Storm took his cell phone and dialed a number. "I want to check in with Kate."

Storm waited. His cousin Karen answered.

"Hello, Karen. This is Derek. How's your mom doing?" Storm

listened, nodding.

"Good. She needs rest. How are you and Patricia holding up? Is there anything I can do?" More nods.

"Okay. I promised Pete that I'd visit to check in on you all and I was planning on being there about four. Is that okay?" Storm listened.

"Sure. You bet. Is it okay if I bring Lisa? She's the lady you met this morning at the funeral, Pete's partner." Storm listened and grinned.

"Thanks, Karen. We'll be there at four to give you all a hug. See you soon. Bye." "Kate's asleep. Patricia gave her a sedative. Karen said four o'clock is fine. She'd like to meet you again so she can see you without tears in her eyes."

"That's understandable. It's terrible to lose a loved one."

They sat silently, reflecting on the sad situation.

"Derek, you said Patricia gave Kate a sedative. Is Patricia a doctor?"

"Yes, an oncologist. Karen's a doctor too, but I don't recall her specialty. They all worked together, not far from here."

"Where's their house?"

"It's twenty minutes east of here. Hampton Manors, or something like that. I have the directions."

"I'm sad for their loss, and yours. Pete told me your Uncle Dan was a kind man. Who would want to murder him? It's disgraceful."

Storm just nodded, melancholic. Lisa changed the subject.

"How long have you been doing Kung Fu, Derek?"

"My father started training me when I was six. He taught me the stances, strikes, forms, leverages, throws and weapons. On certain days, we'd wear our black uniforms and put white chalk on our fingers. Then we'd use our fingertips to strike certain pressure points and check the chalk marks. Other days, we'd dress in white and use colored markers to simulate knives. You could tell where you'd been cut by the marks. Let me tell you something. Any one who thinks they can get into a knife fight and not be cut is nuts. No one is that good. Not even the Masters. If you're in a knife fight, you're gonna get cut. It's vicious."

"Do you go to competitions?"

Storm shook his head. "No. Competition is good for developing the combat spirit, but it teaches bad technique. A tournament has to have rules. You can't gouge eyes, bite, crush windpipes or snap necks. Rules are fine for tournaments but in the real world there are no rules. In the real world, rules get you killed. Warriors will fight the way they've been trained. If they've been trained to obey rules, they'll fight that way.

That's why I chose San Soo. It doesn't honor rules. It's a true warrior art. Don't get me wrong. The other arts are very effective and I've seen many outstanding fighters come from them. The art doesn't make the warrior. The warrior makes the warrior. It's in the heart."

Lisa nodded. "If I'm not mistaken, San Soo means 'scattering hands'."

"You know, I'm not sure. I heard that from some one else. I don't recall Master Chin ever mentioning it."

"What do you do to develop the inner spirit, you know, for serenity and peace?"

"I study the bible and pray. It clears my mind and helps me focus. Sounds like an oxymoron, doesn't it?"

Lisa smiled.

The waitress appeared with their meal. Lisa expertly pinched a large portion with her chopsticks and offered it to Storm. He gladly accepted and did the same for her, though not with as much finesse.

∞

The plan was simple. Rebel retrieved a briefcase and suitcase. He then checked into the hotel, posing as a businessman. Once he reached his room, he called Yankee. Slash hustled up to the room while Yankee maintained vigil on the Foxtrots.

Once Slash reached Rebel's room, he opened a panel on the TV, cut a few wires and replaced the panel. He confirmed it was out of order.

Rebel dialed the front desk.

"Howdy, this is Mr. Davis, room 908. I just checked in. The TV isn't working. Could you send someone up to have a look?" Rebel nodded and gave Slash the thumbs up. "Thank you, ma'am. You have a splendid day."

"They're sending maintenance."

Slash called Yankee. "Yeah, Yank. Maintenance is on the way. I'll call you as soon as we get it."

The mercenaries made adjustments to the room. Rebel placed the closed suitcase on a luggage stand as Slash scattered papers on the desk. Rebel arranged the chairs and turned on the lamp. They removed their trench coats and suit jackets, tossed them on the bed and rolled up their sleeves. They stashed their radios inside the suitcase. Rebel lit a cigarette and flopped into a chair.

A soft knock announced the maintenance man. Rebel opened the door and was greeted by a friendly man in a work uniform with a pushcart in tow. He had a spare TV, tools and spare parts on the cart.

"Are you having some difficulty with the TV, sir?"

"Yes. Thank you for coming so quickly. Come in." Rebel held the door open. "The TV doesn't have power and I checked the cord. It's plugged in."

"All right, sir. I'll take a look."

Rebel turned to Slash. "So Jeff. Where are we on the Parmenter contract?"

Slash took his cue and launched into a phony business discussion. "We're good. Their samples met the specs exactly and our first payment is on the fourteenth. Johnson said production starts tomorrow."

"Good. All we have to do now is get the summaries in for the quarterly reports. You know how those bean counters get."

Slash chuckled as if they had an inside joke.

The maintenance man fiddled with the TV for two minutes and decided it was beyond his scope. "Sir, I'll have to swap out this TV. This one'll have to go into the shop. I'll have you a working TV in about three minutes."

"Good. We'll still have time to catch the financial reports." Slash played his role to the hilt.

The maintenance man lifted the spare TV. Slash walked over to help.

"Here. Let me help. Don't want you to hurt your back"

They set the TV next to the broken one and the maintenance man bent over the dresser to gather the wires. Slash bumped into him as Rebel lifted the master key card from the janitor's pouch. It was an old ploy.

"Pardon me," apologized Slash. "Now I'm in the way."

"No bother, sir. You were trying to help and I appreciate it," grunted the technician, as he bent over the dresser.

Rebel's cell phone rang. "This is Davis."

Rebel listened. "That's good news. Just to let you know, we have the contract squared away and can begin operations any time."

Rebel listened more. "Okay. Great! We'll get right on it and keep you informed, sir." Rebel replaced his phone and informed Slash, "That was the Vice-President. He just gave us authorization to start production." Slash understood that Yankee had given them the green light.

The maintenance man tested the new TV. He smiled and handed the remote to Rebel, who slipped him a ten spot.

"I appreciate you responding so quickly."

"Well, thank you, sir. Just let me get this old TV onto the cart and I'll leave you gentlemen to your business."

Slash was way ahead of him and already had the sabotaged set on the cart. "Thank you, sir. You gentlemen have a nice day."

The maintenance man took the cart in tow and eased it out the door as Rebel held it for him. "Have a nice day, sir."

"Thank you. Y'all do the same." Rebel placed the DO NOT DISTURB sign on the door and closed it.

"Yankee said the Foxtrots are having lunch two blocks away. Let's go."

Slash grabbed the radios and tossed Rebel's to him. "I'll do the entry and you watch the elevators. We'll go to 614 first. What's that other room number?"

"712."

"Right. You got the card?"

Rebel gave it to Slash. He tested it in the lock of Rebel's door. It worked. Rebel grabbed their jackets and tossed Slash's to him. They headed for the stairs.

∞

"Derek, why were you wearing the blindfold?"

"What blindfold?"

"You know, you were practicing your swordsmanship blindfolded."

"Oh, that." Storm nodded. "It's a training method my father taught me. By being blindfolded, I tune in my other senses. It sharpens the hearing, smell, balance and sense of direction."

"Just like a blind person develops more acute senses."

"That's the theory. Also, it helps to develop perception of chi, or energy fields, that are in every living thing."

"Interesting. You're an internalist."

"That's a term I haven't heard since I trained with Master Chin. Yes, I'm a believer in chi and it's internal applications. How are you aware of it? Most doctors in this country pass it off as oriental mysticism."

"I'm Chinese, remember? Our culture was instrumental in developing the concept. What do you know of the meridians?"

"Oh, a test? Let's see. The human body isn't just a physical form. Electrical impulses flow through us. These impulses form fields of energy that flow through and around our bodies, much like the field around a magnet. The size and intensity of these fields vary by individual. Have you ever sensed someone behind you, even though you didn't see, hear or smell anything?"

"Yes."

"So have I. My father was the first to teach me. Later, Master Chin taught me ways to develop it. The meridians are the paths of the flow of this energy. When two energy fields touch, they create a disturbance, like two magnets. I believe a perceptive internalist can sense the disturbance in the energy flow." Storm rubbed his left shoulder and shrugged.

"What's wrong with your shoulder?"

"Just a little reminder of my Iraqi adventure. My shoulder was dislocated. The infraspinitus and subscapularis bug me occasionally."

Lisa got up and stepped to Storm's side. "How is it you know the names of these muscles?" She rubbed firmly around and down his left shoulder blade. Storm shivered, excited by her touch.

"I've had a lot of training. I'm also a licensed massage therapist and holistic health practitioner. Anatomy is a required subject matter for licensing."

Lisa continued her massage. "How did you get interested in that?"

"Master Chin. He told me the traditional lifestyles of warriors in ancient China were very different than today. In ancient times, the village warriors were the monks. They had the training to understand the human body. They were not only warriors but the healers and spiritual leaders as well. The same meridians and pressure points used in combat are the ones used to perform healing. So I decided if I was going to be a real Kung Fu artist, I needed to learn the healing aspects, just like the ancient monks."

Lisa completed her massage and placed her hand on Storm's head. "You are quite interesting."

"So are you." Storm scooped up the check and helped Lisa with her jacket.

"It's time to visit Kate."

∞

Entry was a piece of cake. Rebel watched the hall. As soon as Slash entered room 614, he mounted his earpiece and radio mike and turned on his radio. "This is Slash, I'm on station."

The room was a carbon copy of Rebel's but smelled like a whorehouse. It was obviously the chick's room.

"What's the status on the Foxtrots?" asked Slash, as he shuffled through Lisa's suitcase.

"They're still eating," reported Yankee.

Slash was intrigued by her lingerie and imagined what she looked like in it. But he knew he had to move on. He checked the bathroom and was amazed at the array of bottles, tubes, containers and vials. The counter was filled with them.

He went to the closet and searched the hang-up bag. *"This chick has more clothes than a department store. How does she keep track of all this shit?"* He shuffled through her clothes, admiring the silky, colorful dresses and scarves.

"Christ, she's got a mink jacket, too."

"What's that?" asked Yankee.

Slash had accidentally keyed his radio. "Disregard."

"Let's get a move on, guys," ordered Yankee.

Slash reached into her overcoat. Bingo. Airline tickets. He opened the ticket jacket.

"Rebel, write this down: Pacific West flight 903 to Las Vegas, tomorrow, two-thirty. Seat 16C."

"Viva Las Vegas, baby."

CHAPTER VIII

MODE SHIFTS

Hormuz, Persia: 1294, A.D. Campfires warmed and illuminated the voyagers. A pistol shot pierced the calm and a flaming arrow, loosed from somewhere over the dark waters, arced high in the air and landed in their camp, announcing the arrival the remainder of the fleet. Cheers resounded. Pistol shots rang out, weapons hoisted to celebrate victory.

"The Almighty has saved us, again," observed Maffeo.

"Indeed."

"We are most blessed," added nephew Marco.

The merchants embraced and patted each other's backs as they gave thanks.

Commander Sun and his interpreter approached.

"Masters," intoned Su, "Commander Sun expresses his relief that you are safe."

Niccolo noticed the Commander's ghastly wound.

"My Lord! What happened to the Commander's eye?"

"The Commander was wounded in battle, Master."

"Please inform the Commander that we regret his injury and the loss of his warriors, and give our thanks."

Su nodded and translated. The merchants bowed to the Commander. Surprised, Commander Sun bowed deeply in return and said something to Su.

"The Commander says he is honored. Thank you."

Maffeo extracted a large, uncut ruby from his tunic, showed it to his brother and presented it to Sun. He addressed Su. "Tell the Commander that his valiant actions have saved many lives and our estate. We offer this gem as gratitude."

Commander Sun looked at the uncut stone, not sure of what it was. As Su translated, the Commander's good eye widened and he looked at Su to be certain he heard correctly. Su nodded confirmation. The Commander stood erect, accepted the stone and bowed deeply again. They respectfully returned his bow.

Sun said something to Maffeo. Su translated. "The Commander says, 'The Masters are most generous and thank you'." The brothers smiled and slapped Sun on the back.

"Let us celebrate!"

"Fetch the plum wine," yelled Niccolo. Su yelled the Masters's orders in Chinese. Cheers resounded. Crewmen ran to fetch the wine. Within minutes, a dozen casks were opened, the wine quickly flowed.

Officer Wang assigned eight warriors to guard the perimeter. He ordered eight others to make arrows to replenish the company supply and then he joined the command party at their campfire.

Chang approached Commander Sun and whispered to him. Sun nodded and turned his face toward the fire. They exchanged words as Chang fussed over the wound. He applied an herbal concoction and a bandage. Sun gritted his teeth, muttering harsh words that were obviously curses. Chang ignored the Commander's protests.

Chang poured a potion into Sun's wine and said something to him. The Commander cast a furtive glance and asked a question. Chang responded sternly. Su fell over backwards, laughing.

"What have we missed?" asked Niccolo.

Su was laughing so hard he couldn't respond. The Commander's good eye shot daggers at him. Sun raised the cup and swallowed the contents. He threw the cup into the fire, disgusted.

Su recovered. "Master, the Commander asked what potion Chang put into his wine. Chang say, 'Not potion. Is goat urine! Now drink it'."

The Venetians roared with laughter. "Oh, my! The mighty Commander is forced… to drink… *goat piss*!"

Su, in a whisper, asked Chang what he had actually put into the wine and got the truth. He translated for the Masters. "Chang say it was opium elixir to numb the pain." Another round of laughter sounded.

Su noticed Sun's glaring eye. His laughter fractured into wheezes and his smile disappeared. He knelt before the Commander with trepidation and bowed all the way to the ground. The flummoxed Commander lightened his mood as Chang told him the truth. Sun's mood shifted from disgust, to uncertainty, then humor. He chuckled a bit, then a lot. He slapped Su on the back. The interpreter rose, forgiven, smiling and elated that his head was still attached. Another round of chuckles swept the group and the relieved Su fetched a fresh cup of wine for the Commander.

Crewman arrived with food. The steaming hot crocks were passed around. Another crewman brought a fresh cask of plum wine. They eagerly imbibed, especially the Commander. He suffered less pain as the evening wore on.

In his opium stupor, Sun related through Su, how the *Sea Wind* had taken a cannon shot through the hull and sunk, taking its gold to the bottom. He also expressed his remorse at losing the entire contingent and cargo of *Sea Spray* and setting her adrift. The Commander was proud of his valiant men.

The Masters assessed the damage to the vessels and the remaining cargo and stores. Three of the ships were in need of repairs. The dangers of continuing their voyage by sea were weighed against the risks of traveling over land. There were probably more pirates on the seas, as the Khan's protective reach did not extend that far. However, on land, Mongol control stretched all the way to Eastern Europe. They would enjoy the Khan's protection all the way to Constantinople. They had a golden tablet, inscribed with the Khan's edict to grant them safe passage or suffer certain death.

The brothers decided to caravan overland to Constantinople. From there, they could take to sea again and reach Venice across the Mediterranean Sea. The Commander's company of warriors could return home. The junks, with their crews, could return by sea.

Surprisingly, it wasn't Sun who passed out first. It was Wang, the feisty second-in-command. Little did he know of the praises bestowed upon him by the Commander.

One by one, the merchants, crewmen, passengers and warriors drifted off to sleep. Maffeo, Chang and Su were the last awake. Maffeo took another large, uncut ruby and placed it into Officer Wang's hand. He closed Wang's fingers around it.

"Thank you, my valiant friend. Sleep well."

As Maffeo and Su dozed, Chang finished his wine. He had related to the Masters his concern for the Commander's wound. What he had not mentioned was his disappointment at not finding his journal tablets that he had entrusted to the *Sea Spray*'s Captain. He determined to inscribe replacements.

Fate had other plans though, and Chang Li Suk perished in an accident soon after, taking his vast healing knowledge to the grave.

Las Vegas, 2002: Bravo had dispatched Yankee to Las Vegas immediately after learning of Storm and Chen's destination. Yankee caught the last flight of the day, bringing equipment and pistols in his checked baggage. He rented a four-wheel drive SUV and spent the night at a hotel. He would meet the others at the airport.

Rebel and Slash had tailed the marks and took their same flight. They were to link up with Yankee at the Las Vegas airport and tail the Foxtrot female to Peter Flynn. Since Sparks still hadn't cracked the encryption program, they had to risk tail surveillance because their employer was putting heat on Bravo.

Yankee's cell phone rang. "Yeah! Where are you guys?"

"We're on the upper level in the terminal, approaching the escalators to baggage claim. Where are you?"

"Bottom of the escalators."

"Good. The Foxtrots are eight yards in front of us. He's dressed in green and she's lookin' fine in pink and black."

"Good. Did Sparks get their vehicle data?"

"Yeah. Just the guy, not the broad. There's nothing on her. But we've got his tag number and address."

"Give me his address." Yankee wrote Storm's address on his note pad and referred to a street map. It wasn't detailed but it gave him an idea where Storm lived; Henderson.

Storm and Lisa walked side by side in the queue to baggage claim. The terminal was busy and noisy.

"So when are you going to have that tablet translated?"

"As soon as I get you back to Pete tomorrow."

"Why tomorrow?"

"Because I'm too tired to drive tonight. You shouldn't either."

"Well then, where am I staying?"

"My place. There's a comfortable spare bedroom, just for you." Storm raised one eyebrow.

Lisa felt a spark of anticipation.

"You'll be safer at my place than trying to drive by yourself. Remember, my first priority is to get you safely home. We'll get a fresh start in the morning."

Lisa was puzzled. He was either genuinely tired or he had designs on her, she wasn't sure which. Maybe this was his way of creating an opportunity to get intimate with her. She hoped so. She wanted him to make a move. She decided to entice him into making that move.

Storm, not oblivious to Lisa's suspicions, changed the subject. "You're certain your brother can interpret that tablet?"

"Uh… yes. Lawrence is an expert on Oriental art, especially Chinese."

Their turn for the escalator came.

"Good. I'll fly to San Fran and see him."

"Great!" She hesitated, "Derek, you need to know something about Lawrence. He's… well…"

"Gay?"

Lisa frowned. "I was going to say 'sensitive', but since you put it that way, yes, he's gay. You guessed that just by listening on the phone?"

"I put a few things together, like San Francisco, art history, museum curator, the lilt in his voice; so I guessed he's gay. So what?"

"He's sensitive, too."

Storm flashed a reassuring smile. "Don't fret, Lisa. I'll be nice. I have nothing against gays."

Lisa looked relieved. She wasn't sure how Storm would react upon meeting her effeminate brother.

"Besides, I can swish and glide with the best of them."

A mental image of Storm swishing, limp-wrist, seemed so silly she burst out laughing. She gathered his arm in hers, pressed her breast onto his arm and placed her head onto his shoulder. *"Phase One."*

The sensation of her full, soft breast on his arm was not lost to Storm. He felt his desire rising, but this was neither the time nor the place.

At the bottom of the escalator, they weaved through a maze of limousine drivers and tour guides and searched out the baggage carousel.

∞

The mercenaries followed Storm's truck to his apartment complex. They saw the entrance gate close eight seconds after Storm's truck passed through. It wasn't long before another vehicle entered and Rebel pulled close behind it, pretended to punch in a code number and piggy-backed the vehicle through the gate. They parked where they could keep vigil on Storm's vehicle and apartment.

"I don't see what's so dangerous about this guy," stated Slash.

"I don't either," replied Yankee. "But the Colonel thinks so."

Storm's apartment door opened and the Foxtrot female emerged. "Check this."

The Foxtrot female walked to a red SUV. She unlocked the vehicle, removed a small case, locked it and returned to the apartment.

"Bingo."

Slash smiled. "It can't be this easy."

Yankee exited and snatched his cell phone. He speed dialed Bravo. Sparks answered.

"Sparks, it's Yankee. I thought I dialed the Colonel."

"You did, but he's sleeping. Should I wake him?"

"Hell no! Not unless you've got a death wish. I just wanted to let him know we've located the Foxtrot male's den and the female's wheels. I'm going to her SUV now to get the plate. Got a pencil?"

"Yeah. Go."

Yankee read off the California registration.

"I'll check it out. What's your status?"

"We're camped out in the parking lot of his apartment complex. They're in the apartment and their vehicles are parked here. As soon as they move, I'll call you."

"Roger that. I'll let the Colonel know. So long."

Yankee returned to his vehicle, keeping to the shadows.

"Should we go into the apartment after they go to sleep?"

"No way. Our orders are to tail them. But maybe I'll have a look inside her car. Who knows? Maybe she left a map hanging around."

∞

After dinner, they slumped on the sofa to relax and watch TV. Lisa found the news depressing. "*It's time for Phase Two.*" She yawned.

"I'm going to have a nice hot bubble bath."

"You see? You are too tired to drive tonight."

"I guess so. I'm going down to my car. I'll be back in a few."

"I'll be here." He waited for her to close the door and then he went to the window. She went to her SUV, retrieved a small case and returned uneventfully. He was back on the couch by the time she entered. He flicked the TV remote, looking for something interesting.

Lisa was in the bathroom over an hour before she emerged. She wore an alluring black robe and matching slippers with short heels. Her hair and makeup were perfect and her perfume was intoxicating.

She walked to the couch and sank into it, crossing her beautiful legs, allowing the robe to part just enough to reveal her smooth thighs. Storm noticed but pretended not to. He kept reminding himself of his primary duty. After that, he would *definitely* hit on her. He decided his best defense was a cold shower. He headed for the bathroom.

Lisa wasted no time. She switched off the TV and slipped a romantic music CD into the stereo, pulled a candle from her case, lit it and turned off the lamp. She pulled out a bottle of red wine, poured two glasses and set them on the coffee table. She sat on the couch and experimented with several enticing poses, selecting the one she thought made her the most desirable.

She had barely completed her preparations when Storm emerged, toweling his hair. He stopped in mid-stride, noticed the wine, candle, soft music and God's most beautiful creation since Eve.

"I thought maybe we could give each other a massage," Lisa said seductively.

Storm went back to the bathroom.

"Derek! Where are you going?"

"That shower wasn't nearly cold enough."

Lisa sighed. "*This calls for Phase Three.*"

∞

Yankee eased through the shadows.

He scanned a red-filtered flashlight around the interior of Lisa's SUV. Just girly stuff.

"I'm gonna deactivate the alarm and get in. Are we good to go?"

"You're clear, Yank."

Yankee dropped under the vehicle. It took him two minutes to locate the correct wires and attach alligator clips. He made a cut, re-routed a second line to the ground and disconnected the horn and headlight couplings. He arose, pulled out his lock pick and attacked the front passenger door. He had it open in fifteen seconds. The interior light came on. He reached for the switch and turned it off. He searched the glove compartment.

"Yank, you got company," warned Rebel.

Headlights swept across the parking lot, briefly illuminating Yankee with his hand in the cookie jar. The car pulled into a spot near the manager's office and shut down. A man emerged, looked briefly in his direction and disappeared into the office.

"Shit! That was close."

"No shit."

Yankee stuffed the contents of the glove compartment back in. He reset the interior light switch, locked the door and closed it. He dropped, reconnected the headlight and horn couplings, reset the ground wire and spliced the cut wire. He removed the alligator clips, shoved them into his pocket and headed for the shadows.

∞

Storm and Chen cleaned the breakfast dishes together as they discussed their plans to get to Helendale. Storm thought they should take both of their vehicles, but Lisa insisted on both of them riding in hers; that was Phase Three.

"How do I get back?"

"You can stay with Pete, or *me*, and I'll drive you back on Friday. I'm planning a Vegas weekend." The phrase she left unspoken was, "in your apartment."

The idea appealed to Storm. "I guess I could take a few days off. Mark will run the studio. It'd be good to have company for the long drives, too."

"Good. It's settled. You'll stay at my place. There's a spare bedroom, just for you." Lisa raised one eyebrow, mimicking Storm's gesture of the day before.

"Touché." He leaned close and whispered into her ear, "I am *so* looking forward to it."

She dropped an unfinished pan into the sink. "Let's go." She planted a deliciously lustful kiss on his lips, pressed her supple form to him and then abruptly turned for the door. "Are you coming?"

"You have no idea."

They gathered their luggage and locked the apartment. They went to Lisa's SUV and began loading the luggage. The apartment manger approached.

"Good morning, Derek."

"Good morning, Tom."

The manager glanced around as if looking for someone. "Where's your buddy?"

Storm was puzzled. "What buddy?"

"The big guy who was in this car last night. I assumed it was one of your friends."

Storm's neck hair bristled. "When was this?"

"About ten-thirty."

"What did he look like?"

The manager scratched his head, trying to recall. "Oh, big guy, over six foot, dark hair, built like a brick shithouse. I thought maybe it was one of your Kung Fu buddies."

"Probably not. This is Lisa's car. Tom, this is Dr. Lisa Chen. Lisa, this is Tom, my apartment manager." They shook hands.

"I'm sorry, Derek. I thought the car belonged to this guy so I didn't think nothin' of it."

"That's okay, Tom. Thanks for letting me know."

"You bet."

Lisa checked the interior. "Someone moved my cosmetics bag."

"Is anything missing?"

"No, I don't think so."

"Should we call the police?"

"No, thanks, Tom," replied Storm. "If there's nothing missing, there's really nothing to report." "*It would just be a hassle. Why would someone break in and not steal something?*"

Storm shifted into recon mode and glanced around the lot. "Lisa, lock the truck and come back to the apartment with me. No questions, please. Excuse us, Tom."

Lisa did as requested. Storm and Lisa returned to his apartment. He closed the door behind them. Storm rushed to the bathroom and emerged with a small mirror and a flashlight. A large handgun was tucked into his waistband.

"Give me the keys, Lisa."

"What's going on, Derek?"

"Could be nothing. Lock the door and stay in here until I get back." Storm jogged to the SUV, unlocking it with the fob. He dropped on the pavement and flashed the light under the chassis. He used the mirror to reflect light up into the engine compartment and wheel wells. He didn't see anything suspicious. He checked behind the bumpers, nothing there either. He opened the driver's door and popped the hood. He scanned the edges of the hood and raised it slowly. He searched around the engine block. Everything looked normal. He closed the hood.

A thought occurred. He dropped again and checked the fuel and brake lines. There were no signs of sabotage, tracking devices or explosives.

He opened the rear hatch and unloaded the baggage. He searched the interior. He found nothing.

He re-loaded the luggage, locked the vehicle and returned to his apartment. Lisa opened the door for him.

"What was all that about, Derek?"

"I wondered why someone would break into a vehicle and not steal anything. Maybe he was looking for cash and didn't find any. Anyway, the vehicle seems fine, so we'll get going. Get some water while I get a few things."

"Certainly." Lisa headed for the kitchen. Storm disappeared into his bedroom. He emerged wearing a hip-length vest and carrying a long, slender case.

"Are we ready now?" asked Lisa.

"Yeah. Give me one of those jugs. You drive. I want to be able to look around."

"What's in the case?"

"This? It's a C-R-A."

"What's a C-R-A?"

"Criminal Repellent Apparatus." He grinned.

"Is it legal?"

"Not in Commie~fornia, so it'll be our little secret. Let's hit the road."

∞

"Get a load of this shit," said Rebel. "He's bringing a rifle!"

"What the…?"

"Your Mama!"

The Foxtrots crossed the parking lot.

"Give me those." Yankee snatched the binoculars from Rebel. He focused on Storm's case. Sure enough, it was a rifle case; a case for a large caliber, heavy rifle.

Rebel added, "That case ain't for a .22!"

"Shit!" exclaimed Yankee. Slash and Rebel weren't pleased either. "We didn't bring rifles." Yankee lowered the glasses, sighed and looked down. He was engrossed in problem solving and the others knew not to disturb him. His lips tightened. "Rebel, hang back far enough so they don't make us. We'll be in deep shit if he unloads with that thing."

"No shit!" exclaimed Slash.

∞

Lisa took the wheel as Storm maintained vigil. He constantly checked behind. He didn't detect any tail during their turn onto the Interstate 15 Southbound. A dozen vehicles trailed behind them, but that wasn't unusual. What would be unusual is if a vehicle tailed them taking the back roads.

"Lisa, take the next exit to Pahrump."

"Isn't the Interstate faster?"

"Yes, but I want to see if any one is tailing us."

Lisa looked nervous. He rubbed her shoulder. "It's okay. I'm just being cautious."

Lisa smiled weakly.

"Besides, you're under the protection of Derek the Red Storm." Her smile widened.

Lisa exited onto Highway 160. Storm saw two vehicles follow. Immediately behind them was a blue Honda with a lone woman at the wheel. About a mile behind her was a green SUV. Storm disregarded the Honda as a threat, but he couldn't ascertain how many occupants were in the green SUV.

The long highway to Pahrump had few major road junctions between the Interstate and the town of Pahrump, an hour drive. The road climbed a ten-mile incline to the top of Mountain Springs Summit, just north of Mount Potosi.

"Anything, Derek?"

"Nope." He lied. He was concerned about the green SUV. It maintained its distance. The blue Honda was tailgating them. "Just do the speed limit."

Shortly after cresting the summit, the Honda passed them and sped away. Storm began a silent count as they passed a road sign, counting the number of seconds for the green SUV to pass the same point. A minute later, the SUV passed the road sign. It was a mile behind.

"Lisa, we're looking for Highway 372. It'll turn left in Pahrump. In Shoshone, we'll take another left onto Highway 127. That'll take us into Baker. We'll pick up the Fifteen again."

"What if we're being tailed?"

"I have a plan."

∞

Storm pointed out the turn at Pahrump. She casually took the turn and accelerated to the speed limit. Storm saw the green SUV make the turn also. He sighed. "So, Lisa, have you ever done any Grand Prix racing?"

∞

"Shit. They spotted us. Don't lose them." Yankee was concerned. If they lost the Foxtrots, the Colonel would stick his boot so far up his ass he'd choke on it.

∞

Storm grabbed the rifle case and removed an ugly, black, heavy rifle.

Lisa was amazed. It looked very lethal and it wasn't even loaded yet. Storm inserted a magazine, racked a round into the chamber and checked the safety. He flipped up a sight at the back of the receiver.

"What is that?"

Storm flashed his crooked smile. "This, lovely doctor, is a Fabrique-Nationale FN/FAL, L1A1 Sporter. It's a thirty caliber, 7.62 millimeter, twenty-round capacity, semi-automatic rifle. Legal in all states, except Commie-fornia. Maximum effective range with iron sights is four hundred fifty meters. Maximum range is eight hundred. It weighs eleven pounds fully loaded with Winchester 150 grain Silvertips, which just happens to be what's in it now. And there's two hundred more where they came from."

Lisa gave him a blank stare. "Am I going to need earplugs?"

∞

"Damn it!" Yankee slammed his fist on the dash.

"Son of a bitch. They're goin' rabbit, Reb," observed Slash.

Rebel already had the pedal to the floorboard. The red SUV had rounded a blind bend a minute ago, but when they rounded it, the target vehicle had opened the distance to almost two miles. They had to be running a hundred miles an hour.

"Don't lose them, Rebel. The Colonel will have our balls for breakfast," warned Slash. The speedometer registered one hundred fifteen. They were closing.

∞

Lisa focused on the road. She had never driven over eighty-five miles an hour in her life, and that had been on a six-lane highway. She was doing over one hundred on a skinny two lane undivided highway. She also knew the SUV was top heavy and rolled easily.

"You're doing great, Lisa. We've got a two-mile lead. But he's pushed it up. We're definitely being tailed."

Sagebrush, tumbleweeds and Joshua trees flashed past. The engine roared. She noticed dwellings ahead. "Derek, there's a town ahead."

"That's Shoshone. Take a left at the intersection. Blow through the STOP sign."

"Are you sure?"

"Yes. Take a left, get lined up on the road, then floor it."

Lisa did as she was told. She held the pedal to the floor until she couldn't stand it any more. She braked, turned and blew through the intersection on two wheels. Her tires screeched and left huge, smoking deposits. The vehicle fishtailed and Lisa adeptly compensated, realigned and punched the accelerator to the floor. They surged ahead, bouncing Storm off the door and seat back.

"Hoooo-aaaah! Way to go, Doc! You must have done some valet parking in a previous life."

Lisa was terrified but Storm's quip tickled her. She shook her head as the speedometer passed ninety. Storm watched the pursuit vehicle take the intersection. The pursuer gained ground accelerating out of the turn. Storm reasoned the pursuer had a more powerful vehicle. If so, they wouldn't be able to outrun them to Baker. He searched for a spot to implement his plan.

∞

"No, Rebel!"

"Oh shit!"

Rebel stood on the brakes at the last second, the tires screeched and the front lurched down. Yankee was thrown into the dash, Slash into the back of the front seat. Rebel whipped the wheel, they fishtailed right and he punched the accelerator to the floor. They came out of the turn, accelerating through forty miles an hour, perfectly lined up with the road. They had gained two hundred yards on the Foxtrots.

Yankee regained his composure and noticed how much ground they had gained. "Rebel, you're the *man!*"

Rebel howled a loud war hoot.

The engine roared, powering them at one hundred fifteen miles an hour. They were closing. Yankee figured they'd catch them in ten miles.

Slash figured what was on Yankee's mind. "Well, discreet tail is blown. We go to back up?"

"Yeah. We don't have a choice. We've got to catch her."

"Yeah. I hope she's fun at a party."

The mercenaries laughed at the thought of having Lisa Chen. Rebel drove faster.

∞

There it was, shaped like a magnificent breast jutting proudly from a supine vixen. An isolated mountain peak appeared to their right, eight miles ahead. Storm assessed it. It was the high ground, dominating the surrounding terrain for miles. It had excellent fields of fire, unobstructed views of the terrain below. There was minimal cover below and large outcroppings near the crest, good cover for themselves. No one could approach the peak unobserved. It was perfect.

Storm looked over his shoulder. They had closed within a mile. They were gaining two to three hundred yards every mile. They'd be overtaken before Baker. It was time to fight.

"Lisa, do you see that mountain ahead to the right?"

"Yeah."

"When we get close, find a dirt trail to get up there. It's the best place to make a stand."

"We can't outrun him?"

"No. He'll catch us before we reach Baker. I'll have to fight. I won't let him get you. You understand?"

Lisa nodded without taking her eyes from the road. Her heart was pounding and her adrenaline surged. She had never had this kind of rush. "Should we call the police?"

"All they'd do is arrest you for reckless driving and me for having an assault rifle, which it's not. We're better off without them. Besides, there's no cell signal. I checked."

Storm checked behind frequently. They were still gaining. He massaged her shoulder. "You're doin' great, Lisa. Hang in there, hon."

His affectionate reassurance bolstered her. She believed Storm would take whatever measures were necessary to protect her, no matter how risky or extreme.

Storm saw a dirt trail leading to the mountain. He waited for the appropriate moment. He glanced back again. They were only half a mile behind, confirming his estimates.

"Okay, Lisa. Slow down. Take the next dirt road on the right."

She eased off the pedal and slowed to eighty as she searched for the dirt road.

"There it is." Storm pointed.

Lisa braked and whipped the wheel right. The tires protested as they locked. She mashed the gas pedal to the floor. They surged to seventy miles an hour, bouncing on the rough trail. Lisa desperately clung to the wheel. Storm braced himself.

The pursuit vehicle followed. Storm lost sight of it in their dust trail.

∞

"You lookin' forward to a piece, Reb?"

Rebel smiled, not taking his eyes from the road.

"Good goin', Reb," commented Slash. "Maybe you won't have to settle for sloppy seconds." They laughed.

"Hey! They're turnin' on that dirt road."

Yankee saw the dust plume from the target as it raced toward a mountain off to the right. They immediately figured out Storm's plan.

"Shit! He's heading for high ground. Rebel, catch that son of a bitch."

"You got it."

Rebel repeated his brake, whip and slam maneuver that had worked so well back at Shoshone. The SUV screeched, fishtailed, slid across some dirt and accelerated up the dirt road. The dust cloud from the target obscured their view, but they knew they were gaining because the dust cloud was getting thicker. Rebel flipped on the windshield washers. They careened and swerved from one side of the trail to the other, barely in control. The grade increased rapidly, then the road disappeared. They were airborne. Rebel held the wheel straight. The dust cloud disappeared and they could see.

"Hold on!" yelled Rebel.

"Oh, shiiiit!"

The SUV hit hard, careened off a small boulder and rolled to a stop straight ahead. The mercenaries shook the cobwebs out and scanned the terrain.

"Well, ain't that some shit," said Slash. He pointed over Yankee's right shoulder. The target was two hundred yards away, off the trail in a thin dust cloud, upside down, its wheels spinning.

∞

Neither of them saw the bump until the last second. They were traveling at thirty miles an hour when she spotted it. She reacted instinctively, hitting the brakes and turning the wheel. It was the wrong thing to do.

"Oh shit! Hang on, Derek!" Storm was watching behind when the SUV took flight. It veered to the right, the front dropped and impacted hard on the left fender. The air bags exploded as it flipped onto its roof. The windshield and front windows shattered, pellets sprayed the interior.

Storm was dazed and his left shoulder hurt. It was difficult to breathe. The deflated air bag splayed over his face. Storm grabbed his K-Bar knife, strapped to his ankle. He cut away the air bag.

"Lisa! Lisa!" She didn't respond. He felt for her pulse. It was strong and steady. She was unconscious. He didn't dare move her. He turned off the ignition. He cut away the air bag from Lisa's beautiful face. She was breathing without difficulty.

He heard the other vehicle approaching. He un-strapped and crawled. He searched for his rifle and found it. He grabbed two spare magazines, ran thirty yards and took cover in a small depression.

Storm saw the pursuit vehicle go airborne, emerge from their dust trail and land upright. It hit front wheels first, plowing a huge cloud of dirt and gradually came to a stop off the opposite side of the trail. It sat there in a cloud of settling dust. Storm saw three men inside. He readied his rifle as he glanced at Lisa's vehicle, trying to determine if she had recovered yet. His anger welled. It wasn't uncontrolled rage. It was a cold, calculated wrath that would soon release a shit storm; combat mode.

∞

Rebel steered toward the target. Glass shards pelted them. Loud, sharp cracks from a high-powered rifle boomed as lethal projectiles penetrated the vehicle. They hunkered down as web-shaped cracks filled the windows.

"Rebel! Get us the hell out of here!"

Rebel whipped the wheel in the opposite direction and slammed the gas pedal. The SUV bounced violently across the rough ground. Rebel changed course every five seconds, serpentining wildly to make them a difficult target. Bullets penetrated the doors, fenders and windows. Glass, metal and plastic showered them as Storm's rifle delivered his wrath.

"Holy shit!" A bullet smashed through the rear door, grazed Slash's shoulder and hot plastic pellets imbedded in his neck. "I'm hit! Rebel, firewall this damned thing."

The SUV, looking like green Swiss cheese, careened wildly. There was a brief respite and Yankee guessed correctly that Storm was reloading.

"Reb, head down the hill, get us out of his range." Within seconds, more rounds impacted. Rebel resumed the serpentine maneuvers, but this guy was good, too good. The rounds kept impacting. No ordinary marksman should be able to put that many rounds into such a difficult target. *"This guy has lethal talent straight from hell."*

∞

Storm had fired as soon as they moved toward Lisa. He squeezed off round after round, peppering the target with deadly projectiles. The bad guys apparently understood Storm's muzzle velocity message. The vehicle immediately reversed course and high-tailed away. Storm continued to fire as it careened wildly. Its dust trail obscured his aim, but dust wouldn't stop 150 grains of seething, supersonic vengeance. He fired one well aimed round after another. The rifle barrel smoked as flashes sparked from the muzzle. The heavy, crass odor of cordite filled the air, invigorating him.

The bolt locked aft. The magazine was empty. Storm rapidly ejected the spent magazine and slammed home a new one. He racked the bolt forward. He resumed his furious assault until he emptied that magazine, too. By that time, they were out of range. He figured his last two rounds had fallen short. He safed the rifle, ejected the second spent magazine and loaded the third one. He racked the bolt forward to chamber the next round.

Storm picked up his ejected magazines, blew the dust out of them and ran back to Lisa, glancing over his shoulder to make sure the bad guys stayed out of range. They were. *"Yeah. They got the message."*

∞

The impacts thankfully ceased. Yankee and Slash lifted from the floor while Rebel drove the battered SUV another five hundred yards toward the highway, well out of range. The mercenaries brushed the shards of glass and plastic from themselves and cursed loudly. They knew they were lucky to be alive.

"I'm gonna skewer that son of a bitch."

"Take a number, Slash. I want his balls fried in oil," stated Yankee.

"Deal! I'll slice 'em off for you."

The mercs painfully climbed out. They had numerous bruises and cuts. They assessed their injuries, keeping a cautious watch up the hill.

Slash was not as badly injured as he first believed. The bullet had creased his shoulder muscle but it hadn't hit bone. Rebel and Yankee stripped off their shirts and used their tees for bandages. Rebel suffered the most cuts; his hands, neck and head were covered. He had been the most exposed. As Slash and Rebel treated each other, Yankee walked around the hammered transport.

"...thirty-six, thirty-seven, thirty-eight friggin' bullet holes! Who is this guy, Davy Crockett reincarnate?"

"Thirty-eight rounds on target? I thought I did a better job than that."

"You did fine, Reb. None of us could have done it better. Now I understand why the Colonel said to avoid engagement."

Rebel walked around the SUV. "Hoooey! The rental agent is gonna be *pissed*."

"Forget that. I'm afraid of what the Colonel's gonna do when he finds out." The uncertainty in Yankee's expression was apparent.

∞

"Derek... Derek?"

"I'm right here, babe." Storm caressed her head.

Lisa moaned. "I feel like crap."

"But you look gorgeous. Are you injured?"

She smiled weakly, suspecting he was full of manure. Her hair was a mess. She could only imagine what her makeup looked like. "My left ankle hurts. I think it's sprained."

"How's your neck?"

She moved her neck around. "A little sore, but nothing seems to be broken."

"Okay. You're the doctor. Do you think it's okay to get you out of that harness?"

"I think so. Just do it slowly. I can't tell yet if I have internal injuries. Are you okay?"

"I'm fine. In fact, I was thinking about taking you dancing tonight."

She laughed and then moaned. "Oh, don't make me laugh. My ribs hurt."

"All right. No jokes. Let me get you out." He braced her shoulders and released the belt clip. She settled onto Storm's arm and he gently lowered her. He eased her legs down and stretched them across the vehicle. She moaned when he repositioned her left leg. Her ankle was swollen.

"What happened? The last thing I remember, the car was flying."

"Good memory. Well, gravity won. We hit hard and flipped over."

"Where's the other car?"

"They didn't appreciate my hospitality and ran away. I guess my social skills need work. But seriously, they're a mile down the hill, but they haven't left."

Lisa nodded. "Derek. Did you call me 'babe,' as in 'sweetheart?'"

He caressed her cheek and gazed into her dark, imploring eyes. "Yes, I did. Babe." He placed a tender kiss on her eager lips. She passionately received his offering and wrapped her arm around his neck and pulled him to her, wanting to feel his strong body encircling her. They embraced tenderly. Their caresses caused shivers and aroused them.

But they both knew they were still in jeopardy. There were men nearby that wanted them. Storm regretfully, slowly, broke off their kiss. They held each other, stroking each other's face, confirming their new, unspoken commitment.

"Lisa, I don't want this moment to end. No woman has ever captivated me the way you do. But there are men out there that could kill us."

Lisa nodded. A tear dripped from her right eye and she sniffed. "You're right, Derek. Do what you have to. But know this. I'm looking forward to calling you 'lover'."

Storm flashed his crooked smile. He kissed her forehead. He grabbed his rifle, crawled out and verified the men were still beyond range.

"Okay, Lisa. I'm going to pull you out by your shoulders. You ready?"

"Yes. Be careful of my ankle."

Storm grabbed from underneath her armpits and gently pulled her out. "Rest a minute. I'm going to rummage through the vehicle to see what we can use. Keep an eye on the creeps. If they move toward us, let me know."

Lisa nodded and rolled onto her side. Storm crawled into the vehicle and shuffled through their luggage. He removed a tan jacket from Lisa's bag and tossed it to her. He removed his old Army field jacket from his bag. He gathered his rifle magazines and searched for the water jugs. He found them. They were smashed open. Storm frowned, then poured the remnant of one jug into the other and capped it. They had about one quart of water. Storm selected some warm clothing. He also grabbed two of his tee shirts to use as bandages or signals. An evasion plan formed in his mind.

"What do you want me to do with this?" Lisa inquired about the jacket.

"It's camouflage, babe. It blends with the desert."

Lisa nodded, slipped her arms into the sleeves and snugged it to her. "What are we going to do?"

Storm emerged with the salvaged items and sat next to Lisa, facing the threat sector. "We'll stay here until dark, unless they make a move. After dark, we'll move around the backside of this mountain and disappear." "*I hope they don't have night vision.*"

"I don't know if I can walk."

"Well, sweetie, I'll just have to carry you. You can whisper your erotic fantasies into my ear." Storm wiggled his eyebrows, making her laugh.

"Ow. I told you, don't make me laugh. My ribs hurt."

"Here. Let me take a look."

Lisa pulled up her blouse. There was a large bruise on her left side.

"Does it hurt when you breathe?"

"No. Only when you make me laugh. I don't think the rib is broken, but it's certainly dislocated."

"We'll have to be careful about that. Meanwhile, let me get a splint on your ankle."

∞

"Shit. No cell signal. What are they doin', Reb?"

Rebel observed through the binoculars. Only one of the lenses was functional; a bullet had demolished the other. "They're hunkered down, lickin' their wounds. Looks like the female is injured."

"She alive?"

"Yeah. She's movin' around, but I haven't seen her on her feet yet."

"Maybe we caught a break. If she's immobile, they can't get far. That'll give us time to regroup, maybe flank them after dark."

Slash nodded. Yankee paced back and forth, looking at the ground. "Okay, here's the plan."

Rebel and Slash listened.

Rebel gave his sidearm and spare magazines to Slash. Yankee tossed Slash a canteen and a bottle of cola. Slash removed the binoculars from Rebel's neck. He stuffed the extra pistol into the back of his waistband and slung the binoculars around his own neck. He gathered the spare magazines and liquids and made a nest in a nearby depression. They donned their radios and established communication.

"Okay. We're off. See you in two hours."

Slash grinned, "I'll be right here, or on their ass."

∞

Storm watched intently as the green SUV departed. He saw two of their pursuers in it. He could only guess where the third one was.

The vehicle headed down the incline toward the main road, leaving a dusty wake. He reasoned they didn't have rifles; otherwise they would have tried to flank them already.

Storm saw the pursuit vehicle turn back toward Shoshone. If that were so, they wouldn't be back for more than an hour.

He squatted behind the SUV. "They left one man behind to keep an eye on us and I think I know where he is. We'll wait here about fifteen minutes. Let's see if he gets impatient and tries to approach. If he does, I'll put him down and we'll escape. If he doesn't, we'll move to higher ground. After it gets dark, we'll sneak around the back side and trek off into the desert."

Lisa nodded and rested her head on Storm. She rubbed his aching shoulder. He said, "You know, I've got a comfortable spot in the desert, a few ounces of water, my rifle and a beautiful woman by my side. Life just doesn't get any better."

Lisa giggled. Storm amused her with his facetious quips and metaphors. She kissed his cheek. He pinched her bottom. She squealed. She hadn't felt this silly since she'd been in high school.

∞

"What? You assholes!" Yankee recoiled from the phone. "You better get this situation under control, Yankee, or I'll put my fist so far up your ass, you'll be begging me to rip out your tongue. You sons of bitches! You call yourself 'professionals?' You better get this damned situation under control. Do you understand?"

"Absolutely, sir. You can count on it."

"I *am* counting on it."

"Yes, sir. We're gonna head back as soon as we pick up some supplies. It would help if we had some rifles and night vision and the long-range radios. There's no cell signal out here. I'm calling from a pay phone."

"Which way were they headed?"

"South."

"We'll be there tomorrow and set up headquarters near Vegas. Make sure you don't lose them. Got it?"

∞

Light reflected off something shiny. Storm guessed it came from a binocular lens. Whatever it was, it revealed their adversary's position. He turned onto his back to evaluate the terrain behind them.

"What's wrong, Derek?"

"I'm just planning our evasion route. Do you feel up to a little walk?"

"I'll try."

He assisted her to her feet and let her balance against the vehicle. He slung his rifle over his shoulder, gathered their supplies and arched her arm around his neck.

"See that outcropping of boulders up to the left, just above the one that looks like a huge football?" Lisa scanned the mountain.

"Yes."

"That's where we're going. We're gonna keep the truck between us and him so he won't see us… I hope."

Lisa gingerly stepped with her injured leg. She winced in pain as she put half her weight onto it. "Derek, I can't walk."

"Okay, doll. Let me set you down." He eased her to the ground. "I have an idea." He crawled into the vehicle, rummaged around and emerged with several thick shirts. "We'll tie these around our knees and crawl up there on our hands and knees. That'll keep all the weight off your ankle and we'll stay low. If we do it right, he won't see us."

"Get my green bag. I have Ibuprofen in there."

Storm grabbed her bag and handed it to her. Lisa found the bottle, downed four pills and stuck the bottle into her pocket. "Okay. I'm ready."

They slowly crawled toward their objective. Storm lugged the rifle, ammo, water and snacks. He frequently checked behind, adjusting their course to keep their upturned SUV between them and the bad guy. Every so often Lisa would moan, but she never complained. She was a trooper.

They crawled non-stop for half an hour. They rolled onto their backs for a welcomed rest. Storm offered her the water. She shook her head. "I'm fine."

Storm nodded and smiled. "You rest. I'm going to see if our shadow has moved." She nodded and laid back.

Storm flattened to the ground and crawled into a nearby wash. He inched his way down the wash until he could see around the vehicle. He twice saw reflections. The observer hadn't moved. There was a good chance he hadn't seen them crawl away.

Storm crawled back to Lisa. As he emerged from the wash, he took in the vision of her resting. She was magnificent. He crawled next to her, rested on his elbow and looked at her face. She had her eyes closed. Her steady breathing made her chest rise and fall in a slow, soothing rhythm. Her hair splayed around her head like a jet-black halo. Small beads of perspiration glistened on her skin like sequins.

"Are you staring at me, Derek?"

"Absolutely."

"That's not polite." She opened her dark, absorbing eyes.

Storm chuckled. "My goodness. This from the same woman who took a one-hour bubble bath, dressed in a very sexy robe and slippers, exposed her cleavage and thighs all the way up to... the sofa, and now I'm not supposed to look at you? Well too bad, little miss hypocrite. You're just too damned gorgeous not to look at."

He kissed her passionately. She responded in kind. They embraced, fondling and caressing each other in places they hadn't touched before. Their desire heightened. They fumbled at buttons, zippers and snaps, racing to remove each other's clothes. Lisa was the victor. She tore Storm's shirt open and practically shred his tee, running her hands teasingly over his chest. Storm made a photo-finish second and used their clothing as a cushion. They meshed into a passionate being of one: entwined, entangled, enveloped, enthralled.

∞

The exhausted lovers rested, eyes closed, breathing heavily and perspiring. It was exactly the wrong activity in a desert survival situation, but nature is nature.

"Thank you, lover."

He squeezed her hand. "Thank you, doll. The pleasure was mine."

Storm sat up and grabbed the water bottle. He took a swig and offered it to Lisa. She gladly imbibed.

Storm saw the green SUV approaching along the main road.

"We better get moving. The party-crashers are back."

Lisa capped the bottle. They hurriedly put on their clothes, kissing frequently. Storm secured their kneepads and gathered their gear. They crawled for the hideout, relaxed.

∞

The SUV skidded to a stop. Slash stood and climbed in to get out of the ninety-five degree sun. He was expecting air-conditioning. "Let me guess. He hit the air-conditioner."

"Yup, nicked the low pressure line," replied Rebel. "It quit an hour ago."

"What's their status?"

"No change. I saw the woman try to walk, but the guy had to catch her. She's definitely impaired. I haven't seen any movement since then."

"How long ago was that?"

Slash checked his watch. "Fifty-six minutes ago."

Yankee took the binoculars and scanned the red SUV. He didn't see any movement. He didn't know that if he had been fifteen feet to his right, he would have seen two people on their hands and knees, crawling behind a large rock outcropping, a hundred and sixty-two yards beyond.

CHAPTER IX

TREK

The adversaries maintained their distance. Lisa peeked around the rock and confirmed she also counted three of them.

The outcrop, halfway up the mountainside, provided them with some shade. They assessed their water supply and agreed to ration it. They took turns catnapping. If all went according to plan, it was going to be a long night and they needed rest.

The shadows grew longer and darker. With the setting sun and the mountain behind them, they were well hidden in shadow. The pursuers were still in the hot sunlight, easy to see. Storm felt comfortable napping while Lisa watched. The pursuers were so far away, he'd have ample time to react and the fields of fire were optimum for long-range engagement.

"Derek. It's dark. Wake up."

"I'm awake. What's the status on our party-crashers?"

"I can't see them, but ten minutes ago they were still in the same place."

"Good. If we can't see them, they can't see us." He didn't mention his concern about night vision devices. He planned to evade as if they had them. "How's your ankle?"

"I took more ibuprofen. I can bear it."

Storm nodded. He stroked her cheek. "You're amazing, Lisa." She kissed his caressing hand.

"It's time to move." Storm rose and peered around rock. The moon was in its new phase, leaving the desert in total darkness. He couldn't see the adversaries or even the upended SUV, only the stars. Lisa tested her bad leg. She still couldn't put her weight on it. She would have to use Storm as a crutch or he would have to carry her.

Storm shouldered the rifle and handed the water bottle to Lisa. He turned his back to her and squatted down. "All aboard," he chimed, impersonating a railroad conductor.

Lisa hopped on. Storm shucked her high up his back.

"Off we go."

"Where are we going?"

"To visit some buddies of mine."

∞

"Slash, you're up the middle. Rebel, you flank left and I'll take the right. Keep low and quiet. Check the radios."

They checked the reception.

"It's okay to kill him but we need her alive." The others nodded. "If any one becomes engaged, seek cover, the others flank him and put his flame out. Let's move out."

The rental soldiers fanned out several hundred yards and advanced on the inverted SUV. They jogged at first, not worried about weapons fire. As they closed on the objective, they employed their stealth footwork and maneuver.

The advance up the incline went quickly for the first two hundred yards, then it slowed to half speed. Their senses keyed into every smell and sound. Their pace slowed again as they closed another hundred yards. The gentle wind masked the sound of their footsteps, but likewise, they couldn't hear any movement or voices.

They covered another two hundred yards and again slowed, using the radios to keep line abreast. They could hear the occasional rustling of wildlife. They subdued the urge to use their flashlights. They were fearful of the Mojave Green rattlesnake, nocturnal native to this desert. It was an aggressive night stalker and its venom, a highly lethal neurotoxin, attacked the human central nervous system. A full-blown dose could cause death from respiratory failure.

They closed within fifty yards of the target, within range of their handguns. They could now return fire. They were surprised, but pleased, they had not drawn Storm's rifle fire. They paused to assess the objective.

"Any movement?"

"Rebel, negative."

"Slash, negative."

"Me neither. Rebel, you and I are gonna flank uphill. Slash, stay low and cover us. Let's move out."

The flankers swung wide on opposite sides of the objective, their pistols held on target with both hands, their feet cautiously feeling the terrain. They expected rifle shots at any second, but they never came. As they closed within twenty yards, Yankee flashed his light at the truck. Rebel and Slash followed suit.

"You've got to be *shitting* me."

∞

Lisa saw four sets of yellow eyes to her left.

"Derek, there are some critters out there, to the left."

"I know." He huffed, tired from the exertion. "Four coyotes looking for a meal."

"Will they attack us?"

Storm gulped more air, advancing another step. "No. We're too big. They won't approach unless we sit down. Even then, I doubt they'd attack. They're just curious to see if we have any snacks."

"Snacks?"

"Yeah. Like a cat or a small dog."

Storm estimated they had averaged about one mile per hour. They hadn't heard or seen the pursuers. He was growing weary.

"Lisa, I have to put you down." He squatted and gently put her feet on the ground. She managed to bear her weight.

"Derek, if we could fashion some crutches, I could probably walk on my own. We'd move faster."

"Yeah. Good idea. You stay here but don't sit down. The coyotes might come closer. I'll find some wood."

Storm produced his Colt .45 from under his vest. He cocked a round into the chamber and checked the safety. He showed Lisa how to flip the safety off and point the weapon. "Don't shoot unless they attack, which they shouldn't. And for God's sake, don't shoot me. Identify the target before you shoot. It will be *real* loud and the bad guys will hear it, so don't fire unless you absolutely have to."

"Okay."

Storm walked off into the darkness. She could hear him moving around. She could hear the coyotes circling and sometimes see their eyes, but they kept a wide berth. Something brushed against her leg. She flinched and stepped on her bad foot and collapsed. She gasped as she fell. Her ankle hurt like hell and she moaned.

Storm was by her side in seconds. "What happened? Are you okay?"

Lisa took several deep breaths. "Something brushed my leg and scared me. I hurt my ankle again."

Storm checked her ankle bindings. "We'll rest here for a while. Hopefully, the pain will subside." He rubbed her shoulder and caressed her. "Don't worry. We'll get through this."

"I have no doubt." She massaged her strong leg.

Storm removed his field jacket, rolled it into a ball and placed it behind Lisa. "Here, lean back."

Lisa leaned back and Storm sat next to her. He grabbed a Joshua tree limb he had salvaged and began carving with his knife.

"You found something for crutches?"

"Just one. I'll find another one as we go." He chopped and carved, fashioning the branch into a crude crutch.

"Derek, how far do we have to go?"

"Well... if we're where I think we are, about twenty miles to reach the Army."

"Why the Army?"

"We can't risk returning to the highway. The bad guys would find us. However, the Army's National Training Center, Fort Irwin, is about twenty miles that way." Storm pointed with the knife. "There are always ground units there for desert combat training."

"But why the Army? Shouldn't we find a town and call the police?"

"There aren't any towns within thirty-five miles and they're on the highway. We need to go where they won't follow. There's nothing but desert between here and Fort Irwin. Even their SUV can't hack this terrain, so they most likely won't follow us. If they try to follow on foot, they'll have to answer to me." He patted his rifle.

"What about water?"

"That's the big problem. I figure we can get by for another day if we rest during daylight and travel at night. If we double our pace, I think we can make Fort Irwin by dawn, day after tomorrow."

Storm finished the crutch by wrapping a tee shirt around the top.

Lisa marveled at the celestial display overhead. The desert night sky, uncontaminated by manmade lights, revealed wonders she had never seen. "You know, if my ankle didn't hurt and we had a bottle of wine, this might qualify as a romantic date. Look at those stars."

Storm glanced at the heavens. "Yes. It's amazing. It makes me realize how small I am." He leaned toward Lisa. Their lips met in a soft kiss.

"Interesting. You'll kiss me now, when I'm a mess. But last night, when I was looking my very sexy best, you didn't even try."

"Don't think I didn't want to. We need to move on."

Storm assisted her to her feet and placed the crutch under her armpit. He donned his field jacket, slung his rifle and gathered the water bottle.

"You ever done a three-legged race?"

"Oh, yeah. When I was a kid."

"Good. I'll strap your injured leg to my right leg. Use the crutch for balance. We'll sequence our steps so you can keep the weight off your bad leg. Let's do it."

Storm wrapped his belt around their thighs. Lisa used the crutch for balance. They moved on, awkwardly at first. But they soon developed a rhythm, hobbling deeper into the desert, like some alien three-legged creature.

∞

"They crawled off this way," informed Rebel, following their tracks with his flashlight.

"That bastard is smart. He kept the car between us and them so we couldn't see 'em crawl up the mountain." Slash was gaining more respect for Storm.

"Not smart enough to erase the tracks."

"Don't get your hopes up, Yank," cautioned Rebel. "If they went into those rocks, the tracks will disappear."

Slash and Yankee followed Rebel as he led them up the mountainside. Sure enough, one hundred and twenty yards later, the sand dissipated and the tracks vanished.

"Shit! The tracks end here. We might not find any more 'til mornin'."

Yankee contemplated. "They can't be traveling more than one to two miles an hour, so they can't get far. Is there any chance they slipped by us in the dark?"

"I don't think so," responded Slash. "Nothin' came down that mountain during daylight and we fanned out pretty good after dark."

"Could be they're in those rocks up yonder, waitin' to pick us off."

"Good point. We can't flail around here until daylight. He could be laying an ambush." Yankee glanced down again, immersed in thought. He knew Storm was Infantry trained, a squad leader, decorated for valor in combat and an outstanding marksman. To underestimate him further could be disastrous. Their best chance of finding them would come when the team arrived with all of their weapons and equipment.

"The Colonel isn't gonna like this. No, sir. He isn't gonna like this at all."

∾

The cool night air was a blessing. Lisa and Storm had increased their pace without sacrificing too much perspiration. They were hungry, but the biggest threat was dehydration. They made steady progress, with Storm keeping a mental count of their paces and distance traveled. Every two hours they rested for ten minutes. They sat down for their third rest of the night.

"How long before sunrise?"

Storm checked his watch. "About an hour and a half. If we cover another mile or two, we'll be doing great." He lied. He had no assurances of being rescued according to any timetable, real or imaginary. "Once it's light, we'll find shelter. Hopefully, by dawn tomorrow we'll run into an Army unit. They'll have water and food. They'll help us." Storm turned on his cell phone and checked for signal. He wasn't surprised. It had none. He turned it off and stuffed it into his pocket.

"How's the ankle?"

"It still hurts but I can go on." Lisa snuggled next to him and rested her head on his chest. He wrapped his arm around her. Lisa yawned and infected Storm.

"We best not fall asleep. Do you feel ready?"

"Yeah. Let's go."

They struggled to their feet again, sequenced their steps and hobbled.

Las Vegas: "Yankee, I swear, if I had the time, I'd skin your ass and mount it." Trigger and Sparks looked the other way, pretending not to hear the ass chewing.

"Yes, sir. I'm sorry." Yankee, appropriately chastised, stared at the ground outside McCarran airport. "What do you want us to do now, Colonel?"

"First, get two new SUV's and abandon that piece of shit." The

Colonel nodded at the bullet-riddled vehicle. "That thing will draw every cop in town. I'm surprised you made it this far. Did Storm do that?"

"Yes, sir. The son of a bitch can shoot."

Bravo huffed. "That's not all he's good at. That's why I told you to avoid engagement. He's cunning and talented. I've seen it first-hand."

Yankee nodded.

"All right. Get the new vehicles, four-wheel drives. Trigger. Sparks. Get the gear. Where the hell's Slash?"

"He's checkin' out the location for the Ops Center."

"Good. As soon as we get set up, you show me where you lost them. I've got an idea. And the cost is coming out of your paychecks."

Mojave Desert: At daybreak, Storm found a dry wash running into the just as dry Amargosa River. Along the edge was a hollow area under a stone overhang. It was a good shelter.

He smoothed an area large enough for both of them. He settled Lisa into the hollow and gathered tumbleweeds. He placed them at the entrance and spread his field jacket over their inside, enlarging their shade. He tucked his head inside. "Time to finish the water."

Lisa uncapped the bottle and took a small swig. She handed it to Storm. "You finish it, Derek."

Storm noticed she drank only a fourth of it. "You need more, Lisa."

"No, Derek. You need more than I do. You're a lot bigger and you're bearing the load. You can carry me but I can't carry you. We have to keep you healthy. I'm the doctor and I'm ordering you to drink it."

Storm couldn't argue with her logic. He took a big swig but left a swallow. "I'm good. Here, finish it."

Lisa gave him a scolding look. "You are stubborn."

"I'm Irish. Finish the water. I'm good. Really."

Lisa relented.

"You rest. I'm going to the river."

"What river?"

Storm smiled. "That wide wash we crossed a while ago is the Amargosa River. It's dry on the surface. But sometimes, a few feet under, water flows through the sand. I'm gonna dig down and see if there's any water."

"How do know that?"

"I used to be stationed here. I did some survival training and instruction."

"Is the water drinkable?"

"Yeah. It's pretty well filtered by the sand. It's not the greatest tasting but it'll keep us alive."

"How long will you be gone?"

"No more than an hour. Here, take the Colt." He handed it to her. "Same rules apply. Don't shoot unless you have to and identify your target first."

Lisa nodded. Storm headed down the wash. He was weary after being awake all night. Hunger and thirst were sapping his strength. He hoped to find enough water to get them through another day. The sun was already hot. Storm reasoned that if he spent more than an hour searching, he'd be wasting perspiration and energy that he should be saving. One hour, he would give it one hour.

∾

The Bell helicopter flew southbound over Highway 127, five hundred feet above ground. Bravo had hired the copter and pilot for the day on the pretense of searching for a Hollywood location to shoot a desert scene for a movie. He sat in the left front and Yankee sat in the back, directly behind the pilot. In a case next to Yankee was a high-powered, scoped rifle.

Bravo inserted his team radio earpiece into his left ear, keeping it hidden from the pilot. Yankee wore his radio also. They communicated to each other over the team radio without the pilot's knowledge. They communicated with the pilot via the ship's intercom.

The endless desert passed beneath at eighty knots. Yankee pointed out landmarks. They came upon Lisa's overturned SUV. "There's the SUV, off to the right. We lost their tracks about a hundred yards west, up the hill."

Bravo nodded. He instructed the pilot to fly south.

The pilot nodded and pressed on to Baker. Bravo and Yankee searched with binoculars.

Upon reaching Baker, Bravo had the pilot head northbound on a track slightly west of their original course. They spent another hour flying toward Shoshone, not finding any sign of them. Bravo had the pilot reverse course again and fly a track further west.

∾

Storm was sound asleep. His venture to find water had proven fruitless. He had selected a likely spot but didn't find even a hint of moisture. The strong sun took its toll, but he refused to quit until he reached his deadline. When it arrived, he gathered his gear and a tree limb and went back to Lisa. She was sleeping when he arrived.

He climbed in next to her, careful to not awaken her. He removed the Colt from her relaxed fingers, kissed her on the cheek and holstered the pistol. He drifted off to sleep, not aware of a blue and white helicopter ten miles to the east.

∞

The helicopter completed its northbound track and reversed course again, working further west, edging their way toward Fort Irwin.

"Are you sure they didn't slip by you and go east?"

"I don't see how, Colonel. We had them in sight until dark and then we fanned out. They had to go over that ridgeline, west. If they went north or south, we'd have seen them."

Bravo nodded. "They can't get far on foot. Keep looking."

∞

The unmistakable air-chopping sound alerted Lisa. She rubbed the sleep from her eyes and shook Storm.

"Derek. I hear a helicopter."

"Huh?"

"I hear a helicopter."

The hair on Storm's neck bristled. It didn't sound like an Apache or Blackhawk. "It's not an Army chopper."

The sound grew louder. Storm peered out. It was two miles east at low altitude, headed north. It was a blue and white commercial chopper.

"Should we signal it?"

"No. It's a commercial helicopter. Looks like they're searching for something. Probably us. It could be the bad guys."

Lisa was disappointed. "Could it be a Sheriff's helicopter?"

"No. They use a different kind. That one's definitely a commercial version for tours, aerial photos and searches. There aren't any tours out here and there sure as hell isn't anything to photograph. They're searching. And I'll bet it's us they're searching for. Go back to sleep."

He set to work, chopping and carving at the branch he had retrieved near the river. He fashioned a second crutch for Lisa.

∞

The chopper completed another northbound leg abeam Shoshone and

Bravo had the pilot reverse course and track south and further west.

The pilot informed, "I can't fly much farther south than the Amargosa River on this new track and we have to climb up to fifteen hundred feet."

"Why's that?"

"Straight ahead is Death Valley National Monument. No flights below fifteen hundred feet are allowed. A few miles beyond that is Fort Irwin. It's highly restricted airspace. Only military aircraft allowed."

"Show me." The pilot passed him the chart. He tapped his finger on it to indicate their present position. Bravo read the Restricted Airspace notes, confirming the pilot's statements.

He handed the chart back, glanced over his shoulder and gave Yankee a look that could have melted steel.

Twice, the same helicopter appeared from the north, got within a mile of them and then abruptly turned away. It was at a higher altitude than before. It kept its distance from Fort Irwin. If it had been an official search, the Army would have granted a waiver to fly within the area.

Storm and Lisa waited for dusk before crawling out. They had a lot more ground to cover and they needed an early start. They didn't know it, but during the evening they had traversed the southern end of Death Valley.

The full day of rest helped them both, even though they were thirsty and hungry. Lisa especially benefited. The swelling had diminished considerably. She knew it would swell again once they began their trek. But to start, it was much better.

"How ya feelin', China doll?"

"Hungry. Do you know of a good Chinese restaurant nearby?"

Storm chuckled. "As a matter of fact, I do. It's that way." He pointed toward Fort Irwin. "And a nice, cold Mai Tai sounds real good about now." He didn't tell her the restaurant he had in mind was well beyond Fort Irwin.

He set Lisa on her crutches, gathered their gear and they headed southwest.

"Do you think we'll be found by morning?"

The optimist Storm emerged. "Absolutely. Once we crossed the river, we made it more than half way. The edge of the training area is only a few miles. There's bound to be a patrol or a battalion out in the field. They'll get us to civilization."

"Our tax dollars at work."

"That's right. God bless the United States Army and those who serve." Storm wished he were still in the Army, part of a Special Forces Alpha Team. He missed the camaraderie of working with dedicated professionals. He missed the acrid smell of cordite and the staccato of automatic weapons fire. He missed the vigorous physical training and the tactical exercises. But most, he missed his friend Luke Hale. Storm felt kinship with Luke deeper than that of his own brother. He suspected the same of Luke.

"Derek?"

"Yeah?"

"After this, will we see each other?"

Storm smiled and looked at the beautiful, inquiring face. He felt a special relationship developing with her. "Lisa, you couldn't scare me away with a howitzer. You're stuck with me."

Lisa looked relieved and smiled back. "If you call that being stuck, then stick me every day."

Storm laughed.

"What's so funny?"

"Now who's making sexual innuendos?"

Lisa realized her unintentional pun and laughed. "Yeah. That too!"

"Okay. Enough foreplay. Just keep crutchin', China doll. Just keep crutchin'."

Las Vegas: Yankee was on Bravo's shit list and kept a wide berth. Sparks had the electronics gear all set up. Trigger had recovered and was on his feet. He still looked weak, though.

Rebel and Slash also avoided the Colonel. They too had screwed up, letting the Foxtrots escape. But it was Yankee who bore the responsibility. He had been in charge.

The Colonel hovered over Sparks, who was trying to crack the computer encryption and having no luck.

"Damn it! Colonel, it ain't gonna happen without a mainframe. We don't have the horsepower."

Bravo, impatient but understanding, paced the room. Trigger sensed the Colonel's frustration and left. Sparks didn't have that luxury.

Yankee was in the next room, cleaning weapons.

"What's up, Trig? How you feelin'?"

"Better. But these wounds itch like hell."

"That means they're healing, or so I was told when I was wounded in Mogadishu."

"I hope you're right 'cause I'm goin' stir-crazy. I need some action."

"Combat or fluff?"

"Both."

The mercenary brothers chuckled.

"What's got the Colonel riled now?"

"That encryption program has Sparks stumped. Shit, man, if he can't break it, I don't know who can."

Yankee summoned his courage and went to the Ops Center. The Colonel was pacing the floor. He knocked.

"Come!"

"Pardon me, Colonel, but I had an idea."

"What is it, Yankee?"

"Sir, we haven't had a look inside Storm's apartment. Maybe there's a computer or something that can point us to the lab."

Bravo looked at Yankee and nodded. "Now you're thinking. Take Rebel and Sparks. If this pans out, you're off my shit list."

"Yes, sir." Sparks followed Yankee out the door, right on his heels.

Yankee retrieved his pistol and yelled down the hallway, "Rebel, on me. We've got a mission."

∞

Thankfully, there was a slight breeze. Lisa and Storm had significantly increased their pace. Storm estimated they had averaged two miles an hour.

They stopped for their second rest of the evening. Storm eased her down, unloaded his burden and sat next to her.

"How you doing, sweetie?"

"Pretty good, but my ankle's throbbing again. I need more ibuprofen."

"Can you swallow those pills without water?"

"I'll have to."

Storm leaned back to reach inside his pocket for the bottle and received a dozen pricks into his back.

"Ow. What the hell?" He sat up and turned his back toward Lisa. "Something stuck me between the shoulder blades. Take a look."

Lisa couldn't see in the darkness. "I don't see anything. Was it a scorpion?"

"No, I don't think so. I got stuck a dozen times. Must be needles or briars."

Lisa rubbed her hand across his back and felt numerous protrusions. "I think they're cactus needles."

"That makes sense. See if you can pull them out."

Lisa pulled one but her hand slipped off the smooth, slender barb. She tried again, having the same result. "I can't get a grip. My fingers aren't strong enough."

"Okay. Hold on." He fished in another pocket and produced a collapsible, multi-tool device. He opened it, exposing pliers, and handed it to her. "Try this. Make sure you get a good grip on it before you pull."

"As you wish, Doctor Storm," she answered sarcastically.

"Sorry. I keep forgetting you're a doctor."

"Uh-huh. I noticed that." She took a firm hold on one of the needles, leaned into Storm and stuck her tongue into his ear. His reaction provided the distraction she wanted and she yanked the barb from his back. The mixed pain and pleasure caused an unusual sensation.

"Whew, lady. You sure know how to show a guy a good time."

"Oh good. Because there's more where that came from." Just as Storm began to laugh, Lisa pulled another needle. Storm couldn't help laughing harder. Between her ingenious quips, sexual innuendos and erotic manipulations, he was astounded that pain could feel so good. After three minutes of delightful torture, she kissed him and rubbed his back.

Storm recovered from his laughter and they kissed. The irritation in his back seemed non-existent. His head swam with the ecstasy.

"You know, Lisa, that was the most enjoyable medical procedure I have ever endured."

He couldn't see her face clearly but he knew she was smiling.

Storm took the shirt from one of her crutches and wrapped it around his left hand.

"What are you doing?"

"Well, it's hard to hold a cactus without gloves."

"Why are you going to hold a cactus?"

Storm drew his knife. "There's moisture in them there cacti. And this is how you skin it." He plunged his knife into the small cactus. He cautiously held the top with his wrapped hand as he sliced a cone-shaped piece from its top. He lifted it, sniffed and noted there were no foul odors. He licked the meat. It tasted slightly bitter and had a milky sappiness. That was normal for a barrel cactus. This was one exception to the rule of avoiding milky, sappy fluids. He bit into the meat and sucked out the sap. The moisture invigorated him. He cut off another piece and prepared it for Lisa.

"It's a little bitter but it's edible."

She bit into it and wrinkled her nose, but she sucked the liquid. The moisture felt wonderful on her parched tongue and throat.

When Lisa finished, he sliced vertically into the cactus, making numerous radial cuts. He sliced off two pieces and handed one to Lisa. They sucked the moisture. Storm gathered the used pieces and put them back inside the cactus. He sliced off two more pieces.

Before they consumed the last two pieces, Storm handed Lisa the ibuprofen. She removed four pills, tossed them into her mouth and sucked the juice from her last piece. Storm took two pills and attacked his final piece.

Storm placed all of the pieces inside the cactus. He found an oval shaped rock, cleaned it off and mashed the innards into pulp. He took a pen, unscrewed it, removed the ink cartridge, and offered it to Lisa.

"Here. Use this as a straw. Get as much juice as you can."

"What about you?"

"I'm good. Remember? You let me have most of the water yesterday."

Lisa nodded. She leaned over the cactus and drew the juice. She left some for Storm.

She gave him the pen. "Your turn."

Storm took the pen and drew about two teaspoons of liquid. He sat up and patted his stomach. "Oh, boy. I think I ate too much."

"Me too."

They chuckled.

"Maybe there's another around here."

They searched for several minutes, not finding any more barrel cacti. But Lisa found something else.

"Derek, there's a cactus over here, but it's different." Storm trotted toward Lisa's voice.

"Count out loud so I can find you."

"One, two…"

Storm located her by six. He squatted and examined the cactus.

"Is that good?"

"It sure is, doll face. That's a prickly pear and it's in bloom. We can eat the fruits and tap the stem. Good work." Storm sliced ten fruits from the tips. He peeled one, sniffed it and then licked it. There were no foul odors or tastes. He took a small bite. The familiar, bland taste and pulpy texture assured him that he had identified it correctly. The fruits were edible. He peeled all of the fruits and gave half of them to Lisa. She chewed on the morsels.

"Needs cinnamon."

Storm chuckled as he devoured one. They consumed the fruits as if they were cheeseburgers. Their flavor wouldn't win any culinary awards, but their moisture and bulk would provide them with energy. Once they finished, Storm scraped prickers from the stem, pierced it with his knife, and inserted the pen into the cut.

"Okay, Lisa. Suck out the juice, but be careful not to let your face touch the cactus." Lisa did as instructed, yielding a few ounces of chlorophyll-tasting water. Storm drained it once she was done.

They felt renewed.

"Now, if we only had an agave plant."

"Why's that?"

"We could use the roots to make Tequila."

∞

Yankee sauntered up to Storm's apartment, picked the lock, signaled Rebel and Sparks and slipped inside. Once in, they closed the door and turned on the lights. They were amazed at the array of Chinese weaponry.

"Who is this guy?" wondered Slash aloud. He was familiar with most of the blades, but there were several weapons that puzzled him. They were odd, combining features of several weapons. He wondered about their practicality and how they were used.

Each man took a separate room and they tore the place apart. They didn't care if they left a mess. They only needed to be quiet.

Every drawer was emptied, every cabinet searched, every box opened. They left the refrigerator and freezer wide open. Yankee searched Storm's desk. The search went on for twenty minutes.

Finding nothing, Yankee decided to steal Storm's computer and phone bills. He stuffed the bills into his pocket and disconnected the computer, hefted the stack and instructed the others to exit.

"Looks like it's gonna be up to you, Sparks."

They completely overlooked the Chinese artifacts on Storm's mantle.

∞

They were tired, thirsty and hungry. As dawn came, the stars faded.

Storm took a bearing on a hilltop.

"Okay, Lisa. We'll head for that hill." He pointed. They trudged along, tired, parched.

"How much further, Derek?"

"Can't say. I know we're inside the training area. I recognize the landmarks. If we keep going, I know we'll be rescued. Can you make it another two hours?"

Lisa nodded. She kept moving. Their pace had slowed, but they hadn't yet faltered. They needed water soon. Their lips were chapped and cracked. Their nostrils were dry. Their tongues and throats were parched. They were severely dehydrated. They had to reach relief soon or seek shelter for another day.

Lisa was in agony. Her ankle throbbed and her ribcage hurt. The crutches had chafed her armpits. Sand had penetrated her every crevice. She desperately wanted more ibuprofen but she couldn't summon enough saliva to wet the head of a pin. The pills would choke her. But she never complained. There was nothing he could do about it. They needed water.

The sun emerged. Within minutes, its intense heat enveloped them. They concentrated on each step. They hadn't talked much for three hours. They were too exhausted and dehydrated. Their voices were raspy. They advanced one step at a time. Each step took the effort of ten.

Another hour passed in silence. Storm's felt the sand's heat through his boots. He knew Lisa's feet had to feel just as badly. He felt terrible, not just physically, but also emotionally. This magnificent woman was depending upon him and he was failing.

He shook off the defeatism. *"Damn it! Nobody defeats Derek the Red. Nobody! Not even the damned Mojave Desert."* He was determined to complete his mission and make love to this woman again. She deserved a lot better than a desert quickie.

"I need to rest," declared Lisa. Her appearance told him there was no room for disagreement. Besides, he needed rest too.

He helped her to the ground. She stretched out. Storm propped the crutches in the sand and draped his field jacket over them, creating a shade for their heads. He brushed sand from her face and kissed her nose.

Lisa pulled out her cell phone and turned it on. Its battery power was very low. There was no signal. She turned it off. "No signal."

Storm nodded. He tried to recall if any one had ever had cell reception in the training area. He remembered there were several incidences of soldiers calling their wives, but he couldn't recall exactly where.

"If we can make it around that hill, we might be able to get a signal. I think the cell relays are in Baker and Barstow. That hill may be blocking the signal."

The hill was two miles away. It would take extraordinary effort to get around it in the heat. But if they didn't try, they'd die.

"Okay. Give me a few more minutes."

They rested and remained silent another five minutes.

"Derek. You can travel faster without me. Maybe you should leave me here and go get help."

"Absolutely not. I've *never* left a man behind and I'm not gonna start now. We make it together or we don't make it at all. And we're going to make it."

She squeezed his hand. Those reassuring words were all she needed. It confirmed her value to him. He would die out here with her rather than leave her behind. This man loved her; and she loved him.

Helendale: Pete was worried. They had departed Vegas two days ago. They should have been here the night before last, but he hadn't heard a word.

He called Lisa's condo. Then he tried her cell phone and only got her voicemail. He left a brief message and hung up. He called Derek's apartment and got the answering machine. He left no message. Then he tried Derek's cell. No answer.

He knew they had reached Vegas without a problem. Derek had called him.

He called Derek's studio. A young man answered.

"Hello. This is Pete Flynn. I'm calling for Derek Storm. Is he there?"

"No, sir. This is Mark Long, his assistant. Derek said he had to go to California."

"Okay. That's what I understood but I haven't heard from them. He hasn't been there?"

"No, sir. The last I spoke with him was on the phone."

"All right. If he should call you, would you please ask him to call me as soon as possible?"

"I'd be glad to. Have a good day, sir."

"You, too, Mr. Long."

Pete disconnected. It was unlike Derek. "*What happened?*"

Fort Irwin: Lisa collapsed. Storm dropped to his knees. He took her into his arms and assessed her. Her pulse was weak, her breathing shallow. She wasn't perspiring. She was suffering heat exhaustion. He was losing her.

"Dear, Lord. Please. Help me save her." He regretted making her walk those last three miles. *"She could have been resting. But no, I had to march her to death."* He prayed again. "Lord, give me strength. Let me save her."

Storm summoned his remaining strength, lifted Lisa awkwardly and struggled to get her across his shoulders. It was called the Fireman's Carry, an effective way to carry an unconscious person. Holding her by one leg and one arm, Storm struggled to his feet. He shifted her weight forward and walked toward the main post, thirty miles distant.

"Please, Lord. I just need a little help."

Storm concentrated and prayed with every step. His legs were weak, his balance dubious. He was light-headed. He noticed he wasn't perspiring much. It wouldn't be long before he suffered heat exhaustion, or stroke.

"Please, God. Just a little help." Storm labored under the burden but he would not quit. His body might, but his mind wouldn't. All he needed was a little blessing. *"Please God, help move my legs. If you'll pick them up, I'll put them down. Please send us help."*

Storm moved on. He strained to maintain balance. Twice he stumbled, fell to a knee and labored to rise again. *"Please, God. Send help."*

Storm was dizzy. His knees buckled and he dropped, still holding Lisa precariously balanced on his shoulders. He thought he was delirious. He stared blankly at a blinding light in front of him. It was bright, like the sun. But it couldn't be the sun. The sun was way overhead. The light roared and sand blasted his skin.

"Please, Lord. Save her." Storm lost consciousness, believing the last thing he saw was an angel of God. He collapsed onto the sand.

CHAPTER X

RECOVERIES

Las Vegas: Bravo paced the Ops Center with his cell phone to his ear. "Doc, it means what I said. The subjects eluded our tail. But we've identified them and know where to look. We find them, we find the lab."

"Just how does one elude a tail in the desert, Colonel? The visibility out there must be twenty miles," challenged Rushton.

"You ever been in a desert, Doc?"

"No, but I watch the nature channels."

Bravo rolled his eyes. "Let me tell you something. It's vast, like the ocean, only there are a lot more places to hide."

"I'll have to take your word for it."

"I guess so. I wouldn't presume to tell you how to operate."

"I get your point, Colonel. What's next?"

"We believe the objective is in the California desert. We've got phone bills with some unlisted California numbers. We're gonna check into those. As for the encryption, I'm still massaging my contacts. Also, the female was injured. We're gonna check the hospitals. We're not out of leads and unless you have some dire deadline, we've got time." There was a long silence. "*Screw him. He doesn't have a clue about covert operations.*" "Well, Doc. Do we press on? Or do you think you can find someone better?"

"No, Colonel. I'm certain there's no one better. I'm just… disappointed. I was hoping to have the protocol by now."

"We'll get it, Doc. Just have some faith."

"Okay, Colonel. Get it soon."

"I'll be in contact." Bravo snapped the phone closed. He went to the living room, where the men were evaluating Storm's phone bills and contacting hospitals around Barstow.

"Any luck?"

Slash and Rebel shook their heads. Yankee handed Bravo one of the bills. "There may be something here, Colonel. The highlighted numbers are High Desert exchanges, but they're listed to some phony company with a private mailing box in San Bernardino. They're dead ends. The other one," he pointed, "is a sat-com number, not a cell."

"Sat-com? You mean satellite? That's pretty expensive. Whose is it?"

Yankee handed him a slip of paper. It had a name on it.

Bravo snatched the bat phone, hit speed dial and waited.

"This is Titan, key two-four-seven-four-two. Patch for Bio's, desk thirteen." Bravo stared at the name as he waited.

"This is Titan. I need a background workup on a Hale, Lucien Hale."

Suva, Fiji, South Pacific: The stunning young blonde gathered her luggage and cleared the Customs desk. She had just quit her boring brokerage job in Seattle to spend time with her family.

She was dressed in tight shorts, sandals and halter-top. Her sunglasses perched on the crown of her head, ready for action. The sun assaulted her as she exited the terminal. She slid her sunglasses down.

"Amber, over here sweetie." She turned toward the familiar voice, a voice from a man she loved.

"Dad!"

Amber Hale, twenty-five year old daughter of Luke and Heather Hale, ran to her dad. They embraced and kissed.

"It's good to see you. You look good. How's the boyfriend?"

"We broke up. I can't stand a man who can't stand a women who can think for herself."

Luke chuckled. "Yeah. There's a lot of that going around." He draped his arm over her shoulders and gave her a squeeze. "Let me get your bags."

"Where's Mom?"

"She's on the *Vixen*. The helicopter only holds two, so I'll fly you to the ship as soon as we get your bags loaded. The cocktails are waiting."

"Where's the helicopter?"

"Just around the corner. Follow me."

Fort Irwin: Water cooled his face and washed away the crust of perspiration and sand. A damp towel was placed over his head and around his neck.

Storm was vaguely aware of the presence of beings. Voices mingled, their words unintelligible. "*Angels?*" His vision was blurred and he had a terrible headache. His mouth and throat were still parched.

A hand raised his head as a canteen was placed at his lips. Storm took a small amount of water and swilled it. He moistened his chapped lips with his tongue. He took more water, swilled it, gargled and spat it out. He grasped the canteen from the angel and tipped it up. He took a full mouthful and swallowed. Water had never tasted so good.

"Lisa. Where's Lisa? Who are you?" His vision was still blurred.

"The medic is taking care of her. Have more water."

He did. His vision began to clear. He could see some definition on the angel's face. She was pretty and she had brown hair; and she wore an Army uniform with medical insignia.

"You're the Army."

"Yes. I'm Lieutenant Winston, a nurse with the Air Cav."

"How did you find us?"

"One of our patrols spotted you and radioed us. You're on Fort Irwin."

"Thank God. He answered my prayers. How's Lisa?"

"She's in the chopper. We had to get her out of the sun. My partner is working on her now. It looks like she has heat exhaustion and a broken ankle."

"Sprained, we think. She's a doctor."

Storm took another large swallow. He felt better with every passing minute. He noticed the Lieutenant had positioned herself to shade his head from the sun. Fortified, he attempted to rise.

"You should lay still for a few more minutes."

He weakly shook his head. "No. I have to see Lisa."

He rose with the assistance of his Heaven-sent rescuer. He saw the chopper, a Blackhawk, thirty yards away, the sun glinting off its windscreen. He realized the brilliant light he had seen must have been the reflection. God had sent help just as he had asked. They were just angels of a different kind.

Storm slogged to the chopper. A medic had Lisa in the shade, wrapped in wet towels. He dabbed her chapped lips with a wet cloth and dripped cold water onto her head. There was a field IV in her arm. Storm noticed an ice chest, water bottles and towels.

He climbed in, followed by the Lieutenant. She took an ice-cold towel and draped it over Storm's head and neck. The icy, wet cloth rapidly cooled him.

"Nice of you to bring ice."

She nodded. "We always bring it out here. Heat exhaustion and dehydration are always a threat."

Lisa stirred and mumbled.

"She'll be okay," stated the medic.

"How long have you been out here?"

"Two days. We walked about thirty miles."

"Where did you come from?"

"Somewhere south of Shoshone. Our vehicle crashed in the desert and this was our closest sanctuary." He didn't tell her why.

"You mean from the northeast? You walked through Death Valley?"

"Could be. I didn't have a map. Have you seen my rifle?"

Winston shook her head.

The chopper's engine revved. The rotors spun faster and they lifted off, rotated southwest and headed for the main post.

"We're taking you to the Infirmary. We'll get you fixed up," she yelled.

Storm gave her a thumb-up and nodded. "Thanks," he yelled back. "*And thank you, God. I owe you a big one.*"

Fiji: The *Serene Vixen* anchored off Viti Levu. The helicopter ride was a thrill for Amber. It was her first time in a helicopter. The flight gave her and Luke time to catch up on family events. She was curious about the hole in the windscreen.

"Oh. Bird strike." Amber looked at him suspiciously.

"What kind of bird is shaped like that?"

"The copper-jacketed hollow point. A very small, hard, fast-flying bird. It's hard to tell once they smash into the glass. They make a real mess."

She wasn't buying his malarkey for a minute.

Luke was quite proud of Amber. She was diligent, adventurous, intelligent and beautiful, just like her mother.

Amber was anxious to see the ship for the first time and she was slightly envious that Pierce had beaten her to it.

She was impressed by its beauty, awed by its size. It was truly a cruiser's dream.

"She's magnificent."

Luke hovered just aft of the helipad. He flew a slow circle around the *Vixen*, letting Amber view her from all sides. The bridge crew waved from the wheelhouse as they passed. Luke completed the circle and hovered over the pad.

"Tour's over, time for cocktails." He gently set the chopper on the helipad as Dave Welch trotted out to chain it down. Luke shut down the engine and unbuckled. Amber followed suit.

"Hey, boss. How was the…" Dave stopped in mid-sentence. He got an eyeful of Amber and became speechless. Luke grinned. She had that effect on young men, old one's too.

"Hello," said Amber sweetly. She smiled and extended her hand, "I'm Amber Hale."

Dave raised his hand. "H…hello. I'm… Dave."

"Nice to meet you."

Luke intervened for the sake of the love-struck mechanic. "Dave is our ship's mechanic and machinist. Top notch. His last name is Welch."

"How nice. You must do a good job because the ship is beautiful. Maybe you can show me around later?" Her sparkling smile dazzled him.

"I… I'd be delighted."

"Great. I'm looking forward to it. But right now, I have to go see my Mom. I'll see you later, okay?"

"Uh, sure. Sure."

Luke snapped his fingers in Dave's face, chuckling. "Earth to Dave. Earth to Dave. See that the chopper gets chained down and my daughter's bags are taken to stateroom eight. That is all."

Dave, mouth agape, nodded. Amber followed Luke toward the starboard ladder, casting a flirtatious glance back at Dave.

"He's cute."

Fort Irwin: "Pete. It's Derek."

"Sweet Jesus, lad. Where have you been? I've been worried sick. Are you okay?"

"I'm fine. Lisa suffered heat exhaustion but she's recovering nicely, thanks to the Lord and the U.S. Army."

"The Army? Where are you?"

"Fort Irwin. Can you come get us?"

"Absolutely. How's Lisa?"

"Like I said, she's recovering. Nothing that water and food can't cure. She's got bruised ribs and a badly sprained ankle, though. She'll have to stay off it for a while."

"What happened?"

Storm gathered his thoughts. "Pete, they tried to grab her."

"Who tried to grab her?"

"I don't know, but I'll bet it's the bastards who murdered Dan."

"How did they find you?"

"They probably tailed us from the funeral. I didn't spot them until we were on the way to your place. We made a dash down 127 but we crashed in the desert. Lisa sprained her ankle and bruised her ribs. We trekked through Death Valley for two nights and the Army rescued us about five hours ago."

"When should I come get you?"

"First thing in the morning. Lisa will need the full night to rest and re-hydrate."

"Okay. Let me get a phone number so I can call in the morning."

Storm read the telephone number to Pete. "I'll be standing by at that number from 0700 on. Give me a ring when you're about to leave. I'll ask the Infirmary Commander to notify the gate."

"Okay, I'll do that. By the way, where's Lisa's car? Can we send the auto club?"

Storm grinned. "No. It's totaled."

"That's too bad. The important thing is you're safe. Take real good care of her, Derek. I'll call you in the morning."

"Good night, Pete."

Storm replaced the receiver. He reached over and caressed Lisa's face. He thought about the pursuers. Were they Dan's murderers? What would they do if they found Lisa? Or Pete? What if they found the lab? What would happen to the protocol if they got it? A thousand people died from cancer every day in this country; thousands more worldwide. And these bastards were killing people to prevent the cure from happening. And they tried to harm Lisa, his Lisa.

Storm couldn't mark it on a timetable, but he resolved he was going to make them pay, big time.

Fiji: The welcome aboard party was a success. The crew received Amber with warmth, especially the single men. They all took an immediate interest in her. Luke wasn't concerned. Amber was her own woman and she knew how to handle men, not in a manipulative way, but in a practical sense.

The crew snorkeled and scuba-dived, raced around on jet-skis, dove from the helipad, drank beer and slathered on sun block by the quart. Caroline enjoyed Amber's company. It was nice to have another young female around the predominantly testosterone-infected crew.

"These guys eat too much red meat," commented Caroline. Her husband, Paul, had taken position on the helipad in preparation for a high-dive. He jumped, tucked and twisted. He sliced into the water with very little splash. Amber, Caroline, Heather and Conchetta applauded as he surfaced. Other crewmembers held up scorecards. Without a doubt, Paul was the best high-diver on the vessel.

Amber took a turn at the platform. With every male eye watching her, she made a performance of preparing for her dive. She stretched and posed, breathed deeply as if she were focusing all of her concentration. Then she jumped, flailed her arms and legs, held her nose and splashed into the ocean. When she surfaced, the men cheered and held up their scorecards. She scored perfect tens.

Luke and Salty preferred to shoot clay targets off the port side. Luke stood by the launcher. The Skipper readied his shotgun. "Pull!" Luke pulled the release and two clay targets hurled over the water like Frisbees. Salty engaged the first in one second, blasting it into a dozen fragments. The second succumbed one second later.

"Geez, Skipper. You're four up on me. I only have two shots left. There's no way I can beat you."

"Don't give up. You can still narrow the gap."

"Who said anything about giving up?"

Salty chuckled as he cleared his weapon. "Sorry, boss. Lost my head." He reloaded the launcher for Luke.

"Skip the boss stuff, Skipper. There's nobody here but us. Call me Luke. I feel more comfortable thinking of you as a friend than an employee. If you want to call me 'boss' when the crew's around, fine. But I always want to know your opinions. Never hold anything back. Okay? I need your experience and wisdom." Luke loaded two shot shells, levered the breech closed and placed it to his shoulder. "Pull!"

Two clay targets launched. Luke engaged the first, shattering it into pieces. He lined up on the second, estimated the lead and squeezed. The shotgun recoiled. His second shot missed by inches. He was hell-on-wheels with a rifle, but Salty was definitely the better marksman with a shotgun.

"Three," said Salty.

Luke looked out over the water, disappointed. He fished three Cuban Robustos from his humidor and handed them over. The Skipper graciously accepted the delicacies, placed one in his humidor, one in his mouth and offered one to Luke. They bit off the caps, spat them overboard and torched the aromatic cylinders.

"Okay," said Salty.

"Okay what?"

"You said to not hold back and not to call you 'boss' unless the crew's around. Maybe I should have said, 'Okay, Luke'."

Helendale: Storm and Pete pulled into the driveway at Lisa's condo. Storm honked the horn. The blinds parted, revealing Lisa's face. Her expression was precious. Her eyes widened and her mouth hung open. She was obviously impressed.

Pete smiled. "I think she approves."

Storm pulled the keys from the ignition. Lisa came out, braced by her crutches. "Pete, you didn't! A Hummer! No way!"

Storm handed over the keys to her yellow Hummer. It was a used vehicle, but it was a desire she had previously mentioned to Storm.

Lisa hugged Pete and kissed Storm full on the lips.

"Oh, thank you, Pete. Thank you. It's beautiful."

It was the first time Pete had seen them kiss. "I deduce that you two are an item."

Lisa beamed. Storm blushed. She kissed him on the cheek.

"I told you. She has a great personality."

"You also told me she was four foot nine."

Lisa admired the Hummer. She eased into the driver's seat, obviously delighted. "I'm going to look good in this."

Storm grinned. "China doll, you'd look good in a garbage truck."

Lisa blew a kiss at him. "Isn't he sweet?"

"Derek, why don't you get Lisa inside and I'll put the Hummer in the garage. Let's have lunch."

"I'll buy," quipped Lisa. Storm escorted her into the condo. Pete parked the Hummer.

Storm prepared sandwiches. Lisa sat comfortably at the table, watching him work. Pete entered through the garage.

"I'm glad the two of you are okay. But I'm concerned about our safety. I don't think this thing is over. If those men trailed you all the way from Portland, they're determined. Sooner or later, they'll find us."

"I agree. You two need to keep a very low profile. Take a different route to and from the lab every day, even if you have to drive miles out of your way. Keep your vehicles in the garages and make sure you don't have a tail before you turn down your street. If you do spot one, try to get to a police station. Until we deal with these guys, we're all at risk. Did you get that firearms training, Pete?"

"Yup. Bought a new pistol, too. A .40 caliber. I like it."

"Good. Practice with it until you can make a head shot at ten yards in low light. Lisa needs training too."

Lisa was apprehensive. "I've never even held a gun. I'm afraid of them."

"Sorry, sweetie. But the time has come for you to learn. I'm not Superman and I can't be everywhere at once. You need to be able to defend yourself."

"Well, if you stick around, I'll make it worth your while." She tilted her head seductively and gave him a wink.

Now Pete was blushing.

"That sounds real tempting, China doll. But how am I gonna get to San Fran if I stay here?"

"Why San Fran?"

"Lisa's brother is a Chinese art historian. He lives in San Fran. We need to get that artifact translated."

"Remember, Pete?" The tablet that described Mesothelioma?"

"Oh, right. Wouldn't that be something, finding an ancient cure for cancer that's been lost for centuries."

Suva, Fiji: Amber insisted on sampling the nightlife in the capital. Luke agreed to take her, Heather and several crewmen ashore in the launch.

They decided on a large, beachfront lounge. It was on the beach and featured a large, open-air bar with seating under the stars. The youngsters frolicked on the beach, the ladies looking splendid in their bikinis, the men going shirtless, taking every opportunity to flex their muscles.

Luke and Heather chose to dance inside, spending hours in each other's arms. The younger crewmen, not having any success at garnering Amber's attention, eagerly stalked other young beauties.

Amber took an interest in a gentleman who appeared to be mid-thirties, average looking, medium height and stocky build. He had a pleasant smile. Heather noticed them sitting across the café.

"Looks like Amber found some one interesting."

Luke turned and nodded. "I hope she's having a good time."

"Luke?"

"Yeah, babe?"

"How long is Amber going to be with us?"

"Indefinitely. I made her an offer she couldn't refuse."

"What did you do, Lucien Hale?"

"Uh-oh. You used my whole name. I'm in trouble now."

"No. I just want to know what you did."

Luke smiled. Neither Luke nor Amber had discussed the arrangement yet with Heather.

"Since I was spending so much time managing our accounts, I made a deal with Amber. If she agreed to stay on with the *Vixen* and manage the accounts, she'd have room and board free. I figured she'd be better at it than I am. Besides, I want to enjoy retirement. I don't want to slave over financial accounts. She agreed."

"That's great. I hope she's with us for quite a while."

"Me, too. And she's welcome to take her leave any time she chooses, no strings. Besides, it's entertaining watching all those young studs make fools of themselves vying for her attention."

They laughed.

Amber approached their table.

"Hi, Mom. Hi, Dad. Are you having fun?"

"Oh, yes, dear," answered Heather. Luke pulled out a chair for her.

"What happened to that man who was sitting with you?"

"He went the rest room. He'll be back. I'd like you to meet him. He's nice."

"What's his name?" asked Luke.

"Drake. He's from Oregon and likes the outdoors. He's thirty-three."

"What does he do for a living?"

"He's an entrepreneur. He's never been married and he's here alone on vacation."

The man approached the table.

"Oh, Mom and Dad, this is Drake. Drake, Heather and Luke Hale, my parents."

The gentleman extended his hand to Luke, "How do you do, sir. I'm pleased to meet the parents of such a wonderful and lovely lady."

"Nice to meet you too, Drake."

"I can see where Amber gets her beauty and charms," he said to Heather.

"Thank you. You're very kind."

"Please join us, Drake." He thanked Luke for the invitation and selected the seat closest to Amber.

"Amber tells us you're from Oregon. Beautiful country."

"Yes. It is. I was born and raised in Grants Pass, the southern part of the state."

"How long have you been in Fiji?" asked Heather.

"Six days. I have eight days left for my vacation. Amber told me you folks live on a yacht."

"Yes. We retired a while ago and decided to cruise the world. The ship is anchored off the north point. It's the large one with its lights on." Luke pointed.

"Oh, that one. I saw you steam into harbor. That is a magnificent vessel. You must be proud. I imagine you have all sorts of neat equipment for navigation and communication on board. How do you keep in touch with home?"

"We have satellite communications. Unfortunately, I have to be within a few hundred yards of the ship to use the phone. But we can send e-mail. For ship to shore, we use these." Luke held up a portable radio.

"That's great. It's the dickens trying to call the states from here. My sister wanted me to call her from Fiji, said it would give her something to dream about. But I haven't been able to get a line to the States yet."

"Well, you're welcome to come to the ship with us and call," offered Heather.

Drake looked dumbfounded. "Really. That would thrill me more than my sister. I'd love to see your ship."

"Well, join us in the launch when we head back. We have a spare stateroom. You can stay the night."

"This is a dream, right? Some one pinch me."

Amber obliged and laughed.

"Ow. I guess it's not. Well, thank you, Mrs. Hale, and you too, Mr. Hale. I appreciate it. Are you sure it's not an imposition?"

"Think nothing of it."

"Drake, I'm sorry but I don't recall your last name," said Luke.

"Oh, I forgot my manners. I'm sorry. My last name is Kress, K-R-E-S-S."

CHAPTER XI

SUPPRESSION

Las Vegas: Lisa had Storm use her Hummer to return to Vegas. She wanted to go with him, but Storm and Pete convinced her she needed to keep a low profile and stay off her ankle.

Storm had been fortunate to recover his rifle. A patrol at Fort Irwin had found it and delivered it to the Command Post, who in turn had notified him. They allowed him to retrieve it on his way back to Vegas.

The long drive gave Storm time to think. He wasn't concerned about being spotted on the highway since he was in a new vehicle, but he was wary of returning to his apartment to get the artifacts. He would have to thoroughly recon the area before going to his apartment. If the bastards were there, he'd smoke them. If not, he'd sneak in, get the artifacts, spend the evening at Mark Long's, then catch a flight to San Francisco the next day.

He timed his drive so he would arrive after dark. Storm parked at the local convenience store. He purchased a flashlight, batteries and a bottle of water. He returned to the Hummer and retrieved his Colt and spare magazines.

Storm slipped into the shadows and headed toward the rear of his complex. His combat senses heightened as he got closer. He could feel every rock underfoot, every branch that brushed him, hear every unusual sound, smell every unusual odor. He was mentally prepared for combat. He wanted the bastards to be there. He wanted them to suffer his justice.

Not the phony justice of courts, but real justice.

Storm wound his way through the high shrubs that bordered the rear wall. He selected a dark spot to peek over. There was no one in sight, only unoccupied vehicles. He gave particular attention to the shadows.

Storm traversed prone across the top, minimizing his silhouette. He silently eased down the inside. He listened intently. The only movement was a cat prowling around the dumpster. He moved left and waited in the shadows, allowing his night vision to adapt.

Storm circled the complex, cautiously working toward his building. He was careful not to disturb branches or jostle shrubs. He looked at every parked vehicle. He moved five yards at a time, from the concealment of one tree or shrub to another, keeping to the shadows, the wall at his back to minimize his search sectors.

He reached the corner of his building and moved to its rear. He flattened to the ground and peered around the back corner. The rear side was clear.

Storm returned to the front corner and peeked. The parking lot and walk were vacant. He fished in his pocket for his apartment key. There was no practical, noiseless way of getting to his second floor apartment, other than the walk and stairs. He waited two minutes before committing.

He hustled down the sidewalk and traversed the stairs rapidly and silently, employing the fast, light footwork that his father and Master Chin had taught him. He moved with the grace and stealth of a cat stalking its prey. He took the stairs two at a time, placing his feet close to the side braces to minimize noise. He squatted below the balcony wall and crept to his apartment. He inspected the door, checking for forced entry and booby-traps. There were none he could detect. He tested the handle. It was locked, just as he had left it. He slipped the key into the deadbolt and it unlocked smoothly. He quietly removed the key and stuffed it into his pocket, grabbed his Colt and eased the door open. He lay prone and scanned the interior.

There was a sour odor. It smelled like garbage. He cocked the Colt, quietly listening, smelling, observing. He could see his furniture and the weapons on the wall. A very dim light backlit the kitchen counter and spilled over into the living room. The hall, bedrooms and bath were pitch dark. He could see the artifacts on the mantle. He summoned his sense of presence, hoping to detect the energy field of anyone inside, but nothing registered.

Had he exaggerated the danger? Was there someone really trying to kill him? If so, would they be bold enough to try and ambush him in his own apartment?

His combat senses told him there was danger. Regardless, he had to get the artifacts. He had to commit. And if the killers were here, he'd get retribution.

Storm steeled his nerves. He rose and crept low, rapidly cleared the doorway, placed his back to the wall and quietly closed the door. He relocated immediately against the wall and behind the thick arm of his sofa. There was no sensation of foreign presence. No sign of movement. No sound. No foreign odors. But somebody had tossed the place. The refrigerator light provided a glimpse of the disorder. It also explained the smell of garbage.

Storm made his move. He edged toward the fireplace, alternately watching the hall and the door. He reached for the artifacts and froze. The hair on his neck bristled. He sensed a presence, close, very close.

Storm pivoted and swung his right hand in a clockwise arc, making solid contact with a head or shoulder. A painful grunt emitted from a stealthy adversary. Storm pivoted in a crouch and thrust a left uppercut into the groin of the dimly lit aggressor. He made solid contact.

"Ugghhh!" The aggressor dropped something and it hit the floor with a loud thud.

A red laser dot appeared on the wall and swerved toward him. Storm dove behind the coffee table as he snapped a Colt shot in the direction of the laser. Storm's thunderous Colt blasted, quickly answered by two sound-suppressed shots from his bedroom, both missed.

The man Storm had punched recovered and jumped on him, fought for his Colt and punched Storm in the head. Storm saw stars but instinctively recovered, twisted his hips, blocked the thug's second punch and then plunged his left thumb deep into the man's right eye socket. The thug screamed and his head recoiled backwards. It was exactly the reaction Storm wanted. He gripped the man's head with his left hand, his thumb jammed knuckle-deep into the socket, dropped his Colt, grasped the man's jaw with his right hand and twisted his head back, down and counter-clockwise.

Cr-cr-crack. " Ugh." The grotesque sound of cervical vertebrae shattering could be heard clearly. The thug went immediately limp and collapsed, dead. Storm jumped over the corpse and reached for his Colt. Two more silenced shots spat at him from the bedroom, both hitting the corpse. Storm couldn't reach his Colt without exposing himself.

"Give it up, Storm," yelled a man from the bedroom. "You're covered. Put your hands up." The second adversary shuffled into the hall and placed the laser on Storm. "Put your hands up!"

Storm could see the silhouette of the gunman.

"Okay. You got me. I'm raising my hands."

"Get up! On your knees and cross your legs. Now! Hands on top of your head."

Storm could hear the neighbors stirring. The cops would be on the way soon.

Storm rose to his knees and raised his hands.

"What's goin' on out there?" yelled a neighbor. It was a distraction that Storm hoped for.

Faster than a hell-dispatched wraith, Storm reached behind his neck, inside his vest and grabbed a five-inch long shaken, a sharpened, balanced metal throwing spike, and he launched it. The shaken ripped through the air with fierce velocity and accuracy. It impaled into the thug's neck. He screamed and pulled the spike from his neck as he squeezed off another shot. But Storm had already jumped over the corpse and grabbed his Colt. Storm sent two thunderous 230-grain slugs sizzling at the killer. The wounded gunman retreated through Storm's bedroom and crashed through the window. Glass shattered and scattered. He rolled across the roof and jumped over the edge.

Storm reloaded his Colt and pursued, but he had disappeared. Sirens and flashing lights were approaching from the main road. Storm realized the cops would take him into custody if they found a dead man in his apartment, even if it was self-defense. He ran to the fireplace, grabbed the artifacts, then locked his apartment door and closed the refrigerator door to kill the light. He wanted it as dark as possible inside when the cops came so he would have more time to escape, while they were trying to figure out what to do.

The corpse was bloody. He ran to his bedroom, exited through the window and escaped down the roof. He noticed a blood trail and grinned. He jumped down and slipped into the darkness. His mental calculator tallied the score; killers, one; Storm, one. There were more to go and he wished he had a live one to interrogate.

∞

"Where's Rebel?"

Yankee collapsed to his knees, blood spewed from his neck and his right arm. He was agitated. The team members had never seen him so rattled.

"Storm killed him! I heard his damned neck snap from twenty feet away. He's dead, Colonel!"

Slash and Trigger balanced him. Sparks came running with the medical kit.

"Lie down, Yankee. Trigger, get him patched up. Before you pass out, Yankee, tell me how he got you and Rebel."

Yankee was hyperventilating. "Rebel snuck up on him in the dark... but the guy... I don't know... must have sensed him or smelled him... cause Rebel didn't make a sound... Next thing I know, Storm pistol whipped Reb... and punched him in the balls. I took several shots... but the guy moves so freakin' fast... Next thing I know, I heard Rebel's neck snap... no doubt in my mind... I got the drop on Storm... but somehow, he got a knife and threw it into my neck... Shit, is he fast. I had the laser right on his chest... and he still speared me. I've *never* seen anyone move that fast. It ain't *human*!"

Bravo saw his stunned men and the terror in Yankee's eyes. His men had grossly underestimated Storm, not once, but twice. And this time it had cost them dearly. "I warned you guys. Now maybe you'll believe me. Storm is no pussy. I'd trade any three of you for him."

The men, insulted, steeled themselves and puffed out their chests.

"You just give me a crack at him, Colonel," challenged Slash. "I'll bring you his balls on a silver platter."

"All he needs is a good double-tap between the eyes," bragged Trigger.

"Enough bravado. Trigger, get Yankee patched up. Slash and Sparks, go get Rebel's body and sterilize the apartment."

"Yes, sir."

Bravo grabbed the bat phone hit speed dial.

"This is Titan, key two-four-seven-four-two. Patch for OpsPer, desk nine."

"Desk nine. State request, Titan."

"One agent down, probably permanent. I need a replacement."

"Specialties required?"

"Standard weapons, demo. Specials: transport, hand-to-hand."

"OpsPer copies, Titan. Candidate will be in touch, standard procedure."

"Good. Patch me back to Central."

"Central, go ahead, Titan."

"Patch for Crypto. Desk Two."

"Crypto, desk two. State request, Titan."

"Is Hydra there?"

"One sec."

Bravo waited for fifteen seconds. Another familiar voice answered.

"Titan, this is Hydra. State request."

"Is the line secure?"

"Line secure. State request."

"I've got an agent down and a replacement on request. My team has hit a snag and I'm in special need of decrypt. Can you accommodate?"

"That depends. What's the decrypt?"

"128-bit commercial. We need your talent and will compensate accordingly."

"Doesn't Bole Weevil usually handle these for you?"

"He hasn't cooperated lately. How about it? We'll make it worth your while."

There was a long silence. "It'll have to be time-permitting. Any pressing invalidates the agreement, payment in cash."

Bravo swallowed his pride. "Agreed. How much?"

Fiji Islands: Kress was fascinated by the communications suite aboard the *Vixen*. Luke gave him some instruction and privacy.

In truth, Kress didn't have a sister. When he saw the *Vixen*, he figured it had sophisticated communications. He observed their launch come ashore, spotted Amber and schemed to befriend her.

He had figured correctly. The satellite phone and modem were easy to use. Kress dialed an international number and waited.

"Tel-Tech, Linda. How may I direct your call?"

"This is Kress. Tara Northam's office, please."

"Certainly. One moment."

Cheery music played over the connection as he was placed on hold.

"This is Tara."

"Tara, it's Kress."

"Where are you?"

"Fiji. Vacation, remember? Did you get that information?"

"Oh, I'm fine. How are you? And yes, I have the information."

"Sorry. Communications here suck. I had to con my way onto some spoiled babe's yacht to get access to a satellite phone. So, are you gonna give me the info?"

"It's going to cost you."

"Whatever you say." Kress copied the data. "Did that package get delivered to the FBI?"

"Yes. What are you so nervous about?"

"Nervous? Those guys tried to blow me up. I'd be an idiot if I wasn't nervous."

San Francisco: Storm's flight to San Fran had been uneventful. Storm rented a car and drove to China Town. He didn't see any tail.

Storm trotted up the stairs to the museum entrance. There was a sales booth inside the door, a young Chinese girl caged within. She was young and pretty.

Storm smiled. "Hi there. Do you speak English?"

"Sure do. How can I help you?"

"My name is Derek Storm and I have an appointment to see Lawrence Chen."

"Oh, yes. Mr. Chen, he's *so* sweet. He told me you'd be coming. Go upstairs. His office is the last door on the right. I'll let him know you're coming."

"Thank you. Have a splendid day."

Storm couldn't help chuckling at the way the girl had emphasized how sweet Mr. Chen was. *"I'll just bet he's real sweet."*

Storm knocked on the door. He could hear the pitter-patter of sandaled feet swishing to the door. It opened.

"Heeeellllloooo! You must be Derek. Come in." The melodious greeting tickled Storm. I'm Lisa's brother, Lawrence." He held his hand out like a starlet. Storm gave it a gentle shake, grinning pleasantly.

"Nice to meet you, Lawrence. I'm Derek."

Lawrence looked Storm from top to bottom. "You certainly are. You're exactly as Lisa described."

"Did she tell you I'm straight?"

"Yes. She did. But I suppose it's Lisa's gain. You know, when we were teenagers, she was always trying to steal my boyfriends, the little hussy." Lawrence effeminately slapped Storm on the chest. "Ooooh. Nice pectorals. Come in and show me the artifacts."

Storm couldn't help laughing at his audacious musings. The guy was funny.

"Thanks for seeing me." Storm placed his wrapped bundle on Lawrence's desk and revealed them.

"Oh my!" Lawrence selected the round jade piece Storm had fashioned into a medallion. He ran his fingers over it and turned it over. He read the engravings on both sides. "Yes. Uh-huh. Very good." He set the medallion down and lifted the metal tablet, perusing both sides. "These are quite interesting, Derek. May I call you 'Derek'?"

"Certainly. Do you think these are authentic?"

"It's hard to say for certain with such a cursory examination, but I think they represent the art and style of the Yuan Dynasty, the Mongol Khans who ruled between 1264 and 1368 A.D. Of course, on the Chinese calendar, they were referred to differently, but that's beside the point, isn't it? The artistry of that jade carving is magnificent. It looks to be the work of one of Kublai Khan's artisans, perhaps Li Weng Su or Chiang Dek. Beautiful. Where did you find them?"

"Iraq. 1991. They were in a small, wooden chest, inside the remains of a Chinese ship buried in the sand near the Euphrates River."

"Iraq? The only Chinese ships west of India that I'm aware of, during the Yuan Dynasty, were in the second expedition of the Polo's. How unusual. I'll have to consult my friend Guido, in Venice. We went to college together. He's an art historian too. He's very knowledgeable about Italian art. Oh, is he hysterical. You'd love him. Anyway, he's an expert on the Polo's. They were from Venice, you know. Maybe he can shed some light on the matter."

"Can you translate those inscriptions?"

"Oh, heaven's yes. Let's have a look." Lawrence studied the medallion. "This one states,

'By the strength of the eternal Heaven, holy be the Khan's name. Let him that pays him not reverence be killed'.

This is clearly an edict from the Khan that the bearer was to be granted safe passage, otherwise the transgressor would suffer death. It's a travel pass, issued only to people very close to the Khan. They were most often inscribed on golden tablets, but sometimes on jade amulets such as this." Lawrence turned it over. "That's odd."

"What?"

"The reverse states, "By decree of Kublai.""

"What's the significance?"

"It indicates that this amulet was specifically ordered by Kublai Khan for presentation to a specific party. Usually, these passes made no mention of which Khan had made the decree, but this one is specific, Kublai Khan. That means if it's genuine, and I have no reason to suspect otherwise, that this amulet dates before 1294 A.D., the year Kublai Khan died." Lawrence withdrew a huge magnifying glass from his desk drawer and closely examined the jade. "Beautiful. And fascinating. Iraq. Who could have thought it?"

"Lisa was primarily interested in the tablet inscriptions. She thinks it refers to asbestos cancer."

Lawrence placed the medallion on his desk and took up the metal tablet. "Tablets such as this were used to record events or journals because they're durable. It states,

'I, Chang Li Suk, healer of Uighuristan, inscribe this record of the internal growth disease peculiar to our village. Any who are of concern, may these tablets withstand the ages and benefit our descendants with good health and long life.

For many cycles and generations, the people of Uighuristan village have suffered an illness inside their bodies. Strange growths, starting small and grow larger, attach to the lungs and internal organs. These growths become of size to stop blood, air and energy to lungs or cause the sufferer to breathe heavily and have heart surrender.

Growths have been observed to spread from one organ to other organs, passing of time, and cause suffering in the new organ.

One generation observed, that mostly those working at or living near the village asbestos market suffered. Those living away from asbestos market do not seem to acquire the internal growths. Many of those who worked at the market, but lived away from it acquired the growths, yet their families did not.

This indicates that some element in the production and handling of asbestos may be a cause of the internal growths. Lungs affected most, perhaps element carried through air.

Some believe these growths caused by spirits of the ancients, as many ancients suffered, but I do not believe this.

My observations as healer being 313 moon cycles as

I inscribe these tablets, I have discovered a treatment to prevent and sometimes reduce the growths while they are small. Some growths have reduced completely, not to return.

This treatment serves the village well and is plentiful.

Steadily consume each day...'"

Lawrence placed down the glass. "That's it. There are obviously more tablets. The text made several references to multiple tablets and ends in mid-sentence. Is this the only one you found?"

"Yeah. At the time, I had other things on my mind. There was one other carved jade sculpture of some building, but I gifted it to the man who rescued me."

"A building? I'd be very interested in examining that. Can you arrange it?"

"I suppose so. I'll give him a call."

"Wonderful. I'm looking forward to it."

"So, what about the transcripts?"

"Tell you what, gorgeous. Let me put together a typed translation for you, no charge of course. Can you leave these with me for a few days?"

"Sorry, Lawrence. I'd rather not have them out of my sight for too long. And I have to catch a flight this evening."

"No problem, Derek. I'll just take some digital photos. I'll make the transcript from those and fax a copy to Lisa. How's that, my muscled friend?"

"That works for me, Lawrence. How long will it take?"

Lawrence pulled a digital camera from his desk. "Voila. A little French vernacular, if you please. They'll be done within minutes. I'll link them into my computer and translate them right off the screen. I'll have it to Lisa by tomorrow morning and you can take the artifacts back with you. But I really would like to study them for an hour and get a second opinion."

"Okay. I have time for that."

"Gooood. It's a shame you won't be in town tonight. A friend is having a party. I guaranty you'd be the belle of the ball. Are you sure you can't stay?"

Storm laughed silently. "Sorry, Lawrence. I appreciate the offer but I'm interested in Lisa."

"You should be. She is darling. Daddy's princess. Wait until you meet Daddy. He'll like you. He likes manly men."

"Thanks, Lawrence. I'll look forward to meeting him and seeing the translation. I'll see what I can do to get the other sculpture."

"Excellent. Why don't you take a complimentary tour of the museum and give me about an hour?"

"Thank you. I'll do that. Do I need a pass?"

"Oh no. I'll just call down. You go enjoy and come back in an hour. Enjoy, hunky."

Storm took his leave, thanking Lawrence for the free tour. He called Lisa on his cell.

"Hello?"

"Lisa. It's Derek. I met with your brother. He needs an hour to authenticate the artifacts, but he translated the text on the tablet. Just as you thought, it refers to a disease caused by asbestos. There seem to be other tablets. The one mentioned a treatment, but it didn't get to the particulars. The text indicates there are more."

"So it is about Mesothelioma. That's incredible. If these tablets are authentic, we could be looking at a link to the cure. We might have to find those other tablets."

"By we, you mean me? Do you expect me to go back to Iraq?"

"You're so sweet, Derek. I knew you would do it."

Storm knew he was being manipulated. *"What foolish things men do for love."*

Shangdu, China: December, 1295 A.D.

Standing before Emperor Chengzong, grandson and successor of Kublai Khan, Commander Sun was disappointed to learn that Kublai Khan had passed to the great heaven a year ago. Sun had been close to Kublai Khan, who had personally commissioned him to escort the Venetian Masters back to Europe.

He and his warriors had completed their mission and returned overland to China. He reported to the Khan's Summer Palace in Shangdu, only to learn that Kublai Khan, grandson of the great Genghis Khan, had died.

Emperor Chenzong, seeing Sun's eye injury, deemed him ready for retirement. He decreed that Sun should serve out the remainder of his life as the Emperor's Prefect to govern a small district of the inland. Sun accepted the Khan's edict, albeit regretfully, and served honorably.

In Sun's mind, the governance of a small district was not a suitable job for a dedicated warrior commander. He found the routine boring. He used his plentiful spare time to reminisce and revel in his victories. It was his memories that kept him alive.

Sun decided to record his exploits. He wrote his memoirs on parchment scrolls in minute detail. During his long retirement, Sun read the memoirs frequently. In his late years, he referred to the scrolls less frequently as his health declined. Sensing his impending death, he implored his youngest son, Kick Leong, to take the scrolls to the Khan's scribes at Cambaluc, and ask them to preserve them in the archives as a favor to an old warrior.

So it was done.

Boston: Present Day

Rushton answered the phone.

"Doctor, this is Congresswoman Iris Stakemore. The national office of the Good Works Political Action Committee has just informed me of the recent generous contribution of the NOMP. I want to thank you for your generosity and see if there is anything my office can do for you."

"You're welcomed, Congresswoman. May I ask from where you are calling?"

"I'm on my private cell. You may speak freely."

"Wonderful." He signaled to Raas and Miller. "Congresswoman, I have two associates present, fellow board members of NOMP who authorized the donation. May I put this on speakerphone?"

"You may, Doctor." Rushton pressed a button.

"We're on speaker, Congresswoman. Please proceed."

"To the NOMP Board of Directors, I offer my thanks and appreciation for the one million dollar donation to the Good Works PAC. Your generosity will enable my office to continue our fight for equitable medical care in America. If we can be of assistance to you, please let me know."

"Congresswoman, this is Dr. Raas. Thank you for expressing your appreciation."

"This is Nurse Claudia Miller, Congresswoman. I too would like to offer my thanks for calling. It means a lot to us."

"You're most gracious. I felt it best to contact you personally. A contribution of that magnitude deserves personal recognition. How may my office assist you?"

Rushton grabbed the cordless receiver, automatically silencing the speaker. "We're on closed connection again, Congresswoman. The speaker is off. We have a delicate matter that could be injurious and embarrassing for the NOMP. We believe your office can be of assistance."

"I see. Please explain."

"An extortionist has mailed, what he claims, 'incriminating evidence' to the FBI office in Portland. Of course, this man is a con artist and he attempted to extort money from the NOMP based upon some ludicrous assertions. However, if these accusations were to come to light, they could be highly embarrassing. We'd be wrapped up in legal battles for years, even though there's nothing to these accusations. Our financial resources would be needlessly drained, resources that could be used for lobbying efforts and such."

The tacit implications were not lost to Stakemore. If NOMP were to suffer financially, her contributions from them would cease.

"How may my office be of assistance?"

"As I said, this material was supposedly delivered to the Portland FBI by a con man. If these baseless allegations were to come to light during an investigation, NOMP could be damaged."

"Are you asking me to squelch a federal investigation?"

"There isn't an investigation yet, Congresswoman. If it could be nipped in the bud before it becomes one, there's no harm done, no law broken. Hell, the PR campaign and legal fees could drive NOMP broke."

There was a long silence. "It's risky business to go poking around a federal investigation. I'm afraid I'll have to decline."

Rushton frowned and signaled thumb-down to Raas and Miller. Raas pounded his fist on his knee. Miller smirked and signaled Rushton to give her the phone. Rushton, puzzled, handed the phone to her.

"Congresswoman, this is Claudia Miller again. Does the name Evan Caruthers mean anything to you?"

There was even a longer silence as Rushton and Raas looked at each other quizzically. Miller strolled arrogantly to the opposite corner of the office and whispered into the phone. She finally smiled and disconnected.

"Just like a woman. She changed her mind." Her cagey smirk said it all.

CHAPTER XII

SEARCHES

Las Vegas: "Derek! It's been two years. How're you doing?" greeted Mike Starr.

"I'm great, Mike. How's the family?"

"Great! Brenda's still doing volunteer work and the kids are growing like weeds. How's your studio doing?"

"Terrific. I have ninety-two full-time students, mostly cops and military people. My assistant is running the studio. I haven't been there in two weeks."

"Taking a vacation?"

"No. I've been to a funeral, met a magnificent woman with whom I wandered Death Valley for several days, been shot at, and, oh yes, snapped a guy's neck with my bare hands. Not exactly a vacation."

"Seriously? You broke a guy's neck?"

"Yeah. He spit on the sidewalk."

"You're pulling my middle leg."

"Yeah. I am. The bastard was in my apartment and tried to kill me. Another guy shot at me. It was him or me. He may have been one of the bastards who murdered my Uncle Dan."

"Christ, Derek! Your uncle was murdered? Why?"

"Someone's trying to find my uncle's lab and steal his cancer research."

"Bastards! Is he near a cure?"

"I think so. But he needs some information linked with those artifacts

I found in Iraq."

"You don't say. My folks died from cancer and I've had two close calls. Fortunately, we got them early."

"Thank God for that. It seems like everyone knows someone who's died from cancer. That's why Pete and Lisa are working so hard. They think they're close. We've discovered that one of those artifacts made reference to a cure. Do you still have that sculpture I gave you?"

"Absolutely. I'd never part with it."

"Have you had it authenticated?"

"Uh, no. It's never occurred to me. Do you think it might have some link?"

"We don't know. That's why I'm calling. I've consulted an art historian. He thinks they're genuine. He'd like to examine the one I gave you and see if there's a connection."

"You bet."

"Do you have a digital camera and Internet?"

"I have teenagers, of course I do."

"Can you get some digital images and e-mail them?"

"Sure. I'll do it right now. Give me the guy's e-mail address."

Storm referred to Lawrence's business card and read the e-mail address to Starr.

"Got it, Derek. I'll take care of it."

"Great. Thanks Mike."

"You bet. Check six, wingman. I'm here if you need me."

Boston: The reorganization caused turmoil. Rushton and his cronies had displaced their adversaries from every vital national position. Melanie had been transferred from the Operations Committee to Budget & Finance. Raas passed it off as a promotion, but that was a crock of manure. It confirmed they were attempting something devious.

Melanie devoted her spare time digging into the computer files. She discovered sensitive files had been transferred to other committees and she didn't have access. The cronies had been thorough.

Melanie befriended one of the computer analysts. They were of like minds. They schemed to put a back door into the file security program. Their initial attempts proved unsuccessful and Deirdre, the analyst, nearly got caught with her hand in the cookie jar during her second attempt. It took four attempts for her to install a successful program. She was still working on a program to hack into Rushton's personal files. Melanie checked her watch. "I have to get back to my office before they get suspicious. If you find anything, make a copy and call my cell."

Deirdre nodded without glancing up.

Melanie patted her on the back and headed for her office. She was careful to avoid being spotted coming out of the computer center and once she entered the main office, she made sure she was noticed. She constantly considered alibis.

Melanie closed her office door. She sat, checked her e-mail and opened a message.

"Oh my God!"

It stated,

"Dr. Rushton hired me to break into the research laboratory of Doctors Peter and Daniel Flynn of Portland, Oregon. Rushton paid $5,000 cash on February 14th. He wanted me to steal the research materials and ransack the lab. He double-crossed me and failed to pay the other $5,000. Instead, he hired mercenaries to kill me. I've gone underground. I was given your name and e-mail as a trustworthy contact. Are you game?

Signed,

Ghost."

Las Vegas: The five-foot seven-inch mercenary stood before the assembled Bravo team. By outward appearance, he didn't seem to be what he claimed. He was short, of medium build, and his blue eyes conveyed tenderness, not determination. His soft-spoken manner reminded them of a preacher, not a mercenary. They all had doubts.

Bravo perused his credentials. "Firearms and demolitions. Do you have driving skills?"

"Oy, Colonel."

"You served with the Regiment?"

"Oy, Colonel. Seven years in the SAS," meaning the British Special Air Service, the elite British equivalent of the U.S. Army Rangers and Navy Seals.

"You don't sound Brit," challenged Trigger.

"I'm not. I'm Welsh by ancestry, born and bred in New Zealand."

"What's your code name?"

"Percy."

All, except Bravo, laughed at the sissy name.

Slash manipulated his favorite switchblade. "Why did you chose Percy for a code name?"

The man smirked at Slash. "Because I like to kick the shit out of people who make fun of it."

Not to be intimidated, Slash deftly twirled his switchblade between his skilled fingers and flipped his middle finger.

"How about hand-to-hand?" inquired Bravo.

Percy looked at the table where Bravo sat. He glanced ominously at the team, suddenly pivoted, yelled and sank into a deep squat as he hammered his fist down through the solid oak table. A jagged six-inch square broke off and ricocheted off the floor.

That caught their attention.

"Pretty impressive," complimented Trigger. "Especially for a little guy."

Percy smiled. "It's not in the muscles, mate. It's in the physical dynamics. Any more questions?"

They all nodded approvingly.

"Welcome to Bravo team... Percy."

Helendale: Storm parked Lisa's Hummer a mile away from the lab, hidden from the road. He hiked around the hills and called ahead to let Pete know he was inbound.

He crawled under the back fence, out of view from the road. He made a mental note to check the sensors that were supposed to monitor that section.

He entered through the main entrance and noticed Pete's S-10 parked much further in. With the new bay lights on, Storm could see a tunnel entrance beyond the loading dock. The entrance was perpendicular to the main loading area, in a previously dark corner. Storm hadn't noticed it before and approached it with curiosity. He peeked inside but couldn't see beyond thirty yards. It was large enough to drive a small truck through.

Pete's voice came from behind. "We saw you crawl under the fence on the closed-circuit."

"Hello Pete. Good to know it's working. What's this tunnel?"

Pete scratched his head. "I'm not sure. I discovered it yesterday. I figured I'd ask you to check it out."

"I'll do that. We need to find out where it goes. It could be a chink in the security."

"Geez. I hadn't thought of that."

They headed for the lab. The test animals were making a ruckus.

"The trip to San Fran went well, I understand."

"Yeah. Lisa's brother believes they're genuine. Unfortunately, the treatment wasn't on that tablet. He thinks there are others. We may have to go find them. I don't even know if that's possible. There's going to be another war in Iraq. Soon."

Pete nodded.

"How's the research going?"

Lisa was sitting in a chair, her injured leg propped up, studying analysis data.

"Welcome back, Derek. I missed you." She gave him a wink.

"Hello doll. I missed you too." They kissed passionately, embarrassing Pete. He cleared his throat to remind them he was still there.

"Sorry Pete," apologized Storm. Lisa wasn't sorry. She discreetly groped Storm's buttock.

"To answer your question, the research has stagnated. The DDCG enzyme works to a point, but we haven't figured out how to control the consumption rates. The mice and chimps are suffering side effects."

Lisa added, "We're missing something. We haven't been able to regulate the enzymes once they've dissolved the tumors. They're eating into healthy tissues and causing diarrhea, nausea and vomiting. The solution's too strong, but when we reduce the ratio or the dosage, it's not effective. There has to be something that can moderate the enzymes. We just haven't found it."

Storm contemplated. "Didn't you say that an increase in DDCG would stop the enzymes?"

Pete responded, "We were mistaken. It wasn't the DDCG. It must have been something else. The additional DDCG made them sick. And without it, the enzymes continue to eat into healthy tissues."

"That's why we're experimenting with mix ratios and dosages. We haven't found a balance or even know if there is one." Lisa tapped a few keys on the computer and changed the subject. "So, what did you think of my brother?"

Storm chuckled. "He's a character. He told me you were always trying to steal his boyfriends."

Lisa's jaw dropped. "That little bitch! *He* was the one trying to steal *my* boyfriends. I'll bet he even propositioned you."

Storm nodded and Pete laughed.

"Yes he did. He's not bashful, that's for sure."

"I'm not surprised. I had to have Daddy straighten him out more than once. Boy! Am I going to give him a piece of my mind?"

Storm flashed his crooked smile.

Pete cleared his throat again. "Sorry to interrupt, lovebirds. Derek, would you explore that tunnel?"

Storm kissed Lisa's forehead. "You bet. Where's the flashlight?"

Boston, Mass: Melanie reflected upon the anonymous e-mail. Was Rushton underhanded enough to do those things?

Her cell phone rang.

"Melanie. It's Deirdre. We're in, honey."

"Really? Will they be able to tell?"

"As long as we don't change any data, they won't be able to tell. I've tested it four times. I'm certain."

"You're good, Deirdre. I'm taking you out for dinner."

"Girlfriend, that sounds great."

"Can I access the files from my office?"

"Yes. Just be sure you're not in there at the same time he is. He'll be able to tell."

"Okay. How about from home?"

"No. External access is tracked by the security section. That program's in a separate partition and I haven't attacked it yet. So don't use your home computer until I tell you."

"Okay. How do I get in?"

Helendale: The tunnel was longer than Storm suspected. He estimated he had walked a mile. There were no side halls or junctions. It was a dark winding tube, crisscrossed with spider webs. The air was stagnant.

Storm was glad he had brought water. He paused to wipe his brow and take a drink. He noticed several mice scurry through the beam of his flashlight. He trained his light on them. The beam flashed across a steel framework.

Storm scanned the light, revealing a large steel door with a padlock on it. He studied its surroundings, finding an antiquated electrical panel. He followed the conduit and found it connected to a huge electric hydraulic pump, guarded by a large Black Widow.

The arachnid scampered from the light and Storm cleared its web away. He checked the hydraulic tank. The fluid was very low. Storm flipped the master lever on the electrical panel.

Several indicator lights illuminated. He located the button to start the pump and pressed it. It screeched in protest. Finally, it overcame the resistance and hummed. The pressure was very low, probably due to the low fluid quantity. Storm switched off the power to prevent the pump from burning up.

He studied the electrical panel. He brushed away the thick dust and sneezed as it invaded his nostrils. He could distinguish faded decals on the panel. One button was labeled OPEN, another CLOSE, another LOCK and another OFF.

Storm studied the door mechanism. The hydraulic actuators were connected to the bottom of the door, which appeared to open vertically and outward. He realized what the door was for. It was a secret vehicle entrance to the bunker. The good news was it was secured from the inside. The better news was that it could be used as an alternate entry or emergency escape.

Boston: Melanie saw Rushton and Raas leave for lunch. She used the opportunity to hack into Rushton's personal computer files. For fifteen minutes she scoured file after file, not finding anything suspicious. She began checking files with obscure names. Some contained personal notes, family data, schedules and appointments, contacts and inter-office memos.

The search was tedious but Melanie felt vibrant. It was exciting. She felt like a spy. She imagined being contacted by a handsome British Intelligence agent, to whom she remitted the evidence, thereby saving the republic from corruption.

Melanie opened an obscure file and noticed it contained data on off-budget expenditures. She analyzed the data. One entry was for $5,000. It was the exact date the anonymous e-mail had stated. The DESCRIPTION field was blank. The TYPE field merely stated 'cash.'

"Bingo."

Helendale: "It's an alternate entrance. It's padlocked from the inside but it's a huge steel door that operates by an electrical hydraulic pump," asserted Storm.

"Does it work?"

"Yeah. I tested it. It struggled at first but it worked."

"That must have been the power surge," suggested Lisa.

"What power surge?"

Pete answered, "About ten minutes ago we had a brownout. The lights dimmed, the generator kicked into high gear and the computers crashed."

"Oh, crap. I didn't think about that. Sorry. Are the computers okay?"

"Yeah. They rebooted without much trouble."

Storm sighed relief. "We'll have to isolate that pump from the main power before we use it again. I'll also need bolt cutters, five gallons of hydraulic fluid and a fifty-five gallon drum of WD-40."

"I'll put them on my shopping list."

"No go," said Lisa, staring at the computer screen. Pete leaned over her shoulder.

"Pete, we're at the lowest effective mix ratio and dosage, but the enzyme rates are still way too high. It's not going to work."

Pete reviewed the data and nodded. "We're stuck. It could take years to find a catalyst."

Pete and Lisa looked frustrated, so close but yet so far.

"The other tablets."

Pete shook his head. "I don't think that's an option, Derek. It's not feasible."

"Oh, it's feasible all right. I know exactly where and what to look for."

"Derek, what if there aren't any more tablets? War is imminent. Even if you could get into Iraq, how will you get out? And how do we finance it?"

"Pete, we'll never know if we don't look. They might still be there."

"After twelve years? It's not worth the risk."

"Why not? They were there seven hundred years before I found them. Another twelve shouldn't make a difference. They can't get up and run away and that wreck is in a remote part of Iraq. They're still there. I don't know how I know it, but I know they're still there."

Pete still had reservations. "Even so, how are we going to fund it? I don't have that kind of money. And neither do you."

Storm flashed his crooked smile and his eyes sparkled. "No, I don't. But I know someone who does." Storm took a swig of water. "And he *loves* a challenge."

CHAPTER XIII

DISCOVERIES

Helendale: Storm opened with one of Hale's ancestral dialects. "Comment ca va, Luc?"

"Derek, good to hear from you."

"How's retirement?"

"It suits me. I finally found something I'm exceptionally good at."

Storm laughed. "Yeah right! I've never known you to do anything less than exceptionally well. You were my best student. Have you been practicing?"

"At least four times a week. How's your studio doing?"

"Terrific. Ninety-two students. You remember Mark Long? He's a black sash now. He's running it for me while I'm on this quest."

"Mark's a good man. What quest?"

Storm explained.

"You mean those things on your mantle? Good God!" Hale's father had died of cancer in '99, as well as several of his aunts and uncles. One of his brothers was terminally ill of it. The prospect of a cure held his interest.

"Yup. That tablet makes reference to a treatment but there are subsequent tablets that describe the formula. My uncle's research has hit a wall and he thinks they might provide a clue. I have to find them."

"Sweet Jesus! You're not thinking about going back to Iraq, are you?"

"Exactly."

"You're nuts. There's gonna be another war. Troops are already on the way. Isn't one war enough for you?"

"I know, Luke. But if those tablets get destroyed, the cure could be lost forever. It's worth the risk."

There was a long silence. "You're really committed to this?"

"Luke, what quality of man would I be knowing there's a possible cure for cancer but ignoring it for my own safety?"

That struck Hale's core, just as Storm knew it would. Luke felt ashamed. What more noble motive could a man have than to risk his life for his fellow man?"

"Derek, what's your thinking?"

"I need to infiltrate into Iraq, find the tablets and exfiltrate."

"By yourself?"

"If I have to."

"You *are not* going by yourself. I'm going with you."

Storm sighed relief. "I was hoping you'd say that. There's no one I'd rather have watching my back."

"Nor you mine. Besides, retirement is boring. I could use an adrenaline rush. I'll call you back in an hour. Don't do anything without me."

Fiji: Luke stood on the helipad, gazing. His expression was blank but his sharp mind was working on a scenario thousands of miles away.

"Something wrong, boss?" asked Dave.

The weather was kicking up. Ominous dark-bottomed, cumulus clouds formed to the east. It was time for the *Vixen* to move on.

"We're fine, Dave. Something requires my attention. Please get the chopper lashed down. We'll be moving out soon."

"Aye-aye."

Luke stuffed the satellite phone into his pocket and keyed his radio.

"Skipper, this is Luke."

"Go ahead, boss."

"Have the crew assemble in the main salon in fifteen minutes. Is Mr. Kress still aboard?"

"No sir. Paul took him ashore."

"Did Amber go with them?"

"No, just Mr. Kress."

"Copy that. Is Paul back?"

"Affirmative."

"Thanks. Inform the crew. Mandatory, all hands."

∞

The salon was noisy. The crewmembers were excited, expecting another party. Amber was the last to arrive.

"All present, Mr. Hale," reported Salty.

All heads turned toward Luke.

"I've just been informed of a matter that requires my personal attention. The *Vixen* will be moving out soon. We'll be heading for Manila and then the Persian Gulf."

Gasps issued from the crew.

"The Persian Gulf!"

"There's a war coming!"

"Why?"

"What for?"

"I didn't sign up for this!"

"This isn't a warship."

"SILENCE!" boomed the Skipper. In a more temperate tone, he continued. "The ship's Master is speaking. Mr. Hale will address your concerns as soon as he explains his thoughts. Go ahead, boss."

They were appropriately shocked, and silent. The crew had never heard the Captain yell before. They looked apprehensive.

"Calm down folks. I have no intention of taking the ship into a combat zone. But I do need to get it into the Persian Gulf so I can fly the chopper ashore."

"Why is that, honey?" asked Heather.

"There are some ancient artifacts there that describe a cure for cancer. My friend Derek Storm, and I, are going to find those artifacts and get them to the States. They must be found. Derek knows exactly where they are."

"Where's that?" inquired Paul Thomas.

Luke hesitated and glanced around the table. "Southern Iraq."

There were more gasps and shaking heads.

"The ship will stand off hundreds of miles from the combat zone. Only Derek and I will fly ashore. None of you will go into harm's way. I cannot compel any of you to go, nor do I want to. Any who want to bow out, I understand and I'll respect your decision. I'll put you ashore at Manila, pay for your hotel, or I'll buy you an airline ticket to Los Angeles. It's your decision and you have until we reach Manila to decide."

"I'm staying," declared Paul.

"Me too," Caroline stated, slightly uncertain.

"I go where you do, honey," declared Heather. She rose, stood behind Luke and placed her hands on his shoulders.

"Me too, Dad," Amber yawned.

"I'll go," declared Dave.

All but two agreed. The uncertain pair elected to reach Manila before deciding.

"Skipper, you haven't said much," noted Luke.

The grizzled, retired Navy Captain grinned, stoked up a stogie and fanned the cloud. "No one on this crew is going into the Persian Gulf without me at the helm. I'm the only one with experience in the region. You couldn't pry me from this ship with a crow bar."

Luke gratefully smiled. "This is a noble undertaking. Thank you gang. You're the best crew a Master could hope for. God bless you all."

"Does this mean we get more rifle practice?" joked Paul.

Luke chuckled. "As much as you want. Any more questions?"

No one responded.

"Okay. Let's make way for Manila. I'll be on the bridge. I have planning to do."

Helendale: Storm answered his cell.

"It's Luke, lad. We're in for an adventure."

"Hoo-ah! I knew you couldn't pass up a challenge."

"I'm that predictable?"

"You're not predictable, Luke. You're dependable. There's a big difference."

"Well, thanks lad. Listen. Can you get to Manila?"

"Is that where you are now?"

"Not yet. We just weighed anchor in Fiji. We're en route. We'll pick you up there, refuel, re-supply, then head for the gulf."

"You're gonna take your ship into the gulf?"

"Unless you have a better idea."

"Me? You're the tactician and the guy with all the money. I'm just grunt trigger puller."

"You're too modest. Can you get to Manila or not?"

"Hang on." Storm held his hand over the phone and addressed Pete and Lisa. "Can we get me to Manila to rendezvous with Luke?"

Lisa nodded. "Yes. I'll call my father. You can hop one of his air freighters."

"Luke, I can get to Manila but I don't know when. I'll get back to you."

"No sweat. It'll take us five days to get there. Get me your flight info and I'll meet you there."

"How are we going to infiltrate and exfiltrate?"

"I have a helicopter. It carries two and has a cargo pod. I'm working on a plan. And I have the expert assistance of an old sea dog. We'll have it figured out before we reach the Gulf. You just get to Manila and we'll take it from there."

"Great! I'm looking forward to seeing you again, partner."

"Same here, lad."

"Okay." Storm snapped the cell closed. "It's on. He's going with me. Greater love hath no man."

Lisa was already on her cell. "Daddy. It's Lisa." She giggled at what must have been a clever response. "I miss you too. How's Mom?" She smiled and nodded.

"Daddy, I have a favor to ask." Lisa explained the situation, leaving out the parts about the car chase and her heat exhaustion. "...so, if we don't find those tablets, our research is dead. Derek knows he can find the tablets but we need to get him to Manila so he can join up with his friend. Can he hop a flight to Manila?"

Lisa beamed and nodded affirmation. She grabbed a pen and scribbled on a note pad.

"Uh-huh. Yes. Okay. I've got it, Dad. Thank you so much. What's that?"

Lisa beamed brighter. "Daddy, you are so wonderful. Thank you from all of us. Yes, he's handsome. I'm anxious for Derek and Pete to meet you. They're wonderful. I love you. Give Mom a hug and kiss for me. Bye."

"Dad said he'd be delighted to help and he's looking forward to meeting you both. He said to give him a few minutes so he can call Central Dispatch."

"He has that kind of pull?" asked Pete.

"He owns an international air freight company," stated Storm. "He has the clout."

Lisa smiled and raised one eyebrow. "I'll call Dispatch in a few minutes."

"How fortuitous."

"Daddy also said he'll contribute money for the research."

Pete and Storm were incredulous. They smiled, shook hands and both kissed Lisa's forehead.

Pete said, "You be sure to tell your father that I, we, deeply appreciate his generosity. This calls for a celebration." He hustled off to fetch some beverages.

Storm and Lisa embraced and kissed.

"Derek, I've found a real jewel in you. You be careful."

"Don't worry, Lisa. With you and Pete backing me, and Luke at my side, I'll be back before you know it."

"Luke is that good?"

Storm nodded as he stroked her face. "He's that good."

Boston: Melanie answered her cell phone.

"Melanie. It's Deirdre. Have you seen Rushton's files yet?"

"Yesterday. I found one unusual disbursement. I haven't had an opportunity since."

"Well, girlfriend, I stayed late last night. I found one peculiar file that looked like off-budget disbursements but I'm not a finance guru. You should have a look at it."

"Okay. I will. What's the file name?"

"Get this: Squash2', S-Q-U-A-S-H-2. It sounds like a racquetball schedule."

"Or a plan to suppress something."

"I couldn't make sense of it."

"Hmm. I'll check it out, Deirdre. But I can't do it until he's gone. Have you seen Raas's or Miller's files?"

"Oh yes, honey, and are they boring? Those two don't have lives. I didn't see anything suspicious. Concentrate on Rushton. My supervisor's coming. Got to go."

The connection broke abruptly. Melanie hoped that Deirdre wasn't discovered. She'd have to wait for her to call her back. She sighed, exasperated.

"Suspense is hell."

Las Vegas: "Did we get the info on the chick?"

"Yes sir. But it's not current: no employer, no current address or phone, no utility bills. She must have crawled into the same hole with Flynn. Nothing current on him either."

"Any word from Slash and Percy?" Bravo had assigned them to

keep an eye on the Foxtrot female's wrecked SUV, thinking they'd try to recover it.

"They checked in two hours ago. They searched through the wreck but they didn't find anything."

"What about Storm's computer?"

"Same shit. Password protected and encrypted."

Bravo shook his head. "What about Trigger and Yankee?" He had dispatched them to stand vigil on Storm's vehicle and apartment.

"They checked in twenty minutes ago. Nothing. And the cops still have the apartment taped off."

"Dammit!" Bravo paced the Ops Center.

"Oh, I almost forgot. The bio on Hale came through." Sparks clicked the mouse button. The printer spit out four pages.

Bravo snatched each page as it emerged. His eyebrows arched as he read the second page.

"I know who this guy is," he stated, half surprised.

Sparks looked inquisitive.

"I've never met him but he was a Special Forces NCO on an A Team whose Executive Officer executed a couple of spies without a trial. The X-O was brought up on charges and convicted by General court-martial. He went to Leavenworth. Hale was one of seven NCOs who testified. He's got ethics."

"How's he linked to Storm?"

"I don't know. They didn't serve together." He tossed the pages onto the table and rubbed his chin. "But we're gonna find out."

Boston: Melanie noticed Rushton leave early, so she wandered by his secretary's desk while she was in the restroom and glimpsed Rushton's schedule. He had a dinner appointment that evening.

"Good. I'll have an hour before anyone gets suspicious."

Deirdre's work was superb. Melanie found it easy to access the files from her office terminal, peruse their contents and not leave any trace.

As Deirdre mentioned, SQUASH2 looked unusual. There were numerous mysterious entries. They had to be off-budget disbursements. Question was, where they NOMP funds; and if so, to whom did they go and for what purpose?

There were substantial amounts listed. Several entries were allocated to an entity titled 'Bravo.' No purpose was listed. Several other disbursements went to 'GWPAC.' There was no purpose stated for it either.

"Hmmm." Melanie wished she could make a copy of that file. However, that could only be done from Rushton's terminal with his password.

Melanie copied down the pertinent info from SQUASH2 so she could close that file and search others.

A knock on her door startled her.

"Miss Taylor?"

"Who is it?"

The door opened and George, the kindly old security guard, poked his head inside.

"Just me, Miss Taylor, making my rounds. Is everything okay?"

"Oh, fine. Thanks for checking, George."

"Working late? A pretty young lady like you should be at home in the company of a good man."

Melanie smiled. "Aren't you sweet, and yes, I should go home soon. Thanks, George."

"You bet, Miss Taylor. If you'd like an escort to the parking garage, just give me a yell."

"Thanks, George. I'll take you up on that as soon as I'm done."

"Okay. Just call when you're ready." George smiled and disappeared outside the door, closing it softly.

Melanie returned to the computer. She searched several other files, finding nothing. Then an idea occurred. She opened a budget file and scrolled down. She found two entries that matched the dates and amounts of the mystery disbursements. One for 'Research' for $100,000, which corresponded with the payment to 'Bravo.' The second matched exactly a payment to 'GWPAC.'

Melanie clicked on the entry for 'Research'. Expanded data popped up.

"BoD authorizes, 23 yay-12 nay, $100,000 for investigation of viability of ParaZyme 2000 Protocol," she whispered. *"I remember this vote but what is 'Bravo,' and what does that have to do with ParaZyme 2000?"*

Melanie copied that file onto a disk and closed it. She clicked on the entry for 'GWPAC.' The expanded data appeared.

"BoD authorizes, 17 yay - 16 nay - 2 absent, $250,000 contribution to Good Works Political Action Committee."

"I don't remember this," she declared. She clicked open the meeting minutes and scanned the attendance roster. Her name was one of the two listed as absent. "No wonder. That bastard scheduled this vote while Karen Bourne and I were on vacation. Who's Good Works PAC?"

Melanie closed the minutes file and clicked open a drop menu. She selected the PAC address book and opened it. She scrolled down to Good Works PAC and clicked open the expanded data.

"Good Works PAC. Washington, D.C. Primary beneficiary: Iris Stakemore."

"That bastard! He rammed this vote through to one of the most corrupt people on the hill. No wonder he waited until Karen and I were out of town. He knew we'd vote against it."

Melanie checked her handwritten notes from SQUASH2. "And another million dollars to her, off-budget and unauthorized by the Board." She clicked open the NOMP bank account files, selected the checking account and accessed its history. She scrolled down. There it was. An electronic transfer for *two million dollars*, made on that date, to the Special Lobby account controlled by the Executive Committee, namely Rushton, Raas, and Miller. Melanie copied the file and closed it.

"What are they up to?"

She re-accessed Rushton's personal partition and called up a menu of folders. She scanned the list. She found a folder named 'Reference' and opened it. It was full of innocuous references to medical journals, by-laws, family data, birthdays, and 'Misc.' She clicked open 'Misc.'

The file contained just what it said. And one of them was titled 'Bravo.'

"Aha." She scrolled through the data. Her jaw dropped.

"No way!"

She wrote, nervous and excited at the same time. It dawned on her that the information she was reading could get her killed.

Kona, Hawaii: Kress entered a coffee shop and ordered a decaf. He chose a seat near a power outlet and a phone jack. Kress unloaded his laptop and connected it. He sipped decaf as the laptop powered up.

The e-mail alert sounded. He was astounded to see a reply from Melanie Taylor. He clicked on the message.

It stated she wanted specific information about the Flynn burglary and Rushton, facts that only the actual burglar could know. She also asked why he had chosen to contact her rather than the police.

Kress tapped out a detailed reply. He sent it into etherspace and sipped his decaf.

"Let her chew on that."

Las Vegas: The classes at Storm's studio had progressed smoothly. Mark Long ran the studio like an expert. Nine students warmed up for the afternoon class.

Storm would be pleased to know the enrollment had increased by one. A thirty-year-old computer salesman had enrolled and purchased a uniform. He informed Mark that he had had some training in the military, but he was anxious to learn San Soo. He had heard from an acquaintance that it was a practical defense art.

"Oh, who's that?" inquired Mark.

"A guy by the name of Hale," replied the new student.

"You mean Luke Hale?"

"Yeah, that's him. Do you know him?"

"You bet. He trained with us for years. He's a second-degree black belt."

"Oy. That he is, mate."

"Well, let's introduce you to the class, Percy."

Boston: "What do you mean you won't investigate?" asked Melanie. "I just informed you of evidence of major malfeasance at NOMP, with interstate implications, burglary and murder."

"Look, Miss," replied the Boston FBI agent, "those crimes aren't the FBI's jurisdiction. Our hands are tied. Call the local police."

"Well, what about the illegal political contributions? Isn't that a federal matter?"

"That falls under the Federal Elections Commission, the FEC. The FBI only investigates if the FEC files a complaint. I suggest you contact them. Sorry we can't be of help, but as I said, our hands are tied."

Melanie sighed, exasperated. "All right. I'll do that." She disconnected her cell and tossed it onto the kitchen counter, disgusted.

She was upset. She had knowledge of crimes that could get her killed and the FBI wouldn't investigate. And there was no way Portland PD or the FEC could protect her. She was out in the cold, vulnerable. She needed to talk to someone.

She dialed Deirdre's home number. There was no answer.

Melanie turned on her computer. She had four new messages. She scanned the list. She selected a message from the professed burglar. It contained details, as she had requested. Rushton's unlisted cell number was included.

Melanie assessed the details. She didn't know Rushton's cell number. He only gave it to his secretary and confidantes. She wasn't one. Melanie printed the message and got dressed.

She couldn't call Rushton's number from her home number or cell. He might have caller ID or *69. If it was his number, she didn't want him to know she had it. And if it was his number, it proved that the anonymous e-mailer had access to him.

Melanie took the printout, her keys and two quarters. She ran out of her apartment, down the stairs and out to a pay phone at the street corner. She pumped the quarters into the phone. Her heart was thumping. She dialed the number. It was answered on the fourth ring.

"Hello?"

Melanie thought she recognized Rushton's voice but she wasn't certain. She was nervous and her hands were shaking. She disguised her voice.

"Good evening, Dr. Rushton. This is Susan Smith with the Marketers Polling Service. Would you be willing to participate in our poll regarding consumer products?"

"Lady, this is an unlisted number. How did you get it?" It was definitely Rushton. She could even sense his malevolence through the connection.

"This is Doctor Ardmore Rushton, isn't it?"

"Yes, it is. I'm not interested and don't call this number again."

"Sorry for the inconvenience. Good night."

It *was* Rushton's number. And the burglar had it.

Melanie was bursting at the seams. She walked rapidly back to her apartment, crying and shaking her hands. She felt alone and vulnerable. She needed someone to protect her, comfort her. She needed a hero.

Manila, The Philippines: A pair of blue-green, smiling Irish eyes scanned the international freight terminal. Storm had just cleared the Customs desk with the pilots that had flown him from Honolulu. He thanked them and headed for the sidewalk, searching for Luke. He had no problem spotting the muscular, white man among the shorter, darker-skinned Philipinos.

"Luke!" Storm crossed the street and hugged Hale. They slapped each other on the back.

"Damn. It's good to see you, Derek."

"You too."

"How was your flight?"

"Great! I hopped one from Ontario, California to Honolulu, and another from there."

"So tell me about this new lady. What's her name?"

"Lisa Chen. She's a doctor and she's gorgeous, funny, you know… witty. Her Dad's Chinese and her Mom was a former Miss Nevada. She thinks I'm a terrific lover."

"Sounds like you're a blessed man."

"Hoo-ah."

"You're looking pretty solid."

"So do you. I'd say you've been practicing."

"Four times a week," confirmed Luke.

"Been teaching any?"

"Yes. A couple days a week the ship's mechanic and one of the deck hands train with me. I've promoted them to yellow belt. They're getting pretty good."

"Good. I want to meet them. And we'll get you cranked up for your third-degree test. Damn! I'm looking forward to open workout with you again. I miss it."

"Me too, lad. Let's head for the chopper. You must be tired. I'll fly you to my cruising retirement home."

"I get to ride *inside*, right? You're not gonna make me hang on a FAST rope, are you?" He referred to a thick line that Special Ops troops used to slide down from an airborne helicopter during tactical insertions.

Luke laughed. "No, Derek. You get to ride up front, like a big boy."

"Good. I'm getting too old for that commando stuff."

Portland: "Detectives. Sergeant Krenna."

"Hello. My name is Melanie. Please don't transfer me or put me on hold. You're the fourth person I've spoken to and I keep getting disconnected."

"Okay ma'am. How can I help you?"

"As I said, my name is Melanie, and I have information pertaining to the Flynn lab burglary and the murder of Dr. Daniel Flynn. Are you the person investigating those crimes?"

Krenna snapped his fingers at Lewis and pointed at the phone.

"Yes ma'am. I'm the lead detective. I'm going to have my partner listen in. Okay?"

"Okay."

He nodded to Lewis. "Do you mind if we record this?"

There was hesitation. "I'd prefer if you didn't. I fear for my life and I don't want my voice recorded."

"I understand, ma'am. You said your name is Melanie?"

"Yes."

"May we get your last name?"

"Just Melanie for now. I'm very scared. I hope you understand?"

"Yes, Melanie. I do. Are you in Portland? We can provide you with protection."

"No, I'm not. You can't help me, at least that way. I think I can help your investigation, but I have a question first."

"Go ahead."

"Was there a gun vault in the Flynn lab?"

Las Vegas: "You were right, Colonel," reported Percy. "Hale trained with Storm. The instructor confirmed it."

Bravo nodded. "That's the link. They're Kung Fu buddies. Maybe we can find Storm and the lab through Hale." Bravo scanned the information on Hale. He had retired from an airline job in October of 2001 and disappeared.

"Sparks, link into the Financial Crimes Network and see if there's any data on Hale. Also, check health records. See if anyone in his family has a chronic health problem or special medication needs. I want to know where this guy is, his dog's name, bowel movements, everything."

Sparks nodded and trotted off to the Ops Center.

"Good work, Percy. Go to those classes every day and see if you can learn where they are."

"Oy, Colonel."

Bravo heard the bat phone ring in the Ops Center. He heard Sparks answer it. He came running with the phone.

"Colonel, it's Hydra."

"About friggin' time." He took the phone. "This is Titan."

"Titan, this is Hydra. We're in. Check your e-mail."

"Excellent. I knew I could count on you. Thanks."

"You're welcome. Just remember, you didn't get this data from me."

"What data?"

"Exactly!" The connection went dead.

Portland: Krenna was amazed at the wealth of Melanie's information. The details confirmed that her source had first-hand knowledge. The unlisted phone number of one Doctor Ardmore Rushton of the NOMP was also significant. And the information in the NOMP computers, if it was true, indicated that Rushton had hired mercenaries to get Flynn's research.

But without printouts for evidence, it wasn't enough to obtain a search warrant.

Krenna contacted the Portland FBI and was connected with Special Agent McLarry. He related the information, emphasizing the interstate aspect in an effort to get the FBI involved.

"What do you mean, you'll take it under advisement? Interstate crimes are your jurisdiction, not to mention conspiracy, which is a federal felony." Krenna was pissed off. McLarry was spouting one lame excuse after another.

"You don't understand, Sergeant. There are... political considerations."

"What? This is bullshit."

"Sergeant, I can't speak on the record."

Krenna rolled his eyes. "Okay, Agent McLarry. Please explain it, off the record." He heard McLarry sigh.

"Okay. Off the record. Some weeks ago we received accusations from an anonymous source, linking the NOMP to the Flynn burglary. As soon as we started to dig into it, we got stuffed by the Justice Department. We were ordered to keep 'hands-off.' This certain official made it clear that any agent who violated that order would be subject to termination."

Krenna was speechless. There was a long silence.

"Sergeant, are you there?"

"Apparently not, Agent McLarry. Good day."

Las Vegas: The Bravo team gathered around Sparks at the computer. The download from Hydra seemed to have no end.

"Christ, Sparks. Won't that thing go any faster?" demanded Trigger.

"Patience, my huge Afro comrade. An artist cannot be rushed."

"Artist my ass. Picasso you ain't."

"Mate, get a grip," Percy jibed at Sparks.

"C'mon Sparks. Make that thing crank," urged Yankee.

Bravo grinned and let the banter take its course. Rushton had called the previous evening and he had nothing positive to report. His patience was wearing thin and he let Bravo have an earful.

"About time," declared Yankee.

"How many files are there, Sparks?"

"Two-dozen, Colonel."

"All right. As each file prints out, assign it to one of the men, including me. We'll see what we find."

"Yes sir."

Sparks assigned the files. Each man grabbed several and left the room.

A yell came from the den. "Got something, Colonel." Yankee came running into the Ops Room and thrust papers at the Colonel.

"What ya got?" Bravo read the information at the tip of Yankee's finger. It was a personal mailbox address in Victorville, California.

"Sparks, what file is this from?" Sparks noted the title and referenced his monitor.

"It's from the attorney's folder. It's an address book file. What's the name?"

"Basic Holding Trust."

Sparks tapped keys and clicked the mouse. Then he yelled, "Who's got the file named TRUSFIN9?"

Percy yelled back, "I do, mate. What's the fuss?"

"The Colonel needs it."

Within seconds, Percy stood before Bravo and presented him with the printout. "By your command, sir."

"Thanks Percy." Bravo studied it with Yankee looking past his shoulder.

"There Colonel," indicated Yankee. He pointed to a reference.

"Payments monthly, fifteenth each month to Basic Holding Trust from Corridor Holdings Trust." Bravo's eyebrows arched.

"Corridor. That's the name Flynn mentioned. That's it." Bravo tapped his finger on the papers and gazed into the distance. "This has to be where Flynn gets his funds. They have to be near Victorville, wherever that is. Yankee, get me a map of California."

Yankee bounded across the Ops Room, grabbed a road Atlas and opened to the California pages. He handed it to Bravo.

Bravo located the small city on the map.

"It's thirty miles south of Barstow. Now it makes sense."

He flopped the map on the table and pointed. "Vegas, Storm's home and business. Here's Victorville. Here's where we lost them after the car chase. The lab must be near Victorville."

"Makes sense, Colonel," confirmed Yankee.

Slash sauntered into the Ops room, scratching his head as he stared at his printout. "Anyone know what the hell is a *Serene Vixen?*"

CHAPTER XIV

SCHEMES

South China Sea: The storm had Salty Skibba's undivided attention. Two days out of Manila, the *Vixen* had cut across the outer edge of a tropical low-pressure area. It wasn't yet a monsoon but it had the potential. Rough twelve-foot seas battered the ship and the winds frequently gusted to sixty knots. Heavy rain poured down nearly horizontally, striking with the force of ice cubes. Occasionally it hailed. The beautiful ship heaved high on the waves and dove steeply into the troughs. The ride was quite rough.

"This'll be a hell of a blow in a few days," said the Skipper as he studied the weather fax printout. He pointed at the center of the enormous low-pressure area, eighty nautical miles southeast of their position. "See here?" He ran his finger along a high-pressure ridge, perpendicular to and southwest of the storm center.

Luke studied the printout, very familiar with its symbols from decades of aviation experience. "Looks like the upper level winds and that high-pressure ridge will steer the storm away from us. Is that the way you read it, Skipper?"

"That's my read. We'll be good by tomorrow night but the Philippines are in for a soaking. Seven knots is as fast as I dare go in these seas."

"How's the crew holding up?"

"Well, Caroline's sea-sick. She's never experienced weather like this, at sea anyway. She was pretty green around the gills last I saw her."

Luke grinned in sympathy. "So's Amber. She hasn't been out of her stateroom all day. Poor kids. How's our Dramamine supply?"

"We're good. Mrs. Hale stocked up before we left Manila."

"I'm glad she thinks about those things. All I worry about is fuel and ammo." The Skipper laughed.

Storm entered the wheelhouse from the outside. He struggled to close the hatch against the winds but finally muscled it closed. "Hoo-ah! If that were sand instead of rain, I'd think I was back in Saudi." He chuckled as he shed his dripping slicker and hung it on a rack next to the hatch.

"Why didn't you come up the interior stairs?" asked Luke. "You could have been blown overboard and no one would have known."

"What stairs?"

Hale pointed to a stairwell at the back of the wheelhouse that descended into the crew lounge. "Those stairs," he smirked.

"Oops. My bad." They chuckled. "So what's the word? Is this going to get better or worse?"

The Skipper answered. "We'll be out of this by tomorrow night. It shouldn't get much worse. We're cutting across the edge of the storm and moving away from the center."

"Good." Storm held his hand to his cheek like a startled debutante. "All this wind is raising Cain with my delicate complexion." Everyone on the bridge broke out in laughter. It was typical Storm humor.

"Keep the bow into the waves, Mr. Pell," commanded the Skipper to the young helmsman, Terry Pell.

"Aye-aye, Skipper. Steering bow into the waves."

"Have you guys had lunch yet?" asked Luke.

"Haven't had time," answered Salty.

"I'll ask Connie to whip up some sandwiches."

"That sounds great, Mr. Hale. Thanks," answered Terry.

"You bet. How about you, Skipper?"

Without looking up from his chart, the Captain answered, "Much obliged, boss. Thanks."

"Sandwiches it is. We'll be back in a few." Luke and Storm descended the inner stairwell and made their way toward the galley, jibing each other all the way.

Once they were safely out of earshot, Terry said, "Skipper?"

"Yes, Mr. Pell?"

"Are we going to be okay in the Persian Gulf?"

The Captain looked up from his chart. "We'll be fine, son. The boss won't put the ship or the crew into jeopardy. He's assured me of that. Not only that, he said he'd defer to my judgment. He won't risk us or this ship." He returned to his chart and mumbled, "I can't say that for him and Mr. Storm, though."

Victorville: Hot, brisk winds blew out of the south, sending sand and debris skyward and reducing visibility to five miles, even though there wasn't a cloud in the sky. The one hundred ten degree temperature pummeled everything exposed to it.

A gray Ford SUV and a gray Chevy Van pulled into the driveway of the Bravo team's newly relocated safe house. The single-story rental sat in a sparsely populated area near Adelanto and the former George Air Force Base. Dozens of abandoned jetliners and cargo planes could be seen parked on the huge ramp a mile away.

Slash and Percy came out of the house. Bravo had dispatched them to secure the new house.

"Welcome to your new quarters," said Slash. "Four bedrooms, two and a half baths, full kitchen *and* a pool."

"No shit?" said Yankee. "A pool?"

"Won't do you much good, mate," intoned Percy. "You've still that wound on your neck."

"Screw that. I'm going in." He noticed Bravo's stern gaze. "Right after we get the gear unloaded."

Bravo went inside with Sparks, leaving the rest to unload. Sparks dutifully kept pace behind Bravo as he assessed the layout. Bravo pointed at a nook off the kitchen. "Set up the Ops Center there, Sparks." The search for Dan Flynn's lab now had a new center of gravity.

Straight of Malacca, Malaysia: *Serene Vixen* had finally cleared the heavy seas and increased speed to eighteen knots. The ship had rounded the Malay Peninsula slightly behind schedule but all were grateful to be clear of the heaving waters. At their current speed, the motion-sickness rate was kept to a minimum. Caroline and Amber especially were grateful.

Hale and Storm were ensconced in the main salon, chugging beers and munching appetizers, watching Fox News via satellite. The reports showed the United States and Great Britain military build-up in the Gulf was well in progress. The furor over the 9-11 atrocity had fueled the war on terrorism. The reports of terrorist training camps within Iraq raised their hackles.

"Damned United Nations," swore Storm. "If it weren't for them, we would have kicked Saddam's ass out in '91. Now our boys are gonna have to go in there again. God help them."

Luke added two cents. "And you know that bastard has been providing money, weapons and sanctuary to terrorist groups. That alone justifies pounding his ass. The Weapons of Mass Destruction argument is merely gravy on the potatoes."

A loud continuous blast shattered the calm. Both jumped to their feet, startled.

"What's that?" Storm yelled over the blare.

"It's the emergency claxon. Something's wrong." Luke dashed forward through the main dining salon and outside to the stairs leading up to the wheelhouse. Storm was right on his heels.

Bullets ricocheted off the steel hull right below them. The sound of the automatic weapon that fired them followed, from the direction of the starboard bow. Hale and Storm dove for cover behind the thick steel gunwale as more projectiles peppered the hull and superstructure.

"What the hell is going on?"

"Maybe my ship doesn't meet the local zoning standards."

Several of the crew opened up with automatic weapons, returning fire. "Way to go, Salty!" yelled Luke. He bounded up the stairs. Storm was right on his tail.

Paul Thomas was at the top deck weapons locker, slamming a magazine into an FN/FAL. He tossed the rifle to Luke, who snatched it and handed it to Storm. More bullets peppered the *Vixen* and they all ducked. Thick fiberglass splinters and glass shards spewed around them. Luke saw the damage to his ship and became extremely pissed.

Paul tossed Luke's Bushmaster rifle to him and grabbed an FN/FAL for himself. He tossed spare magazines to each of the men.

"What's going on, Paul?" yelled Luke, his heart thumping, not from fear, but adrenaline.

"Pirates. I think they mean to commandeer the ship."

"Commandeer *my* ship. *Big* mistake!"

"The Skipper said they've been paralleling us for half an hour. He didn't think much of it until he saw they had weapons."

More bullets chewed up the superstructure and were answered by Hale's crew.

"All right," yelled Storm. "They want to play? Let's play!" He ran down the stairs and dove for cover behind the gunwale. Hale and Thomas followed. Hale made a quick assessment of the pirate ship. It was closing off the starboard beam. The vessel was wood and Hale spotted at least two gunners. Hale and Thomas dove behind the gunwale and spread out.

Luke yelled out his targeting plan. "On my call. Ready?"

All heads nodded as more bullets ricocheted off the hull. Dave Welch opened up from the stern of the ship with another Bushmaster.

"Now!"

In unison Storm, Hale, and Thomas popped up above the gunwale. Storm took quick aim and emptied his magazine on full auto in a single burst. The bullets tracked directly at the pirate's wheelhouse, chewing the structure into pieces. Glass shattered and wood splintered as Storm's harbingers of lethal disaffection delivered his wrath.

Likewise, Paul Thomas emptied his magazine in a single automatic burst, into the wooden hull slightly aft amidships. Wooden chunks spewed from the structure as .30 caliber rounds punished the engine compartment. Within seconds dark, oily smoke plumed from the compartment and the ship immediately lost headway.

Hale scoped the pirate gunner on the bow, estimated the boat's speed, adjusted his sight placement and squeezed the trigger once. The Bushmaster spit out a sharp crack. One fifty-five grain, supersonic messenger of death sizzled across the one hundred-seventy yard range between the two ships in .23 seconds. The hot penetrator pierced the target's left cheek and sliced into his spinal cord right below the V-2 vertebrae; it was instant death.

Hale scoped the second target even before the first one had collapsed. Another pirate stood atop the wheelhouse, nervously reloading his rifle and gaping at the carnage around him. He never finished his reload. Crack! Splat! He went down, persuaded by another of Luke's supersonic sizzlers.

Other pirates ran around excitedly. Some had weapons. One grabbed the rifle dropped by Luke's first target.

"Well Paul, you wanted more rifle practice," yelled Luke as he pointed at the pirate ship. "So practice."

Paul grinned and slammed another magazine into his rifle. All along the length of the *Vixen*, automatic rifles spit hot, copper-jacketed slugs at the pirates. Welch, Thomas, Storm, Hale, Pell and the Skipper hammered the beleaguered vessel. By the time they were done, it looked like the aftermath of the St. Valentine's Day Massacre.

The smoking rifle barrels sizzled and an acrid odor filled the air.

Luke inhaled deeply. "Damn! I love the aroma of cordite. It smells like… freedom."

The pirates had severely underestimated the tenacity of Hale's crew. It had cost them dearly. They would never pirate the high seas again.

In a Texas accent Storm yelled, "Ah want y'all to know there's a new sheriff in town. And his name is Luke Hale."

Luke grinned like a jackal. "Cocktails anyone?"

Kona, Hawaii: Kress made his daily visit to the coffee shop, bought a decaf and hooked up his computer. He was pleased to find another message from Melanie Taylor. He clicked it open.

The message stated that she had verified the information he had provided and believed that Kress was who he claimed. She had information for him if he was willing to share information with her. It also expressed her fear of being discovered and harmed.

Kress took note of her fears but he also perceived that she was anxious to learn more. He tapped out a reply, warning of political corruption that had suppressed the evidence he had sent to the Portland FBI. He sent the message into etherspace.

He enjoyed his decaf, played on his computer and watched the pretty girls go by. He thought about going on one of those submarine dives to get photos of the beautiful tropical fish.

The e-mail alert sounded. He clicked open the e-mail program and saw a reply from Melanie. He clicked it open.

It stated that Rushton had paid NOMP funds to Congresswoman Iris Stakemore, who in turn referred him to someone named 'Bravo.' Rushton then retained this Bravo to steal the ParaZyme 2000 research, then paid Stakemore an additional $1 million to suppress an FBI investigation.

"*Stakemore.*" He wasn't surprised. She had a sleazy reputation. Hushed rumors about her and her dirty PAC had been circulating for years. To date, nothing could be proven. She was too slick. So far.

"*Who is this Bravo guy?*"

Indian Ocean: The *Vixen* cruised the smooth ocean at her economical cruise speed of twenty-three knots. Storm, Hale, Welch, and Thomas were taking advantage of the smooth ride to get in a good Kung Fu workout in the gym while Heather, Amber, and Caroline exercised on the cardio machines. All seven of them were dripping with perspiration, the men sweating, the ladies glistening.

Luke respectfully deferred to Storm to run the class and he put them through a vigorous warm-up regimen. The forty-minute workout concluded with a torturous drill that Storm called 'the deck of cards.' He pulled out a deck of playing cards, shuffled them and placed them face down at his feet.

"Push-up position," he commanded. All the men dropped to the floor. "It's time for the killer. But remember, pain is just weakness leaving the body," he declared with a diabolical laugh.

Storm flipped over the first card, revealing a nine. He called out the number and in unison, they pumped out nine push-ups, counting loudly with each repetition. Storm flipped the next card and called out, "Seven." The men rolled onto their backs and executed seven stomach crunches in unison.

The next card was an Ace. "Fifteen," called out Storm, laughing like a crazy man. Welch groaned. The men rolled back to the push-up position and pumped out fifteen more push-ups. And so it went, card after card, alternating push-ups and crunches.

Halfway through the deck, Dave Welch ran out of steam and collapsed. Paul Thomas lasted another four cards.

Luke had only once ever made it through the entire deck, six years ago, at age forty-four. He hadn't been able to get out of his chair for three days after that episode. In fact, he had puked right on Storm's studio floor after he had finished.

Luke gave the drill his best effort but his left arm gave out on the forty-third card and he collapsed, exhausted. Storm laughed again between his counts.

Storm continued flipping the cards and pumping out the exercises, counting loudly with each perfect repetition. As usual, he completed the entire deck, sprang to his feet as if just getting started and yelled, "Hoo-ah." Everyone was in awe of his stamina.

"All right, lads," he said. "Get some water and lay out the mats." The men took a break to hydrate and laugh about how sore they were. Luke finished his water and pulled out the thick, blue gymnastic mats from a wall locker. Paul and Dave unfolded the mats and placed them on the floor, forming a large square.

Storm clapped his hands twice, signaling lesson time. The men gathered around him.

"Today's lesson is the Rainbow Throw. This technique works best on an adversary attacking from your flank. With the assistance of Sifu Luke, I'll demonstrate.

Storm and Hale rendered each other the informal San Soo salute, signifying respect for each other. Storm nodded and Luke launched a full-speed attack from Storm's left side. Wraith-like, Storm quickly pivoted left and crouched. He thrust both his fists into Luke's body, his uppermost fist into the solar plexus, the other into his groin. Storm yelled loudly as the punches landed, releasing explosive power.

The Double Dragon punches halted Luke's advance, knocking the wind out of him. Storm grabbed Luke's belt and jacket, kicked out his feet, dropped to the mat on his back and threw Luke over him. Luke's body arched over him and slammed onto the mat. The impact expelled what little wind Luke had left.

He was completely winded, dizzy, ears ringing and gasping for air. Storm immediately maneuvered atop Luke's back, locking his legs and neck in a submission chokehold.

Amber, Paul and Dave were shocked at the brutal slam. Heather had seen it all before and knew Luke was okay. He was turning blue, struggling for air. He tapped Storm's arm with his free hand and Storm immediately released him.

"You okay, Luke?" Hale nodded, still choking. He'd taken worse beatings from his instructor. And Storm had taken similar beatings from him. They were rugged men.

Luke caught his breath, flopped onto his back, rotated his shoulders and hips and kicked himself into an upright fighting stance, still slightly winded. He rendered a salute to Storm, who reverently returned it.

"Thank you, Sifu Luke. Catch your breath and we'll demo it in slow motion."

"I'm ready, Sifu," reported Luke, showing his Kung Fu warrior spirit to recover and fight.

Storm continued. "Excellent. Now lads, you saw Sifu Luke thrown across my supine form, his body describing an arc, like a rainbow. That's where the technique gets it name. What makes this technique work is the dynamic principle called 'drop weight.' By forcefully dropping my weight below his center of gravity and pulling his weight forward and down, taking his balance, his mass plus my drop weight plus any forward inertia from his attack are all added together synergistically, like one plus one equals three, and translated into a very violent takedown. As you saw, Sifu Luke was severely winded. That throw wasn't even full force and it wasn't on a hard surface. Imagine otherwise."

"Now, the counter to the attack is evasion. The squat and pivot into a semi-knee drop stance lowers your profile, moves your head below the plane of attack. The initial pivot also provides the power for the Double Dragon punches into the solar plexus and groin. Even if the blows don't completely halt the advance, you translate any remaining inertia into the throw. You grab his belt and his jacket above the waist, the higher the better. Then you kick out your feet and drop on your back. This pulls him off balance and then you throw him across your body and slam him to the ground. Then you follow through with submission or kill, whichever the situation demands. Sifu Luke and I will now demonstrate again in slow motion. Watch closely."

Storm nodded and Luke launched into a half-speed attack. This time, Storm responded at half-speed and paused at every critical point to explain and let the students observe. Three more slow-motion demos provided them with all of the critical knowledge to employ the technique properly.

Then Storm had the yellow belts pair up with a black belt and practice the technique slowly, emphasizing correct application rather than speed. They repeated the maneuver ten times from each side, then, when he was certain they had the concept, he paired them together to practice with each other. He could see Luke was getting beat up and wanted him to take a break.

"How you doing, old boy?"

"I'm not as young as I used to be. You rang my bell pretty good on that first takedown."

"Sorry."

"No. Don't be sorry. They have to learn to do it properly."

Storm slapped Luke on the back. "Well, it's your turn to bounce me around. You ready?"

"Yup. Let's do it."

Luke practiced the throw on Storm for five minutes before the Skipper stuck his head in the door. "Ten o'clock, boss."

"Thanks Skipper. We'll start planning in thirty minutes in the main salon."

"Aye, aye."

∞

After refreshing showers, Hale and Storm met Skibba in the main salon. The Skipper had already erected a folding table at one of the long, leather-cushioned, curved bench seats. Numerous charts, maps, tablets, calculators, and reference manuals were arrayed on the table. He had even gathered the performance data for the helicopter, saving Luke the trip.

Paul Thomas cautiously entered.

"Excuse me Mr. Hale, Skipper. Would you mind if I participate? I'd like to help."

"Absolutely Paul."

Paul smiled and took a seat next to Storm. "That was one hell of a workout, Mr. Storm."

"Thanks Paul. And call me Derek. Welcome. And thanks for offering your assistance. What's your background?"

"I was in the Navy four years, Salvage and Recovery Engineer."

"Hoo-ah! It's good to have another military mind. We've got Army, Navy, and Air Force talent, the Combined Force Concept."

The men munched on sandwiches as they began their session. Salty got right to the point. "First, what's the objective?"

Storm pulled an old land navigation map from his back left pocket. He couldn't speak with his mouth full of food. He placed the map on the table and carefully unfolded it. It was scorched and ragged along two edges. Luke recognized it.

"That's your map from the Persian Gulf War, isn't it?"

Storm swallowed. "Aye, it is." Storm pointed to a highlighted mark on the map. "This is the approximate location of the buried shipwreck, where I found the artifacts. It's about seventy miles upriver from the mouth of the Euphrates and about two hundred meters west of it. It sits in a huge bomb trench from a B-52 strike. There aren't any towns or villages within fifteen miles. It's remote."

"What's so important about these artifacts?" asked Paul.

Storm answered. "They describe an ancient Chinese treatment for cancer. I have the first of the tablets, which describes the ailment, and it makes reference to subsequent tablets that describe the treatment." Storm pulled his tablet from his rear pocket and handed it to Paul.

Paul gingerly took the tablet and studied both sides. "This is Chinese?"

"Yep. I had it translated several weeks ago by two experts. They verified its authenticity."

Luke interjected. "So, our objective is to recover the companions to this tablet and get the data back to the States. Hopefully, researchers can make use of it and develop a cure for cancer."

"I see," declared Paul, whose aunt had succumbed to the disease some years ago.

"Boss, how close do we have to get to get the chopper within range?" asked the Skipper.

"I figure we'll have the *Vixen* lay offshore southeast of Kuwait City a hundred miles or so. Derek and I will fly to the port and refuel. Then we'll fly a low-level route to the objective, try to locate the shipwreck and the artifacts, then back to Kuwait, refuel again, and then return to the ship."

"Okay," said the Skipper. "That covers the overall concept. Let's get to the specifics. First, the Persian Gulf is strewn with mines, particularly the northern end of it. We don't have any mine detecting equipment. We may not be able to get closer than a hundred fifty miles to Kuwait. That's a hell of a long way to fly a single-engine chopper over water. You sure you want to do that? You're not thirty any more, boss, no offense."

"None taken, Skipper. If that's what has to be done, then we'll just have to do it. I don't want the ship or crew put in danger. Derek and I know the risks. It's our choice."

"What about infiltration by boat?"

Luke shook his head. "Too risky. There'll likely be armed patrols on the river. And there's not much room to maneuver on the river. Evasion would be extremely difficult if we get intercepted."

"I agree," added Storm. "The Iraqi regime is paranoid and keeps the populace under control with patrols and terror squads. There's no way we'd make it past all the villages on the river without being intercepted. The terror squads are especially brutal in the southern part of the country. The Shiite Muslims aren't aligned with Saddam, who claims to be Sunni Muslim. He keeps them under his boot with thug terror squads. They're thick as mosquitoes in that area."

All heads nodded.

Luke continued. "By chopper, we can avoid populated areas and military compounds, use the whole sky for evasive tactics and alter our course as necessary. And it's faster. I think we stand a better chance airborne."

"I see your point," deferred Salty. "You know air and land warfare better than I. How can I help?"

"Your knowledge of the Gulf is extremely important. Just get us as close to Kuwait City as you deem safely feasible. The rest is up to Derek and me."

The Skipper nodded, leaned back and pulled a stogie from his breast pocket. "You got it. Now, what about logistics?"

The planning session went on for six hours, addressing a hundred considerations: weapons, ammo, fuel, water, food, counter-measures, communications, navigation, special equipment, documents, clearances, evasive tactics, tools, contingencies, outbreak of war, chemical and biological weapons.

At the conclusion of the session, Storm pulled Luke aside. "What if the Iraqi's launch jet fighters to shoot us down?"

Luke grinned and winked.

Boston: After numerous days of anxiety, Melanie decided she needed to get a grip on her fears. Her anxiety was showing at work and several co-workers had asked her what was wrong. She passed it off as a family matter.

As soon as she arrived home, she called Iowa to talk with her parents. She didn't reveal the specifics of her discoveries, but she discussed the general nature of her concerns. The conversation provided her with reinforcement from her stalwartly, honest parents.

Melanie felt fortified and supported. She elected to face the unknown and do the right thing. She dropped to her knees and prayed, something she hadn't done for several years. She sought Divine help, protection and strength to be righteous.

Melanie rose and went to her computer. She called up her Internet home page and clicked the cursor to the entry box for the search engine. She typed in FEDERAL ELECTIONS COMMISSION and hit the ENTER button.

Kona: "Tara, it's Kress."

"Well, well. Still in Fiji?"

"Nope. Hawaii. The big island."

"So when do you get back?"

"Next week. I have four days left."

"Well, there'll be a pile of work for you."

"Thanks. Just what I wanted to hear."

"So, what's up?" inquired Tara.

"I need some info on a bad guy."

"Worse than you?"

"Much! He gives pond scum a bad name."

"I see. So, what's in it for me?"

Kress sighed. "And you women call us men opportunists. What do you want, Tara?"

"Oh, let's see: flowers, dinner, Las Vegas and kinky hot sex."

Kress sighed again. "You're shameless, woman. And insatiable. What do you think I am?"

"Does the word 'stud' have any meaning?"

Kress chuckled. It wasn't often he was categorized as such. "Okay, you hussy. You win."

"Good. I plan to collect as soon as you get back."

"Not so fast, hot pants. Not until you come through on your end."

"Mmmm. I like the way you chose your words."

Kress rolled his eyes. "So, are you gonna get the information or not? My vacation clock is ticking here."

"Kress," she responded, disgusted. "You really know how to sweep a girl *onto* her feet. Give me the name."

Boston: "Finally some good news," Rushton said into his cell.

"We're close, Doc," assured Bravo. "We've located the objective's financial source and we've got a twenty-four/seven watch on it. Sooner or later, someone's gonna show, then we got 'em. It could be a couple of weeks, though. We have information that he receives his funds on the fifteenth of each month."

"Good work, Colonel. I'm looking forward to hearing more good news."

"Okay Doc. I'll keep you posted."

Rushton broke the connection.

"What's the deal, Ard?" asked Raas.

"Our operatives have traced Flynn's finances to some jerkwater town in the California desert. They have his mailbox under observation. They think he'll pick up his money on the fifteenth. We'll have to cool our jets until then."

"At least we have breathing room," noted Miller. "Our Congress critter came through. The FBI investigation is on hold."

"I wonder how she pulled that off?" said Rushton.

"Who cares, as long as she did," declared Raas. "I'm still trying to figure out why, after she was so reluctant?"

"Well," said Miller as she slowly pumped her crossed leg. "It seems a certain Congress critter has a deep, dark secret that she wants kept under the carpet."

"And what might that be?" asked Raas.

"All in good time, Doctor." She winked.

Indian Ocean: The repairs of the damage from the pirate attack had gone well. The *Vixen* had numerous dents in her steel hull from bullet impacts; there were no penetrations. The crew filled in the dents with auto body filler, sanded it and repainted the damaged sections.

The fiberglass superstructure proved to be another matter. There was a lot of glass and fiberglass to clean up. Most of the bullets had penetrated both sides of the cabin walls, so they had two holes to repair for every bullet. Some paneling and cushions inside the salons had been punctured, as well as some cabinets.

Luke assessed the finishing touches in the dining salon. The crew had been meticulous in patching the holes, but the cushions and cabinets would have to wait until they reached a port where he could have them repaired or replaced.

"Just be thankful no one was hurt," remarked Skibba as he puffed on his cigar.

"I am," said Luke. "I'm glad God's watching over us."

"How do you know that?" asked Dave Welch as he finished patching the last hole in the fiberglass.

"We don't *know* it," interjected Storm. "We *believe* it. That's why it's called 'faith.' We believe He watches over the righteous. Mind you, I'm not declaring that the Almighty has deemed me to be righteous, but merely that we are on a righteous journey for the benefit of all mankind."

"Well said, my tipsy Irish friend," jibed Luke as he slapped Storm on the back. "Let's go check out the chopper."

Storm, Hale and Skibba headed for the helipad, leaving the crew to the repair work.

They found Paul putting the finishing touches on a new paint job for Luke's chopper. The previously white and red whirlybird was now a muted tan color, with foot-high, black letters, F-N-C, stenciled on each side. The rotor blades had been sanded down to the bare metal and painted the same tan color.

"F-N-C?" asked Derek.

"Yup."

"What's that stand for?"

"That's our cover. Fox News Channel, my favorite."

"What?"

"We're gonna be disguised as journalists going to report on an archeological site. Actually, it's not far from the truth." Luke grinned and slapped the back of his hand on Storm's chest.

"Ow! You brute," Storm replied like an effeminate gay guy. "I'll slap you, bitch."

Paul gave Storm a funny look. He was still trying to adjust to Storm's unusual brand of humor.

"He's kidding," Luke said.

"Hard to tell," intoned Salty, "he's so good at it." Salty puffed his stogie while the others had a good laugh.

"Did you and Dave get those modifications done for me?" inquired Luke.

Paul nodded and wiped his hands on a rag. He walked around the chopper and the others followed. He pointed to a molded box just above the engine exhaust. "See that sponson? That's your chaff dispenser. The door is electrically activated by a switch on the console. When the door is open, the squibs are armed. They're fired by the little button Dave installed on the cyclic."

"How many chaff shots?"

"Eight. The first press fires the first squib, the second fires the second, and so on."

"What's chaff?" asked Storm.

Luke replied. "It's shredded aluminum foil bundles. When the squib fires, it blows a cloud of foil behind the chopper, making a false radar target. It confuses the pulse radars of older jet fighters and the radar or laser fusing on missiles. Theoretically, the warheads should explode behind the chopper, although it won't work against American fighter radars. But it should handle anything the Iraqi's throw at us."

Paul pointed to a bulbous fiberglass container he had molded onto the top of the tail rotor's vertical stabilizer. "That's your emitter ejector."

"Now what?" asked Storm.

Luke smiled. "Air-to-air missiles and SAMs come in two varieties, radar-guided and heat-seekers. The chaff will handle the radar missiles, these emitters provide defensive counter-measure against heat-seekers."

"So they generate heat?"

"Nope." Luke smirked. "Heat-seeker is a misnomer. They don't actually seek heat. They track very specific radio frequencies that correspond to heat from engine exhaust. So, I designed battery-powered emitters that transmit electronic signals in a very specific micron range that simulate the radio frequency of engine exhaust. It's amazing what you can order from Radio Shack." Luke took pleasure in stunning his best friend.

Paul added, "The emitter batteries are activated when they're deployed. Each one is wired to a lever in the cockpit, four emitters, four levers. When you lift the lever up, it releases a tiny drogue parachute, it drags the emitter from its tube, which closes the battery circuit and then it transmits the frequency until it floats to the ground and the battery dies, decoying the missile."

Storm nodded. "So where are the deflector shields and photon torpedoes?"

Washington, D.C.: The offices of the Federal Elections Commission were quite busy due to the ongoing House and Senate election campaigns. The entire U.S. House of Representatives, all four hundred thirty-five seats, was up for election every two years. One third of the Senate, thirty-three seats, was also on the polling block at the same time.

Sandra Dillers, supervisor of the Commission's Compliance Section, sat at her desk, which was stacked high with seven piles of documents. It was her job to oversee the federal employees who processed the waves of compliance documents of every candidate and their associated PAC's.

The job had its periods of lull, as well as periods of overwhelming activity. This was definitely one of the latter.

The noise level in the outer office was unbearable. Workers from every section yelled across the room to other sections, demanding some document or reference. Office machines whirred and clacked. PA announcements blared every few minutes and phones rang non-stop. Sandra had to close her office door to hear herself think. But her office only had single-pane windows to the outer office and much of the cacophony vibrated right through them.

Sandra methodically worked her way through the voluminous stacks. The IN piles were still four times the size of the OUT pile.

There was a knock on her door.

"Come in."

The door opened and Sandra's supervisor, Kathy Zimmerman, entered. She looked very concerned and held an 'Eyes Only' folder.

"What's up, Kathy?"

"Sandra, what does your section have on Congresswoman Stakemore and her PAC?"

"Let me check." Sandra referred to her computer and tapped a few keys. "Floyd Katz has those. Let me give him a ring."

"Please ask him to bring in all the files."

"Sure." Sandra hit the intercom button and dialed a four-digit number.

"Floyd, it's Sandra. Do you have the files for Congresswoman Stakemore and Good Works PAC?"

A response, indiscernible to Zimmerman, came through the line.

"Good," said Sandra. "Please bring all of them to my office. Thanks." She punched off the intercom. "They'll be here in a minute. What's going on?"

"I'll wait until the files get here. This needs to be kept low-profile."

"I understand. Would you like some coffee?"

"Oh. Thanks, no, hon. If I have any more coffee, my bladder will float away." She smiled courteously.

A knock on the door announced Floyd's arrival.

"Come in, Floyd."

The young federal worker poked his head in. "The Stakemore files, Ms. Dillers." He entered and handed the files to Sandra.

"Thank you, Floyd. Please close the door when you leave."

"You're welcome, Ms. Dillers. You and Ms. Zimmerman have a good day." The ladies thanked him in unison as he gently closed the door.

"What's up, Kathy?"

Zimmerman inhaled and sighed. "Sandra, we received some disturbing information last night about the Congresswoman and her PAC. The information came from anonymous sources within the National Organization of Medical Professionals, detailing huge, undeclared contributions to her PAC for illegal purposes. It's very disturbing."

Kathy handed the 'Eyes Only' folder to Sandra, who immediately opened it and read. Seconds later, she looked up with eyes as big as saucers.

Straight of Hormuz, Persian Gulf: The scenery was predominantly militaristic and industrial. Uncounted oil tankers, freighters and naval vessels from dozens of nations transited or patrolled the Gulf. The presence of U.S., Great Britain, and Saudi warships and patrol craft gave ample evidence of an upcoming conflict.

As the *Vixen* steamed northwest up the Gulf, several Saudi and American patrol boats approached the elegant motor yacht to have a look-see. The U.S. flag waved proudly from her mast, hopefully providing warm fuzzy feelings to the military personnel on the boats.

Heather, Amber and Caroline, all in tight, revealing swimsuits, manned the gunwales, blew kisses and waved to the men. The façade had the desired effect. The beautiful women disarmed the wary sailors, who waved back and blew wolf-whistles at them.

The patrol boats paced the yacht for miles so the men could ogle the beauties. Several of the American sailors made marriage proposals to the women. The ladies simply responded with waves and kisses from afar. Neither of the patrol boats attempted to stop the yacht.

Fifteen miles later, the boats sped off and were replaced by another U.S. patrol craft from the north. The façade was repeated several times as the *Vixen* transited through each sector.

The further north they motored, the denser became the sea traffic. Huge cargo vessels could be seen at each port and through his powerful binoculars, the Skipper could see tanks and Infantry vehicles being off-loaded. "There's definitely going to be another storm," commenting to Hale and Storm. "Abrams tanks, Bradley tracks, Hummers, mobile artillery pieces; this ain't no love-in."

U.S. Navy F-14 Tomcats patrolled overhead, probably flying Combat Air Patrol, CAP, to cover their carrier fleet.

"Take a look at that beauty," said Salty. He gave the binoculars to Luke and pointed to a huge ship on the northern horizon. Luke peered through the optics. It was an aircraft carrier flying U.S. colors. Luke could see aircraft launching from its catapults and choppers circling the area.

"What are the choppers for?"

"One is for Rescue, in case a catapult goes cold and dumps a jet into the sea. The other is a sub hunter. The surface Navy has a phobia about enemy subs and they go to extreme measures to keep them clear of the A-O."

Luke gave the binoculars to Storm and he looked. "God bless the U.S. Navy. What are all those ships around the carrier?"

"Various combat and support ships: missile cruisers, destroyers, tankers, supply ships. They all protect and support the carrier group."

"Which carrier is it?" asked Luke.

"I can't tell from this distance, boss. And we won't get close enough to find out. Trust me."

"How much longer until we reach station?" asked Storm.

Salty referred to the ship's master clock and his navigation chart. "We'll be on station by early morning."

Storm and Hale looked at each other.

"The chopper launches at dawn, Skipper. Please inform the crew. Derek and I have to go finalize our preparations."

"Aye, aye, sir. We'll have her ready to go."

Storm and Hale exited the wheelhouse. Salty waited for fifteen seconds for Luke to get completely out of sight and earshot. He grabbed the satellite phone, punched in a thirteen-digit number and pressed SEND. He waited two rings for an answer.

"Hello, Delores. This is Walt. How have you been?"

"Well, Walt Skibba, you old sea goat. Are you still available? I need a good sailor."

"No, Delores. I'm spoken for. The sea is my mistress, but I hope you find a worthy salt to keep you warm at night."

"You always did play hard to get," said Delores, Skibba's second ex-wife. "I miss you."

"Well, thanks, doll. I miss you, too. But I have an ulterior motive for calling."

"And what might that be?"

"I need to speak to your boss, Admiral Bennett."

CHAPTER XV

OPERATION EUREKA

Southern Iraq: Luke figured they would have twenty-five minutes of fuel to search for the shipwreck, fly back to the port and land with a reserve of ten minutes fuel. It would be tight.

"Twenty-five minutes on-station. That's not much, Derek."

"Hopefully, I'll be able to recognize the exact spot. With the GPS, we should get close enough for me to recall the exact location."

"That would depend upon how accurately you marked the map, now, wouldn't it?"

"Hey, this is Derek you're talking to."

"Okay. Don't be so… sensitive, sweet cheeks."

Storm assumed his pseudo-gay persona. "I'm going to slap you, Mister Smarty Pants."

"Sissy."

Storm chuckled.

"Time to check in."

Storm called the ship and spoke into the satellite phone. "Skipper. We're feet dry. We'll keep you posted." Storm disconnected. "They've got good data-link track on us and confirmed 'feet dry'." The code phrase informed all that the chopper was over land in hostile territory.

The low cloud cover that stretched inland from the gulf worked in their favor. It was high enough for Luke to fly comfortably at thirty feet AGL, yet low enough to discourage jet fighters from swooping down on them blindly from above. It made them a difficult target to identify visually.

As Luke flew, Storm scanned ahead with binoculars, giving Luke advance notice of Iraqi troop positions. There was quite a bit of military activity due to the impending conflict. Luke maneuvered to avoid entanglements, keeping a close eye on the terrain and the radar detector he had modified to receive military radar bandwidths.

The radio erupted with a loud transmission on the emergency frequency. "Unknown rider! Unknown rider tracking three-two-zero, low altitude, twenty-four miles north-northwest of Kuwait City V-O-R. This is Rambler zero-six on Guard. Identify."

Luke referred to his chart. "Shit! They've spotted us already."

"Who's that?"

"AWACS."

The transmission was repeated with more urgency.

"Unknown rider! This is Rambler zero-six. Identify or be engaged! You are violating the southern No-Fly Zone."

"Uh-oh. That doesn't sound good."

"It's not," confirmed Luke. "We're in the No-Fly Zone, so you can bet there's a couple of F-15's up there looking to stuff heat-seekers up our ass if we don't identify ourselves."

The radar detector audio alarm screeched and every light on its display lit up like a Christmas tree.

Without removing the binoculars from his eyes, Storm asked, "Why is that little black box screaming at us like we're about to die?"

"Must be that time of the month," Luke yelled into the intercom. The radar detector confirmed there was at least one targeting radar locked-on to the chopper. He couldn't tell if it was from an airborne interceptor or a Patriot missile site. Either way, it wasn't good news. If they didn't identify themselves, they would be splashed, shot down.

Luke transmitted. "Rambler zero-six, this is unknown rider, twenty-five northwest of Kuwait V-O-R on VHF Guard."

"Unknown rider, identify."

"This is unknown rider, call sign Foxtrot November Charlie. This is a civilian helicopter carrying journalists to an archeological site upriver. We are not armed. Negative hostile intentions. How copy?"

"Fox November Charlie, this is Rambler zero-six. State origin, destination and purpose."

"This is Fox November Charlie. Origin, Port of Kuwait, destination, archeological site seventy miles northwest the mouth of the Euphrates.

We are not armed. Negative hostile intentions. We're journalists. How copy? Over."

"This is Rambler zero-six. Do you have clearance? Authenticate Zulu-Papa."

"This is Fox November Charlie. We're civilians. Negative authentication. I say again. We're civilians and unarmed. Hold your damned fire. We're taxpayers, damn it!"

Storm laughed his ass off. "Yeah, that's good. I'm sure they'll check our status with the IRS before they blow our asses out of the sky."

Luke laughed with him. "It's worth a try."

The chopper violently rolled left as a hard, turbulent downdraft hammered it. Luke struggled with the controls, using every ounce of his skill to avoid ground collision. A loud roar vibrated through the chopper as a USAF F-15C Eagle screamed by slightly overhead. The wake of the jet's engines put the chopper out of control. Luke milked the power and the flight controls for everything they could produce, barely avoiding impact.

The chopper recovered level coordinated flight just a few feet from the ground. Luke's heart was in his throat. He had been wrong about the cloud layer protecting them from fighters.

"Rambler, this is Fox November Charlie. I hope that Eagle driver got a good V-I-D. He almost splashed us with his jet wash. Don't do that again. We're civilians in an unarmed civilian chopper. Tell the fighter jock KNOCK IT OFF and SEPARATE."

Having been a fighter pilot himself, Luke used their standard lexicon. 'Splash' means an air-to-air kill. 'Jet wash' referred to wake turbulence. 'Knock it off' signified the end of an engagement. 'Separate' meant to fly away from the target. 'VID' meant visual identification.

The F-15 circled to the south beneath the cloud layer, preparing to make another pass.

"Fox November, this is Rambler zero-six. Copy. We have V-I-D. Break. Mustang four-one, V-I-D complete, separate, vector two-niner-five, climb angels base minus four."

The last they saw of the F-15, it had abruptly leveled its wings and surged up into the cloud layer, two miles south of them.

"What was all that gibberish?"

"The Weapons Director told him to separate, fly heading 295 degrees and climb to some specific altitude."

"So it's all over?"

"It's all over."

"Good. I need to change underwear."

Luke sniffed the air. "Yeah, you do."

The radio crackled again. "Fox November Charlie. This is Rambler zero-six. V-I-D confirms non-hostile. Contact Rambler two-four on one-three-three point one-five, squawk mode three, six-four-two-five for flight following. Good luck."

Luke scribbled the numbers on the windscreen with a grease pencil and responded, "Fox November, contact Rambler two-four on one-three-three point one-five and squawk six-four-two-five. Thanks, zero-six, Fox November, out."

Luke switched on his transponder and set the Mode 3 code at 6425 and then tuned his VHF COM radio to 133.15 Mega Hertz. He pressed the transmit button.

"Rambler two-four, Rambler two-four, this is Foxtrot November Charlie, thirty northwest of Kuwait VOR, in the weeds. Request flight following."

"Roger, Fox November. This is Rambler two-four, radar contact. I have your request and will provide flight following, time permitting."

"Thank you much, Rambler." He addressed Storm via intercom. "We've got a guardian angel."

"Well, that was fun." Storm continued his scan.

"Yeah. It was."

"And now I know why you fighter jocks are bald. It's all the close calls. Picture it, the autopsy reports would have read CAUSE OF DEATH: DIRT. Those fighter jocks are pretty good, zipping around down here at five hundred miles an hour."

"They're the best," confirmed Luke. "Doesn't matter what branch, Air Force, Navy, Marines, Army. All of our aviators are superbly trained, disciplined and bold. Manly men."

"That was an impressive save on your part, too," complimented Storm.

"Yep. I'm one of the best," said Luke without a hint of modesty. Fact be known, he was.

They intercepted the Euphrates, zigged and zagged upriver, steadily closing on the objective. Forty miles to go to a seven hundred year old metal tablet inscribed with the medical hope of mankind.

A pair of dark brown eyes beneath a bushy unibrow forehead peered through Russian-made binoculars at an odd-looking helicopter several miles distant. It was flying away. The owner of the dark eyes put down his optics, shouldered his AK-47 and picked up a field telephone. He made a report to his headquarters, in Arabic.

Persian Gulf: The *Vixen*'s wheelhouse was crowded but quiet. Nerves were on edge.

"Where are they?" asked Heather, looking past the Skipper's arm at the data-link display. She could see the display but couldn't interpret it.

"About two miles from the objective," answered Skibba. "They've passed the exact coordinates twice in the last ten minutes. Looks like they're still searching. The chopper's been going back and forth in a search pattern for…" he referred to his watch, "sixteen minutes."

Amber took her mother's hand and rested her head on her shoulder. "They'll be okay, Mom," she said, not totally convinced herself.

"They just stopped," noted Salty.

"They've landed?"

"Can't tell, Mrs. Hale. They could be hovering."

"Why?" wondered Amber, aloud.

"Could be they're at the spot, but maybe they aren't certain." The Skipper didn't mention the other consideration. They could be trying to hide.

Southern Iraq: The hot, gusty afternoon winds had kicked up, making the air turbulent and reducing the visibility to two miles. The cloud cover had evaporated as they moved inland. Luke skillfully eased the controls, constantly adjusting to keep the chopper on an even keel.

Storm thought it would be easy to identify the bomb trench he had been stranded in during '91. Unfortunately, the area was strewn with dozens of long, deep bomb trenches, remnants of the massive B-52 and B-1 bomber strikes during the Persian Gulf War. For thirty-eight days, coalition bombers pounded Iraqi Army positions in this area, shaping the battlefield in preparation for the ground offensive. The massive carpet-bombing campaign had accomplished its purpose, evidenced by the short, one hundred hour ground offensive.

The bomb trenches looked amazingly similar, the area was pockmarked with them, some overlapping others.

"How much time left?" asked Storm.

"Nine minutes."

Storm shook his head and continued his search.

The minutes ticked by, exhausting work for Luke, a frustrating search for Storm. The fuel quantity gauge kept creeping lower. As long as the engine was running, time was their adversary.

As much as the fuel, Luke was concerned about the amount of sand being ingested by the engine. He constantly monitored the engine and gearbox RPM, temperatures and torque. He had noticed a distinct degradation of performance during the past hour but didn't mention it to Storm. He wanted him focusing on the objective.

"Water," said Luke via intercom. He didn't dare remove his hands from the controls in the gusty winds. Storm grabbed a plastic tube and stuffed it into Luke's open mouth. The tube was connected to a five-gallon water container beneath Storm's seat. Luke sucked the refreshing liquid, taking a large portion and nodded for Storm to remove it.

Luke was getting muscle cramps in his legs.

"Derek, I'm gonna set down in this trench for a minute. I need to stretch my legs." Storm nodded and Luke eased the chopper down below the rim of the elongated crater. Once below the rim, the stiff winds abated, but the rotor downwash kicked up a maelstrom of sand, obscuring the visibility. Luke focused intently, trying to determine their altitude above the ground. It was like flying in a bowl of cream soup.

Finally, the chopper touched down and Luke cut the power to idle. They removed their headsets, unbuckled and climbed out. The temperature was over a hundred degrees. They were drenched with perspiration. Sand crusted around their eyes, noses and mouths.

"You sure know how to pick a vacation spot," yelled Luke above the engine noise. Storm smiled and gave him an 'okay' sign.

They stretched, took a suck of water and climbed back in. Luke revved the engine, kicking up the maelstrom again. The chopper got airborne and they resumed their search.

Storm checked his watch. They were out of time.

"Damn it," he yelled into the intercom. "We're at bingo time. Luke glanced at the clock and the fuel gauge. Derek was right.

"We'll give it five more minutes. That will only leave us a five-minute reserve. I'm okay with it if you are."

Storm nodded.

Persian Gulf: Things were tense on the bridge. All hands were gathered in the wheelhouse, eager for updates. The suspense made the air thick.

"They're moving again." Salty checked his watch and monitored the GPS display. He pressed buttons on its control panel and studied the data. He checked his watch again.

"They're still moving north."

"How much time do they have left?" asked Amber.

"None." Heather chewed her nails.

"Are they headed back yet?" asked Paul.

"Nope. Still headed north."

"Maybe they lost track of time," posed Caroline. "Should we call them?"

The Skipper pulled a cigar from his pocket. "Young lady, that's Luke Hale you're talking about. He and Mr. Storm know exactly what time it is. And even though we don't know what they're doing, they do. It wouldn't be a good idea to try cooking in their kitchen."

"Oh." Caroline got the message.

Paul eased close to the Skipper and whispered, "They're cutting into their fuel reserve."

The Skipper blew a cloud of smoke. "I know."

Southern Iraq: Luke climbed the chopper to 200 feet AGL, giving Storm a better view of the terrain. Each minute clicked by with excruciating speed, thinning their margin for safe return.

The clock ticked into their fifth minute, their frustration grew. Forty seconds left, only enough time to check one, maybe two more bomb trenches. The next trench was void. Hale continued north, heading for the next one, twenty seconds remaining.

"Fifteen seconds," yelled Hale. Storm focused on the next trench, eager to see its bottom.

"Ten seconds."

The far end came into view. Each second they flew north, more of the trench was exposed. Storm could see about half of the bottom.

"Five seconds. Three, two, one, time's up."

Storm slapped Hale on the shoulder. He pointed into the trench, slightly ahead and left. An armored personnel carrier lie on its side inside the trench. Storm smiled widely and nodded. "That's it!"

Luke descended the helicopter into the trench, swirling another maelstrom of sand. He set the copter down gently. Storm was unbuckled and outside before the skids touched ground.

He ran full speed to the capsized track as Luke let the chopper idle. Sand was piled halfway up both sides of the Bradley. Storm brushed away the crust from the front corner, exposing an identification number.

It was his old Bradley. "*Thank God*." He waved at Luke and flashed a thumb up.

Luke shut down the engine, unbuckled and ran to the damaged Bradley.

"That's it, Luke! My old squad vehicle! We found it!" Hale had never seen Storm so excited. Storm wrapped his arms around Hale and lifted him off the ground. They smiled and laughed.

"This is where you were stranded?"

"Yup!"

"You sure know how to pick 'em. I hope you have better taste in women."

"Let's get the equipment. The ship should be right over there." Storm pointed to a pile of wooden rubble, partly covered by sand, sixty yards west of the track.

"That pile of sticks is the Chinese ship?"

"Part of it. Trust me." Storm ran back to the chopper.

Hale walked.

Persian Gulf: The satellite phone rang. All hands crowded around. "This is Skibba."

His concerned look turned into a smile. "That's good to hear, boss. I'll let everyone know." He called out loudly, "They found the site. They're safe and the chopper's in good shape."

A cheer roared through the wheelhouse.

"Did you hear that, boss?" He smiled and nodded. "Very good. We'll be standing by." The Skipper put the phone down and announced, "They're in the right place. They're starting to dig."

Another round of cheers blasted the wheelhouse.

Southern Iraq: Twelve years of wind and sand had reclaimed the entire shipwreck. The western embankment of the trench had eroded and collapsed, enveloping the boat again. Not a piece of it was exposed, other than the parts Storm had used as a signal fire. But Storm knew its location in relation to the Bradley and the pile of burned wood.

Luke took a minute to call the ship and apprise them of their status. Then he helped Storm unload the gear. Once they had their weapons ready, Hale informed Storm that he was going to tend to the chopper. Sand had to be cleared from the filters, oil and coolant levels checked and replenished and sand cleared from the cockpit. Once he got into it, Luke was alarmed at how dirty the oil and gearbox fluids looked. They would have to be completely purged and replaced as soon as they returned to the ship.

As Hale worked on their transport, Storm dug furiously at the site. It was backbreaking work, one shovel-full at a time.

Knowing they were in hostile territory, Luke kept a sharp vigil. He knew there would be no respite for them should they be captured. They would be relentlessly tortured and executed as spies. The current Iraqi regime was notorious for its abuses.

When he finished servicing the chopper, Luke shouldered his Bushmaster and climbed to the rim of the trench. He scanned the horizon but the visibility was only three to four miles, depending on which direction he looked. There wasn't much to see.

Reasonably certain they were unobserved, Hale descended into the trench. Storm had managed to move five or six cubic yards of sand by himself. Luke plunged his shovel into the sand and struck something solid. It turned out to be a rock.

Storm plunged his shovel in. It hit something solid also, but he sensed it was something other than a rock. He glanced at Luke, his eyes gleamed with hope. He shoveled aside more sand and exposed a thick, rotted, dark piece of wood. It had obviously been shaped by hand.

"That's the ship," said Storm. Luke scooped more sand. In minutes, they could distinguish a definite shape to the object.

Hale scooped away more sand, exposing part of another plank, a wider, thicker one. There were characters carved into the wood, oriental characters.

"I didn't notice that before."

Luke dropped the shovel and grabbed the digital camera from his pocket. He took images of the characters from several angles. He connected the camera to the satellite phone and dialed the connection for his powerful Mac computer in his office stateroom on the ship. He transferred the image data via satellite.

Storm studied the images in the digital camera. "I wonder what it says?"

Persian Gulf: The crew anxiously crowded around Caroline as she entered the wheelhouse, yelling about the digital images.

Caroline and Amber had run down to Luke's stateroom office as soon as they received word that he was transmitting. Amber sat at Luke's computer and printed out dozens of copies of the images of Storm standing at the stern of the ship, and close-ups of the bold, elaborate characters engraved into the wood.

Caroline passed out the photos, enjoying the oohs and aahs of her shipmates as they caught their first glimpses of what Hale and Storm were seeing first-hand.

"Well, I'll be damned," declared Salty. "They actually found it."

"They sure did!" exclaimed Terry Pell.

"That's amazing."

"A seven hundred year old ship. Imagine."

"Incredible."

The comments carried on for minutes, disrupting the wheelhouse. The Skipper had to put his foot down to regain order. "All right, people. Everyone grab a few photos and man your posts. We still have people behind enemy lines and a ship to run."

The crewmen didn't argue. Dutifully, they cleared the bridge and paraded off, images in hand. They were all excited, joyous, feeling privileged to be part of what could be the most significant medical discovery of mankind.

Heather still chewed her nails.

Southern Iraq: Hale and Storm exposed more of the ship. They shoveled for an hour in the one hundred degree heat without stopping. Then they took a water break. Luke wiped the sweat from his brow. They guzzled more water and fanned themselves.

"This heat is a bitch. Was it like this when you were in the war?"

"No. It was mostly cold."

"Well, let's get that tablet and go home."

"Amen, brother."

They gulped more water and plunged back into their dig. It didn't take long for Storm to recognize something.

"See that corner piece?"

"Yeah. You recognize it?"

"It's the doorframe to the aft cabin."

"Is that good?"

"You bet," assured Storm. "That's where I found the wooden chest."

"What wooden chest?"

"The little box that had the artifacts in it."

"You mean it's right in there?"

"Yup. We just have to dig it out."

"All right. Let's kick this pig and make beer call." They dug rapidly, alternating their plunges and throws, quickly displacing years of built-up sand. Their shovels hit more solid objects; planks, separated from the ribs of the hull.

"More to the right," instructed Storm. "The box should be a few feet more in that direction." He pointed. They laboriously shoveled away more sand. They dripped with perspiration, panted and wiped their brows with their hats and sleeves.

The digging became more difficult; sand from the embankment slid down and filled the space they had just cleared.

"Derek, let's take some of those planks…"

"… and brace the bank," finished Storm. "I was thinking the same thing."

The men dropped their shovels and hefted a large plank. It took the efforts of both to lift the board, set it into place and secure it above the excavation. They secured six planks into place and resumed shoveling.

Minutes later, Storm's shovel hit another solid object, but softer than the planks. His eyes got wide and he grinned. Storm plunged to his knees and dug with his hands as Luke removed his hat and wiped his brow. Storm relentlessly scooped handfuls of sand away from the object. His fingers struck the object. It felt like wood. He dug and scooped with renewed vigor, exposing an object made of wood, a lighter shade than the ship planks.

Storm scooped away more sand, exposing a metal fitting attached to the wood. Storm scooped and brushed away more sand, his hands hot from the effort. The metal fitting was an ornate corner piece nailed to the wood. With each scoop, more dimensions were revealed. Storm plunged both arms elbow deep into the hot sand, grabbed hold of the box and pulled it free.

"Hoo-ah!"

"All right!"

Storm set the chest on the ground and they ran their hands over it. They were awed. They were touching history, more than seven hundred years of it.

The wooden chest appeared plain, but the metal clasps, hinges and corner fittings were ornately shaped and engraved. Luke noticed slats missing from the back.

"Looks like some one broke into it already."

"Yeah, me. I used those slats to splint my broken arm. That's when I found the artifacts."

"Well, are you going to check inside or just stare at it?" S m i l i n g, Storm tipped the box and shook it. Some rotted cloth and rough, colored stones poured out with the sand. Luke gathered the stones and Storm shook the chest again. A jade piece fell out. Something else, something heavy and dense, rattled inside.

Luke examined the stones, uncertain of their type or value and stuffed them into his vest pocket. Storm tossed him the jade piece and he tucked that away too.

Storm looked up. "The moment of truth." Luke readied his digital camera as Storm reached inside. He felt something metal. It was solid and dense and approximately the same feel and dimensions of the original tablet. He twisted his wrist several ways, trying to position it so he could remove it through the hole. Out came a sand encrusted, foot-long, four-inch wide, half-inch thick slab of metal. Storm brushed and blew the sand from both sides, which were covered with inscriptions. The characters were very similar to the ones on the original. Storm reached inside the chest. It was empty.

Storm held up the tablet like a trophy he had just won. "Eureka!"

Hale snapped digital images of Storm, the derelict vessel and close-ups of both sides of the tablet. "I hope that's what we think it is, partner."

"Me too."

They laughed and smiled, patted each other on the back and reveled in their good fortune.

Luke pondered. "Ever wondered how a thirteenth century Chinese junk came to be buried in Iraq?"

"Lots. But I never lost sleep over it." Storm tucked the tablet in his safari vest.

"I'll notify the ship and transmit the data."

"Great. I'll start loading the gear."

Hale connected the digital camera to the satellite phone and transmitted as Storm packed their equipment. He shuttled back to the chopper, having to walk past his old Bradley. The sad memory of his fallen comrades plagued him. He fought the urge to look inside it, knowing the bodies had been recovered, returned to the States and received military hero funerals.

Storm grabbed another load of gear. Luke was still in the middle of his data transmission. As Storm lifted the equipment, a dozen spits of sand exploded around his feet and the distinctive thwa-thwa-thwa of an AK-47 on full auto-fire pierced the calm. Hale and Storm jumped in place and turned to face the noisy gunfire. They found themselves eighty yards from an Iraqi Army Sergeant holding a smoking AK. And he had four of his buddies for company.

Persian Gulf: Amber was excited. She heard Caroline enter the stateroom behind her.

"Caroline, my Dad's sending new data. Look at these images."

Caroline peered at the new images on the huge monitor. They were clear, colorful and highly defined.

"Wow. Look at that."

"Incredible, isn't it? They're seven hundred years old. I've never touched anything that old, have you?"

"Only my great grandfather," joked Caroline.

The data stream flowed for several minutes. Amber processed the images as quickly as they completed download. She printed the images by the dozens.

Caroline grabbed a stack and headed out the door to distribute them.

"Uh, oh!"

Caroline stopped abruptly and returned to the office.

"What's wrong?"

"I don't know. The download just stopped in the middle of transmission. It didn't finish. The connection is still active."

"Computer malfunction?"

"No. No error messages. The data stream just stopped." They looked at each other, anxious.

Southern Iraq: "Damn. I forgot to check in with Immigration. Did you do it?" asked Storm sarcastically.

"Slipped my mind, lad. Maybe that's why they're pissed?"

The Sergeant yelled at them in Arabic, which neither of them understood. Storm and Hale looked at each other, shrugged their shoulders and pretended that nothing was amiss.

The Sergeant yelled again. Storm and Hale shrugged their shoulders and put on their dumb faces. The Sergeant fired another warning shot past them and the soldiers advanced at a fast pace. The Sergeant pointed his rifle at Luke's satellite phone and then at the ground.

"I think he wants you to drop the phone, Luke."

Luke pointed at the phone, the Sergeant again yelled and signaled him to drop it. He did. The wire connecting the phone to the digital camera disconnected and dangled from Luke's pocket.

These soldiers had little training in taking custody of hostile prisoners. They advanced on the Americans, mistake number one, in a tight, line-abreast rank, mistake number two, made no attempt to split, mistake number three, nor flank them, mistake number four.

The soldiers closed within ten yards. Storm and Hale avoided making any abrupt moves, even though their rifles were within arm's reach, out of sight.

The squad leader said something to his men. One of them gave him a furtive look and hesitantly lowered his rifle, slung it over his shoulder, muzzle up and raised his hands in the air; mistake number five.

"Oh, look," laughed Storm. "He's surrendering."

"I believe you're right, lad. Let's graciously accept his surrender and relieve him of his rifle."

Hale and Storm walked casually toward the soldiers, smiling, closing to seven yards before the Sergeant yelled again. They were at optimum range. The soldier with the raised arms pumped them down and up again, repeating what the Sergeant said.

"I think they want us to raise our hands," said Storm. He glanced at Luke, his eyes twinkled a tacit message.

"I've got the two on the right," said Luke, smiling at them.

Hale and Storm slowly raised their hands and placed them behind their heads. The Sergeant said something to his men. Two more of them shouldered their rifles and advanced.

"How about now?" asked Luke quietly, through tightly clenched, smiling teeth.

"Okay. Now!"

With amazing speed, both San Soo warriors crouched low, reached into hidden sheaths in the neckbands of their vests and extracted a shaken in each hand. They simultaneously launched the sharpened steel throwing spikes at their four respective targets. The balanced throwing spikes split the air with fierce velocity.

Storm's right shaken caught the Sergeant completely off guard, penetrated his left eye and disappeared into his skull. He dropped backward, lifeless. Storm's left shaken pierced deeply into the second soldier's throat. The man tried to yell, but his larynx was pierced. He dropped his rifle, grabbed his throat and staggered, gurgling loudly.

Hale's right shaken sank deeply into the groin of the third soldier, who screamed in agony, dropped to his knees, grabbed at his mutilated genitals and doubled over. His left shaken missed his intended target, striking two inches high, into the bladder of the fourth soldier. Hale made a mental note to practice his left-handed throwing skills. The wounded soldier grabbed at the spike, but it was buried too deeply to be removed without surgery. He collapsed to his knees, down to a shoulder and then curled into a ball, screaming in agony.

The fifth soldier, caught with his arms up and rifle slung, got a close up inspection of Storm's right boot. Storm closed the distance in two seconds and launched into a flying roundhouse kick. His boot made solid contact with the man's face, emitting a spine-tingling 'thwock'. Hale heard the man's neck snap. The soldier went down, most likely dead; Storm just had that effect on some people.

Luke engaged in 'follow-through.' Hale drew his Colt .45 ACP from a hidden holster. He rapid-fired two rounds into the staggering soldier, pumped two into the kneeling one, and then two into the one balled up around his groin. Americans, five; Iraqis, zero.

Bullets sprayed the sand around Hale as the staccato of machinegun fire echoed through the trench. One bullet creased his left calf as he dove for cover behind the sand pile he and Storm had created. A truck with a fixed-mount machinegun, five hundred meters away, atop the eastern rim of the trench, hammered away at them.

Storm ran a zigzag pattern toward the capsized Bradley. Bullets sprayed the sand and rocks at his feet, flinging stone splinters into his legs. He dove behind the destroyed track. "Shit!" He crawled to the far end and peeked around the corner. The gunner opened up on him again. Storm rolled back behind cover.

"Hey, Luke! You want a piece of this?"

"Nope," yelled the former Green Beret and then murmured to himself, "I want all of it."

"*What the…?*" It wasn't like Luke to turn down some action. "*What's he up to?*"

Hale grabbed his Bushmaster and peeked around the sand pile. He saw the Iraqi gunner peppering the Bradley, keeping Storm pinned down. Luke raised his rifle and thumbed off the safety. He had to take out that gunner before he nailed Storm or shot up the chopper.

Luke scoped center-mass on the enemy gunner. He adjusted his breathing and carefully squeezed the trigger. Just as he squeezed, the target moved rapidly from the view of his scope. His shot missed. He looked over the scope. The truck was on the move, closing fast along the eastern rim of the trench. They were attempting to flank them. The gunner continued to spray rounds at Storm as the truck kicked up a huge dust cloud.

Luke revised his plan. He scoped the driver and rapid-fired nine rounds. He saw his supersonic messengers impact in a tight pattern on the truck's windshield. The vehicle slowed rapidly, turned toward the rim and its front wheels went over the edge. The truck hung there, suspended by the sand, its rear wheels spinning.

Luke scoped the gunner's head and squeezed off four rounds. The last three proved unnecessary.

"Got him!"

"About time, you old fart." Storm jumped to his feet and brushed himself off. The measure was more symbolic than substantive. He still looked filthy.

"Quit grousing and suck it up."

"Your Mama."

"Wimp."

The buddies walked to each other, hugged and slapped backs.

"Let's get the hell out of here before the Islamic Jihad show up," recommended Storm.

"Are you okay?"

"Yeah, nothing serious. How about you?"

"Ah, he winged my leg but we don't have time for a pity party. Let's round up the phone and the weapons and get going. You've got the tablet, right?"

Storm patted his vest pocket. "Let's go." Storm grabbed the satellite phone and his rifle. "What about the other gear?"

"Leave it. Another patrol could be here any minute." Luke limped to the chopper and strapped in. He cranked the engine without doing any preflight. He felt like they were on borrowed time.

Storm secured Luke's rifle behind their seats and held his in his lap. The chopper was airborne in two minutes, rotated to a heading of 145 degrees and climbed above the sand maelstrom and the trench. Luke cruised the chopper at its most economical speed at thirty feet AGL, making their way toward freedom.

"Call the ship. Let them know our status, then hook up the camera and retransmit the imagery data."

"Right." Storm reached into Luke's leg pocket and grabbed the camera. He notified the *Vixen* and relayed the digital images as Hale coordinated on the radio with the AWACS.

"I have one suggestion," stated Storm.

"What's that?"

"We need to work on your left-handed throwing skills." Storm smirked.

Luke flashed him an ungracious finger.

Persian Gulf: Paul couldn't take his eyes off of the GPS display.

"*What's taking them so long?*" He was growing concerned. He knew they had found the tablet and contacted the ship, but they hadn't moved from the excavation site. At least, the chopper hadn't. And Amber said the data transmission had been interrupted mid-stream but the satellite connection was still open. They weren't answering the phone. Something was wrong. But what?

Paul stared at the display, praying for sign of movement. It was like trying to locate a stationary fly on a piece of raisin bread. He refused to believe that Luke had been killed, or worse, captured. It couldn't be. It mustn't be. Luke had risked his life and his ship to save him from the DEA thugs in Cabo. Who knows what horrors he would have been subjected to in a Mexican prison. He owed Luke, big time.

It moved! He saw the symbol move. The chopper symbol and the data block flashed three times, indicating a change of status. The chopper was in motion again.

"They're airborne!" A loud cheer boomed in the wheelhouse. High fives slapped and shouts of relief predominated.

The Skipper walked to Paul's side, looked over his shoulder and confirmed the data.

"This calls for a cigar." The fair warning cleared out half the crew, as usual. Salty stoked another of his Cuban luxuries.

The satellite phone rang. Paul beat the Skipper to it.

"Vixen. Go ahead." He heard the chopper's thwopping rhythm in the background.

"Hello, Paul. It's Derek. We're airborne. We should be clear of hostile territory in seventy minutes. We have the tablet."

"It's them. They have the tablet and they're on the way out!" There were more shouts. "Are you guys okay?"

"We're both slightly wounded. Nothing serious. We'll be okay."

"Wounded by what?"

"Wounded? Who was wounded?" demanded Heather.

"Bullets. What else?" answered Storm.

"They're okay, Mrs. Hale. Mr. Storm says it's not serious."

Heather gave him a look that could have frozen a volcano. "Give me the phone, Paul."

Realizing he was no match for Heather's potential wrath, he handed it over.

"Derek, it's Heather. Who's wounded?"

"We both are, but they're just scratches. Nothing that a couple of band-aids can't fix. Really. Forget I mentioned it."

"You better not be lying to me Derek, or I'll have you neutered."

"Ouch. You sure know hospitality," Storm responded, laughing. "Really. We're both okay, Heather. And stop chewing your nails."

Heather took her hand from her mouth.

Storm asked, "Is the Skipper there?"

"Luke's okay?"

"For the last time, he's fine. Who do you think is flying this chopper?"

Heather relented and handed the phone to the Skipper.

"Skibba."

"Howdy, Skipper. It's Derek. We're airborne."

"So we heard. When you get back you can tell us your war story."

"Will do. But right now, make sure the computer's cranked up. I'm gonna retransmit the imagery data. We should be clear of hostile ground in a little over an hour. We'll call you when we reach safe airspace."

"Copy that. The computer's good to go. We'll be standing by. Watch your asses."

"I'd rather watch Amber's."

The Skipper rolled his eyes. He hit the intercom button for Luke's office. "Miss Hale, the satellite data is coming through. Your father is on his way home."

"Thank God! We're ready."

Southern Iraq: The radar detector screeched a loud, low pulse rate tone. It's display lit up like a department store window.

"Shit! Radar lock!" Storm and Hale scanned the horizon.

Luke transmitted. "Rambler two-four, this is Fox November. We're radar-locked. Is there a friendly on us?"

"Negative, Fox November. No airborne friendlies or hostiles in your sector. Keep me posted."

"Roger that." Luke hit the chaff dispenser button once, blowing a chaff cloud behind the helicopter and then he randomly changed his heading and altitude every five seconds. His counter-measure and evasive maneuvers worked. The targeting radar lost its lock-on and the detector went silent and blank. Luke continued his evasive tactics for another minute, dispensed another chaff bundle at 200 feet and swooped the chopper back down to thirty feet.

"How much farther?" He had delegated navigation responsibility to Storm while he concentrated on the evasive maneuvers.

"Thirty-two miles to the Kuwaiti border."

"That would be one hell of a hike if they nailed us."

"No kidding."

The radar detector screeched again.

"Shit!" Luke climbed the chopper, popped the third chaff bundle, changed course again and descended rapidly to twenty feet. The radar didn't break lock this time. The detector continued screeching. Hale popped the fourth bundle and changed course and climbed to one hundred feet. It had no effect.

The detector went into frenzy, the pulse rate increased to a fast pace and the pitch frequency increased.

"SAM launch!" yelled Hale. "Find it!" He dispensed the fifth chaff bundle and descended to ten feet and changed heading, pushing the chopper to maximum speed.

Storm spotted a smoke trail coming at them from their left rear, low on the horizon. "Left eight o'clock, Luke. Closing fast."

Luke banked hard left to face the missile. A second smoke trail appeared in the distance from the same direction.

"Second launch!" yelled Storm.

Luke didn't answer. His heart was pumping overtime. His adrenaline surged. Luke steeled his nerves and focused intently on the first missile, which was closing at Mach two.

"It's coming right at us," said Storm, calmly. He had absolute faith in his buddy.

"Easy lad. Not yet." Luke's mental calculator clicked off the precise timing necessary. "Hang on!"

Luke whipped the chopper into a violent right turn and popped the sixth chaff bundle. The detector pulse rate was so fast it was a steady tone, impact was imminent. The severe turn put a tremendous load on the rotor blades and the red OVER-TORQUE warning light flashed in protest. Luke was flying the chopper to its extreme limits.

The abrupt maneuvers worked. The first missile overshot and exploded in the chaff cloud. The shock wave from the explosion buffeted the chopper violently and Luke struggled to keep it under control while trying to keep the second missile in sight.

The chopper's left skid skipped off the ground and kicked up a dust cloud, made worse by the rotor wash. It couldn't be helped. The chopper was stretched to its limit.

The sand cloud obscured their vision and they both lost sight of the second missile, *the* major sin of aerial combat. The detector pulse rate tone increased rapidly again. The second missile was closing fast.

Luke was left with only an act of desperation. He popped the seventh bundle of chaff and reversed course so rapidly, the chopper flew backwards. He cut the power to idle and the chopper slammed to the ground. The impact jarred them to the bone and Luke heard one of the skid struts crack.

The detector went silent. They heard the roar of a rocket motor pass close overhead and felt the shockwave of the supersonic missile as it passed. A tremendous explosion blasted above the ground, some distance away. Its violent concussion buffeted the chopper and peppered it with shrapnel and debris. They held onto the frame as the machine rocked sideways, its main rotor blades just inches from the ground. If they impacted, the chopper would be wrecked and they'd be in for a long walk, if they weren't killed.

God must have intervened. The pressure wave subsided and the chopper slammed back down. The detector was silent.

"Hoo-ah! That was close. Good work, old fart."

Hale accepted the left-handed compliment. "Thanks. Better than Six Flags, eh?"

Storm flashed his crooked smile. "What say we get out of here?"

"No kidding. All that maneuvering chewed up a lot of fuel."

Luke revved the engine and lifted off blindly in the sand cloud and climbed just high enough to get them above it. The chopper was vibrating harder than usual. Even Storm noticed it.

"What's all that vibration?"

"Some debris must have hit the rotor blades. They're out of balance. There's nothing we can do about it now. As long as it doesn't get worse, we should be able to reach Kuwait."

"How's our fuel?"

"Not good. We've got enough to get out of Iraq, but not enough reach the port."

"How many of those chaff things do we have left?"

"One. Let's hope we don't have to use it. Also, I heard one of the struts crack when we hit back there. She won't bear another impact like that. We'd crash and burn."

The radio crackled. "Foxtrot November, Rambler two-four. What's your status?"

"This is Fox November. We were engaged by two radar SAMs, SA-6's. They were launched eight miles northeast of our position. It was a close call. We had to go to slow-motion replay for a ruling."

"Copy that, Fox November. We have a backtrack fix on that site. They'll be getting airmail from our fast movers in about two minutes."

"God bless the U.S. Air Force."

"Roger that, Fox November. We're tracking you. Keep me posted," replied the AWACS controller.

"Wilco. And thanks for the help."

"My pleasure. Keep low and check six."

Hale questioned Storm. "How far to Kuwait?"

"Twenty-six miles."

Hale looked at the fuel quantity gauge and the fuel flow indicator. He mentally calculated their minutes of fuel remaining. "Derek, we're in for a walk."

"Whatever." Storm was cavalier, grinning from ear to ear. "I know a good restaurant in Kuwait. Great seafood."

The chopper continued its off-balance flight with both of them giggling, covering their nervousness.

Persian Gulf: The chopper's symbol danced in a tight zigzag pattern on the GPS display. The data block indicated numerous, erratic course changes and altitude excursions. Paul didn't know what to make of it.

"Skipper?"

Skibba stepped to Paul's side and studied the display. "Looks like evasive maneuvers," he whispered. "Keep your voice down, Paul. I don't want Mrs. Hale to get alarmed."

"Aye, aye," Paul whispered back.

They monitored the display intently. The helicopter symbol danced erratically and the flight data changed rapidly, but neither indicated progress toward Kuwait. The chopper was maneuvering wildly in a tight area.

"Evasive maneuvers from what?" whispered Paul.

"No telling. Keep me posted."

Paul nodded and the Skipper went to his navigation chart and commanded, "Mr. Pell, all ahead half, maintain ten knots. Steer course three-two-two."

Pell responded instantly. The yacht's huge engines revved up, the ship shuddered momentarily and eased through the water.

Skibba keyed his portable radio. "Mr. Welch, report to the bridge ASAP."

"On the way, Skipper."

"Skipper, our speed is ten knots, steady on course three-two-two," reported Pell.

"Very good. Maintain course and speed."

"Aye, aye, sir."

"Skipper," whispered Paul.

Skibba casually walked to the GPS station, aware of Heather nervously watching from outside. "What do you have, Mr. Thomas?"

"They've stopped. They're still thirty miles inside Iraq."

Skibba studied the data.

"What do you think, Skipper?"

"Don't know. We just have to grit our teeth and wait for them to call."

The data block flashed. The chopper symbol rotated and indicated movement toward Kuwait. Both men sighed relief.

Dave Welch entered the wheelhouse. "I'm here, Skipper."

"Excellent. I want you and Mr. Thomas to take station on the bow. Take binoculars and keep a sharp lookout for dark shadows under the surface. Report to me immediately by radio if you spot any, no matter how insignificant you think they are."

Dave scratched his head. "What are we looking for, Skipper?"

"Sea mines. Now get the binoculars and radios. Go."

"Yes, sir."

"Aye, aye, sir." They ran off.

The satellite phone chimed.

"Skibba."

"Hi, Skipper. It's Derek."

"Good to hear from you. What's your status, Mr. Storm?"

"We're okay. We had some scary missile dodging to do. It used up a lot of fuel. Luke says we've got enough to get clear of hostile territory but not enough to reach the refuel point."

"I figured that. I've ordered the ship to move closer to the refuel stop and I'm going to see if I can pull a few strings with the Navy. Watch your ass and keep in touch. How's the chopper holding up?"

"She's vibrating like an X-rated motel bed," Storm declared, laughing.

"How's the boss?"

"The old gray boy just ain't what he used to be. He says he's okay but I can tell he's exhausted from dodging SAMs."

"Was it close?"

"Well, when we left the ship, I had red-brown hair and white underwear. Now it's the opposite."

Skibba laughed. "Thanks for that vivid word picture. You'll pardon me if I don't share it with the others over the dinner table."

Storm laughed. "That's okay, Skipper. I've got it covered."

"You silver-tongued devil. That'll have the women hanging all over you."

"Hoo-ah. Hey, gotta go. We'll be in touch."

"Later. Skibba out."

The Skipper disconnected, dialed another number and pressed SEND.

"Delores, it's Walt. I need to speak with Admiral Bennett again, it's urgent."

Southern Iraq: "Break left! Break left!"

Hale slammed the vibrating chopper into a violent left bank, spotted a missile smoke trail and jinked the chopper away from its path. There was no warning from the radar detector. The missile was a heat-seeker.

"Flare!" yelled Hale.

Storm flipped up one emitter lever, spitting out one of the electronic transmitters. The emitter cleared its tube, began transmitting its deceptive signal and floated toward the ground. Luke rotated the chopper's exhaust away from the missile, attempting to hide the heat source from the missile's seeker head.

A second missile launched from their right flank. Luke spotted the flash and the smoke trail, several miles away.

"Second launch! Flare!" Storm flipped up the second lever.

The first missile took to the first decoy and zipped past the chopper without detonating. Hale rotated the heavily vibrating chopper to hide the exhaust from the second missile. The second missile bit off on the second decoy, passing well behind and below the helicopter.

The bubble windscreen exploded in their faces. Bullets and Plexiglas shards sprayed through the cockpit. Luke jinked the chopper wildly to spoil the aimed fire coming at them from some ground troops, three hundred meters to the east. Their faces, arms and torsos were peppered with the hot, sharp plastic. More bullets hit the engine compartment.

Hale jinked the chopper, zigzagged, climbed and dove away from the gunfire at the chopper's maximum attainable speed, which was constantly reducing. The chopper controls were sluggish. Their responsiveness was dropping off as the wounded whirlybird lumbered away from the hostiles.

Another SAM launched from their left, half a mile away. Storm spotted it. Without order, he flipped up the third lever. "Missile launch! Nine o'clock!"

Hale turned the flailing chopper left. "Flare!"

"Already away!"

The Russian-manufactured, shoulder-fired piece of crap guided on the decoy and impacted the ground past the chopper, its explosion focused away from them. Several more bullets impacted the chopper. Oily, black smoke poured from the engine compartment.

"We're smoking!" yelled Storm.

Luke figured that. He could smell it, the oil quantity and pressure were slowly decreasing and the red OVER-TORQUE warning light flashed.

Storm aimed his rifle out the left door and unleashed a hellish burst of thirty-caliber slugs at the hostiles. His spent cartridges ricocheted around the cockpit as the air within became thick with cordite.

Luke assessed their situation. He headed the chopper southeast, away from the hostiles to the opposite side of the river. The heavily wounded bird struggled to remain airborne, spewing hot, oily smoke in its wake, providing an effective smoke screen between them and the hostiles.

Luke transmitted. "Rambler two-four, this is Fox November! We're taking fire! We've been hit and we're going down! Mark our position! Two American souls on board!"

"Fox November, this is Rambler two-four. Copy, you're going down. Two souls. Say intentions and…" The radio went dead.

"Hang on!"

Storm braced himself on the frame as Luke fought with the marginally responsive controls. The chopper cleared the opposite riverbank by inches. The engine chugged, sputtered, backfired and then exploded. Flames burst out from the engine compartment.

"We're on fire!" yelled Storm.

"Roger that!" The red FIRE WARNING light flashed.

The engine took the rest of the day off. The rotors slowed and the bird plunged to the ground south of the river and plowed a huge spray of sand as the skid struts snapped and collapsed. The chopper rolled onto its right side. The whirling rotor blades successively smacked into the ground and shattered, throwing sharp debris in all directions. The tail boom impacted and snapped off, sending the tail rotor airborne, a lethal Frisbee. The bubble cockpit tumbled and rolled like a lopsided football. The fuel tanks erupted. Fiery plumes enveloped the cockpit.

CHAPTER XVI

EGRESS

Persian Gulf: The *Vixen* cautiously cruised deeper into the gulf. Thomas and Welch were at the bow, scanning intently for signs of sea mines. The fleets of oil tankers, freighters and naval ships grew thicker with every mile.

"Come starboard to three-three-one, Mr. Pell."

"Aye, aye. Three-three-one."

Skibba gave wide berth to the U.S. Navy aircraft carrier group off their port bow.

He glimpsed the GPS display and saw the chopper symbol moving erratically again. He pressed a button on its control panel and studied the flight data block. The chopper was changing course and altitude every few seconds and then it described a tight circle and edged southeast. The symbol crossed the overlay marker for the river and disappeared. The data block went blank. There was only one explanation. They were down in hostile territory, with no covering force.

"Oh, shit!"

Southern Iraq: The impact wrenched Storm's back, renewing his twelve-year-old injury. The pain shot straight through his spine. The chopper tumbled, throwing charts, equipment and debris around the bubble. Storm felt like a seed inside a maraca. Flames flashed through the cockpit, singeing his hair and exposed skin. By some stroke of destiny, the flames abated quickly.

The bubble came to rest on its right side with Storm on top of Luke. Fire still burned around the engine compartment and acrid smoke from burning oil and rubber-coated wiring choked him.

Luke appeared to be dead.

"Luke. Luke!"

Hale didn't respond and hung limply in his harness.

"No! Please, God! Don't take Luke."

Storm quickly unbuckled and reached for his friend. He was breathing and had a steady pulse. "Thank you, Lord."

Storm drew his .45 and shot three holes through the lower windscreen. He fought through his back pain and repositioned. He kicked out a large piece of the windscreen and painfully climbed out the top of the rubble. He carefully slid to the ground, went to the front and pulled away pieces of the shattered windscreen.

He resisted the pain, coughed from the thick smoke, reached inside and unbuckled Luke's harness. Luke's limp form slid to the bottom. Storm struggled to move Luke into position for extraction. He managed to get him rotated, grasped his safari vest by the epaulets and dragged him thirty yards clear of the burning chopper, his back protesting all the way.

Storm noticed that Luke had two nasty bumps on his head. Luke had been fighting to maintain control of the chopper all the way to impact and didn't have a chance to brace.

Storm returned to the chopper. He retrieved their rifles, ammo magazines, first-aid kit, GPS, map and the five-gallon water can. He was reliving his survival experience of twelve years ago. "My travel agent is gonna hear about this."

Storm heard automatic rifle fire coming from the opposite side of the river but he couldn't see over the embankment. He crouched and jogged to the riverbank, upwind of the burning chopper. He flattened himself on the bank and painfully crawled to the crest, his rifle at the ready. He was careful not to kick up a dust trail.

Storm cautiously peeked over the crest. He saw four Iraqi soldiers on the opposite bank, yelling and pointing at the smoke column from the burning chopper.

"Duh! These guys are stupid." The hostiles stood upright, silhouetted above the horizon, providing perfect targets. Two of them were armed with AKs, one with an RPG launcher and one with a pistol.

Fortunately, the river was too wide and the current too swift for them to attempt forging. *"Good old Luke. Even under intense fire with a severely damaged bird, he placed a daunting natural obstacle between us and them. He's still got a lot of Infantry left in him."*

Storm estimated the range, two hundred forty meters. He figured he could take out two of them before they could take cover. He eased his rifle to his shoulder, selected single shot, and took aim on the soldier holding the pistol, most likely their leader. He concentrated, then smoothly squeezed off one round.

Crack! One hundred fifty grains of copper-jacketed lead launched across the river, hit the target center-mass and knocked him backwards.

Crack! Storm's second shot had the same effect on the soldier holding the RPG. One soldier dove for cover at the sound of the first shot. The other one was either stupid or in shock. He looked at one dead comrade, then the other. It cost him.

Crack!

"Three for three. Damn, I'm good." Storm struggled to a low crouch and relocated fifty yards downwind. His back protested every movement.

He heard several long bursts of fire from an AK. The remaining soldier was firing wildly toward Storm's previous position.

Storm eased himself to the top of the bank and cautiously peeked over. Apparently, the lone soldier had not been trained well. He hadn't relocated after firing and Storm spotted him immediately. He saw the man's helmet poke above the bank as he fired at a phantom target.

Storm considered his shot option. It would be a low probability shot, a head shot at two hundred forty meters without a scope. And it would give away his position. Then it was just a matter of who had more ammo, superior tactics, or more reinforcements.

"Did you leave any for me?"

Storm nearly jumped out of his skin. Luke had regained his senses and stealthily crept up behind Storm.

"Jesus, man! I nearly had an out-of-body experience."

"You didn't sense me?"

"Not that time. Your stealth technique is getting better."

Hale eased his singed, bleeding body to the ground and crawled up the bank.

"What's our situation, lad?"

"We *had* four armed hostiles… until three minutes ago. There's one more, eleven o'clock, prone defilade, peeking over the opposite bank, two hundred forty meters. That's too far for a head shot with this." He patted to his un-scoped rifle.

Luke grinned like a predator who had just found a meal and patted his rifle. "Let's see what Mr. Bushmaster has to say about it." Storm flashed an evil grin, knowing what was in store for the lone Iraqi.

Luke eased to the crest. Storm noticed he was bleeding from his left calf and the back of his left shoulder. His hair was singed, his skin burned. He looked like hammered, bloody dog shit but he hadn't uttered one word of complaint. He was a true warrior.

Luke peeked over the bank, spotted the target and raised his rifle. He inhaled, gripped the rifle, adjusted his aim, let his breath out half way and then held it.

Crack!

Luke looked through the scope and then rolled over to face Storm. "Two hundred forty-*six* meters, Derek," corrected Hale. "Two hundred forty-*six*."

"Get him?"

Luke gave Storm a condescending look.

Storm's evil grin returned. He rose and brushed himself off. "Forget I asked. I should know better."

Persian Gulf: "Mr. Pell, all ahead two-thirds, maintain twenty-three knots, steer course three-one-niner."

"Aye, aye, sir." Terry eased the throttles forward and turned the wheel right.

The Skipper needed to move the *Vixen* another eighty miles closer to the port of Kuwait. He had received assurances from Admiral Bennett's staff that the gulf was clear of sea mines and hostile watercraft to that point. And since several of the staff officers had previously served under Skibba's command, they respected him and promised to keep him advised of further developments.

Skibba transmitted on his portable radio. "Mr. Thomas, Mr. Welch. The lanes are clear, you may stand down."

They faced the wheelhouse and waved acknowledgement. Welch headed for the stern and Thomas returned to the bridge.

"Anything I can do, Skipper?" asked Paul as he entered the wheelhouse. Skibba signaled 'come-here.' Paul closed to the Skipper's side.

"Paul," he whispered, "The GPS data from the chopper went blank right in front of my eyes. Just before it disappeared, it was losing speed and altitude and tracking erratically. I think they're down inside Iraq."

"Jesus! How far?"

The Skipper pointed to the navigation chart. "The last fix I had was here," he indicated with the point of his calipers. "They're about nineteen miles from the border. If they're down, they're in for a long walk."

Paul nodded seriously. "Does Mrs. Hale know?"

"No. And I want to keep it that way, for now. Maybe we'll hear from them soon."

"Can the Navy or the Air Force pick them up?"

Skibba shook his head. "Not for civilians, who by their own choice, entered Iraq illegally. I spoke with my former boss in the Pentagon, Admiral Bennett. Current policy prohibits rescue of 'stupid civilians,' his words. They'll only dispatch Search and Rescue for downed pilots enforcing the No-Fly Zone. The good news is, if the Iraqis send aircraft after them, the Air Force will shoot them down. At least they have cover from airborne threats. The bad news is they'll have to fend for themselves against hostile ground forces until they reach the border or the gulf."

Paul nodded, looking glum. "There has to be something we can do, Skipper."

"All we can do right now is move closer to Kuwait. We can close another eighty miles before we have to be concerned about seaborne threats. The Admiral's staff has promised to keep me apprised of any changes. So, until we hear from the Admiral's staff or Mr. Hale, that's all we can do. They're on their own."

Paul sighed. "God, help them."

Southern Iraq: The temperature soared over one hundred degrees and the sun pounded their burned skin. Hale and Storm returned to the wreck and retrieved their scorched hats and sunglasses. Storm found a tube of sun block. They smeared generous amounts on their exposed skin. It was a painful experience, considering their sand-covered, first-degree burns.

"Whew!" exclaimed Storm, laughing. "I haven't had a sandpaper massage since I trained Mistress Dominique." He smeared lotion on his singed neck, laughing through the discomfort and passed the tube to Luke.

"Let me have a look at your wounds," said Storm.

"Check my left shoulder. Something bit me." Luke turned his back to Storm as he applied lotion to his scorched face.

Storm ran his hand over Storm's bloodied shoulder and felt a metal fragment.

"Ouch. That's it."

A thin metal shard was impaled in Luke's shoulder blade. "Hold still. I need disinfectant and bandages." Storm fished through the medical kit, found the supplies and braced Luke's shoulder.

"Okay, hold still. Oops."

"Oops, wha..?" Storm pulled the shard while Luke was distracted, a trick he had learned from Lisa during their desert trek.

"Got it." He tossed it away, applied disinfectant and covered the wound with tape strips. "You'll need stitches when we get back. How does it feel?"

"Like I got stabbed. There any painkillers in the kit?"

"Just Ibuprofen. Want some?"

"Yeah. A double dose."

Storm found the bottle and tossed it to Luke. He downed four tablets and tossed the bottle into the kit.

Then Storm went to work on Luke's calf. A bullet had creased his muscle, leaving a narrow, shallow gouge. He disinfected it and covered it with strips. "You might need stitches there too."

"Thanks. How about you, Derek. Any wounds?"

"Just burns and some rock splinters in my legs. My back took the worst of it. I took some Ibuprofen already. There's not much more we can do."

"Where are we?"

Storm extracted his map and the GPS. He knelt carefully, keeping his back straight and tossed the map onto the sand. Luke placed rocks on the corners to anchor them from the wind. Storm scanned back and forth from the GPS to the map and pointed with his index finger. "GPS shows us here. The Kuwaiti border is seventeen and a half miles, bearing one-one-niner."

"Seventeen miles. Oh joy," stated Luke sarcastically.

"Hey old sport, Lisa and I already had our desert survival practice last month. I need another one like a hole in the head."

"I hear you. With our wounds, seventeen miles in this heat will probably kill us. Me for sure. We need a better plan." Luke knelt by the map. He made some rough measurements with his fingers and ran mental calculations. "I've got an idea."

Storm edged closer.

Hale outlined his plan. "What do you think?"

"Risky. If the villagers spot us, they might report us to the Army."

"So you'd rather haul all this stuff seventeen miles?"

"No, I just said it's risky."

"Nobody lives forever."

Storm nodded. "Okay, Luke. You're the tactician. Let's do it."

Persian Gulf: The satellite phone rang.

"Skibba."

"Don't pay the ransom, Skipper. We're still on the lam."

"Good Lord, Luke. You had us worried. What happened?"

"We were shot down. We're injured, but mobile, mean and armed."

"What's your twenty?"

"We're a mile southeast of the wreck."

"The chopper's wrecked?"

"The old bird has reached her final resting place. Anyway, here's our plan." Salty listened intently as Luke detailed their escape route. Skibba gave Luke assurances that he would pull whatever strings he could.

"I appreciate that, Skipper. The hard part will be informing Heather and Amber. Can you do that for me? I need to get off the phone to save its battery."

"You bet, boss. I'll break it to them easy. And we'll have a twenty-four/seven watch on this phone until you're safe."

"Did you get the image data?"

"Affirmative. Amber has already e-mailed them."

"Terrific. And just in case we don't make it back, you know where to send the transcript, right?"

"Affirmative. And you're going to make it back. Skibba has spoken."

Luke laughed. "Yes, I believe we will. Gotta go. Battery's low. Hale out." He stuffed the phone onto his vest.

"They received the data and sent it to your wanna-be lover in San Fran," he informed Storm.

"Good. Mission accomplished."

Luke nodded. "Now all we have to do is get out alive."

"No challenge for a couple of old warriors."

"You know where we can find some?"

"Some what?"

"Old warriors." Luke picked up the water can and the medical kit. Storm gingerly squatted and grabbed his map.

"Ready to hike, old warrior?" teased Storm.

"Liberty is that way." Luke pointed.

Washington, D.C.: "I don't see that we have a choice, Sandra. Huge unreported contributions, hiring mercenaries to murder a doctor?" Kathy Zimmerman shook her head. "This needs to be reported to the House Ethics Committee. I'm not going to risk my job."

Sandra Dillers agreed but still had questions. "The Majority Whip will be very interested. But do we have enough evidence? These are just unconfirmed allegations."

"You have a point. Call NOMP. See if you can confirm the dates and amounts of these donations and include your findings in the report."

"Should I ask them about 'Bravo'?"

Zimmerman shook her head. "No, hon. It might make them suspicious and jeopardize our informants. We need to keep them safe so they can testify before the committee."

Sandra bit her bottom lip and nodded apprehensively. The nastiest part of her job was just beginning.

Southern Iraq: The trek played hell on the two Americans. The temperature exceeded a hundred degrees and there was no cloud cover or shade. Wind-blown sand pelted their exposed, burned skin.

Their progress was slow and tactically sound. Luke limped but he refused to allow Storm to carry the heavy gear, fearing further injury to his friend's back. They covered two miles during the first hour. They didn't have the option of lying low in the shade during the day and traveling at night, per survival doctrine. They had to get clear of the chopper wreckage before more troops arrived.

They chose their route carefully, staying on rocky terrain as much as possible to hide their tracks. It made for slow, strenuous travel, but it was necessary. Where they couldn't avoid soft ground, they deceptively changed course. Once certain they weren't leaving tracks, they resumed their original course.

It took four hours to reach a marshy area at the outskirts of a river village. They quietly eased into water and hid amongst tall marsh grass.

The cool water felt good on their punished skin.

They were careful not to jostle reeds, which would function as waving flags, revealing their position. They were equally cautious not to alarm the waterfowl. The cormorants stayed close to shore in the shallow water, while the ducks preferred the deeper water. They chose a path between the groups of birds, wading chest deep with their heavy rifles at the ready.

The sun was low on the horizon, twilight encroached. The darkness would be their friend but twilight was not. It was feeding time for the fish and they suspected there would be numerous anglers about, trying to snare an evening meal. They elected to find a hiding spot until dark.

Storm led the way, wading slowly. Luke struggled silently behind him, trying to keep his rifle, gas mask and medical kit high and dry. Storm had cleverly rigged the water can, which was only one-third full, low on Luke's back. The trapped air in the can provided buoyancy and Storm strapped the medical kit and Luke's gas mask above it. The buoyant can held them above the water and lightened the load. Luke was grateful for Storm's ingenuity since his wounded leg and shoulder were giving him as much pain as Storm's back was giving him. At least the marsh water was providing some welcomed body temperature regulation.

Some voices, speaking Arabic, came from their one o'clock. Storm held up his open hand. They froze. The voices sounded close, thirty or forty feet. Storm signed Luke to stay put. They crouched nose-deep into the marsh. Storm eased forward and peeked through the grass.

He spotted three people standing knee-deep in the marsh. They were civilians, apparently a father and his two teenage sons. They were casting lines from crudely fashioned poles. They seemed intent on their fishing. They showed no awareness of the Americans. They had no firearms or weapons that Storm could see.

Storm dismissed them as an immediate threat, but he was wary of them. They could sound an alarm and troops might come running. He slowly back-stepped to Luke. He pointed to a heavily grassed area closer to shore and signaled 'Rest.' Hale gave a shallow nod and they eased to the prospective hideout. They slowly imbedded themselves in the tall grass and lay in the shallow water.

They silently removed Luke's load, quenched their thirst and munched the last of their food. There was nothing more to do but rest and wait for their friend, the night.

∞

The cool night air was a blessing. Storm and Hale remained hidden in the marsh until 10 p.m. Then they waded down river toward the village. It wasn't long before they came upon a rotting wooden dock. It had seven boats of various sizes tied to it.

Luke knelt in the high grass as Storm went to the dock and selected the smallest of the boats, untied it and pulled it into the shallow water. They transferred the gear into it. Luke had Storm get in the boat and lie down, then he pushed the boat into deeper water, crawled in and paddled to the center of the river where the current was fastest.

Passing the village, Hale kept them in the shadows, gently paddling downstream. They maintained silence and kept low.

Hale estimated the current at two knots. At that rate, they would reach their planned exit point in four hours. All they had to do was avoid patrols.

After many silent hours, Storm broke the quiet. "I feel guilty," he whispered.

"Me too. After this is over, I'll have to find the man who owns this boat and pay him for it."

Persian Gulf: "I'm sorry, Walt," said Admiral Clarence Bennett. "We can't do anything while they're in Iraq. If they make it to Kuwait or the gulf, we can send Search and Rescue. Until then, my hands are tied. We can't intrude onto foreign soil without specific orders from CinC." The Admiral was referring to the Commander-in-Chief, the President.

Skibba's heart sank but he knew Bennett was right. And with a military build-up in progress, there were many itchy trigger fingers on both sides of the border. "I understand, Admiral. Thanks for talking to me. I appreciate it."

"Any time, Walt. My line is always open to the best missile cruiser Captain I ever had. You keep in touch. And one more thing."

"What's that, sir?"

"Be sure to call me when those men are safe. I'd like to know."

"Wilco, Admiral. Thanks again." Out of respect, Skibba held the line open until the Admiral disconnected.

Paul stepped to the Skipper's side. They stared into the darkness of the gulf. Somewhere out there, on the ground in hostile territory, were two brave men. And Skibba was pissed that he had no way to get them out.

"How far are we from Kuwait, Skipper?"

"Sixteen miles. That's as close as the port authorities will allow us."

The glow of the lights from Kuwait City could be seen over the northwest horizon. The running lights of multitudes of ships crisscrossed the gulf. The *Vixen* moored out of the traffic lanes but they were still a nuisance to the harbormasters of Kuwait, who were frantically trying to accommodate the plethora of military support vessels.

Dave Welch entered. "Reporting for watch, Skipper."

"Thanks, Dave. Caroline's on after you. I'm going to my cabin. Wake me immediately if you hear from the military or Mr. Hale."

"Aye, aye, sir. I have the con."

Skibba took the outside stairs to the lower deck. He breathed in the salty air, relishing the freedom of being at sea. He missed the satisfaction and prestige of commanding a missile cruiser, but he enjoyed being in command of one of the finest private motor yachts in the world. The only way life could be better was if the boss and Derek made it home safely. He said a silent prayer and entered his stateroom.

Southern Iraq: The sound of a truck being downshifted cut across the water. A glow of light appeared at their one o'clock, several hundred yards ahead. Storm checked his map. There were no roads, villages or ports indicated at that location. He signaled Hale to head for shore.

Hale paddled to the south riverbank. They elected to recon the area before proceeding. They were still a mile short of where they intended to embark. They pulled the boat ashore and covered it with foliage. They left the medical kit and water can near the boat and stealthily maneuvered to a sand ridge near the light and noise.

Storm peeked over the ridge and spotted the glow of a cigarette. It was a hundred yards away, being puffed by a soldier inside a camouflaged, open-air bunker. The bunker was at the end of a road that paralleled the river and dead-ended at a gate next to the bunker. A truck was parked at the gate, idling, its headlights off. It was an eighteen-wheeler with a flat bed trailer. The bed was stacked with large drums. They were covered by large tarps.

A rumble shook the ground, Hale and Storm dropped prone. Huge camouflaged doors swung open to their right two o'clock, revealing a road ramp going underground. Dim light glowed from inside the ramp area. They could see the ramp but not directly into the underground area.

Hale slapped Storm on the shoulder and thumbed right. Storm

nodded. They crouched and soft-stepped along the ridge toward the ramp. A huge truck emerged from the ramp, its lights extinguished. They dropped again.

The truck was like the other one but its trailer was empty. They watched as the truck drove to the gate, parked and idled. Out hopped the driver. He was wearing a *gas mask*. Hale and Storm looked at each other.

The driver of the inbound truck jumped out. The drivers swapped trucks and the guard raised the gate barriers. Hale slapped Storm's shoulder again and thumbed right. They repositioned as the noise of the trucks covered them.

They flopped to the ground where they had a view directly into the underground facility. It was cavernous. There was a loading dock stacked with columns of fifty-five gallon drums with Biohazard labels on them, forklifts moving other drums and numerous personnel working. They were all wearing gas masks and full bio-chemical warfare suits: gas masks, hoods, gloves, boots, the works.

Hale and Storm held their breath and donned their gas masks, pressed their palms over the exhalation ports and blew hard into the masks. The air inside the masks cleared through the seals, displaced by the air they had just exhaled. They pressed their palms over the inlet ports on the masks and inhaled, testing the seal on the masks. Luke's mask didn't seal correctly the first time, so he tightened the straps and repeated the procedure. Satisfied, they flashed each other thumbs-up.

They observed the activity. Workers shuttled pallets of drums with forklifts, unloading them from the inbound trailer. Others relocated empty drums with hand trucks. Others stacked wooden boxes, resembling artillery ammunition crates, on another trailer.

They noticed a variety of vehicles. One vehicle resembled an RV. There were drums connected to it by thick hoses and steel valve fittings. Another vehicle resembled a radar control van for a surface-to-air missile site.

Hale looked at Storm through the Plexiglas faceplate of his mask and said, "Oh, oh." Storm nodded, knowing the implications.

Storm and Hale agreed it wouldn't be healthy to stick around, nor would it be wise to try to paddle past on the river. The guard bunker provided the sentry with a good view of the river. They returned to the boat, retrieved their gear, and headed across the desert.

Persian Gulf: Skibba awoke before sunrise. His sleep had been restless, worried. He showered, grabbed his portable radio, pocket humidor and headed for the wheelhouse.

He found Paul Thomas in the Captain's chair, his head bobbing from drowsiness. Skibba wasn't surprised. Paul had volunteered to stand a double watch so Terry Pell could get a full night's rest.

Skibba tapped him. "Paul, you're relieved. Go get some shuteye."

Paul snapped awake and rubbed his eyes. "Mornin' Skipper."

"Good morning. Any news from Mr. Hale?"

Paul shook his head regretfully. "Not a word."

"Okay. I have the con. Go get some sleep."

Paul nodded and surrendered the Captain's chair. He gathered his coffee mug and headed for the warmth of Caroline.

Skibba patrolled the bridge, monitoring every status panel. He wanted to do more but there was no more he could do without risking the ship and crew, and that wasn't his call to make.

Southern Iraq: Traveling across open desert in broad daylight presented Storm and Hale with several problems.

First, it was hotter than hell. Second, there were very few places to hide and there where a lot more hostiles as they got closer to the border. Third, there were probably land mines between them and the border.

They had covered a lot of ground but it was too risky to continue in broad daylight. They sought the cover of a wash to conceal themselves.

They dug a small cave into the sidewall of the wash, crawled inside, then piled sand and rocks around them for camouflage.

"We'll rest and wait until dark," recommended Hale.

"You do realize if the SCUDs start flying or the coalition forces advance, we're in prime position to have our asses carpet-bombed?"

"Yeah. I know. How far to the border?"

"Four and a half miles. I don't know how many past that to reach friendly forces."

"We might not have to reach friendly forces. All we have to do is get over the border alive. Then we can call for rescue."

Storm agreed. "It's gonna be slow in the dark. We keep running into more troops. I hope they don't have night vision."

Boston: "Hello, Doctor Rushton? This is Sandra Dillers with the Federal Elections Commission in Washington, D.C. If you could spare a few minutes, I'd like to verify some recent contributions by your organization."

"I suppose we can accommodate the FEC, Miss Dillers. I hope we haven't done anything wrong."

"Oh, goodness no, Doctor. It's merely a routine verification. It's a congressionally imposed requirement for the FEC to call and verify contributions that exceed a certain amount. There's no onus associated with it. We simply verify that the recipients are reporting accurately. That's all."

"Well, as I said, Miss Dillers, we'll be glad to assist the FEC in its duties. How can I help?"

"Congresswoman Iris Stakemore and the Good Works PAC have reported generous contributions from NOMP. We just need to verify those dates and amounts."

"Certainly." Rushton tapped a few keys on his computer and clicked the mouse. "What dates are you checking?"

Sandra stated the dates and asked Rushton to confirm the amounts.

"Yes, Miss Dillers. Those dates show we donated two-hundred fifty thousand and another one million."

"That's what we're showing, Doctor." She lied.

"Good. Because that's what our data is showing in the computer."

"Oh, good. Then everything is fine. That's all I needed to know. Thank you for your cooperation, Doctor. Have a nice day."

"You have a nice day, too. Good-bye." Rushton hung up and thought nothing more of the call.

Southern Iraq: The noise was deafening. A half-dozen Iraqi tracked vehicles maneuvered around the wash.

They weren't merely passing by; they were preparing defiladed defensive positions. Through their limited view, they counted six vehicles. One, an American-made M-113, 1970's vintage, parked at the edge of the wash directly opposite them. Five soldiers, armed with AK's, dismounted and scurried around, seeking cover positions away from the vehicle. Two of them jumped into the wash, twenty feet away. They made enough noise to wake the dead.

Storm and Hale slowly drew their .45's and thumbed off the safeties.

"This would not be a good time to fart," whispered Storm.

Hale chuckled softly. They'd be in a hell of a mess if the soldier's detected them. They were cornered. If the soldiers stayed through the night, their opportunity for escape would be almost nil. The Americans had been without food all day and they had only a half-gallon of water left. The only things they had plenty of were ammunition and guts.

Storm checked his watch. It was only four o'clock, three hours until dark. It must have also been time for the flies to feed because dozens of them zeroed in on their bloody wounds.

"We need to revise our plan," whispered Hale.

Persian Gulf: "Skipper. I want the truth. Where's my husband?" Heather had Skibba cornered in the galley.

Skibba sighed. "I don't know, Mrs. Hale. We heard from them yesterday afternoon. The chopper is out of commission. They're walking to the Kuwaiti border. Once they reach Kuwait, U.S. forces can pick them up. Luke said his phone battery was low, so he would call once they reach Kuwait. Once they call, CentCom will send a chopper to get them."

"Who's Zincon?"

"CentCom, Mrs. Hale. Central Command, the Army's headquarters. As soon as they call, they'll be picked up."

"They haven't checked in for twenty-four hours?"

"No ma'am. Luke said the phone battery was low, so he'll call when they're clear."

"And what if they don't get clear?" Heather was distraught. Tears streamed from her eyes. Her hands shook.

The Skipper glanced down, frustrated. He commanded no resources to retrieve Hale and Storm. He looked directly into Heather's eyes.

"He'll call, Mrs. Hale. That's Luke out there. There's few like him. And he has a damned good partner. They'll call."

Southern Iraq: They waited until 0230 a.m. Even though they were hungry, wounded and smelly, they were rested and pumped up for action.

Storm silently dug out of their cubbyhole. He carefully lifted each rock and relocated it. It took him twenty minutes to clear a path. The opening was just large enough to crawl through. He eased out, stifling the urge to moan from the pain in his back. Hale covered him with his .45, poking the barrel through a gap between several rocks.

Storm cleared the hole, holstered his .45 and eased his FN out while keeping a wary eye on the sleeping Iraqis across the wash.

Hale passed his Bushmaster out. Then he handed out the water can and the medical kit. Storm silently placed them aside and Luke crawled out.

Luke stretched up on his tiptoes, peeked over the banks of the wash and scanned full-circle. The scant moonlight provided enough illumination for him to assess the Iraqi positions.

He knelt in the sand and diagrammed the scenario. He drew a jagged line, representing the wash. Then he pointed at the APC, held up six fingers, and dotted their relative positions in the sand. Then he pointed at the sleeping soldiers and dotted the sand in a dozen spots, indicating their positions.

Storm signaled 'okay.' Hale handed Storm his last shaken. Storm placed his rifle on the ground, took Hale's shaken and drew his last one. With a steel spike in each hand, he soft-stepped toward the sleeping soldiers. He approached them from behind as Hale covered him.

Storm crept up behind the first soldier, placed the shaken an inch from the man's right ear, then plunged the sharpened point deep into his ear canal. The spike impaled his brain, instant death. The man hardly moved, made no sounds.

Storm slowly extracted the shaken; blood dripped from it and his hand. The second soldier stirred. Storm froze. Hale aimed at the APC. The soldier settled down and Storm repeated the lethal procedure. Storm removed the spike and wiped it and his hand on the dead soldier's jacket. He signaled 'okay.'

Luke flashed 'okay' back. Storm softly jogged back to the hole. He grabbed his rifle and the medical kit. Hale hefted the water can. They silently crossed the wash and set down the gear. Hale boosted Storm up the embankment. Storm edged prone next to the APC. Hale passed up the gear and weapons, then scaled the steep wall. Storm provided cover with his rifle.

With Storm in the lead, they crawled to the rear of the M-113. Hale was familiar with it. It was a diesel-powered, dual-tracked vehicle, used for carrying Infantrymen into combat. It had limited water fording capability, decent range, sported a 7.62 mm machinegun mounted at the commander's hatch, a rear loading ramp with integral personnel hatch and was controlled by steering and brake levers rather than a steering wheel.

Luke had crewed M-113s during the early seventies, his years in the Armored Cavalry. He knew he could drive the thing if he could remember how to start the engine.

Storm crawled to the rear corner, peeked around and rapidly retracted. He signaled 'one' and a slash across the throat. Hale knew what was coming.

Storm cautiously set down his rifle and drew a shaken. He reached around the corner, grabbed a sleeping soldier by the throat and squeezed, crushing his larynx. He abruptly yanked the startled man around the corner and plunged the shaken upwards into the man's neck at the base of his skull. The spike pierced the man's spinal cord, causing instantaneous silent death. The soldier gave one violent twitch, then went limp.

Storm dragged the body along the side of the track and dropped it. He whispered, "The ramp is down." Hale nodded.

Storm crawled back to the open ramp and peeked inside. A dim red dome light cast an eerie glow about the interior. He counted four soldiers inside, six AKs, one RPG with reloads and a box of Russian hand grenades.

All four soldiers were asleep, a cardinal sin for combat infantry. Two of them weren't wearing boots. They were sleeping on the side benches, snoring. The vehicle commander was slumped against the engine firewall, sound asleep and drooling. There was a fourth soldier sleeping atop a stack of duffel bags, aft of the commander's seat.

Storm withdrew and faced Hale. He signaled 'four,' 'sleep,' and another slash across the throat. He handed Hale the bloody shaken. Storm pointed at himself, signaled 'two' and pointed his thumb to the right. Then he pointed at Hale, held up two fingers and pointed his thumb left. Hale nodded. Storm drew his shaken.

Storm grabbed his rifle and medical kit. Hale grabbed the water can. They soft-stepped to the ramp.

Storm's heart pounded as his adrenaline kicked in. The same went for Luke. They were nervous but ready to do whatever they had to do.

They tread silently up the ramp and quietly set their gear inside. The interior smelled horrendous. It reeked of body odor and urine. These men hadn't had showers in weeks.

They approached the sleeping soldiers without looking directly at them. It was a stealth technique they had practiced many times, to avoid casting their life-energy onto their prey, alerting them to their presence. The Masters had taught that most humans could sense when they are being closely watched, even when asleep. They were not going to risk that and performed the technique exactly as the San Soo

Masters had taught.

Storm moved forward to the vehicle commander. Hale chose the man on the duffels. Storm held up three fingers. Hale nodded. Storm folded down one finger at a time. As soon as the last finger folded, both men grabbed their prey by their throats and plunged the shakens into their ears. The bodies twitched, but they died silently.

They repositioned to their secondary targets. This time, Storm raised only one finger. Storm's finger folded and he plunged the shaken into the target's ear. Hale's target was on his right side, facing away from him, with his arm over his head. Hale grasped the man's throat from behind and jammed the spike under the base of his skull. The man twitched violently and struggled, so Hale jammed it deeper and pried it around. The soldier went limp.

Hale felt nauseated. It was the first time he had ever killed men with a shaken. He puked on the dead soldier and spit out the bile. He wiped his mouth with his sleeve and grabbed the water can. He sucked a mouthful of water, sloshed it quietly and spit it out.

Storm patted him on the back and whispered, "I almost puked when I did the first one."

Hale felt better. "I wish I had an antacid."

Storm fanned the air. "I'd settle for a breath mint," he teased, grinning from ear to ear.

"Eat shit." Luke grabbed his rifle.

"Up yours." Storm grabbed his.

"Kiss my ass." Luke grabbed the water can.

"Smells better than your breath." Storm grabbed the medical kit.

"Or your B.O."

"Look who's calling the kettle black."

The hushed verbal jousting raised their spirits. Storm removed the dead soldier from the commander's seat and tossed him on the duffels. "Do you know how to raise the ramp?"

"It's been thirty years but I remember the engine needs to be running. It uses hydraulic pressure."

"Can you get this sucker cranked up?"

"Give me a couple of minutes." Hale lumbered to the driver's seat, left of the engine compartment.

"Can this thing take a hit from an RPG?" asked Storm.

"I don't recall. Let's not find out. We'll leave the top hatches open to prevent over-pressure if we take a hit. Besides, this place could use some fresh air."

Hale climbed into the driver's seat. The space seemed smaller than he remembered as he squeezed past the left control console. "*Or my ass is bulkier.*"

Storm stood guard inside the ramp. Luke reviewed the instruments and controls. It had been a long time.

"Yes. Master Switch, ramp control, start switch, lights, shift lever, accelerator, steering levers," he quietly recalled. Louder, to Storm, "I've got it, Derek."

"Good. Don't crank it yet." Storm disappeared outside, down the ramp. He softly trotted around the track, checking for obstacles, then returned.

"Luke," he whispered loudly, "there's a sand dune right in front of us. You'll have to back up about ten feet and pivot forty-five degrees right to get around it."

"Roger that. Let me know when you're ready."

Storm flashed an 'okay' and stood up through the commander's hatch. He scanned around the vehicle and noticed two more sleeping soldiers in a foxhole. They were the closest threat. They would have to be dispatched to Allah before Luke cranked the machine. Storm noticed five more APCs to their right, the closest approximately ninety yards west.

Storm gently lowered himself, careful not to aggravate his back. "Luke, we've got two bandits sleeping, four o'clock, fifteen yards. I'll be right back."

Storm disappeared. Hale hustled from the driver's seat, clawed his way past the smelly dead soldiers and grabbed his rifle to provide cover. By the time he reached the ramp, Storm was back, holding his bloody shaken.

"Let's go." He walked right past Luke.

Luke shook his head and struggled his way back to the driver's station as Storm wiped off his shaken and manned the commander's hatch. They put on headsets and talked through the vehicle's intercom. Storm turned on the radio and monitored the frequency. It was silent. The Iraqis were probably asleep.

"Okay Luke. Any time you're ready."

Luke flipped on the electrical Master switch and dimmed the instrument lights. The battery voltage looked strong and the fuel quantity indicated two-thirds full, more than enough. Luke hit the starter switch.

The powerful diesel motor cranked, spewing black smoke from its exhaust stack.

The engine rumbled and Luke pressed the accelerator to rev up the RPM. He immediately raised the ramp. The high RPM quickly produced the necessary hydraulic pressure, the ramp swung shut and Luke jammed the shift lever into reverse. The track surged backward ten feet; Luke pulled the left brake lever back, locking the left track, which pivoted the nose right. At forty-five degrees of turn, he locked back the right lever, shifted into FORWARD, released both steering levers forward and slammed the accelerator to the floor. The engine roared and the APC lurched forward as Luke yelled, "Let's kick this pig!"

"Hoo-aah!"

The APC loudly sped away, kicking up twin sprays of sand in its wake. The radio came alive with excited Arabic chatter.

"We woke them up," yelled Storm.

Automatic machinegun fire arced toward them, tracers giving evidence. Rounds splashed off the sides and top of the APC, motivating Storm to keep his head inside the hatch.

"They're pissed," yelled Storm. "I heard them call 9-1-1 and report us for grand theft, APC." He laughed loudly.

An explosion blasted on the right side, then one on the left. Two more impacted near the right, another on the left. Storm guessed RPG rounds were being fired at them. The track rolled and vibrated with the concussion of each blast. Luke held the accelerator to the floor, randomly changed course every ten seconds and generally headed south, toward the border.

All of the weapons fire was coming from their rear. Luke flipped on the headlights. The RPG rounds began falling short; they had driven out of range.

It occurred to Storm that they were racing directly at U.S. forces in an enemy combat vehicle. He grabbed the Iraqi squad leader's dead body, tore open his jacket and shirt, then ripped the smelly tee shirt from the torso. It was the closest thing he could find to a white flag. He climbed to the hatch, grabbed the radio antenna, pulled it down and tightly tied the tee shirt to it.

The careening APC jostled him repeatedly, sending his back muscles into spasm. He fought the pain, disconnected the hatch machinegun from its mount and tossed it overboard.

A huge explosion blasted thirty yards ahead to their left.

"Shit!" yelled Storm. "Incoming Luke! Get us out of here."

"No shit, Sherlock." Hale was already on it. A barrage of high-explosive artillery rounds hammered the desert all around them. The M-113 rocked and bounced wildly as shrapnel and concussions pummeled them. Luke swerved and dodged the craters, keeping the pedal floored, subjecting Storm to a painful ride. Debris rained down. Luke propelled the wildly careening APC through dense smoke and sand plumes.

"How far?" yelled Luke into the intercom.

Storm glanced at the GPS but he couldn't read the display; the APC was bouncing around too much. "Can't tell. Just keep it floored and head south."

Luke had no compass at the driver's station, nor could he see any stars through the dense smoke. "Which way is south?"

"Eleven o'clock."

Luke pulled back the left steering lever, turning the APC left, estimated thirty degrees of course change, released the lever, and let the powerful diesel propel them at full speed. The turn took them away from the artillery barrage. Storm peeked out the hatch. The rounds were still falling, but well to their rear. He sighed in relief. It was too soon.

There was a twenty second respite, then more artillery rounds splashed to their rear, but each successive round hit closer to them. The hostiles were 'walking their fire' to the target. And they were the target.

A shell impacted thirty yards to their left, exploded and rained down debris. They had the range.

"Serpentine, Luke!"

Hale resumed the evasive zigzags, randomly changing direction every ten seconds. Every time he jammed back one of the control levers, the APC lurched, throwing Storm around. More shells exploded around the APC, it bounded wildly.

A shell hit close to the left side and knocked the APC onto its right track, balanced precariously on the verge of capsizing. Instinctively, Hale pulled back the right lever, locking the right track. The inertia pivoted the APC right and slammed the left track back to the ground, hard, throwing Storm face-to-face with one of the dead soldiers.

"Holy shit! Luke, put the spurs to her."

Hale didn't need to be told. He had already released the levers forward and slammed the accelerator to the floor. The APC lurched forward again as Hale intently stared through the periscope visors, desperately trying to maneuver around craters and gullies. The thick smoke impeded his view, which was already extremely limited through the periscopes. He felt he was as much a passenger as a driver.

Minutes of ceaseless pounding had them convinced they were going to die. The explosions repeatedly hammered the APC, rocking it violently like a bucking bronco. Storm was thrown forward behind the driver's station, yanking him from his headset.

The air cleared. Hale could see stars and the headlights revealed terrain. "Which way is south?"

Storm aligned the GPS with the front of the APC and read the compass heading. "Twenty degrees right," he yelled into Hale's ear. Luke pulled the right lever back and headed south. The ride smoothed a bit. The shelling had ceased.

"I hope that's the last of it," yelled Storm.

"Amen."

A red tracer round from a large cannon arced across their path from the left. It exploded harmlessly two hundred yards to their right. Dozens of sets of headlights illuminated in front of them. Machinegun tracer bullets impacted into the desert thirty yards to their front. They were facing a semi-circle of armored vehicles, their lights and cannons focused on them. They had nowhere to go.

"Oh shit!" Luke locked both levers full aft, stopping. "They got us. It's been great knowing you, Derek." He killed the lights and lowered the ramp.

"You too, my friend. God bless." Storm grabbed their rifles and Russian hand grenades. He passed the Bushmaster and three grenades to Luke, then readied his weapons. They hustled to the ramp. They shook hands and slapped each other's back.

"I'll see you on the other side," said Luke.

"Ditto." They weren't talking about the border.

Hale hefted the RPG and grabbed several rocket grenades. They ran down the ramp and split, Hale going right, Storm left. They serpentined as they ran away from the APC, fearing a tank round would impact at any second. They expected machinegun fire but none came. They dove into depressions, trying to get as low as possible. They were fifty yards apart and could see each other in the spray of headlights.

Storm aimed his rifle across the front of Hale's position, covering him. Hale hurried, nervously trying to remember how to load and operate the RPG. He hadn't fired one since he had been in Special

Forces, thirty years ago. Once accomplished, he aimed his rifle across the front of Storm's position. With interlocking fields of fire, the hostiles would have to penetrate through two lanes of firepower to get at either of them. Even though their tactic was only symbolic against armor, it was the best defense they could mount, and they were determined to make the most of it, each to his dying breath.

CHAPTER XVII

RETURNS

Storm's heart pumped like an overloaded compressor. Ditto for Hale. They covered each other while burrowing deeper into the sand. It was three minutes before they realized no one was shooting at them. Other than the rumble of the idling armored vehicles, it was quiet.

"Mr. Hale? Mr. Storm?"

"*What the… English?*" Storm was confused. "*And how could they know our names?*" "Did you call me, Luke?"

"No. Did you call me?"

"Negative. What's going on?"

"Mr. Hale? Mr. Storm?" The voice came from the direction of the armored formation. A man walked into the spill of the headlights; he held a white flag.

"Who's there?" challenged Storm, taking aim.

"Hold your fire. Are you Mr. Hale?"

"No. Who are you?"

"Captain Robert Walker, United States Army. To whom am I speaking?"

"Where are we?"

"Kuwait. You're two clicks inside Kuwait."

Storm and Hale sighed, tears welled in their eyes. They had made it. Luke lowered his rifle and stood. "I'm Hale."

"I'm Storm."

Luke trotted to the Army Captain. "Are we glad to see you!" Luke vigorously pumped the Captain's hand.

Storm walked up and hugged Luke, then shook the Captain's hand.

"I'm glad we found you, sirs. We've been expecting you."

Persian Gulf: The satellite phone rang. Terry dashed to the communications console.

"Vixen, this is Terry."

"Terry! It's good to hear your voice."

"Mr. Hale! Where are you?"

"Mr. Storm and I are getting some medical attention. We're in Kuwait and we're safe. We have the artifacts. Let everyone know we'll be back to the ship this afternoon."

"With all due respect, sir, you're gonna have to do that yourself. Please don't hang up or Mrs. Hale will have me keelhauled."

Luke laughed. He knew Terry was right. Heather would be stalking about like a loup-garrou, a werewolf, looking for something to kill. "Okay. I'll hang on. Wake them up."

"Thanks, sir." Terry hit the PA button. "Attention all hands. Attention all hands. This is the bridge. Mr. Hale and Mr. Storm are alive and well. I say again, they're alive and well."

"I'll take the phone, Terry." Heather stood behind Pell, tears in her eyes and a relieved look on her weary face.

Northern Kuwait: "Yep. We're fine, honey. The Army found us and we're getting some medical attention. We'll be back to the ship this afternoon. I love you, too." Luke blew a kiss into the phone, disconnected and handed it to Storm. He immediately dialed Lisa's cell, figuring it was 3:30 p.m. in California and she was probably at work in the lab.

The battalion medics cleaned and dressed their wounds and tended to Storm's injured back. They put stitches into Hale's gashes. Derek rested on a field cot as they girdled his back with a brace.

"Captain Walker, how did you know we were headed your way?" inquired Luke.

"Division G-2 received a fax from CentCom stating that two American civilians had been shot down in a private helicopter, and were going to cross the desert to the border."

Hale realized that Salty must have yanked a few strings and informed CentCom of their plan. *God bless him.*

Captain Walker continued. "We were advised to be on the alert for you, either on foot, possibly by vehicle. When our forward observation posts spotted an APC flying a white flag and dodging an artillery barrage, we suspected it was you. We fired rounds across your bow to get your attention."

"That was one of our tanks?"

"Yes sir. We needed to get you stopped before you ran over any of our soldiers."

"Ah. Thank God for that. I'd never be able to sleep with that kind of guilt."

"That was impressive work you did," complimented Walker.

"What work?"

"Subduing the sentries and stealing the APC. That took guts."

"How did you know we subdued sentries?"

"We have our sources," answered Walker, with a sly wink. "You hungry, sir?"

"I'm famished. We ran out of food yesterday."

"We'll fix you up, sir." Walker turned to a cigarette-smoking Sergeant at the tent opening. "Sergeant Gillespie, see if the mess tent can rustle up a couple of hot meals for these taxpayers."

The Sergeant nodded and disappeared into the darkness.

"Thank you, Captain. We appreciate the hospitality." Luke placed a friendly hand on the Captain's shoulder. "Listen, Captain, there's something your Intel people need to know about." Hale went to Storm's cot. He was talking all lovey-dovey with Lisa. Painkillers had made him giddy. Luke pointed at his map. Storm flashed an 'okay' without breaking the stride of his phone conversation. Luke pulled the map, unfolded it and informed Captain Walker of the Iraqi biochemical depot.

Helendale: "Pete, they're safe! And they found the tablet!"

Pete came running. "That's great! They're okay?"

"Yes. He'll be coming home soon. He took digital photos and sent them to my brother. We should have a translation soon."

"That's terrific. I'm anxious to see what this ancient treatment is." Pete shook his head in disbelief. "Is that Derek on the phone?"

"Yes. Want to talk with him?"

"Absolutely."

Lisa presented Pete her cell.

"Hello, Derek? It's Pete. How are you, lad?"

"Hi Pete. We got banged up a bit, but overall we're good. I re-injured my back."

"How serious?"

"It's just muscular. I won't need surgery again, just some T-L-C."

"He needs T-L-C, Doctor Chen. Isn't that your specialty?"

Lisa flashed a mischievous smile.

"Lisa says she's going to be on you like a cheap suit."

Lisa slapped his arm. "You're bad, Peter. Give me my phone."

Storm laughed. He was anxious to get back to her and Pete.

"Hello sweetie," she purred. "I can't wait for you to get home."

"Me too. Can you arrange to get me home from Kuwait City?"

"I'll check and get back to you."

Storm gave her Luke's personal satellite number.

"Got it. I'll get right back to you. I love you." She blew a kiss into the phone.

"You too. I'll be waiting."

Lisa disconnected. "Oh, Pete. This is great news. I'm going to make arrangements for Derek and then I'm calling Lawrence and ask him to put a rush on that translation."

Kuwait City: The Army had been magnificent. They stitched Luke's wounds, cleaned and bandaged Storm's, and braced his back. They also treated their burns. They even fed them, gave them clean clothes and provided hot showers.

The food was better than Hale had remembered from his time in the Army. The troops looked muscular and energetic.

3rd Infantry Division HQ sent two Intelligence officers to interview them about the biochemical depot. They took copious notes and asked pertinent questions. Storm and Hale answered truthfully without embellishment. The officers were grateful for the information and promised to arrange transport to Kuwait City.

They were good to their word. Thirty minutes later, a Hummer arrived to take them to civilization.

The driver loaded their gear and rifles. The drive to Kuwait City was an hour. The driver was fascinated by their adventure. Approaching the city, Storm handed his blood-encrusted shaken to Luke.

"I won't get this through airport security."

Hale took it and tucked into the sheath in his vest. "You're going to the airport?"

"Yeah. Lisa made arrangements for me to hop a cargo flight."

"Bullshit! You're not riding a jump seat halfway around the world with your back in that condition." Luke plugged his satellite phone into the Hummer and dialed.

"Skipper, it's Luke. Could you do me a favor?" He instructed Skibba to buy a First Class airline ticket for Storm.

Persian Gulf: The noise and vibration inside the Sea King helicopter rattled Hale to the bones. Walt Skibba had significant pull with the Navy.

After dropping Storm at the airport, the driver took Hale to the port helipad. The Navy chopper was waiting for him. The crew briefed Hale on emergency procedures and got him strapped in. They lifted off and headed for the *Vixen*.

The helicopter was too large for the *Vixen*'s helipad, so they planned to lower Luke on a winch.

Hale stared out the door, reliving the past three days. He had never felt more alive, or blessed. He closed his eyes and offered thanks to God.

When he opened his eyes, he saw the silhouette of the *Vixen* on the horizon; it was home.

The crew chief whistled. "Wow. That's one beauty of a ship. That's yours, sir?"

Luke nodded, "With God's blessings, yes. And thanks. She is a beauty."

As the chopper approached the ship, Luke spotted Heather, Amber and the entire crew on the upper deck, waving and jumping wildly. Confetti flew. A banner was strung across the back of the helipad; WELCOME BACK LUKE & DEREK.

The Rescue man clipped a snap link to Luke's harness. As Luke stepped to the open door, the Rescue man asked, "Who's Derek, sir?"

A tear came to Luke's eye. He grinned. "He's my friend."

Helendale: Lisa opened the e-mail from her brother.

> Greets sis,
> The digital images were fascinating. I would like to examine the tablet when Mr. Muscles returns. Can you arrange that? Thanks sweetie.

The translation is in the attachment. Good luck. I hope
it helps.
Love
Lawrence

Lisa tapped out a thoughtful reply and sent it. Then she opened the
attachment. The translation was there.

"Pete. Come see this." She printed copies of the text.

Pete entered the safe room. "What's up?"

"The transcript just came in."

Pete took the first copy from the printer and studied it. Lisa read it
on screen.

"... nine portions of green tea, prepared as described.
Take water of one moon cycle having magnet and silver
coin immersed. Heat water, not boil, to hot. Insert one
crushed walnut and one portion green tea. Insert hot
water. Sufferer must consume entire portion while warm,
not cold, not boil. Consume nine portions each cycle of
light. Do not consume after light. Sleepless result. Stop
treatment for nerves quiver, sleepless, nails turn white,
hair fall out, or stomach nervous. When nails normal
and stomach not nervous, start again, five portions early
each light cycle, for one moon cycle. Increase portion
by another for each light cycle, for one moon cycle.
When nails white, remove one portion for light cycle.
Steady consume this amount of portions each light cycle.
This treatment stops the internal growth disease. Most
sufferers return normal healthy. So says Chang Li Suk,
healer of Uiguristan. Reverence to Khan.

"Interesting," stated Pete. "The mention of magnetically charged
silver in the water reminds me of what the pioneers did in the 19th
century. They would toss a silver coin into their water barrels to keep
the water fresh. And colloidal silver has been around for millennia. It's
claimed to have beneficial health properties. I wonder what the green
tea and the walnuts are about?"

"Let's see what the analysis software has." Lisa tapped a few keys
and clicked the mouse. A search page appeared. She typed in WALNUTS
and tapped the ENTER key. A reference page popped up. It listed the

element and mineral contents. They scanned the list.

"My goodness," declared Pete. He pointed to an element halfway down the list. It said, SELENIUM, high in content, second only to Brazil nuts. "Selenium is an ingredient of antioxidant enzymes. It's essential for the immune system and the thyroid."

Lisa added, "I'm aware of studies showing that it lowers incidences of prostate, colorectal and lung cancers. Intriguing, yes?"

"But what's with the green tea?"

Lisa returned to the search page, typed in GREEN TEA, and hit ENTER. Another reference page appeared. They scanned the data.

"Here," pointed Lisa. "Selenium has also been found to greatly increase the anti-cancer effectiveness of green tea," she read aloud.

"Interesting," stated Pete. "The Chinese healer used the selenium in the walnuts to enhance the green tea. Combined with the charged silver, perhaps he really hit upon a combination that eliminates unhealthy cells from the body."

"How so?"

"Let's say that healthy cells carry a positive energy charge and unhealthy cells, such as cancer, are either negatively charged or dead. It stands to reason that the negatively charged unhealthy cells would be attracted to the positively charged silver and expelled with the silver through the skin and excretion."

Lisa pondered the concept, then added, "And by ridding the unhealthy cells, the green tea and selenium boost the immune system and it overtakes the disease. The body cures itself."

"Sounds plausible. Which makes me wonder how the DDCG had effect." They read further into the data. The last finding provided a possible answer.

Pete read out loud, "…EGCG, epigallocatechin gallate, was shown to disrupt the cell cycle in human colon cancer cells." Pete stood up, staring into the distance.

"What is it, Pete?"

"EGCG and DDCG are the same family of polyphenols. They both suppress cancer cell function. But we know that the DDCG has harmful side-effects in large doses and it isn't potent enough in small doses."

"It has to be in the combination, Pete. I think we need to experiment with this formula."

"I agree. We need to order colloidal silver, green tea extract and a large supply of selenium."

"We need a big magnet, too."

Persian Gulf: The master stateroom was decorated in rich colors and materials. Frilly garments hung from sconces and hooks, feather boas adorned light fixtures and sexy artwork hung from the bulkheads. Lace-trimmed lampshades accented the gilded gold, burgundy colored walls and a heavy, antique brass headboard dominated the king-size, satin covered bed. Luke called it 'French Bordello' decor. It was very erotic and it was his and Heather's favorite retreat.

Anticipating Luke's arrival, Heather had turned down the bed, perfumed the sheets, fluffed the frilly pillows, lit the scented candles and put on soft jazz. She wore sexy lingerie beneath her conservative clothes.

She gave Luke an hour with the crew, knowing there had to be a celebration. But at the first opportunity, she grabbed him by the belt and seductively nuzzled his ear. "It's time for a *real* welcome home, darling."

They retreated to the stateroom. The crew avoided the passageway to their suite. Their lovemaking was passionate. They giggled as they tried to stifle their sounds of passion, but their endeavor was obvious, embarrassing Amber. The younger crewmen chuckled and cast teasing glances her way.

"How gross? Everyone knows my parents are having sex."

Salty reigned in the least tactful of the crewmen by assigning them duties. It was time to leave the gulf.

Ontario, California: It was a beautiful sunny day and Lisa anticipated spending all of it with Derek. She had a special treat in store. The drive home up the Cajon Pass normally took an hour. But she had a feeling they wouldn't make it all the way home without stopping. In fact, she wouldn't be surprised if they had to stop before they reached the pass.

Storm was the first passenger to emerge from the jet bridge. His crooked smile melted her.

"Derek!" She ran into his greeting arms. They embraced tightly and kissed deeply.

"Let's get your luggage," she urged.

"Don't have any. So let's just get going."

They ran the length of the hall, hand-in-hand, weaving through the throng of passengers, out the security checkpoint, down the escalator and out to the short-term lot. Lisa led him to the Hummer.

They embraced again. They wanted each other in every way imaginable.

"Let's go," urged Lisa. Storm grinned. She unlocked the Hummer with the remote as she ran around to the driver's side. They buckled in. Lisa started the engine, quickly backed out and drove for the exit.

They weren't even to the highway before she laid her hand seductively on his thigh.

"Got something in mind, China doll?"

She was right. They didn't make it to the Cajon Pass before they had to stop. It wasn't even close.

Indian Ocean: The salt air invigorated Luke. He, Heather and Amber casually paraded the length and breadth of the *Vixen*, savoring her splendor as she split the smooth waters.

The crew was happy to have Luke back and relieved to be leaving the Persian Gulf. They were looking forward to exploring Mauritius, the *Vixen*'s next destination.

"Dinner should be ready soon," remarked Heather. "Connie's preparing blackened redfish, scalloped potatoes, creamed asparagus and my special spinach-strawberry salad."

"Mmm. Sounds good."

"Enjoy yourself, dear. I'm going to the galley to help Connie."

"You bet, honey. I'll be there for dinner." Luke gave Heather a peck on the lips and a discreet pat on her tush.

"I'll help," added Amber. Luke gave her a peck on the cheek. "Bye, Dad." The ladies headed for the galley, leaving Luke on the helipad. He missed his helicopter. The ship looked as if a part were missing. He missed Derek too.

He fished into his pocket and removed the gemstones and jade disc they had discovered. The stones were colored, one a deep red, the other green. Luke guessed that one was a ruby and the other emerald. He made a mental note to have them appraised, cut and polished.

The jade disc caught his interest. It appeared to be a match for the one Storm had made into a necklace. He had worn it for many years. It was a symbol of Storm's personality, part of his identity. There was no other man Luke wanted by his side if he was in a scrape; events had confirmed that.

Luke resolved to make the amulet into a medallion, exactly like Storm's, and to wear it around his neck, exactly like Storm.

Victorville: Percy and Trigger munched doughnuts and sipped coffee as they maintained vigil across the street from Dr. Flynn's mailbox station. The establishment was a private business, offering personal mail and shipping services. It was in a strip mall on Seventh Street, the main drag. The business offered twenty-four hour access to its mailbox clients, requiring the Bravo team to maintain a twenty-four/seven watch.

Percy and Trigger parked across the street, in the lot of a twenty-four hour gas station and convenience store. They parked off to the side, allowing rapid exit and an unobstructed view through the mail store windows. It was a simple matter to survey the mailboxes through binoculars; the lobby was well lit.

They were better prepared than their first encounter with Storm. They carried their usual side arms, now equipped with silencers and laser sights, stun guns, a taser, spotting scope, submachine guns and scoped rifles. Trigger even brought an M-72 LAW, a recoilless Light Antitank Weapon, which fired an unguided, high explosive rocket capable of taking out an armored car. They were ready.

The early morning weather was very comfortable. The winds were light and the temperature mid-sixties. Visibility was unlimited.

Trigger sipped his coffee and checked his watch; it was three thirty-three a.m. It was boring, especially the graveyard shift. Hardly anyone entered the mail store between 2300 and 0700.

Surprisingly, the convenience store was busy. Truckers, sanitation workers and road maintenance crews provided a steady flow of customers.

The Bravo team had stenciled the logo of a well-known security company on their SUV's, providing them with a cover should the local police take an interest. Sparks had even manufactured phony, but credible, ID cards.

An old green Toyota hatchback pulled into the strip mall. Percy tapped Trigger's arm. " 'Ave a look, mate."

Trigger set down his coffee and grabbed the binoculars. The occupant emerged and walked into the mail store.

" 'E's makin' for the proper row."

Trigger peered through the binoculars. The elderly man shuffled to the row where Flynn's box was located. The man, who appeared

Mexican, was definitely not Flynn, Storm or the chick doctor. The man casually looked around and inserted a key into a mailbox lock. Trigger concentrated, zoomed and re-focused.

"That's it, Percy. This guy must be Flynn's courier. It sure as hell ain't Flynn or Storm."

"Oy mate. What say we get some snapshots?" Percy lifted a camera with a telephoto lens and snapped numerous photos of the Toyota and the courier as he exited the store.

"Get the license plate?"

"Oy mate."

Trigger zoomed and focused on the license plate. He scribbled the registration and vehicle description on his notepad.

The courier climbed into his vehicle and drove off. He turned north on Seventh Street. Percy started the SUV and followed, keeping a discreet distance.

At the end of the street, the courier turned left onto old Route 66. Percy casually followed. Trigger concentrated on keeping the vehicle in sight.

The winding drive along the two-lane road seemed to take forever. Passing a little town named Oro Grande, Trigger speed-dialed Sparks on his cell. He wasn't surprised it took six rings for Sparks to answer.

"Hello?"

"Sparks. Wake up. It's Trigger."

"What's up?"

"A courier just cleaned out the mailbox. We're tailing him. It's an old Mexican guy in a green Toyota hatchback. He's heading northbound on 66. We just passed a town called Oro Grande."

"Should I wake the Colonel?"

"Uh, not yet. Let's see where this takes us. But for insurance, get Yankee and Slash on the road for backup."

"Okay. Good idea. I'll have them call you for rendezvous."

"Good man. If we turn up something, we'll call."

"Okay. I'll inform the Colonel when he wakes up."

"Roger that." Trigger snapped his cell shut and clipped it to his belt.

The road paralleled the usually dry Mojave River. There were some lush areas adjacent to the river but mostly it was sparsely populated hills and desert.

The long drive passed a biker's bar, some modest homes, trailer parks, and a resort community called Silver Lakes in the town of Helendale.

Just north of the Silver Lakes turnoff, the road wound through some hills, finally turning northeast toward Barstow.

"Christ. This guy's heading for Bedouin country."

"Oy mate."

The Toyota made a left turn. Percy killed the headlights and turned onto the same road. The street sign read INDIAN TRAIL.

The Toyota crossed a set of railroad tracks, then across the Mojave River bed, turned a bend in the road and stopped at an array of mailboxes. Percy coasted to the side of the road without touching the brakes; it kept the brake lights from illuminating.

Trigger saw the man exit the car, cross through its headlights and place envelopes into the bottom right mailbox. The man returned to the vehicle and drove away.

As Trigger kept the Toyota in sight, Percy sped to the mailboxes, jammed the shift into PARK and ran to the box. It had no identification on it. He opened it, grabbed the mail and hustled to the glow of the SUV's interior dome light. He checked the addresses on the envelopes.

"They're all addressed to Corridor Holdings, Trigger."

"That's it. This is a dead drop."

"Oy. We just got closer." Percy returned the mail to the box and closed it. He jogged back to the driver's side and climbed in.

"All right," said Trigger. "Let's find a place to stakeout this box."

"Right-O, mate."

They had no inkling they were only one mile from the lab.

San Francisco, California: "I'm doing splendidly, sissy," declared Lawrence. "And how might you be?"

"Great. That translation has put our research back on track."

"Oh goodie. I'm happy for you. How is that hunky boyfriend of yours?"

"Derek is just hunky," she giggled.

"Is he back yet?"

"Oh, yes. He arrived yesterday. In fact, he's here now."

"Oh, goodie. He can listen in. I think he'll be interested in what I've learned from my Italian friend, Guido."

"Sure. Let me hook up my cell to the speakerphone." Lawrence heard some commotion, then heard Lisa call out, "Derek. Pete. Lawrence is on the phone and he has important information for us. Come listen." There was more commotion and a click.

"Okay, Lawrence. You're on speakerphone and we're all here."

"Salutations one and all. It's Lawrence calling from lovely San Francisco and I have some exciting news for you."

Storm answered, "Go ahead, Lawrence. We're all ears."

"You're *much* more than that, you hunk." Lawrence couldn't hear it, but Storm laughed silently. "But anyway, I've learned some interesting details from my Italian friend, Guido, you know, the art historian in Venice. He is *such* a party animal."

They laughed at Lawrence's descriptive commentary.

"Guido is an expert on the Polo expeditions and he told me that during the Polo's second expedition, the really long one in which Marco accompanied them, they lost several ships in the vicinity of the Persian Gulf. The expedition was escorted by Chinese soldiers commanded by Sun Dek Yee. After escorting the Polo's to Constantinople, Commander Sun returned to China with his men in 1295 A.D. The Commander learned that his Imperial benefactor, the great Kublai Khan, had died the year prior. Then, the new Emperor assigned Commander Sun to serve as a district Prefect during his retirement. During that period, Sun wrote his memoirs and left detailed descriptions of his exploits."

Lawrence paused briefly. "It seems that the expedition was sailing in a fleet of Chinese ships in the vicinity of the Straight of Hormuz when they were beset by pirates. The pirates sank one of their vessels, named *Sea Wind*. Sun wrote that most of the crew were saved, however the ship went to the bottom with a rather large cargo of gold bullion and coins. It has never been located."

"Wow. A treasure hunt," intoned Storm sarcastically.

Lawrence continued. "Well, Sun was injured during that battle, but he recovered. He lost one of his eyes, I'm told. But here's the really interesting part. The second ship they lost was named *Sea Spray*. Sun's account states that the pirates murdered the entire ship's complement and looted the cargo. By the time the Chinese recovered the ship, it was a total loss, so they set it adrift in the gulf."

"That's interesting Lawrence. But what makes that important?" asked Storm.

"Valid question, my muscled friend. Remember the digital images you took of the buried ship?"

"Yeah?"

"On the stern of the junk, the big plank with the Chinese characters carved out?"

"Yeah?"

"That engraving is the name of the ship."

There was a long silence. Lawrence could feel the tension, the anticipation, right through the radio waves. He was savoring the moment.

Pete couldn't stand the suspense. "Get on with it, man."

"Oh, party pooper. Very well." Lawrence inhaled for effect. "The name of the ship that Derek found is... *Sea Spray.*"

Lawrence had to recoil from the phone. The shouts of excitement hurt his ear. He held the phone at a comfortable distance until the cacophony subsided.

"So chances are that the artifacts are genuine?" posed Lisa.

"It certainly supports that conclusion," answered Lawrence. "Also, Commander Sun's memoirs specifically mention the name of a healer who joined the expedition and became Sun's personal attendant."

"Let me guess," said Pete. "Chang Li Suk?"

"Give that man a cigar."

"So these tablets are the real thing," said Lisa, amazed.

"It appears so, sweetie. And the final information I want to pass on is this. Guido says that when Marco Polo died, the estate he left to his wife and children was only half as large as he had claimed. There was supposedly a vast treasure of jewels and gold that the Polo's hid somewhere in the Mediterranean. After departing Constantinople by ships, they were caught in a storm. Some of the ships were damaged too badly to sail, so they are rumored to have stashed half of their treasure on one of the Greek Isles with the intention of returning to retrieve it at a later date."

"Shortly after they returned to Venice, war broke out against the city-state of Genoa. Marco was captured and imprisoned. That's when he disclosed his exploits to a fellow prisoner, a writer, who penned "The Adventures of Marco Polo.""

"Intriguing," stated Storm.

"Yes, it is," affirmed Lawrence. "The truly enticing part is that the Polos never had an opportunity to recover their stash before they died. Legend has it that it's still hidden somewhere in the Greek Isles."

CHAPTER XVIII

MURDER IN MIND

Washington, D.C.: Sandra Dillers walked down the hall to her supervisor's office. She carried the records for Congresswoman Stakemore and her Good Works PAC, along with her Report of Findings.

Stakemore's PAC had failed to report the enormous contributions of the NOMP. Actually, one was unreported, the other under-reported. The Chairman of the NOMP Board himself had confirmed the anonymous allegations. They were going to have some explaining to do.

Sandra knocked on Kathy's door and entered.

Kathy Zimmerman gazed up from her desk.

"It's all here, Kathy, the complete package for the Ethics Committee."

Portland: The weather was pleasant and sunny. Kress regretted having to spend the day indoors, shuffling through piles of papers that had stacked up during his vacation. He would rather have been fishing or back in Fiji. Or better yet, on that yacht with the rich babe, what was her name? Amber something. He recalled the ship's name, *Serene Vixen.* Then he recalled. Hale, their family name was Hale.

The intercom squawked. "Kress?"

"What is it, Tara?"

"Have you checked your e-mail? The in-file is full and it's re-routing your excess to mine."

"Okay. Don't get your pantyhose in a wad."

"Brat."

Kress turned to his computer. Tara was right. "Shit. Seventy-one messages," he mumbled. He scanned the list and deleted the SPAM. That thinned it out. He transferred others to hold files, deleted a few more and replied to others. At the thirty-second message, he recognized Melanie's e-mail address. He clicked on it.

"Ghost,

I sent the information to the FEC. FBI will not investigate. Maybe FEC can do something. These people have to be stopped. Wish me luck.

Melanie

PS: If anything happens to me, please come forward and reveal all you know about Rushton. He and Stakemore are thick as thieves."

"Holy shit, girl."

Kress drummed his fingers. There wasn't much he could do. Kress hit the intercom button. "Tara, did we come up with anything on 'Bravo'?"

"Nope. Dead end."

"How about Iris Stakemore?"

"Just the unclassified stuff."

"Okay. Thanks."

Kress had a hard choice to make. Should he risk himself to help Taylor or should he maintain a low profile? He knew what the safe option was but his conscience wouldn't allow him to choose it. He got her involved. He couldn't leave her suspended on a high wire without a net.

Kress tapped out a reply to Taylor and sent it. He braced his elbows on his desk and flopped his head into his palms.

"I can't believe I'm doing this."

Helendale: Pete studied the specimen samples. He could hardly believe his eyes.

"Lisa, check the microscope and tell me what you see."

Lisa leaned into the instrument. She studied the comparative samples.

"What am I looking for, Pete?"

"See if the cancerous cells appear active."

"Yes they are. But barely."

"That's my judgment too. I think we've disrupted their replication cycle." Pete noted the time and marked it on his chart. "Is there any change in the control group?"

"They still seem active."

Pete switched slides. "Now take a look at this sample."

Lisa looked. "Those cells are very active, perhaps twenty percent more. Is that the control group?"

"No. Those are the healthy cells subjected to the protocol. Here are the control group's healthy cells." Pete switched slides again.

Lisa peered in. "Looks normal." She stood up and smiled.

Pete's smile greeted her. "That was my conclusion. Now, I'm going to switch slides again. Tell me if you see any group overtaking another."

Pete swapped slides. She instantly saw the difference. "The healthy cells are strong. They're repelling the cancerous cells. It works, Pete." She stood.

"Good. We're at a consensus. I think we've stopped the cancerous growth and strengthened the healthy cells. There's more."

Pete placed two slides of identical cancerous cells under the device. Lisa leaned into the instrument again. Pete took a vial from the bench and shook it.

"Watch closely. Both slides are from the same control group specimen. I'm going to add one drop of the protocol solution to the slide on the right."

Lisa saw the drop of fluid appear and meld into the sample. The original sample remained in its active cycle. The treated sample showed immediate effect. The cancerous cells were becoming lethargic. The healthy cells became more vigorous.

"That's amazing Pete. The effect is instantaneous. The original sample is still in its growth cycle but the treated sample is disrupted. You've done it."

Lisa cleared a space for Pete. He looked into the scope again. He studied the results for a moment and came up smiling. "It works," he declared proudly.

"What's next?"

"Now we have to duplicate the test results with more specimens. We'll need at least a dozen tests with results that can be duplicated. Then we can proceed to live specimens to check side-effects."

Pete glowed with anticipation. Lisa hugged him.

∞

Storm put the finishing touches to the tunnel entry door and its hydraulic mechanism. Pete's handyman had re-routed the electrical power so the hydraulic pump and its control panel ran off a separate generator. That modification would prevent power surges to the lab equipment. The handyman had also installed floodlights.

A loud rumble shook the ground. Storm braced himself against the wall, fearing an earthquake. The vibration built up slowly. It grew louder and more intense. It seemed to originate overhead. Storm heard the blast of an air horn, then another, followed by two shorter blasts.

The vibration reached a crescendo that rattled Storm's bones. Dirt shook from the walls and ceiling and clouded the air. The flood lights rattled and blinked, casting an eerie strobe light effect.

The racket slowly subsided, leaving a dirty mess. Storm coughed and sneezed, not finding relief from the irritating, stagnant air. He pulled his tee shirt over his face to filter the air.

He flipped the lever to power the hydraulic pump, then pressed the START button. The pump surged, then stabilized at high RPM. The pressure climbed into the green arc on the gauge, 3000 to 3300 psi. Storm pressed the UNLOCK button. Two jackscrew bolts turned and slid outward from the edges of the door. He pressed the OPEN button. The hydraulic pressure dropped slightly and the pump automatically increased RPM, boosting the pressure back into the green arc.

The door squealed as the actuators overcame their decades of stagnant inertia. Light appeared through the bottom of the exit.

Storm generously applied more lubricant to the actuators and lift mechanism. The heavy door slowly swung outward and upward, pivoting on huge hinges at its top. Brilliant sunlight and fresh air entered the tunnel. Storm lowered his tee shirt and wiped the grime from his face.

He stepped outside, squinting as he scanned full circle. Railroad tracks ran directly over the tunnel entrance. A crossing was two hundred yards to the north. That explained the air horn. Trains used the horns at crossings to warn drivers of their approach.

A hard-packed dirt trail ran parallel to the tracks. It stretched for miles, passing the crossing to the north, past the tunnel entrance and past a dirt underpass a hundred yards to the south.

Storm climbed the embankment to the tracks. He scanned the area. Both the dirt road underpass and the paved crossing ran east for a quarter mile, all the way to the old Route 66. He turned to descend the slope and stopped in his tracks.

"*Son-of-a-gun.*" The outer surface of the tunnel door was covered with gravel and sagebrush. It was camouflaged! It looked exactly like the embankment.

"*It's a secret entrance.*"

Moonlight Bay, Mauritius: The *Vixen* anchored off the west coast of Mauritius Island. It was the smaller of two islands, the other being Reunion, just off the east coast of the huge island of Madagascar. The small islands were French possessions.

The weather was splendid for water activities. It was sunny, hot and humid. After the stresses of the Persian Gulf, the crew eagerly took to the refreshing waters. Some were darting about on jet skis and wave runners. Others used the launch to parasail. Others dove from the helipad, while some went ashore for snorkeling or shopping. Everyone was having a great time.

The satellite phone rang. Salty pulled it from his pocket and answered. "Vixen. This is Captain Skibba."

"Salty. It's Derek. How goes it?"

"I'm fine, Mr. Storm. Did you get to California okay?"

"Sure did. Thanks for asking. It's a beautiful night here in the desert. The stars are amazing."

"I know what you mean. Would you like to speak with Mr. Hale?"

"Certainly. Is he about?"

"Right next to me. Hold on." He passed the phone to Luke.

"I hear you made it home okay."

"Sure did. Thanks for the first class ticket."

"My pleasure, lad. How's the back?"

"Still gets spasms but otherwise okay. I'm calling to update you. Lisa's brother called yesterday and had an interesting tale about that ship and the artifacts. It verifies their authenticity and get this; that ship was named *Sea Spray* and was part of the second Polo expedition. It was set adrift in the Persian Gulf in 1294 A.D."

"No kidding?"

"That's not the half of it." Storm briefed Luke on the Polo estate, the artifacts and the cancer research.

Hale listened closely, allowing Storm to talk away. "So tell me again about this Polo treasure."

Washington, D.C.: Stakemore was madder than a neutered rooster in a henhouse. Her temper was legendary and she had the reputation of shooting the messenger, even throwing things at them. Those who knew her always delivered bad news by e-mail. Any other mode was too risky.

She had just received e-mail from a source within the House Ethics Committee. The message stated that evidence had been submitted to the committee from the FEC. It concerned contributions to her PAC from a certain organization, and allegations of attempting to influence a federal investigation regarding interstate crimes.

"That son-of-a-bitch Rushton. He's the only one who could have given the FEC that information. Or maybe there's a leak in NOMP."

She considered her predicament. The House Ethics Committee was chaired by the House Majority Whip, the second highest-ranking Congressman of the opposing party. He was merciless in policing ethics violations. And since she was a member of the minority party, he would take extensive measures to rake her over the coals.

She would have to pressure Rushton to get rid of the problem. Otherwise, she'd be subpoenaed to appear before the committee and be subjected to embarrassing, probing cross-examination. She would be disgraced, censured, perhaps even expelled from the House, maybe even end up in prison. And if Rushton were the problem, she would have to get rid of him.

The FEC sources must not be allowed to testify. They must never have the opportunity to jeopardize her. They had to be neutralized, permanently.

She grabbed her cell phone.

Boston: "But Congresswoman, you can't expect me to conduct a witch hunt for some nebulous characters and… neutralize them. I'm a doctor," declared Rushton indignantly.

"Don't give me that doctor shit, Doctor. Miller coerced me into squelching that investigation. Do you know the risks I had to take for that? Of course not. Now the House Ethics Committee is on my ass. Do you realize what could happen if I'm subpoenaed? Does the word 'prison' inspire you?"

Rushton considered her statements. He knew he had to play ball or he could be living in a 6 by 8 foot birdcage for a long time. "Congresswoman, how can I help?"

Stakemore outlined her demands as Rushton rubbed his temple. He shouldn't be hearing this from a member of Congress, but he was.

Stakemore had no qualms about quashing any threat. *"This is a hell of a mess."*

Finally, the Potomac windbag came up for air. "Madame, you are diabolical. It will be done. I don't see that we have a choice."

"Correct, Doctor. You don't! So do it!" The connection went dead. Her unspoken threat was tacitly understood.

Helendale: From a hill a mile away, Storm viewed the area around Pete's dead drop through his binoculars. His mission was to retrieve Pete's mail.

He noticed an SUV turn off Indian Trail onto a dirt road. It went westbound two hundred yards and turned into the desert, weaving slowly between large junipers and sagebrush.

It stopped and a large man exited the passenger side. He walked northeast and began tiptoeing, as if stalking something.

Storm scanned left and spotted the probable target. An identical SUV was parked between some large junipers, facing the mailbox array. Storm hadn't noticed it before. *"Reconnaissance definitely pays off."*

Storm observed the stalker again. He recalled this man. He was one of those who had pursued Lisa and him near Fort Irwin. Storm now knew the rules of the game. These were the killers, and they were on to Pete's dead drop.

Storm bided his time and observed. They were too far away to engage with his rifle. Nor could he approach them in Pete's truck; they had unobstructed fields of fire. And approach on foot against professional killers was foolishly suicidal. Taking them out now was not an option.

Storm observed the stalker as he soft-stepped toward the parked vehicle and withdrew a knife. It's polished steel blade flashed in the sunlight. The killer rounded the rear corner of the SUV, crouched and crept to the driver's door. The driver appeared to be asleep. He saw the stalker reach for the open window.

Slash silently crept up behind the SUV. He could make out one figure inside but he suspected there was another inside or close by. The target was leaning back on the headrest. Slash guessed he was asleep.

"Dead meat." Slash muffled the noise of his switchblade as he clicked it open. He soft-stepped closer and noticed the driver's window was open.

"This is gonna be easy." He shifted the blade to his left hand and

squatted as he rounded the left rear corner of the vehicle. The side mirror reflected the target's face. He was sleeping. Slash eased forward, planning to get his blade to the victim's throat.

He raised the blade and reached through the window. The door burst open, deflecting his blade and slamming into his knee. The intended victim grabbed Slash's left wrist and violently twisted it outwards with so much force Slash had to throw himself into a cartwheel to prevent his elbow from being broken.

His adversary released his grip and jumped out, jammed his right knee into Slash's groin and harshly grasped his throat, his thumb dug into the side of his Adam's apple. The pain in his groin and throat was excruciating. He howled. The adversary thrust the fingers of his free hand at Slash's eyes, stopping just short of gouging into them. He posed them there as a warning.

"You might try less after-shave, mate," teased Percy. "You smell as a tart; it woke me up." Percy laughed, released his grip and helped Slash to his feet.

Slash coughed reflexively from the poke in the throat. He shook his head and chuckled, having new respect for Percy. There were damned few people who could subdue him when he had a blade in his hand. The New Zealander was good, very good.

Trigger stepped from behind a nearby juniper, zipping up his fly and chuckling. "Looks like Percy got the best of you, man. Pretty impressive for a runt."

Slash rubbed his sore groin and retrieved his blade. "Whew, man," he rasped, massaging his throat. "You're good. I gotta hand it to you." Slash extended his hand, Percy accepted it and they shook. It was official. Slash had finally accepted Percy as a card-carrying member of the Bravo team.

Yankee drove up in the other SUV, shoved it into PARK and climbed out. "Glad to see you boys are playing well with others." His shit-eating grin let Slash know he had seen the whole episode.

Slash routinely tried to sneak up on fellow team members to see if he could catch them off guard. It was rare that any of them could stop him before he got his blade to their throats. He used this drill to keep the others on their toes and taunt them with his prowess. But Percy was no sucker and had just proved it.

∽

From his hilltop perch, Storm observed the door burst open; the stalker was caught off guard and subjected to a violent supination takedown. The vehicle occupant very skillfully manipulated the stalker into submission, stopping just short of gouging his eyes out.

The sudden halt of the maiming strike told Storm that he was observing a spontaneous drill, designed to taunt and test comrades-in-arms. These men were definitely combat trained; the intended prey was particularly proficient with unarmed defense techniques. He had just subdued an armed opponent who outweighed him by fifty pounds, from a position of disadvantage.

He focused on the victor. He was about Storm's height but lacked Storm's barrel chest and thick arms. But he certainly had a thorough knowledge of physical dynamics and would be a worthy adversary hand-to-hand, if it ever came to that. Storm focused on the man's face. He didn't recognize him.

Nor did he recognize the huge black man who emerged from behind a large juniper, zipping up his fly. But he did recall the man who drove the SUV. It was one of the pursuers from the previous month. This was no coincidence.

Storm's plan formed. He lowered the glasses and smirked. He climbed into Pete's truck and started it. He hefted his FN rifle, checked the magazine was properly seated, pulled back the bolt lever and released it, chambering the first of twenty 7.62 mm rounds. He checked the safety engaged, placed it on the floor and drew his Colt. He tapped the magazine, ensuring proper seating, pulled back the slide and released it, racking the first of seven rounds into the chamber. He patted his vest, checking that his spare magazines and shaken were secure. He clicked on the Colt's thumb safety and holstered it.

"It time to play."

Storm shifted into DRIVE and headed down the hill toward the intersection of Wild Road and Indian Trail. He got a running start, blew through the STOP sign and floored the gas. The powerful VORTEC V-6 engine accelerated the light truck rapidly to seventy miles an hour.

∞

Percy and Trigger had been up all night. Yankee and Slash had just arrived for their shift to watch the dead drop. The mail was still there, untouched for three days. Apparently, Flynn wasn't hard pressed for cash.

A green Chevy S-10 rounded the corner from Wild Road. The truck sped along Indian Trail as if making a non-stop dash for the highway.

It suddenly braked hard, swerved across the road and skidded to a stop abeam the mailbox cluster. The truck blocked the team's view; they couldn't see which box the driver opened.

"We've got a customer," Yankee informed them. Trigger dashed around the SUV to get his binoculars. The others ran and jumped into their vehicles.

The S-10 sped off and rounded the eastbound curve toward 66. Trigger didn't get to the binoculars in time; the S-10 had only been at the boxes for three seconds.

∞

Storm waited until the last second, stood on the brakes and swerved across the road. The S-10 slid to a stop abeam the dead drop. Storm flipped open the lid, grabbed the envelopes and tossed them on the floor, flipped the lid closed and floored the accelerator.

The rear wheels spun in the sand, the truck fishtailed and he steered for the asphalt. The rear tires found traction and the pickup vaulted ahead at full power, southbound on Indian Trial. Storm steered it around the eastbound bend toward the 66. In his mirrors, he noticed the killers were in hot pursuit. He had a half-mile lead and unless God dealt them a wild card, they didn't stand a chance of catching him.

∞

"Shit!" yelled Yankee. He and Slash jumped into their idling SUV. He grabbed the portable radio. "Radio check. Yankee's up."

"Oy mate. Five by five."

"We'll pursue the S-10. You guys check the mailbox."

"Oy."

Yankee floored the gas, spinning the rear wheels and spewing sand behind them. He drove like a madman, cutting diagonally across the desert for Indian Trail. Slash braced for the rough ride, struggling to keep the pickup in sight. The SUV bounced repeatedly, swerving around tall sage and junipers.

Percy and Trigger made a similar dash for the mailbox cluster. They spanned the two hundred yards in forty seconds. Percy swung the SUV broadside to the boxes and slammed the brakes. The vehicle slid to a hard stop abeam them, tossing Trigger into the dashboard. He didn't even grunt.

Trigger threw open his door and dashed to the boxes. He flung open the lid to the dead drop.

"The mail is gone!" He dashed back to the SUV.

Percy keyed the radio. "S-10 has the mail. I say again, the S-10 has the mail."

Slash responded. "Roger that. We're in pursuit. Target just turned north on 66."

As soon as Trigger was in, Percy floored the gas, cut the wheel hard left and fishtailed it to reverse course and join the pursuit.

∞

The S-10 went airborne over the railroad tracks and bottomed out as it landed on the other side. Sparks flew from underneath as loud scraping pierced Storm's ears. "Sorry, Pete," he apologized in absentia. Storm kept the pedal floored until it was time to negotiate the turn onto 66.

He hit the brakes and slowed. He turned left, the cargo bed slid right. The tires squealed and smoked, leaving black rubber marks, evidence of their protest. He slammed the gas pedal to the floor as he blew through the STOP sign. The truck zoomed north on 66. He glanced over his left shoulder. He had opened the distance.

∞

Yankee whipped the wheel left and floored the gas. The SUV rounded the corner onto 66, tilting onto its right wheels. The tires screamed and smoked, working hard to maintain traction. The powerful V-8 revved as the transmission downshifted into passing gear and the SUV accelerated. The SUV straightened and lurched as the left wheels lowered and found traction.

"Shit," yelled Yankee. He didn't know if he could catch the S-10. "If we lose this bastard, my ass is gonna be barbecued." There was no assurance or consolation from Slash. He knew what the Colonel's reaction would be.

"That ain't no doctor drivin' that S-10."

Yankee glanced at Slash, then back to the road. "Storm. Frigging Storm!" Slash nodded, drew his side arm, racked a round into the chamber and checked the laser. He holstered it and snatched an MP-5 9mm submachine gun from the floor. He readied that too.

"It's time to lay down the L.A.W.," declared Yankee. Slash gave him a furtive glance, then jumped to the rear seat, reached into the cargo space and threw off a canvass tarp. He snatched the M-72 Light Antitank Weapon. He extended the telescoping launcher tube. The rocket motor and trigger armed automatically and spring-loaded stadia sights popped up.

Slash lowered the right rear window and leaned out with the weapon.

He placed the launcher to his shoulder and rested his right cheek against the tube. He closed his left eye, lined up the sights on the fleeing pickup and gauged the range. It was a perfect sight picture.

"Adios, shitbag." He squeezed down the trigger, the rocket motor ignited, blasting hot gas. The rocket thrust clear of the muzzle and streaked toward its target, trailing a dense gray smoke trail. It tracked perfectly.

"Say 'Good night, Gracie'," yelled Yankee.

∞

The SUV had closed some distance but Storm wasn't alarmed. He checked his mirrors. Both SUV's were back there.

"*No sweat.*" Storm's intended turnoff was ahead on the left. He had the truck speeding over ninety miles per hour.

Storm noticed an eighteen-wheeler rig coming from the opposite direction and estimated the timing. He eased off the gas, intending to turn onto a dirt road right after the rig passed it.

He glimpsed the mirrors again. The passenger in the lead vehicle was leaning out the right side. He had some kind of weapon on his shoulder. Storm saw a flash and a blast of smoke. A projectile with a bright flame and gray smoke trail streaked at him. He instantly recognized what it was.

Storm made a quick recalculation. He slammed the brake pedal, the tires screeched as the truck nosed down. He whipped the wheel left, steering across the path of the oncoming rig.

The shocked rig driver stood on his brakes and hit the horn. The loud horn blast and the rig's screeching tires increased intensity as the rig and the pickup hurtled toward each other at an alarming rate. The trailer fishtailed into the opposite lane.

The S-10 barely cleared the rig's lane in time. They passed within a foot. Storm fought the steering wheel, trying to avoid collision and plunging into the roadside wash.

The rig passed head-on to Storm's right. A huge explosion tore through its trailer; a dense field of smoke, fire and debris blew into Storm's path. He held the wheel steady, floored the gas and powered through it. Smoke, flames and debris invaded the cab.

He was through it. He realized the rocket must have impacted the rig's trailer, destroying its cargo.

"Oh, Lucy. You've got some 'splaining to do." He decelerated and turned onto the dirt road. He reached up and pressed a button on a remote control.

∞

"Oh, shit!" Yankee stood on the brakes. The SUV violently nosed down; the tires squealed and smoked, leaving thick black rubber skid marks. Slash was thrown hard into the back of the front seat.

"Ugh! Damn it!"

The trailer swerved into their lane and the rocket slammed into it midway. The thin metal trailer wall was no match for the high explosive, nor was its cargo. The resulting explosion blasted debris for two hundred feet. The S-10 disappeared around the rig's right side.

The SUV and the rig came to a stop abeam each other, facing opposite directions. The shocked rig driver looked down at Yankee, who looked up at him. The man was as white as a ghost.

"Hell of a morning for a drive, eh Bucko?"

Yankee slammed the shift lever into REVERSE, peeled rubber, slammed it into DRIVE and whipped the SUV in front of the rig. Percy and Trigger passed them at full gallop, almost clipping them. They raced down the dirt shoulder where the S-10 had vanished. Yankee stomped the gas and fell into close trail with them.

Percy hooked a left onto a dirt road. Yankee followed, easing off the gas because the dirt cloud obscured his view.

Percy's SUV hauled ass down the trail. They rocketed through a railroad underpass and turned a bend. He eased off the gas and coasted.

"Where the hell did he go?" Trigger was astounded.

"Got me, mate. 'E just up and vanished."

Yankee's SUV turned the bend and pulled alongside. "Where is he?" he yelled through the window.

"Beats us, Yank. He disappeared."

The SUV's stopped side by side. All four mercs got out and scanned in all directions. There wasn't a trace of the S-10. They all shrugged their shoulders or threw their hands in the air.

Yankee put his head into his hands. "The Colonel is going to kick my ass."

∞

The tunnel door slammed shut. Storm eased the pickup through the tunnel and parked it in the loading bay.

He gathered Pete's mail and headed for the lab. Storm bounded up the stairs, crossed the loading dock and hustled down the corridor. He went into the lab, where Lisa was working.

"Hi, China doll. What are you doing here so early?"

"Hello lover." She reached up to receive his kiss. Storm pecked her on the lips.

"Is Pete here yet?"

"What's wrong Derek?"

He sighed. He didn't want to alarm her but he knew he had to inform her about the threat. "Remember the guys who chased us last month? I just saw two of them and they had company. They had Pete's dead drop under surveillance and chased me. We need to raise our security status. Is Pete here?"

"He's in the office." Lisa looked apprehensive.

"I'll be right back, sweetie. I need to talk to Pete." He stroked her face. Then he left.

Pete was in the safe room office.

"Morning Derek."

"Morning Pete. Here's your mail." Storm placed it on his desk. "Pete. We have a problem."

His uncle looked up. "What problem?"

"The goons who chased me and Lisa last month are in the area. They know where your drop is; they had it under surveillance. But I managed to evade them."

"You're certain it was them?"

"Absolutely. We need to notch up our security."

"I see." Pete pondered. "The only way they could know about the dead drop was if they followed Senor Martinez. I'll have to change the mailbox and the drop."

"That would be a good idea."

"What's a good idea?" Lisa had entered behind Storm.

"Changing Pete's mail arrangements."

"Are you sure those are the men who chased us?"

"No doubt. I recognized two of them. There are at least four of them and they've got some serious firepower. They fired an antitank rocket at me."

"My Lord!" exclaimed Pete.

"These men are serious bad news. We need to assess our security, right now."

"Okay, Derek. I'll leave that to you. Just let me know what to change."

Boston: Rushton, Raas, and Miller were gathered in Miller's office. Rushton had just briefed them on his conversation with Stakemore.

"You're surprised she's calling in markers?" asked Miller.

"Claudia, this isn't calling in markers. She's demanding we commit premeditated murder."

"What happens if we refuse?" asked Raas.

"She takes us down with her."

"So we dance or die," concluded Miller.

"In a nutshell."

The silence made the air thick. They swilled and sipped their drinks.

"How did the FEC get the information if Stakemore didn't report it?" posed Raas.

They looked at one another with suspicion.

"Don't look at me," said Rushton. "What would I have to gain by incriminating myself?"

"That goes for all of us," asserted Miller. Raas nodded affirmation.

They laid aside their suspicions. They couldn't be the informants. It made no sense.

"Okay," continued Raas. "If it wasn't one of us, who was it?"

"And how did they get the information?" added Miller.

"It had to be someone who gained access to my personal files. That's the only place that information is stored. Even the Board of Directors doesn't have it."

"So, besides you, Ard, who has access to your files?" asked Miller.

"I thought I was the only one. But apparently someone else has hacked in. But who?"

"It's obvious," responded Miller. "Miss Goody-Two-Shoes."

Raas challenged. "I don't see how. We transferred and coded all of the sensitive files when we banished her to the finance committee. She doesn't have access to shit."

"Not necessarily," responded Miller. "I've noticed she's become chummy with Deirdre Towns."

"Deirdre in the computer section?" said Rushton, seeking clarification.

Miller nodded and sipped her drink.

Rushton nodded. "We need to find out." Rushton sipped his drink then added, "And how they did it."

Helendale: Pete stared through the microscope. The slides from the control group appeared unchanged. The cancerous cells from the treated specimens were definitely disrupted. Pete switched slides and examined the sample from another treated specimen. So far, so good. He repeated the process for a dozen samples. He smiled and stood proudly.

"Doctor Chen, if you would be so kind as to verify my observations?" Pete held out an open hand, inviting Lisa to gaze into the instrument.

Lisa could tell by his smile that the results were positive. She leaned to the device and observed. Pete switched the slides at her every confirmation. All twelve of the treated samples showed positive dramatic results.

Lisa rose from the bench and smiled. "You did it, Pete! It works!" She gave him a hug.

"*We* did it, Lisa. Along with Derek. It was a team effort."

"What's next?"

"First, we issue a press release and get the medical community to duplicate the results through independent sources. Then we need to find human volunteers for the FDA approval process."

Victorville: The mood at the safe house was sullen. Yankee was bedridden from the beating Bravo had administered. He had two black eyes, a broken nose, bruised ribs and battered abdominal muscles. The Colonel had beaten him until he collapsed. Trigger and Slash had hauled him to his bunk and patched him up.

"He's lucky his carcass isn't on my trophy wall. Let that be an example to the rest of you. No more screw-ups!"

The Ops room was uncomfortably quiet.

"Yankee is relieved. Slash is the new XO. Any questions?"

Percy raised his hand.

"What Percy?"

"Colonel, how do we find them now? They'll move their mailbox and change the drop."

"I'm aware of that. The lab has to be near Helendale. That's where the truck disappeared. They have to get their groceries somewhere. We're going to patrol that town. There are a couple of grocery stores, a Post Office, a bank and restaurants. We know one of them drives a green S-10. We know what they look like. Someone in that town must know them. So you guys get off your asses and find them. That includes you, Sparks."

"Yes sir."

Slash inquired, "And when we find them, we tail them?"

"No." Bravo paused. "Kill them."

Boston: Raas entered Rushton's office and closed the door. "Guess what I found?"

Rushton turned in his chair. "What?"

Raas tossed a folder onto Rushton's desk. He grabbed it and opened it. It was a printout of a computer program. "What's this?"

"A backdoor program to hack into secure files."

"Is that how it was done?"

"Yup." Raas pointed at the folder. "I checked with the computer security section. That program was inserted without authorization two weeks ago."

"Who did it?"

"Terminal 4DC2C8, the workstation of Deirdre Towns."

"She's the one who hacked my files?"

"No. She merely inserted the program. Your files were accessed from several terminals. The most interesting one was terminal 7239F8."

"And that belongs to…?"

"Melanie Taylor."

"Then Claudia was right."

"It appears so."

"If she leaks this to the board or testifies in Congress, we're screwed." Rushton sat silently.

"There is a solution, Ard."

Rushton nodded. Melanie Taylor had to be silenced, permanently and irrevocably silenced.

CHAPTER XIX

KNIGHT STORM

American News Service
New Hope for Cancer Victims: The U.S. Medical Research Association reported today the discovery of a possible cure for cancer. From a secret research lab, Drs. Peter Flynn and Lisa Chen, developers of the treatment, have reported positive results of a cancer treatment, designated ParaZyme 2000, which has been found to be effective on most forms of cancerous and pre-cancerous cells in mice and primates.

"The results are conclusive and amazing," claimed Dr. Flynn. "The protocol worked in every case of primate cancer, halting the cancer's ability to invade healthy cells, reducing, even eliminating tumors, and boosting the body's immune system."

Dr. Lisa Chen, co-researcher stated, "Cancer cell disruption is complete by using the ParaZyme 2000 protocol. Not only have the tests been positive, they've been a medical miracle. The few side-effects observed have been minor and treatable with over-the-counter products."

The USMRA report states that the treatment has proved successful in all cases of mice and primates tested. The Doctors are having their test results duplicated by independent laboratories. They are currently seeking human volunteers and FDA approval.

"We've made amazing progress in one year," declared Dr. Flynn, "thanks to some recently discovered information and the exploits of some associates. We look forward to the day when our first human patient is cured."

To learn more, go to parazyme2000.com.

The press release hit all of the major news services, networks, newspapers and periodicals. In just one day there were 147,000 hits on the website, a virtual avalanche. E-mail responses from researchers worldwide were encouraging, offering their services to duplicate and verify their work.

The number of volunteers was staggering. Requests came from all around the world, overloading their ISP. It just showed the level of hope of those suffering from that tragic malady.

Pete and Lisa were confident the treatment would test successfully on humans. The only side effects they noted in the test animals were some minor watery bowel movements. But that was to be expected. That was one of the body's natural means of evacuating toxins and waste. The skin and bladder were others.

As much as they enjoyed the notoriety, they still had much work to do. The process of FDA approval was as daunting as the discovery itself. The federal government thrived on regulations and red tape. It seemed the FDA was more interested in protecting its regulatory empire than helping people. "Death by bureaucracy" was Pete's term for it. That's why so many Americans went to foreign countries for the latest medical treatments. The FDA often prevented them from being made available in the U.S.

On top of all that, Pete and Lisa had to maintain a low profile. There were forces out there that wanted to sabotage their work, or worse.

Boston: Melanie browsed the morning edition of The Globe. An article in the Health section caught her attention. She read it casually until she noted the term ParaZyme 2000. She recalled the name and that of Dr. Flynn. It was the name of the doctor murdered in Portland. She wondered if they were related.

She continued reading. The protocol was effective; they were about to start the FDA approval process. There was a website listed.

She stared out the window. She had to know if the doctors were related. Melanie turned to her computer and typed in the web address for the ParaZyme site. Its home page appeared. She searched various pages, absorbing the material. She found a history page and studied it. A copy of the press release published in the NOMP official journal was there. The article mentioned the names of both Peter and Daniel Flynn; they were brothers.

She stared out the window again. Their lab in Portland had been burglarized by the man calling himself 'Ghost.' The Flynn's must have relocated the lab, because the most recent press release stated it was in a secret location. Dan Flynn had been murdered shortly thereafter, probably by the thugs Rushton had hired. Now they were trying to steal his research. It all fit.

Her cell phone beckoned.

"Taylor."

"Melanie, it's Deirdre. We've got a problem."

"What?"

"Raas was in here yesterday sniffing around like a mutt at a fire hydrant. He spent an hour with my supervisor. It's the only hour he's ever spent down here in the eight years I've been here. Something's up. My supervisor and Raas were on the computer the whole time and when I came into work today, that back door program I installed had been uninstalled."

"It's gone?"

"Completely. Not a trace. Not only that, I'm locked out of a lot of sensitive programs and my supervisor wants me in his office at ten o'clock. I think I'm going to be fired."

"Oh no. I'm so sorry, Deirdre."

"Look, sweetie. I'm not blind or deaf and you weren't holding a gun to my head. I knew there was that risk."

"I am so sorry, Deidre."

"That's okay, honey. It's just a job. You better watch your tail. They can't fire you, but they're up to no good. I have to go. The super is coming." The connection abruptly ceased.

The jig was up. Deirdre was right. She was an elected board member and they couldn't fire her. But they might try something more drastic.

Melanie's hands quivered.

It was Friday. She could leave work early and spend the weekend out of town. *"That's what I'll do."*

But what about the cancer treatment? It and the lives of the researchers were threatened. If Rushton ever got control of it, it wouldn't see the light of day.

Melanie called up a generic ISP and created an e-mail account under a phony name. Then she returned to the ParaZyme website and clicked on the hyperlink CONTACT US. She typed a message, used the phony e-mail as the return address and clicked SEND.

∞

Rushton read the morning paper. It didn't take him long to spot the press release from Pete Flynn. He read it and fumed.

He was on his cell to Bravo in seconds. His opening was abrupt. "I don't give a shit if it's five in the morning in California, Colonel. We need to talk."

"Okay Doc. Why are your knickers in a twist?"

"Have you read the morning paper? That research you were supposed to appropriate is successful and has just gone public."

"Well then, that's good news."

"No it's not! There's no way to suppress it now."

"Are you telling me to abandon the search? Because if you are, you're nuts. I'm not giving up. I have *never* failed a mission and I'm not going to start now. My reputation is on the line. Storm has put some kinks in my plan, even killed one of my men. This mission isn't over until I say it's over and that's not until we get the research and I kill Storm."

"That's not good enough, Colonel. You screwed around too long. Your gravy train has left the station."

"Okay Doc. We can shut down. But there are no refunds."

"I don't need a refund."

"Then what do you want?"

"I want it stopped."

"No. My reputation is higher priority than your fears. I'm going to find that lab, destroy it and kill them all. If you won't pay any more, that's fine. My reputation will be intact."

Rushton paused. "You're going to do it anyway?"

"I just said that. Did I stutter?"

Rushton paused again. "Since you're determined to carry this through, let's discuss a new contract."

"I'm listening."

"If you can find and destroy the lab by the end of next week, I'll make it worth your while."

Bravo paused. The probability of finding the lab within a week was pretty good. "Why one week, Doc?"

"It will take at least that long for the independent labs to get the materials and formula to duplicate the research. Once it's in their hands, there's no suppressing it. Before then, its destruction might still have some value. After that, all bets are off."

Bravo was silent. Rushton knew he was evaluating the proposal. "Okay Doc. Two hundred large, cash, if the objective is destroyed by close of business, Pacific Time next Friday."

"Agreed. Now get it done."

Helendale: Pete and Lisa were overwhelmed by the volume of e-mails. As soon as they cleared space in the storage, it filled up instantly. They issued a generic blast response to all senders. They only had time to select the most promising messages to issue individual responses.

Lisa rubbed her eyes and yawned. She had been reading e-mails for five hours. She would continue until lunchtime, then spend the afternoon on research. She returned to her tedious task.

The subject line of a message caught her attention. DANGER. KILLERS AFTER PZ 2000. She clicked open the message.

FROM: FLORENCE NIGHTINGALE
DEAR DR FLYNN,
ELEMENTS OF MEDICAL COMMUNITY HAVE HIRED KILLERS TO LOCATE YOU AND YOUR LAB. SERIOUS DANGER. PLEASE CONTACT ME. THIS IS NOT A HOAX. I HAVE INFO ABOUT YOUR BROTHER'S MURDER. POLITICAL CORRUPTION INVOLVED.
F.N.

"Pete, look at this."

"What?" Pete read the e-mail over her shoulder.

"Is this some kind of sick joke?"

"I don't think so. She mentions Dan's murder. Question is, whose side is she on? Is it even a she? It could just be a way to smoke us out."

"What do you want to do, Pete?"

Pete shook his head. "I'm torn. I don't want the killers to find us, but I want to know who's responsible for Dan's murder." Pete stared at the floor, perplexed. His eyes welled with tears.

Lisa felt compassion for him. He was a kind but lonely man. Lisa rose from her chair and embraced him.

"I'm very sorry, Pete. It must be terrible losing your loved ones. You're not alone. Derek and I are here and we love you."

Pete gently hugged her and sobbed. The emotional stress was catching up to him. He had suppressed the grief too long.

"What's wrong?"

Storm had entered the office and noticed Lisa consoling his sobbing uncle.

"We just received an alarming e-mail. It's on my monitor." She stroked Pete's back and head.

Storm stepped to her desk and read the message. His emotions came to the surface too. His eyes teared and his Irish blood boiled.

"Lisa, send a reply. Give her your cell number and tell her to ask for Daniel. I want to see what she knows."

Boston: The conspirators gathered in Rushton's office. He presented them with the newspaper article regarding the ParaZyme 2000.

"Shit," exclaimed Raas. "We'll have to spread some money around the FDA to make sure it's not successful."

"Correct," affirmed Rushton. "Maybe the FDA can stonewall long enough for Bravo to locate the lab and destroy it. I gave him one week."

"How much?" inquired Miller.

"Two hundred, cash," he answered. Then to Raas, "How much do you think we'll need to keep the FDA in line?"

Raas thought about it. "For the half-dozen critical players, about twenty grand each."

Rushton nodded. "We've got enough in the Executive Fund to cover Bravo and the FDA. Let's make it happen. This could be our last chance."

Helendale: Storm was in the cargo bay checking the fluids and tires on the vehicles. He had backed them to the loading dock for rapid evacuation.

He had also improved their lab and home security. He installed a crude periscope near the tunnel door. It would allow them to scan the area outside before they opened it. He also installed motion sensors along the dirt trail.

Their daily transportation requirements were the biggest challenge.

The killers had seen Pete's S-10, so they carpooled to and from the lab in Lisa's Hummer.

Lisa came out to the loading dock with her cell phone. "For you, lover. A lady asking for Daniel."

"This is Daniel. How can I help you?"

"Daniel, this is Florence. I'm following through on a message I sent to Dr. Peter Flynn. Are you the person to whom I need to speak?"

"Yes I am. We're interested in hearing your information about the death of Daniel Flynn."

"Good. I know who's responsible."

"Can you fax or e-mail it to us?"

There was a long hesitation. "Uh… Daniel, I believe my life is in danger. I have to be very careful to whom I reveal this information. I'm very scared. I hope you understand."

Storm could sense her trepidation. "I see. You're telling me that you're uncomfortable with sending us the information."

"Yes. I'm sorry. I want the right people to have the evidence, but only the right people. I want this information to get to Dr. Flynn, personally."

Storm saw her point. "Tell you what, Florence. Call back in ten minutes. You'll speak directly to Dr. Flynn. He'll discuss it with you. I'm sure we can work out some arrangement. How does that sound?"

Florence paused again. "Okay. I'll call back in ten minutes." The connection went dead.

Storm was a little frustrated.

"What is it, Derek?"

Storm slowly shook his head. "That woman sounds very scared. I believe she knows something and wants us to know about it but she's afraid. She'll only speak to Pete."

Storm headed for the office. Pete was at his desk.

"Something up, Derek?"

"Yeah. Florence Nightingale just called. She'll be calling back in ten minutes to speak with you."

"Why me?"

"She sounds scared. I believe she has information about the killers and Dan's murder but she won't discuss it with me. I thought you might be able to convince her. She doesn't want to risk sending it electronically, so maybe a personal meeting is in order."

"Why won't she fax it?"

"I'm not sure. Maybe she's afraid it will fall into the wrong hands, or maybe she wants to verify ID, or maybe she just needs a hug. Who knows? She's female."

"Chauvinist."

"Thanks." Storm smiled.

They devised a scenario to hopefully satisfy the woman, keep her safe, keep them safe and get the information.

All they had to do was convince her of it.

Mauritius: The satellite phone woke Luke. He glanced at the alarm clock. "*Who's calling at this hour?*"

"This is Luke."

"Good morning."

"Hello Derek. I'm glad to hear from you, even if it is four o'clock in the morning."

"Oh, sorry. I forgot about the time difference."

Luke rolled out of bed and pulled on swim trunks. "That's okay lad. What's going on?" Luke left the stateroom so Heather could sleep. He walked up to the main deck as Storm filled him in. The night air was hot and humid, quite a difference from the air-conditioned stateroom.

"Luke, we have a lead on the people responsible for my Uncle Dan's murder. However, the lady with the information won't discuss it over the phone or fax it. She wants to meet in person in Boston, Monday night. I'd like to have some backup in case it's a setup."

Luke checked the day and date on his watch. "Yeah. I can be there Monday. Can you meet me at Logan Airport?"

"Yeah. I'm flying there tomorrow. I'm linking up with the pilot who rescued me during Desert Storm."

"Can he be your backup?"

"No. He's an airline pilot. He's out of town Monday night."

"Okay. It's a date. I'll call you back with my flight arrangements."

"Great. And thanks, Luke. You're the best friend a man could have."

"Same goes for you, partner. I'll be there. The Jade Gang rides again."

"The Jade Gang?"

"You'll see."

Boston: It was a cold afternoon at Logan Airport. Luke had spent the past two days airborne, taking three flights to get from Mauritius to Boston, through Europe. He should have been exhausted, but he managed to get some sleep in a plush first-class seat on the segment crossing the Atlantic.

"Luke."

Storm was in a crowd, his arm held high. Smiles came to their faces. They greeted each other with strong handshakes, hugs and slaps on the backs.

"Thanks for coming, Luke."

"You bet. The Jade Gang rides again."

"What's this Jade Gang you keep mentioning?"

"Remember the outlaw James Gang? We're the Jade Gang." Luke smiled and reached under his shirt. He pulled out the jade medallion. Storm reached under his shirt and pulled out his. They were a match.

"The Jade Gang," murmured Storm pensively. "It fits." They let the medallions hang outside their shirts and smiled.

"I hope you brought a heavy coat. It's as cold as a witch's tit outside."

"No. I don't keep one on the ship. I'll have to buy one. You have wheels?"

"Yeah. My buddy Mike lent me one of his cars. Let's get you a coat, then we've got some recon to do."

∞

The meeting place Florence had selected was an Irish pub. It occupied a corner, so it had exits to sidewalks on two sides. Luke also spotted an exit from the kitchen. Storm checked the restrooms; there were no outlets.

It was a typical Irish pub. The décor was dark with mahogany wood wall panels and bar, lots of greenery, dim lighting, a stage, kitchen and an extensive bar.

Storm positioned himself to observe the bartender and the counter spaces behind the bar. He noticed a 12 gauge pump shotgun within easy reach from the cash register. He and Luke nursed a couple of beers before scouting outside.

They studied the approaches and fields of fire. There were several streets to monitor, rooftops and a subway station. It would be a challenge for two men.

Storm figured they would arrive at the pub an hour early, eat dinner separately and nurse beers until Florence showed, if she appeared at all.

"How are you going to recognize her?"

"She's supposed to be alone and carry a single red rose. She'll recognize me by this piece of yellow paper in my shirt pocket."

"Okay. Let's discuss contingencies."

The food at the pub was excellent. The service was good too. The rush hour crowd was cheery and boisterous. Pretty lasses hustled pitchers of beer, teasing and taunting the local gentry, all in good fun. Storm and Hale felt right at home: cold beer, good food, pretty lasses and lots of laughs.

Storm sat at a table with his back to a wall. Luke sat at the opposite end of the bar. They could watch each other's avenues of approach. Luke could also monitor the bar and part of the kitchen. They nursed their beers and pretended not to be aware of each other. They joked with the locals and chatted up the barmaids. They appeared jovial, without a care in the world.

They were surprised when, at the appointed hour, a pretty young woman entered the pub. She wore a black overcoat, hat, gloves and she carried a single long-stemmed red rose. Whoever set this up for her must have never taken Spy 101. You *never* show up on time. You either show up very early and recon, or you make the other party wait for an hour or two, and see what their assets are when they get frustrated and leave. But you never show at the appointed time.

Storm waited until the lady looked in his direction, then he casually lifted the yellow paper, folded it and tucked it into his shirt pocket. He looked out the window. The lady approached him.

"Would you be Derek Storm?"

She obviously had no covert training. *"No wonder she's so scared."* She was shaking. He scanned the bar and the sidewalks; Luke rubbed his eye, signaling all clear.

"Yes. I'm Derek Storm. You must be Florence."

"Yes."

"Please sit." Storm rose, smiled and held a chair out for her. "You have nothing to fear from me, Florence. I'm a close friend of Pete Flynn. He should have given you my name."

"Yes. Thank you." She sat. Storm sat. "I was told to expect a Derek Storm, so before we begin, may I see your driver's license?" Storm wasn't aware of it, but Florence had pressed 9-1-1 on her cell phone and had her finger on the SEND button, ready to press it at the first sign of trouble.

"No problem." Storm withdrew his wallet, removed his Nevada license and slid it across the table. "I have a passport as well."

"Please," she said, as she studied his license. Storm produced his passport and handed it to her with a disarming smile. Florence seemed to relax after examining both documents. She politely handed them back.

"Thank you. I feel a little better."

"Good." Storm tucked away his documents. "I understand you have some information for Dr. Flynn."

"Yes. The information must get to Dr. Flynn. Can you assure me of that?"

"I guarantee it. Pete and I are very close. That's why he asked me to meet you. I'm one of the few people he can trust."

Florence nodded. "Okay. I'll go get the documents. I'll be back in a few moments?"

"You didn't mention money. How much are you asking for the information?"

Florence looked shocked. It had never occurred to her to ask for money. "I… I don't want money. I just want to do the right thing. The people responsible for this mess have to be brought to justice, but the FBI won't investigate. There's political corruption involved. It's way above my head. Maybe Dr. Flynn will know what to do with the information."

"So you're doing this simply because it's the right thing to do?"

"Yes. It's the way I was raised."

Storm smiled. "Lassie, you're a true gem. God bless you and those that raised you."

Florence blushed. "I… I'll go get the documents. I'll be back in a few moments."

"Smart lady," complimented Storm, "not to bring them in here with you."

"I thought it best." She was still nervous.

Storm studied her face. She was young, very pretty. Not the eye-popping beauty that Lisa was, but very pretty.

"Your accent isn't Bostonian. You sound more Midwest."

"Good guess. I'll get that information now."

"Shall I come along?"

Florence hesitated. "No. I'd feel better if you remained here. It will only be a few moments. I'll come back, give a large envelope to the hostess and then I'll leave. You can get the envelope from the hostess after I've departed."

Storm issued a tight smile. "If that puts you at ease, it works for me."

"Thank you. I'll return soon."

Storm glanced Hale's way. Luke rubbed his eye, all clear. Florence rose and headed for the front door. Storm scanned the sidewalks. Most of the rush hour crowd had dissipated. There were only four people on the street.

As she turned right on the sidewalk, Storm noticed a seedy-looking character taking interest in her. The man was smoking a cigarette. He looked like he had missed the appointment with his razor four days running. He wore a navy blue watch cap pulled down over the tops of his ears, brown boots, dirty tan corduroys and a black faux-leather winter jacket, no gloves. *"Quite the fashion icon."*

The man tossed his cigarette into the gutter and followed Florence. Storm's neck hair bristled.

Storm thumbed his nose and flashed a closed fist with one finger extended. Luke caught the signals; something smells, hold tight for one minute. Storm tossed a tip onto the table and walked casually to the exit. Outside, he turned right, caught Luke's all clear signal and saw the suspect cross the street and round the corner of an adjacent building. Florence was nowhere to be seen.

Storm gauged the traffic and dashed across the street. He ran to the end of the block and peeked around the corner. It was an alley leading to the entrance of a parking structure. He saw the suspect turn right at mid-alley, toward the parking garage. Storm rounded the corner, pressed his back to the wall and counted to ten. Then he peeked around the corner at the pub. There were no tails; Luke exited the pub.

He waved at Luke and Luke waved back. He had his back.

∞

The broad was inside the pub. Sean 'Blackjack' O'Reilly smoked a Marlboro and watched her from the sidewalk. Blackjack had been hired to locate this broad and make her less of a problem, for whom and why, he didn't know and didn't care. He was being paid three thousand, cash. That could buy a lot of cocaine and meth, his best friends. He had been provided with the broad's name, address, phone number, vehicle registration and photo. It couldn't be any easier.

He had planned to do her at her apartment but she hadn't been home all weekend, which pissed him off. He had wasted the whole weekend staking it out. He tracked her down at work this morning. He located her car in the NOMP parking garage. It was an easy matter to park near the garage exit and wait. When she left work, he tailed her to the pub.

She was seated at a table with some guy sporting a goatee and a ponytail. The man smiled a lot but he looked rugged. Blackjack figured it wouldn't be wise to tangle with him. He had a real confident air about him and Blackjack was into easy money.

The broad talked with the man, then she got up and left by herself. She walked toward the garage where she had parked her car.

Blackjack took a final drag on his cancer weed and flicked it into the gutter. He fell into a loose tail on the broad. She crossed the street to the garage. He waited until she entered the alley before he crossed. He knew where she was going.

He would ambush her as she reached her car, knock her unconscious, carry her to his car, dump her in the trunk, then wrap her with duct tape. A nice drive to the Cape would culminate in a night of debauchery, then he would slit her throat and dump her body in a river to be washed out to sea. Then he would return to Boston and collect the second half of his fee; it was easy money.

The broad went to the elevator. Her car was parked on the next level up. "*Perfect.*" Blackjack hustled up the stairs. The broad would have to wait for the elevator, giving him time to get into position. He was up the stairs in seconds and snuck into position behind his car, two down from the broad's. There was no one around.

Blackjack unlocked his car trunk and left it ajar. He hid behind his car. The broad would have to pass the front of his car to get to hers.

The elevator chimed, the doors opened and out came the broad. As predicted, she walked past the front. He heard her unlock her car with a remote. He eased closer to her car. He peeked under the bumper and palmed his blackjack.

Her feet pointed to the front of the car, he eased around the corner toward her back. She seemed unaware of him. He raised the blackjack…

∞

Storm saw the suspect watch Florence go to the elevator, then race up adjacent stairs.

"*This scum is up to no good.*"

Storm silently raced up the stairs, seconds behind the suspect. At the second floor, he dropped down and spotted the suspect's boots and corduroys by looking under the cars. Storm soft-stepped around several parked vehicles.

The elevator bell chimed and Florence emerged. She turned left and walked down the line of parked vehicles. The creep peeked under a bumper. Storm saw his plan. Florence turned away, the perp made his move.

Storm soft-stepped triple time behind the perp. The assailant raised the blackjack.

Storm snatched his arm in mid-strike, grabbed the wrist with both hands, twisted it inward and pivoted counterclockwise. There was no mercy, no stopping short and no waiting for a cry of submission. The perp howled in pain as his arm broke at the elbow. The ugly sound of snapping bones pierced the quiet. Storm threw him backwards violently, slamming him on the floor.

Storm wasn't through. He flexed the wrist until it was ninety degrees to its forearm, then he pushed all of his weight down, snapping the bones. The perp howled and cried. Storm jammed his left knee into the perp's back, released his shattered arm, then clasped both hands below the man's chin and yanked it up, stopping just short of snapping his neck. The creep was completely at his mercy.

Florence was startled. She turned around and screamed. "What's going on?"

Luke came running up. He spotted Florence between two cars, looking at the ground, stupefied. He ran to her.

She saw Luke and cringed. "Don't hurt me."

"It's okay, Florence. He's with me."

Storm's affirmation reached her. She began to cry. Luke flashed her a compassionate smile and opened his arms to her.

"It's okay, angel. We're here to help. You're safe."

Florence looked unsure. Storm nodded. She looked relieved, the tears flowed heavier and she fell into Luke's embrace. He kissed her forehead and stroked her hair as if he were consoling his own daughter.

"Let's find out what this creep had in mind." Storm twisted the man's head. "What were you up to?"

The perp's eyeballs rolled in their sockets; sweat covered his upper lip, his color was flushed. He was in shock, on the verge of passing out. Too bad for him.

"I said, what were you going to do?"

"I... I... was paid to... kill her," he managed to mumble.

"Who hired you?"

"Willie the Whack."

"Who's Willie the Whack? What's his real name?"

"I don't know."

"Why does he want her dead?"

"Don't know... someone just... wants her dead."

Luke asked Florence, "Do you recognize this man?"

She shook her head. She didn't want to look at him.

"This guy's a waste of protoplasm," opined Luke.

"I agree." Storm released the man's neck, snatched his unbroken wrist and twisted it outward. He extended the fingers backwards to their limit. The painful manipulation motivated the creep to his feet, moaning in pain. Storm cranked the leverage harder and dragged the creep, on his tiptoes, around the far side of a concrete column, out of sight of Florence.

Luke covered Florence's ears with his hands. He didn't want her to hear what was coming.

As soon as Storm had the killer out of sight, he slammed him into the column with a one-knuckle punch into his solar plexus. The creep wheezed and sank to his knees. Storm released his grip on the wrist, speared his spread fingers into the man's eyes, tilted his head back and twisted it violently. The perp's scream was cut short. Vertebrae snapped like knuckles cracking. It was over. The creep collapsed. Storm dragged the body to his car, opened the trunk, tossed the body in and slammed the trunk closed.

"How's the view now, creep?"

Florence observed Storm as he approached.

"I'm sorry to be blunt Florence, but it's obvious someone wants you dead. That gives special credence to your information. Now, someone has murdered my Uncle Dan and they're trying to murder my Uncle Pete. I want to know who's responsible and I want to know right now."

"The Flynns are your uncles?"

Storm nodded. "Do we get the information or not?"

She shivered and nodded. "My name isn't Florence."

"We figured that. Give me something useful."

"My name is Melanie Taylor. I'm a board member of the National Organization of Medical Professionals."

"The medical association that prevented the socialist takeover of the health care system?" asked Luke.

She nodded, tears streaming. "I have evidence in my car. Senior members of the NOMP board of directors plan to kill Peter Flynn and destroy his lab."

"Please get it," demanded Storm.

Melanie opened her car door, reached inside and pulled out a briefcase. She handed it to Storm. He grabbed it, flopped it onto the trunk and opened it. He took a large envelope from inside and tore it open. He began reading. He spent minutes absorbing the material. Meanwhile, Luke rubbed Melanie's back, attempting to soothe her.

Storm asked, "These people, Rushton, Raas and Miller, you know where they work and what they look like?" He tossed the papers into the briefcase and slammed it shut.

"Yes."

Storm turned away and walked, pensive. Luke had seen him like this before. He called it 'caving,' the time when a man had to retreat into his emotional cave to sort things out. He often did it himself and knew to let the process reach its conclusion uninterrupted.

Storm faced them. "Can you get us photos of them, their work schedules and a layout of the building?"

She nodded again. "Yes."

Storm retreated again, deep in thought.

"Is he okay?" she asked Luke, sobbing.

Hale nodded. "He's fine. But hell hath no fury," he pointed to his friend, "like an avenging Storm."

CHAPTER XX

PURE PURSUIT

The Omni Hotel was down the street from the historic Boston Common, along the tourist thoroughfare known as Freedom Trail. It occupied a very old building with a rich history. The hotel had been renovated many times, but it kept its colonial flavor and aura of historical significance. It had plush lobby décor, rich furnishings and high caliber clientele. Presidential candidates had patronized its accommodations over many decades.

Storm escorted Melanie to his sixth floor room. Hale had reservations for a suite and registered at the front desk. They transferred Melanie to Hale's suite, where she would have her own accommodations.

After getting settled in, they gathered in the living area. Luke prepared cocktails from the mini-bar and put Melanie at ease.

"You can rest easy now."

Storm added, "We're aware of the threat to my uncle. We just didn't know who was responsible. Now we can take appropriate measures."

Melanie sipped her vodka nervously. "I hope so. I've tried getting the FBI to investigate, but they won't touch it. It's like I latched onto some contagious disease."

Storm swigged his beer. "How did you learn that information?"

"I had help from someone who lost her job over it."

Storm nodded. "I'm sorry to hear that. Just be thankful it wasn't more severe. People have been tortured and murdered, nearly you included. And call me Derek."

Melanie proffered an uneasy smile. "Okay Derek." She faced Luke. "I'm sorry sir, but I don't recall your name."

Luke downed his whiskey and water and placed the glass on a coffee table. "My name is Luke Hale. I'm married with children your age. I'm independently wealthy and mostly retired." Luke informed her of his and Storm's history.

"I see." She sipped her drink. "You're best friends."

"More than that," informed Storm. "I would die to save that man's life." He pointed to Hale.

"And I his."

Melanie had no response. She could not recall a single girlfriend of whom she could make that claim.

Storm continued. "We're not unique, Melanie. We're just men. Once men have shared combat together, they become brothers, bonded to one another."

They told her of their military and martial arts experience. She listened intently, impressed.

"Okay. You convinced me. If you can protect me, I can help stop those bastards."

Storm said, "We need photos of them, a floor plan of the building and their work schedules. We also need specifics about security, emergency exits, video cameras…"

The list went on. Melanie took notes while Hale took notes of her answers. She revealed Stakemore's participation in the conspiracy. The men decided to deal with the bitch after the NOMP conspirators were taken down.

The session went on until Melanie felt the need to retire. She retreated to her room while Hale and Storm plotted.

"What's your end game, Derek?"

Storm's evil twin emerged. He used Luke's satellite phone to call Lisa. They exchanged chitchat for a few minutes, then Derek got to the point.

"Lisa, I need you to overnight express some things to me in Boston. Got a pencil?"

∞

Miller sat in Rushton's office, sipping coffee as Rushton read the paper.

"I haven't seen Melanie yet today," he said casually.

"Me neither. Maybe she's had an unfortunate accident."

"We should be so lucky." He sipped his coffee. His cell phone rang.

"Doctor Rushton." He heard a lot of background noise; it sounded like traffic.

"Doctor, this is Iris Stakemore."

"Yes Congresswoman," he said for Miller's benefit. "What's all that noise?"

"I'm at a public phone. There's a lot of traffic. I'm sorry."

"Quite all right. What can we do for you?"

"Doctor, is it safe to talk on this line?"

Rushton was surprised. "Yes, unless you know something I don't."

"No. That's good. I just received word that the House Ethics Committee is going to convene a hearing in two weeks. It involves a certain member of Congress and the committee is making preparations for major press coverage. NOMP contributions to a certain PAC have come into question. Not only that, a source has confirmed they know about Bravo, Dan Flynn's murder and interference with an FBI investigation."

She took a breath. "They have hard evidence, the kind that's difficult to refute. They have copies of e-mails, records of disbursements from NOMP, copies of audio-tapes, even sworn affidavits." Stakemore was excited and breathing rapidly, panicked.

"Testimony from whom?"

"I don't know, unnamed witnesses. That's all the source could discover. The committee is playing their cards close to the vest. And to top it off, an intern of a certain Congress member ratted out to the committee so she could get a better job with the Majority Whip, the sniveling little bitch opportunist."

Rushton rolled his eyes. *If that isn't the pot calling the kettle black.*

"Calm down, madam. There has to be a way to deal with this."

"Doctor, need I point out, if the committee convenes a hearing, the subject will be subpoenaed to testify. In the face of the evidence, the subject will be disgraced, censured, maybe even expelled from the House, or worse, slapped in leg irons."

"Madam, calm down. Take some deep breaths. Do you have a Valium?"

"I don't want a frigging Valium!"

Rushton recoiled from the phone. "See here, Doctor. A certain Congress member's ass is on the line. And so is yours. What do you think will happen if the subject gets prosecuted? Who will protect you from the FBI?"

"I see your point. Give me a moment. Please stay on the line." Rushton brought Miller up to speed.

"What do we do?"

Raas entered and closed the door. Rushton told him to have a seat and briefed him.

"Madam Congresswoman, I want to put this discussion on speaker so my associates can help work this out. Is that all right?"

"If you must."

"We're on speaker now, Congresswoman. Dr. Raas and Nurse Miller are listening. Please proceed."

"As I mentioned, if the subject is called to testify, NOMP will be in jeopardy too. My thoughts are this: if the subject were to disappear, the committee will have no one to question. Congress has no jurisdiction over NOMP. They can order you to appear, but you have no obligation to answer their questions. NOMP is a private organization and you're all private citizens."

"Go on."

"I suggest the subject disappear, permanently. But that will take money."

Raas intoned, "And that buys insurance to protect NOMP?"

"Exactly."

"Pardon me, madam," interjected Miller. "But if the subject vanishes, won't the FBI investigate anyway?"

"No. The subject will still be able to pull strings under the table. Not so from a prison cell. And keep in mind the consequences of conspiracy, bribery, kidnapping, murder and civil rights violations."

Rushton glanced around the room. The consensus was obvious.

"How much would be required for the subject to vanish?"

"Six million, cash."

Rushton considered the huge amount. He decided not to answer, fearing a recording.

"Madam, I'll have to get back to you. This requires further evaluation by our Executive committee. Good day." He pressed the END button.

"What are you doing, Ard?" asked Raas, incredulous.

"Just cool your jets." Rushton pressed the speed dial for Stakemore's personal cell. It was answered immediately.

"Hello?"

Rushton blurted out, "Don't talk, just listen. Our company wishes to be the fund manager for the retirement plan you have selected. You will be contacted soon by one of our account representatives to discuss investment options. Good day." He ended the call abruptly.

"Christ!" exclaimed Miller. "Six million dollars. That will blow the rest of the year's lobbying budget."

"I know."

Raas added, "And the Executive fund won't cover it. We'll need a special authorization from the board."

"I know. Fortunately, we control the majority. Get the word out to our supporters. Have them meet here in one hour. We'll get them on board and call a special meeting of the board for tomorrow."

∽

Melanie took Tuesday off work at Hale's request. They spent the day planning. They determined they would have a higher probability of success if they could catch them all together. For that, they needed their schedules, as well as information about NOMP security systems. They decided Melanie should return to work on Wednesday to get the information. It was the only way.

Luke accompanied Melanie that day. He posed as her father. He was the right age and no one at NOMP had ever met him or her real father. He could reasonably pass as her biological father.

Luke's presence was two-fold. Primarily, he was there to protect Melanie. Secondly, he could assess the layout and security measures.

Melanie introduced Luke as her father to the security guards and office workers as they went to her office. Once inside, Luke had Melanie place all of her family photos into a drawer.

"Hide them all. It's less to explain if someone comes in."

"Good idea." She had learned to trust his judgment.

Melanie guarded the door as Luke scanned her office for bugs and recording devices.

Satisfied it was clean, Luke took station at the door and Melanie went to work on the computer. It didn't take her long to find the data they needed.

She called up the photos of Rushton, Raas and Miller and printed three copies of each. As they processed, she grabbed an empty folder from a drawer. As the sheets came off the printer, she placed them into the file.

Next, she accessed the floor plan. She printed three copies and placed them into the file. Then she called up their schedules and noticed something.

"Luke, come see this."

He walked to her desk. He whispered, "Call me Dad, even in here. Someone might overhear."

"Oh, right. Sorry, Dad." She highlighted an entry on the screen. "Rushton has called for a special meeting of the board today at ten thirty. It's a vote on a special lobbying disbursement so it involves more than two million dollars, otherwise he could have authorized it himself."

"How convenient."

"I have to attend that meeting, but you can't."

Luke considered it. "I can't protect you in there, but they aren't likely to hurt you in front of witnesses. You should be safe. While you're in there, I'll wander around the building and check out the security."

"We'll need to get you a special VISITOR pass. You still can't get into the restricted areas though."

"What are the restricted areas?"

"The maintenance rooms, conference rooms, offices, the security operations room and the computer center. You can pretty much wander the halls, stairs and the open spaces."

"That should be enough." A thought occurred to him. "If you introduced me to the Security Supervisor, would he allow your kind old dad into the operations center? It would give me a good look at their camera coverage."

"That might be possible. We'll check on that when we get your pass."

Melanie printed copies of the schedules and tucked them into the folder.

Getting the VISITOR pass was a simple signature exercise. The guard didn't even ask Luke for ID. Melanie simply introduced him as her father and explained that she had to attend a board meeting. She didn't want her poor dad to have to wait in her office, so could he have a pass and wander the building?

The Security Chief was gracious. He agreed to escort her dad to the operations center. Melanie made a show of hugging and kissing her dad before dashing off. Luke dutifully hugged her and pecked her on the cheek.

"Your daughter is a lovely, kind lady, Mr. Taylor. It's always a pleasure to speak with her."

"Thank you, Chief. Her mother and I are very proud of her."

The Chief smiled. "It's obvious she adores you. I wish I had that kind of relationship with my daughter."

Luke tried to sympathize. It was easy for him to transpose his relationships with his daughters to Melanie. They had many of the same qualities. He could only imagine what it was like not to have closeness of kin.

They reached the security center. A sign was posted on the thick, metal door. SECURITY OPERATIONS, AUTHORIZED PERSONNEL ONLY.

The Chief swiped a magnetic card and pressed a six-digit code onto a cipher lock keypad. The lock clicked and the Chief pushed the door inward, allowing Luke to enter.

The room was smaller than Luke expected. It was dark with dim indirect lighting reflecting from the ceiling. There was only one guard, seated at a control console, flanked by eight closed-circuit monitors. All monitors appeared to be functional, switching images at sporadic intervals.

"Mr. Duncan, this is Miss Taylor's father, Mr. Vincent Taylor."

Luke shook hands with Duncan.

The Chief continued, "Miss Taylor has to attend a board meeting. Let Mr. Taylor observe the operations while she's in the meeting."

"Certainly. Welcome, Mr. Taylor."

"Thank you, Mr. Duncan."

"Mr. Taylor, enjoy the show and feel free to roam the unrestricted areas. Remember, smile for the cameras." He pointed to the monitors. "Mr. Duncan will give you an overview of the operation."

Luke smiled and shook the Chief's hand. "Thanks, Chief. I promise not to be a bother."

"It's a pleasure. No bother at all. Enjoy."

"Thanks again."

The Chief departed. Duncan pulled a roller chair toward Luke.

"Have a seat, Mr. Taylor. I'll run you through our setup."

"Thank you." Luke sat.

"Call me Larry."

"Okay Larry. Call me Vince."

"Yes sir, Vince."

Luke chuckled. "Not Sir Vince. Just Vince."

"Okay Vince."

Duncan spent ten minutes explaining the NOMP security system, showing camera coverage, console controls, lighting, recording, etc. Luke made extensive mental notes, smiling as he acted fascinated.

Storm was in his hotel room on the phone to Mike Starr.

"Then it's agreed," said Storm. "I'll get the jade sculpture to San Fran, then I'll get it right back to you."

"Sounds good, Derek. Man, what a find. I'm glad you and your buddy got out of Iraq unscathed."

"Me too. On the next matter, I'd like to ask your help, Mike."

"What's up?"

Storm summarized his plan and asked for help with weapons, equipment and transportation.

"I can do better than that. I have a type rating in a G-5."

"What's a G-5?"

"A Gulfstream five. It's a large corporate jet. It has intercontinental range and plenty of room to carry the load you're talking about. We can lease one from the executive airport across town. I know the owner."

"That sounds great. When can you get it?"

"Any time between now and Saturday. All I need is the date and destination."

"Super. I know the destination, but the date is still a question mark. I'll know more by this evening."

"Good. Let me know as soon as possible."

"Super. Thanks Mike."

"You bet. Talk to you later. Bye."

The plan was ready. All they needed was time-on-target.

Luke was in Melanie's office when she returned. He was seated at her desk, writing notes.

"Did you have a nice look around, Dad?" She closed the door.

"Yup. How did the meeting go?"

"Curious. They were surprised to see me."

Luke huffed. "Not surprising. They're probably the ones who hired the goon to knock you off. They expected you to be dead by now."

"How regal of them?"

"Quite." Luke vacated her seat.

Melanie sat. "That meeting was bizarre."

"Explain."

"The sole item on the agenda was a request for six million dollars for some nebulous lobbying endeavor. Rushton said it was an emergency appropriation to protect NOMP from Congressional action. But he wouldn't reveal what action or whom the funds were for. It sounded underhanded. I voted NO, but the measure passed. There goes six million hard-earned dollars, to whom and for what, I don't know. At least my conscience is clear." She sighed. "Did you get what you needed?"

Luke nodded. "Let's get back to the hotel."

Melanie's cell phone rang.

"Hello?"

"Melanie, it's Deirdre. How are you, hon?"

"I'm good. I've been more worried about you. Where are you?"

"I'm at home. The kids are in school and John's at work."

"I'm sorry you lost your job."

"Not to worry. I'll find another one. Besides, I can use a few weeks off."

"You're taking it better than I would."

"Well, thanks. You're a sweetheart. But let me get to the reason I called. Do you remember when I told you that we couldn't access the personal files from external sources?"

"Yes. Raas found it and had it purged."

"That was the internal access program. They didn't find the one I installed the day I was fired."

"You didn't."

"I did. And I've been into Rushton's personal files, right here from home. Was there a board meeting this morning?"

"Yes. We just adjourned."

"Was there a six million dollar appropriation vote?"

"Uh huh."

"Guess what? Rushton authorized that disbursement before the meeting, in cash."

"When did he do that?"

"Last night. He even scheduled a courier for tonight at six p.m."

"To whom is the courier taking the money?"

"I'm not sure. The file said I-S pension."

"*I-S, Iris Stakemore. The money was a bribe.*" "All six million is going to I-S pension?"

"That's what the file indicates."

"What courier?"

"SECURE BONDED COURIERS."

"At six p.m. tonight?"

"Right. In Rushton's office."

"But we don't know where it's going?"

"Correct. The file didn't say. But there was another tidbit that seemed interesting."

"What?"

"Six cash disbursements, twenty thousand each, from the Executive Committee Fund to the FDA for P-Z 2000."

"P-Z 2000. ParaZyme 2000. Those bastards are bribing the FDA."

"It appears so. The Executive Committee is meeting in Rushton's office tonight at five-thirty."

"Deirdre, you're a doll. Thanks for the information." Melanie took a deep breath as she chose her words. "Deirdre, there's something you need to know."

"What's that, hon?"

"Someone tried to kill me Monday night. I think it's connected to Rushton."

"Oh my God!"

"I'm okay. I've got some guardian angels." She smiled at Luke. "But to be safe, maybe you and the kids should leave town for a few days. There's something in the works to deal with the problem."

"What are you going to do, Mel?"

"I can't say any more. You get out of Boston for a few days."

"Oh my God! I never thought of that. Look honey, I'm gonna take your advice and get the kids out of school. Got to go. You be careful."

"I will. Stay in touch."

Melanie disconnected and told Luke everything.

"We move tonight. Call Derek and give him the details. I've got some arrangements to make."

"Melanie dialed Storm's hotel room and Luke called the *Vixen* on his satellite phone.

"Skipper. It's Luke. Got a pen and paper? Good. Here's what I need you to do." Luke outlined the plan.

At the conclusion, the Skipper responded, "It'll be done, boss. And I know just the place."

Helendale: The mercenaries had scoured the entire Helendale area. Thus far, it had been fruitless. Several shop owners had recognized the photos, but none knew their names or whereabouts.

Slash and Trigger patrolled the town. They reasoned that Chen and Flynn lived somewhere nearby and sooner or later, they or the S-10 would be spotted at the shopping center.

Trigger steered their SUV into the shopping center from Vista Road, heading for a Mexican restaurant at the end of the row of shops. Slash noted a yellow Hummer parked near the bank's ATM. It was a nice rig with black bumpers and headlight guards, convertible top and splashguards.

"Check out that Hummer," he said as they cruised past it.

Trigger twisted in his seat. "Nice wheels. Looks a lot more comfortable than the ones we drove in the Army."

"No shit. My kidneys still remember their service."

A slender, longhaired woman came out of the bank. She was stunning. She had dark hair, tight figure, great legs and... Oriental features. Slash's jaw dropped. He gawked and pointed.

"It's her, Trig!"

"Where?"

"Coming out of the bank." Trigger twisted in his seat again. They saw Lisa walk to the Hummer.

"Shit! She's getting into the Hummer. Turn around, Trigger."

Trigger tried to whip the SUV around the bend to the next lane, but a car backed out right in front of him. He hit the horn but the old lady driver paid him no mind and leisurely continued backing out. Trigger slammed the shift into REVERSE and attempted to back up, but another vehicle was right on his tail.

Slash watched the Hummer. It backed out and sped out to Vista Road. Slash lost sight of it as it passed behind a breakfast diner.

"Shit! She getting' away, Trigger. Move this thing."

Trigger slammed the shift into DRIVE and eased on the gas. He nosed forward until the SUV's bumper crunched the trunk of the old lady's car, then he stomped the gas pedal. Both vehicles surged forward. Trigger saw the old lady freeze. He pushed her car forward and cut his wheel hard left. The old lady's Pontiac slammed into a parked car and the SUV's rear tires burned rubber. They pushed the Pontiac's tail sideways, scraped the Pontiac's rear fender and squeezed around the tight corner. Slash flipped the bird at the old lady and the SUV sped around the corner.

Trigger floored the gas. He didn't even try for the exit. He drove straight across the lot, the SUV launched over some concrete parking blocks, across the sidewalk and off the curb. Trigger cut hard right onto Vista Road but the Hummer was not in sight. He raced to the intersection at Helendale Road and braked.

"Where the frig did she go?"

Slash caught a glimpse of yellow rounding a bend on Helendale Road.

"Left! Left!"

Trigger floored the gas and blew through the four-way STOP. They careened around the corner, leaving several cars askew in the intersection, their horns blaring.

Trigger accelerated to ninety miles an hour. They streaked for a mile without letting up.

Slash searched with binoculars. The Hummer turned right, just past a horse corral. She had at least a mile lead on them.

Trigger kept the pedal floored until the last second, hit the brakes hard and whipped around the corner onto the same road. The sign read WILD RD. They slid onto the opposite shoulder, kicked up a sand cloud and regained the pavement a hundred yards further.

"This is Wild Road," commented Slash. "This comes out near the dead drop on Indian Trail."

Trigger had the gas pedal floored but they couldn't gain ground. The narrow bumpy road made several sharp turns. Trigger had to slow to fifteen miles an hour at each turn to keep from slamming into fences.

After they rounded a third curve, they crested a ridgeline. The road turned into a mile long downhill straightaway all the way to Indian Trail. The Hummer had vanished.

∞

Lisa heard a car horn blare behind her. She turned and saw a gray SUV bracketed between two vehicles. Its passenger was pointing at her and the driver was making vulgar gestures to the driver in front.

"*Gray SUV*," "Shit!"

Lisa threw her purse into the Hummer and jumped in. She jammed the key into the ignition and started the engine. She shifted to REVERSE and backed out. She shifted to DRIVE and sped away.

"*Where do I go?*" She almost panicked. "*Home. No! Don't go home. Police station. No. Too far away. The lab. Okay. The lab.*"

She turned right onto Vista and immediately left on Helendale Road. She floored the accelerator and dashed past the golf course, horse stables and RV Park. She sped to ninety miles an hour as she fished through her purse for her revolver. She wasn't afraid of it now, but she still wished Derek were there.

A quick check in her mirrors confirmed the SUV was in pursuit, far behind. The secret tunnel was farther away than the main entrance. They might catch her before she could reach it. The main entrance would have to do. It was off a dirt trail over a ridge, hidden from Wild Road.

Lisa slowed as she came abeam a horse corral. She whipped right onto Wild Road. The tires squealed but she ignored their protest. She straightened the wheel and floored the gas. She glanced right and noticed the SUV had not gained any ground.

The first of three sharp curves was coming up and she slowed. She smoothly rounded the first and second curves, but not the third. She drove straight off the road, across a patch of wild grass and onto a trail. She engaged the four-wheel drive and powered up the rocky incline and descended behind the ridgeline. She drove several hundred yards to the lab. As soon as she cleared the gate, she pressed the remote, closing the gate and arming the security system.

She drove straight into the loading bay and pressed another button. The bunker doors swung closed. She turned off the Hummer and heard the bunker doors latch.

Her heart rate was off the charts and she was shaking. She placed her head into her hands and cried.

"Derek. I need you."

Boston: Luke sent Storm and Melanie shopping. They bought an off-the-rack black suit, white dress shirt, black shoes and a conservative tie for Storm. They also purchased supplies and equipment. As soon as they returned to the hotel, Melanie hemmed the trousers for Storm.

Luke contacted the courier company, told them he was calling from NOMP and that there had been a change of itinerary. The courier would not be required this evening. The dispatcher accepted the ersatz cancellation graciously and Luke assured her that their company was still NOMP's courier of choice.

Storm suited up as Melanie and Luke inventoried their supplies and gear: duct tape, Nyquil, socks and one unopened overnight express package.

A knock came on Luke's suite door. Storm answered. A man carrying a large gym bag entered and shook Storm's hand.

"Luke. Melanie. I'd like you to meet Mike Starr, the pilot who directed my rescue during Desert Storm."

"Hello, Mike. I'm Luke Hale." They smiled and shook hands.

"I'm Melanie Taylor."

Starr said, "I understand you're the courageous lady who revealed all this hubbub."

Melanie blushed. "I guess so."

"Well, thank you for coming forward. It takes a strong person to take action in the face of evil."

"I'm not all that courageous."

Luke interjected. "A statesman, Edmond Burke I believe, once said, 'All that is required for evil to triumph is that a few good men do nothing.' What you've done takes courage. We admire you for that."

Melanie was flattered. Until now, she didn't realize how much these men respected her.

"You look quite dapper, Derek," noted Starr.

"Thank you. I see you brought some goodies."

Starr smiled. "I did." He set the bag on a sofa, unzipped it and pulled out two huge, holstered handguns.

"Holy shit!" exclaimed Luke. "What are those?"

"They're .44 Auto-Mags." Starr grinned widely, proud of his matched set of chrome plated, semi-automatic pistols.

"Are those handguns or do we need tripods?" joked Storm.

Starr passed one to Storm. Derek stripped his jacket, checked the weapon safety and chamber, then hefted it, aiming at a vase across the room. "Night sights, nice application. Damn, this thing is heavy."

"Good thing. The recoil would be unbearable if they weren't."

Storm strapped on the holster and donned his jacket. The huge rig made an obvious bulge. "I'll have to speak with my tailor about that."

"Clothing tailor or Melanie Taylor?" she quipped. The men chuckled.

Starr reached into the bag and produced a Kimber semi-auto. He handed it to Luke. "I understand you're a .45 man."

"You heard correctly. Thanks." Luke took the weapon, checked the chamber and safety.

"I don't have a holster for it yet. It's brand new."

"That's fine. I'm a waistband kind of guy." Luke stowed the piece behind his back.

Starr went into the gym bag again. He removed a cardboard box.

"What's that?" inquired Melanie.

Starr opened the lid and removed an object covered with bubble wrap. He removed the wrapping, revealing a carved jade sculpture.

"That's beautiful," she declared. "Where did it come from?"

"China," answered Storm, "but it took the scenic route through Iraq."

The men chuckled at Melanie's puzzled look. Storm explained the significance of the piece.

"Wow."

Starr wrapped the sculpture and boxed it. He presented the box to Storm.

"I'll get this right back to you, Mike."

"You bet. Now, last but not least." Starr reached into the bag and removed Tasers, a stun gun, two cans of pepper spray and four walkie-talkies. The avengers distributed the gear.

Starr concluded, "The G-5 is standing by. All I have to do is file the flight plan."

"How about wheels?" asked Storm.

"One van in the parking lot down the street, courtesy of my neighbor."

"Great."

Hale checked his watch, 5:12 p.m. "It's show time, folks."

Starr said, "Time to go pure pursuit."

Hale smiled. Storm and Taylor looked puzzled.

"It's fighter pilot terminology," explained Luke. "When a fighter is pursuing a target to shoot a heat-seeking missile, he points his nose behind the bandit to slide behind him, that's called lag pursuit."

Starr continued, "And if you want to close range or cut him off, you point your nose in front of him. That's called lead pursuit."

Hale finished the lesson. "And when you're ready to blow his ass out of the sky, you point your nose directly at his tailpipe and press the launch trigger. The skinny white wingman does the rest. That's pure pursuit."

Storm and Melanie understood.

Storm remarked, "I guess it's time to go pure pursuit."

Helendale: Pete consoled Lisa. She had had enough of high-speed car chases. And she was tired of being an entrée on the menu. She needed relief. So did Pete.

"It too dangerous to go out now. We need to stay in the bunker. We'll be safe until Derek returns."

"I still wish he were here."

"Me too, Lisa. But he can't be everywhere at once. We'll manage. We have everything we need to hold out for a week."

"What about the police? Can't they do anything?"

"I've already discussed it with the Sheriff's Department. They can patrol the area but they have a large territory to cover and they can't spend all their time out here. They can only respond if a crime is committed. They aren't security guards. But I'll call and update them. We'll just have to hunker down until Derek returns. He'll deal with them."

Lisa nodded and wiped her tears. "I'm going to call Derek." She needed more than anything to hear his voice.

Boston: The avengers arrived at the NOMP building at 5:49 p.m. Starr drove the van and Storm sat in the front passenger seat. Hale and Taylor sat in back.

Starr eased to the curb at the front entrance. Storm hopped out and entered the lobby. Starr drove to the rear and parked near an exit door.

Storm approached the lobby security guard.

"Bonded Courier. I have a six o'clock appointment with Dr. Rushton."

The guard noticed the bulge under Storm's left armpit.

"Packing heat for this one, eh?"

Storm smiled. "We take our work seriously." Storm flashed open his jacket. The guard got a good look at the chrome-plated hardware and whistled.

"I guess you do." He referred to an access roster on his desk. "Bonded Courier, Dr. Rushton, six o'clock. Okay. Please sign the log."

Storm endorsed a phony name.

"Do you know how to get to Dr. Rushton's office, Mr. Cleary?"

"Top floor to the left?"

"Yes sir. The elevators are to your right."

"Thank you. Have a good evening."

"You too, sir."

Storm waited at the elevators and nodded politely at the guard. Elevator doors opened. Storm entered and rode to the top floor. He exited and turned left.

The layout was exactly as Melanie had described. He headed for

Rushton's office, noting the closed-circuit cameras.

Rushton's door was open. Storm heard three distinct voices. He knocked on the doorframe.

"Bonded Courier for Dr. Rushton."

"Come in and close the door."

Storm complied. He faced them. He recognized all three from the photos. His blood boiled. These were the people responsible for Dan's murder, the impetus behind the killers who threatened Pete and Lisa. He could kill all three of them right now without firing a shot. But that would be too good for these scum. But they were going down, hard. They were going to suffer painful, slow deaths.

Rushton glanced at his watch. "Right on time. Good man."

"That's what you pay for, right Doctor?"

"Yes. Let's get down to business." Rushton pointed at a large steel case on his desktop. It had dual steel combination locks. "This package must be delivered tonight. You're booked on the 8 p.m. Atlantic Shuttle flight to Dulles Airport." He slid an airline ticket across the desk. Storm glimpsed it and tucked it into his jacket. "Take this to Dulles, where you will proceed to the Red Star Rental Car parking lot. At 1 a.m., you will rendezvous at slot G-37 and give this case to a lady who will identify herself as 'Flowers.' Ask no questions. Once you've handed over the case, your mission is complete. Clear?"

"Yes sir: 8 p.m., Atlantic Shuttle, Dulles Airport, Red Star Car Rental, G-37, 1 a.m., Flowers, no questions."

"Good man." Rushton pulled a wad of currency from his pocket. Storm lifted the heavy case. Rushton peeled off three crisp C notes and handed them to Storm. "We're counting on you."

"Consider it done, Doctor." Storm took the cash and pocketed it. "Thank you. Unless you have something further, I'll be on my way."

"That's it. Good night. Please close the door on the way out."

Storm nodded and left. He closed the door and immediately sidestepped out of view of the security cameras. He tucked an earpiece into his left ear and keyed the walkie-talkie.

"Bingo, three. Good to go."

∞

In the van, Luke heard Storm's transmission. "He's got positive ID on them. Let's go."

Hale and Starr exited and hid in the shadows near the rear exit. The door opened two minutes later.

Hale and Starr rushed in and silently followed Storm through a back hallway. They went to a service elevator where there were no security cameras. They rode to the second-highest floor, then down another camera-less service hallway to a stairwell. They trotted up to the top floor.

Storm paused at the door and signaled STOP. He cracked the door open and assessed a security camera. It was in mid-sweep. He closed the door and checked his watch. Twelve seconds later, he cracked the door. He signaled GO.

The crusaders dashed silently through the door, along the near wall and hid behind a desk outside Rushton's office. They heard voices inside and the mention of Stakemore's name.

Storm checked his watch again. Luke crosschecked his. Storm held up five fingers. Starr and Hale nodded. Storm folded down a finger with each passing second. When his fist closed, Hale flung open Rushton's door, they rushed inside and Storm closed and locked it.

"What's this?"

"What the…?"

"Who are you?"

Starr and Hale shot Raas and Miller with Taser darts and juiced them. Storm leveled his Auto-Mag at Rushton.

"Hands up. Now!"

Rushton thrust his arms up.

"If you even twitch, I'll blow your head off."

"Is… this a… a robbery?"

"Shut up." Storm cocked the Auto-Mag's hammer.

Starr pulled duct tape from his bag and tossed a roll to Luke. Starr and Hale taped the groggy Raas and Miller around their ankles and knees. Then they taped their hands behind their backs and wound tape all the way around them at elbow level.

Hale soaked two socks with Nyquil and stuffed them into their mouths. Starr taped their mouths shut. They had the choice of swallowing the Nyquil or suffocating. They made the right choice.

They turned to Rushton. The huge bore of Storm's portable artillery piece had Rushton's complete attention.

Starr grabbed Rushton's arms and taped his wrists behind his back, then he wound the tape around his torso and elbows. Hale grabbed the doctor by the scruff of his neck and pulled him to his feet. Rushton winced from the pain of Luke's talon-like grip.

"Stand up, asshole."

Rushton struggled to his feet. Starr kicked his left ankle.

"Ow."

"Put your feet together."

Rushton hesitated. Luke was in no mood for defiance. He thrust his fingertips into Rushton's liver, grabbed his bottom right rib and pulled. An ugly snap issued as the rib broke. Starr stuffed a sock into Rushton's mouth to smother the impending scream.

"Put your feet together or he'll break another one," threatened Storm. Rushton immediately complied; the defiance had gone out of him. Tears streamed from his eyes.

Starr taped his ankles and knees together and shoved him into the chair.

Storm's fierce look of disdain and the pain nearly caused Rushton to faint. Storm placed the gun's muzzle between Rushton's eyes.

"Now Doctor, we're going to play twenty questions. If we don't get answers we like, my associate is going to break more of your bones. He's very good at it. I trained him myself. Now, we're going to remove the gag. If you yell, we'll snap your neck. Nod if you understand."

Rushton closed his eyes and nodded. Perspiration formed on his forehead and upper lip. He was ready to puke.

Luke grasped the doctor's head and yanked it back, then twisted it to its limit. Further rotation would induce pain and blinding flashes of light. Extreme rotation would break it.

Starr removed the gag. The doctor gasped for air.

"First, what's in the steel case?"

"Money."

"How much?"

"Six million."

"Who's it for?"

"I'm not supposed to say."

Luke twisted the neck. A sharp pain shot through Rushton's neck. White flashes appeared in his eyes.

"We don't like that answer. Last time. Who's the money for?"

"Ah! Ah! Iris Stakemore." Luke eased the pressure.

"The bitch Congress critter?"

"Yes."

"What's the money for?"

"A payoff."

"For what?"

"To keep her quiet."

"About what?"

"Some work and … referrals she did for us."

"What work?"

Rushton hesitated. Luke twisted.

"Ah! Ah! Okay. She referred us to some mercenaries."

"For what purpose?"

"Ah! To obtain research materials." Luke eased his grip.

"ParaZyme 2000?"

"Yes."

"Did the mercenaries kill Dan Flynn?"

"Yes."

"Did you tell them to kill him?"

"No! No! That was Bravo's idea."

"Who's Bravo?"

"Colonel Bravo. He's the boss of the team."

"What does he look like?"

"Huge guy: six foot five, two hundred sixty or seventy pounds, solid muscle. Short brown hair, buzz cut. Two scars on his left cheek. Brown eyes, wide shoulders and thick arms."

That description didn't trigger Storm's memory.

"Did Bravo kill Dan Flynn?"

"I don't know. I only know it was his idea."

"What are Bravo's orders?"

"Find the research lab."

"And do what?"

Rushton hesitated. Luke twisted.

"Ah! Ah! Destroy the lab."

"And what about Pete Flynn?"

"I think he means to kill him too." It took all of Storm's discipline to keep from squeezing the trigger. Luke peered into Storm's eyes and recognized the look.

"Sifu," said Luke. Storm glanced at Hale. Luke shook his head. He knew Storm wanted revenge, but killing Rushton in his own office would cause major problems.

Storm focused and resumed the interrogation. "Can you call off Bravo?"

"No. I already tried."

"Why not?"

"He's turned it into a personal vendetta. He's after some guy named Storm."

"Why?"

"Storm killed one of his men and has foiled his plans. He also said that the guy could recognize him. His reputation is at stake."

"What does that have to do with Pete Flynn?"

"Storm is Flynn's nephew. His research assistant is Storm's girlfriend. He said he has to kill them to get at Storm and kill him, otherwise he'd be looking over his shoulder the rest of his life."

Storm round-housed his left elbow into Rushton's temple. The blow knocked him to the floor, unconscious.

"Bravo is right," remarked Storm. "He *will* have to watch over his shoulder for the rest of his life."

CHAPTER XXI

SURPRISE

Lugging three unconscious bodies to the stairway, unobserved by the cameras, down a flight of stairs and to the service elevator was no small chore. The doctors were heavy. Miller was a little plush on the bottom also.

At the rear exit, they dumped them unceremoniously into the rear of the van. Starr eased the van along the rear alley, turned into traffic and headed for the executive airport.

Luke's satellite phone rang.

"Hello?"

"Hello. This is Lisa Chen. Is Derek Storm with you?"

"Yes, one moment." He handed the phone to Storm. "It's for you, lover boy."

"Hello?"

There was a long silence as Storm spent several minutes listening. He inquired, "Can you guys pull this off without me?"

Starr shook his head. "No way. After we drop off the bundles, I'll need help flying back."

"Can you fly me to California after the drop?"

"Yeah. I'll just need help getting it across the Atlantic."

Storm spoke into the phone. "Listen, Lisa. I'll be there in three days. Go into lockdown. I'll deal with those bastards when I get back. I'll check in every chance I get."

Storm listened.

"I love you too. Good-bye." Storm disconnected and returned Luke's phone.

"What's going on, Derek?"

"The killers spotted Lisa and chased her. She's scared but she and Pete are in the bunker. They should be okay for a week or so."

Luke nodded. "Where's that case Rushton gave you?"

"Back here. Why?"

"The courier was going to deliver that payoff tonight."

"What are you getting at?"

"We can grab Stakemore tonight."

"Yeah, why not?" agreed Storm, as he held up the last sock gag. "I'd hate to waste this."

∞

The Executive Airport was a casual operation. There wasn't much security. Starr flashed his airline ID at the gate guard, drove through the gate and parked right next to a Gulfstream. He backed the van to the jet's entry door.

"That's our bird. You guys load the cargo while I file the flight plan. We'll leave in twenty minutes."

Storm scanned the ramp. It was well lit but there was shadow between the van and the jet.

Starr opened the entry door and hustled to the operations center. Storm and Hale grabbed Rushton by the armpits and legs. They hauled him to the rear of the cabin. They tossed him into a seat next to the lavatory and strapped him in.

They repeated the process with Raas and Miller. Melanie parked the van, locked it and returned to the jet. Starr arrived, his kit bag in hand. Melanie tossed him the van keys.

They boarded, Starr closed the door and took his station in the command pilot's seat. Hale strapped into the right seat. Storm and Melanie strapped into passenger seats in the cabin.

Starr ran through his cockpit checks. Luke, not familiar with the G-5, helped with basic stuff: radios, navigation equipment, and pressurization. He called for ATC clearance to Dulles as Starr started the engines. When Starr was ready, Hale called for taxi and takeoff clearance.

"Gulfstream Six-Tango, wind two-zero-zero at twelve, you are cleared for takeoff."

Seconds later, the G-5 zoomed for altitude, slipping gracefully through the humid night sky, destination KIAD, Dulles Airport.

An hour later, they touched down gently on the centerline of Runway 19 Right at Dulles. Starr eased the nose wheel to the runway, pulled up the engine reverse levers and gently applied the brakes. The jet slowed. Hale called out the airspeed as they decelerated.

"One hundred knots. Eighty knots."

Starr eased the reverse levers to idle power.

"Sixty knots."

Starr stowed the reversers, increased brake pressure and steered left along the centerline for a high-speed exit.

"Dulles Ground, Gulfstream Six-Tango, clear of One-Niner-Right for the Execjet ramp."

"Six-Tango, Dulles Ground. Give way to the American seven-six at Taxiway Delta, then taxi to the ramp."

Luke acknowledged. An American Airlines Boeing 767-300ER taxied across their front and turned into the D Concourse ramp. Starr eased up the left throttle and passed well behind it.

"I'm taking down the right engine, Luke."

"Roger that."

To save fuel, Starr cut the fuel to the right engine. The G-5 taxied nicely on one engine. As the right engine wound down, its electrical generator automatically transferred its load to the left engine's generator.

Starr maneuvered the jet onto the Execjet ramp and lined up on a parking line. A ground service employee with lighted wands guided them to a stop. The ground man plugged in a cable from a portable generator and signaled Mike to shut down the left engine. Starr shut it down and the portable generator picked up the entire electrical load.

Starr and Hale executed the Parking checklist and went to the cabin. Starr lowered the entry stairs and went to file the next segment of their flight plan.

Storm briefed Melanie on use of the stun gun and told her to use it if they regained consciousness. She had no qualms about it.

Storm and Hale discussed their plan to snatch Stakemore.

"I think she'll be close by," opined Hale, "since there's six million in cash at stake. She won't want that money out of her sight."

"I wouldn't either. I'll bet she sends a lackey to fetch it while she watches from a distance."

"My thoughts exactly."

Storm crossed his arms on his chest. "As soon as Mike gets back, we'll do a little recon."

Starr was back within twenty minutes. He had filed the flight plan and gathered food and beverages for the long flight. He passed up the boxes and climbed the entry stairs.

"Good news. The ride across the Atlantic should be smooth with tailwinds all the way. We're filed for takeoff at 0130 local time."

"Perfect," stated Luke. "Hopefully, we'll have Thunder Thighs in custody."

Starr smirked. "I take it you don't like her."

"What's not to like? She's like a greasy chicken dinner: two fat thighs, two small breasts and two left wings." Everyone chuckled.

"Mr. Hale," said a shocked Melanie, "you're a rascal."

"Thank you, pretty lady. I think she epitomizes what's wrong with many of our elected officials. They're destroying our liberties for their own selfish motives: greed and power."

"Yeah," agreed Storm. "That's why I believe in term limits. One term in office, the second term in prison." They chuckled again.

"It's recon time," announced Storm.

Luke dialed his satellite phone. He called the car rental company and ordered a minivan. He also requested transportation to take them to the rental counter.

Fifteen minutes later a shuttle bus appeared at the gate. Storm and Hale boarded and rode it to the rental counter. Luke rented a vehicle and charged it to a credit card from one of his business trusts. There was no way to trace it back to him.

He and Storm went out to the lot, located the vehicle and readied their gear. They cruised the lot and located space G-37. It was occupied by a Ford Taurus.

They spent the next hour scouting the lot and the surrounding area. There was only one entrance and one exit. They made note of the lighting, shadows, blind spots, avenues of approach and escape. They selected a parking spot in the shadows that gave them a good view of the entrance, exit and space G-37.

Luke killed the interior lights so they wouldn't illuminate when they opened the doors. They rechecked their weapons and gear and called Mike to advise him of their status.

Storm and Hale plugged earpieces into their walkie-talkies and made a radio check. Then Storm casually walked to space G-37 where they made another radio check. All was good, so he returned to the minivan.

Hale checked his watch. It was 11:36 p.m. They had eighty-four minutes to rendezvous time.

Luke parked the minivan down the street from the lot entrance. They could drive into the lot, if necessary, while keeping an eye on the exit at the same time.

Twenty minutes prior to rendezvous, Storm took the case and strolled into the lot. He waited in the shadows. He could see the drop point, the entry, exit and the minivan.

"Radio check."

"Lima Charlie, how me?" responded Luke.

"Lima Charlie." Loud and clear.

Storm rechecked his AutoMag, Taser and pepper spray.

"How's the weather out there?"

"Cold as a witch's tit. At least the wind isn't too bad."

"I'll keep the heater going for you."

"Thanks. I'll need it. That and a stiff shot of bourbon."

"Too bad we don't have any," lamented Luke.

"Not so. The jet has a wet bar in the cabin. I spotted a bottle of Jack Daniels in the rack."

"I thought you'd prefer Irish whiskey."

"Beggars can't be choosers."

A vehicle rounded a bend and approached from the opposite direction from Luke.

"We've got company from the east." He killed the minivan ignition and ducked behind the dashboard.

"Roger that. In sight."

A black Lincoln limousine pulled to the opposite side of the street and parked short of the lot entrance. Its headlights extinguished.

Luke peeked over the dashboard. The limo was fifty-five yards ahead, facing his direction, on the opposite side of the road.

"If that's them, they're twelve minutes early," Storm said.

The limo had smoked windows in the rear. Luke could distinguish the driver but he couldn't tell how many people were in the back. The minutes ticked by.

"I wonder what they're waiting for?" asked Storm. "Do you see any tails or flanks?"

"Negative. Do you?"

"Negative."

"Maybe they're just punctual."

"Let's hope so."

Three minutes prior to rendezvous, the limo's rear right passenger door opened and the interior lights came on.

Luke reported, "Male driver, two females and one male in the back."

"Copy that."

A man stepped out, leaned back inside the limo for a moment, emerged and closed the door. He walked toward the lot.

"Male from the rear is heading for the lot."

"Roger. In sight. Let's go Option Charlie."

"Copy that. We're go, Option Charlie."

The man walked into the lot and wandered around. It didn't appear to be recon, merely unfamiliarity. Besides, it was too late for recon. It was a dead giveaway that he wasn't a professional. The man finally located the G row and swished toward space 37.

"I think this guy is gay," transmitted Storm. "Look at the way he walks."

Hale chuckled. "If he's not, then he's practicing Lady-with-a-Fan technique. Or he's got a very bad rash."

Storm chuckled. "Any tails or flanks?"

"Negative."

"Negative here too. Option Charlie's a go."

"I'm on the move." Luke slid out the rear hatch and slinked into the tree line, stealth Infantry mode.

Storm eased out of the shadows and slowly headed for the rendezvous, his head on a swivel. The contact didn't spot him until he was within a car length. The young man was startled.

"Easy, fella," assured Storm. "I'm with Bonded Courier. I have a package to deliver."

"V... very well. I'll take it." The kid was obviously very gay and very nervous.

"I was told to expect a lady. Who are you?"

The kid looked really nervous now. Normally, Storm would have expected an ambush but he could sense no danger; there was just this wimpy kid and the limo, which Luke had covered. He whispered into the radio, "Alpha check?"

"Your six is clear."

Storm addressed the lad again. "Okay, son. This is the last time I'm going to ask. If I don't get the correct answer, I'm leaving with this case." Storm lifted the case to emphasize his point. "Now, who are you?"

"F... Flowers?"

"Are you asking me or telling me?"

"N... no sir. I'm Flowers, David Flowers."

Storm smiled. "That's the right answer. Here's your case." Storm approached and gave him the case. The kid took hold but as soon as Storm released his grip, the kid lost his and dropped it.

The kid smiled nervously, as if to say 'oops.' He bent over like a woman, dialed combinations into the locks and opened the case. It was filled with five hundred dollar bills, bundled in neat stacks.

"All good?" asked Storm.

"Y... yes. Thank you." He closed and latched the lid. When he looked up, he was staring down the bore of Storm's AutoMag. He wet his pants and began to cry. "Please don't hurt me. Please."

"Relax son. This is just for show. I'm not going to hurt you." He didn't enjoy tormenting the youngster but it was necessary to implement Option Charlie. Storm lifted the case.

∞

The limo driver's door opened and he stepped out, facing the lot. He reached under his coat and withdrew a fistful of Glock. He felt two sharps stabs into his back and then an electrical jolt that made his teeth clench and his body spasm. He dropped the Glock, staggered and collapsed.

Luke released the Taser trigger, raced to the driver's door and jumped in, facing the occupants in the rear. Iris Stakemore and an unknown woman were in the back. Luke leveled his .45 at them. "Let's play Simon Says. I'm Simon and I say freeze." The shocked women complied. "Simon says place the palms of your hands on the roof." They complied nervously. "Very good. I can see you've played this game before."

"Who are you?" asked the unknown woman.

"Simon says shut up." Luke aimed his .45 at her. He said into his radio, "Option Charlie, phase two complete. Bundle is tight."

Storm acknowledged. "Okay, son, let's go back to the limo. You passed the test."

"W... what test?"

"This test." Storm holstered his pistol. "This was just a test. Your boss wanted to know how well you follow instructions under pressure. You did fine."

"Really?"

"Really." Storm lied. "Let's go back to the limo. I have to report to your boss."

The young man turned toward the limo, his crotch and right leg were soaked in urine. Storm placed a friendly arm around his shoulders, attempting to put him at ease. As they walked toward the limo, the kid's right shoe squished every time he placed his weight on it. The poor guy was walking in his own piss.

Luke taped and gagged the women and the driver and extinguished the interior lights. He loaded the unconscious driver into the front seat and climbed into the rear.

Storm opened the rear door and ushered the young man inside. When he stooped to enter, Luke snatched him in and Storm followed, locking the door.

The lad saw the new stranger and the two bound women. He was puzzled and afraid.

"What are you going to do?"

"We're not going to hurt you, kid," assured Storm. "We're just taking the Congresswoman for a little vacation."

Luke taped the kid's ankles and knees together, then his arms and torso. Storm slapped duct tape over his mouth.

Storm positioned the youngster and the unknown woman on the floor, facing each other and taped their ankles, knees and necks together.

"They make a cute couple, don't they?" observed Storm.

"Yeah. One of those December-May romances."

"Did you do the NyQuil bit on Stakemore?"

"Absolutely. She'll be out soon," informed Luke. "Time to get the wheels." He exited and fetched the minivan.

Five minutes later, they had Stakemore's limp plump body loaded through the minivan's rear hatch. Hale pulled the vehicle up the road and parked in shadows.

Storm drove the limo in the opposite direction a hundred yards and parked it in the woods. He locked the doors with the fob and threw the keys away. He ran to the minivan and hopped in.

∞

Mike was at the entry gate as planned, talking with the security guard. Hale pulled the minivan to the gate and lowered the window.

"Howdy Mike. I told you we'd make it on time."

"Hey, hey. There they are." To the guard, he said, "These are my passengers. You can let them in."

"Yes sir." The guard opened the gate. Starr climbed into the back seat.

"Have a good night, sir."

"You as well," answered Luke. "Good night."

Luke drove to the G-5 and backed it to the entry stairs. Storm and Starr hopped out, opened the rear hatch, threw a blanket over Stakemore and hauled her fat ass into the cabin. Storm strapped her into a seat as Starr headed for the cockpit.

Luke parked the minivan near the operations building, tossed the keys under the passenger seat, leaving the vehicle unlocked. He trotted to the jet as Starr started the engines. Luke hustled into the cockpit while Storm closed the entry door.

Luke phoned the rental car company and told them where to pick up their minivan and where to find the keys.

Storm stuck his head into the cockpit. "We're ready back here." He pulled off a set of latex gloves and tossed them into a trash bag.

"Okay Derek," answered Mike. "You ready, Luke?"

"Almost." Hale shed his gloves and tossed them into the trash. "Now I'm ready."

Helendale: Pete didn't like what he saw on the security monitors. Two men were on the hill just west of the bunker, searching. One of them had a rifle, the other had binoculars.

An hour earlier, through the tunnel periscope, he had spotted two other armed men. They were driving a gray SUV with a damaged side panel.

The prospects were bleak. The killers were getting closer. The FDA was erecting roadblocks, demanding practically every scrap of research data before they agreed to verification by independent researchers. The thousands of test volunteers were suffering 'death by bureaucracy.' Lisa was depressed and Pete's back was in knots. He wished for two things: Derek to return and an antacid tablet.

Enroute to Haifa, Israel: As soon as the jet was airborne from Dulles, Storm opened the overnight express package from Lisa. He removed two smaller cardboard boxes. In one box was a syringe. The other contained two capped vials filled with a grotesque concoction.

"What's that?" Melanie asked.

Storm frowned. "You don't want to know. Why don't you see if Mike and Luke need some coffee?"

Melanie nodded sadly. She headed for the galley.

Storm inserted the syringe through one of the vial caps and extracted half of its contents, then he purged the air from it. He pushed Stakemore upright in her seat and opened the lower part of her blouse. He felt for her bottom right rib and pushed his fingers into her abdomen. He located her liver, inserted the syringe and injected the entire contents. Stakemore winced but didn't waken.

Storm repeated the procedure on the others. He was done by the time they had reached cruise altitude over the Atlantic.

For the rest of the flight to France, they took shifts manning the cockpit. Storm relieved Luke in the co-pilot's seat so he could rest.

Mike flew halfway across the Atlantic. Storm learned a lot about aerial navigation, radio communications, fuel burn and timing as they crossed each navigation waypoint.

At the halfway point, Storm went back to wake Luke and Melanie. He brewed a fresh pot of coffee for them and checked the security of their cargo.

Luke and Melanie crewed the second shift, with Luke in the commander's seat. He instructed Melanie how to assist him. She was tired but she was eager to help and to see jet flight from the pilot's perspective. She was amazed at how quickly sunrise came while flying eastbound.

Ten minutes prior to their descent, Melanie awakened Mike. The professional pilots took over for the descent, approach and landing in southern France.

Starr talked Luke through the landing procedures and handling characteristics for the G-5. Luke touched it down softly on the runway centerline as if he'd had a thousand landings in the G-5.

It was a simple refueling stop in France, so they weren't too concerned about Customs. Neither were the authorities. Starr filled out some paperwork, declaring nothing. The officials didn't even walk out to the aircraft to inspect, however they kept a close eye on it until it was airborne again.

The second leg to Israel was more demanding. They had to circumnavigate several large thunderstorm fronts and the ride was turbulent. They bounced around in moderate chop for an hour, south of Greece.

Luke flew the approach and landing at an airfield outside of Haifa.

After the landing rollout, Starr taxied the jet to a remote ramp cluttered with corporate jets and general aviation aircraft. The Customs officials were already there and walked toward the G-5. Luke got on his satellite phone.

"Salty, it's Luke. Where are you?"

"We're at the maintenance hanger on the south side of the field."

"Is the hanger clear?"

"As you requested. It cost you twenty thousand in greenbacks but they agreed and are awaiting your arrival."

"Great. We have the hanger in sight. Is the transportation ready?"

"Good to go."

"Great. Keep the line open and stand by." Luke turned to Starr. "They're ready."

Starr nodded. He pressed the transmit switch, "Ground Control, this is Gulfstream Six-Tango on the general aviation ramp."

"Go ahead, Six-Tango."

"Six-Tango, we have hot brakes and need to taxi to the maintenance hanger to cool them off. We need to taxi now, before the tires blow."

"Copy that, Six-Tango. Is Customs inspection complete?"

"Negative. I'll wave them off. We must taxi now." Starr opened his side window, waved and yelled at the Customs officials.

"Stay clear. Hot brakes. The tires could blow." He transmitted to the Tower again, "Ground Control, this is Six-Tango. We must taxi to the hanger now or the tires will blow."

"Six-Tango, are you declaring an emergency?"

"Okay, have it your way. Six-Tango is declaring an emergency for hot brakes, possible fire hazard. I'm taxiing to the south hanger now. Tell Customs to meet us there."

Starr eased the throttles forward and turned the G-5 toward the maintenance hanger. He waved off the Customs officers again.

The Tower finally acknowledged. "Six-Tango. Understand you have declared an emergency for hot brakes. You are cleared to taxi to the south maintenance hanger. Fire equipment is responding."

Hale turned to Storm. "We're heading for the hanger. The fire trucks and Customs will meet us there. Get them to the front door, quick."

"Right." Storm ran to the back of the cabin and dragged each unconscious body forward. He piled them in a haphazard heap near the entry door.

Starr taxied into the open hanger, following the commands of a guide man. He shut down the engines while the ground crew closed the hanger doors part way, chocked the wheels and placed air duct hoses in front of the main wheels. The hoses blew cold air across the brakes to cool them.

Storm threw open the entry door. He tossed out each flaccid body onto the waiting shoulders of Salty Skibba, Paul Thomas, Terry Pell and Dave Welch. They in turn dumped them unceremoniously into the rear of a tan Ford van, slammed the doors shut, jumped in and sped away.

Melanie straightened the cabin, hiding all evidence of the abductees. The firearms, jade sculpture, syringe and vials were in a hidden compartment behind the wet bar's water tank.

The van was out of sight by the time the fire trucks arrived. The firemen scurried around the aircraft, hauling hoses into the hanger and taking position, ready to spray the wheels if they caught fire.

Starr made a show of repeatedly going to the cockpit to check the brake temperatures. Five minutes later, he poked his head out the entry door and yelled, "All clear. Brake temperatures are normal. You can terminate the emergency."

The Fire Chief waved off his men and notified the Tower. The firemen gathered their equipment and prepared to return to the firehouse.

Two Customs officers approached. They looked grim. Starr disarmed them with a smile and an apology.

"Sorry for the inconvenience, gentlemen. We had very hot brakes and I feared they might blow the tires or catch fire. I had to keep you clear so you wouldn't be injured." He extended his hand and shook with each of them. "We're safe now. Come on aboard. The aircraft is yours for inspection."

The Customs officers spent ten minutes inspecting the jet and the occupant's baggage. All seemed in order, so they bid good day and departed.

As soon as they were out of sight, Luke called the Skipper. "We're clear. Pick us up at the curb."

The avengers gathered at the front of the jet.

Luke said, "Mike, it was a real pleasure to meet you. Thanks for letting me fly that beautiful machine. She handles like a dream and our plan couldn't have succeeded without your help. Thanks." They shook hands.

"You're welcome, Luke. I was glad to help. Come visit us in Cambridge some time."

"It's a deal. And I'd like you to visit my yacht."

"I'm looking forward to it." Starr turned to Melanie. "Well, I guess this is it, young lady. God bless you. You'll be safe with Luke for a few weeks. When you get back to Boston, be sure to give me a call."

"I will. And thank you." She gave Starr a hug and kissed his cheek. She turned to Storm. "Derek, thank you for saving my life. Please keep in touch."

"I'll do that. And thank you for bringing this conspiracy to light. It wouldn't have been possible without your courage." Storm gave Melanie a hug and a peck on her cheek.

She wouldn't let him get off that easily. She flung her arms around his neck and kissed him full on the lips. She pressed her supple body against him.

Storm was embarrassed. "Wow! That's some going-away present."

Melanie whispered into his ear, "There's a lot more where that came from. Thank you." She gave him a look that couldn't be mistaken for anything but desire. They slowly released from their embrace. Melanie's adoration for Storm was evident. He was her white knight.

Storm regained his composure and faced Luke. "It looks like the Jade Gang has completed phase three."

Luke grinned and nodded. "Phase four will be complete in a few days. You have my word. You be careful and check six. I'll make certain these jerks get their just rewards." Luke gave Storm a knowing wink. They grasped hands and embraced, slapping each other on the back.

"Adios, amigo," said Storm. "I have to get back ASAP. The hounds are still in the hunt."

"I hear you. Give me a call if you need reinforcements."

"I will. Keep in touch."

"You know I will." Tears welled in Luke's eyes. He was going to miss his friend, again.

Starr and Storm returned to the G-5. Melanie and Luke headed for their rendezvous at the Immigrations counter, then to the van. There was still work to do, phase four.

Helendale: "What do you make of that, mate?" Percy and Yankee stood on a hilltop looking eastward. Percy handed his binoculars to Yankee and pointed to a chain link fence to the east. "Second hill, south slope at the base."

Yankee took the binoculars and scanned the slope. "I see a fence in a depression between two ridge spurs. Is that it?"

"Oy, mate. Look real close to the slope. I thought I made out a concrete structure."

Yankee adjusted. "Yeah. There's something there."

"What say we have a look, mate?"

∞

The security alarm triggered. It made a low toned, intermittent buzzing sound; the motion sensors had detected something.

Lisa glanced up, saw the number four sensor blinking and looked to the closed-circuit monitors. Two armed men were approaching the fence. She didn't recognize them.

Pete entered the safe room. "I heard the alarm. What's up?"

"There are two armed men near the fence."

Pete observed the monitor. They were armed all right, one with a pistol, the other with a scoped rifle. He grabbed his cell phone and dialed the Sheriff's Department. "Lisa, do you recognize them?"

"No."

"Me neither." Pete spoke into the phone, "Yes, this is Dr. Flynn. Is Sergeant Crane available? Yes. I'll wait." Pete and Lisa observed the monitor.

"Hello, Sergeant Crane. This is Dr. Pete Flynn out in Helendale. We spoke before about stalkers who were searching for my laboratory."

He paused.

"Yes. The one north of Wild Road. We have two suspicious armed men nearby. One has a rifle, the other a pistol. Do you have a unit nearby?"

Pete listened.

"Very good. Thank you. I'll give you my cell number. Your Deputy can call when he gets close. We'll keep a watch on them. Thank you." Pete disconnected. "A Deputy will be here in about twelve minutes."

"Good." Lisa nervously checked the security status board. All exits were closed and locked, except for the interior door between the loading bay and the corridor.

"They're climbing the fence," noted Pete. He strapped on his new pistol and grabbed the twelve gauge.

∞

"That's curious," said Yankee. "Closed-circuit cameras inside the fence. Isn't that downright inhospitable?"

"I don't know about you, mate, but I can't tolerate an ungracious host." Percy climbed the fence, Yankee followed.

They dropped inside and inspected the cameras.

"The cables are encased in steel conduit," observed Yankee. "It would take a metal saw to cut through that."

"Or a demo charge. Or we could just shoot out the cameras."

"Look," pointed Yankee. "Motion sensors. Someone knows we're here."

"They don't seem too concerned about it, mate. No alarms, no angry landlord."

"Not yet. Keep your eyes peeled."

Percy walked down the spur and peeked over the ridge. "Here, mate."

Yankee joined him. They angled down the steep incline and examined the structure. It was the corner of a concrete bunker. It was slightly crumbled and the tips of steel reinforcing bars were exposed.

"Shit!" exclaimed Yankee. "Steel reinforced concrete. It looks pretty thick. Let's get a look around the corner."

As he had guessed, the concrete looked to be about two feet thick.

"Get a gander at these, mate." Percy slapped his hand on a huge, thick steel door.

"Christ! It would take a dozen LAWs to get through that."

"Somebody is serious about keeping out trespassers."

Yankee noticed a security camera slew and focus on them. "Whoever's in there has an interest in us now. Look over your right shoulder."

Percy took a glance. "Oy. They're interested, but not enough to come out."

"Or invite us in."

"Can't see why, mate. I had a bath yesterday."

Yankee chuckled but his grin disappeared when he looked over Percy's shoulder. A police car was approaching on Indian Trail, a mile away, its lights flashing.

"Time to go, Kiwi. The heat's inbound."

Percy whipped around and spotted the car.

"Okay, mate. Let's take our leave."

∞

Pete slewed the camera to focus on the trespassers. He began recording.

Lisa was on Pete's cell, talking to the inbound Deputy. "Yes, two men, inside the fence at the entrance doors. The larger man is dressed all in tan and has a rifle. The smaller man has a beige jacket and blue jeans. Both are wearing baseball caps and have dark hair."

Lisa listened.

"Okay, thank you. I'll keep the line open." She addressed Pete. "The Deputy is a mile away."

"They're leaving," noted Pete. "They must have spotted the police car." Pete switched images from camera to camera, following the trespassers as they returned the way they came.

"They're climbing the fence, they're leaving."

Lisa repeated the information to the Deputy, then listened. "The Deputy wants to know which direction they're going."

"West, into the hills."

Lisa relayed the information.

The trespassers disappeared. By the time the Deputy arrived they were nowhere to be seen. The Deputy searched the area on foot with Pete, to no avail. There was nothing more to do.

Pete thanked the Deputy for responding so quickly. The officer departed and filed his report on the trespassers, probable hunters.

Mediterranean Sea: The *Vixen* dropped anchor near a remote uninhabited island. It was just a small rock poking above the sea. It was less than a square mile in area, had limited vegetation, but it was covered with thousands of sea birds and their prolific piles of droppings. The island was officially the possession of Greece but it was so small and remote no other land mass could be seen from it. It was also forty miles from the nearest shipping lanes.

Skibba knew of this island from his time in the Navy. He was a Lieutenant on a survey ship, decades ago, assigned to survey the island and the waters surrounding it. He had been the officer in charge of a landing party. It was a hot, miserable, rugged hunk of volcanic rock, practically barren, except for the birds, their droppings and one small fresh water pond on its west side. 'Hell on earth' was Salty's summary of it.

The crew had stocked the launch with MREs. Paul and Dave Welch motored the launch to the island and unloaded them. They were back to the ship in forty minutes.

Welch secured the launch to the *Vixen*'s transom, Paul remained at the helm. Welch, Skibba and Hale loaded the abductees into the launch. They had been sequestered in the yacht's forecastle for three days, subsisting on water and bread. They had no idea where they were, what day it was, or even what hemisphere they were in. They reeked of body odor, urine and feces.

Hale jumped into the launch, armed with two shotguns and his .45. He passed a shotgun to Paul and gave the shove-off signal. Salty and Dave tossed the lines aboard the launch and pushed her away.

Paul piloted the launch to the island. Not a word was spoken. Hale secured the launch to a rock. He cut the tape around Stakemore's ankles and knees. "Christ, woman. You've got ankles like a cow. Stand up."

He grasped her flabby upper arm and hauled her to her feet. He ripped the tape covering her eyes. She squinted and blinked rapidly.

"Step ashore." As Hale balanced her, she stepped into the water and waded ashore.

"Turn around." She obeyed. Fear was written all over her face. "Stay put or my man will blow you away." Paul leveled the shotgun at her.

Hale repeated the process with Miller, then Raas, then Rushton. They stood in an uneven line facing the boat.

Thomas covered them as Luke walked behind and cut them free. "Remove your gags." They did so as Hale returned to the boat. He addressed them.

"Attention, ladies and gentlemen. The endeavor you are about to undertake is brought to you courtesy of Dr. Daniel Flynn. We know that you are the people responsible for his murder."

"I don't know what you're talking about," declared Stakemore.

"Oh, shut up, you pretentious cow," blurted Miller.

"How dare you?"

BLAM!

They jumped. Luke had fired his shotgun into the air to get their attention. He pumped another shell into the chamber.

"Pay attention. You are on a remote island in the Pacific," he lied. He knew they had no idea where they were. "The closest land is three hundred seventy-seven miles away. The closest shipping lanes are a hundred fifty miles." More lies. "That pile of packets over there," he pointed, "is food. It should last you about three months. There's fresh water on the other side of the island."

"You mean to maroon us here?" Raas was astounded.

"Yes, we are stranding you here. Not only that, you've all been injected with cancer."

"Cancer?" replied Miller.

"Cancer? What form?" inquired Rushton.

"What?"

"Good Lord," invoked Miller.

Luke leveled his shotgun at them. "Yes, cancer. Metastasized pancreatic cancer, I believe. I'm told it's very fast. Being doctors, you'd probably know better than I. Just the same, I think it's a fitting tribute to you all. Your kind are boils on the ass of humanity."

"You can't do this!" yelled Stakemore.

"We just did. It's exactly what you have done to others. Good people are dying because of your sick lust for power and greed."

"We haven't killed anyone," protested Raas.

"Oh, no?" challenged Luke. "Dan Flynn was tortured and murdered. Derek Storm was almost killed in his own apartment. He and Dr. Chen almost died in Death Valley while eluding your killers. Melanie Taylor was almost raped and murdered. Pete Flynn and his assistant have to live like moles, hiding from your hired guns. And more decent people are dying as I speak, because you bribed the FDA to block the ParaZyme 2000 research. We have the evidence, so don't play innocent to me, you slimy bastards."

"Who are you?" yelled Miller. "We didn't do anything to you."

"No, you haven't. Not yet. But my brother is dying of bone cancer right now. If you people hadn't stalled the research, he might have stood a chance. Now it's too late." A tear ebbed from Luke's right eye.

"So you're going to abandon us here, with cancer and no hope of medical treatment?" demanded Rushton.

"Bingo. And to answer the lady's previous question, I'm a close friend of Derek Storm, the nephew of Dan Flynn. This is payback."

"Look, whoever you are. Don't do this," pleaded Rushton. "What do you want? We can get you money, millions. Just take us back."

Luke glared Rushton a look of cold, seething disgust. He slowly shook his head. "Not no, but 'hell no.' This is about justice, not money. I gave my solemn word to see this through."

"But this is not right," protested Raas.

"You want to stand on righteousness, Doctor? Have you ever heard of the biblical principle 'Reap what you sow?' How about the Golden Rule, 'Do unto others as you would have them do unto you?' Or maybe Hammurabi's law, 'An eye for an eye, tooth for a tooth'?"

"What does that have to do with anything?"

"You don't see it? You're as bankrupt of morals and ethics as the devil. Thousands of people are dying from cancer because you people have inhibited development of the cure. Now you'll get to experience that fate. You'll reap what you have sown."

"You can't do this," blurted Stakemore. "I'm a Congresswoman."

"Shut up, you sick twisted pervert," yelled Miller.

"I will not. I demand he return us home."

"We have cancer," murmured Raas, mesmerized.

"You're responsible for this," yelled Stakemore, pointing at Rushton.

"Oh, shut up," he yelled back. They were losing it.

"I will not shut up! I'm a Congresswoman!"

"Bullshit!" screamed Miller.

"I am too."

"Don't give me that shit," screamed Miller, getting right into Stakemore's face. "You're nothing but a perverted, twisted freak!"

"Shut up!"

"In fact," yelled Miller, turning away from Stakemore, "she's not even a SHE!"

CHAPTER XXI

FIRE IN THE HOLE

"Shut up! Shut up, you filthy bitch!" shrieked Stakemore. She ran up behind Miller and punched her in the back of her head. Miller stumbled forward, turned and punched Stakemore squarely in her face. She went down backwards, crying, holding her broken bloody nose.

Miller stood over her defiantly, her hands on her hips. She looked down, disgusted.

"Your dirty little secret is out now."

"What are you talking about?" asked Rushton.

"She is not Iris Stakemore. She is a he."

"A transvestite?"

"No! Please, don't," pleaded Stakemore.

"No. A trans-sexual. He bought the boobs, hormones and voice box job, but… he still has his dick."

"No. Please." Stakemore whimpered and cried.

Miller enjoyed the torment. "It's real name is Evan Caruthers. Nineteen years ago, *Mister* Caruthers was a second grade school teacher. He was arrested for molesting a seven-year-old boy. There wasn't enough evidence to convict him, so he was released. To escape the stigma of being an accused pedophile, dear Evan started a sex change operation. He changed his identity to Iris Stakemore. Only, he couldn't part with his penis. I guess it was just too precious."

"How do you know all this?" inquired Raas.

"The child he molested was my nephew."

Caruthers-Stakemore broke down completely, fell face down into the sand and cried.

"I've heard enough of this soap opera horseshit," Luke said cynically to Paul. "Let's get back to the ship."

"Aye-aye, boss."

Hale loosed the bow line and pushed the boat free of the rock. Paul started the motor and steered for the *Vixen.*

"What a bunch of warped bastards," remarked Paul.

"No shit. But I'll be able to sleep well knowing that they're receiving perfect justice."

Paul nodded. "What's next, boss?"

"Back to Haifa. Something at that airfield caught my eye."

Helendale: It was still dark, early morning and the Bravo team had the bunker surrounded.

Their research revealed it had been constructed in the forties and abandoned by the Army shortly after WW II. There were no surviving blueprints or schematics for it. They had been lost or destroyed long ago. Bravo's team had little idea of its dimensions or internal layout.

The only records Sparks could find were in the San Bernardino County Recorder's Office. The complex had been sold twice, most recently to a blind holding trust without any tax identification number. The trust officers were unknown. The tax statements were addressed to a second blind trust with a private mailbox address in Apple Valley, a town nearby.

Bravo's instincts told him that Peter Flynn and his lab were inside that bunker. Lisa Chen might be in there, perhaps even Storm. He was resolute. He had to kill them all and destroy that lab or his reputation would be in the toilet. His ego wouldn't allow that.

Bravo's team had probed the area two nights in a row, testing reactions and assessing the security devices. They had located many of the sensors and cameras. The cops had come calling twice but the mercenaries had eluded them. They were no match for Bravo's skilled team.

Yankee had discovered a weakness in the bunker's security system. There was one area where the motion sensors were mounted outside the fence at ground level. But they lacked overlapping coverage. Yankee thought it might be possible to approach from behind the sensors and render one of them useless. It would take hours but it would allow the team unannounced access into the compound.

Under cover of darkness, Yankee slithered up behind the sensors. On the blind side of one sensor, he placed a bed of cotton. On that, he placed a large water-filled condom. Then he rested one edge of a cardboard box, open end down, onto the condom. He eased the box over the sensor and slowly placed its opposite edge on the ground. He pinched a tiny hole in the top of the condom, allowing the water to drip out slowly. As the condom deflated, it very slowly lowered the box over the motion sensor without triggering it.

As the condom slowly deflated, Bravo's men carefully moved amongst the sagebrush and junipers and flanked the bunker. They all took station according to Bravo's plan.

With only one hour until sunrise, the team was in position, anticipating the signal from Bravo to commence the raid.

It was going to be a blast.

∞

The flights back from the Middle East and Europe had been long but uneventful. Storm and Starr had managed to get some sleep while crossing the Atlantic, taking shifts monitoring the controls while the autopilot flew the aircraft. The technical gadgets in the cockpit fascinated Storm.

They landed at dawn, at the Southern California Logistics Airfield, formerly George Air Force Base. Mike was beat. He needed sleep before soloing the G-5 back to Boston.

Storm called Pete's handyman for a ride to Helendale. He didn't want Pete or Lisa to leave the bunker. The handyman, Rick, was glad to be of service. He drove to the airfield, picked them up and drove them to Lisa's condo. Storm and Starr thanked him and went inside.

Starr collapsed onto Lisa's couch, exhausted. Storm didn't have that luxury. He gathered his gear, weapons and supplies. Then he called Lisa.

As expected, she was in the bunker.

"Hello, China doll."

"Derek! It's good to hear your voice. Where are you?"

"At your condo. How are you guys doing?"

"We're safe but we're going stir crazy. We haven't left this bunker for days. I was getting worried about you."

"I'm doing great. I'm on my way but I didn't see your Hummer."

"Oh. Uh, it's in here."

"Pete's truck too?"

"Yes."

"I'll just have to hump it to the lab on foot. It'll take an hour or so."

"I can hardly wait. Those men have been snooping around. We called the cops but they turned up nothing. They're getting tired of responding every time we call."

"How often have they been around?"

"Three times. They came twice in the middle of the night."

Storm didn't like the sound of that. They were probing, preparing for something.

"Okay. I'll be there in an hour. I'll come to the main entrance after I scout the area. You guys stay put."

"We will. And Derek?"

"Yeah?"

"I missed you something awful."

"I missed you too, Lisa. I'll be there soon." Storm blew her a kiss and hung up.

He left Starr sound asleep and set out. It was a beautiful morning for a walk, Infantry style. The weather was perfect: not too hot, not too cold, and not too windy. It was perfect for a four-mile hike.

∞

It took ninety-seven minutes for the box to cover the motion sensor. Bravo had Yankee positioned on the eastern spur with an M-16 rifle. His job was to cover the bunker entrance, observe for alternate exits and provide backup for Trigger.

Trigger was positioned at the southern tip of the western spur. He was armed with three anti-tank rockets and his favorite sniper rifle, an accurized M-14 with a Leatherwood sniping scope, the type many Marine snipers had used in Viet Nam. He commanded a ninety-degree field of fire covering the trail from Wild Road. The only obstruction was a ridge two hundred yards to his south. His assignment was to engage and destroy any police vehicles that came up the trail.

Bravo, Slash, Sparks and Percy used bolt cutters to slice through the fence behind the disabled motion sensor. Once inside, they spray painted the security camera lenses.

They lugged Semtex plastic explosive into the compound. Percy, Slash and Sparks set breaching charges on the hinges and latch of the right entry door. Sparks connected electronic remote detonators to the charges and informed Bravo they were ready.

The assault team retreated back through the fence and sought cover.

Bravo keyed his mike. "Radio check."

"Yankee loud and clear."

"Trigger, Lima Charlie."

"Alpha check?"

"All clear," whispered Trigger.

"Good to go."

"Package is ready. Twenty seconds, mark."

They installed foam earplugs and made love to the ground. Sparks held the remote detonator transmitter, flipped open a red guard over a key port, inserted a key and turned it a quarter-twist clockwise. A red light illuminated. It was armed. He gave Bravo a thumb-up and flipped open a second red guard, exposing a red button.

Bravo checked his watch. He held up five fingers, then four, then three, two, one.

"Fire in the hole!"

Sparks pushed the red button.

∞

Pete and Lisa were knocked off their feet. A huge explosion blasted into the bunker. Shrapnel, debris, dirt and smoke filled the loading bay, shattering the windows on Lisa's Hummer and smashing it with chunks of steel and concrete. It was trashed.

Pete's ears were ringing and his bones ached. Lisa was sprawled unconscious on the lab room floor. Pete struggled to his feet. The room was spinning and his muscles felt like gelatin. He dropped to his hands and knees for stability and crawled under the smoke layer to Lisa.

Pete fought the urge to vomit and grabbed Lisa under her armpits. He dragged her down the corridor and into the safe room. He placed her on a cot, grabbed his shotgun and pistol and peeked out into the corridor. The lights were blown out. It was dark and smoky. He eased down the corridor to the loading bay, bracing himself on the wall. He peeked into the loading bay.

It was a mess. Daylight shined through one of the doors. It was off its hinges, laying askew in the frame. A man crawled through the hole.

Still dazed, Pete raised the shotgun. The man emerged and stood up.

"Freeze!"

The man dove behind the Hummer. A second man appeared in the hole and sprayed a burst of automatic fire. Bullets ricocheted off the concrete walls as Pete ducked back. The gunfire was loud and reverberated off the walls.

Pete peeked around the corner again and fired two shotgun blasts. He retreated to the safe room and hit the switch to close the door. The heavy steel door slid along its guide track and into the frame on the opposite side. Pete slid the locking bars across and latched them down.

Another loud explosion ripped through the corridor.

He and Lisa were locked in. They were safe but they also had no escape route. It was definitely time to call the cops.

∞

Storm instinctively dropped when he heard the explosion. It sounded similar to the five hundred pound aerial bombs he had heard during the Gulf War. A huge debris cloud rose above the hill about a mile ahead.

"The lab! Holy shit!" Storm tripled his pace. He warmed quickly, laboring under his heavy load of weapons, ammo and water. He heard automatic weapons fire.

∞

Percy was first through the breach. He cleared the door, a man yelled at him. He dove behind a yellow Hummer.

Slash heard the yell, saw Percy dive, stuck his rifle and head into the breach and noticed a man pointing a shotgun at Percy. He unleashed a burst to cover the Kiwi.

Two shotgun blasts responded, missing high and wide. Percy pulled the pin on a fragmentation grenade and lobbed it into the corridor.

"Frag out!" He and Slash ducked and covered their heads. The grenade bounced of the far corridor wall and tumbled inside. It exploded seconds later, ringing their ears.

"Press! Move out!" commanded Bravo as he crawled through the breach. Percy stood and fired a burst at the corridor from his M-16. Slash quickly advanced along the east wall leading to the loading dock.

Bravo cleared the breach and took position next to Percy. "I'll cover, Percy. Advance."

"Oy, Colonel." He flanked left and aimed his rifle at the corridor. Bravo covered him with his MP-5 submachine gun.

Percy aligned with the corridor and peered in. It was smoky and dark but he could see it was vacant.

"Clear, mate."

Slash took the cue, rolled onto the loading dock and rushed into the corridor. He dove to the floor and covered the hall.

"Clear!"

Percy and Bravo hustled in past Slash and hugged the walls. They searched the rooms. An open room to the right appeared to be the lab. Dozens of test animals jumped around in their cages and screeched at them. A closed door on the opposite side turned out to be a utility closet.

Only one door remained, at the end of the corridor. It was a heavy gauge steel door set into a reinforced steel frame.

Bravo slapped the door twice. It was thick and dense.

"Shit!" He spoke into the radio. "Sparks, we need twenty pounds of Semtex, ASAP."

∾

Lisa came to with a splitting headache and ringing ears. Pete was on his cell phone. He slapped it closed, clipped it to his belt and pumped another shell into his shotgun.

"What happened?"

"The killers are inside the bunker. They blew up the doors and they're in the corridor. We're locked in. The Sheriff's units are on the way, ETA ten minutes. How are you?"

"I have a pounding headache."

They heard two firm slaps on the door and a man with a deep voice cursed.

"What should we do, Pete?"

"Help me move the desks to make a shelter. They might have more explosives."

∾

Storm approached the crest of the hill just west of the lab. He flopped to the ground, using the butt of his rifle stock to break his dive. He was four hundred yards from the bunker.

He removed his binoculars and scanned the area. He couldn't detect any movement or see the lab entrance. It was on the opposite side of the spur. There was still a dust cloud hovering above the depression. That had to be the source of the blast.

Storm heard sirens from the southeast. He scanned toward Indian Trail and saw two police vehicles, lights flashing, blazing down the road. They were separated by several hundred yards and had to be going eighty miles an hour on the rough road.

"The cavalry has arrived."

∾

"We have company," advised Trigger.

"Roger that," answered Sparks. The team radios failed to penetrate the bunker, as they had suspected, so Sparks was stationed at the breach to relay messages.

The lead Deputy vehicle rounded the corner onto Wild Road and raced toward the trail to the bunker. Trigger prepared his rockets. He extended the first tube, arming the rocket motor igniter and raising the pop-up sights. He laid it aside and prepared another. He mounted it to his shoulder and sighted down the trail.

The lead Deputy vehicle slowed and turned north onto the trail. Trigger lined up the sights for a two hundred yard head-on shot.

The fuzz-mobile bounced along the rocky trail, disappeared momentarily and re-appeared as it crested the ridge exactly where Trigger expected. Trigger squeezed down on the firing button. A blast issued from the rear of the tube and the armor piercing, high explosive rocket streaked at the vehicle.

∾

Deputy Donald Platter slowed to make the turn to Dr. Flynn's lab. It was the third time this week he had responded to this location.

"*This Doc is getting to be a pain in the ass.*"

He noticed a thin dust cloud near the bunker but didn't make the connection. He advanced up the trail as quickly as the rough ride would allow, twenty miles an hour. The vehicle crested a small ridge and he saw a gray smoke trail behind a brightly burning object, streaking directly at him.

"Oh, shit!"

The rocket slammed into the engine compartment. There was a blinding flash. It was the last thing Deputy Platter ever saw.

∾

Storm spotted the back-blast from a rocket motor and saw a rocket launch to the southeast. It slammed into the lead Deputy vehicle and exploded. The car caught fire, exited the trail to its right and rolled inverted. The car was consumed by a fireball.

"Son of a bitch!"

Storm focused the binoculars. He spotted movement under a juniper bush. A black man in desert camouflage was hidden beneath the bush, facing the trail. He was preparing to fire another LAW.

Storm dropped the binoculars and grabbed his FN. The second Deputy vehicle was rounding the turn onto the trail.

Storm carefully aimed at the black man's back. It was a four hundred yard shot on a prone target, very low probability of a hit, but there was no time for precise sniping.

Storm squeezed the trigger six times, rapid fire, hoping to distract the gunner. With luck, one of the rounds might hit.

∞

Bullets splashed the rocks around Trigger. He covered and yelled into the radio, "Yankee, I'm taking fire. Cover me."

"From where? I don't see anything." Yankee could hear a heavy battle rifle discharging its lethal loads, but it was coming from the far side of the opposite spur. He had no shot.

"Behind me somewhere. Smoke his ass!" The second Deputy's vehicle was about to crest the ridge. It came. Trigger aimed.

"Adios, motherfu…"

∞

Storm saw the black man cover up during his salvo, then resume his task, apparently uninjured.

"Damn!" He re-aimed, this time firing ten rounds. The man went limp. Storm grabbed his binoculars. The man was wounded, hopefully dead.

Storm rose and crested the spur. Automatic weapons fire sounded. Storm dropped.

He realized the rounds were not aimed at him but at the newly arrived Deputy.

∞

"*What the…?*" Deputy Esai Garcia crested the ridge and spotted the source of the black smoke. Deputy Platter's vehicle was upside down, off the trail, ablaze.

He stood on the brakes and the vehicle skidded. He slapped the shift lever into REVERSE and floored the gas. A spray of bullets hammered the engine compartment, fenders and windows. Glass shards pelted him and a bullet grazed his neck.

"Madre de Dios!" The car reversed far enough to put the ridge between the attacker and him. The salvo stopped. Unfortunately, so did the engine.

Garcia grabbed the radio mike and pressed the transmit button. It was dead. He tried his portable radio. "Central, this is Four-Baker-Nineteen! Shots fired! Officer down! Officer needs assistance, code three! Automatic weapons fire! Send SWAT! Send SWAT!"

The radio worked but there was no response. He was too far out in the boonies.

"Screw this!" Garcia grabbed his shotgun from the console bracket and popped the car trunk. He flung the door open, crouched, ran to the trunk and retrieved an M-16 and spare magazines.

He hustled right and raced up the incline. Near the top, he dove to the ground, loaded the M-16 and racked a round into the shotgun.

He peeked over the ridge.

∞

"How much longer?" prodded Bravo.

"Four, maybe five minutes, Colonel," answered Percy. He was working furiously to set two demolition charges to blow the safe room door. They hadn't anticipated such an obstacle and it had taken some time for Sparks and Slash to retrieve the explosives.

"Trigger, come in," they heard Sparks transmit.

"What? Oh, shit," they heard him transmit. "Colonel, Yankee says Trigger is down. One cop car totaled, another disabled. One Deputy believed dead. Yankee has the other pinned down."

"Copy that, Sparks. Keep me posted."

"Roger that."

"Make it a rush job, Percy."

Trouble was they didn't know they were in a lot more trouble than they knew. They had become the prey.

∞

Storm saw the Deputy poke his head above the ridgeline. Automatic weapons fire spewed from under a large bush on the eastern spur. Another assassin had the Deputy pinned down from an elevated position.

The Deputy bravely returned fire. "*Good man.*" The assassin fired again. More automatic weapons fire came from around the corner of the bunker, near the entrance, but Storm couldn't see exactly where. There were at least two assassins outside the bunker, an undetermined number inside. And they were after Lisa and Pete.

"*No time like the present.*"

He aimed at the assassin on the eastern spur, three hundred yards distant. It was another tough shot on a prone target. Storm sighted and controlled his breathing. He smoothly squeezed the trigger. BLAM. The round impacted short. Storm aimed again and fired.

∞

"*Now what?*" Deputy Garcia heard two M-16's firing at him. Someone else fired two high-powered rifle shots, but not at him.

He rolled right, crouched, ran thirty yards and dropped. He peeked over the ridge. A burst of M-16 fire raked the ridge near his previous position. A man inside the bunker was trying to nail him.

Garcia noted that the gunman on the eastern spur didn't fire. He saw a slumped form under the bush.

"*I hope he's out of it. But who took him out?*"

He aimed at the bunker, noticed movement to the left of it and held his fire. A lone figure was moving rapidly along the spur. He carried a large battle rifle, moving confidently, quickly and gracefully, like a jaguar ready to pounce.

Garcia had seen this technique before, during the Gulf War as a Marine. Whoever that guy was, he knew what he was doing.

∽

Storm flanked to the blind side of the west spur and maneuvered above the bunker entrance. He looked down and saw an M-16 poking out through the breach. It fired occasional bursts at the Deputy.

Storm set aside his FN and drew his bayonet, strapped to his right ankle. "*It's Ginsu time, asshole.*"

∽

"Yankee, come in," demanded Sparks.

He could see him but he wasn't moving, firing or responding.

"Yankee's down."

"God damn it," answered Bravo. "What's going on out there?"

"There's a cop out here with an M-16 but I don't think he's the one who shot Yankee. I know he didn't take out Trigger. We must have a wild card, Colonel."

"*Storm. It has to be.*" "Hold what you've got, Sparks. We're almost ready."

There was no answer.

"Sparks? Sparks?"

∽

Storm leapt from ledge. His right foot slammed down on the M-16's barrel, wrenching it from the assassin's hands. Faster than a wraith from hell, Storm reached inside the breach, snatched the assassin's hair, yanked back his head and thrust the bayonet fully into his throat and twisted.

The assassin was shocked by the lightening fast assault. His eyes opened wide. Blood gushed from his throat, spraying Storm's arm and shoulder. The killer's eyes rolled back. He gurgled, sputtered and died.

Storm withdrew the bayonet, wiped it on the dead man's jacket and stowed it. It was time to have a look inside.

A solo figure attired in desert camouflage stood on a hilltop a mile west of the bunker. He observed the melee through an expensive pair of binoculars. He was unarmed but he had an intense interest in the drama unfolding at the bunker.

Men were firing automatic weapons at each other. A cop car was blown to pieces and a lone, daring figure leapt from the top of the bunker, out of sight. It was one hell of a firefight.

The mysterious observer put down the optics and quietly munched on a snack bar. He finished it and unhooked a cell phone from his belt. He speed dialed a long distance number and waited.

"Yeah, Spider. It's me. I'm on location. Our informant was right. Patch me through to the Director."

"Sparks?" Still no answer. Bravo's hair bristled.

"Percy, go check on Sparks. Slash will run the wires."

"Oy, Colonel." Percy handed the wire to Slash, grabbed his rifle and headed for the entrance. He peeked into the loading bay. Sparks was lying in a bloody heap inside the breach.

"Sparks is down, Colonel."

"What the hell is going on? Keep us covered, Percy. We're coming out."

"Oy."

Slash unreeled twin strands of wire as he and Bravo backed down the corridor. They didn't have any more remote detonators, so they'd have to blow the charges the old-fashioned way with a hand-cranked dynamo.

Bullets ricocheted off the walls as the staccato of an M-16 on full rock-and-roll echoed. They dropped to the deck, Percy returned fire. Someone was behind the Hummer.

Storm streamed another burst at them. Return fire responded. Storm leveled the rifle again and squeezed. It spit two rounds and jammed.

"Shit!" He tossed it and drew his .45. Then he heard a 'pling' sound.

"*Uh oh.*" He recognized the distinctive sound of a grenade handle being released. He dove to the floor and covered.

BOOM! A bone-jarring concussion reverberated through the loading bay. Shrapnel, dirt and debris ricocheted off the walls. Thick, acrid smoke filled the air.

Storm shook out the cobwebs and peeked around the Hummer's flattened rear wheels. Three men came from the corridor. One of them was giving orders, one fired a burst at the Hummer, the third was unreeling demolition wires. That could mean only one thing.

"*Disapproved!*" He took aim at the man giving orders. BLAM. Two hundred thirty grains of copper-jacketed lead slammed through the target's right shoulder, spraying a blood pattern onto the wall behind him.

Bravo went down. "Shit! I'm hit. Finish the job. Blow it! Blow it!"

Percy emptied a full magazine of .223 caliber supersonic sizzlers at Storm. Storm rolled to the front of the Hummer and selected another target.

BLAM. The round caught the target in his hip. He dropped the wires and went down, screaming.

Bravo yelled, "We're hit, Percy. Cover us."

"Oy, Colonel. Toss me some ammo."

Bravo didn't have the same ammo as Percy. He reached into Slash's ammo pouch and pulled out two magazines of .223 rounds. He tossed the first one at Percy, who snatched it from mid-air. Bravo tossed the second one.

BLAM.

The second magazine was blown away, inches from Percy's outstretched fingers.

"You son of a whore." Percy shook his fingers reflexively. He ejected his spent magazine and slammed home the one he caught. He smacked the rifle's bolt release and sprayed a burst at Storm.

BLAM.

A .45 slug slammed into Percy's rifle, tearing it from his grip and rendering it useless. His hands stung.

"Son of a bitch!" Percy pulled his Beretta and returned fire.

POP. POP. POP. Percy's 9mm shots sounded insignificant compared to the booming .45 slugs from Storm's hand cannon.

Bravo strapped a field dressing over his gaping shoulder wound. "STORM?"

Storm didn't respond. That was stupid Hollywood stuff. Only a moron brought verbiage to a gunfight. Not that he thought the killer was a moron. He guessed he was calling his name purely for psychological effect. Or he was stalling.

Percy noticed a truck.

"Colonel, there's a truck behind you. See if the keys are in it. I'll cover."

Bravo rolled onto his stomach. Sure enough, there was a green Chevy S-10 sitting inside the entrance to a tunnel. He struggled to his feet and zigzagged to it.

BLAM. BLAM. POP. BLAM. POP. POP. BLAM. Storm's magazine was empty. Clack, click, shink. Percy recognized the sound; the adversary was reloading. Percy turned the corner and fired. POP. POP. POP.

The rounds hit the Hummer or splashed the wall behind it.

Bravo reached the S-10 and spotted the key in the ignition. The truck was already facing into the tunnel, all the better for a quick retreat.

Bravo struggled back to Slash. He grabbed the detonator wires and reached for the dynamo.

BLAM.

It disappeared under his hand. There went their last chance to blow the lab. Bravo dove back for cover.

"Storm, you son of a bitch. I'm gonna rip your head off and shove it up your ass."

POP.

Bravo dragged Slash to the S-10. The gunfight raged as Percy covered their withdrawal.

Bravo yelled, "Percy, SUNSET, TOBOGGAN." Those were the code words for busted operation and egress.

"Oy, SUNSET, TOBOGGAN." Percy reloaded, fired again, then ran along the dock for the tunnel. Automatic rifle fire sprayed the wall in front of him. He stopped so quickly it almost reversed time.

"FREEZE! Deputy Sheriff! Drop your weapons!"

Percy froze, his back to the Deputy. He raised his hands. "BOOMERANG, Colonel," he yelled, the code word to escape.

The Deputy crawled through the breach and drew down on the assassin. He didn't notice Storm on the ground at the opposite end of the Hummer, covered in debris.

The Deputy yelled at Percy, "Drop your weapons! Now!" The assassin dropped his pistol.

"Place your hands on top of your head and interlock your fingers." The assassin obeyed. The Deputy sure-stepped toward his collar, too close for Storm's comfort. Storm elected to remain an observer rather than move and be mistaken for one of the killers.

They heard the S-10 start and shift into gear. It sped away through the tunnel. The Deputy glanced toward the sound. That's all it took.

Like a whirlwind, Percy spun off the dock and kicked away the Deputy's rifle. The killer crashed down on the Deputy, slamming his right forearm into his left clavicle. Storm heard the collar bone snap, the Deputy screamed and went down backwards under the lightening-fast onslaught. He dropped his rifle and grabbed at his broken bone. The assassin reached to his belt and withdrew a combat knife.

Storm couldn't remain an observer. He aimed and squeezed the trigger. Nothing happened, a misfire; bad ammo. The Deputy couldn't afford the time it would take Storm to clear the round, reload and re-aim.

Storm leapt to his feet and charged, the killer had his knife ready to skewer the injured Deputy.

The killer heard Storm's footsteps and turned. Storm launched into a flying kick and his right foot kicked the knife from the killer's hand. Storm's momentum slammed him into the killer and his left knee plowed into the killer's abdomen. He went down backwards, winded. But he back rolled immediately and pushed up onto his feet, ready to fight.

Storm recognized him. It was the killer who had subdued his knife-wielding buddy at the dead drop last week. Storm knew he was in for a fight.

"C'mon, mate. Let's 'ave a go."

"Your move." It was a ruse. Storm launched a left sidekick at the killer's genitals and came up short. The killer slid backwards but he leaned forward. Storm pivoted hard clockwise and slammed a left punch to his jaw.

The killer staggered. Storm was all over him. He unleashed a flurry of punches, elbows and knee strikes, but the killer was good. Only two of Storm's strikes landed, those only partly. The assassin's counters and blocks were fast and forceful. He was very highly skilled.

The killer counter-attacked with a volley of kicks, knee strikes and punches. A roundhouse kick caught Storm in his left ribcage; it hurt like hell, partly winding him.

Storm recognized the man's fighting style. It was an Indonesian art that used a large working circle for flashy, powerful kicks and punches. The man liked to kick high at Storm's head and ribs. Those strikes could be devastating.

There were weaknesses in the style, though. High kicks left the combatant exposed to low attacks, and once a skilled adversary got under it and inside the power circle, he could pummel the opponent with elbow strikes and punches.

Storm and the assassin exchanged blows for a full minute: punches, kicks, finger stabs, claws, elbows. Most were blocked, countered or evaded. They assessed each other, looking for openings.

The killer led with a left punch at Storm's face. Storm evaded and the killer attempted to plant a right roundhouse kick to his head. Storm squatted under the kick, slid forward, exhaled forcefully, sank his mass low to increase power, and punched down into the killer's groin.

The killer recoiled and bent over. Storm pivoted right, catching him on the jaw with the back of his elbow and simultaneously slammed his left open palm into the killer's solar plexus. The killer staggered. Storm pivoted left and again dropped his full mass. His right elbow crashed through the killer's clavicle, the bone snapped, giving him a taste of what he'd done to the Deputy. Storm pivoted right and thrust his extended left fingers into the killer's eye sockets, hooked his fingers down behind his cheekbones, pulled and pivoted left as he slammed his open right palm against the killer's forehead.

"YAH!"

The equal, opposing forces ripped the killer's cheekbones from their connections. The killer gasped and collapsed.

Storm wasn't sure if he was dead yet, but he sure wasn't getting up again in this lifetime. The killer's brain had slid out of its cranial nest and compressed his upper palate on the top of his windpipe, disrupting all of his air and motor functions. He was a motionless lump at Storm's feet.

Storm checked the wounded Deputy. He was unconscious but alive.

"Freeze! Hands up!"

Storm, exhausted, panting like a champion racehorse, looked toward the breach. A third Deputy had arrived and drawn down on him.

"I'm on your side." He raised his arms.

"Then we won't have any problems if you do as I say. Turn around and get on your knees. Cross your legs and lean back."

Storm complied. The Deputy approached and slapped cuffs around Storm's wrists. "What's going on here?"

"That guy," Storm nodded at the assassin, "attacked your Deputy. He has a broken left collar bone and probably needs a change of underwear."

"Are you a wise ass?"

"No. The last thing he saw before he passed out was that guy getting ready to stick him with that K-Bar. I saved his life."

"Yeah. Says you."

"Deputy, it's the truth. There's something else I know that you don't."

"So thrill me."

"There's a demolition charge set to blow in that corridor. Unless you know how to disarm it, I suggest you let me."

That got the Deputy's attention. "How much time do we have?"

"I don't know, so you better decide quickly."

The Deputy nearly had an out-of-body experience. He looked at the wires, at Storm, at the wounded Deputy, at the K-Bar, at the dead guy.

"Times a wastin'."

The Deputy rolled his eyes. "Aw shit!" He holstered his 9mm and grabbed the chain between Storm's cuffs. "Okay. Let's have a look. If you're scamming me, your gonna feel my baton up your ass."

"You smooth talker, you."

He ushered Storm up the loading dock stairs, pulled his flashlight and shined it down the corridor. They followed the wires. They were connected to two explosive charges mounted on the left side of the safe room door.

Storm whistled. "Semtex. Nasty stuff. It's plastic explosive."

"What? Like C-4?"

Storm nodded. "Very similar. It'll kill us if it blows."

The Deputy's out-of-body experience resumed. He looked around, confused.

Storm kicked the door twice. "Pete? Lisa? It's Derek. Are you in there?"

"Derek? Derek! Thank God! We're here. I'll open the door."

"NO! Get back. There are two explosive charges on the door. I have to defuse them. Is Pete in there?"

"I'm here."

"Get back and find cover. And tell this Deputy to release me so I can defuse this stuff."

CHAPTER XXIII

TRAPPED

Haifa: It wasn't as attractive as its predecessor but it would fill the bill. It was an old Hughes helicopter, what the U.S. Army designated as OH-6. Its silhouette resembled an egg on the end of a stick with a beanie cap on top. It was painted in desert camouflage colors. After its long service with the Israeli armed forces, its military insignia and markings had been painted over.

The venerable OH-6 was military surplus, having served its useful life as a combat machine. It was pockmarked with patched bullet holes and dents, and its Plexiglas windscreens were slightly crazed from wind-blown sand. But she was a rugged, reliable aircraft and she was for sale.

Luke scrutinized the maintenance and flight logs. The machine had a history of superb maintenance and reliability, at least on paper.

Dave Welch was elbow deep under her engine cowling, in search of fluid leaks. He hadn't found any yet.

"There's no such thing as a used engine without a leak. I'm going to find it, Mr. Hale. Trust me."

Luke chuckled. Dave wouldn't give the machine his okay until he was satisfied he'd fly in it himself.

The salesman approached. "How is your inspection going, Mr. Hale? Do you like the helicopter?"

Luke rose and shook hands.

"So far, so good. The log books seem to be in order and my mechanic is frustrated that he can't find any leaks." They chuckled.

"He won't find any. Our mechanics went over her with a fine-toothed comb. She's completely airworthy."

Luke nodded. "Mordechai, let's get a pilot out here for a test drive. Then maybe we'll talk some numbers."

Helendale: Storm was pissed at the Sheriff's Department. The Deputies had arrested him and charged him with possession of an unregistered 'assault rifle.' His semi-automatic FN was completely legal in Nevada, but Commie-fornia had its own definition; any firearm that was black and ugly was deemed an 'assault weapon.'

The fact that Storm had saved Deputy Garcia's life, twice, had little bearing on the matter. The pricks had arrested him anyway. The third Deputy might have been smoked too, had Storm not engaged the killers.

They hauled him into town in handcuffs in the rear of a patrol car. They fingerprinted, photographed and booked him. He was locked up overnight with the local drunks and miscreants, a wonderful experience. *"Whoever coined the phrase, 'The police officer is your friend,' was either a liar or a naïve moron."*

Pete had to borrow a vehicle to drive into town for Storm's arraignment. Lisa's Hummer was totaled and the S-10 was AWOL.

At Storm's arraignment, the judge had agreed to release Storm into Pete's custody upon posting $5,000 bail. Pete forked over the money, the cops released Storm and they returned to Helendale.

During the drive home, Pete encouraged Storm to skip town.

"What about the bail money, Pete?"

"Derek, you can't find those killers or protect us if you're locked up. Five grand is a small price to pay for our security. It's only money."

Lisa had been surprised to find a strange man sleeping on her couch. In all the commotion, Storm had forgotten about Mike and neglected to tell her. After Storm had defused the explosives, the Deputy slapped the cuffs back on and whisked him to the patrol car. Lisa didn't even have the opportunity to give him a hug.

Mike was as surprised as Lisa. He awoke to a gorgeous woman pointing a pistol in his face. Mike recovered and politely introduced himself. After a few questions, Lisa was satisfied and put away her pistol, apologizing. She fixed a meal as she explained Storm's predicament. Mike was not pleased. He was glad to hear Pete was handling it. Lisa thanked him for his help and arranged a ride to the airfield for him. By the time Storm was released from jail, Mike was long gone.

Pete, Lisa and Storm enjoyed a pleasant dinner but they were still edgy. There were still two killers on the loose.

After dinner, Pete politely excused himself and returned to his condo. Lisa and Storm enjoyed each other for a long, slow, erotic time. They exhausted themselves and lounged in each other's arms for hours. They decided that Lisa needed a vacation and that Storm needed to get out of Commie-fornia, as Pete had advised.

Lisa fell off to sleep. Storm tried, but something kept gnawing at him. One of the men he shot in the bunker was vaguely familiar.

Victorville: After abandoning Flynn's S-10, Bravo and Slash stole an old Pontiac and returned to their safe house. Bravo dropped Slash at the house and dumped the car several blocks away.

Bravo called his contacts for medical assistance. He and Slash would have to lick their wounds until it arrived.

Bravo attempted to contact Rushton but there was no answer and his messages went unanswered. He had a shoulder wound that would take a month to heal and Slash had a similarly serious wound in his hip. Three of his men were suspected dead, Sparks for certain, and Percy's disposition was unknown. Bravo frequently checked the team's voicemail messages but there were none.

The local newspaper reported on the raid the following day. It claimed that one Deputy had been killed, one injured, two Sheriff's vehicles were destroyed and four unknown men with automatic weapons were found dead at the scene. Derek Storm had been arrested and charged with possession of an unregistered assault rifle.

If Bravo hadn't been so thrashed, he would have thought it amusing that Storm had been the one arrested. But that bastard had killed or wounded every member of his team and scuttled his reputation.

There was going to be payback. "This isn't over yet, Storm," he murmured. "*Not by a long shot.*"

Boston: With Rushton, Raas, and Miller out of the picture, Melanie felt secure enough to return to Boston. Before she departed, Hale encouraged her to take the case of bribe money. After all, it belonged to the members of NOMP.

Melanie wanted to accept but she couldn't figure out how to smuggle six million dollars cash back into the United States. The Customs officials would suspect her as a drug dealer, lock her up and confiscate the money for good old Uncle Sam.

Melanie was also concerned about all of the expenses Luke had incurred. The jet had cost a bundle to lease and fuel, and Luke had laid out twenty grand for the hanger gambit in Haifa. She offered to reimburse him from the cash hoard but Luke wouldn't hear of it.

Amber hit upon a solution. They could deposit the cash into a foreign account, payable in Swiss Francs. Melanie could return to the U.S. unencumbered. The money could earn interest for several months or until the current NOMP regime was ousted. Then they would return the funds by wire transfer. Luke could keep the interest earned and any gain from the exchange rate.

It was a stellar idea. They agreed to it and Luke put her on a flight to Boston.

When she returned to work, everyone was curious about where she had been. They thought she had disappeared with Rushton, Raas and Miller. Melanie explained that her father had taken ill and she had to go home, didn't they get the message? Yes, her father was fine now.

Melanie denied any knowledge of Rushton's whereabouts or the six million dollars. On the outside, she pretended to be as mystified as everyone else, but on the inside she was throwing a party.

Three weeks later:

Mediterranean Sea: Luke had purchased the OH-6, paid for lessons, earned a type rating, bought spare parts, then flew it to the *Vixen*.

They anchored off Haifa until they took delivery of some specialized electronic equipment. Amber had searched the Internet and found some sonar equipment and an instrument that measured the density of solid structures. Its advertisement claimed it was highly effective at locating aquifers, underground caverns and spaces under collapsed buildings, where survivors might be. Luke figured it was worth try.

Equipped with their new gadgets, the cruisers set course to the Greek Isles.

Once they reached Greece, Storm and Lisa joined them for a vacation. Lisa's father had generously provided airline tickets. They were happy to get away from the stress of the lab and the killers. Pete, ever the lab rat, decided to stay and make arrangements to put the lab back in order, then visit the family in Portland. He needed a break too.

Lisa met the Hales and crew for the first time. She fit right in.

Lisa contacted her brother and asked for details about the Polo treasure. Lawrence lacked specific information, so he gave Lisa the e-mail address for his party animal buddy, Guido.

Unfortunately, Guido had very little in the way of specifics. In e-mail to Lisa, he stated there was only one written reference from a third-hand source, a friend of a friend of Maffeo Polo. An old, hand-scribed letter made an obscure reference to an underwater cavern on an undisclosed island in the Med, with an octagonal shaped rock over the entrance.

The crew held a brainstorming session. They imagined themselves as the Polos, sailing across the Med from Constantinople in rickety wooden ships. They figured the rag-tag fleet wouldn't have ventured far from the mainland because the ships would have been heavily laden and sluggish to maneuver. They would also be in frequent need of repair and re-supply.

The group elected to bypass the outer islands; they were too far from the mainland. They also bypassed inhabited islands; the inhabitants would have discovered the treasure long ago. There was no evidence of such an event in their research. They also eliminated the larger inner islands; those were too often frequented by tourists and their guides.

They had searched dozens of isles amongst the hundreds there. They viewed the search as much a vacation as they did an endeavor, taking time to engage in leisure activities and treasure hunt at their whim.

Luke used the chopper to search while Paul and Caroline preferred to search in the launch. Everyone volunteered to ride in the chopper or the launch whenever a likely island was targeted. Everyone participated, either conducting the search or supporting it from the ship.

Luke took a day to relax. He settled in the main salon and tuned in Fox News. It featured an article about the mysterious disappearance of Congresswoman Iris Stakemore, who recently came under scrutiny for questionable campaign finance practices. The news article gave a brief summary of her political career and mentioned she had been a 'no show' at the House Ethics Committee hearing on the matter. The FBI was investigating.

But that was dwarfed by bigger news. The second Gulf War had started in Iraq. U.S. and coalition forces were penetrating deeply into the country, advancing rapidly, pummeling the hapless forces of

Saddam Hussein.

That news triggered Luke's memory. *"I need to go back there after it settles down and pay that villager for the boat we stole."*

Victorville: "Looking good, Titan," declared the doctor, as he taped a fresh bandage over Bravo's wound.

Doc 'Profile,' as he was known in the covert community, had been dispatched by a secret federal agency. He was an expert at providing medical treatment for shadow personnel and keeping it a secret, low profile.

"Good. How's Slash?"

"He's healing well. The infection is under control and he should be mobile in a few days. You'll both be back in service soon. Until I give you the word, no unnecessary stretching or exercise or we'll have to start over. Clear?"

"Clear. Thanks, Doc."

"Just doing my job, Titan. We have to get you boys back in operation. There's nasty shit going down in the Middle East and your talents are needed." The doctor gave Bravo a wink. "I'll be back in two days. Rest."

Bravo nodded. Doc Profile packed his kit and took his leave.

Bravo was still seething. Storm had derailed his gravy train, his planned retirement. His Army pension was insufficient for the lifestyle he craved: warm sunny skies, white sandy beaches, Caribbean breezes and nubile, smooth-skinned nymphs catering to his every whim and lusty desire.

"Frigging Storm," he lamented. He was determined to smoke his ass if it was the last thing he did.

Bravo figured that Storm had a connection to the disappearance of Rushton and Stakemore. He also had to have a base of operation.

Several times, he and Slash had driven past the bunker to see if Storm was hanging around. All they saw were armed security guards and work crews. Flynn and Chen were nowhere to be seen either, only the hired help.

Frustrated, Bravo went to the living room. Slash was watching TV.

"Slash, turn that shit off. We're gonna go back through the Flynn files."

Slash clicked off the TV. Bravo slapped a pile of files in front of him. "Let's get to it."

They scanned through the documents. Fifteen minutes later, Slash found something.

"Hey Colonel. Remember this?" He handed Bravo a phone bill.

Bravo perused the statement. "Yeah! Good work, Slash." He snatched the bat phone and dialed.

"This is Titan. Key two-four-seven-four-two. Patch me into Research, desk six, priority amber." He waited.

"This is Titan. I need research on a SatCOM number, the owner and current whereabouts." He read the number aloud; it was registered to the *Serene Vixen*.

Unnamed Island, Greece: The marooned urbanites were having a rough go at survival. None of them had the slightest iota of basic survival skills; it took them a week to make a fire.

They didn't have much to occupy their time besides eating MREs and blaming each other. There were often loud, heated arguments and they spent much of their time isolated from one another rather than working as a team.

The obnoxious Caruthers-Stakemore was the primary instigator of most arguments. As a result, she became the pariah and the group banished her. Miller had even threatened to kill him/her.

Not accustomed to being ignored, Caruthers-Stakemore repeatedly returned to the group and behaved, for a while. Then the nagging bitch persona would emerge and the arguments would begin again. Now was such a time.

"I have HAD it!" screamed Miller. "If I hear one more complaint from you, I'll bash your freaking head in."

"You wouldn't dare."

That was the final straw. Miller grabbed sand and threw it into Stakemore's face. Miller charged. They screamed as Miller tackled him/her. The angry pair tumbled, thrashing at each other, clawing, scratching, biting and pulling hair. Rushton and Raas did not intervene.

Stakemore got the advantage, rolled Miller onto her back and pummeled her face. Miller countered with a poke into Stakemore's eye. The trans-sexual recoiled, screamed and rolled off Miller.

Miller quickly exploited. She rolled to her feet and kicked Stakemore in the face. It was a stunning blow; she collapsed onto her hands and knees.

Miller grabbed a large rock with both hands, raised it and slammed the back of Stakemore's head. They all heard her skull crack.

Caruthers-Stakemore flopped limp onto the sand. Blood gushed from a gaping wound in the back of her skull. The rock left a deep, wide depression in her cranium. Bone fragments protruded from the scalp and Miller was close enough to see gray brain matter.

Miller lifted the rock again. "And this is for my nephew." She slammed the rock onto Stakemore's head again. The ugly 'thwuck' sound made Raas and Rushton wince.

Evan Caruthers, a.k.a. Iris Stakemore, was no more.

Greek Isle #44: Another fruitless week passed for the treasure hunters. They had searched eight more small islands. At least they were having fun.

At the ninth island, Paul Thomas detected an underground anomaly that might be an underground cavern. He and Terry donned scuba gear and dove on the site. They emerged twelve minutes later, excited.

Amber and Dave were in the launch.

"Did you find something?" asked Amber.

Terry removed his mouthpiece. "There's a tunnel down there. It has a large entrance but it's dark inside. Call your dad and ask him to bring some underwater lights."

Twenty minutes later, Luke and Storm hovered beside the launch and lowered two powerful halogen undersea lights.

"Where's this tunnel?" Luke radioed.

Terry answered, "Directly below that wedge-shaped crevice on the cliff."

"Okay. We'll scout above. Good luck and be careful."

"You too, boss."

Luke flew to the cliff at wave top level. Storm scanned the face for a possible entry.

Terry and Paul strapped on their tanks and went into the sea. Amber suited up and joined them.

Luke hovered at the base of the cliff and traversed slowly across the face for a hundred yards, then he climbed twenty feet and reversed direction, forming a raster search pattern. He traversed the chopper across the face of the cliff, climbing with each pass.

"Keep a sharp eye out for Guido's octagon," Hale reminded.

Terry, Paul and Amber entered the tunnel, guided by the powerful lights. It was large and went deep into the island. The group stayed close and ventured farther in. Fifty yards in, the tunnel narrowed, creating a Venturi effect. The current increased dramatically to squeeze through the narrow space and pushed them further into the tunnel.

The unexpected rush swept them deeper under the island. The tunnel narrowed even more, the current increased and the divers found themselves trapped in a current stronger that their abilities. They crashed into one another, the current became turbulent. They bounced off the walls and spun in circles. They grabbed for each other, trying to stay together. Terry's light smashed against a wall and extinguished.

They were swept deeper under sea level. They could feel the pressure building in their ears and sinuses. They breathed harder, struggling to regain control.

The tunnel narrowed more and jammed them into a ball. The current increased and dragged them deeper. They heard thunderous rhythmic pounding. They struggled to untangle. Terry got free and was sucked through a narrow choke point. Amber and Paul followed, not by choice.

The pounding noise grew more intense, the current and turbulence tripled. They were being sucked toward the source of the noise. They tumbled and spun, hopelessly riding the current. They tucked into fetal positions. All they could do was ride the current and hope for the best.

∾

The raster scan progressed smoothly.

"Luke, come left and climb a bit."

Luke eased the chopper to where Storm pointed. Fifteen feet below the precipice was a small shelf of rock at the base of a steep slope. It was dotted with shrubs of various sizes.

"See that large bush with the red flowers?"

"Yes."

"What's that behind it?"

A huge, partly exposed, odd-shaped rock lie against the incline. It had unnatural angles on its left side, as if shaped by hand. The right side was covered with dirt and the bush obscured part of it.

"Could that be an octagon?"

Luke studied it as he hovered. "It's worth a look. I'll take us to the top. Get a fix as we crest the rim."

Luke climbed the chopper to the top and set down on a flat area twenty feet from the edge. He shut down the engine and they released their harnesses. As Luke completed his shutdown checklist, Storm gathered gear to rappel down the cliff.

Storm used a short length of rope to make a harness. He tied it around his waist, then looped the loose ends between his legs and tied them off to the line at his hips. It was a field expedient harness known as a Swiss seat.

He clipped a snap link to the front of the harness and donned thick leather gloves. Luke secured a line to a chopper strut and tested it. Satisfied, he passed the line to Storm. He looped it twice through the snap link and pulled it behind his back with his right hand. He leaned his full weight back to test it.

"Okay. Here's the belay line." Luke attached an additional line to Storm's harness and passed the opposite end twice around another of the chopper's struts. Then he secured himself to the chopper, donned leather gloves and grabbed the belay line. His job would be to brake Storm's fall in the event of a mishap.

Storm backed to the edge of the cliff, feeding the rope through the snap link. At the edge, he tossed the free end over. He grasped the rope with his right hand and jammed it to the small of his back, locking it against his hip. He leaned his full weight on the line again. It tested secure.

Storm eased his grip and leaned over the edge, using his left hand as a guide and his right hand as the brake. He spread his legs wide. "Good to go."

"Rappel away."

Storm pushed off the cliff and eased his grip. He zoomed down, covering the distance in two bounds. He was level with the shelf. He braked the rope behind his back, halting his descent, slightly left of the shelf. "Moving right," he yelled.

"Moving right." Luke saw the lines skitter along the edge as Storm traversed.

Storm reached the shelf and found enough footing to stand. "Secure belay."

Luke reeled in the belay line until it had no slack, then he backed it off a few feet to give Storm some slack. He tied the rope to the chopper. "Belay secure. Test it."

Storm maintained his grip on the rappel rope and yanked on the belay line with his left hand. He slowly transferred his full weight from one rope to the other. It tested secure. He released his grip on the rappel rope. "Belay is secure."

Luke untied and ran to the cliff. He flopped to the ground and crept to the edge. It was a long way down, more than a hundred feet. Waves pounded and swirled on the rocks, creating a foggy mist. White marine birds buzzed at them, squawking and fluttering warnings to get away from their nests. Storm and Hale ignored them. They were a nuisance, not a threat.

Storm studied the strange rock. It was a large slab, seven feet in diameter and nearly a foot thick. The shallow ledge and the short incline provided enough support for Storm to maneuver around the rock without having to hold his line.

He could hear a muffled, rhythmic noise, booming. It sounded like it was coming from under the slab. Storm placed his ear to the edge of the slab. He felt a rush of air and the noise grew louder.

Storm dug at the edge of the slab with his gloved hands. The airflow and noise increased. Storm pulled his flashlight and examined the spot. There was a gap between the back of the slab and the face of the incline. Storm scooped away more rocks and dirt. The booming grew louder. He flashed his light under the slab. "There's a tunnel here."

"What shape is the slab?"

Storm moved right. He traced the edge of the slab with his gloved hand, scraping away dirt and rocks, revealing more of the stone's dimension and shape. He pushed away the bush and reached behind it. The final edge revealed itself.

"Ha! It's an octagon!"

"No shit?"

"No shit. It is definitely an octagon."

They were elated. Yet they had no idea of the drama unfolding in the bowels of the underwater tunnel below. Nor did they notice a fishing boat offshore.

∞

They tumbled and ricocheted off the walls and each other. The current was tearing them apart. They were battered and bruised, nearing the limit of their endurance.

Paul's hose punctured and air bubbled out at an alarming rate. His breathing became labored. He sucked harder, the volume diminished. He sucked again and got a mouthful of seawater. His air was gone!

He spit out the mouthpiece and held his breath. He was getting light headed, his lungs wanted to burst. Panic assaulted, but he refused to relinquish control. An eternity passed.

He had to find air, now. He cut away his weight belt. His only chances were to find an air pocket or buddy breathe with Amber or Terry.

Paul popped to the surface like a cork and banged his head on a low overhang. He was stunned and exhaled. A loud booming noise echoed. He gasped for air and was rewarded.

Air! It was slightly stale but it was breathable.

"Paul!"

He heard Terry's yell over the booming racket. He coughed and sputtered. There was splashing behind him. He didn't have the energy to look.

Terry and Amber swam up behind him, grabbed his harness and towed him to a ledge. It was dark, except for the glow of Paul's lamp.

Terry climbed onto the ledge as Amber steadied Paul. Terry grabbed him and hoisted him up. Amber climbed up. They removed Paul's gear as he coughed up seawater and vomit.

"Are you all right?" asked Amber.

Paul nodded even though he was retching. After a minute, he recovered. "I'll be okay. Lord, I don't ever want to do that again. That's as close as I've ever been to drowning."

"What happened?"

"My air hose got punctured." He coughed and spit out more water and bile.

Amber gently rubbed his back.

"Check that out," yelled Terry above the ruckus. He pointed the light across an underground lake. As each successive wave surged into the chamber through the tunnel, it crashed into the far wall, climbed its face and pounded against the bottom of an overhanging layer of rock. An orifice in the overhang spewed frothy seawater, creating the booming noise with each successive surge. It was a naturally formed blowhole, thundering a booming rhythm and creating a permanent mist in the chamber.

"That explains all the racket," yelled Amber.

Terry scanned their surroundings. The cavern was wide and tall. It had layered rings of overhangs extending all the way to the top, about seventy feet above. There wasn't any daylight. There were bats hanging inverted along the ceiling and the bottoms of the uppermost ledges.

"How are we going to get out of here?" yelled Terry.

∞

"Dave, we found an octagonal slab up here. It's covering a tunnel into the cliff."

"No kidding?"

"No kidding. Derek says he can't see the end of the tunnel but it goes in at least thirty yards. The slab is massive. We're going to need some strong backs with crowbars and a hydraulic jack. We're going to fly back to the ship and fetch the gear. What's the status on the dive party?"

"Not a word. They've been down for fourteen minutes. They have another sixteen minutes of air."

"Okay. Give me a call when you hear from them. We're heading for the ship."

∾

"Good question," yelled Amber. They had no food, no fresh water and only fifty feet of rope. The cavern walls were slimy and practically smooth, not climbable.

"That current is too strong. We can't get out that way," yelled Paul.

"Well," hollered Terry, " the good news is we have air. And those bats have some way out of here."

"But it's probably way at the top," hollered Amber. "How are we going to get up there?"

Terry scratched his head and Paul looked down. They were stumped.

"When's low tide, Mr. Helmsman?" yelled Paul.

Terry checked his watch. "Six and a half hours. What do you have in mind?"

"I'm the strongest swimmer. If we haven't been found by then, I'll try to go back out the tunnel."

"That's suicide," hollered Amber.

Paul gave her a sorry look. "What choice do we have?"

∾

Hale and Storm assembled the gear and recruited volunteers to move the slab. They crowded into the chopper. Luke lifted off and headed for the cliff with the heavy load.

"Chopper, this is Dave. Come in."

"Go ahead."

"Boss, it's been thirty minutes since the dive party went under. They haven't surfaced. I'm worried."

Storm and Hale looked at each other.

"Did they go into the tunnel?"

"I think so."

Luke wasn't certain what to do. The radio crackled again, this time from the Skipper. "Chopper, come back to the ship and get me to the launch. They might need help."

Hale whipped the chopper around. By the time he landed, Salty and Heather were running under the blades to climb aboard. Salty carried two sets of diving gear, tossed them on and told the two crewmen to get off. He helped Heather aboard and climbed in.

"Go!" he yelled.

Luke lifted off and pushed the chopper as fast as it would go. They reached the launch and Salty lowered the dive gear to Dave. Then Luke slipped the chopper a few feet sideways and Salty jumped into the water. Heather grabbed the door frame and prepared to jump.

"Where are you going?"

"After our daughter." She was gone before Luke could protest. Luke shook his head. She was Scottish and redheaded. There was no arguing with her.

"Chopper's going topside again to find a way in from the top," Luke radioed to the launch. To Derek he yelled, "I hope Paul was right about there being a cavern."

∞

"Vixen, this is Terry. Come in." His tenth transmission went unanswered. The radio waves were not penetrating the rock.

"Save it, Terry," yelled Paul. "We might need it later."

Terry turned off the radio. "We should probably turn the light off too."

Paul agreed.

"Just a second," hollered Amber. "I have an idea." She grabbed Paul's empty air tanks and partly submerged them in the water. She withdrew her dive knife and straddled the tanks. "I'll take the first shift." She banged the knife on the tanks. Tang-tang-tang, bong, bong, bong, tang-tang-tang. She repeated the sequence.

"S-O-S," recognized Terry. The tapping and pounding sent sound waves through the cavern and the underwater tunnel.

"Clever lady," yelled Paul. "I'm glad she's on our side."

Terry yelled back, "Let's hope they hear it." He flicked off the light.

∞

Storm rappelled down first. Luke lowered the equipment, then he rappelled down with Storm belaying from below.

Storm used a shovel to dig a footing for the hydraulic jack. Hale wedged the jack between the footing and the back of the slab, inserted the handle and pumped for all he was worth.

Five minutes into it, Storm relieved him.

"You ain't the man you used to be, my friend."

Luke panted. "Wait until you turn fifty, smart ass." Storm laughed and pumped for all his worth. Amber was precious to her dad. Terry and Paul were like family. That made them precious to Storm as well.

The slab moved. Dirt and rocks near its base cascaded down the cliff and splashed into the foamy waves. Storm renewed his effort. The slab slid some more. Storm panted and perspired.

"My turn." Luke tapped him and Storm came off, tag team style. Luke pumped with renewed vigor. The slab inched away from the face. It hung by the thinnest of margins. Hale pumped again and again. The jack stopped.

"Damn!"

"What?"

"The jack is fully extended. Find a flat rock." Luke opened the jack's release valve and compressed the cylinder rod.

Storm scanned the cliff. There were no loose flat rocks. "I'll have to go topside." He unclipped his rappel line, grabbed the belay line and scaled the cliff hand over hand. His powerful arms and legs pushed him over the top in less than a minute. A minute later, he descended on his rappel line.

Storm reached into his trouser pocket and extracted a flat rock. "Just what the doctor ordered."

"Perfect."

Storm held the rock against the slope and Hale jammed the jack into the gap and pumped it. As soon as the jack put tension on the rock, Storm released it. Luke pumped furiously for two minutes. The flat rock began to crack and crumble, but the slab didn't budge.

"Come on you son-of-a-bitch. Give."

Storm grabbed a crow bar, jammed it behind the slab and leveraged his weight into it. He pushed his mass on the bar, Hale pumped. The slab budged. Dirt and rocks cascaded down the cliff. It budged more.

Both men were straining.

"On three," grunted Storm.

"Okay. One, two, threeeeee."

Storm reached deep into his internal chi and focused his energy into the crow bar. Hale pumped hard.

The slab slid, teetered and broke free. Its base slid away from the shelf. The men jumped away. A small avalanche of debris tumbled down the cliff. The slab cleared the shelf and fell. It smacked the cliff, tumbled and broke into several pieces, plunging into the sea.

Storm lost his footing and followed it. Luke grabbed for his belay line. The nylon rope stretched to its limit under Storm's weight, rebounded slightly and slammed him into the cliff.

"Hang on," yelled Luke.

"That had occurred to me."

The belay line held. Luke swung Storm toward the face. He grabbed and found a foothold.

"Okay. Climbing."

"Climb on." Luke took up the slack as Storm ascended.

Storm was winded by the time he completed the twenty-foot climb. They took a short breather and sat in front of the exposed opening. Cool, moist air flowed from the tunnel.

Luke flashed a light into the jagged-walled tunnel. It descended into the cliff for fifty yards and appeared to bend down and to the right. It looked large enough for both of them to enter in tandem.

"No time... like the present," panted Storm.

Luke radioed the launch. "Dave, any word on the divers?"

"Yeah. The Skipper and Mrs. Hale just surfaced. They found the underwater tunnel but the Skipper said the current is too strong inside. He had to pull Mrs. Hale out and she's pissed. The Skipper thinks they may have been sucked in and trapped."

"We found a small tunnel up here. We're going in."

"Roger that. I'll inform them."

"Let's go," said Storm.

"I'll go. It's my daughter and crew in there. I need you here to relay messages. Stick close to the entrance and rest."

"You sure, Luke? You're not thirty anymore."

Luke winked. "Neither are you." He plunged into the tunnel.

"But I'm a hell of a lot closer to it than you are, you stubborn old fart."

∞

"My turn," said Terry. He flipped on the light. Amber relinquished her station.

Terry drew his dive knife and took position. He began tapping and pounding. Paul flicked off the light.

∾

Luke's flashlight provided full view of the narrow tunnel. He crawled on his hands and knees and rounded the bend. The tunnel descended steeply and made another bend to the left twenty yards ahead.

"How you doing, Luke?"

"Real good."

Luke reached the second bend. The slope increased but the walls widened. Luke elevated to a crouch and worked his way down.

He heard noise. Between the booming pulses, he thought he heard metal banging on metal. He advanced. The thunder grew louder and so did the metal sound. Ting-ting-ting, bong, bong, bong, ting-ting-ting, WHOOSH, ting-ting-ting, bong, bong, bong, ting-ting-ting, WHOOSH.

"Amber, Paul, Terry?"

WHOOSH.

He descended down the tube. The whooshing thunder and the tapping grew louder. Luke slipped on the slick floor. He fell on his butt and slid down the tube like a water park ride. He was forcefully deposited on his butt thirty yards later.

"Ugh! Lord, thanks for giving me a fat ass." He struggled to his feet and rubbed his tailbone.

"Luke, how're you doing?"

"Good. I hear someone tapping S-O-S."

"Want me to come down?"

"Give me a minute."

Luke scanned his flashlight. He was no longer in the tunnel. He was in a cave. He heard squeaking sounds above. He flashed the light. Bats, thousands of them.

∾

"What's that?" yelled Paul.

"What?"

"What?"

"I thought I saw a light flash off the ceiling. There it is again. It's a flashlight! HELLO."

Terry hammered on the tanks. Amber yelled for help. Paul clicked on the light and flashed it across the ceiling like a car lot beacon.

∞

Luke heard a voice. The metal pounding changed rhythm and intensified. A bright light flashed across the ceiling from below.

"HELP! WE'RE DOWN HERE!"

"Amber? It's Dad. Where are you?"

"Down here. Down here."

Luke followed the light beacon downward. It went below the ledge he stood on. He lowered himself to the ledge, crept to the edge and peeked over. The light below focused on a curvaceous figure in a bright yellow wet suit, Amber's wet suit.

"Amber, it's Dad. Are you guys okay?"

"We're okay but we can't get out."

"Are Paul and Terry with you?"

"Yes, we're all here." The men stepped into the beam of Luke's flashlight and waved.

"Help is here. I'm going to get some equipment. Hold tight. I'll be back soon."

Luke flashed his light around the cavern and made note of the equipment he would need. He ascended the tube, yelling to Storm all the way.

∞

They were elated. Amber jumped up and down, hugged both of them and kissed them full on their lips. Terry was thrilled. Paul hoped Caroline didn't find out.

∞

Storm relayed the good news and relayed Luke's instructions. He wanted the launch to return to the ship and he would meet them there in the chopper.

Storm remained behind at the tunnel entrance.

Within a half hour, Luke had returned with the Skipper, Heather, Dave and the equipment.

When Luke descended the cliff to re-enter the tunnel, Storm wouldn't hear of it. "You are NOT going into that tunnel, old man. I don't care if it is your daughter down there. You're the only one who can fly that chopper and it's our only way back to the ship. If anything happens to you, we're all screwed. So you get your old raggedy ass back up top and wait by the chopper." Storm was smiling as he delivered the command.

Luke knew he was right. One slip and the crew and his family would be stranded for some time.

"We've got it under control," assured Storm, patting him on the back.

Heather entered the tunnel.

"Where are you going?"

"After our daughter." She was gone before he could protest. He looked at Storm, Dave and Salty. They shrugged their shoulders, hefted the gear and entered the tunnel.

∞

"That's them, all right." Slash set down the binoculars.

Bravo nodded.

From their rented fishing boat, they had confirmed the identity of the elegant motor yacht, the *Serene Vixen*. Their radio scanner intercepted every transmission between the parties. The names Luke, Derek and Lisa had been transmitted numerous times.

"One thing has me puzzled."

"What's that, Colonel?"

"Why would some rich guy and Storm have an interest in a cave covered by a rock shaped like an octagon?"

∞

The rescue progressed. Storm located a sound stalagmite and secured the ends of several ropes around it. He attached a covered basket to the free ends and lowered it to the stranded divers. The basket contained MREs, canteens of fresh water, climbing harnesses, flashlights, spare batteries and bulbs and snap links.

The divers ate the MREs as the rescue party prepared to hoist them to safety.

Being the lightest, most feminine and the boss's daughter, they sent Amber up first. Dave anchored the lines as Skibba, Storm and Heather hoisted her.

There was a veritable homecoming party on the top ledge as Amber was pulled to safety. She hugged and kissed everyone, especially Dave.

Next up were the scuba gear and the basket.

They needed Terry topside to help hoist Paul. He went up next.

Finally, with all available hands pulling their guts out, they hoisted the two hundred thirty pound Paul Thomas. As he crested the top overhang, he pulled himself over.

The panting rescuers relaxed, wiped their brows and guzzled water.

Storm smiled and announced, "Time for beer call."

The band gathered their equipment as they chattered.

Dave felt the need to relieve his bladder so he snuck off to a dark crevice. He tripped over something in the dark as he unzipped his fly. He went down, landed on something hard and bruised his shin.

"Oh, damn."

"What's wrong?"

"Where's Dave?"

"I'm over here." He was laying on something, rubbing his shin. Something smelled musty, moldy.

The Skipper flashed his light toward Dave's voice. He was sprawled face down atop some bulky objects covered by a rotted tarp.

"What did you find, Dave?" asked Storm.

"Hell if I know. It smells. Help me up."

Storm extended a hand. Dave recovered.

The Skipper snatched the tarp and tossed it aside. The party focused their lights into the crevice. They were staring at six large, old wooden trunks, two human skeletons in body armor and an assortment of crossbows, swords and some very unusual weaponry.

CHAPTER XXIV

JUST HANGING AROUND

Rushton and Raas figured out how to rig a deadfall trap for sea birds. They used rocks and sticks for its structure, spoiled shellfish as bait. They managed to catch two birds. They plucked and gutted the waterfowl and roasted them over an open fire on a crude spit.

The birds were loaded with fat and foul tasting. The taste was not just bad, it was awful. All three of them spit it out. They weren't that desperate yet.

Raas and Miller were beginning to feel the first effects of the malignancy spreading inside them. They experienced abdominal cramps and acute diarrhea. Rushton knew it wouldn't be long before he became symptomatic too.

Their outlook was bleak. They hadn't seen even one ship since they were marooned. The only aircraft they saw were so far overhead they could barely see the plane. There was no way for anyone aboard to spot them. They had no communication with the world.

Stakemore's body was covered with rocks and served as a constant reminder of their collective destiny. Their only consolation was the ever-increasing pile of bird dung accumulating on her grave. They thought it a fitting tribute to her. They still couldn't see through their own hypocrisy.

Treasure Island: "Say what?" yelled Luke into the tunnel. Dave came into view around the topmost bend. He was so excited and jabbering so fast, Luke couldn't understand a word he was yelling.

"Easy Dave. Slow down. I didn't understand what you said." Luke pulled Dave from the tunnel. He was nearly out of breath. Luke secured a belay line to his harness.

"What's up?"

"We rescued all three of them, Mr. Hale. We even saved the scuba gear. And guess what?" Dave eyes widened and he hopped up and down on one leg as he nodded his head.

"Spit it out, man."

Dave danced in place and turned a rotation. "There is a shit load of treasure down there."

"Really?"

"No shit, boss. It's incredible! There are six huge trunks filled with gold, silver, statues, jade, coins, you name it. It's the kind of stuff you see in pirate movies. It's just incredible."

"Well, I'll be. Everyone is safe?"

"Yeah. They're fine. Oh! There are two dead guys down there."

"Dead guys? Like, recently dead?"

"Oh no. Sorry. I meant skeletons. They're dressed in some kind of uniforms with shields and crossbows, that sort of stuff. Mr. Storm knows what the weapons are, but I don't. Go have a look."

Luke handed the radio to Dave, unhooked his belay line and plunged into the tunnel. He rapidly scrambled down the tube, lost his footing again and slid the last few yards on his butt.

"Ugh! Damn!" He turned to the slippery tube. "That's two. You do that again and I'll have you walled in."

Flashlights shined on him. The gang was having a good laugh at his misadventure. Paul extended a hand and helped him to his feet. Luke rubbed his sore tailbone. "I guess there's a price to pay for everything."

"You can bet on it," confirmed Storm, "so you stay away from the ledge, you clumsy old fart."

Hale and Storm draped their arms over each other's shoulder and laughed. The crew laughed with them. They were in good spirits, even the divers.

Luke looked into the lights. "Amber!" He opened his arms.

"Dad." She stepped into his embrace.

"Are you okay?"

"Just fine." She kissed his cheek.

Luke turned to Paul and Terry, shook their hands and patted their backs. "You boys okay?"

"We're fine, Mr. Hale."

"Yup. Thanks for finding us."

"You bet. You guys are family."

Smiles and chuckles predominated.

"Well, the precious cargo is safe," declared Luke.

"And so is the Polo treasure," added Storm.

Luke looked around. "So where is it?"

The group parted, forming a channel for the boss. Terry focused the halogen light.

"Taa-daa," announced Amber. The powerful light illuminated a vision right out of a Hollywood movie. Luke stopped in his tracks. There were six large wooden trunks, opened, filled to their brims with all manner of valuable booty. Luke whistled and removed his hat.

"Quite a sight, eh, boss?" admired Salty.

"Yeah. Somebody pinch me."

Heather accommodated, right on his sore tush. "Ow. I was speaking metaphorically dear."

"I know." She whispered into his ear, "It's just that your butt is so cute it deserved a good pinch."

Luke smiled and subtly wiggled his eyebrows at her.

"Do we have a camera?" asked Amber.

"No," Storm answered. "This was a rescue mission. But that's a good idea. We should record this and document it."

"Good idea. We'll bring the camcorder and a spotlight when we come back. Right now, we need to figure out how to get this stuff out of here."

Paul, the marine engineer, already had a project in mind. Storm examined the skeletons, their uniforms and weaponry.

"They're Chinese, maybe Mongolian. Leather and metal body armor, crossbows, swords, pudao, all Chinese," he informed Luke.

Amber approached from behind. "Where's Dave?"

Luke answered, "He topside manning the radio."

What they didn't know was Dave was on the radio, blabbing everything he knew about the treasure to the excited ladies on the ship; and blabbing to everyone else monitoring the frequency.

∞

Bravo smirked. "Can you believe that? A treasure?"

"Sounds too good to be true," commented Slash. He guzzled beer from a can.

Bravo pondered.

"What do you want to do, Colonel?"

"What do I want to do? What do I want to do? Storm wiped out my team, ruined my retirement and you're asking what I want to do?"

Slash halted mid-guzzle and swiped his mouth with his arm. "Sorry, Colonel. I meant, when do you want to kill Storm?"

Bravo peered through the binoculars. "Right after we secure our new retirement fund."

"You mean steal their treasure? I love it. Just say when."

"Right after they load it onto their ship."

∾

Luke flew the chopper to the ship, bringing Salty, Heather and Paul with him. Salty didn't like to be away from the ship any more than necessary while she was out of port. Paul needed to round up the retrieval equipment and Heather wanted to plan a fancy celebration dinner.

As soon as the chopper set down on the pad, Connie, Lisa and Caroline came running. Caroline gave Paul a big hug and kiss. Lisa wanted to know if Derek was all right and Connie wanted to hear more about the treasure. Heather told her all about it as they headed for the galley.

Salty, wanting to be aware of every facet of the Vixen's status, patrolled the ship before going to the bridge. Caroline helped Paul gather the gear. Luke fetched weapons, ammo, lights and video equipment. He figured they would have to post guards around the clock until the treasure was recovered.

∾

A small pleasure craft piloted by a solitary figure cruised slowly from behind an adjacent island. It eased into the smooth, shallow waters a mile west of the *Vixen.*

The pilot stopped the motor and tossed the bow anchor overboard. He donned a snorkel mask and fins and dove off the bow, following the anchor chain to the bottom. He inspected the anchor, repositioned it for a firmer hold, surfaced and boarded the boat.

The loner removed his snorkel gear and toweled dry. Then he prepared a fishing pole and cast the line. He put on a pair of dark sunglasses and took a seat facing the white yacht and a fishing boat anchored a mile to its east.

∾

Paul had given a lot of thought to the recovery of the treasure. The smaller delicate items could be carried up through the tube tunnel and shuttled to the ship by chopper. However, the trunks were too large and the gold too heavy for them to be extracted that way.

Paul had a clever concept. "We'll use portable coolers."

"How?" asked Storm.

"We'll lash three coolers together. Two of them will be sealed airtight, like air tanks. The third will be loaded with cargo until they reach neutral buoyancy. We'll attach the coolers to a tow cable from the launch and feed them into the underwater tunnel. We'll need one diver outside to feed the coolers into the tunnel and one inside to retrieve them. The strongest diver will have to be outside, secured to the launch. And he has to stay out of that current."

"That would be me," volunteered Dave.

"And I'll take the inside," offered Terry.

"Good. We take the small objects topside through the upper tunnel and the boss will shuttle them to the ship by chopper. Then he'll offload, refuel and re-supply as necessary. Now, we can send up the weapons, armor and a lot of the jewels that way."

The group nodded.

Paul continued. "The heavy, bulky stuff will have to go out underwater in the coolers. We'll shoot a bracket mount into the ceiling and rig a block and tackle to it. Then we'll sift through the booty and lower it to the bottom ledge. From there, we'll load it into the cooler until the load achieves neutral buoyancy and the launch will tow it out through the tunnel. The outside diver will attach a marker buoy to it and the launch crew will haul it aboard. When the launch gets close to its maximum displacement, they'll head for the ship, transfer the load and return."

Everyone acknowledged.

"How long do you figure this will take, Paul?" asked Terry.

"Hard to say. A few days. It'll be back-breaking work."

"Why can't we just haul the trunks out through the tunnel?" inquired Luke.

"Several reasons, boss. First, they're extremely heavy. I doubt our tackle can handle the weight. Second, they have sharp corners. They'll get snagged on the walls in the tunnel and there are lots of sharp snags. I've got the scars to prove it. Third, those trunks are very old and I question their structural integrity. They'll break apart when they hit the tunnel walls and we'll lose the entire load. They'll have to stay behind."

Luke nodded. "Well, it sounds like you've got it covered. How about we get started?"

"Hoo-ah," added Storm.

∞

The first attempt didn't go as well as planned. The block and tackle gave way half way down and the load crashed to the lowest ledge, nearly crushing Storm and Terry.

Paul reassessed the tackle and determined that the volcanic rock ceiling was too porous to hold the weight. He asked Luke to fly back to the ship and bring back a welding torch and some angled steel.

Three hours later, they had a functional, hand powered, swiveling crane. The crew on the top level sifted through the bounty, loaded it into a sturdy basket, swiveled the load over the ledge and lowered it. Storm and Terry transferred it into the cooler, sent the empty basket back to the top and signaled the launch to tow by tightening the cable and pounding on it three times with a pipe.

The launch crew did their part.

The sifting crew found some interesting artifacts mixed in with the coins and jewels. There were several gold and bronze statuettes, jade sculptures and bolts of elaborately patterned, decayed silk.

By the end of the first day, the cruisers had developed a smooth tempo to the operation and recovered a third of the treasure. By the end of the second day, they had recovered another third.

The weather that night began to deteriorate. The Skipper radioed Luke with the forecast. A storm front was shaping up to the southwest and heading their way. It would be upon them by the following evening. Luke descended into the cavern to inform the crew.

The crew decided to take shifts and work later that evening and start earlier the next morning. They wanted to complete the recovery before the storm hit. He returned to the chopper, radioed the launch crew and received the same response. The work went on into the night.

The morning brought choppy seas and a red sky. The anticipated storm could be seen off in the distance, the forecast had it reaching their location by late afternoon.

The late shift had recovered a good portion of the bounty the previous night and they were now back at the ship catching up on their rest. The early shift took over and dug into their work.

"We'll be done in four or five hours," Paul assured Luke.

"I hope so. That storm front is moving this way, cell tops are 35,000 feet with wind gusts to sixty knots and half inch hail possible. We need to have the chopper and the launch battened down before it hits."

"I hear you, boss. We'll be done by then."

"Good. I'll see you down below."

Paul rappelled down the cliff to the tunnel entrance as Luke belayed from above. After Paul had disconnected and entered the tunnel, Luke radioed the ship.

"Go ahead, boss," answered Skibba.

"What's the status of the ship?"

"I've ordered the crew to start securing and batten down. How's it going on that end?"

"Paul thinks we'll be done in time."

"All good," answered Skibba. "I noticed our little friends headed for harbor." The Skipper made reference to the two smaller boats that had anchored near them for several days. Both were gone, leaving the *Vixen* the only ship in the vicinity.

Or so they thought.

"That's it," yelled Storm from the bottom of the cavern. "The last load is on its way out. Haul me up."

Luke tossed a line down. With two lines running through the block, Hale could pull from the top and Storm from below, combining their strength to lift Storm to the top level.

Luke had already flown the others back to the ship. All that remained were the launch crew, himself and Storm. The launch would return to the ship as soon as they pulled the coolers aboard.

Storm stepped onto the top ledge as Hale swiveled the crane.

"How much of this equipment do you want to take back?"

Luke thought about it. "The tanks, torch, the block and tackle. The crane can stay."

They disassembled the rigging, unaware of a man at the top of the cliff, elbow deep into the chopper's engine compartment.

∾

Slash kept a sharp eye on the cliff as he worked inside the engine compartment. He had already cut two electrical lines to the fuel control and left them spaced closely together so they would arc when the ignition was turned on. He was now taking a wrench to the fuel line above the severed wires. He backed off the coupling until a slight steady drip of fuel ebbed from it.

Slash smirked and chuckled. The chopper would burst into flames as soon as they tried to crank the engine. He silently closed and latched the cowling and tossed the wrench into a tool pouch.

He checked the cliff again, stood back and admired his work; sabotage, one of his favorites.

He grabbed the tool pouch and headed for his boat, beached on the far side of the small island.

"Wait until they try to climb those ropes."

∞

Storm exited the tunnel first and secured the belay line to his harness. He gave it a tug. It held.

"Okay, hand out the equipment." Hale passed out the gear and crawled from the hole for the last time. He secured a line to his harness and tugged. It held.

"Okay, I'm up," declared Storm. "I'll toss the line down for the equipment."

Storm began to climb the face. It was only fifteen feet to the top but the final ten were sheer cliff. Storm alternately searched for finger holds and toeholds as he pulled himself up the face. He came to a spot where there was no convenient handhold. He reached his right hand higher and stretched. He felt a hold with his fingertips but he wasn't high enough to get a firm grip on it. He would have to jump a little to reach it and sacrifice his toeholds.

Storm jumped. He caught the hold firmly, grabbed his right wrist with his left hand and pulled himself higher with both arms. He felt with his boots to find a toehold.

The handhold gave out. Storm flattened against the cliff, he lost traction and plummeted.

"Oh shit! Below!"

He fell past Luke, bounced off the cliff and reached the end of the belay line. The nylon rope stretched to its limit and stopped him with a sudden jolt, seven feet below Luke. The jolt wrenched his back.

"Ugh!"

"Derek! Hang on! I'm coming."

The rope slipped, Storm fell a few more feet.

"The line's slipping. Grab it, Luke."

The rope slipped again. Then it released completely, its end whipped over the edge of the cliff. Storm plunged, the rope in trail.

Luke made a desperate lunge. He snatched the line with both hands, praying his belay line would hold them both and that he could hang on to Storm's rope.

Hale's short fall reached the end of his line. It stretched quickly and jerked him to a stop. Storm was still in free fall, frantically clawing at the cliff.

Hale rapidly tossed the loose end over his shoulder, around his back and grabbed it to his front with both hands. "This is gonna hurt," he winced.

Storm's rope reached its full stretch and jerked down onto Luke's shoulder.

"Aah! Aah! Hang on, Derek. I've got your line."

Storm slammed against the cliff hard, bounced off and slammed again. He fought for control, a footing, a handhold, anything.

Luke strained under the tension of Storm's line as it tried to slice into his shoulder. His belay line slipped. They both dropped four feet and endured another bone-jarring jolt.

"My line's giving way, Derek. Find a hold. Quickly!"

"The thought had crossed my mind." He slammed against the cliff again. He reached, grabbed. His fingers found sanctuary. He pulled to the cliff and found footholds. "Thank you, God."

Luke's line slipped again. He fell several feet, but he refused to release Storm's belay.

"Luke. I'm good. Tie off the line to your harness."

Luke hurried and did so. He reached for the cliff. Just as he got hold and pulled to the face, the line gave. Luke's belay line came whipping over the cliff and plummeted, slapping Storm across his back.

"Uh oh. Not good."

Hale made love to the cliff. They were both clinging precariously to the cliff by their fingers and toes, connected to each other by a single line, thirty feet from the top and a hundred feet above the frothing surf and rocks below. And there wasn't a soul topside to help them.

∞

Bravo had been aboard the *Vixen* for two hours. He had donned scuba gear and loaded a waterproof bag with weapons, ammo and supplies. Then he had Slash motor past the yacht and head for the opposite side of the island. As the boat passed two hundred yards abeam the yacht, Bravo went over the blind side and swam to the ship underwater from astern.

He had surfaced next to the transom walk and silently boarded. He stalked forward unobserved.

The first crew member he encountered was Connie, preparing the table in the dining salon. He crept up behind her and clamped his massive hand over her mouth.

"If you yell, I'll kill you and everyone on this ship. Blink twice if you understand." Terrified, she did. He lifted the petite lady without a problem and took her to a lower level stateroom. There, he gagged her and taped her to an immobile stand.

He continued his search. He next came upon Heather, Amber and Lisa, sunbathing on the helipad. They had their eyes closed and weren't alerted to his presence until his hulk immersed them in shadow. When they opened their eyes, they were staring down the barrel of his MP-5.

Bravo issued the same warning as he had Connie, then slapped tape over their mouths and around their wrists. The startled women complied with his orders with hardly a sound. He ushered them to the same stateroom.

And so it went. In small groups, sometimes individually, Bravo subdued the entire complement of the *Vixen*, from stern to bow, bottom to top.

After securing the Skipper, who was alone on the bridge, Bravo took a head count. There were only four to go, the two future crispy critters in the chopper and the two in the launch, and it was inbound.

∞

Dave and Terry were laughing and slapping high fives as they winched the launch into its storage bay.

"We're rich, man!" exclaimed Dave.

"Oh yeah! Cold margaritas, sunny beaches, large bank accounts, our own boat." Dave secured the winch.

"Thank you boys." A deep, menacing voice chilled their enthusiasm. They turned.

A mountain of a man stood in the passageway. He was huge, six-six and two hundred sixty pounds of rippling muscle. He looked exceptionally mean and he had a machine gun aimed at them.

"Now put your hands over your heads and I won't blow you away."

The surprised youngsters obeyed.

"W… who are you?" asked Dave.

"Did I give you permission to speak, dickhead?"

They shook their heads.

"Then shut up and get on the floor, arms and legs spread."

The lads complied.

Bravo slapped tape over their mouths and bound their wrists behind their backs. He jerked them to their feet.

"Now, if either of you snot-nosed ass wipes gives me the least bit of resistance, I'll kill you both. Understand?"

They nodded.

"Very good. Let's join the crew in stateroom four." He shoved them toward the passageway. He turned on his portable radio. "Slash, come in."

"Here, Colonel."

"Objective secure. Bring her in."

∞

Luke hauled up the loose line with one hand. He tied the end into a tight knot and wedged it into a fracture in the cliff face. He gave it a tug, then another.

"*It's not a piton but it'll have to do.*" He wished he had a few pitons, iron mountaineering spikes, and a hammer to drive them in.

It had been twenty-five years since his days in Special Forces, the last time he had done any serious mountaineering. Even back then it had been tough, strenuous work. And back then he had been in a lot better shape and much better equipped.

He yelled down to Storm, twenty feet below, "Climbing."

"Roger. Climb on." There wasn't much Storm could do other than hang on for dear life and pray. If either of them should fall, it was over for both of them.

Luke struggled up the face, one terrifying foot after another. His body shook from the strain and the adrenaline rush. He willed himself to live, to see Heather, Amber and the crew again. "*Climb, man.*"

"If you go any slower we'll miss cocktail hour," yelled Storm, trying to make light of their predicament.

"Don't make me laugh, wise ass, or we're both fish food."

"Up yours."

"You wish."

"Kiss my Irish ass."

"Not in this lifetime."

"And you said there wasn't anything you wouldn't do for me."

They chuckled, trying to subdue their fears.

Luke struggled on, inching higher up the face.

"*Only a few more feet to the ledge,*" Luke encouraged himself. He couldn't reach the shelf. The line connecting him to Storm went taught. There was no slack.

"I'm at the end of my rope, Derek. Literally."

"Did you reach the shelf?"

"No. You'll have to climb to give me some slack."

Storm took two deep breaths. "*Courage lad.*" "Okay. Climbing."

Luke wedged his clenched fist into a fracture, making as solid an anchor for them as he could. "Climb on."

Storm struggled up the face. Fortune and God smiled on him. He found adequate holds, scaling the cliff one strenuous foot at a time. He managed to climb twenty feet in ten minutes. He was exhausted, but he had made it up to the spot where Luke had anchored the knotted rope. He freed the knot and let it drop.

"Anchor knot's clear. Pull it up."

Luke hauled it up single-handed and wedged the knot into the fracture above him. He removed his sore, bruised fist. Even through the leather glove, his knuckles were lacerated and bleeding. He tested the rope anchor twice.

"Okay. I'm climbing."

Storm wedged his fist into a crevice. "Climb on."

Hale pushed up the face and reached the shelf at the tunnel entrance. "*Careful now. Don't get careless.*" He knew from experience that many mishaps occurred at the brink of reaching the objective because the climber became anxious and careless. He crested the shelf and scurried to safety near the tunnel.

He wasted no time securing his line to a rock. He had to help Storm up the face and knew he was tired.

"Belay secure. Any time, Derek."

Storm took more deep breaths and resumed his ascent. He labored, but faster this time. Luke was able to assist in pulling him up. As Storm neared the shelf, Hale pulled on the rope. Storm swung his leg onto the shelf and Luke grabbed his harness. He pulled. Storm was atop the ledge, tired but deeply thankful.

They rested as they panted and willed their breathing back to normalcy. They looked across the sea at the *Vixen.* A fishing boat very similar to the one that had anchored near the ship earlier, now motored around the corner of the island. It was moving fast and they saw it pull along side the yacht.

"I wonder what that's about?" Luke was quizzical.

"I can't imagine. But I don't like the look of it."

"We better get to the chopper. Ready?"

Storm nodded. "You go first. And watch out for that top step. It's a doozie."

∞

"What do suppose this does?" Slash poised his finger over a button on the ship's navigation console.

"I don't know. Unless it's labeled SELF-DESTRUCT, give it a push." Bravo's smirk and quip gave Slash reason to laugh.

Slash pushed the button and a screen on the NAV display flashed on.

"Interesting." Bravo studied the screen. "It's a moving-map display. I've seen them on GPS units in the field. This one is obviously for maritime navigation. Quite a gadget."

"If we punch in coordinates, will it tell us how to get there?"

"I don't know. Look around. Maybe there's an operator's manual somewhere. I'll figure out how to start the engines."

Slash rummaged through the cabinets and lockers. "What are we gonna do with the hostages?"

Bravo looked over the top of his sunglasses and issued an evil grin. "Shark bait, eh?"

"As soon as we get to deep water. I don't want them found. That'll teach Storm not to lock horns with me. That is, if they don't fall off the cliff or blow up in the chopper."

The mercenaries laughed. They had possession of a huge motor yacht and a priceless treasure. Retirement was not just over the horizon, it was underfoot.

∞

Luke finally reached the top of the cliff, secured a line to the chopper strut and tested it four times. He tossed it down to Storm.

The gusty winds at the front of the approaching storm blew over them. Storm didn't hesitate to grab the line and he scaled the cliff with Luke's assistance.

They untied their ropes and jumped into the chopper. Storm buckled in as Luke flipped on the battery switch and ran through his preflight checks. He was ready to hit the ignition.

"Hey, the ship's moving."

Luke looked up. Sure enough, the *Vixen* was under way, leaving a huge foaming wake in trail.

Luke keyed the radio, "Vixen, this is Luke. Come in."

There was no response. "Vixen, this is Luke. Come in."

Silence. Hale and Storm looked at each other.

The wind gusted again. Luke's eyebrows arched. He flipped off the battery switch. The chopper's electrical system went dormant.

"What's wrong?"

"I smell fuel." They both un-strapped and hustled to the engine compartment. Luke opened the cowling. A puddle of fuel streamed out.

"Shit! We've got a fuel leak," remarked Storm.

"Some one's been screwing around in here. This bird was fine this morning. Dave checked it. He'd never miss a leak of that magnitude."

Luke glanced toward the *Vixen*. She was moving southwest at full bore, directly into the approaching thunderstorm.

CHAPTER XXV

AVENGING STORM

S torm stripped his shirt and ripped off his tee shirt. "Do we have any tools?"

"Yeah." Luke hustled and retrieved a tool sack from the cockpit.

Storm put his attention to the engine. "Found it."

Luke looked in. "Someone clipped the safety wires and backed off the fuel line coupling to the control unit."

"At least they didn't cut it. We can tighten her down. Got a crescent wrench?"

Luke handed him the wrench. Storm took it and wondered, "Why didn't they cut the line?"

"That would have been too obvious. I'd have spotted the puddle or smelled the fumes sooner than I did. Someone was real subtle about this for a reason."

"There. She's tight." Storm sopped up the excess fuel with his shirt and checked for other leaks. "Give it a few minutes. Let the wind evaporate the rest of it."

Luke nodded. He looked toward his ship, now just a white speck in the distance. His family and crew were disappearing. His heart sank.

"You know," he thought aloud, "what good is a tiny fuel leak like that without an ignition source?"

"I see your point," answered Storm. He tossed away the fuel-soaked shirt and looked under the cowling again. "Help me look for cut wires."

Hale and Storm systematically traced every electrical wire to its origin and connection.

"Found one," declared Storm. Luke hustled to his side.

"Where?"

"Right here, below the coupling I just tightened."

"That's the igniter box." Luke reached in and felt around. "There's another clipped wire back here. There are needle-nosed pliers and electrical tape in the bag."

Storm grabbed the bag and searched. He produced a set of dykes and the tape. He tossed the dykes to Luke. He quickly trimmed the ends of the severed wires and twisted them together. Storm bit off two pieces of tape and wrapped the twists.

Luke tossed the dykes into the sack and ran to the cockpit. He flipped on the battery switch and hit the ignition. The engine sparked.

"Let's go."

Storm slammed the cowling closed and latched it, grabbed the tool kit and jumped in. Luke strapped in.

The chopper's engine and rotors were up to speed in a minute. Luke revved it and lifted off. He rotated toward his ship and revved the chopper to full power. The chopper cleared the cliff and Luke nosed it over toward the sea below. The chopper quickly gained speed and Luke leveled her off at wave top level, pushing her to redline speed.

"Vixen, this is Luke. Come in."

Silence.

"Vixen, come in. This is Luke."

Still no response. The *Vixen* steamed directly toward the storm front. Huge, dark cumulonimbus clouds loomed ahead. Heavy rain poured out their bottoms, obscuring the horizon. Sunlight was waning.

"Can this thing go any faster?"

"Nope. Any faster and the retreating blade will stall. We'd flip over and crash."

Storm looked disappointed. He tapped his foot and drummed his fingers, anxious to do something. He drew his .45 and racked a round into the chamber, cocked the hammer, thumbed up the safety and holstered it.

The chopper closed rapidly on the ship. The air became more turbulent and the seas heavier as they closed on the weather front. The rain started, light at first, then it quickly became heavy.

They approached the ship from astern. They lost sight of her for a moment as she passed through some heavy rain. Luke climbed the chopper to fifty feet.

"Can you land on the pad?"

"It'll be tough in this turbulence. It'll depend on how much the ship is pitching and rolling."

The yacht came into view a quarter mile ahead. Luke could see its deck pitching way beyond the limit of safety. The ship was into eight foot seas and the heavy rain soaked them through the door-less cockpit openings.

The chopper closed on the *Vixen*. Luke slowed to match her speed and hovered over the pad. The chopper buffeted and bounced in the turbulence. The yacht heaved and rolled in the rough sea.

"There's no way I can land and we're low on fuel."

Storm un-strapped. "We'll have to jump."

"I can't. If I release the cyclic, she'll crash and kill us."

Storm was incredulous. "What are you going to do?"

Luke shrugged his shoulders. He was exhausted from the cliff and fighting the severe weather for control of the chopper. "Get going. I can't hold this hover forever."

Storm stood on the skid and held the door frame as Luke closed to the pad as closely as he dared, ten feet. Storm timed his leap.

Luke glanced toward his friend. He was gone.

"God be with you, my friend."

Storm hit the pad like a ton of bricks. The heavy rain hammered down on him and made the deck slick. He sprawled across the heaving helipad, trying to catch his breath from the bone-jarring impact.

He recovered and drew his Colt. He stood and ambled toward cover. A huge wave hit the ship and washed across the pad. The ship's bow planed into the air and the stern dropped away under him as the ship listed twenty degrees.

Storm fell onto the deck as it rose to meet him. He banged his head on the deck, slid toward the port edge and lost his grip on the .45.

Lightening flashed, thunder instantly boomed. Storm felt himself sliding over the edge. He willed his fingernails to find purchase in the steel pad but there was none. He slid over the edge. He fell. He grabbed. Contact!

"Ugh!" He slammed against the steel hull. He hung from a rail by his left hand. The .45 fell past him. He grabbed for it but missed. It was consigned to the deep.

For the third time today he was hanging precariously. The ship heaved again, a wave crashed over the gunwale, slamming him into the hull.

"Please God. Just a little help."

He grabbed his left wrist with his right hand and pulled himself up. "Aaaaah!" He was inches away from reaching the rail with his right hand. His left hand was tiring.

∞

The chopper wasn't designed to take such a pounding. The heavy turbulence buffeted the whirlybird wildly as it paced the ship, running out of fuel. Luke knew he didn't have enough fuel to reach land, so he stayed with the ship, hoping it would slow down and find calmer seas, soon.

He saw Storm slide over the opposite side of the helipad.

"God, no!" He whipped the chopper across the *Vixen*'s stern. Storm was hanging from a railing by one arm. He was getting pounded by the waves and pelted by the rain. If he fell into the sea, he'd be sucked under into the propellers.

"Dear Lord, give him strength, give him help. Please!"

There was nothing Luke could do for Derek, except pray.

∞

Another wave crushed Storm against the hull. Lightening cracked, thunder ripped. The charged air particles made Storm's hair bristle. He was losing focus. A memory of training with his father came to mind. His father had said, *"In the trouble, find the calm space and go there with your mind. In the calm, see all but watch nothing. You will find your focus. Focus, Derek."*

Storm eased his mind and sought the calm. He visualized himself in Lisa's arms, tranquility, peace. He felt a sudden peace, a sense of well-being. His mind reached the calm arena, all distractions shut out: no lightening, no thunder, no waves.

Storm focused all of his life force into his arms and exerted a blood-curdling yell. He exploded with a burst of energy and lifted into a one-armed pull up, grabbed the rail with his right hand and pulled himself over. He landed on the stairs outside the launch storage bay below the helipad. He breathed heavily, soaked and exhausted.

"Thanks, Dad."

∞

"This should be good enough," commented Bravo. "They'll never be found in these heavy seas." He pulled the throttles back to one-third speed. "It's time to dispose of our burdensome hosts."

Slash issued an evil smile, held up his switchblade and clicked it open. "I'm on it."

"Don't make a mess. I want to keep this boat."

Slash thrust a sloppy salute at Bravo and headed down the stairs for the stateroom level.

"Retirement, here we come."

∞

Storm cautiously worked forward on the ship. There was no one in sight. He made his way to an arms locker but it was locked and he didn't have a key.

"The staterooms. Luke keeps some weapons down there unlocked." He went to the stairs and descended to the stateroom level. He dripped rainwater but it couldn't be helped. He traversed the passageway toward his and Lisa's stateroom, number four. He found it padlocked from the outside. He tested the doorknob, locked.

"What the hell?"

He placed his ear to the door. He heard muffled groans and sobs from inside. He tugged on the padlock. It was secure. The noise excited whoever was inside. The groans turned into muffled yells. He recognized Lisa's muffled voice. It sounded like the whole crew was in there.

"A crowbar. The machine shop." He knew it was down one level, just forward of the engine room.

∞

Slash worked aft through the crew lounge, galley and dining salon. His arrogant smirk faded as he noticed a trail of water on the salon floor. It wasn't from Bravo or him, they were bone dry.

He readied his switchblade and followed the trail. It made a fork at the stairwell, one trail going down the stairs, the other coming through the main salon.

He heard a rhythmic whop-whop-whop interspersed with the sounds of the surf and thunderclaps. He glanced out the windows. He saw the chopper.

"What the hell?" He radioed Bravo. "Colonel. That chopper is following us and some one is on board."

"Shit! Deal with it, Slash. Forget what I said about making a mess. Keep me posted."

∞

Storm was about to round the corner to the stairs. His neck hair bristled! He flung himself backwards. A knife slashed across his right pectoral and bicep, slicing open shallow wounds. Storm launched into a back roll and pushed upright into his San Soo fighting stance.

A huge man with a mean, smirking face, buzz cut and rippling muscles entered the passageway from the stairs. He brandished a long switchblade.

"You are one stubborn son-of-a-bitch."

"Oh?"

The thug wasn't in the mood for chitchat. He lunged at Storm's midsection and sliced up toward his face. Storm stepped inside the thrust and blocked with a hard down windmill block.

"Yah! Hah!" Storm slammed the back of his right elbow into the killer's face and side-kicked his groin. He staggered, Storm exploited it, exploding with a furious flurry of punches, elbow strikes and kicks. The man was solid, he wouldn't go down, but he was stunned and retreating.

The killer tried to slice at Storm's face, but Storm blocked and snatched the knife-wielding arm, planted a kick into his liver, slapped the palm of his left hand across the edge of the killer's hand and pivoted to his right. The killer's right arm twisted but it didn't break; his arm was too massive. The pronation leverage took the killer's balance and he bent over, dropping the knife.

Storm kicked at his head but the killer countered with a left block and somersaulted, unlocking Storm's manipulation. The killer punched at Storm's groin, but Storm intercepted the fist with a cross kick.

The killer rolled upright and glared at Storm.

"I'm gonna pound you and gut you for the Colonel." He lunged at Storm with an extended front kick at his knee. Storm evaded. He lunged again and missed. The smaller man was too fast for him. He eyed the knife on the floor.

"You won't live to get it," growled Storm.

The killer scowled and charged. Storm counter-attacked: right block, left block, left palm to the chin, right open hand to the throat, left knee to the groin, right forearm hammer to the neck.

The killer staggered but he wouldn't go down. He launched at Storm again. Storm unleashed: right block, left punch to the solar plexus, right punch to the spleen, left knee to the bladder, right claw across his eyes, left front kick to the stomach.

The killer staggered back, bloodied, bruised and dazed. Storm advanced. The killer turned left and ran up the stairs. Storm pursued.

On the next level, the killer raced into the main salon. Storm launched into a flying drop kick, caught the killer squarely in the back and sent him flying over a couch. The assailant crashed through a coffee table as Storm dropped onto his back and slapped his arms to the deck to absorb the shock of the fall. Storm hand-sprang to his feet.

The killer recovered sluggishly and shook out the cobwebs. He dashed to a bulkhead and snatched one of Luke's prized displays from its mount, a Japanese katana, a Samurai sword. He drew the long sharp, combat-hardened steel blade from its scabbard. He glared at Storm and threw the scabbard at him. Storm caught it and tossed it aside.

The killer growled, "I told you I'm gonna gut you, bad."

"You also said you were going to pound me to pulp. Here I am."

Storm's provocation had the desired effect. The killer advanced and swept the blade in a fast, skillful figure-eight pattern, then held it pointed at Storm, still advancing.

The display told Storm a lot about the killer. He had fluid motion with the blade, correct grip and controlled, balanced posture. He was well-trained and disciplined with the blade.

Storm dashed to the opposite bulkhead, the killer pursued. Storm grabbed another of Luke's weapons from its wall mount; it was a thin, curved-blade Chinese broadsword, the one Storm had presented to Luke upon his promotion to black belt.

This was going to be a fight to a steely death. The Japanese katana was longer and stronger than the Chinese sword. But Storm's blade was lighter, more flexible and easier to wield.

Storm turned and faced the killer. He halted, maintaining his perfect posture.

"Pretty sword," smirked the killer. "But can it fight?"

"Come find out."

The killer advanced.

Blades whistled as they sliced the air and collided: ching, clang, bling, bling, clang, ching, prang, whish, whish. Neither scored a hit.

They circled counter-clockwise, their faces grim with concentration, focused on each other's centerline and shoulders, watching for the opponent's next move.

The killer kicked away an end table and attacked. The blades flashed again, their speed leaving light trails in their wake: whoosh, clang, cling, cling… bling, pling, clang, clang, ching, whish, plang, ching… plang, ching, ching.

Storm assessed the killer's technique. He liked to strike from low to high and back to low. It was an unusual style, but very effective against the average swordsman. But Storm was not average, not by a long shot.

The killer advanced again. The blades flashed like a steel whirlwind. The killer grunted as he launched each strike. He was becoming frustrated with Storm's skilled counters, a good sign. Storm knew that frustration caused mistakes and in this game, mistakes were invariably fatal.

The killer sliced at Storm's neck. Storm committed. He dropped flat under the arc of the blade and drop-kicked at the killer's front knee. He caught it just right. Crack!

"Aaaah!" The thug went down on his back, in pain. Storm rolled to his feet and crouched, his hands above his head, his sword guarding his back.

The killer moaned and raised his katana to cover as he tried to regain his feet. He couldn't. His knee was broken.

Storm closed the distance and slapped away the katana with the side of his blade. He thrust the broadsword sideways at the killer's throat and stopped just short of piercing the villainous creep.

"Who else is on this ship?"

"Screw you!"

Storm pressed the blade and it sliced into his throat slightly. "How many men are with you?"

"Aaah. Kiss my ass."

"Good-bye, asshole."

POW!

A pistol shot ripped the sword from Storm's hand.

"Hello Mr. Storm." A huge man with a deep voice, buzz cut and a mean, carved face glared at him from the entrance of the dining salon. It was the man from the bunker, the one Storm suspected of being Colonel Bravo. He looked down at the subdued swordsman and recognized him too.

"You're the scum who raided my uncle's lab."

The Colonel smirked. "Bravo Storm. You recognized me. I'm Colonel Bravo."

"I don't think so," challenged Storm. "I know you. Don't I…

Major Whitcup?"

Bravo showed no emotion. "That's Colonel Whitcup, United States Army, Retired. Good memory, Storm. Too good. That's one of the reasons I have to put a bullet in your head, just like I did your uncle."

"You killed my Uncle Dan?"

"Good-bye, Storm."

Storm dove. Bravo fired and missed. Storm rolled. Bravo fired again. Again.

Storm was desperate. He had little cover and no firearm. He rolled, faked one direction, lunged another and dove behind the wet bar. The onslaught of bullets kept coming.

Clack, clatter. Storm recognized the sound. Bravo had just ejected a spent magazine to reload. Storm made a dash for the exit. Bravo slapped in a fresh magazine and released the slide. He aimed.

"*This is it,*" thought Storm. He dove for the exit.

Bravo squeezed. A hand appeared from behind him and deflected the gun. POW.

Storm rolled through the exit. He heard a scuffle in the salon. He peeked in.

A stranger had entered behind Bravo and made a grab for the gun. The stranger pounded furiously on the huge mercenary but his blows had little effect. They grappled for the weapon, dancing in a lethal circle.

The valiant smaller man was no match for the hardened killer. Bravo gained the advantage quickly and landed several crushing blows. He freed the gun and shot the stranger in the gut. He went down.

Storm couldn't let him die. He charged across the salon while Bravo had his back turned and dropped kicked. The gun went flying and Bravo went tumbling into the dining salon, smashing into chairs and the table. Glasses and dishes crashed and splattered.

Storm ducked back into the main salon. The killer swordsman was trying to regain his feet. Storm reached for a wall display, grabbed a Chinese hook sword and threw it sidearm at the injured killer. The sharp multi-edged blade sizzled across the room like a renegade saw blade and sliced into the killer's throat. He staggered, gurgled and dropped to his knees, blood spewing from his severed carotid artery. Death was seconds away. He collapsed.

A massive hand grabbed Storm's left shoulder from behind and whirled him around. Instinctively, Storm covered, squatted and pivoted into the spin, increasing his power. Storm slammed a one-knuckle uppercut punch into Bravo's groin. He bent over and gasped in shock. Storm kneed his face. Bravo recoiled upright. Storm unleashed: knee, elbow, punch, kick. This guy was harder to bring down than the other one. Every blow Storm launched hit its target solidly, but the monster wouldn't drop.

Bravo blocked two blows and head butted Storm. He staggered. They both staggered.

Through his bloodied, torn face, Bravo growled, "You should have died in the desert. You should have died at the dead drop, or in the bunker or fallen off the cliff, or blown up in your sissy friend's chopper. I'm gonna kill you if it's the last thing I do."

Bravo charged, they exchanged blows and entangled. They grappled for advantage, trying to snap each other's bones.

Straining, Storm taunted Bravo. "Just think of me as a chronic hemorrhoid, Whitcup. A pain in the ass that just keeps coming back. And Luke is no sissy. Count on it."

"You ain't coming back from this." Bravo landed an elbow that winded Storm. He pushed Storm away and launched kicks at him with his massive legs.

Storm evaded most, countered some, but Bravo landed one to his liver. Fists and hammer blows followed. Storm blocked and countered to his best, but this man was larger, faster and more powerful in his dynamics than the other killer. Blows landed to Storm's neck, he saw white flashes, signs of impending unconsciousness. Storm went down on his hands and knees. Bravo pummeled him. Storm was losing awareness. Once that was gone, so was his life, and all those locked downstairs. Bravo kicked at Storm's head and ribs.

"Focus, Derek. Go to the calm place and focus." Storm dropped and rolled onto his back. He thrust a heel kick up into Bravo's groin that lifted him off the floor.

"Uuugh!" Bravo staggered backwards, bending over and holding his crotch. Storm scissors-kicked upright and side kicked Bravo's head. Side kick groin, side kick head, roundhouse shin kick to his knee; it was like kicking a tree trunk, but Bravo buckled slightly, swung back wildly and missed.

Storm kicked him in the stomach, bouncing him off a door to the outside deck. Bravo kicked but Storm evaded inside to Bravo's centerline. Storm turned it loose, his Kung Fu warrior spirit unleashed like a demon from hell: right kick knee, right kick groin, right kick opposite knee, right punch temple, pivot, right chop throat, left palm solar plexus, left knee groin, pivot, right roundhouse elbow to the jaw.

Bravo spun around, stunned by the onslaught of the dragon-possessed adversary. He staggered as he reached for the door handle and tried to get to the outside deck. Storm helped him through with a kick into the small of Bravo's back. The frame shattered, the door came off its hinges as Bravo crashed through it and landed chest down on the gunwale outside. Bravo grabbed the railing, barely conscious.

Storm pursued. The heavy rain pelted them and the ship heaved in the heavy seas. Storm ignored the weather and hammered his elbow down on Bravo's spine. Crack! Bravo yelled and slumped chest down on the rail. Thunder boomed, the ship heaved and tossed Storm against the outer bulkhead. His head banged on a protrusion, the emergency equipment sponson.

He had an idea. He opened the sponson, grabbed a thin orange cylinder, removed an end cap and pulled an exposed ring. The flare ignited and sparked intensely red.

Storm wound up like a fast-pitch softball champion. "Fire in the hole!" He thrust the burning flare through Bravo's trousers into his rectum.

"Aaaaaaaah!"

Bravo arched his back as he screamed, a scream that came all the way up from his boots. Storm reached his right hand over the top of Bravo's head, dug his fingers into Bravo's eye sockets, hooked them behind his skull bone and placed his left forearm across the back of Bravo's neck. Storm violently surged his left forearm forward and his right hand back, yelling loudly to maximize his power.

"Yah!" CR,CR, CRACK! "That's for Uncle Dan, you murderous bastard!" The huge, muscled mercenary went limp, his head dangling at a bizarre angle.

Storm lifted Bravo's legs and leveraged him overboard. Bravo's lifeless body splashed into the heaving sea, the flare still burning. "Now that's hot shit."

Storm heard the chopper. It pulled alongside the ship. Luke had the interior lights on and flashed him a hand signal. He was almost out of fuel.

The chopper's engine sputtered. Correction, he was completely out of fuel. The engine chugged, the rotors slowed and the chopper banked away from the ship. It descended lower, lower.

A huge wave lifted the *Vixen*, passed and welled up to catch the chopper. It sucked the machine into its mass.

Luke was down. And the ship was still underway.

∞

Luke had paced the ship and constantly fought the gusty winds for control of the craft. The chopper vibrated, rolled and yawed wildly as each gust slammed it. Twice, micro-bursts, violent downdrafts at the center of the embedded thunderstorm cells, had stalled the rotors, nearly dropping him into the turbulent sea.

Luke had no hope of returning to terra firma. It wasn't looking too good for landing on the ship, either. The heavy rain had soaked the helipad, making it slippery. Even if he had the fuel and the ship slowed, the heaving seas would toss the chopper right off the pad.

Ten minutes went by without any indication from Storm. Luke prayed for him, and himself. He was in one hell of a jam.

The chopper was extremely low on fuel. The amber FUEL LEVEL LOW warning light taunted him. He couldn't jump onto the ship. That gambit had almost killed Storm. Besides, if he released the cyclic control, the chopper would crash and kill him before he could get clear. There was only one option. He was committed to ditching in the white caps. He was waiting for the last possible moment.

A man crashed through the door from the dining salon. Storm appeared and slammed his elbow into the man's back. A wave hit the ship and slammed Storm against a bulkhead. Hale saw him open a sponson and remove something.

Luke saw a flash of red light and Storm shoved a flare up the guy's butt. "*Ooh. That's got to hurt,*" winced Luke. Storm snapped the man's neck and heaved him overboard.

Luke turned on the interior lights. Storm looked at him. Luke friction-locked the collective with his left hand and held his thumb to his lips and tilted his head back as if drinking. Then he flashed a thumb down. He was out of fuel.

The engine sputtered, he lost altitude. It chugged. The transmission wound down, the rotors slowed, the generator dropped off line. His instruments went dead.

"*This is it. Lord, help me.*" He nosed the chopper away from the ship. It descended and lost speed. A huge wave crested and slapped the machine like a fly swatter.

The craft inverted, the rotor blades snapped as they hit the water. Debris flew in all directions and the chopper went underwater upside down.

Luke released the controls. He was a mere passenger now, holding his breath in a sinking death trap.

∾

"God, no!" Storm became frantic. He had to get the ship stopped and rescue Luke but he needed help, fast. He grabbed three life preservers and tossed them overboard to mark the spot where Luke went down. He checked his watch, noted the time.

He ran back inside. The wounded stranger lay on the floor, bleeding, holding his right side.

"Stranger, I don't know who you are but I owe you my life."

Grimacing, he replied, "Thank me later. There's no one driving this boat and we're headed for the shipping lanes."

Storm examined the man's wound. He raced to a linen cabinet, snatched some white cloth napkins and tossed them to the stranger.

"Plug the hole with those. We have a doctor on board. I'll send her up."

Storm bounded down the stairs two levels to the machine shop and searched for a crow bar. He didn't find one, so he grabbed a ball peen hammer and raced back up to the staterooms. In the passageway, he snatched the killer's abandoned switchblade while on the run and dashed for stateroom four.

He charged at the door with the hammer raised and slammed it down on the lock. The lock, latch and door frame shattered. He kicked the door in.

The entire ship's complement was piled askew, bound, gagged and blindfolded. Storm cut the Skipper loose first, talking a mile a minute as he did.

"Skipper, Luke has crashed in the sea behind us. No one's at the helm and we're headed for the shipping lanes."

"Cut me loose. I have to get to the bridge."

Once freed, Skibba raced from the room.

Next, Storm freed Lisa. "There's a strange man in the dining salon upstairs. He's been shot near his appendix and needs a doctor. He saved my life, so take care of him and don't worry about the dead guy impersonating a Pez dispenser. Go."

Lisa planted a quick kiss on Storm's lips and ran out. Storm cut away the wrist bindings on the others and allowed them to free themselves. He ran down the passageway, bounded up the stairs and raced for the bridge.

∞

The chopper sank deeper. There were no air pockets to buoy it. Luke flashed back to his water survival training in the Air Force. Even though banged up and disoriented, he calmly un-strapped and pushed himself free of the sinking chopper.

It was dark. He couldn't tell which way was up. *"Follow the air bubbles,"* he remembered. He exhaled some. Bubbles rolled from his lips, past his neck and over his shoulder. He rotated and followed them. He tried to kick, but his left leg hurt and wouldn't respond; it was broken. He arched his back and porpoised, struggling to reach the surface.

He had a nasty bump on his head and felt dizzy. He needed precious air. His lungs screamed for relief, to expel their toxic contents and renew.

He thrust with his arms as he porpoised. There was dim light above. Air, get to the surface.

Something floated above. He couldn't tell what it was, if it was submerged or surfaced. He reached for it. *"The survival pack!"* He frantically grabbed it, felt around, found a tee handle and yanked it.

A large gush of carbon dioxide discharged and inflated the survival raft. Luke held on for dear life as the raft ballooned to its full shape and whisked toward the surface. He exhaled small amounts of air as he ascended to relieve some of the pressure on his aching lungs. *"Take me to the air."*

The water rolled and frothed. He knew he was approaching the surface. *"Hold on lungs. Just a little more. Please, God."*

He broke the surface, his lungs practically exploded through his nose and mouth. A large wave crashed over him, submerging him again. He desperately clung to the raft. They surfaced again. He sucked in the precious life sustaining gasses. Rain and hail pelted him but he didn't care. He had air.

The storm was relentless, as if dispatched by hell's minions. Forty knot gusts ripped across the sea, waves heaved him into the air and crashed down, hail pelted him.

Exhausted, battered, Luke fought to take in air as the seawater competed for access to his windpipe. He turned his back to the waves and struggled to climb aboard the raft but couldn't.

Flash! Crack! Lightening struck the water a hundred yards away.

Luke reached down and untied his boots; they were dragging him down. It was a strenuous endeavor, particularly the one on his broken leg. He persevered through the pain.

Free of the boots, he pulled his shirttails free to allow the water to drain. He emptied his pockets. He did everything he could think of to lighten his load.

He attempted to board the raft.

"Come on! Give it to me God!"

He must have heard. Another large wave lifted him, crested and suspended him momentarily in midair. Luke snatched the raft under his hips. As he dropped, the raft impacted and bounced his legs inside. The pain in his leg amplified.

"Aah! Aah! Thank you, Lord. Ah. Ask and you shall receive."

Luke regained composure. He felt around the outside rim of the raft and located a nylon line. He reeled it in and was rewarded with a waterproof pack attached to its end. He hauled it aboard, contesting with the crashing waves for its possession.

With the pack secure, Luke felt around the interior rim, located a sectioned fiberglass rod and screwed the sections together. He snapped the base into a rubber support in the middle of the raft bottom. He pulled up a skirt attached to the inside rim, lifted it over his head and snapped it to the top of the rod. He repeated the process three more times, completing a water-resistant covering over him. The protective cover gave him respite from the elements and prevented the raft from getting swamped.

The heavy waves rolled and heaved the diminutive vessel, but it always stabilized upright. "Thank you."

He searched through the equipment pack. He found a light beacon. He pulled a plug from its housing, opened a flap in the skirt and immersed the beacon in the sea. The water energized a circuit and it flashed. He clipped the beacon to a steel D-ring on the outside rim and closed the flap. Hopefully, the beacon would alert passing ships to his presence.

Luke removed a hand-powered pump from the pack, placed the suction end in the pool of seawater under his butt and fed the drain tube through a small opening in the skirt. He vigorously squeezed the pump, sucking the water back into the sea where it would feel more at home.

It was completely dark now. But the storm wasn't ready to sleep.

Hale removed an emergency radio from the pack and turned it on. It was preset to an emergency frequency.

"Vixen, this is Luke. Come in."

Silence. He tried again with the same negative result. He turned off the squelch switch. A blare of scratchy static assured him it was working.

"Vixen, come in. This is Luke on emergency frequency." No response, only static. He checked the battery level. It was only at half power. "Later," he lamented. He turned it off to conserve the battery.

He leaned back and assessed his condition. He was exhausted, dehydrated and hungry. His left leg was broken just above the ankle. He was bleeding from his forehead and his left shoulder was hyper-extended. He had no medical supplies. Other than that, he was in great shape.

He closed his eyes and wondered how Storm and the crew had fared. Then he passed out.

∾

Skibba made an all out run for the bridge. He quickly assessed the ship's status. They were on a collision course with a huge container freighter. There was no question as to who would win that clash of masses.

Skibba immediately clicked off the autopilot, shoved the throttles forward and wheeled in full starboard rudder. The *Vixen* responded. Her bow came hard starboard and she listed twelve degrees to port. Waves hammered at her. It was not the textbook solution of cutting through heavy seas but they had no choice. The freighter loomed larger in the wheelhouse windows.

Skibba hit the P.A. "All hands, brace for collision. All hands, brace for collision." Skibba held on for all he was worth as the yacht heaved, listed, turned and plunged.

Storm bounced off the bulkheads as he clamored up the steps to the bridge.

"Skipper. Luke's in trouble. We have to go back and find him."

Without looking, Skibba replied, "I heard you the first time, sir. First things first."

Storm looked out the window and noticed what had monopolized the Skipper's attention. "Holy shit!"

"Brace! Brace! Brace!" yelled Skibba into the P.A. He hit the alarm bell, signaling collision warning.

Storm's eyes grew wide as the freighter and the yacht closed range. "This is gonna be close!" He grabbed the console and braced.

The ships passed head-on with mere feet between their port beams. The *Vixen* hit the freighter's wake and rolled side to side. A large wave crashed across her upper decks, heaved her, then dropped them. They rode the wake and the waves for a minute, then Skibba reversed course and headed back for Luke.

Terry Pell struggled up to the bridge. "Reporting for duty, Skipper."

"Take the helm, Mr. Pell. Come hard about starboard. Steer course zero-four-five, make our speed twelve knots."

Pell grabbed the wheel as he acknowledged the orders.

"How far back is Mr. Hale?"

Storm checked his watch. "Eleven minutes. I tossed some life preservers over to mark the spot."

"Good man." Skibba did some quick mental calculations. He went to the navigation console, noted their GPS position, then went to his chart table. He placed his calipers on the chart, noted the time, estimated speed and computed a distance. He swiveled the calipers to another spot on the chart. He flopped a straight edge down and drew a pencil line between the two points.

"Mr. Pell, steer course zero-four-nine degrees and make your speed eighteen knots."

"Aye aye, sir. Steer zero-four-nine, make speed eighteen knots."

Skibba returned to the P.A. "All hands, man your stations. Man overboard. This is not a drill. Man your stations. Man overboard."

∞

Amber and Heather climbed the stairs carefully as the ship listed and plunged. They entered the dining salon to assist Lisa. The place was a wreck. Chairs were broken, glasses and dishes shattered, tables up-ended, the outside door was off its hinges, sea water gushed in, there were bullet holes in the bulkheads and blood was in prolific supply.

Lisa was hunched over a man on the floor near the passageway between the dining salon and the main salon. There was a pool of blood on the floor and bloody handprints on the wall. They approached Lisa from behind and saw the wounded man's face.

"Drake?"

"Drake?"

He coughed. "Hello, Amber, Mrs. Hale."

"What are you doing here?"

"Oh?" Cough. "Long story. I'll tell you later." His eyes rolled back and he passed out.

"Quick," said Lisa. "Help me get him onto the dining table." The women grabbed Kress and labored to get him onto the table. Heather swept the table clear of the remaining dishes and allowed them to crash to the floor.

Dr. Lisa took charge. "Amber, come here. Press down hard on this towel and don't let up. We have to stop the bleeding. Heather, turn on all the lights, get a lot of clean towels and two large bowls of hot water. I have to run down to the Infirmary."

Heather went to the wall and flicked on all the light switches. She noticed the nearly decapitated man in the main salon, a huge pool of blood beneath him. Blood splatters patterned the walls and furniture around him.

"Oooo! What happened to him?"

Lisa ran past Heather and down the stairs. "I'm guessing that's Derek's handiwork. I can tell by the sword sticking out of his neck."

Heather shook her head. "Men... speaking of which, where's Luke?"

∞

The *Vixen* paralleled the freighter's course northeast, gaining on it.

"Skipper, our course is steady zero-four-nine degrees, speed is eighteen knots."

"Excellent Mr. Pell. Maintain course and speed."

"Aye, sir."

The ship heaved and rolled, closing on the location where the chopper went down. But so was the freighter.

Skibba shook his head. He went to the P.A. again. "All hands, man forward stations. Man the searchlights and search for wreckage."

"How's our time?" asked Storm.

"Eight minutes to go. But we have to get there before that freighter. Mr. Pell, make our speed twenty-one knots."

"Aye, sir. Make speed twenty-one knots." He shoved the throttles forward.

"What can I do, Skipper?"

"Nothing here, Mr. Storm. You can help search forward if you care to." By the time Skibba looked around, Storm was gone.

∞

Lisa hurriedly prepared the makeshift operating table as Amber and Heather catered her every order.

"You know this man?"

"He was a guest on the ship when we were in Fiji," answered Amber.

"Can you help him?" asked Heather.

"I think so. The bullet penetrated just below his appendix. He's lost a lot of blood. See if he has ID with his blood type on it."

Heather searched Kress's pockets.

"Amber, get that table lamp, find an extension cord and put it on the table right here," Lisa pointed. "I need more light."

∞

All available hands were on the ship's bow, tied in and wearing life vests. They scanned with searchlights and binoculars, fighting the elements. Storm came running forward with a large black FN rifle with a large round device mounted on its receiver.

As he reached the bow, he handed the rifle to Paul. "Paul, hold this while I tie in."

"What's this for?"

"Night vision scope. It might be our best hope of spotting Luke."

Paul arched his eyebrows. "Good thinking."

Storm completed the tie-in and took the rifle. He flipped on the scope and raised the rifle to his shoulder.

"Come on, Luke. Be there."

∞

"Damn!" exclaimed Skibba. The freighter was heading for the exact spot they had to search.

"Mr. Pell, full speed ahead. We have to warn off that freighter."

Terry's eyeballs opened wide. At twenty-one knots in these rough seas, it was taking every ounce of his skill to maintain control of the ship. Full speed would be a real stretch of his abilities. "Aye sir. Full speed ahead." He shoved the throttles full forward.

Skibba went to the P.A. "Mr. Welch, report to the engine room." Skibba wanted the mechanic at his normal duty station, monitoring the engines. He was going to push the *Vixen* to her limits.

Skibba hit the P.A. again. "Miss Thomas, focus your light on the stern of that freighter."

Skibba raised his binoculars and looked through. A searchlight on the ship's starboard bow flashed across the freighter's stern, returned and stabilized. Skibba caught the name and hit the P.A.

"Thank you Miss Thomas. Resume search."

Skibba grabbed the radio mike. "This is motor yacht *Serene Vixen* hailing freighter *Lung Pao* on emergency frequency. This is *Serene Vixen* hailing *Lung Pao*. Come in."

There was no response.

∞

The powerful halogen searchlights swept the waters well ahead of the *Vixen* and the freighter as the yacht cut across the freighter's wake. Storm scanned a ninety degree arc across their bows. He checked his watch.

"Shit! Come on, Luke. Give me a sign."

∾

A loud rumbling sound awakened Luke.

"That's machinery. A ship!"

He threw open the skirt flap and nearly wished he hadn't. A large ship was bearing down directly at him.

∾

Storm thought he saw a flash of light through the night scope. Another one. Yes! It was an emergency light beacon. He stabilized the rifle as much as possible. There was another flash.

"A raft! Ten degrees right. Two miles."

Paul repeated Storm's report into the radio. They heard the Skipper on the P.A. "Search party, all lights ten degrees starboard. Ten degrees starboard. Raft in the water. Two miles."

Skibba had mixed feelings. He was elated to learn about the raft, but distressed that it was right in the path of the freighter.

He grabbed the radio mike as the yacht nudged ahead of the freighter. "This is *Serene Vixen* hailing *Lung Pao* on emergency frequency. *Serene Vixen* hailing *Lung Pao* on emergency frequency."

There wasn't any response.

"Mr. Pell, get us ahead of that freighter. We're going to cut across her bows and veer her off."

The Skipper couldn't see the look of terror on Terry's face. He was maxed out; nonetheless, he obeyed. "Aye sir. Full speed, prepare to cross the freighter's bow on your command."

Skibba grabbed a flare pistol, hurried to the wheelhouse door and fired it into the air. The red flare whistled into the stormy night, streaking across the path of *Lung Pao*. He ran back to the communications console, grabbed a hand-held signal lamp and squeezed its trigger button. He flashed the signal directly at the freighter's bridge.

A signal from the freighter's bridge flashed back. Acknowledgement! "Finally!"

Skibba dropped the lamp and grabbed the radio mike. "This is *Serene Vixen* hailing *Lung Pao* on emergency frequency. Come in please."

A response came back in a foreign language. Skibba made out the words 'Lung Pao,' but he didn't understand the rest.

"This is *Serene Vixen* hailing *Lung Pao*. Come in."

A different voice came over the radio in broken English. "*Serene Vixen*, this *Lung Pao*. What is nature emergency?"

"This is Captain Skibba of the yacht *Serene Vixen*. We have a man overboard in a raft, directly off your bow. Please cut your engines and turn hard starboard, hard starboard."

"Roger. Man overboard. Hard starboard."

"I hope it's not too late."

Luke was conflicted. Should he swim or remain in the raft?

The freighter loomed larger, the waves swelled. Luke knew he wouldn't make much headway with his broken leg and hyper-extended shoulder. He'd most likely get sucked into the ship's propellers and diced into fish food. The raft was his only flotations device. He elected to stay put.

"God, I know I'm an unworthy pain in your backside, but please, just one more blessing."

The freighter bore down. Its engine noise stopped, the bow turned away, slightly at first, then more.

Spotlights from behind the raft illuminated the area. The freighter approached. Luke sealed the flap, hunkered down and grabbed the inner rim straps.

"Okay, Lord! It's up to You."

The *Vixen's* spotlights located the tossing raft and stabilized on it as best they could. Both ships were slowing, but their momentums still carried them toward the raft with alarming speed. *Lung Pao* veered to starboard, *Vixen* to port.

One hundred yards to go. Storm saw the freighter turning but it was still drifting toward the raft. He knew they would collide.

The crew watched in horror as the freighter's port beam slammed the vulnerable raft. It heaved and bounced off the freighter's hull. Popping sounds reached across the sea as the raft burst, inverted and submerged beneath a wave.

Storm couldn't stand it any more. He snatched a toss ring, made a running start and dove over the starboard bow into the turbid waters fifteen beet below.

"Man overboard!" yelled Paul. He radioed the bridge. "Skipper, Mr. Storm dove in."

∞

"Here she comes."

The raft rose on the freighter's bow wave and impacted against her hull. Three of the raft's four inflation tubes popped loudly, punctured by sharp barnacles.

The raft bounced away from the hull and rolled inverted. A wave crashed down on it and tossed Luke around like a seed in a dry gourd. His broken leg issued its protest. The raft submerged.

Seawater instantly filled the interior. Luke struggled to hold his breath against the suffocating onslaught. He struggled blindly in the submerged darkness, trying to locate the flap to escape. Temporal distortion invaded his mind. Everything seemed to be happening in slow motion. It was taking too long.

Luke was tired and hadn't caught a full breath before being submerged. His lungs screamed for more air, his heart pounded away at ramming speed. His fingers searched frantically. The fiberglass support rod had snapped and a sharp end pierced his right thigh. Pain. He fought the urge to yell and lose his precious air.

Velcro! The flap! He tore an opening and spread it. He clasped his hands as if to pray, sliced them through the gap and spread his elbows to widen it.

"Air! Now!" his lungs demanded. Hale painfully pushed his torso through the opening but the rod protruding from his thigh snagged the skirt. He couldn't separate from the raft.

His brain screamed at him. *"Air! Now! Or I'm outta here!"* Luke's spirit wouldn't allow him to quit. He fumbled with the snag, the collapsed skirt wrapped around his arm, entangling him more.

"Come on!" He was losing awareness. His fingers refused to follow orders. His legs couldn't kick. His arms wouldn't paddle. There was no more control of his motor functions. His mind told him not to quit, but his old body had its limits.

Air trickled from his nose and lips. Seawater seeped in. Tunnel vision, darkness. *"I love you, Heather."* His hearing faded. All went black. He sensed an intensely bright white light at the end of a long, dark tunnel. He was being swept toward the light.

∞

A powerful arm reached around Luke's torso and hauled him to the surface. The raft dragged along behind them.

Storm broke the surface, exhaled forcefully and sucked in a huge breath. He kept Luke's head above the water, gripped him around his chest from behind and squeezed hard. A long stream of seawater spewed from his nose and mouth. Storm released and squeezed again. More water came up. He squeezed a third time. No water.

Storm placed his mouth on Luke's and blew hard, trying to inflate his lungs. Nothing. He felt for a pulse. None.

A wave crashed over them. Storm felt for the pulse again but couldn't detect one.

"Come on, Luke!" Storm reclined Hale and hammered down on his chest, right over his heart. He felt for a pulse again and another wave crashed over them.

A heartbeat! The jumpstart worked. Storm placed his ear close to Luke's nose. No breath. He held Luke's nose and blew into his mouth again. Another wave crashed over them.

"Come on, Luke! I know you can hear me. Breathe!" He blew into Hale's mouth again.

Hale coughed and regurgitated. Seawater and vomit came out. Storm rinsed his mouth with seawater and spit it out.

Luke was breathing. It was shallow but he was breathing. Another wave crashed over them. Storm protected Luke's air passage. He was still unconscious. A toss ring landed in the water four feet away.

"Behind you, Derek. Grab the toss ring." Paul had jumped in and swam up behind them to help. They towed Luke to the ring and hung on as the crew hauled them all to the ship.

∾

It had been an exhausting, adrenaline-draining day for everyone. The *Vixen* had been stretched to her limits too.

The storm had finally passed, allowing Lisa to perform surgery on Kress. The storm left a trail of wispy clouds and light seas in its wake.

Lisa was able to extract the bullet, stop the bleeding and get Kress stabilized, thanks to the help of Heather and Amber, who both had the same blood type as Kress. Transfusions from them kept him alive until Lisa could stop the bleeding.

Then she had attended to Luke. He was a mess. Fortunately, he was unconscious when they recovered him, so she used the opportunity to set his broken leg bone and stitch his forehead. Storm had done a great job of resuscitating him and all he really needed now was rest and nourishment. Storm and Paul carried him to his stateroom as Heather trailed along, sobbing but thankful.

Kress awoke shortly after dawn. Sunlight flashed into the main salon, where they had transferred him after the surgery.

"He's awake," said Amber, waking Lisa.

Lisa rubbed her eyes and yawned. "Okay. Let's get some coffee and do a post-op check." She padded barefoot to the groggy Kress. Storm rose from his couch and joined them.

"How are you doing, Mr. Kress?"

"Pain. But I'm still alive, unless I'm staring at angels."

Lisa checked his dressing and his wound. "We've removed the bullet and stopped the bleeding. That's the good news."

"What's the bad news?" he slurred.

"Well, as you can see, this isn't a hospital and we don't have the latest in surgical equipment. The work I did here can be described as meatball surgery. It's enough to get you stabilized but not the recommended level of treatment for proper recovery. We're heading for Greece to get you into a proper hospital. You have an interesting scar on your stomach now. I'm sorry about that, it couldn't be helped."

"Not to worry, Doc. Chicks love scars and the stories that go with them." He coughed. He took the beautiful doctor's hand. "Thank you."

"It's me who should be thanking you."

Kress looked puzzled. He didn't understand.

"I'm told you saved my boyfriend's life. Thank you."

Amber's curiosity took over. "Drake, how did you end up here? The last time we saw you was in Fiji."

"Oh. First off, my real name is Darren Kress, not Drake."

Now Amber was puzzled. "Why the fake name?"

Kress smiled weakly. "I'm an undercover investigator for the Department of Health and Human Services. I was assigned to investigate a Medicare fraud ring in Portland last year when we got wind of a plot to sabotage Dr. Flynn's cancer research."

"That's Derek's uncle, my boss," informed Lisa.

Kress continued. "We suspected that elements of the National Organization of Medical Professionals were behind it."

"Why didn't you arrest them?" asked Lisa.

"Well, I'm not a law enforcement officer, just an investigator. I'm not authorized to carry firearms or arrest people. I only investigate and report my findings to the higher-ups. They determine if they want the FBI to investigate. Secondly, I didn't have any credible evidence to turn over to the FBI until after Dan Flynn was murdered. By that time, a certain corrupt Congresswoman had quashed the Justice Department and they squelched the FBI."

"Stakemore," confirmed the battered and bandaged Storm.

Kress nodded. "I'm sorry, sir. I don't believe we've met."

"Sorry." Storm extended a hand. "I'm Derek Storm, Dan Flynn's nephew."

"So, you're Derek Storm? I see. I'm sorry. I wish I had known what those mercenaries were up to before…" his voice tapered off.

"I understand. It's not your fault."

"But how did you get *here*?" Amber asked again.

"An informant in one of the Intelligence agencies tipped us off about this band of mercenaries named the 'Bravo' team. Their leader, Colonel Bravo, has a notorious reputation for getting the job done with… extreme brutality."

"His real name was Colonel James Whitcup," interjected Storm, "retired from the Army. I knew him as a Major during the Persian Gulf War. He worked in the Division G-level staff. And you can refer to him in the past tense. He's dead. I snapped his neck last night and threw him overboard with a rocket up his ass."

"You're thorough, aren't you?" replied Kress, trying not to laugh. "You nailed all of them."

Storm was puzzled. "How do you know that?"

Kress smiled weakly. "I observed the raid on the bunker. I was trying to locate Bravo's team when I stumbled upon the raid and you showed up. I was unarmed as usual, and had no way of helping other than calling the police. The next day, I read the details in the newspaper. That was some mighty fine action under fire, Mr. Storm. I'm in awe of you." They shook hands again.

Exasperated, Amber again asked, "But how did you get *here*, on the *Vixen*?"

"Oh." Kress smiled and squeezed Amber's hand. "After Derek wiped out most of Bravo's team, I tried to trail the last two, but I lost them. Last week, our informant, someone who Bravo had double-crossed previously, notified us that they flew to the Med, so I picked up their trail here. They rented a fishing boat and shadowed your ship. I rented a boat too, tailed them and watched them watch you."

"So those were the two boats back at the island?"

"Correct." Kress coughed and gulped.

"Here. Have some water," said Lisa. She raised his head for him to swallow.

"Ah. Thanks." He gulped and continued. "When I saw one of the men don scuba gear and go over the side, I suspected they were making a move on Dr. Chen. So I followed their boat to the opposite side of the island. The thug on the boat beached it and ran up the hill. He was gone for half an hour, so I hid my boat and stowed away in his."

"That must have been when they sabotaged our ropes and the chopper," reasoned Storm.

"I can't speak to that, Mr. Storm. But when the killer returned to the boat, he drove to this ship. I snuck aboard the yacht when they weren't looking."

Storm grinned and nodded. "I'm glad you did. Thanks for saving my life."

"Glad to do it, especially to nail those bastards. By the way, the conspirators and Congresswoman Stakemore have mysteriously disappeared. The FBI is looking for them."

"Gee, I wonder what happened to them?" said Lisa, giving Storm a teasing glance.

Storm smiled back and wrapped his arms around her. "We may never know, China Doll. We may never know."

EPILOGUE

Southern Iraq: It had taken months for Luke's broken leg to heal. When the day came to cut off the cast, he wasted no time diving into the ocean, relishing his freedom from the annoying encumbrance. He spent an hour in the water, swimming, floating, dreaming and reminiscing. He remembered something he had to do.

Most of the hostilities had subsided in Iraq; enough that Luke felt it was safe to return. He took a commercial flight to Kuwait City, hired a limousine and returned to the little village on the Euphrates where he and Storm had appropriated a certain wooden boat.

Luke had the driver make inquiries around the village to determine the name and whereabouts of any villager who had lost a boat just prior to the start of the war. One name kept popping up.

They located the man. Luke asked the driver to explain what happened and what he wanted to do to rectify the matter. The villager became ecstatic, hugged Luke as Arabs do, and kissed him on both cheeks.

Two days later, Luke was back with a brand new twenty-foot fiberglass fishing boat with an outboard motor, a supply of fuel and a full set of fishing gear. He presented the boat to the astounded villager.

As Luke bid farewell to the man and his family, he gave the villager an envelope. The man was curious and looked inside. It was stuffed with enough Iraqi and Kuwaiti currency to compensate him for a year's worth of revenue. The villager was beside himself and made excited remarks to his family, his arms waving animated gestures. The man embraced

Luke again as his wife and children looked on.

Luke shook hands with him, bid farewell to the family and returned to the *Vixen*, content that he had done the righteous deed.

MONTHS LATER

Off Martha's Vineyard, Atlantic Ocean: It was a beautiful August afternoon. Sunshine, light waves and warm breezes dominated the weather as the contingent of the *Vixen* frolicked on the ship and in the ocean.

The wave runners and parasail were popular with the crew and guests; the party was in full swing. Loud music blared from the ship's audio system. People ran around, laid around, dove, wrestled, played cards, ate and drank to their hearts content.

Storm, Lisa, Pete Flynn, Melanie Taylor, her new beau Steve, Mike Starr and his wife Brenda, had all joined the Hales and crew for the festivities.

Darren Kress's wound had healed and he eventually returned to his job. Luke had invited him but Kress had pressing business in Portland. HSS had finally nabbed the Welfare fraud ring they had targeted and Kress had to appear in federal court as a witness. Luke offered him a rain check, gladly accepted.

Luke stood on the helipad, admiring his new Bell Jet Ranger helicopter. She was a beauty, painted in white, blue and gold. He gazed out over the ocean as Heather sneaked up behind him, laid her head on his shoulder and squeezed his buttock. "What are you thinking about?"

Luke turned and kissed her tenderly. "I was just thinking how fortunate we are. We have a nice family, we're financially secure, I have a wonderful wife and good friends."

"Yes. We're blessed."

"My leg healed fine, I have a new chopper…"

"And I have a magnificent husband." She kissed him. "You know, Pete Flynn is an interesting man, so intelligent and compassionate."

"Yes. He told me that several independent labs have verified his cancer cure and human testing is going to begin soon. He said the FBI busted six FDA weasels who took bribes to hush it up."

"Thank God. Did you talk with Melanie yet?"

"Not yet. How's she doing?"

"Very good. She told me that once the press reported the conspiracy,

NOMP was flooded with wrongful death lawsuits. They're broke, declaring bankruptcy."

"Oh, that's good." Luke smiled and laughed. "That proves there is God and He is righteous."

"Melanie mentioned she wants to use the six million to found a new organization, but not for control of the medical practices. She envisions it more as a clearinghouse for medical information. She wants to avoid lobbying and politics."

Luke's smile widened. "God bless her. She has a good heart."

"Yes, she does. I think she's sweet on Derek, too."

Luke chuckled. "She'll have to take a number. Lisa has dibs, I think."

"I know. But she is adorable. Her boyfriend seems nice too."

"Yeah, I met him downstairs. Big guy. I think he's a hockey player. Did you see the scars on his face?"

Heather nodded. "Melanie says it gives him character." They chuckled.

"Yeah, he's a rugged guy. I think that's him on the parasail." Luke pointed at the parachute being towed by the launch.

"Luke, I'm proud of you." Her adoration reflected in her eyes.

"How's that?"

"You could have kept all that treasure, split it with the crew and no one would have known."

The cruisers had held a conference amongst themselves. They discussed their options regarding the disposition of the Polo treasure and reached a consensus.

They agreed that all of the artifacts having historic or artistic value should be gifted to museums in Italy and China, where they belonged. That included the statuettes, jade carvings, sculptures, minted coins, jewelry and the Chinese weaponry and body armor. Some tattered, decayed parchment manuscripts were also found and gifted.

As for the bullion and loose gemstones, they were salvaged bounty. They had no historic or artistic value, only monetary.

The crew decided to pay for all of the expenses Luke incurred for their expedition and buy him a new helicopter, and then they divided the remainder equally amongst themselves. It came out to be a smidge over two million dollars per participant.

Luke and Heather donated their shares to charities, the first of which was Pete and Lisa's research.

"Yeah," agreed Luke. "I'm glad we've made a contribution to history." He gave her a hug. "Well, I should go below and be sociable."

"Yes, let's." They headed for the stairs.

"Do you think Derek and Lisa will get married?"

Luke rolled his eyes.

∞

Storm and Lisa lounged on the sundeck, catching rays.

"Derek, what are you going to do about your Kung Fu studio?"

"I've already worked a deal with Mark Long. I'm going to sell him the business and let him pay for it monthly. He jumped for joy. He's only twenty-four and he owns his own business now."

"That's great. What about your apartment?"

"Whoa. Too hot there! There was a dead guy in it, remember? Although, I wish I could recover my weapons and certificates, my military decorations, photos, you know, the personal stuff. I suppose I'll just have to let it go. It's too risky to go back. I'm the one who made the dead guy."

"Go back and explain it."

"No way. All that would happen is that I'd be arrested and put on trial for who knows what crime, even though I was just defending myself. I'm not guilty. I'm not going to waste my time to prove it. That bastard deserved it."

"You really have a way with people."

"Oh, very funny Doctor." He flicked his towel at her bottom.

She flinched and laughed. "Where are you going to live?" she asked tantalizingly.

"Is this the live-in question?"

"Absolutely not. I don't shack up. I'm not that kind of girl." She batted her beautiful eyelashes at him.

"That's right. I forgot. You're a newly wealthy doctor princess. No, I'm not living in Commie-fornia."

"Well?"

"Well what?"

"Where are you going to live?"

Storm sighed. "Well, I suppose now's as good a time as any."

"What?"

"Heather and Luke have invited me to live on the *Vixen*."

"You're kidding. When will we ever see each other?"

"Oh, frequently, China doll. We're millionaires now. And this is a ship. It travels from one place to another on water. And there's this new invention called the airplane. They use it to fly from one place to another. I hear it's quite the rage."

It was Lisa's turn to snap a towel. "Brat."

Storm laughed. "Don't worry, Lisa. I plan to see you frequently. I love you. I just can't risk going back to California for any extended length of time."

They sipped their cocktails.

Storm had a thought. "You know, you could live here."

Lisa shook her head. "No. The Hales didn't invite me, they invited you."

Storm snapped his fingers several times, "Earth to Lisa. One word from me to Luke and you're in."

Lisa thought about it and shook her head. "I can't abandon the research. Pete is counting on me and we've come so far. No. I have to see it through."

"How about when it's done?"

"Leukemia."

"Leukemia?"

"Yes. We need a cure for leukemia. The memories I have of those poor, suffering children still haunt me. I know I can make a contribution."

Storm smiled widely. "You are the most magnificent woman I have ever met. God bless you."

"Thanks. And I love you too." She blew a kiss at him. Storm pretended to catch it and placed it on his lips.

He rubbed his stomach. "I'm hungry. How about you?"

"I could use a bite."

"Let's see what's on the buffet."

Luke and Heather were enjoying a pleasant conversation with Mike and Brenda Starr in the main salon.

Paul came running up. "Mr. Hale, I'm sorry to interrupt but the Skipper would like you to call the bridge."

"What's it about, Paul?"

"Something to do with the Coast Guard."

"Thanks." Luke picked up the phone and pressed the intercom button. "Skipper. It's Luke. What's up?"

"There's a Coast Guard ship approaching the port bow, two miles out. They hailed the ship and said they want to speak with you. They mentioned you and Paul by name. I don't like the sound of it."

"Okay. I'll be right there. Keep the ship on normal status. We don't want to alarm the guests."

"Aye, sir."

Luke replaced the phone and tried not to look concerned.

"What's wrong?" inquired Heather.

"Coast Guard. They probably want to do an inspection or something. You all enjoy. I'll take care of it. Paul, would you accompany me to the bridge?"

"Absolutely, Mr. Hale."

They headed forward. Storm and Lisa were coming down the stairs and Luke intercepted them.

He smiled. "Hi lovebirds. I don't want to be a party pooper Lisa, but would you mind if I borrow Derek for a few minutes?"

"Oh, not at all. You boys have fun."

Luke had a minute to assess the situation, develop a plan and brief the bridge party. The Coast Guard vessel pulled along side the *Vixen*. The huge yacht dwarfed the forty-foot vessel.

Storm tossed a ladder over the gunwale and climbed up the ladder to the bridge as Guardsmen placed rubber cushions between the hulls of the ships. A Coast Guard Lieutenant and three men in suits stood on the patrol craft deck.

Luke looked down from the bridge deck. "What is this, a raid?"

"No sir," answered the Lieutenant.

"An inspection?"

"No sir. May we come aboard?"

Ordinarily, Luke would have refused but he was curious. "You may come aboard as long as you understand that every person on this vessel explicitly reserves all of their constitutional rights without prejudice to any of those rights. Do you understand?"

The puzzled Lieutenant looked at the suited men. They looked disgusted but nodded.

The Lieutenant yelled up, "Yes sir. We understand. Permission to come aboard?"

"Permission granted with the reservation to revoke such at any time. If you agree, you may come aboard."

Two of the three suits nodded their heads in disgust. The third looked dumbfounded.

"Agreed," yelled the Lieutenant. "Thank you, sir." The officer scaled the ladder first, followed by the suits. Once over the gunwale, they climbed the ladder to the bridge level.

Storm politely offered assistance as they reached the top deck.

Luke opened. "I recognize the uniform, rank and insignia of the Coast Guard. God bless you and your crew, Lieutenant. I have great respect for the Coast Guard and those who serve it." Luke extended his hand to the officer.

"Thank you, sir. I will convey your sentiments to my crew."

"Who are these gentlemen?"

The oldest looking man reached inside his coat. Luke noticed Storm tense and prepare to pounce. The man extracted a leather folio and flipped it open.

"I'm Agent Smithson, D-E-A. These are Special Agents Laramie and Doss, F-B-I." The others flashed their credentials and extended their hands to shake. Luke ignored their gesture.

"*Special* agents. Yes, well, I'm sure your parents are all very proud of you. What business do the DEA and FBI have on this ship?" Luke glared directly into the eyes of the DEA man. He didn't like what he saw. Something about this guy bothered him, a lot.

The feds stuffed away their credentials. "Are you Mr. Lucien Hale?"

"I have the right to remain silent."

The Lieutenant looked uncomfortable as the feds glanced at one another. They weren't accustomed to this type of reception.

The DEA man continued. "Is there a Paul Thomas on board?"

"I have the right to remain silent." Another round of glances. One of the FBI agents reached into his coat. Storm was behind him in a flash and placed his palm on the back of the man's right shoulder.

"Go slowly," he quietly advised the fed. The visitors just had their anxiety level bumped up a notch.

The FBI man slowly withdrew a paper from his jacket and unfolded it. He showed it to the others. Storm could see it was a copy of an old photo of Luke in his Green Beret uniform. He was thirty pounds heavier now, with less hair, but it was undeniably him.

"It's him," nodded the DEA agent. "Mr. Hale, we'd like to have a word with you and Paul Thomas about the disappearance of two of our agents in Cabo San Lucas last year."

"I didn't say I was Luke Hale. I have the right to remain silent. If you want to discuss this, let's step into the wheelhouse so we don't alarm my guests."

Luke led the way. Salty and Paul were already inside. Storm brought up the rear and closed the door behind them. Luke turned and faced the feds. "Okay, gentlemen. First, I have a few questions."

"Go ahead, Mr. Hale."

"I never said I was Mr. Hale, remember?"

The DEA man got frustrated and blurted out, "Are any of you Paul Thomas?" No one answered. They just issued indifferent stares.

"Agent whatever-your-name-was…"

"Smithson."

"Agent Smithson, you will address me and only me or you will leave this ship. Understood?"

"You're not cooperating, Mr. Hale."

"Do you have a warrant?"

The feds didn't answer. One shook his head.

"Do you have probable cause to board this vessel?"

"No sir," replied the youngest agent. "This is not an arrest or search. We have no warrants. It's merely an investigation." The DEA man gave the junior agent a look that could freeze hell. The older FBI man looked disgusted.

Luke replied, "Thank you, Special Agent Doss. At least one of you has some integrity."

"Okay, Mr. Hale," interrupted the DEA agent, "I don't want to make things tough for you, but…"

"But what? Are you trying to intimidate me, you federal weasel? I think you are. Am I being too sensitive or did anyone else take it that way?"

Storm, Thomas and Skibba all nodded. The Lieutenant, knowing he was out of his element, stayed at the back of the group and remained silent. He was clearly uncomfortable with the circumstances. The junior agent looked very nervous. Storm kept a close watch on him as Luke confronted the DEA thug.

Luke declared, "I think it's time for cocktails." The statement puzzled the feds but was a prearranged signal. Thomas and Skibba produced shotguns from behind the console and pumped shells into their chambers. They leveled them at the FBI agents.

The DEA fool reached under his coat.

"NO!" yelled the other feds in unison.

"Ahem."

DEA man looked over his shoulder. Storm had a .45 leveled at his head. "I strongly recommend you cool your jets, Mr. Narc. This one's already chambered."

"You're all under arrest," growled the narc.

"For what?" challenged Luke.

"Assaulting federal officers."

Skibba laughed out loud. "I don't think so. This vessel is three hundred yards beyond U.S. jurisdiction. We're in international waters. Lieutenant, why don't you call your ship and confirm it?"

The officer looked unsure. Luke nodded for him to proceed. Seconds later, he said, "The Captain is correct. We're in international waters."

"Both the Captain and the Lieutenant are correct," confirmed Luke, as he removed his favorite Colt .45 Auto from the arms locker and racked a round into the chamber. "You have no jurisdiction here. So to me, you're not federal officers, just unwelcome intruders."

"What are you going to do?" asked the older FBI agent.

"We're going to usher you back to your boat once we search you for contraband."

"Contraband?"

"Yes. I don't want any of you slimy sneaks planting contraband on this vessel and use it as a pretense to raid us."

"That's preposterous," protested the DEA fool.

The FBI men and the Lieutenant were taken aback. The officer stated emphatically, "We do *not* operate like that, sir."

"I believe you, Lieutenant. My beef is not with you or your crew. As I said earlier, I have great respect for the Coast Guard. Your personnel have always been courteous and professional, you included."

"Then why are you doing this, sir?"

"Just like you, every man on this bridge put many years into military service to defend the Constitution and Bill of Rights. Just like you, we swore an oath to defend it from all enemies, foreign *and* domestic, and to bear true faith and allegiance to the same. That oath is to the Constitution, not to the government or its agents. I'll be damned if I'm going to allow corrupt federal officers to abuse our rights or pervert them for their own purposes. They have forgotten for whom they work. They are not our masters, we are theirs. But I've learned through hard experience that many feds have no regard for the rights of the citizenry, so I distrust pretty much all of them."

"You're not gonna get away with this, Hale," growled the DEA thug.

Luke got right into his face. "You're making too much ruckus for someone who's righteous. Search him."

Storm pushed the DEA creep against the bulkhead. "Assume the position and spread 'em." He glanced to Luke and rolled his eyes, "I've always wanted to do that." He patted down the fed. He removed his firearm and unloaded it, allowing the ammo to clatter to the floor. He replaced the pistol in the holster. He found his spare ammo and tossed that away. He found his back-up pistol strapped to the inside of his left ankle. He unloaded and replaced that too. He found a switchblade taped to his right ankle and tossed that to Thomas. "You won't need that on this ship." He continued frisking the protesting creep. "Hello, what's this?"

The narc's head bobbed as Storm extracted a large clear plastic bag from his left rear pocket. It contained a substantial quantity of a powdery white substance.

Luke walked to Storm. He took the bag and opened the seal. He sniffed at it and recoiled.

"What is this stuff?" DEA man didn't answer. Storm sniffed it and shrugged his shoulders.

"May I?" interjected the senior FBI agent. Luke held the bag for him as he sniffed.

"It's cocaine."

"Thank you, Special Agent Laramie." Luke turned to the DEA fool. "Just what were you thinking when you boarded this ship with this crap, huh?"

"It's for training."

"BULLSHIT! You must think I'm an idiot. No one on this ship has any interest in this shit. You were going to plant it on the ship before you left and use it as a pretense to raid us later, weren't you?"

The loudmouth agent fell silent.

"Smithson, you asshole," growled the senior FBI agent. He was furious. "Mr. Hale, this conduct by a federal officer violates every ethical standard we are sworn to."

"So what? It doesn't stop you federal assholes from doing it. And I never said I was Lucien Hale. Why is it you people can't hear that?"

Agent Laramie smiled, "I hear you, sir. Please don't include us in this jerk's circle. We were sent to accompany him on an investigation, nothing more. We had no idea he possessed cocaine or what his intentions were. In fact, Agent Doss and I had never met him until today." Doss nodded affirmation to Luke.

Laramie stepped to Smithson as he spoke to Luke, "But we'll be glad to place him under arrest." The agent pulled his cuffs and slapped them around Smithson's wrists. "You are under arrest.."

Luke intoned, ".. for violation of section two forty-two of U.S. Code Title eighteen, deprivation of rights under color of law."

Laramie smiled. "Thank you, Mr. Ha.."

"Ah. Ah." Hale raised an eyebrow.

"Thank you, sir." He addressed Smithson, "You have the right to remain silent. Anything you say…." He went through the whole Miranda recital. When he finished, he grabbed the chain between the cuffs and faced Luke.

"Sir, with your permission, we'll take leave of your ship and book this man."

"We're out of U.S. jurisdiction," protested Smithson. "You can't arrest me here."

"Nice try," countered Laramie. "But I personally observed a crime committed by a federal officer and as soon as we set foot on the Coast Guard ship, we'll be in federal territory. I'll just arrest you and read your rights again. And I'm sure Mr… this ship's Master consents to us arresting you on his sovereign vessel."

"You assume correctly, Agent Laramie."

"So Smithson, you're screwed any way you look at it."

"Thank you," said Luke. "And please take this garbage with you." He handed Doss the bag of cocaine.

"Yes sir. We apologize for the inconvenience."

Luke laughed. "Inconvenience? What you refer to as an inconvenience, I see as a threat. The perspective is different through the other side of the window. Isn't it?"

"I guess so. Let's go. Good day sir."

The men returned to the Coast Guard ship and it departed. When it was safely away, the cruisers stowed their firearms.

∾

The sunset was beautiful. The crew gathered on the helipad and admired the spectral display as day gave way to night.

Their dinner had been superb and they cheered Connie as Paul raised the petite lady onto his shoulders. Caroline kissed Paul. Salty and Luke stoked up their Cubans. Lisa and Derek smooched. Heather and Amber hugged their favorite men.

The customary round of toasts ensued. They toasted everything and each other until the champagne ran out.

During a lull, Storm stepped to Luke's side. "How about teaching me to fly that thing?" He nodded at the chopper.

"Okay. Sure."

"When?"

Luke was nearly seeing double from all the booze. "Tomorrow, when we're sober."

"All right! Do you think I can do it?"

"I have no doubt." Luke gazed at the horizon as Storm danced on Cloud Nine. Heather came to Luke's side and they hugged.

"A penny for your thoughts?"

Luke gazed at her lovely Scottish face. "I was just thinking about the *Sea Wind*."

"The what?"

Derek intoned, "The *Sea Wind*? The sunken ship from the Polo expedition?"

Luke nodded. "The one that went to the bottom with a large load of gold." He wiggled his eyebrows.

Storm's eyes widened. "And has *never* been located," he stated emphatically.

"Yeah. That one."

Storm shook his head. "You're nuts, man."

Luke smiled. "Maybe."

- THE END -

Bibliography

1. Biochemical Pharmacology 2002; 63: 2145-9.

2. Biochim Biophys Acta 2002; 1542 (1-3): 209-20

3. Biological Trace Element Research 2002; 86 (2): 177-91

4. Cancer 2002; 86 (10): 1645-51

5. Cancer Epidemiol Biomarkers Preview 2002; 11 (8): 713-8

6. Cancer Letter 2002; 177 (1): 49-56

7. Carcinogenesis 2002; 1307-13

8. FAS Military Analysis Network; www.fas.org/man/dod-101/sys/land/m2.htm

9. International Journal of Oncology 2002 June; 20 (6): 1233-9

10. "Marco Polo and His Travels," Silkroad Foundation, 2000; www.silk-road.com/artl/marcopolo.shtml

11. "Marko Polo and Korcula," Dr. Zivan Filippi; www.korcula.net/mpolo/mpolo6.htm

12. NIH Clinical Center, National Institutes of Health; www.cc.nih.gov/ccc/supplements/selen.html#risks

13. Pancreas 2002; 25: 45-8

14. "Polo, Marco," Encyclopedia Britannica 1997;   www.carmensandiego.com/products/time/marco06/marcopolo.html

15. "Polo, Marco," Microsoft Encarta Online Encyclopedia 2002; http://encarta.msn.com/encyclopedia_761556866/Marco_Polo.html

16. Prostaglandins Leukot Essential Fatty Acids 2002; 66: 519-24

17. Rand McNally Deluxe Road Atlas & Travel Guide, Rand McNally & Company 1993; 11, 33

18. The SAS Survival Handbook, Wiseman, John 'Lofty', Harper Collins 1996; 16-19, 22-26, 30-31, 37, 57-59, 86, 99-101, 103-104, 124-128, 181-183, 187-196, 207, 211-215, 217-218, 236, 246, 254-260

19. United Defense Corporation; www.uniteddefense.com/prod/bradleyM2A3.htm

20. Worldwide Essential Education; www.mcsilver.com.